The Year's Best
Fantasy and
Horror

ALSO EDITED BY ELLEN DATLOW AND TERRI WINDLING

The Year's Best Fantasy: First Annual Collection
The Year's Best Fantasy: Second Annual Collection
The Year's Best Fantasy and Horror: Third Annual Collection
The Year's Best Fantasy and Horror: Fourth Annual Collection
Snow White, Rose Red (forthcoming)

The *Year's Best*
Fantasy and
Horror

FIFTH ANNUAL COLLECTION

Edited by Ellen Datlow
and Terri Windling

ST. MARTIN'S PRESS   NEW YORK

The editors would like to dedicate this book to
Jim Frenkel, the man whose idea this series was,
the person who does much of the dirty work, the
guy who nudzhes us to death. Thanks, Jim.

Library of Congress Catalog Card Number: 91-659320

Paperback ISBN 0-312-07888-9
Hardcover ISBN 0-312-07887-0

First Edition: August 1992

10 9 8 7 6 5 4 3 2 1

A Bluejay Books Production

CONTENTS

Acknowledgments

Many thanks to all the publishers, editors, writers, artists, booksellers, librarians and readers who sent material and recommended favorite titles; and to *Locus, Library Journal* and *Folk Roots* magazines, which are invaluable reference sources. (Anyone wishing to recommend stories, music or art published in 1992 can do so October–December c/o The Endicott Studio, 781 South Calle Escondido, Tucson, AZ 85748.)

Special thanks to the Tucson and Chagford public library staffs, the Book Mark bookstore and Tucson's Book Arts Gallery; to Robert Gould and Charles de Lint for music recommendations; to Lawrence Schimel and Jane Yolen for story recommendations; to Beth Meacham, Tappan King, Robin Hardy and Ellen Steiber; to Rob Killheffer at *Omni*; and in particular to our editor Gordon Van Gelder, our packager Jim Frenkel, our cover artist Tom Canty, to Editorial Assistant Brian McDonald, and my hard-working co-editor and friend Ellen Datlow.

—Terri Windling

I would like to thank Robert Killheffer, Gordon Van Gelder, Lisa Kahlden, Merrilee Heifetz, Keith Ferrell, Linda Marotta, Mike Baker, Matthew Bialer, and Jim Frenkel for all their help and encouragement. Also, a special thank-you to Tom Canty and Terri Windling. Finally, I appreciate all the book publishers and magazine editors who sent material for 1991.

(Please note: It's difficult to cover all nongenre sources of short horror, so should readers see a story or poem from such a source, I'd appreciate their bringing it to my attention. Drop me a line c/o *Omni* Magazine, 1965 Broadway, New York, NY 10023.)

I'd like to acknowledge Charles N. Brown's *Locus* magazine (Locus Publications, P.O. Box 13305, Oakland, CA 94661; $48.00 for a one-year, first-class subscription [12 issues], $35.00 second class) as an invaluable reference source throughout the Summation; and Andrew I. Porter's *Science Fiction Chronicle* (S.F.C., P.O. Box 2730, Brooklyn, NY 11202-0056; $36.00 for a one-year, first-class subscription [12 issues], $30.00 second class), also an invaluable reference source throughout.

—Ellen Datlow

The packager would like to thank Catherine Rockwood and Ross Alvord for their help in making this book possible.

Summation 1991:
Fantasy

> "Creative imagination is more than mere invention. It is that power which creates, out of abstractions, life. It goes to the heart of the unseen, and puts that which is so mysteriously hidden from ordinary mortals into the clear light of their understanding, or at least of their partial understanding. It is more true, perhaps, of writers of fantasy than of any other writers except poets that they struggle with the inexpressible. According to their varying capacities, they are able to evoke ideas and clothe them in symbols, allegory, and dream."
>
> —Lillian H. Smith, Librarian

In this book, it has been our happy task to gather together the works of writers whose capacity to "evoke ideas and clothe them in symbols, allegory and dream" is great indeed. These works are gathered from far and wide: literary reviews and pulp magazines, mainstream fiction collections and genre anthologies, children's literature and foreign works in translation—for fantasy literature is a vast field that spills far beyond the confines of the adult fantasy genre created (as a marketing tool) by modern publishers. Fantasy fiction is as old as the first stories told and written down, as old as its mythic and folkloric bones. It is a field that is as literary as the works of its most eloquent practitioners (Spenser's *Faerie Queen*, Shakespeare's *A Midsummer Night's Dream*, William Morris's *The Defense of Guinevere*, James Thurber's *The Thirteen Clocks*) and at the same time as crassly commercial as a lurid paperback with a big-breasted woman swooning at the feet of a muscle-bound swordsman.

It is not only a preponderance of the latter kind of book that has made the entire fantasy field suspect within the contemporary literary establishment of the late twentieth century, segregating many worthy works of literature into the genre "ghetto," but also a shift in fashionable literary taste, which can be traced to Victorian times when stories with their roots in folktales and oral narratives came to be associated with the lower-class and unlettered segments of society. During the Victorian era fantasy was banished to the nursery and the field of children's literature was born—but it has never been content to stay there. Instead it popped up in "children's books" read avidly by adults (Tolkien's *The Lord of the Rings*, White's *The Once and Future King*), in mainstream novels (Atwood's *The Handmaid's Tale*, Helprin's *A Winter's Tale*); in the popular Magic Realism of Latin-American writers (Marquez's *One Hundred Years of Solitude*, Allende's *Eva Luna*); in the popularity of works by folklorist Joseph Campbell and poet Robert Bly.

In the 1990s, fantasy literature remains a viable, indeed popular, art form—against the bleak backdrop of a publishing industry in decline, a massive American illiteracy rate, and a culture where school-age children spend a staggering average of four hours a day watching television. Newspaper columnist Ellen Goodman recently discussed the differences between "the generation that reads and writes" and "the generation that watches and rewinds. . . . Those of us who are print people—writers and readers—are losing ground to the visual people—producers and viewers. The younger generation gets more of its information and 'infotainment' from television and movies. Less information. More infotainment. The franchise over reality is passing hands."

While genre fiction, even at the best-seller level, does not have nearly the impact or reach of the average movie or television program, it nonetheless plays a vital role in keeping fiction and the love of reading alive in our present culture—particularly among younger readers. This is a responsibility we cannot easily ignore. *The franchise over reality is passing hands.* . . . Fantasy, a literature that goes beyond reality into the imagination—the surreal lands of myth and dream—is nonetheless at its best a literature that tells us much about the real world, and the hearts of the men and women who live in it. "Fantasy," Ursula Le Guin has said, "is a journey. It is a journey into the subconscious mind, just as psychoanalysis is. Like psychoanalysis, it can be dangerous, and it will change you."

The fantasy story, like the mythic stories championed by Joseph Campbell, works with symbols and metaphors that relate directly to modern life, speaking directly and unflinchingly of the hero's quests, the Trickster's tasks and the dark woods we each summon the courage to enter as we take the long journey from birth to death. In a time when the prevalent media fare has become increasingly formulaic, simplistic, jumping with MTV-and-advertising-style editing from image to image to image, it is all the more important for a popular literature to exist that explores the deeper complexities of the human heart, traveling more leisurely through the shadow realms of the soul. Campbell has said the artist is the myth-maker of the modern age. In a field where myth directly infuses modern story, this is a role a fantasy writer must pay attention to—even when, perhaps especially when—the writer's stated goal is to entertain.

One of the most interesting aspects of the fantasy literature written in this country and in this decade is that much of it comes from a large group of writers who know of each other and each other's works. Mass-market book distribution and evolving telecommunications have made this possible, as have computer networks devoted to the discussion of the field, small-press review magazines, academic conferences (like the annual International Conference on the Fantastic, in Florida), and conventions (like the annual Fourth Street Fantasy Convention, in Minneapolis) where writers, artists, publishers, and readers mingle and share their thoughts. In my capacity as an editor working with writers and illustrators across this country and in England, I am struck again and again by the passion and commitment with which these artists approach their craft. When you walk into a bookstore and find the Fantasy section where the works of these writers are segregated away from other works of fiction, the bright colors of look-alike titles and cynically commercial series jump out from the shelves (and the best-sellers lists). But if you look further, and ignore the often-lurid publishing package (over which the author, and indeed the illustrator, have little control), you will find that a fascinating contemporary fantasy literature is being formed (including a distinctively American brand), author by author, story by story, book by book.

Most recently the field has incorporated ideas explored by the Latin-American Magic Realist writers, bringing myth and folkloric motifs into modern and urban settings. At the other end of the spectrum from Urban Fantasy, the Imaginary World brand of fantasy created most memorably by Tolkien, Lewis and Eddison and then by poetic writers like Le Guin, McKillip, Beagle, Cooper, Walton and others in the seventies and early eighties, seemed to grind down to a predictable, derivative formula in the late eighties. This sparked many lively discussions among writers about what exactly makes a superlative fantasy book. Ellen Kushner, a talented prose stylist, has spoken eloquently to decry the kind of derivative works in which a young writer merely mimics his or her favorite author. "We have books based on Tolkien," says Kushner, "and then books based on those books, and then on *those* books . . . like Xerox copies of a Xerox copy, getting increasingly muddy and fuzzy until the original spark is completely gone."

The best fantasy, Kushner and others have stated, must come from the writer's own heart, life and experience. (This is a measure that applies, I believe, to books meant as pure entertainment as well as to ones written with serious literary intent.) "A writer," Cynthia Ozick has written "is dreamed and transfigured into being by spells, wishes, goldfish, silhouettes of trees, boxes of fairy tales dropped in the mud, uncles' and cousins' books, tablets and capsules and powders . . . and then one day you find yourself leaning here, writing on that round glass table salvaged from the Park View Pharmacy—writing this, an impossibility, a summary of who you came to be, where you are now, and where, God knows, is that?" Fantasy, more than other forms of literature, cannot depend on novelty of plot to give it originality, based as it is on the mythic tradition of familiar tales served up anew. The themes that underlie the stories are ancient and familiar ones; what the best writers must bring to these themes to make them fresh, to make them sing again in the reader's imagination, is their own unique voice and point of view.

Anaïs Nin once said (if you'll bear with me for one more quote): "I believe one writes because one has to create a world in which to live." Fantasy is a potent way to reimage the world around us, re-envision its wonders and take us away from it so that we can return and see it anew. What new world shall we create in the future—not only in our books and our genre but, by extension, in our lives, and for the lives of the generation to come? This is a question all fantasy writers address (either consciously or unconsciously); as all writers; and all artists; and all of us who participate in the collective act of the arts as readers, viewers and audience. I hope we can keep this question in mind as we write books, publish books or support those books by our critical selection of one book over another when they sit before us on the bookstore shelves.

Although the corporate publishing industry continues to groan under declining store rack space and sales, the smaller, innovative presses are thriving—which brings me to start the roundup of the year with works I'd recommend tracking down from the smaller companies. Chronicle Books of San Francisco published a gorgeous, fantastical book mixing art and story called *Griffin and Sabine: An Extraordinary Correspondence* by Nick Bantock. This imaginative book follows the developing relationship between a postcard artist and a mysterious island woman through illuminated correspondence. Chronicle not only managed to do a beautiful production job at a reasonable retail price, but were also able to get the book placed on national best-sellers lists, which is quite a feat given distribution networks that still greatly favor the large publishing companies.

Mercury House, also in San Francisco, published the first American edition of *The Start of the End of it All*, collecting Carol Emshwiller's brilliantly quirky short fiction. Mark V. Zeising (Shingletown, CA) published *The Hereafter Gang* by Neal Barrett Jr., a Magic Realist story set in the Texas Panhandle, which I recommend highly. Morrigan published *The Magic Spectacles* by James P. Blaylock, with illustrations by Ferret—a wonderful magical coming-of-age tale. Pulphouse (Eugene, OR) published a Special Winter Holiday issue of *The Hardback Magazine* with good stories by Charles de Lint, Lisa Goldstein, and Kara Dalkey; and their Axolotl Press line published a new "Newford" novella by Charles de Lint, *Our Lady of the Harbour*. Triskell Press (Ottawa) published a lovely chapbook of de Lint's poetry titled *Desert Moments*. Crossing Press (Freedom, CA) published an anthology of original Magic Realist stories by women writers, titled *Dreams in a Minor Key*, edited by Susanna J. Sturgis. Pyx Press (Orem, UT) publishes a small magazine, *Magic Realism*, issued seasonally and edited by C. Daren Butler and Julie Thomas; issue #4 in the fall of 1991 interspersed new stories and poetry with old Celtic fairy tales. Street of Crocodiles (Seattle) published an odd but intriguing collection of Jessica Amanda Salmonson's stories, *Mystic Women: Their Ancient Tales and Legends*. Owlswick Press (Philadelphia) published Avram Davidson's peculiar and wonderful *Adventures of Doctor Eszterhazy*, as well as Keith Roberts's collected *Anita* stories. Johns Hopkins University Press finally (bless them) brought Thomas M. Disch and Charles Naylor's *Neighboring Lives* back into print—a splendid historical novel set in nineteenth-century Chelsea, highly recommended. Donald M. Grant (RI) published a new Peter Straub novella, *Mrs. God*, with beautiful sepia-washed paintings by Rich Berry. Nazraeli Press (published in Germany but distributed in the U.S.) released *Afternoon Nap*, a small, surrealistic book of paintings and text by Fritz Scholder. I highly recommend *Fables* by poet Michael Hannon, previously published by Turkey Press (CA) but unseen until this year. Leonard Baskin's Gehenna Press (MA) published an exquisite hand-printed and hand-bound book by Baskin on the history of the Grotesque. Finally, Edgewood Press (MA) published *The Best of the Rest 1990: The Best SF and Fantasy from the Small Press*, well edited by Steve Pasechnick and Brian Youmans.

As for the larger publishing houses: In last year's volume of this anthology series I noted the dearth of excellent Imaginary World fantasy, and thus we reprinted primarily works of Urban Fantasy and Magic Realism instead. This year, I am happy to report, there is a resurgence of good Imaginary World fantasy in both short fiction and novel form, while the more contemporary forms of fantasy continue to make a strong showing. There were quite a number of good fantasy novels published in 1991. The following is a short list of works you should not miss, showing the diversity of styles and approaches that exists within the current fantasy field (in alphabetical order):

Hunting the Ghost Dancer by A. A. Attanasio (HarperCollins). An evocative, literary fairy tale, set in the prehistoric past.

The Last Voyage of Somebody the Sailor by John Barth (Knopf). A delightful, literary mainstream fantasy about a modern man who finds his way into the world of Sinbad and the Arabian Nights.

The Paper Grail by James P. Blaylock (Ace). Equally delightful, equally literary, this novel by one of the field's best writers involves ancient legendary and strange conspiracies, set in Southern California.

Witch Baby by Francesca Lia Block (HarperCollins). By the author of the wonderful young adult (YA) fantasy *Weetzie Bat*, another fantasy tale set in a punk, surrealist vision of Los Angeles.

The End-of-Everything Man by Tom De Haven (Doubleday). It looks like generic fantasy, but don't be put off. It's much, much more, and will rekindle your sense of wonder.

Murther and Walking Spirits by Robertson Davies (Viking). A mainstream novel from this superlative writer, with distinct fantasy elements. The book is narrated by a character killed off on page 1.

Tam Lin by Pamela Dean (Tor). The Scottish fairy tale and folk ballad "Tam Lin" is recast among the theater majors of a midwestern college campus. A memorable contemporary retelling of the tale by a talented new voice in the field.

The Little Country by Charles de Lint (Morrow). Set in Cornwall among musicians, writers and Cornish villagers, de Lint again weaves modern magic, bringing myth into the contemporary world.

The Architecture of Desire by Mary Gentle (Bantam UK). Complex, dark fantasy set in a skewed version of Cromwell's England. At this rate, Gentle may become the modern successor to Mervyn Peake.

Sherwood by Parke Godwin (Morrow). A thoroughly entertaining historical novel with slight fantasy elements, based on the classic Robin Hood legends—the best of the Robin Hood material to appear in the wake of the recent movies (and far better than either film).

Eight Skilled Gentlemen by Barry Hughart (Doubleday). I've long been a fan of Hughart's Chinese picaresque fantasies—and this is his best so far.

Cloven Hooves by Megan Lindholm (Doubleday). Lindholm is a writer who has not yet received the attention she deserves for her serious, thoughtful and thoroughly adult fantasy works. This novel about a woman's relationship to Pan is set in the author's own native Alaska and Washington State.

Dangerous Spaces by Margaret Mahy (Viking). Mahy is a New Zealand writer of some of the very best young adult fantasy to be published in the last two decades. This moody ghost story shows Mahy at top form.

The Sorceress and the Cygnet by Patricia A. McKillip (Ace). McKillip tops the list of writers working in the Imaginary World area of fantasy fiction. The novel is part fairy tale, part Magic Realism, and pure poetry.

Beauty by Sheri S. Tepper (Doubleday). This dark and intriguing novel falls between the realms of fantasy and science fiction, but working as it does with the themes of fairy tales, I'll include it here—and recommend it highly. Readers with a taste for Angela Carter's fiction should give this one a try.

Death Qualified by Kate Wilhelm (St. Martin's). Wilhelm is a writer who has quietly given the field some of its very best works. This book was published in the St. Martin's mainstream list: a fascinating and thought-provoking courtroom drama involving chaos theory.

In addition to the foregoing books, lovers of good adventure fantasy written with wit and intelligence should be sure not to miss Steven Brust's *The Phoenix Guards* from Tor Books (a fantasy homage to Dumas and Sabatini) or Michael Moorcock's *The Revenge of the Rose* from Ace and Grafton (which Faren Miller aptly described as "sword-and-sorcery à la Dickens with a tip of the hat to Brueghel"). Lovers of fantasy with a humorous bite should check out Terry Pratchett's *Witches Abroad* from Gollancz, or indeed any title by this British author; and Patricia C. Wrede's charming *Dealing with Dragons* from Jane Yolen Books/HBJ.

Sarah Canary by Karen Joy Fowler (Holt), a Magic Realist novel set in the Washington Territory in 1873, has my vote for best first novel of the year. Runners up are: *Gojiro* by Mark Jacobson (Atlantic Monthly), a bizarre and moving fantasy about a boy and a giant mutant lizard. *Moonwise* by Greer Ilene Gilman (Roc) won't be to everyone's taste, but there are passages of prose that read like the finest of poetry. Other notable debuts: *The Illusionists* by Faren Miller (Warner), *The White Mists of Power* by Kristine Kathryn Rusch (Roc), and *The Spiral Dance* by R. Garcia y Robertson (Morrow).

The "Best Peculiar Book" distinction goes to the aforementioned *Griffin and Sabine* by Nick Bantock (Chronicle). The runner-up is *Spring-Heeled Jack* by Phillip Pullman (Knopf), an imaginative YA superhero fantasy mixing prose and cartoons (illustrations by Gary Hovland) based on the nineteenth-century character of the title.

Other 1991 titles particularly recommended, listed by publisher:

From Ace: *Phoenix* by Steven Brust (fifth in the Vlad Taltos series, not to be confused with the aforementioned *Phoenix Guards*).

From Atheneum: *Sing for a Gentle Rain* by James J. Alison (YA time travel about an Indian boy drawn back to the 13th-century Anasazi).

The Black Unicorn by Tanith Lee (excellent YA fantasy in an Arabian Nights–like desert setting).

The House on Parchment Street by Patricia A. McKillip (a reissue of this lovely YA ghost story).

From Avon: *Tours of the Black Clock* by Steve Erickson (reprint of this 1989 surrealistic novel).

Flute Song Magic by Andrea Shettle (a lovely YA fantasy novel, winner of the Flare Books competition for authors between 13 and 18 years of age).

The Dream Compass by Jeff Bredenberg (a quirky but literary and promising first novel, halfway between fantasy and SF).

Lavondyss by Robert Holdstock (the American reprint of this amazing British novel).

Soulsmith by Tom Dietz (an enjoyable coming-of-age novel set in Georgia).

From Baen: *Lion's Heart* by Karen Wehrstein (standard genre fare but this young writer has a mystical, poetic flair.)

Flameweaver by Margaret Ball (a sparkling historical, a cut above the rest).

From Ballantine: *Shaman* by Robert Shea (historical Native American fantasy).

The Collapsing Castle by Haydyn Middleton (first American edition of a Celtic fantasy set in a small English village).

From Bantam: *King of Morning, Queen of Day,* by Ian McDonald (the first two-thirds of this Irish fantasy are excellent and highly recommended).

Great Work of Time by John Crowley (a mass-market publication of this splendid World Fantasy Award–winning novella).

Illusion by Paula Volsky (meatier fare than her previous books; recommended).

From Bantam Skylark: *The Golden Swan* by Marianna Mayer (rewritten Hindu fairy tale with illustrations by Robert Sauber).

Noble-Hearted Kate by Marianna Mayer (rewritten Celtic fairy tale with illustrations by the wonderful Winslow Pels).

From Del Rey: *Perilous Seas* by Dave Duncan (standard fantasy fare, but it takes unexpected turns—and Duncan is always a fine writer).

Yvgenie by C. J. Cherryh (the third book in her series based on Russian history and legend).

From Dell: *The Worm Ouroboros* by E. R. Eddison, with a foreword by Douglas E. Winter, a long critical introduction by Paul Edmund Thomas and a glossary of terms (originally published by Cape in 1922, this is one of the finest fantasy novels of all time. A must read, particularly for those who love the sound of language used well).

From Delacorte: *Song of the Gargoyle* by Zilpha Keatly Snyder (medieval historical novel by an extremely talented writer of YA fantasy).

From Doubleday Foundation: *The Dagger and the Cross* by Judith Tarr (well-written twelfth-century historical fantasy).

Nothing Sacred by Elizabeth Ann Scarborough (futuristic fantasy about a POW nurse in Tibet).

From Harper & Row: *The Dragon's Boy* by Jane Yolen (moving YA Arthurian fantasy).

Dragon Cauldron by Laurence Yep (YA fantasy adventure from this talented author).

From HarperCollins: *Quiver River* by David Carkeet (a terrific coming-of-age story with subtle magic about a vanished Indian tribe, highly recommended).

From Harcourt Brace Jovanovich: *Many Moons* by James Thurber (a reprint of the fairy tale with the 1943 Caldecott Award–winning illustrations by Louis Slobodkin).

Wizard's Hall by Jane Yolen (humorous fantasy for children).

From Holt: *Bronze Mirror* by Jeanette Larsen (uses the history and myths of China to talk about the nature of artistic creation; highly recommended).

Three Times Table by Sara Maitland (good literary fantasy).

From Houghton Mifflin: *Enter Three Witches* by Kate Gilmore (entertaining fantasy about a young New York boy raised by witches).

From Knopf: *The Dust Roads of Monferatto* by Rosetta Loy (a Magic Realist family saga, translated from the Italian).

The Witching Hour by Anne Rice (technically this is horror, but this superb dark fantasy about a family of witches over the centuries is likely to appeal to fantasy readers as well).

Among the Dolls by William Sleator (a reprint of this novella with illustrations by Trina Schart Hyman).

From Macdonald: *Outside the Dog Museum* by Jonathan Carroll (another clever tale, not entirely successful, about the modern shaman Venasque).

From Macmillan Collier: *The Satanic Mill* by Otfried Preussler (a reissue of this excellent fantasy about a young apprentice's experience with evil, translated from the German by Anthea Bell—highly recommended).

Witch House by Evangeline Walton (another reissue, from one of the fantasy field's most beloved writers).

From Methuen: *The Drowners* by Garry Kilworth (a YA ghost story set in nineteenth-century Hampshire by one of England's finest writers).

Black Maria by Diana Wynne Jones (YA fantasy about a witch in an English seaside town, by another of England's finest).

From Morrow: *Chase the Morning* by Michael Scott Rohan (an intriguing fantasy novel set in a quayside bar).

Castle in the Air by Diana Wynne Jones (first American edition of this sequel to *Howl's Moving Castle*).

King of the Dead by R. A. MacAvoy (the second book in her *Lens of the World* trilogy—read it for the prose. Highly recommended).

From Orbit: *Flying Dutch* by Tom Holt (literary fantasy, highly recommended).

From Penguin: *Grimus* by Salman Rushdie (a reprint of this literary fantasy novel by the author of *The Satanic Verses*).

From Pocket: *Witch Hunt* by Devin O'Branagan (an interesting generational saga following a family of witches through three centuries).

From Random House: *Peter Doyle* by John Vernon (a literary alternate history novel about the [nonexistant] relationship between Emily Dickinson and Walt Whitman, and the search for Napolean's penis . . . highly recommended!)

The Annotated Alice by Lewis Carroll (a revised edition, including "The Wasp in the Wig," which was cut from the original publication).

From Roc: *Rats and Gargoyles* by Mary Gentle (first American edition of this splendid dark fantasy).

From Scholastic: *The Promise* by Robert Westall (first American edition of this YA ghost story).

From Simon and Schuster: *The Almanac of the Dead* by Leslie Marmon Silko (a modern Southwestern saga incorporating Native American myths, highly recommended).

The Half Child by Kathleen Herson (historical fantasy about a changeling, set in the seventeenth century).

From Tor: *Mojo and the Pickle Jar* by Douglas Bell (charming Southwestern fantasy novel).

Sadar's Keep by Midori Snyder (second book in an Imaginary World trilogy that is a distinct cut above most in the genre, with terrific character studies).

Mairelon the Magician by Patricia Wrede (charming, witty fantasy set in a magical Regency England).

Street Magic by Michael Reaves (entertaining, thoughtful Urban Fantasy set in L.A.).

From Villard: *Who P-P-Plugged Roger Rabbit?* by Gary K. Wolf (sequel to the fantasy-detective novel *Who Censored Roger Rabbit?*).

From Vintage: *Sexing the Cherry* by Jeanette Winterson (first American edition of this Magic Realist story of a young man's coming-of-age, by a young British writer).

From World's Classics, UK: *Peter Pan in Kensington Gardens* and *Peter and Wendy* by J. M. Barrie, edited and with an introduction by Peter Hollindale (a new combined edition of Barrie's droll, classic tales, with the Arthur Rackham cover).

Nineteen ninety-one saw the publication of excellent work in the area of short fantasy fiction, both within the genre and without. It seems that in fantasy fiction, unlike (alas) mainstream fiction, the short story form is alive and well and commercially supported by the readership. Ellen Datlow and I read a wide variety of material over the course of 1991 to choose the stories for this volume, ranging from genre magazines and anthologies to fanzines, small-press and university reviews and foreign works in translation. The stories selected for the fantasy half of this volume were chosen from: the magazines *Omni*, *Isaac Asimov's Science Fiction Magazine*, *The Magazine of Fantasy & Science Fiction*, *Ellery Queen's Mystery Magazine*, *Weird Tales*, *Pulphouse* and *The New Yorker*; the literary reviews *Grand Street* and *Winter's Tales*; single-author collections published by St. Martin's, Arcade, Random House and Mercury House; an Axolotl Press limited edition; the children's books *Vampires* and *Pish, Posh, Said Hieronymus Bosch*; the anthologies *Full Spectrum 3*, *Catfantastic II*, *A Whisper of Blood*, *Once Upon a Time, The Fantastic Adventures of Robin Hood* and *Colors of a New Day: Writings for South Africa* and translations of foreign works first published in Spanish (from the University of Nebraska Press), French (from Grand Street), Russian (from Abbeville Press), and Japanese (from Kodansha International).

In addition to the stories selected for this volume, the following is a baker's dozen of story collections that are particularly recommended to lovers of good short fiction (alphabetically, by publisher):

From Academy Chicago: *Visions and Imaginings: Classic Fantasy Fiction* edited by Robert H. Boyer and Kenneth J. Zahorski (from the distinguished team of editors who have brought us some of the finest reprint anthologies in the fantasy field).

From Atlantic Monthly: *The Literary Ghost: Great Contemporary Ghost Stories* edited by Larry Dark (a splendid, fat, highly recommended collection of twenty-eight ghostly tales by writers such as John Gardner, Paul Bowles, Muriel Spark, Penelope Lively, Joyce Carol Oates, A. S. Byatt, Fay Weldon, Anne Sexton and Steven Millhauser).

From Dedalus UK: *The Dedalus Book of British Fantasy: The 19th Century* edited by Brian M. Stableford (entries by William Morris, George MacDonald, Disraeli, Edward Lear, Lewis Carroll, Oscar Wilde, Tennyson, Keats, Christina Rossetti and more. Stableford has done a wonderful job; this should be on every fantasy reader's shelf).

Tales of the Wandering Jew edited by Brian M. Stableford (nine reprinted and eleven original stories, plus two poems by Stableford—with particularly good contributions by Steve Rasnic Tem and Ian McDonald).

From Delacorte: *The Door in the Air and Other Stories* by Margaret Mahy (nine stories from this amazing New Zealand writer, with illustrations by Diana Catchpole. Originally published by Dent in 1988, this is its first American edition).

From Dutton: *A Hammock Beneath the Mangoes* edited by Thomas Colchie (an anthology of superlative Latin American stories by Cortázar, Fuentes, Allende, Amada, Márquez and the like. Quite a treat).

From Grafton: *The Bone Forest* by Robert Holdstock (contains one novella set in the same patch of primal English woodland as his World Fantasy Award–winning novel *Mythago Wood*, plus seven other stories).

From Kodansha International: *Beyond the Curve* by Kobo Abe (a collection of excellent, strange Japanese stories in translation, many of them with an existentialist SF and fantasy bent).

From Pantheon: *Shape-Shifter* by Pauline Melville (a collection of twelve literary fantasy stories, reprinted from the 1990 Women's Press edition which won the Manchester Guardian Prize).

From Rutgers University Press: *Green Cane Juicy Flotsam* (stories by Caribbean woman writers, several of them Magic Realist in style).

From St. Martin's Press: *More Shapes Than One* by Fred Chappell (reprint stories and two originals by this unique and gifted Southern writer).

Fires of the Past edited by Anne Devereaux Jordan (thirteen lovely original contemporary fantasy stories about hometowns).

Other notable collections in 1991:

Author's Choice Monthly #22: Hedgework and Guessery by Charles de Lint (magical stories and poems, from Pulphouse); *The Book of the Damned* by Tanith Lee (three wonderful novellas, from The Overlook Press; *The Gilda Stories* by Jewelle Gomez (a cycle of stories about a black lesbian vampire collected from various gay publications, from Firebrand Books); *Vampires* edited by Jane Yolen and Martin H. Greenberg (original YA fiction by a range of up-and-coming writers, from HarperCollins); *Horse Fantastic* and *Catfantastic II* edited by Martin H. Greenberg (enjoyable theme anthologies with original fiction, from Daw); *The Walker Book of Ghost Stories* edited by Susan Hill and illustrated by Angela Barrett (seventeen YA ghost stories, including some originals, from Walker UK); *Great Tales of Jewish Occult and Fantasy: The Dybbuk and 30 Other Classic Stories*, edited by Joachim Neugroshel (a reprint, from Wings); and *Monkey Brain Sushi: New Tastes in Japanese Fiction* edited by Alfred Birnbaum (contains Haruki Murakami, Eri Makino and more, from Kodansha).

A selection of recommended works of nonfiction published in 1991:

All My Roads Before Me: The Diary of C. S. Lewis 1922–1927 edited by Walter Hooper (HBJ).

Wandering Ghost: The Odyssey of Lafcadio Hearn by Jonathan Cott (a biography of the man who brought Japanese literature and legendry to the western world, by Jonathan Cott—whose books are always a treat. Knopf).

Gilbert: The Man Who Was G. K. Chesterton by Michael Coren (Paragon House).

The Design of William Morris' The Earthly Paradise by Florence Saunders Boos (a detailed examination of Morris's epic poem, from The Edwin Mellen Press).

The Magical World of the Inklings by Gareth Knight (a biography of four members of the Inklings: Tolkien, Lewis, Williams and Owen Barfield, from Element, U.K.).

The Land of Narnia by Brian Sibley (a guide to the Narnia series for YA readers, from Harper and Row).

Chicago Days/Hoboken Nights by Daniel M. Pinkwater (a delightful memoir, from Addison-Wesley).

Don't Tell the Grownups by Alison Lurie (a reprint edition of Lurie's collected essays on children's fiction, fantasy and fairy tales, from Avon).

Recommended new works on myth, legend and fairy tales:

The Old Wives' Fairy Tale Book selected and retold by Angela Carter (the last collection put together before Carter's sudden death earlier this year; highly recommended; published by Pantheon. Carter was both a splendid writer and a folklore enthusiast—the fantasy field will sorely miss her).

Spells of Enchantment edited by Jack Zipes (a beautiful, fat collection of fairy tales—complete with a Warwick Goble cover—by one of the major scholars in the field; highly recommended. The volume is published by Viking, and is an excellent source book).

Arabian Nights: The Marvels and Wonders of the Thousand and One Nights, adaptation by Jack Zipes (from the classic Sir Richard Burton translation, published by Penguin).

The Book of Dede Korkut (an edition of the 10th Century Turkish magical epic, from the University of Texas, Austin).

Folktales from India edited by A. K. Ramanujan (the latest edition in the wonderful Pantheon Fairy Tale and Folklore Library, Pantheon/Random House).

Primal Myths: Creation Myths from Around the World by Barbara C. Sproul (from HarperCollins).

Myths of the Dog-Man by David Gordon White (from the University of Chicago Press).

Here All Dwell Free: Stories of the Wounded Feminine by Gertrude Mueller Nelson (a psychological investigation of fairy tale themes in a beautifully designed edition, from Doubleday).

Robin Hood by J. C. Holt (the history of the legend in a revised and expanded edition from Thames and Hudson).

Arthur the King by Graeme Fife (a nicely designed edition tracing the development of Arthurian literature, from Sterling Publishers, NY).

The Encyclopedia of Arthurian Legends by Ronan Coghlan (available from Element, Rockport, MA).

Books by John Matthews, available this year from Aquarian Press/HarperCollins:

An Arthurian Reader (with a lovely Burne-Jones cover).

A Celtic Reader: Selections from Celtic Legends, Scholarship and Story (with a lovely John Duncan cover).

The Song of Taliesin: Stories and Poems from the Books of Broceliande (paperback edition).

Children's picture books are a source of magical fantasy tales as well as of the very best enchanted artwork created today. Harcourt Brace Jovanovich in particular had a plethora of beautiful books this year. Particularly recommended in 1991:

Wings, the story of Icarus retold by Jane Yolen, with gorgeous paintings by Dennis Nolan (HBJ).

The All Jahdu Storybook, fifteen Trickster tales by Newbery winner Virginia Hamilton, with masterful illustrations by Barry Moser (HBJ).

Pish, Posh, Said Hieronymus Bosch by Nancy Willard with exquisitely detailed paintings by Leo and Diane Dillon in the spirit of Bosch himself (HBJ).

Stories for Children by Oscar Wilde. Even if you already own Wilde's fairy tales, take a look at this one for the splendid illustrations by P. J. Lynch (Macmillan).

The Happy Prince and Other Stories by Oscar Wilde. This is a facsimile of the 1913 edition—with the Charles Robinson illustrations—of Wilde's wonderful literary fairy tales. The volume is part of Peter Glassman's beautiful Books of Wonder Series (Morrow).

The Three Princesses: Cinderella, Sleeping Beauty and Snow White. Cooper Edens has interspersed the text with illustrations from over fifty classic editions (by artists like Rackham, Dulac, Dore, Crane and Goble). This doesn't make for a satisfying read or a satisfying book for children, but it is a lovely collection for adult art lovers. (Published by Bantam, it is a compilation of Eden's former Green Tiger Press editions, beautifully designed.)

Jim Henson's The Story-teller is a fine collection of nine fairy tales based on the late Henson's Emmy-winning television series. The stories are retold by Anthony Minghella and beautifully illustrated by Darcy May. It is a lovely tribute to a creative man greatly missed in our field (Knopf).

Another source for interesting artwork is the area of adult comics and graphic novels. The following are several collections I'd recommend for fantasy readers and fine-art lovers new to the adult comics field:

Hawk and Wolverine, text by Walter Simonson and Louise Simonson, art by Kent Williams and the stunning painter Jon J. Muth (Epic).

Black Orchid, text by World Fantasy Award–winner Neil Gaiman and art by World Fantasy Award–winner Dave McKean (DC).

The Sandman Collections, text by Neil Gaiman, art by Sam Keith, Mike Dringenberg, Kelly Jones, Charles Vess, Colleen Doran, Malcolm Jones III (DC).

V for Vendetta, Alan Moore and David Lloyd (DC).

The Love and Rockets Collections, Los Bros. Hernandez (Fantagraphics).

Other art works of interest published in 1991:

The Lord of the Rings, illustrated by Alan Lee. This is a lavish anniversary edition with fifty new paintings by one of the finest watercolorists living today. The publisher's production job washes out some of the beauty of the stunning original paintings, but this is still an edition to be treasured for a lifetime (Unwin Hyman, U.K./Houghton Mifflin, U.S.).

The Telling Line: Essays on Fifteen Contemporary Illustrators by Douglas Martin, discussing children's book illustrators including Michael Foreman and the late Charles Keeping (Delacorte).

The Art of the Fantastic: Latin America 1920–1987, a beautiful, thorough collection, text by Holliday T. Day and Hollister Sturges (Indianapolis Museum of Art).

Leonora Carrington: The Mexico Years (1943–1895), my personal favorite of the year's art books, a slim but lovely edition of the enchanted, fantastical paintings by a woman whose works are too little known (The Mexico Museum in San Francisco, distributed by the University of New Mexico Press).

Anxious Visions: Surrealist Art, lavishly illustrated, with excellent text by Sidea Stitch (Abbeville Press).

The Symbolist Generation: 1870–1910, a fine overview of this era with Rizzoli's usual high quality of art reproduction; text by Pierre-Louis Mathieu (Rizzoli).

Holly Roberts, a collection of the vibrant, mystical works of this contemporary artist who combines oil paint and silverprint photographs. The book is beautifully produced, but it does not quite capture the luminous quality of the work itself. (The Friends of Photography Press, The Ansel Adams Center, San Francisco).

The Aeneid of Virgil, a new translation by Edward McCrorie and art by Luis Ferreira (Donald M. Grant).

The Arthurian Book of Days, an art book with more than seventy medieval illustrations, text by John and Caitlin Matthews (Macmillan).

Berni Wrightson: A Look Back, an interesting, thorough collection of this American artist's work (reprinted by Underwood-Miller from a 1979 edition).

Necronomicon by H. R. Giger, a reprint of the original lavish edition of bizarre paintings by this European artist, with an introduction by horror writer Clive Barker (Morpheus International).

The Rodney Mathews Portfolio, *The Bruce Pennington Portfolio*, *Mark Harrison's Dreamlands*, and *The Chris Foss Portfolio*: these are nicely produced collections of art by British book and record album illustrators, primarily science fiction–related but possibly of interest to fantasy enthusiasts too (Paper Tiger).

Fantasy cover art that stood out from the rest on the shelves in 1991:

Dave McKean's modernistic montage for *Outside the Dog Museum* (by Jonathan Carroll/Macdonald UK). Leo and Diane Dillon's distinctive and decorative work for *Juniper* (by Monica Furlong/Knopf). Trina Schart Hyman for charming work on *Wizard's Hall* (by Jane Yolen/HBJ). Jody Lee's sumptuous, well-designed work for *The Winds of Fate* (by Mercedes Lackey/DAW). Heather Cooper's rich painting for *The Black Unicorn* (by Tanith Lee/Atheneum) and John Collier's for *The Sleep of Stone* (by Louise Cooper/Atheneum)—both part of Byron Preiss' beautifully packaged Dragonflight series. Bruce Jensen for the design of *The Ultimate Werewolf*, *The Ultimate Dracula* and *The Ultimate Frankenstein* (Dell)—another Byron Preiss package. Robert Gould's stunning new Elric painting and design work on *Revenge of the Rose* (by Michael Moorcock/Grafton and Ace). Dennis Nolan's elegant portraiture and design for *Sadar's Keep* (by Midori Snyder/Tor). Thomas Canty's painting and gorgeous design work on *A Whisper of Blood* (by Ellen Datlow/Morrow). Arnie Fenner's distinctive design work for Mark V. Ziesing Books. Michael Whelan's evocative painting for *The Summer Queen* (by Joan D. Vinge/Warner). Rick Berry's painterly portraiture for *Phoenix Guards* (by Steven Brust/Tor). Gerry Grace's lovely painting for *Strands of Starlight* (by Gael Baudino/Orbit UK). Raquel Jarmillo's pre-Raphaelite–influenced jacket painting for *Sarah Canary* (by Karen Joy Fowler/Holt). And Mel Odom's shimmering *Tigana* (by Guy Gavriel Kay/Roc). We are indebted to these and many other cover illustrators for laboring within commercial publishing constraints to bring artistic vision into the fantasy field.

British artist and moviemaker Brian Froud brought splendid new works-in-progress to the Tucson World Fantasy Convention (making a rare convention appearance to support his *Faerieland* series for Bantam Books) which confirmed his place as one of the finest painters of magical works of our time. Charles Vess, David Cherry, Dawn Wilson, Don Maitz, Janny Wurts and Artist Guest of Honor Arlin Robins were among the other artists on hand for that event. Janny Wurts won Best of Show in the convention exhibition; Dave McKean won the World Fantasy Award for Best Artist of 1990; and Charles Vess shared the World Fantasy Award for Best Short Story in 1990 with Neil Gaiman for their comic book *A Midsummer Night's Dream*.

Traditional folk music is of special interest to many fantasy readers because the old ballads, particularly in the English, Irish and Scots folk traditions, are often based on the same folk and fairy tale roots as fantasy fiction. And the current generation of worldbeat musicians, like contemporary fantasy writers, are taking ancient, traditional rhythms and themes and adapting them to a modern age. (New listeners might try *Flight of the Green Linnet: Celtic Music, the Next Generation* as an introduction to the music. Or, if you prefer music with a rock or punk edge to it, I'd suggest starting off with a worldbeat band like Boiled in Lead.)

Ireland's De Dannan has released *1/2 Set in Harlem*, mixing traditional Irish tunes with Klezmer influences and Gospel songs; De Dannan's *A Jacket of Batteries* is also finally available in America. Canada's wild instrumental band Rare Air, billed as "nouveau Celtic pop funk jazz," has released *Space Piper*—although, as always, they are truly best heard live to appreciate the magic they weave. Minneapolis band Boiled in Lead beats Rare Air for wildness, and their release *Orb* is highly recommended, containing a lively variety of ballads and world beat "rock-and-reel." Scotland's Hamish Moore and Dick Lee have released *The Bees Knees*, a mix of Highland pipes, soprano sax, Celtic and jazz influences, virtuoso musicianship and humor. Pentangle, complete with the gorgeous guitar of Bert Jansch and the haunting voice of Jackie McShee but sans founding member John Renbourn, has released *Think of Tomorrow*. Andrew Cronshaw has produced *Circle Dance*, a charity collection with terrific material from Richard Thompson, June Tabor, Fairport Convention, the late Sandy Denny, and others. Cronshaw's own latest release, *Till the Beasts' Returning*, is not so shabby either, featuring enchanted instrumental music on the electric zither, flutes and strings and with one song by June Tabor.

Milladoiro, a band dedicated to Galician music (the Celtic music of Spain) has released *Castellum Honestic*, mixing Galician melodies with the feel of medieval music and a touch of jazz. Montreal's Ad Vielle Que Pourra's new *Come What May* ranges from Breton music to medieval to cajun. Scotland's amazing Capercaillie, with Karen Matheson's haunting vocals, has released *Crosswinds*. Australia's excellent Not Drowning, Waving, mixing jazz and moody rock with Celtic and Australian Aboriginal rhythms, has released *The Little Desert* in this country. Guitarist Mazlyn Jones, from a remote area of Cornwall, has released *Mazlyn Jones*, aptly described by one reviewer as "a mystic carpet ride," drawing on images of the natural world and the fantastic. From Wales, Delyth Evan's *Music for the Celtic Harp* has no surprises but is beautiful listening; also from Wales, Clennig has released *Dwr Glan*, a mixture of old Welsh songs and dances with Breton and Galician music. *Gwerziou & Soniou* by Yann Fanch Kemener contains ten unaccompanied songs in Breton—songs of war, love, religious stories and the supernatural.

Sparky and Rhonda Rucker's *Treasures and Tears* uses music as a teaching tool to preserve Black American folklore; their traditional music is country-folk in flavor, with a touch of soul. The Gypsies are a large ensemble given to mixing Balkan instrumental music with jazz influences and a bit of Klezmer: clarinets, accordions, and gypsy violin. Great fun. Their latest release is *Gypsy Swing*. For lovers of medieval music, imagine medieval music with a punk edge and you'll have Dead Can Dance, whose latest, *Aion*, is their best so far (featuring, as it does, less of the Jim Morrison–like vocals of Brendan Perry and more of the exquisite, eerie, soaring vocals of Lisa Gerrard against a background of tenor and bass viol). Other beautiful women's vocal music, passed on to me courtesy of Charles de Lint, is performed by American singer Connie Dover, and by harpist Loreena McKennit (including lovely versions of Tennyson's *The Lady of Shalott* and Yeats's *Stolen Child*). Track down anything by either of these ladies. Another tip from de Lint is Ireland's Luka Bloom (a.k.a. Barry Moore, brother of Irish folk musician Christy Moore), whose new release, *The Accoustic Bicycle*, is a real treat and contains, God help us, Irish rap.

Music is evident in several works of fantasy fiction this year: Charles de Lint, himself a musician with the Ottawa Celtic band Jump at the Sun, weaves Celtic music into his novel *The Little Country* (Morrow) and his novella *Our Lady of the Harbour* (Axolotl). Elizabeth Ann Scarborough's novels *Phantom Banjo* and *Picking the Ballad's Bones* (Bantam) deal with folk music and the devil, set in modern folk music clubs. Worldbeat music inspired—and is laced throughout—the continuing books of the "punk fantasy" Borderlands series: *Life on the Border*, with stories by musicians de Lint, Ellen Kushner, Midori Snyder and others (Tor), and *Elsewhere*, a Borderlands novel by Will Shetterly—a very moving coming-of-age tale (Jane Yolen Books/HBJ). Writers Emma Bull and Steven Brust are members of the Minneapolis band Cats Laughing, which issued a new version of their first release, *Cats Laughing*; their second release, *Another Way to Travel*, contains a song by Bull featured in *Life on the Border*. Ellen Kushner's novel *Thomas the Rhymer*, based on the English/Scots folk ballad of that name, was released in paperback (Tor); Kushner, a radio d.j. and former folksinger, has put together a performance piece of traditional ballads and text from her novel, which debuted in Boston in 1991. She will be performing the piece in England with folksinger June Tabor this year.

The 1991 World Fantasy Convention was held in Tucson, Arizona, over the weekend of November 1–3. The Guests of Honor were Harlan and Susan Ellison, Stephen R. Donaldson and Arlin Robins. Winners of the World Fantasy Award were as follows: *Thomas the Rhymer* by Ellen Kushner and *Only Begotten Daughter* by James Morrow (tie) for Best Novel; *Bones* by Pat Murphy for Best Novella; "A Midsummer's Night Dream" by Neil Gaiman and Charles Vess for Best Short Fiction; *The Start of the End of It All and Other Stories* by Carol Emshwiller for Best Collection; *Best New Horror* edited by Stephen Jones and Ramsey Campbell for Best Anthology. Special Award/Professional went to Arnie Fenner, designer for Mark V. Ziesing Books; Special Award/Nonprofessional went to *Cemetery Dance* edited by Richard Chizmar. The Life Achievement Award was given to

Ray Russell. The judges of the 1991 awards were: Emma Bull, Orson Scott Card, Richard Laymon, Faren Miller and Darrell Schweitzer. The 1992 World Fantasy Convention will be held in October in Pine Mountain, Georgia. (For membership information, write: WFC'92, Box 148, Clarkston, GA 30021.)

The 1991 British Fantasy Awards were presented at the British Fantasy Convention in London in November. The winners were as follows: Best Novel: *Midnight Sun* by Ramsey Campbell; Best Anthology/Collection: *Best New Horror* edited by Stephen Jones and Ramsey Campbell; Best Short Fiction: "The Man Who Drew Cats" by Michael Marshall Smith; Best Artist: Les Edwards; Small Press: *Dark Dreams* edited by David Cowper Thwaite and Jeff Dempsey; Icarus Award for Best Newcomer: Michael Marshall Smith; Special Award: Dot Lumley, for services to the genre. (For membership information on the 1992 convention, write: UK Fantasy Con, 15 Stanley Road, Morden, Surry, SM4 5DE, UK.)

The 1991 Mythopoeic Awards were presented during the Mythopoeic Society's Annual Conference in San Diego in July. The award for a book-length fantasy "in the spirit of the Inklings" went to *Thomas the Rhymer* by Ellen Kushner; the Mythopoeic Scholarship Award went to *Jack: C. S. Lewis and His Times* by George Sayer. (For information on next year's convention, write: Mythcon XXIII, Box 17440, San Diego, CA 92117.)

The International Conference on the Fantastic in the Arts was held, as always, in Ft. Lauderdale, in March. The Guests of Honor were writer Gene Wolfe, artist Peter Maqua and scholar Brian Attebery. The Crawford Award for Best First Fantasy Novel was awarded at the conference to Michael Scott Rohan for *The Winter of the World* trilogy. (For information on next year's conference, write: ICFA 92, College of Humanities, Florida Atlantic University, Boca Raton, FL 33431.)

The Fourth Street Fantasy Convention was held, as always, in Minneapolis, Minnesota. The Guests of Honor were writer Diana Wynne Jones and publisher Tom Doherty. (For information on next year's convention, write: c/o David Dyer-Bennett, 4242 Minnehaha Ave. S., Minneapolis, MN 55406.)

That's a brief roundup of the year in fantasy; now to the stories themselves.

As always, the list of the very best stories of the year ran longer than we have room to print, even in a fat anthology such as this one. I'd particularly like to recommend you also seek out the following tales: "Now I Lay Me Down to Sleep" by Suzy McKee Charnas (in *A Whisper of Blood*); "Snow on Sugar Mountain" by Elizabeth Hand (in *Full Spectrum 3*); "Venus Rising on Water" by Tanith Lee (in *Isaac Asimov's*, Oct. 1991); "Lighthouse Summer" by Paul Witcover (in *Isaac Asimov's*, April 1991); "Little Miracles, Kept Promises" by Sandra Cisneros (*Woman Hollering Creek and Other Stories*); "The Better Boy" by James P. Blaylock and Tim Powers (in *Isaac Asimov's*, Feb. 1991) and "Fin de Cyclé" by Howard Waldrop (in his story collection *Night of the Cooters*.

I hope you will enjoy the tales that follow as much as I did. Many thanks to all of the authors who allowed us to collect them here.

—Terri Windling

Summation 1991:
Horror

More than any specific event in 1991, the continuing recession proved to have the most impact on publishing. In what has long been held to be a recession-proof industry, the effects were finally being felt both in magazines and books. Despite this, the American SF, fantasy, and horror book publishers seemed to hold their own, with remarkably few changes; this was not so for the nongenre publishers.

A year after the takeover of MCA (including Putnam, Berkley and Ace books) by the Japanese electronics conglomerate Matsushita there have been no perceptible editorial effects.

Harcourt Brace Jovanovich accepted a takeover bid from General Cinema Corp., the fourth largest theater operator in the U.S., after rejecting an earlier smaller offer to bondholders.

Farrar, Straus & Giroux cut its staff by sixteen people, including Linda Healey, the editor brought in four years ago to develop journalistic nonfiction books for the company. Healey has since joined Pantheon, which has been restarted by André Schiffrin as a nonprofit foundation.

The hardcover William Morrow SF, fantasy and horror program edited by David Hartwell and the Avon paperback line edited by John Douglas were combined into one line under the new palindromic imprint of AvoNova with John Douglas as editor. The new Avon-driven hardcover list will appear in the fall of 1992. Avon will do all editorial, advertising and promotional work. They will coordinate with the Morrow production staff; the Morrow sales staff will handle the books. It will have a Morrow imprint; Avon will pay a distribution fee; Carolyn Reidy, President and Publisher of Avon Books and a supporter of SF and fantasy at Avon, left the company late in 1991 to become President and Publisher of the Simon & Schuster Trade Publishing Division. Howard Kaminsky, Chief Executive Officer of the Hearst Trade Books Group is temporarily filling in until someone is appointed to replace Reidy.

On the magazine end, *Aboriginal SF* pulled back to quarterly publication with the final 1991 issue, and has applied for nonprofit status.

General Media, the parent corporation of *Omni*, laid off one hundred twenty employees throughout the corporation in October and moved most of the operations of *Omni* down to Greensboro, NC, with the exception of the fiction department and two senior editors of other departments.

Davis Publications sold *Alfred Hitchcock's Mystery Magazine, Ellery Queen's Mystery Magazine, Analog, Science Fiction and Fact* and *Isaac Asimov's Science Fiction Magazine* to Bantam Doubleday Dell in early January 1992. The four magazines will be added to the Dell Magazines Group, which publishes crossword, horoscope and word game magazines. It was announced that no changes were contemplated in the editorial staff or direction of the four magazines, which will continue to operate out of their own headquarters for at least a year.

On March 1, 1991, Kristine Kathryn Rusch became the sixth editor of *The Magazine of Fantasy and Science Fiction* in its forty-two-year history. Retiring editor Edward L. Ferman remains publisher and art director of the respected monthly digest. In early January 1992 Rusch announced that she was giving up her editorial duties at Pulphouse, although she will remain on the Board of Directors and keep an advisory role. Most of her editorial duties have been taken over by Mark Budz.

Pulphouse: The Magazine, originally announced as a weekly, cut back to a biweekly schedule after only four issues because of the following factors: readers complained that they didn't have time to read a weekly and were worried about the costly subscription price of $95 a year; writers complained that a week on the newsstand would not give enough exposure to their stories; booksellers complained that there wasn't enough time to sell a weekly magazine because most customers only visit a bookstore once a month. The fifth, sixth and seventh issues came out biweekly; as of the eighth issue, the magazine will be issued monthly. On October 21, 1991, Pulphouse became a corporation, with stock, a Board of Directors and a business foundation.

British book and magazine publishing fared far worse than American, being the center of seven major upheavals in and out of the field, some of which were the result of financial problems. Since Robert Maxwell's mysterious death on November 5, 1991, his empire has been in chaos—Macdonald was forced to file for the UK equivalent of bankruptcy protection and was bought by Time Warner, Inc., in February 1992. Meanwhile, Macmillan executives in the U.S. assert that Macmillan Publishing Corp. (U.S.) will not be sold; it is not currently liable for MCC debts.

Reader's Digest UK fired eighty of its full-time staff and thirty part-timers; David & Charles, a Reader's Digest subsidiary, announced cuts of nearly 20 percent, with eighteen employees leaving now and sixteen projected losses through attrition.

Hodder cut 120 of its 640-member staff, while HarperCollins let go sixty, Ladybird cut fifty-four, Random Century cut sixty-six and Faber cut fourteen. Deutsch dismissed its entire sales force; for nonfinancial reasons (at least not directly) all but one member of the editorial staff of The Women's Press resigned, including SF editor Sarah Lefanu. Rumors held that the departures were the result of an "internal putsch," and that The Women's Press may now turn to a more mainstream brand of feminism. Soon after, in a surprise move, Kathy Gale, Pan Books' editorial director of specialist fiction, revealed she was leaving the mass market imprint to become publishing director of The Women's Press. She is corunning the company with plans to expand, develop and redirect the list.

Anthony Cheetham, fired late in 1991 as head of Random Century, has formed Orion Books and bought Weidenfeld & Nicolson and its subsidiaries, Dent and the paperback division of Everyman Library. Deborah Beale, who built the Legend imprint at Century, has joined him as publishing director. She will build a new SF imprint, Millennium, in hardcover, trade paperback and mass market. John Jarrold has left Orbit (MacDonald) to replace Beale at Legend. Malcolm Edwards has been made managing director in charge of fiction for HarperCollins trade division and Jane Johnson has been promoted to editorial director in charge of SF, fantasy and horror.

Fear magazine, Britain's only slick horror movie/short fiction magazine, started a companion all-fiction magazine, *Frighteners*, edited by Oliver Frey. The first issue was published on June 27 and unfortunately, within a week had been pulled from the shelves by many booksellers because of a Graham Masterton story "Eric the Pie," which had a particularly disgusting scene in it. After complaints, the retailers removed all copies of the issue and destroyed most of the 45,000-copy print run. The magazine published three issues—I only saw the first and the fiction was pretty dreadful. Partly as a result of the financial loss incurred by the destruction of the print run, Newsfield Publications, publishers of both *Fear* and *Frighteners*, has gone into liquidation. the mid-September business failure occurred less than a week after John Gilbert resigned his post as editor of *Fear*. *Fear's* publication was suspended after thirty-three issues. The magazine attempted to combine literature and film in equal proportion but later issues were pushed more toward gore by the publisher to increase sales. The fiction was inconsistent throughout, but the magazine was an interesting and useful addition to the horror field. John Gilbert, who owns the title (having leased it to Newsfield), is looking for a publisher to start it up again.

Argus Specialist Publications cancelled *Skeleton Crew* only nine months after it was launched as a rival to *Fear*. The magazine never really recovered from the sacking of its original editor after the first two issues.

More on censorship: on August 31, police seized more than four thousand comics from Manchester, England, publisher Savoy Books. The comics, issue #5 of *Lord Horror*, were considered obscene. In addition, Savoy has been found guilty of publishing an obscene book, the novel version of *Lord Horror* by David Britton. The book and comic is a fictional depiction of the life of the World War II traitor known as "Lord Haw Haw." The decision was made by Manchester Magistrates Court; Savoy plans to appeal. A Canadian subscriber to the American magazine *Iniquities* had the first issue of his subscription seized by Customs as a prohibited item. The offending story dealt with necrophilia. The subscriber planned to challenge the decision but had little hope for a reversal. In July, the Japanese translator of Salman Rushdie's novels was slain by an Iranian attacker and Rushdie's Italian translator survived a similar attack. Although there was an announcement that a consortium of American book publishers would together publish a paperback edition of *The Satanic Verses*, as of the end of February 1992, the group could not come to an agreement to do so.

In other news, a flap developed in Great Britain over the recent best-selling novels of the late V. C. Andrews. Barry Winkelman, managing director of her former publisher, HarperCollins, wrote an open letter to the trade saying the most recent book, *Dawn*, published by Simon & Schuster, was not written by Virginia Andrews but by Andrew Neiderman. The book's cover describes it as "the new Virginia Andrews," but a letter inside from the Andrews family notes that her estate has been working with a "carefully selected writer to expand upon her genius." Simon and Schuster offered a money-back guarantee.

The first World Horror Convention, held in Nashville, TN, Feb. 28–March 3, barely managed to cover costs with only 300 attendees. Writer Guest of Honor was Chelsea Quinn Yarbro, who replaced Clive Barker when he cancelled due to work commitments. Artist Guest of Honor was Jill Bauman. Robert Bloch was honored as Grand Master.

The 1990 Bram Stoker Awards banquet and weekend took place in Redondo Beach, CA, June 21–23. The award winners were: Novel, *Mine* by Robert R. McCammon (Pocket); First novel, *The Revelation* by Bentley Little (St. Martin's); Novelette, "Stephen" by Elizabeth Massie (Borderlands); Short Story, "The Calling" by David B. Silva (Borderlands); Collection, *Four Past Midnight* by Stephen King (Viking); Nonfiction, *Dark Dreamers: Conversations with the Masters of Horror* by Stanley Wiater (Avon); Lifetime achievement award, Hugh B. Cave and Richard Matheson.

The Readercon Small Press Awards were announced in Worcester, MA, at Readercon 4, July 13: Novel, *Red Spider, White Web* by Misha (Morrigan); Magazine Fiction, *Journal Wired*, Mark V. Ziesing and Andy Watson, eds.; Magazine Nonfiction, *The New York Review of Science Fiction*, David Hartwell, et al., eds.; Magazine Design, *Journal Wired*, Andy Watson, design; Collection, *The Brains of Rats* by Michael Blumlein (Scream/Press); Anthology, *When the Black Lotus Blooms*, Elizabeth Saunders, ed. (Unnameable Press); Value in Bookcraft, *Slow Dancing Through Time*, by Gardner Dozois et al. (Ursus/Ziesing); Short work, "Entropy's Bed at Midnight," by Dan Simmons (Lord John Press); Reprint, *The Atrocity Exhibition*, by J. G. Ballard (Re/Search); Nonfiction, *Across the Wounded Galaxies*, by Larry McCaffery (U. of Illinois Press); Jacket Illustration, *H. R. Giger's Biomechanics*, H. R. Giger, illustrator (Morpheus International); Interior Illustrations, *H. R. Giger's Biomechanics*, H. R. Giger, illustrator (Morpheus International).

As in past years, my 1991 novel reading has been peripatetic. The following is a completely biased view of what I've found interesting. I'm particularly delighted to note all the excellent and promising first novels. I've covered few strictly genre titles, as I assume readers will already be aware of them:

Bones by Joyce Thompson (Morrow) is a psychological horror novel about secrets and child abuse. Freddy, a divorced mother, supports two children as a police artist and struggles to be a good and understanding mother. Then her alcoholic father is brutally murdered, his brain stolen and the killer begins a reign of terror on Freddy and her children. Freddy receives pieces of a "novel" which slowly reveal the motivation, if not the identity, of the killer. Although a red herring is introduced in the middle of the novel, and Thompson occasionally gets lost in details, *Bones* is a frightening and fascinating story, intelligently and gracefully written.

Stone City by Mitchell Smith (Signet) is a harrowing suspense novel about a former history professor sent to prison for hit-and-run manslaughter who is coerced, both by the administration and by the leader of the "lifers" (prisoners sentenced to life imprisonment), into investigating two murders in the prison. This novel is far more than just a suspense or a mystery; this is an epic about an average Joe caught in a squeeze who must learn to abide by rules "inside," which are often the antithesis of those in the outside world. It's also a study of prison life that made me rethink the entire prison system. Although lengthy and occasionally overwritten, it's the first book in quite a while that made me want to know what would happen after the book ended. With more promotion than it received, it might have made the best-seller lists. Highly recommended.

Eyes of Prey by John Sandford (Putnam) is the third in a series about Lucas Davenport, serial killer expert extraordinaire, whose home base is Minneapolis. This was better than the last novel (*Shadow Prey*) but not as good as the first (*Rules of Prey*). The best thing about these books is Davenport, a three-dimensional, soul-searching character. A woman is murdered by a "troll" at the behest of her drugged-out doctor husband who is called Dr. Death by his colleagues because of his obsession with the subject. Some nice twists.

Sliver by Ira Levin (Bantam), while not of the caliber of *Rosemary's Baby* or *A Kiss Before Dying*, is better than I expected, considering his more recent attempts at horror/thrillers such as the male wish-fulfillment fantasy *The Stepford Wives* and the predictable *The Boys from Brazil*. *Sliver* is creepy. A rich nut has bought the building he lives in and wires it for sight and sound so he can spy on his neighbors—and manipulate their lives. Levin's writing here is too elliptical; possibly trying to speed up the story, he sacrifices coherence. And the climax is pretty unbelievable.

Chicago Loop by Paul Theroux (Random House) is (like the following novel, *Frisk*) what Bret Easton Ellis's *American Psycho* should have been. A successful businessman, husband and father, living in a Chicago suburb goes nuts. He's already verging on crazy at the start of the novel: he's a compulsive liar, he plays weird sex games with his wife once a month, and he lives a secret life, placing personal ads to meet women. He becomes progressively stranger, murdering (almost unconsciously) a woman he picks up through an ad, then spends the rest of the novel trying to make amends, ultimately attempting to *be* her and get murdered himself. This strange, fast-moving novel by the author of *The Mosquito Coast* and other mainstream books is a fascinating descent into madness.

Frisk by Dennis Cooper (Grove Weidenfeld) opens with thirteen-year-old Dennis observing a series of photographs that seem to show a boy being mutilated. From that moment on, Dennis is obsessed with young male bodies and longs to discover their innermost workings. He either daydreams or actually does—lure, torture and murder young men. Erotic, terrifying, and horrifying. Experimental in style, it's a difficult book to read or to actually enjoy, but definitely worth a look.

Physical Culture by Hillary Johnson (Poseidon, 1989) is a short first novel about a middle-aged accountant in a suburban mattress factory who leads the secret life of a masochist. He is unable to experience "normal" desire throughout his life. Lovely, subtle in its buildup into strangeness, it makes an interesting companion to the Cooper and Theroux.

The Fear in Yesterday's Rings by George C. Chesbro (Mysterious Press) is an excellent addition to the Mongo series. The protagonist is a dwarf who started out in a circus and became a professor and expert in criminology. His former boss has lost the circus and is a broken man. Mongo tries to get it back for him, running into opposition from the current owners. Werewolf murders in the Plains states bring Mongo's expertise into play. A work of science fiction as well as horror, it's thoroughly satisfying.

The Cipher by Kathe Koja (Dell Abyss) is the novel that launched this new horror line. The novel is a wondrous SF/horror journey into the unknown. A black hole is discovered in a storage room of an apartment building by Nicholas Reid and his sometimes girlfriend, Nakota. Nakota is one of the most interesting characters I've encountered in horror fiction. She is hateful—cold, heartless, selfish and vicious—but in a believable way; I was almost cheering by the time she got her just desserts. Nicholas is a poor jerk, poet/video store employee, who basically gets in over his head. Koja's style, always interesting in her short fiction, is occasionally opaque, but she is spectacularly in control here. Once you get hooked by her prose you'll be more than willing to trust her to take you on a fine ride. Constantly surprising. Without a doubt one of the best first horror novels of the year. Highly recommended.

Prodigal by Melanie Tem (Abyss) is another good first novel, this one about family relationships and how they shift as children reach puberty and/or when trauma is experienced by a family. Ethan Brill, eldest of the Brill family's seven children, has disappeared and is feared dead. Before his disappearance he was stealing, lying, taking drugs. . . . The story is told from the point of view of the second oldest sister, Lucy, who is on the verge of puberty. It begins so meticulously to depict the pain and resentment of a surviving child that at first I feared Tem wouldn't be able to pull it off, but the slow buildup works beautifully. Highly recommended.

Tunnelvision by R. Patrick Gates (Abyss). Good characterizations put this serial killer/police procedural a step above the rest. Ivy Delacroix is a bright, friendless young kid brought up by his widowed mother. He meets and befriends a lonely old woman. Bill Gage is a cop haunted by his past. And Wilbur Clayton is the end result of an abused childhood.

Down By the River by Monte Schulz (Viking) is about the repercussions to a small California town where a sixteen-year-old girl is allegedly raped by hoboes in a railyard. The police chief, a refugee from the big city, is unable to prevent a vigilante party from taking action against the transients. An old man is killed, others are wounded and one man escapes. Soon after, it's apparent that the teenage accusers are being stalked and brutally murdered, seemingly for revenge. Published out of genre, *Down By the River* is far more than a serial killer novel—it is an intricate portrait of American small town life. This first novel, rich in detail and characterization, glaringly points out the difference in the quality of the prose of most horror writers as compared to that of more literary writers.

The Man Upstairs by T. L. Parkinson (Dutton) is also an impressive horror novel debut. Recently divorced Michael West moves into a small San Francisco apartment building. Soon afterward, a new neighbor moves in upstairs: a charming, handsome and self-possessed plastic surgeon named Paul Marks. Michael becomes obsessed with Paul's sex life and his own mirror image, withdrawing more and more from the world. A young boy is found dead, a young woman is murdered, and Michael finds himself becoming confused about what is real and what is not. A profoundly disturbing novel about psychosexual obsession, control and loss of self.

Madlands by K. W. Jeter (St. Martin's) is a hard-edged SF novel with horrific elements. It's about an imaginary place called the Madlands—a kind of consensual reality Los Angeles, derived from archival material left after a disaster that has destroyed the real L.A. (if there is such a thing). If people stay too long they lose their pattern discrimination and their human forms are altered in disgusting and grotesque ways—breaking down into earlier life forms. Enjoyable and very Philip K. Dickian.

Sarah Canary by Karen Joy Fowler (Henry Holt) is a crossover novel by a writer of science fiction and fantasy short stories. It's disturbing in the way real-life American racism against the Chinese (and anybody else who is different) in the 1870s is horrific. It's an evocative, picaresque, thought-provoking and historical novel about a young Chinese timber worker who discovers a mysterious Caucasian woman in the forest. He fears she is a ghost lover meant to haunt him, and as other men and women come into contact with Sarah Canary (as he names her) she becomes whatever symbol of womanhood they wish to see. This brilliant first novel has a marvelously fantastic feel to it, along the lines of Peter Carey's *Illywacker*. It opens with one mystery and ends with another. British critic John Clute calls it the "best first contact novel ever written," which is an interesting interpretation. Highly recommended for lovers of the fantastic and good literature.

Gojiro by Mark Jacobson (Atlantic Monthly) is also not horror, despite Gojiro being the infamous movie monster Godzilla. On a remote island populated mostly by lizards, the effects of the atomic bombs dropped on Hiroshima and Nagasaki are felt—a monitor lizard becomes huge and smart and is immediately alienated from his fellows. A young boy in Hiroshima falls into a coma. Somehow Gojiro's cries of loneliness are telepathically "heard," and the boy recovers and travels two thousand miles to join his new-found friend. The novel is about their adventures on the road to Hollywood. A charming, hip, satirical science fiction debut.

Palindrome by Stuart Woods (HarperCollins) is a dark suspense novel that opens powerfully—a beautiful photographer, Liz Barwick, is admitted to a hospital after her doped-up football player husband nearly beats her to death. She divorces him and flees to an idyllic island paradise off the Georgia coast to heal her physical and psychic wounds. There she meets and becomes friends with the owners, including mysterious twin brothers who have not spoken to each other in twenty years. Various threads of the plot converge as her vengeance-bound ex-husband tracks her down and her involvement with one of the twins becomes increasingly strange. A good read despite some believability problems.

Damage by Josephine Hart (Knopf). This debut novel was published to justifiable critical acclaim. In a style as spare and cool as his emotional life, a man tells the story of his own destruction. This novel is a deeply moving, frightening psychological drama of obsession in which the refrain is "Damaged people are dangerous. They know they can survive." For once, the jacket blurbs do a book justice: "A passionate, elegant, ruthless story." I was so caught up in it, I almost missed my subway stop. Read it! One of the best novels of the year published outside the genre.

The Weekend: A Novel of Revenge by Helen Zahavi (Donald I. Fine). This first novel opens with "This is the story of Bella, who woke up one morning and realised she'd had enough," enough of being tormented by lowlife men in Brighton, where she's gone after leaving London and her former life as a prostitute. This is a literate *Ms. 45*, a simply told tale of less than 200 pages that packs a wallop, particularly the last chapter, which universalizes in a surprisingly believable way the most extreme form of conflict between men and women. This might appeal to women more than men, but who knows? It does have a sense of poetic justice for both sexes.

Wilderness by Dennis Danvers (Poseidon) is a fast-paced first novel about Alice White, a woman who has avoided intimacy her entire life of thirty-plus years in order to protect her secret: she is a werewolf. This is not a horror novel, despite its subject matter. It deals with trust, relationships between exes [sic], the relationship between humankind and animals and the accommodations necessary between our wild and domestic natures.

St. Peter's Wolf by Michael Cadnum (Carroll & Graf) is another werewolf novel, with themes, psychology and occasionally even scenes similar to those of *Wilderness*. Yet it is quite a different reading experience. I suspect how the reader reacts to these two novels is dependent on which is read first. I read *St. Peter's Wolf* second and was disappointed. It's denser and it's beautifully written, but the author's love affair with words sometimes gets in the way of the story. The book feels repetitious and there are too many minor characters who have no impact on the story. Also these werewolves seem more and more indestructible and even mystical, losing credence. A sharper focus would have helped.

Sleepwalker by Michael Cadnum (St. Martin's) came out several months before *St. Peter's Wolf*. Although the supernatural plays a large role here, the novel shares more with Cadnum's debut novel, *Nightlight*, in its poetic spareness. Archeologists unearth a twelve-hundred-year-old bog man at a site in York who appears to have been murdered. Two archeologists, former colleagues years before, are brought together, their personal problems and secrets intersecting. The site, rumored to be haunted, becomes more and more dangerous as trivial incidents like tools moving around escalate to unexplained "accidents," and the bog man himself seems to be more mobile than he should be. A good read.

Outside the Dog Museum by Jonathan Carroll (MacDonald–UK/Doubleday) is another magical mystery tour by the author of *Land of Laughs*, *Sleeping in Flame* and other novels. This one concerns an arrogant genius architect named Harry Radcliffe, who, straight out of a nervous breakdown, is commissioned by the Sultan of Saru to build a museum to honor dogs. Radcliffe is not a nice guy but he seems to have been touched by a higher force to experience and possibly create great things. Carroll is an amazing writer, able to create perfect vignettes and stories within stories, but his plotting is occasionally weak. Although *Outside the Dog Museum* is absorbing throughout and the reader hopes Carroll can pull it all together at the end, I found myself thinking about the book afterward and wondering what happened. The book is about creativity, responsibility, God, mysticism, and fate. Despite the serious themes and minor flaws, it is quite a lot of fun to read.

The Drowners by Garry Kilworth (Methuen) is a YA ghost story set in Hampshire, England, on a flood plain. John Timbrel is MasterDrowner for his community—the person who maps out the necessarily exact science of opening and closing the locks for irrigation. One wrong decision means fields and crops are ruined for the season. Against this background a drama is played out between a rich, greedy landowner, his murderous hired hand and Tom Timbrel, the master's apprentice/son. An atmospheric and effective slice of English regional life.

Honour Thy Father by Lesley Glaister (Atheneum). The author won the Somerset Maugham Award for this first novel. It's a disturbing novel about four aged sisters trapped for decades in the Fens of England by an autocratic and psychotic father obsessed with keeping them pure. The vision is very dark, and the play between past and present is well done, but perhaps too literary for some horror fans.

Don't Say a Word by Andrew Klavan (Pocket) is an intricately plotted psychological suspense novel. Klavan is the author of last year's excellent *The Scarred Man*, written under his Keith Peterson pseudonym. Klavan has the ability to draw the reader into his world immediately, no matter how unpleasant his characters.

Nathan Conrad, dubbed "psychiatrist of the damned," is persuaded to take on one more hard-luck case: that of an angelic-looking young woman who has been accused of slicing a man to shreds and then lapsing into catatonia. Meanwhile, Conrad's idyllic personal life is about to be ruptured by two brutal opportunists. An Edgar nominee and a definite page-turner.

The New Neighbor by Ray Garton (Charnel House) is an erotic horror novel with illustrations by J. K. Potter. The new neighbor, a beautiful young woman ('natch) is a succubus who seduces *anyone* she can. There's a lot of masturbation and hot sex in this fairly standard story, but it's a fast, entertaining read. The book looks great—the cover is elegant, the interiors sexy and disturbing. Primarily for collectors of Potter and Garton.

Tender Loving Rage by Alfred Bester (Tafford) is a mainstream suspense novel, never before published, by the late Alfred Bester, author of the classic science fiction novels *The Demolished Man* and *The Stars My Destination*. The time is 1959, the place New York City, where two men fall in love with model Julene Krebs, who displays a completely different personality with each of them. All three characters are haunted by past secrets. On Fire Island just before a hurricane, Julene's past catches up with her and her two lovers. It's a strange, anachronistic little novel with noirish dialogue, Fitzgeraldian characters, wild parties and orgies, talk of discos and Bella Abzug. Despite the weird sense of displacement (I don't know when Bester actually wrote it) it's an interesting thriller.

The M.D.: A Horror Story by Thomas M. Disch (Knopf) is a horror/science fiction novel of power and corruption. The first section of the novel is a joy, with its depiction of what initially seems to be a typical midwestern childhood and the miseries of attending Catholic school. Young Billy Michaels, growing up in Minneapolis in the early seventies, sees a vision of Santa Claus one Christmas.

The vision claims Santa Claus is only one of his many guises and that he is actually Mercury, the pagan God of science and medicine—in this story, an evil god. Billy is tempted by this god to use his brother's homemade caduceus, the winged serpentine emblem of the healer's art. However, as in many fairy and folktales, its use always backfires.

There is a large gap in time from when young Billy tries to do good with the caduceus, always failing, to the middle-aged William, the M.D. of the title, who ultimately becomes a monster, consciously doing evil. Who or what is Mercury really? The devil? But could there be a devil without a positive counterpart? If this god is actually Mercury, then why is he evil? And why don't the other gods in the pantheon make an appearance? Several characters have strong religious beliefs but none of these beliefs seem to have any connection or effect on the Mercury character. Despite these unanswered questions, *The M.D.* is elegantly written, ambitious and absorbing.

Time's Arrow by Martin Amis (Harmony) is a virtuoso performance, a story told backward from a man's death to his birth. The narrator, a doppelgänger imprisoned within Dr. Friendly's body, is a separate consciousness that shares but has no influence on the doctor's life—an innocent. Through the doppelgänger's perceptions, the reader sees history in a completely different light and begins (unlike the doppelgänger) to understand the monstrousness of Dr. Friendly. The resulting novel is thoroughly cerebral rather than emotionally engaging.

Wetbones by John Shirley (Mark V. Ziesing) begins with all the energy, solid characterizations and action that a reader expects of John Shirley. The novel seems at first to be a hard-headed look at Hollywood, but it quickly becomes a cautionary tale about the dangers of any kind of addiction. A weird guy lures young girls away from home and psychically feeds off them until they're used up; a respected Hollywood couple own a ranch that is the nexus of all kinds of perversion and corruption; a recovered alcoholic combs L.A. for his runaway daughter; and two men go after the grail of fame and fortune in the Hollywood film industry. In general, a good combination of street life and splatter that certainly goes over the top in violence. For me, the grisliness became a bit numbing and I felt there was too much explanation of the supernatural elements. Don't even ask what "wet-bones" are—you don't want to know. . . . A good read, and a beautifully designed package by Arnie Fenner.

Bones of Coral by James W. Hall (Knopf) is an intricate mystery that opens with a Miami paramedic responding to a suicide call and discovering the father he hasn't seen in twenty years. The novel focuses on Key West and illegal chemical dumping, and the underside of the high-tech society we embrace. There's a refreshing relationship in which male and female are equal in age and status. (If anything, the woman, a famous soap opera actress, has the edge.) A great read.

Other novels published in 1991 were *The Wild* by Whitley Strieber (Tor), *The Bridge* by John Skipp and Craig Spector (Bantam); *Unearthed* by Ashley McConnell (Diamond); *The Fire Within* by Graham Watkins (Berkley); *Lizzie Borden* by Elizabeth Engstrom (Tor); *Dracula Unbound* by Brian W. Aldiss (HarperCollins); *Lot Lizards* by Ray Garton (Mark V. Ziesing); *Bad Dreams* by Kim Newman (Simon & Schuster–UK); *Ghosts of Wind and Shadow* by Charles de Lint (Axolotl/

Pulphouse); *Steam* by Jay B. Laws (Alyson); *Fetish* a short novel by Edward Bryant (Axolotl/Pulphouse); *The Fetch* by Robert Holdstock (Orbit); *Through a Lens Darkly* by James Cohen (Donald I. Fine); *The Headsman* by James Neal Harvey (Donald I. Fine); *Revealing Angel* by Julia Maclean (St. Martin's); *The Walled Orchard* by Tom Holt (St. Martin's); *Midnight Sun* by Ramsey Campbell (Tor); *Nothing Human* by Ronald Munson (Pocket); *The Burning* by Graham Masterton (Tor); *The Kinder Garden* by Frederick Taylor (Carroll & Graf); *Peter Doyle* by John Vernon (Random House); *The Choiring of the Trees* by Donald Harrington (HBJ); *Maus II* by Art Spiegelman (Pantheon); *Flicker* by Theodore Roszak (Summit); *Phantom* by Susan Kay (Delacorte); *Boy's Life* by Robert R. McCammon (Pocket); *A Dangerous Woman* by Mary McGarry Morris (Viking); *Doctor Sleep* by Madison Smartt Bell (HBJ); *Something Stirs* by Charles L. Grant (Tor); *Imajica* by Clive Barker (HarperCollins); *The Goldbug Variations* by Richard Powers (Morrow); *Murther and Walking Spirits* by Robertson Davies (Viking); *Hangman* by Christopher A. Bohjalian (Carroll & Graf); *The Host* by Peter R. Emshwiller (Bantam); *The Women of Whitechapel and Jack the Ripper* by Paul West (Random House); *Summer of Night* by Dan Simmons (Putnam); *Needful Things* by Stephen King (Viking); *Nightlife* by Brian Hodge (Abyss); and *Mastery* by Kelley Wilde (Abyss).

Anthologies:

In 1991, as in the past four years, original anthologies provided the most consistently well-written and interesting short horror. There were almost thirty anthologies published that were dominated by horror material, plus many anthologies and collections that contained at least some horror.

However, the abundance of original anthologies does not mean that everything is great in the field. Most of these anthologies were commissioned a few years ago, when economic conditions were more favorable and horror as a genre was at its peak. If these anthologies do well, we'll see more, otherwise, not. In no particular order:

Obsessions edited by Gary Raisor (Dark Harvest) is a good collection of wide-ranging obsessions. What stands out about this anthology is that the reader hardly ever remains aware of the theme until she finishes a story—the best way for a "theme" anthology to read. In other words, you're not looking for the theme because the stories are so effective. The standouts are by C. J. Henderson, Charles L. Grant, Al Sarrantonio, A. R. Morlan, and Dan Simmons.

Hotter Blood edited by Jeff Gelb and Michael Garrett (Pocket Books) contains all original stories, and is a considerable improvement in quality over *Hot Blood*. There's more variety, fewer "woman as castrator" or "woman as victim" stories. Could it simply be due to the inclusion of more female contributors? Or is it because the first volume was slammed by some critics for using too many stories with women in stereotypical horror roles? In any case, there are very good stories here by Gary Brandner, Stephen Gallagher, Kiel Stuart, Karl Edward Wagner, and Grant Morrison.

Psycho-Paths edited by Robert Bloch (Tor) is disappointing. Too many psychos meeting other psychos. The best stories are by Dennis Etchison, Gahan Wilson,

Steve Rasnic Tem, Chelsea Quinn Yarbro, Michael Berry, Brad Linaweaver, and Susan Shwartz.

Cold Blood: New Tales of Mystery and Horror edited by Richard T. Chizmar (Mark V. Ziesing) is another disappointment, considering it comes from the editor of the World Fantasy Award–winning small press magazine *Cemetery Dance*. None of the contributors are at their best, although F. Paul Wilson's contribution is very good. Few of the stories pack the punch they should and very few follow through on good ideas.

Under the Fang edited by Robert R. McCammon (Pocket). The first official Horror Writers of America–sponsored anthology does not show off the membership to best advantage. The idea, a shared-world vampire anthology set at a time after vampires have taken over, is not a bad one. Unfortunately, the contributors don't go far enough off the main track and there's little depth to most of the stories. There are some interesting visuals by Nancy A. Collins, an amusing collaboration by Yarbro and Charnas placing their famous vampires in the same century, and a good Thomas F. Monteleone story, but the book is not the showcase it should have been.

Newer York edited by Lawrence Watt-Evans (Roc) is not marketed as a horror anthology, but considering how most outsiders feel about New York, it shouldn't be surprising that there are a number of stories here that verge on the horrific. The best include those by Robert Frazier, Eric Blackburn, Martha Soukup, Laurence M. Janifer, Robert J. Howe, and a collaboration between Warren Murphy and Molly Cochran.

Dead End: City Limits: An Anthology of Urban Fear edited by Paul F. Olson and David B. Silva (St. Martin's), while consistently entertaining, is not as good as their first collaboration, *Post Mortem*. The standouts are by Steve Rasnic Tem, Poppy Z. Brite, Thomas F. Monteleone, and Charles L. Grant.

Dark Voices 3 edited by David Sutton and Stephen Jones (Pan) is disappointing on the whole, with four reprints (one of which appeared in last year's *Year's Best*) out of fourteen stories. Several had predictable third-rate "Twilight Zone" TV plots. The few standouts were by Kathe Koja, Lene Kaaberol, Stephen Laws, and Brian Lumley.

Cafe Purgatorium: Three Novels of Horror and the Fantastic by Dana M. Anderson, Charles de Lint, and Ray Garton (Tor) is in fact three novellas. One, "Dr. Krusadian's Method," is a reprint from the 1990 Ray Garton collection, *Methods of Madness*. Dana M. Anderson is a newcomer who contributes the interesting title novella about a haunted speakeasy. And "Death Leaves an Echo," Charles de Lint's ghost story, rounds out the lovely package. Powerful work by all three writers.

Embracing the Dark edited by Eric Garber (Alyson Publications) contains original and reprint gay and lesbian vampire stories. The best are reprints by Kij Johnson, Nina Kiriki Hoffman, and Peter Robins and the original vignette from Jewelle Gomez's "Gilda" series. The editor's introduction claims he wants to "reject the clichés and invert the metaphors" of heterosexual horror fiction, and further accuses the standard horror novel of glorifying heterosexuality and conversely "punish[ing] any deviation from this heterosexual norm." This condemns a whole genre by its lowest levels of writing. So it is with great irony that I found many of the stories in the volume (at least those by men) basically idealized gay pornography, "gigantic manhood" and all. Too many of the stories are driven by the facts of the characters' sexuality at the expense of plot or atmosphere, a disaster in the horror or suspense genres. Also, the explicitness sometimes works against a story's effectiveness by undercutting the atmosphere of horror. In contrast, Edward Bryant's classic "Dancing Chickens" (not included in the anthology), which contains a sympathetic gay protagonist, juxtaposes an external horror against the personal horror of his protagonist's life, and it knocks most of the stories in this anthology out of the water.

The Bradbury Chronicles: Stories in Honor of Ray Bradbury edited by William F. Nolan and Martin H. Greenberg (Roc). Many of these stories are lovely homages to early Bradbury—and quite faithful to the originals. And therein lies the rub—they are enjoyable as nostalgia pieces but there's not enough originality, although Chad Oliver, Charles L. Grant and F. Paul Wilson make gallant attempts to transcend the theme. It's bad enough when beginning writers are persuaded to "sharecrop" in an established writer's universe, but here is an example of established writers being persuaded to lend their formidable talents to what is essentially a rehashing of another's worldview. Their time and energy would be better spent writing their own material—writing their best and showing how they were influenced as writers, not as imitators of Bradbury.

Tales of the Wandering Jew edited by Brian M. Stableford (Dedalus). Stableford does a good job with a difficult subject. The Wandering Jew of legend is intrinsically an anti-Semitic creation of Christians. The legend goes that a shoemaker taunted or threw something at Jesus while he was walking to his crucifixion and that Jesus cursed the man to live until the second coming. Both the traditional and new stories here could be construed as anti-Semitic in their assumption that the Wandering Jew deserves punishment for his nonbelief, and many of the stories have the wanderer convert to Christianity during his wanderings. The best stories focus on the repercussions of unwanted immortality rather than the religious aspects of the legend. Includes good pieces by Steve Rasnic Tem, Ian McDonald, Robert Irwin, and Geoffrey Farrington.

Cold Shocks edited by Tim Sullivan (Avon) is a satisfying follow-up to *Tropical Chills*, with excellent stories by A. R. Morlan, S. P. Somtow, Graham Masterton, Michael Armstrong and Edward Bryant and very good stories by the rest.

The Ultimate Werewolf edited by Byron Preiss (Dell) is something I expected to dislike, not believing there could be enough different takes on the theme to keep a reader's interest. I was pleasantly surprised. Beginning with a classic reprint by Harlan Ellison, this anthology of mostly originals finds enough variations on the werewolf theme to keep everyone happy. The best were by Nina Kiriki Hoffman, Craig Shaw Gardner, Mel Gilden, Nancy A. Collins, Pat Murphy and a collaboration by A. C. Crispin and Kathleen O'Malley.

The Ultimate Dracula and *The Ultimate Frankenstein* edited by Byron Preiss (Dell). Unfortunately, the negatives I expected from *The Ultimate Werewolf* did show up in these two. The more specific a theme, the more difficult it is to put together interesting stories that play against that theme. For example, the best story in the Frankenstein book (which, as is customary, mistakes the creature for its creator) is by S. P. Somtow, who does not use the traditional characters at all but creates his own erotic nightmare from his imagination and the exoticism of Thailand, his homeland. The Dracula stories would be better if they weren't about Dracula but about vampires in general. There's only so much you can do with the "Father of Darkness" as the actual character. *Boring*, for the most part, with notable exceptions by Dan Simmons, Brad Strickland, Steve Rasnic Tem and Melanie Tem, W. R. Philbrick, John Lutz, and Kristine Kathryn Rusch.

Nightmares on Elm Street: Freddy Krueger's Seven Sweetest Dreams edited by Martin H. Greenberg (St. Martin's) also suffers from too specific a theme. The contributors—talented writers such as Nancy A. Collins, Brian Hodge, Bentley Little and Philip Nutman—bring what they can to a thankless task. Only for die-hard Freddy fans.

Chilled to the Bone edited by Robert T. Garcia (Mayfair Games) is an anthology that has the exact opposite problem. It is based on the idea (I hesitate to call it a theme) that there are bad things out there—demons and vampires and werewolves and other beasties. And there's a secret society that's been fighting these bad things for centuries. Unfortunately, few of the stories reflect this "theme," loose as it is. Apparently, all the stories have to have a note or message that says "beware" of something or someone. That's the extent of their connection. Contributions by some usually excellent writers are especially disappointing. A mess.

Final Shadows edited by Charles L. Grant (Doubleday Foundation) is the concluding volume (double-sized) of the World Fantasy Award–winning anthology series. A mixed-bag ranging from the powerful to the adequate, the best stories are by Brian Lumley (originally published in *Dark Voices* 3 in the UK), Michael Bishop, Jack Cady, Melanie Tem, Stephen Gallagher, Dennis Etchison, Tanith Lee, and the novelette by David Morrell. Oddly, there are no introductions or biographical notes. The cover art gets my nomination for the ugliest of the year.

Borderlands 2 edited by Thomas Monteleone (Borderlands Press/Avon) is disappointing after last year's volume, which produced two of the best stories of the year. Not enough ambition and too much heavy-handedness, but some good, edgy stories by Charles L. Grant, James S. Dorr, Philip Nutman, David B. Silva and Brian Hodge.

Vampires edited by Jane Yolen and Martin H. Greenberg (HarperCollins) is aimed at the young adult audience and as such, is entertaining but not all that horrific. There's one lovely story by Mary Frances Zambreno and a quite moving piece by Mary K. Whittington.

Night Visions 9 (Dark Harvest). Thomas Tessier shines with a novella. In contrast, James Kisner's and Rick Hautala's work in this volume pales beside it. Hautala's work is bloody and vicious but lacks scope and resonance. A disappointing volume in this series.

Thirteen edited by T. Pines (Scholastic) is an all-original YA anthology with some scary stuff by various writers known for their young adult fiction.

The New Gothic edited by Bradford Morrow and Patrick McGrath (Random House) is a beautiful-looking volume with originals and reprints, which tries to separate itself from the horror field by an heroic attempt at obfuscation in the introduction. This is yet another marketing attempt to separate literary writing from popular writing. No go, guys. Peter Straub's early fiction (and some of his current) is firmly based in horror and fantasy (although the excerpt in *The New Gothic* isn't). Joyce Carol Oates has written mainstream, fantasy, science fiction and horror at various times, and certainly McGrath himself veers back and forth between the realistic and the fantastic. The stories in the anthology vary from the bloodless (in the figurative sense) and boring to the quite bloody (literally) and creepy. The best of the originals are by Janice Galloway, Scott Bradfield, Patrick McGrath, and Bradford Morrow.

Masques IV edited by J. N. Williamson (Maclay) is another mixed quality bag. The weakness of this series has always been that the editor crams in too many very short stories, which usually work on only one superficial level, rather than going for fewer but longer and more ambitious works. Despite this, almost half of the twenty-six stories are very good, including those by Ed Gorman, James Kisner, Graham Masterton, David T. Connolly, Darrell Schweitzer, Ray Russell, Kathryn Ptacek, Lois Tilton, Mort Castle, Rick Hautala, and Dan Simmons.

Pulphouse: The Hardback Magazine Issue #10 is a special holiday issue with an especially good horror story by Nina Kiriki Hoffman. #11, the speculative fiction issue, had good horror fiction by Steve Rasnic Tem, Stephanie Perry, and Resa Nelson.

A *Whisper of Blood* edited by Ellen Datlow (Morrow/Berkley) is a follow-up to the vampirism anthology *Blood is Not Enough*. All are original stories, with the exception of three; the anthology attempts to push the limits of vampires and the idea of vampirism to the max. Stories by Pat Cadigan, K. W. Jeter, Karl Edward Wagner, David J. Schow, Kathe Koja, Suzy McKee Charnas and others.

Darklands edited by Nicholas Royle (Egerton Press) was published in a limited edition of 500 copies in Great Britain. There may be a trade edition eventually. Good stories by Stephen Gallagher, Julie Akhurst, Philip Nutman, Brian Howell and Joel Lane.

Copper Star: An Anthology of Southwestern Fantasy, Horror and Science Fiction edited by Bruce D. Arthurs (1991 World Fantasy Convention) is a beautifully produced limited edition hardcover of sixteen stories with illustrations. The book was produced specially for members of the 1991 World Fantasy Convention and has excellent stories by Mike Newland, Edward Bryant, Melanie Tem, Norman Partridge and Jeannette M. Hopper.

Raw Head, Bloody Bones: African-American Tales of the Supernatural selected by Mary E. Lyons (Scribners) is a collection of ethnic folktales. The introduction explains something about the oral tradition of these tales, evolving from stories of lions in Africa to rabbits in America. The tales cover hags (witches), sea serpents, zombies and other supernatural beings. This is charming but not very frightening. It's perfect for young adults around a campfire during a starless night.

Fires of the Past edited by Anne Devereaux Jordan (St. Martin's) is mostly science fiction but has some horrific material by Edward Bryant, Jane Yolen and Kit Reed.

Monkey Brain Sushi: New Tastes in Japanese Fiction edited by Alfred Birnbaum (Kodansha) can only marginally be considered fantasy or horror—a cartoon strip, an S&M story. There is some very weird stuff (including "TV People," by Huraki Murakami, which appeared in last year's volume of *The Year's Best Fantasy and Horror*). What's most interesting to me is how close in flavor it is to the type of hip American fiction being published today—even the S&M.

Tales of the Outré: Writings Celebrating the Centenary of H. P. Lovecraft (Unspeakable Tomes, 1990) is an original anthology of spoof Lovecraft stories, all written under pseudonyms [not seen].

The following original or mostly original anthologies cross genres and also contain some horror: *Dark Crimes* edited by Ed Gorman (Carroll & Graf)—story by Ed Gorman; *Winter's Tales: New Series 7* edited by Robin Baird-Smith (St. Martin's)—stories by Tom Wakefield, Patrick McGrath, Tony Peake, and A. L. Barker; *Revenge* edited by Kate Saunders (Faber & Faber)—stories by Lisa St. Aubin de Terán and Kate Saunders; *Full Spectrum 3* edited by Lou Aronica, Amy Stout and Betsy Mitchell (Doubleday Foundation)—stories by Marcos Donnelly and R. V. Branham; *Writers of the Future Volume VII* edited by Algis Budrys (Bridge)—story by Barry H. Reynolds; *The Fantastic Adventures of Robin Hood* edited by Martin H. Greenberg (Signet)—stories by Steven Rasnic Tem and Nancy A. Collins; *Sword and Sorceresses VIII* edited by Marion Zimmer Bradley (DAW)—stories by Deborah Burros, Jennifer Roberson, Eluki bes Shahar and Jere Dunham; *New Worlds 1* edited by David Garnett (Gollancz)—story by Brian W. Aldiss; *A Hammock Beneath the Mangoes* edited by Thomas Colchie (Dutton)—stories by Moacyr Scliar and Guillarmo Cabrero Infante; *Subtropical Speculations* edited by Rick Wilber and Richard Mathews (Pineapple Press)—story by Joe Taylor; *Invitation to Murder* edited by Ed Gorman and Martin H. Greenberg (Dark Harvest)—stories by Gary Brandner, Billie Sue Mosiman, Kristine Kathryn Rusch and Andrew Vachss; *Unmapped Territories: New Women's Fiction from Japan* edited and translated by Yukiko Tanaka (Women in Translation); *Horse Fantastic* edited by Martin H. Greenberg and Rosalind M. Greenberg (DAW)— story by Jennifer Roberson; *There Won't Be War* edited by Harry Harrison and Bruce McAllister (Tor)—stories by Jack McDevitt, Nancy A. Collins and Gregory Frost; *When the Music's Over* edited by Lewis Shiner (Bantam Spectra); *The Fifth Book of After Midnight Stories* edited by Amy Myers (Robert Hale–UK); *Tales of Magic Realism by Women: Dreams in a Minor Key* edited by Susanna J. Sturgis (The Crossing Press)—story by Stephanie T. Hoppe; *Catfantastic II* edited by Andre Norton and Martin H. Greenberg (DAW)—story by Elizabeth Moon; *A Woman's Eye* edited by Sara Paretsky (Delacorte)—story by Nancy Pickard.

Anthologies containing mostly reprinted material included *I Shudder at Your Touch* (with four originals, including one by Patrick McGrath) edited by Michele Slung (Roc); *The Mammoth Book of Terror* edited by Stephen Jones (Carroll & Graf); *Hollywood Ghosts* edited by Frank D. McSherry, Jr., Charles G. Waugh and Martin H. Greenberg (Rutledge Hill Press); *Civil War Ghosts* edited by Martin Harry Greenberg, Frank McSherry, Jr., and Charles G. Waugh (August House); *The Horror Hall of Fame* edited by Robert Silverberg and Martin H. Greenberg (Carroll & Graf); *Sacred Visions* (with three original stories—an especially good one by Gene Wolfe), edited by Andrew M. Greeley and Michael Cassutt (Tor);

Scarlet Letters: Tales of Adultery from Ellery Queen's Mystery Magazine edited by Eleanor Sullivan (Carroll & Graf)—including stories by Ruth Rendell, Andrew Klavan and Lawrence Block; *Fifty Years of the Best from Ellery Queen* edited by Eleanor Sullivan (Carroll & Graf); *The Best of Pulphouse: The Hardback Magazine* edited by Kristine Kathryn Rusch (St. Martin's); *The Mammoth Book of Ghost Stories 2* edited by Richard Dalby with a preface by Christopher Lee (Carroll & Graf)—including stories by Dickens, Stoker, Wharton, Mary Wilkins, Kingsley Amis and many other, less familiar names; *Arabian Nights* adapted from Richard F. Burton's unexpurgated translation by Jack Zipes (Signet); *Echoes of Valor III* edited by Karl Edward Wagner (Tor); *Masters of Darkness III* edited by Dennis Etchison (Tor); *Classic Tales of Horror and the Supernatural* edited by Bill Pronzini, Barry Malzberg and Martin H. Greenberg (Morrow/Quill); *Crime Classics: The Mystery Story from Poe to the Present* edited by Rex Burns and Mary Rose Sullivan (Viking)—including stories by Chesterton, Hammett, Sayers, Woolrich, Faulkner, Borges and McBain; *Back from the Dead* edited by Martin H. Greenberg and Charles G. Waugh (DAW); *Best New Horror 2* edited by Stephen Jones and Ramsey Campbell (Carroll & Graf); *Alpha Gallery: Selections from the Fantastic Small Press* (write Michael A. Arnzen, Director, SPWAO Publications Dispersal, 1700 Constitution #D–24, Pueblo, CO 81001); *Dark Crimes: Great Noir Fiction from the 40's to the 90's* edited by Ed Gorman, includes two originals (Carroll & Graf)—and stories by Edward Bryant, Evan Hunter, Lawrence Block, Karl Edward Wagner and Andrew Vachss; *New Stories from the Twilight Zone* edited by Martin H. Greenberg (Avon)—includes the classics "Nightcrawlers," "Shatterday," "Dead Run," and "The Last Defender of Camelot"; *The Literary Ghost: Great Contemporary Ghost Stories* edited by Larry Dark (Atlantic Monthly)—a terrific lineup including stories by A. S. Byatt, Patrick McGrath, Anne Sexton, Fay Weldon and Paul Bowles; *The Literary Dog: Great American Dog Stories* edited by Jeanne Schinto (*Atlantic Monthly* 1990, but missed last year)—includes stories by Donald Barthelme, Ann Beattie, Michael Bishop, T. Coraghessan Boyle and Doris Lessing; *The Year's Best Horror Stories XIX* edited by Karl Edward Wagner (DAW); *Spells of Enchantment: The Wondrous Fairy Tales of Western Culture* edited by Jack Zipes (Viking)—a gorgeous package of over 800 pages, including literary fairy tales for adults by everyone from Hans Christian Andersen and Hermann Hesse to Jane Yolen and Stanislaw Lem. Wonderful illustrations; *Victorian Ghost Stories: An Oxford Anthology* selected by Michael Cox and R. A. Gilbert (Oxford University Press); *Die Monster Die!: The World's Worst Horror Fiction* edited by Micki Villa—24 stories from horror comics of the '40s and '50s (Malibu Graphics); *Haunting Christmas Tales* no editor, YA, which include stories by Garry Kilworth and Joan Aiken (Scholastic–UK); *Crime for Christmas* edited by Richard Dalby (O'Mara–UK); *Tales of Witchcraft* edited by Richard Dalby (O'Mara–UK); *The Virago Book of Ghost Stories: The Twentieth Century: Vol. 2* edited by Richard Dalby (Virago–UK); *The Man in Black: Macabre Stories from Fear on Four* anonymous (BBC Books–UK); *A Book of Dreams* edited by Trevor Jones and George P. Townsend—stories from *Dream* and *New Moon* magazines (Weller–UK); *Spooky Sea Stories* edited by Charles G. Waugh, Martin H. Greenberg and Frank D. McSherry (Yankee Books); *The Virago Book of Fairy*

Tales edited by Angela Carter (Virago–UK); *Short Sharp Shocks* edited by Julian Lloyd Webber (Weidenfeld & Nicolson–UK); *The Walker Book of Ghost Stories* edited by Susan Hill (Walker–UK)—YA stories, some original, and illos. by Hill; *Gaslit Nightmares 2* edited by Hugh Lamb—ghost/horror stories from the Victorian and Edwardian periods (Futura–UK); *Strange Tales from the Strand* edited by Jack Adrian—29 ghost/supernatural stories from the past 100 years of *Strand Magazine* (Oxford–UK).

A number of notable collections included horror or crossover material: *The Ends of the Earth* by Lucius Shepard, lavishly illustrated by J. K. Potter (Arkham House). Shepard's second collection includes fantasy such as "The Scalehunter's Beautiful Daughter," horror such as "The Exercise of Faith," and crossover such as "Life of Buddha."

Arkham House also produced Michael Swanwick's first collection, *Gravity's Angels*, including his first sale, "The Feast of St. Janis" up through "Snow Angels," published in 1989. It's a rich mixture of science fiction and fantasy with a dollop of horror. Interior illustrations by Janet Aulisio with cover art by Picasso.

New Life for the Dead, the first collection of stories by Alan Rodgers, was published by Wildside Press. It includes his Bram Stoker award-winning debut story, "The Boy Who Came Back From the Dead," along with other reprints of prose and poetry. The book contains one original story and a few original poems.

Another production of Wildside Press appearing late in 1991 was the first major collection by Nina Kiriki Hoffman, *Courting Disasters and other Strange Affinities*. More than sixty stories are reprinted along with one original.

Beyond the Curve, Kobo Abe's first collection in English (Kodansha), is a fascinating mixture of short fiction by the author of *The Woman of the Dunes*. The stories (some, never before published in English) are weird, surreal and often verge on the horrific.

Sexpunks and Savage Sagas by Richard Sutphen (Spine-Tingling Press) is a self-published triumph of packaging and marketing over content (although I have no idea if the book actually sold). The author is an "occultist" who has decided to turn his attention to horror. I don't think this guy has ever read horror fiction; he seems not to have a clue that he's using every cliché in the book.

Blood by Janice Galloway (Random House) is a mixed bag of weirdness, possibly more literary than horror readers would like. Many of the stories were first published in British and Scottish magazines. Some very dark pieces, including the remarkable "Blood."

Thomas Ligotti's second collection, *Grimscribe: His Lives and Works* (Carroll & Graf) is being marketed by the publisher as a novel. Now this is a writer who should have been included in *The New Gothic*, if gothic is of a certain baroque style (which is one way I would describe it). Several original stories.

J. G. Ballard's *War Fever* (Farrar, Straus & Giroux) came out in the U.S. just as we were going to war with Iraq. The cover jacket includes a photograph of a man who looks like (but isn't) Sadam Hussein. What does this bizarre coincidence mean? Absolutely nothing except that Ballard has always had the knack of plugging into the political sensibilities of his times. Is there any honest-to-goodness horror in this collection? Probably not. But anyone who calls him or herself a lover of horror has a responsibility to be aware of new work by Ballard, who wrote the great "autoerotic" novel, *Crash*, and the infamous story "Why I Want to Fuck Ronald Reagan" way before Reagan's administration was thought to have done the same to our country.

The prolific Joyce Carol Oates's new collection, *Heat* (Dutton) is a dark one, with some stories more overt in their horror than others.

Waking Nightmares, Ramsey Campbell's newest collection (Tor), covers the years 1974 to 1989 and includes material taken for *The Year's Best Fantasy and Horror* series.

Carol Emshwiller's World Fantasy Award–winning collection *The Start of the End of It All* (Mercury House). Emshwiller has crossed between the mainstream and fantasy fields for many years and is finally receiving the recognition her writing deserves. A different version of this collection was published in the UK by the Women's Press with very little distribution. Terrific weird stuff.

The Copper Peacock and other stories by Ruth Rendell (Mysterious Press) shows off the talent of this British master of psychological suspense with nine stories; one especially chilling story, "Mother's Help," is an original.

Author's Choice Monthly: #17, Alan Brennert's *Ma Qui and Other Phantoms*; #18, Joe R. Lansdale's *Stories by Mama Lansdale's Youngest Boy*; #22, Charles de Lint's *Hedgework and Guessery*; #24, J. N. Williamson's *The Naked Flesh of Feeling* (Pulphouse).

And collections not seen: *Seven Strange and Ghostly Tales* by Brian Jacques— YA (Hutchinson–UK); *The Dark Entry and Other Tales* by Kelvin I. Jones (Sir Hugo Books–UK); *On Meeting Witches at Wells* by Judith Gorog—YA (Putnam/ Philomel); *Tales, Weird and Whimsical* by T. M. Lally (Merlin–UK); *The Best Supernatural Stories of John Buchan* by John Buchan (Robert Hale–UK); *The Unsettled Dust* by Robert Aickman (Mandarin); *The Mary Shelley Reader* includes two novels, seven stories, essays, reviews and letters; The *Frankenstein* text is the rare 1818 first edition, not the heavily revised 1831 which is the source of most reprints (Oxford University Press); *Ravenscarne and Other Ghost Stories* by Mary Williams (Piatkus–UK); *The Collected Short Stories of Roald Dahl* (Michael Joseph–UK).

In contrast to the anthology market, the professional magazine market languished. Small-press horror magazines proliferate, but there continue to be very few professional magazine markets for horror. The following is a sampling of the best professional, semiprofessional and small-press magazines:

Weird Tales usually looks good; the spring issue illustrated by Gahan Wilson was particularly interesting. Good stories and poetry by Jessica Amanda Salmonson, Robert Bloch and Henry Kuttner, Ramsey Campbell, Juleen Brantingham, William F. Nolan, Jason van Hollander and Thomas Ligotti. The editors are George H. Scithers and Darrell Schweitzer.

Iniquities, while nicely designed, is still not on a regular schedule and is still inconsistent in its fiction choices. The editorials are a bit too informal for a slick magazine; however, *Iniquities* always has interesting art, including pieces by J. K.

Potter, Alan Clark and Allen K. in recent issues. And there were good stories by
Ramsey Campbell, Elizabeth Massie, Steve Rasnic Tem, Wayne Allen Sallee and
H. Andrew Lynch and Nina Kiriki Hoffman. The editors are Buddy Martinez and
J. F. Gonzales.

The now-defunct *Fear* Magazine published good horror stories by Mike O'Driscoll, John Pritchard, Jeff Vandermeer, Rick Cadger, David Duggins, Huw
Collingbourne, Malcolm Twigg, Robert Neilson and Andrew J. Wilson.

Fantasy Tales, as far as I can tell, only came out with one issue, in the spring.
The cover by J. K. Potter was striking, but the fiction was disappointing, despite
stories by Thomas Ligotti, Neil Gaiman and William F. Nolan (all three reprints).
The editors are Stephen Jones and David Sutton.

Pulphouse, the Weekly Magazine quickly became simply *Pulphouse the Magazine*. Unfortunately it hasn't yet found its feet, although there was a wise change
in cover design after a few issues that used authors' photographs. So far the fiction
has been inconsistent in quality, but there was some good horror by Mark Budz,
Patricia B. Cirone, David J. Schow, Bradley Denton and Steve Perry. The editor
is Dean Wesley Smith.

The Magazine of Fantasy & Science Fiction, which had a change of editors in
March, published excellent horror stories by Wendy Counsil, Kathe Koja, Michael
Lee, Bradley Denton, Elizabeth Engstrom, Terry Bisson, Sally Caves, David
Hoing, Katharine Eliska Kimbriel, Lois Tilton, Lynn S. Hightower, Esther
Friesner, Kristine Kathryn Rusch, Sheri S. Tepper, Mike Resnick, Henry Slesar
and Marc Laidlaw. The editor was Ed Ferman and is now Kristine Kathryn Rusch.

Isaac Asimov's Science Fiction Magazine published notable horror by Ian R.
MacLeod, Kathleen J. Alcalá, Pat Murphy, Jonathan Lethem, Don Webb, Keith
Roberts, Alexander Jablokov, Lawrence Person, Greg Egan, Walter Jon Williams,
Leonard Carpenter, Richard Paul Russo, Connie Willis, S. N. Dyer, Paul Wit-
cover, Peni R. Griffin and Tanith Lee. The editor is Gardner Dozois.

Alfred Hitchcock's Mystery Magazine published horrific stories by Marion M.
Markham, Robert William Klein, John Paxton Sheriff, Gloria Erickson, Peter
Sellers, K. D. Wentworth, James S. Dorr, Tony Richards, Simon P. McCaffery
and William Beechcroft. The editor is Cathleen Jordan.

Ellery Queen's Mystery Magazine published horrific fiction by Virginia Layef-
sky, Sharon Pisacreta, Richard Patrick Gibbons, Joe Gores, Henry Slesar, Clark
Howard, Peter Lovesey and James Powell. For many years the editor was Eleanor
Sullivan. She died of cancer in 1991. The new editor is Janet Hutchings.

Omni published horrific material by Jack Cady, Robert Frazier, J. G. Ballard,
Barry N. Malzberg, Michael Bishop and J. R. Dunn. Fiction editor is myself
(Ellen Datlow).

Interzone published horror by Chris Beckett, Sylvia M. Siddall, Greg Egan,
Garry Kilworth, Diane Mapes, Nicola Griffith, Martha A. Hood, Frances Amery,
David Langford, Ian R. MacLeod and Alan Heaven. The editor is David Pringle.

New Mystery is a slick new magazine that published its first two issues in 1991.
Despite the self-congratulatory tone of the first issue, the fiction is quite impressive
with excellent new stories from the likes of Lawrence Block, Ruth Rendell, Steve
Rasnic Tem, Atoda Takashi, Ardath Mayhar, James S. Dorr, Shizuko Natsuki

and Leslie Alan Horvitz. There's a freshness to the stories that the old warhorses *Hitchcock* and *Ellery Queen* often lack. It should give the two pulps a run for their money. The editor is Charles Raisch.

And the following is a sampling of the best small-press magazines specializing in horror:

Noctulpa became a digest-sized annual and this seems to have been the right decision. *Noctulpa #5*, called *Guignoir and Other Furies* is impressive, with all the fiction worth reading and effective illustrations by Peter H. Gilmore throughout. Look for stories by Lucy Taylor, Norman Partridge, Nancy Holder, Tia Travis and Scott H. Urban. The magazine is edited by George Hatch.

Cemetery Dance, edited by Richard T. Chizmar, is still the small-press magazine to watch since *The Horror Show* died. Good covers (although the spring cover resembles Jill Bauman's cover for an Alan Ryan novel several years ago) and some good fiction by Joseph Coulson and William Relling, Jr., Melanie Tem, Graham Masterton, Steve Rasnic Tem, Ramsey Campbell, G. Kyle White, Steven Spruill, S. K. Epperson, Bentley Little, Gene Michael Higney, Bill Pronzini, Tom Elliott, Nancy Holder, John Shirley and Wayne Allen Sallee.

After Hours, edited by William G. Raley, redesigned its ninth issue, eliminating story illustrations, which allows slightly more room for text. There was excellent fiction in issues 9–11 by Steve Rasnic Tem, Molly Brown, Robert Grey, Cecily Nabors, Steve Antezak, T. G. Som, Suzi K. West, Eric Del Carlo, Warren Brown, John Dowling and Gorman Bechard.

Deathrealm, edited by Mark Rainey, always has good interior art. I felt the fiction was weak this year although there were good stories by Barb Hendee and Jeff Vandermeer. #15 changed from digest-size to large format.

Not One of Us, edited by John Benson, changed to a new computer with issue #7; this makes the type much more legible. This small-sized magazine usually has readable fiction and some good art. In 1991 there was good horror fiction by Gary A. Braunbeck, Mark McLaughlin and Steve Vernon, and good art by Ray Bashom, John Borkowski and Bucky Montgomery.

Prisoners of the Night, an adult vampire magazine edited by Alayne Gelfand, had a cover (on #5) that looked like it belonged on a coloring book. Good fiction (surprising in light of the art) by Robert Grey, Wendy Rathbone and Taerie Bryant.

2AM edited by Gretta M. Anderson continues to look good, with a clean, legible design. The fiction is always literate if not necessarily frightening. Seems to go more for the repellent factor than fear or horror. Relling's column continues to enlighten, entertain and offend. Good fiction by Brian Skinner, Jessica Amanda Salmonson, Earl Murphy and John Coyne.

Grue edited by Peggy Nadramia also continues to look good, with a fall 1991 cover by Rick Lieder. Excellent fiction and poetry by Norman Partridge, Lisa Lepovetsky, Darrell Schweitzer, and Robert Frazier appeared in issues #13 and #14, the latter a poetry supplement.

Tekeli-li! Journal of Terror (since shortened to *Tek!*) is a new fiction and nonfiction magazine edited by Jon B. Cooke. It makes a serious attempt at reviewing horror. Two overlapping film articles by the same contributor should have been combined and I think the piece on *American Psycho* misses the boat, but on the whole it's a good start. Legible type and good-looking art. Good fiction by James Thompson and Douglas Clegg.

Nyctalops, edited by Harry O. Morris, is apparently the last issue of the magazine after a hiatus of seven years. Morris is known for his dark fantasy/horror art, particularly in the small press (although he's beginning to do book covers. I believe he's the cover artist of Ron Dee's *Dusk* and the reprint of Michael McDowell's *Toplin* (both Abyss), the latter of which is illustrated throughout. So it shouldn't be surprising that *Nyctalops* features terrific art by T. M. Caldwell, J. K. Potter, H. E. Fassl and Morris himself. Serious articles and reviews, good fiction and poetry by Thomas Ligotti, Jessica Amanda Salmonson and Kevin Knapp. The letters are quite old, some dating from seven years ago, and probably should have been tossed. But altogether, a lovely package.

Weirdbook, a World Fantasy Award winner, is a Lovecraftian/weird tales magazine that has been lovingly edited by W. Paul Ganley for many years. While much of the material is not to my taste, I thought there were good poems by Joseph Payne Brennan and Ace G. Pilkington and good stories by Jessica Amanda Salmonson and Brian McNaughton.

Tales of the Unanticipated edited by Eric M. Heideman is published every eight months. There was good fiction in issue #8 by Kij Johnson, Martha A. Hood and Jamil Nasir.

Other magazines in and out of the field that published good horror stories or poems were: *Aboriginal SF*; *Amazing Stories*; *Haunts*; *The Nation*; *Figment*; *The Sterling Web*; *Starshore*; *The New Yorker*; *N.Y. Press*; *Aurealis*; *BBR*; *Glamour*; *Argonaut*; *Dark Horizons*; *Eldritch Tales*; *Outlaw Biker's Tattoo Review*; *Xenophilia*; *Twisted*; *Midnight Zoo*; *A Magazine of American Culture*; *Dreams & Nightmares*; *Skeleton Crew*. Authors included Sandra Paradise, A. J. Austin, K. D. Wentworth, Bruce Boston and Robert Frazier, Nina Kiriki Hoffman, Norman Partridge, Jessica Amanda Salmonson, Tom Elliott, Regina deCormier-Shekerjian, Don Webb, Michelle Marr, Octavio Ramos, Jr., Charles Sheffield, Jessica Greenbaum, Ian Frazier, Mike Romath, E. R. Van Helden, Stephen Dedman, Diana Reed, Tod Mecklem, Joyce Carol Oates, George W. Smythe, Peter Relton, Gary A. Braunbeck, Michael Arnzen, Carl Buchanan, Miroslaw Lipinski, Janet Gluckman, Ken Wisman, R. H. W. Dillard, Michael Arnzen, Lawrence Schimel and Nicholas Royle.

Many small-press magazines appear irregularly and are only available through subscription. Here are addresses and prices for some of the better ones. Only U.S. subscription prices are listed. For overseas information, query the publication. I'm including publications unavailable on U.S. newsstands. *Noctulpa*, which comes out each spring, can be ordered from 140 Dickie Avenue, Staten Island, NY 10314. Query for information and price; *Cemetery Dance*, P.O. Box 858, Edgewood, MD 21040, $15 for a one-year subscription (quarterly); *After Hours*, P.O. Box 538, Sunset Beach, CA 90742-0538, $14/one-year subscription (quarterly); *Deathrealm*, 3223-F Regents Park, Greensboro, NC 27405, $15 payable to Mark Rainey for a one-year subscription (quarterly); *Not One of Us*, 44 Shady Lane,

Storrs, CT 06268, $10.50 payable to John Benson for a three-issue subscription; *Prisoners of the Night*, MKSHEF Enterprises, P.O. Box 368, Poway, CA 92074-0368, $12 (one issue, 102 pages); *2AM*, P.O. Box 6754, Rockford, IL 61125-1754, $19 payable to Gretta M. Anderson, publisher, for a one-year subscription (quarterly); *Grue*, Hell's Kitchen Productions, Inc., P.O. Box 370, Times Square Station, New York, NY 10108-0370, $13 payable to Hell's Kitchen Production, Inc. for a three-issue, one-year subscription; *Tek! Journal of Terror*, c/o Jon B. Cooke, 106 Hanover Avenue, Pawtucket, RI 02861, $20 payable to Montilla Publications for a one-year subscription (quarterly); *Haunts*, P.O. Box 3342, Providence, RI 02906-0742, $13 for a one-year subscription (quarterly); *Weirdbook*, W. Paul Ganley, Publisher, Box 149, Buffalo, NY 14226-0149, 7 issues for $25 (no regular schedule, $7.15 per issue); *Midnight Zoo*, 544 Ygnacio Valley Road, #13, P.O. Box 8040, Walnut Creek, CA 94596, $37 for a one-year subscription (seven issues), California residents add 8.25% sales tax; *Tales of the Unanticipated*, P.O. Box 8036, Lake Street Station, Minneapolis, MN 55408, $10 payable to the Minnesota SF Society, for a three-issue subscription; *Eldritch Tales*, Crispin Burnham, *Eldritch Tales*, 1051 Wellington Road, Lawrence, KS 66049, $24 payable to Crispin Burnham for four issues (irregular); *Dreams & Nightmares* (poetry), David C. Kopaska-Merkel, 1300 Kicker Road, Tuscaloosa, AL 35404, $5 for a one-year subscription (quarterly).

For more information on the horror/dark fantasy field subscribe to: *Locus* and *Science Fiction Chronicle*, the oldest and best newsmagazines covering science fiction (primarily), fantasy and horror. They each periodically cover books published, market reports for the U.S. and Great Britain, domestic and foreign publishing news, and convention reports and listings. Ordering information for each are in the acknowledgments at the front of this book. Charles L. Brown is publisher and editor of *Locus* and Andrew I. Porter is editor and publisher of *Science Fiction Chronicle*.

Necrofile: The Review of Horror Fiction, edited by Stefan Dziemianowicz, S. T. Joshi and Michael A. Morrison is published quarterly by Necronomicon Press. This is the first nonacademic publication in recent years (that I'm aware of) to have made a serious effort to deal exclusively with the written horror field in critical terms. The first issue, 28 pages in newsletter format, contains two essays on horror—Ramsey Campbell (who will have a regular column) writes about his negative personal experiences with copy editors and Thomas Ligotti attempts a definition of "weird fiction." There's also a serious, unhysterical review of *American Psycho* putting it into the context of a piece of literature (failure or not) and a piece of horror fiction; a review of Thomas M. Disch's *The M.D.*; and an overall look at the first eight titles from the Dell/Abyss horror line. #2 reviews *Clive Barker's Shadows in Eden*, recent Ramsey Campbell works, Brian Stableford, Michael Cadnum, and Fred Chappell among others. Professional and readable. (Necronomicon Press, 101 Lockwood St., West Warwick, RI 02893. Individual issues are $2.50; a four-issue subscription is $10.00. The magazine will appear in January, April, July and October.)

The Scream Factory edited by Peter Enfantino is trying to be the professional news magazine of the horror field but so far is only partially successful. #7 covers the 1980s in horror. There are numerous lists, some illuminating and fun, others boring. Is it really necessary to list every horror novel published in the U.S. in the 1980s? The "biggest yawns of the '80s" was interesting, as were some of the commentary on trends, hot new writers, and so forth. Usually the only fiction in *The Scream Factory* is the awful Wyrmwood series. Someone please kill it. #6 (to backtrack) is an all-fiction issue of the magazine—the best of the batch is the subtle and moving Douglas Clegg story. The magazine always looks good, with a readable design but the art in #6 is heavy-handed, occasionally even giving away the plot of a story. (*The Scream Factory*, 4884 Pepperwood Way, San Jose, CA 95124. $20 payable to Peter Enfantino for four issues.)

Crime Beat: Newsmagazine of Crime, edited by T. E. D. Klein (former editor of *Twilight Zone Magazine*), fills an obvious niche for true crime addicts. This stylish-looking oversized magazine has illustrations by some former TZ artists and articles ranging from America's ten most dangerous streets, couples who kill and the story of a Jeffrey Dahmer survivor. The tough-talking style is perfect for the crime buff. Found on newsstands (for subscription information, call 800-877-5303).

Carnage Hall #2, edited by David Griffin. I gave this magazine's debut issue in 1989 a glowing review. The delayed second issue appeared in 1991 and although it looks as good as the first, there are some marked differences in content. The editorial and criticism are self-indulgent and occasionally arrogant. Griffin takes up six pages to excoriate Harlan Ellison's piece on fans, "Xenogenesis," and spends another six pages trashing Kathe Koja's writing in general and specifically her first novel, *The Cipher*. Also included is a thin interview with prominent film critic Pauline Kael that gives no insight into her taste or her writing. An experimental piece of fiction, a poem and a interesting piece by Jessica Amanda Salmonson on anthologies round out the issue. The editor needs to rethink his tone and get back on track (*Carnage Hall Magazine*, P.O. Box 7, Esopus, NY 12429, $4.50 payable to David Griffin, for one copy. Published irregularly).

Scavenger's Newsletter, published by Janet Fox, is a monthly containing market reports, minireviews of small-press magazines, advice and letter columns. This booklet-sized 28-page magazine is invaluable for beginning writers of science fiction, fantasy or horror ($11.50/year payable to Janet Fox, 519 Ellinwood, Osage City, KS 66523).

Gila Queen's Guide to Markets, edited by Kathryn Ptacek, is another monthly devoted to giving up-to-date publishing and marketing information in various genres. Magazine-sized, 24 pages ($20/year payable to the *Gila Queen's Guide to Markets* or Kathryn Ptacek, P.O. Box 97, Newtown, NJ 07860).

The New York Review of Science Fiction, published monthly by Dragon Press, edited by David G. Hartwell et al., makes a diligent effort to be a serious critical magazine covering science fiction, horror and fantasy. It features thought-provoking reviews, interesting but sometimes opaque articles, and best of all (for me), "Read this" sidebars—what individual writers are reading. ($25/year, $33 1st class, payable to Dragon Press, P.O. Box 78, Pleasantville, NY 10570.)

Science Fiction Eye, published and edited by Stephen P. Brown, is the most provocative and invigorating nonfiction genre-oriented magazine around. Still on an irregular schedule, the most recent issue has Bruce Sterling covering a computer game–designing conference; Richard Kadrey covering out-of-the-way music; Takayuki Tatsumi, Norio Itoh and Mari Kotani writing about various science fiction topics from a Japanese point of view; and plenty of reviews, letters, and so forth. (*Science Fiction Eye*, P.O. Box 18539, Asheville, NC 28814. Three issues [one year] $10 U.S.; $15 overseas.)

Fangoria, edited by Tony Timpone, is the queen of the gore magazines, now twelve years old, identifiable by its gaudy, gory covers and gaudy, disgusting interiors reveling in all those gooey special effects. I love reading this on the subway. Although the magazine has always provided more coverage of the horror in film than the horror in print, in the last year it has published interesting reviews and serious articles. One issue concentrated on women in horror from "lady splatterpunks" (those who act in the movies) to those who write and edit horror fiction. Can be found on newsstands.

Gauntlet #2 Exploring the Limits of Free Expression, is an annual published and edited by Barry Hoffman. Volume 2 is much better than the first in scope and in addressing both sides of controversial issues. But a lot of the material is dated by the time each *Gauntlet* appears, which is a problem for any annual series. Some critics claim *Gauntlet* preaches to the converted. I disagree, feeling that the intention is not to preach but to inform those interested and concerned with censorship. Also, *Gauntlet* might provide the impetus to confront and fight censorship to those who are unaware of the problem. The fiction *Gauntlet* publishes rarely works for me. It generally seems heavy-handed and preachy. The "Wizard of Oz" story by William Relling, Jr., was supposedly dropped from *Borderlands* by Avon for reasons of censorship; however, the issue seems to be one of copyright or trademark infringement, and while there's some discussion of this, there's not enough. The legalities may be unpleasant but these laws protect the creators of various characters. It would behoove authors to be aware that these same laws could equally protect their own writing in the future. Get your targets straight (and work to change the law if you don't like it). *Gauntlet* is published each March; $8.95/year, $15/2 years payable to *Gauntlet*, Inc. Dept. 91, 309 Powell Road, Springfield, PA 19064.

Psychotronic (video magazine) primarily covers horror videos and horror personalities but also contains interviews and complete filmographies of favorite horror actors, directors and producers; book and music reviews. It contains a wealth of information for the true grade b–z horror fan. A six-issue subscription to this quarterly costs $20, payable to publisher/editor Michael J. Weldon, 151 First Avenue Dept PV, New York, NY 10003.

Mystery Scene, published by Martin H. Greenberg and edited by Ed Gorman covers the mystery and horror genres with articles and autobiographical columns by writers, news items, reviews, columns and so forth. Published bimonthly, it's a good place to get a feel for what's happening in these two genres. My only complaint is that there is too much overlapping and not enough variety in the book reviews. Sometimes one book is reviewed two or three times in one issue. Subscription costs $35 for seven issues, Mystery Enterprises, 3840 Clark Road SE, Cedar Rapids, IA 52403.

* * *

The small specialty press continues to be active, often publishing a limited signed edition for collectors along with a trade edition of a book.

Roadkill Press published reasonably priced limited-edition paperbacks of Joe Lansdale's "On the Far Side of the Cadillac Desert with Dead Folks"; Melanie Tem's chilling original story "Daddy's Side"; Simon Hawke's novel excerpt, "The 9 Lives of Catseye Gomez"; two Roadkill doubles including one with original stories by Wil McCarthy and Gregory R. Hyde, and a second with original stories by Ann K. Schwader and Lucy Taylor; "The Tortuga Hills Gang's Last Ride: The True Story," an original by Nancy A. Collins; a collection of three guest-of-honor speeches by Dan Simmons entitled *Going After the Rubber Chicken* and "Distress Call," by Connie Willis (write Little Bookshop of Horrors, 10380 Ralston Road, Arvada, CO 80004 for information); Ferdogan & Bremer announced *The Black Death*, an occult thriller by Basil Copper with illustrations and jacket art by Stefanie K. Hawks (700 Washington Avenue SE, Suite 50, Minneapolis, MN 55414); Scream/Press published the long-awaited limited *Books of Blood* VI by Clive Barker, illustrations by Harry O. Morris; its sister imprint Dream/Press published an omnibus edition of Richard Matheson's two novels of love and fantasy, *Somewhere in Time* and *What Dreams May Come* (write P.O. Box 481146, Los Angeles, CA 90048 for information); Charnel House published Ray Garton's *The New Neighbor: A Novel of Erotic Horror* with illustrations by J. K. Potter (Charnel House, P.O. Box 633, Lynbrook, NY 11563); Donald M. Grant published Stephen King's *The Dark Tower III: The Wastelands* with illustrations by Ned Dameron and an artist's portfolio of the twelve color illustrations from the book *Mrs. God* by Peter Straub, beautifully illustrated by Rick Berry in a slightly longer (and reportedly the preferred) version of the story than that which appeared in Straub's collection *Houses Without Doors*, Edward McCrorie's new translation of *The Aeneid of Virgil* with art by Luis Ferreira and *The Face in the Abyss* by A. Merritt, illustrations by Ned Dameron (Donald M. Grant, Publisher, Inc., P.O. Box 187, Hampton Falls, NH 03844 for information); Borderlands Press published *Borderlands 2* edited by Thomas F. Monteleone, *Under the Fang* edited by Robert R. McCammon, Joe R. Lansdale's novel *The Magic Wagon* with illustrations by Mark Nelson and cover by Jill Bauman, *No Doors, No Windows*, a collection of dark suspense by Harlan Ellison and *Gauntlet 2* edited by Barry Hoffman (for information write: Borderlands Press, P.O. Box 32333, Baltimore, MD 21208); Wildside Press published Alan Rodgers's first collection, *New Life for the Dead* and Nina Kiriki Hoffman's second collection, *Courting Disasters*. In addition, the press published *Rescue Run* by Anne McCaffrey, *Pink Elephants* by Mike Resnick, *Sir Harold and the Gnome King* by L. Sprague de Camp, *The Armageddon Box* by Robert Weinberg, and *The Black Lodge* by Robert Weinberg. *The White Mists of Power* by Kristine Kathryn Rusch and *Letters to the Alien Publisher*, anonymous, were published by First Books. (For information on all these titles write: The Wildside Press, 37 Fillmore Street, Newark, NJ 07105.) Dark Harvest published the original anthology *Obsessions* edited by Gary Raisor, the first hardcover edition of Robert R. McCammon's novel *They Thirst*, two new novels by F. Paul Wilson: *Reprisal* (the third novel in the series started with *The*

Keep) and *Sibs*, *Night Visions 9* with stories by Thomas Tessier, James Kisner and Rick Hautala, and the "shared crime" anthology *Invitation to Murder* edited by Ed Gorman and Martin H. Greenberg (Dark Harvest, P.O. Box 941, Arlington Heights, IL 60006); Mark V. Ziesing Books published Ray Garton's novel *Lot Lizards*, *Wetbones*, a novel by John Shirley, *Cold Blood*, edited by Richard Chizmar, and *The Hereafter Gang* by Neal Barrett, Jr. (Mark V. Ziesing, P.O. Box 76, Shingletown, CA 96088); Ultramarine Press published a limited edition of Thomas M. Disch's novel *The M.D.: A Horror Story*, in addition to up-to-date author checklists for Thomas M. Disch, Kim Stanley Robinson, Lucius Shepard, Roger Zelazny, Dean R. Koontz and K. W. Jeter, and the Science Fiction and Fantasy paperback first edition: a complete list of all of them (1943–1973, 151 pages) (Ultramarine Publishing Company, Inc., P.O. Box 303, Hastings-on-Hudson, NY 10706); Underwood-Miller published several titles in 1991, including the long awaited *Clive Barker's Shadows in Eden* edited by Stephen Jones and illustrated by Clive Barker, *Ecce and Old Earth* by Jack Vance, *Bernie Wrightson: A Look Back* with commentary by Christopher Zavisa and an introduction by Harlan Ellison, *The Complete Masters of Darkness* edited by Dennis Etchison, *Horror-story Volume Three—The Collector's Edition* edited by Karl Edward Wagner, *Selections from the Exegesis by Philip K. Dick* edited by Laurence Sutin, *The Selected Letters of Philip K. Dick–1974* introduction by William Gibson, and *Computer: Bit Slices from a Life* by Herbert R.J. Grosch. (Underwood-Miller, Inc., 708 Westover Drive, Lancaster, PA 17601); Tartarus Press published chapters 5 and 6 of Arthur Machen's *The Secret Glory*, previously unpublished, and a two-volume trade paperback, *Machenalia: Critical Essays on the Work of Arthur Machen* (Tartarus Press, 51 De Montford Road, Lewes, E. Sussex, BN7 1SS, UK); Necronomicon Press brought out *21 Letters of Ambrose Bierce*, *In Search of Lovecraft* by J. Vernon Shea—six essays on Lovecraft, 13 poems and two stories, *The H. P. Lovecraft Memorial Plaque*, *Witches of the Mind: A Critical Study of Fritz Leiber* by Bruce Byfield, *The Centennial Conference Proceedings* edited by S. T. Joshi, *H. P. Lovecraft Letters to Henry Kuttner* by David E. Schultz and S. T. Joshi (Necronomicon Press, 101 Lockwood St., West Warwick, RI 02893); WSFA Press published their annual Disclave guest of honor collection, this one called *The Edges of Things*, thirteen stories by Lewis Shiner, two of them original (WSFA Press, P.O. Box 19951, Baltimore, MD 21211-0951); Chris Drumm Books published Steve Rasnic Tem's *Celestial Inventory*, a horror novella (Chris Drumm Books, P.O. Box 445, Polk City, IA 50226); Haunted Library published *Absences: Charlie Goode's Ghosts*, a collection of five original stories by Tem about a psychic sleuth (Rosemary Pardoe, Flat One, 36 Hamilton St., Hoole, Chester, England, CH2 3JQ); Starmont published *The Shining Reader*, edited by Anthony Magistrale, *The Devil's Notebook* by Clark Ashton Smith (Starmont House, P.O. Box 851, Mercer Island, WA 98040); Broken Mirrors Press published *Welcome to Reality: The Nightmares of Philip K. Dick* edited by Uwe Anton, *Captain Jack Zodiac*, a novel by Michael Kandel, and *Lafferty in Orbit*, a collection (Broken Mirrors Press, Box 473, Cambridge, MA 02238); Tafford published Alfred Bester's psychological thriller *Tender Loving Rage* (Tafford Publishing, P.O. Box 271804, Houston, TX 77277); and Borgo Press published *Jerzy Kozinski:*

The Literature of Violation by Welch D. Everman (Borgo Press, P.O. Box 2845, San Bernadino, CA 92406).

Graphic Novels:

I Am Legend by Richard Matheson, in four parts. Adapted by Steve Niles and illustrations by Elman Brown (Eclipse). The classic vampire novel, lovingly adapted here, maintains the feel of the original.

M by Fritz Lang, illustrations by Jon J. Muth (Arcane/Eclipse) continuing from last year. Wonderfully evocative and true to the film, which starred Peter Lorre.

Cages by Dave McKean (Tundra) numbers 1–4 (of the projected ten) are interestingly mysterious. The gorgeous covers are more in the McKean style than are the black-and-white interiors, which disappointed me. Seems to be about art and the creative process, but it's not at all clear where it's going.

Hellraiser 3 (Epic) contains three hellraiser stories inspired by Clive Barker's movies. Only the third, "Songs of Metal and Flesh," comes close to capturing the feel of the movies in its perversity, viciousness and graphic depiction of mutilation as prescribed by the Cenobites. Several different artists contribute work—the best is by Bill Sienkewicz—not really part of the stories but grace notes between them. Other artists included are Ted McKeever, A. C. Farley, Scott Hampton and Kevin O'Neill.

Violent Cases by Neil Gaiman and Dave McKean (Tundra) is the color version of this terrific graphic novel, previously only published in England. A new introduction is provided by Gaiman.

Clive Barker's "Son of Celluloid" adapted by Steve Niles and illustrated by Les Edwards (Eclipse) is a very effective rendition of the Barker story about a haunted movie theater in which the "ghost" is the cancer of a dead criminal.

Clive Barker's "Revelations" adapted by Steve Niles and illustrated by Lionel Talaro (Eclipse) is another good-looking Barker adaptation. A murderous couple are forced to reenact the last night of their relationship in the presence of a narrow-minded evangelist and his unhappy wife.

Clive Barker's "The Yattering and Jack" adapted by Steve Niles and illustrated by John Bolton (Eclipse) is the best of all the graphic novelizations I've seen of Barker's work. It combines nastiness with charm and playfulness in both the text and illustrations. Hardcover as well as soft. Highly recommended.

Taboo 5 edited by Stephen R. Bissette (SpiderBaby Graphix and Tundra). This impressive new addition to the series is more consistent in quality and sophistication than the first four issues although there are a couple (Jeff Jones's for one) that are just too obscure or simply don't work.

The S. Clay Wilson piece is quite odd—the introduction, by Bissette, explains that Wilson received a commission to illustrate a letter from a dead man and that the resulting piece was so disgusting no one but *Taboo* would publish it. Furthermore, Wilson is quoted as saying it was "the most odious, satanic, twisted commision [sic] I've ever done." It is unclear from his statement and from Bissette's introduction discussing the "homophobic nausea that informs every panel" who are the homophobes here: the artist who created the work or the person who commissioned it. The work is a very negative visual depiction of what is essentially a love letter. While the letter's text may not reflect many people's sexual tastes, it is neither violent nor homophobic (unless Bissette refers to how the person who commissioned the work wanted it interpreted) and is certainly less repulsive to me as a woman than is most of the woman-hating swill Wilson usually creates. All in all, very strange.

This issue of *Taboo* includes chapter four of *From Hell* (see the following) by Alan Moore and Eddie Campbell. *Taboo Especial*, also out in 1991, is a big disappointment except for the back and front covers by J. K. Potter. Most of the pieces are too obvious.

From Hell: Being a Melodrama in Sixteen Parts by Alan Moore and Eddie Campbell (Mad Love/Tundra) is the compilation of the prologue and first two parts of the series that has been appearing regularly in *Taboo*. Brilliant dissection of Victorian England, using the Jack the Ripper mystery as the focal point. One of the most interesting graphic novels available today. With an appendix by Moore, which distinguishes between fact and fancy and clarifies certain points. Highly recommended.

The Tundra sketchbook series is a good idea that can only be as successful as the various sketchbooks of each individual artist:

#1 *Melting Pot* by Eric Talbot and Kevin Eastman is pretentious, heavy-handed, male adolescent fantasy and not very interesting. #2 *Fetal Brain Tango* by John T. Totleben. An interesting artist experimenting stylistically from the naturalistic to expressionistic. Top notch. #4 *The Rick Bryant Sketchbook* has some nice material, mostly portraits but nothing really exciting, with no commentary at all. In contrast, #5 *Sketchbook* by Charles Vess is astonishing. Vess is best-known to fantasy and horror readers as co-winner of last year's World Fantasy Award with Neil Gaiman for their graphic novel "A Midsummer Night's Dream," from the Sandman series. What really makes this sketchbook special are the notes wherein Vess discusses what he was aiming for, and articulates for the reader the process of creation from idea to finished color work. Bravo. #6 *Screaming Masks Sketchbook and Companion Volume* by Rick McCollum and Bill Anderson is very comic-booky in feel and neither illuminating or ambitious in scope. #7 *Vanitas Paintings Drawings and Ideas* by Jon J. Muth shows a fine artist at work, experimenting with his medium. Thought-provoking. Magnificent. [Sketchbook #3 not seen.]

Art Books:

Pish, Posh, Said Hieronymus Bosch by Nancy Willard and The Dillons (HBJ), is a sumptuous feast for the eyes by Leo and Diane Dillon, two of the best artists the fantasy and science fiction field has ever had. Their son Lee also participates, having created the gorgeous gilt frame that appears throughout the book. An oddly good-natured piece of work considering the seriousness of the art on which it's based. In Bosch's original paintings the creatures/machines were used for torture, yet all the horror is leached from his art in this interpretation. Still, the book is quite beautiful.

Nancy Grossman (Hillwood Art Museum). I was forced to buy this oversized trade paperback when I saw it displayed in B. Dalton's window. The front and back covers are filled by two heads in what look like black bondage masks. Grossman, who first exhibited her leather-covered sculpture heads in 1969, insists that she wasn't even aware of the bondage scene when she conceived of these, but rather was inspired by Frankenstein and the equestrian tack with which she grew up. The book shows her illustrations and paintings as well as the evolution of her sculpting, and indeed she started with leather riding materials formed into intricate tortured-looking monster shapes. Her method of creating the masks is described—she first sculpts raw wood heads, paints or covers them with a red under-mask before dark leather skins are permanently affixed. Fascinating.

Torment in Art: Pain, Violence and Martyrdom by Lionello Puppi (Rizzoli) is a deeply disturbing coffee-table book whose avowed intention is "to give a fully documented account of the complex mechanisms that governed the workings of public executions and of the impact this obsessive and dazzling public spectacle might have had. . . ." The paintings, drawings and etchings have been chosen from the twelfth through nineteenth centuries—a time when public execution in Europe was an event that brought the populace together to view torture and executions as entertainment. The book connects individual paintings to specific, documented executions the artist might have witnessed, to explain the accuracy of the artist's depiction of a particular torture or method of execution. This is death as public spectacle. The book does not try to explain why executions evolved into a private affair and why, with the advent of the guillotine, torture gave way to a quick death for criminals, away from the deliberate infliction of pain. And it never does explain, to my satisfaction, how torture provided a cartharsis for the populace of those times. (The book makes reference to Michel Foucault's book *Discipline and Punishment: The Birth of the Prison* for some possible answers.) For anyone interested in the origin of splatter—here it is. Not cheap at $75, but thought-provoking and lavishly illustrated.

Tales of Edgar Allan Poe illustrated by Barry Moser (Books of Wonder/Morrow) is notable for the color illustrations by Moser, who has done marvelous black-and-white work for *Alice in Wonderland* and *Through the Looking Glass*, *The Wizard of Oz* (with Nancy Reagan as the wicked witch), *Moby Dick*, *The Scarlet Letter*, and many other classics. While I personally prefer his black-and-white etchings, his eighteen watercolors for the Poe are beautiful and powerful. A perfect gift book.

Nuclear Enchantment: Photographs by Patrick Nagatani with an essay by Eugenia Parry Janis (University of New Mexico Press). Nagatani is a Japanese-American born in Chicago thirteen days after Hiroshima, where he had relatives. In 1987 he was drawn to New Mexico, as the nexus of the birth of the nuclear age. His photographic constructions often juxtapose high-tech and Native-American imagery of the area and his work is drenched with unnatural colors, reminiscent of Sandy Skoaglund's green radioactive cats. On the cover you've got a green sky, nuclear workers in protective gear, and bats flying right at you. Satire, fantasy, horror all mix in this SF apocalyptic art.

H. R. Giger's Necronomicon (Morpheus International) is the first hardcover and first U.S. edition of this oversized art book. It opens with an essay on the *fantastique* in art by Clive Barker, and continues with commentary by Giger on his childhood and the various real-life influences on his visionary art (much of it inspired by his nightmares and dreams). Photographs of Giger, from childhood to adulthood with his family and friends, sketches and full-page color paintings of projects including those for Jodorowsky's ill-fated production of the film *Dune* and album cover art for Emerson, Lake and Palmer's *Brain Salad Surgery*. His art is erotic and horrific, as shown by the sets he designed for *Alien*. As beautiful and creepy as last year's *Biomechanics*.

Mary Ellen Mark 25 Years, edited by Marianne Fulton (Bulfinch Press/Little Brown), is a retrospective of her strongest images, including many that are quite justly famous. Included in the book are mostly unpublished photographs of Indian circuses. All the work is black-and-white; Mark was inspired by the black-and-white work of Robert Frank, Henri Cartier-Bresson, Marion Post Wolcott and W. Eugene Smith. She works best in this medium. Many of her photographs have been about people on the fringes of society—inmates of mental institutions (her *Ward 81* series), her prostitutes in *Falkland Road: Prostitutes of Bombay* (which took ten years to obtain financial backing and access to the women), the dying in Calcutta and runaways in Seattle. Powerful photo essays. One hundred thirty tritone illustrations.

Ralph Eugene Meatyard: An American Visionary (Rizzoli) who died in 1972 of cancer, was a photographic contemporary of Minor White and Paul Strand. He moved in a completely different direction from their sharp, "realistic" type of photography. Perhaps because the manipulation of photographic object into phantasms was not then in vogue, his work is rarely mentioned in historical surveys. Meatyard's best work deals with death and decay; his photographs show children in ghostlike poses, in grotesque masks. His final series, "The Family Album of Lucybelle Crater" taken from 1969–1971 pair Meatyard's wife, Madelyn, who appears in each picture, with one of his friends or family members. The two figures are set in informal but staid poses in a suburban setting and each figure wears a mask. Madelyn's mask depicts an old woman with exaggerated, oversized, sad features—the Lucybelle Crater of the title (the name is taken from a Flannery O'Connor story). Worth a look.

Twin Palm Publishers–Twelvetrees Press publishes some wonderfully strange art books. A selection of some of the books they've published in the last few years:

Sleeping Beauty: A History of Memorial Photography in America by Stanley B. Burns, M.D. Between 1830 and 1940 it was not uncommon for people to have postmortem photographs taken of their loved ones. In many of the photos the dead look as if they're merely sleeping, in others there's no effort to disguise blood coming from the nose or mouth, or rashes from whatever disease caused a child's death. Seventy-six color plates. Dr. Burns is an opthalmic surgeon and photographic historian and archivist. He owns 100,000 vintage prints. Twenty thousand of these are early medical photographs from 1839–1920 and make up the largest collection of its kind in the world. Some of these appear in the 1987 book, *Masterpieces of Medical Photography: Selections from the Burns Archive* edited by Joel-Peter Witkin. They include tintypes, daguerreotypes and photographs of wounded Civil War veterans. Both an historical document of medicine and an indictment of war. Not pretty.

In the book *Gods of Earth and Heaven* (also by Joel-Peter Witkin) cadavers, transsexuals and animals are carefully arranged to create a mythology from Witkin's own mind. Second printing. The out-of-print photography book *Joel-Peter Witkin*, which I've seen selling for $200, may be reprinted soon. (Twin Palms Publishers, 2400 North Lake Avenue, Altadena, CA 91001).

Bernie Wrightson: A Look Back edited by Christopher Zavisa (Underwood-Miller) is a lovingly executed retrospective of the comic book artist who created *Swamp Thing*. I first saw Wrightson's work several years ago in a Northampton, Massachusetts, bookstore (coincidentally, the gallery that represents Barry Moser's work is also in Northampton). It was his 1977 black-and-white illustrated version of the great Mary Shelley novel *Frankenstein*. I was struck by the fine detail of his drawings. I knew nothing about the artist, but later learned that he was a contemporary artist. *Bernie Wrightson: A Look Back* showcases, along with Wrightson's illustrations for *Frankenstein* (with sketches, copious notes and alternate versions of scenes), his early work, his experiments in style, technique, and medium—in actuality, his evolution as a multifaceted artist. The book is a hefty 360 pages, lavishly illustrated. Highly recommended.

Nonfiction Books:

Autonomedia publishes (sometimes in conjunction with Semiotext(e)) well-produced attractive paperbacks on a variety of arcane topics, ranging from a reprint of Hakim Bey's book of rants, *T.A.Z. The Temporary Autonomous Zone, Ontological Anarchy, Poetic Terrorism*, to *Horsexe*, a study of the phenomenon of transsexuality by Catherine Millot. *Horsexe* includes some Freudian and semiotic gobbledygook (skip the equations), but it's a fascinating topic and a fascinating essay. Historically there have always been groups that denied their birth gender (in fact, there have been religious cults—the Skoptzy sect of early twentieth-century Russia—that regularly castrated the men, but I don't buy the premise that they wanted to be female, rather that they wanted to keep themselves pure and away from the female) but it wasn't until relatively recently that transsexuality could become a physical reality through science and technology. Some women consider male-to-female transsexuality as just another patriarchal ruse to denigrate women. What frightens and frustrates most women about the male-to-female transsexual is that it seems to reinforce sexual stereotypes "with a view to maintaining women in the conventional, subordinate role from which they were on the point of freeing themselves . . . they gauge femininity in terms of conformity of roles."

Hannibal Lecter, My Father by Kathy Acker (Semiotext(e)—Native Agents Series) is a collection of several short pieces by Acker and an interview with her by Sylvere Lotringer about her life and art. Included is her first piece, written when she was twenty-one. (I call them "pieces" because although mostly fictional they aren't what one would call stories.) Also included is the play *Birth of the Poet* performed at the Brooklyn Academy of Music Next Wave Festival in 1985.

Holy Horrors: An Illustrated History of Religious Murder and Madness by James A. Haught (Prometheus, 1990) is an invaluable complement to *Torment in Art*. It's difficult, in light of the evidence in *Holy Horrors*, to counter the author's argument that religious faith keeps "groups apart, alienated in hostile camps" and that "religious tribalism sets the stage for bloodshed. Without it, young people might adapt to changing times, intermarry and forget historic wounds. But religion enforces separation. . . ." *Holy Horrors* uses some of the same illustrations as *Torment in Art* but puts them into a very different context—torture used in a religious fervor against heretics and infidels, indeed, against anyone with whom the majority religion didn't agree. Haught covers everything from human sacrifice to the massacres of the Crusades, the Sepoy Mutiny, the Nazi Holocaust and the insanity of Jonestown.

Bloodlust: Conversations with Real Vampires by Carol Page (HarperCollins). One's first reaction to the title is, what a great idea! The conversations are with people who *think* they are vampires—they suck or drink blood regularly. Some of them feel the blood keeps them younger-looking but, as the author points out, the majority use blood drinking as a power trip—the persuasion of a "donor" is paramount to the satisfaction. None take it from those unwilling to supply it and no one is hurt physically. Nothing supernatural here. Unfortunately, the people interviewed are basically sad misfits and/or completely nuts but their stories are not very interesting.

Female Perversions: The Temptations of Madame Bovary by Louise J. Kaplan (Doubleday/Anchor). Traditionally, sexual perversion has been considered an exclusively male realm. In the definition most often used by psychoanalysts, "what distinguishes perversion is its quality of desperation and fixity . . . a person . . . has no other choices . . . would otherwise be overwhelmed by anxieties or depression or psychosis." Kaplan's thesis is that "perversions . . . are as much pathologies of gender role identity as they are pathologies of sexuality . . ." and that "these stereotypes are central aspects to perverse strategy." Dr. Kaplan tries to show how certain behaviors of females, including kleptomania, self-mutilation (delicate cutting) trichotillomania—a mania for hair-plucking and anorexia are indeed perversions by her definition. She uses Flaubert's *Madame Bovary* for examples because "on every page . . . there is a fetish of one sort or another." A fascinating, thought-provoking book.

Broken Mirrors, Broken Minds: The Dark Dreams of Dario Argento by Maitland McDonaugh (Sun Tavern Fields–UK) is the first English language book on the Italian master of baroque grand guignol horror films such as *Suspiria* and *Four Flies on Grey Velvet*. Although a serious critical study, it's accessible for those not well-versed in Argento's oeuvre. It made me, whose seen only two of his films, want to see the others. Expensive ($30) but good-looking hardcover with stills from the films, ads and lobby cards.

Shock Xpress: The Essential Guide to Exploitation Cinema edited by Stefan Jaworzyn (Titan Books–UK) is a compilation of six years' worth of old and new material from the British magazine. Includes an illuminating interview with the British censor, an interview with John Waters, and an interesting historical piece about freaks in the cinema starting with Browning's *Freaks* in 1932 (not shown in Great Britain until 1963). Entertaining. They take their schlock very seriously.

Prism of the Night: A Biography of Anne Rice by Katherine M. Ramsland (Dutton) is a must for her fans. A moving portrait of Rice's life and how it relates to her several writing personas using interviews with her friends and family. Included is her relationship with her husband, poet Stan Rice, and the terrible tragedy of their young daughter's leukemia. Ramsland is sensitive to the subject and provides a good overall view of Rice's life and works.

The Thrill of Fear by Walter Kendrick (Grove Weidenfeld) is an erudite, exasperating and often self-contradictory look at the evolution of horrific fiction (Kendrick generally means film, even when he uses the word "fiction," causing much confusion), which is certain to infuriate most horror fans and other supporters. First, Kendrick holds a very narrow view of what he defines as horror—strictly fiction/film meant to convey chills—and that's it. Not discomfort, eeriness or a subtly creeping fear. Kendrick is so patronizing toward the subject, one wonders why he's even interested in writing about it. Furthermore, at whom is the book aimed? Some quotes from the book: ". . . the effects it aims at, no matter how skillfully they are handled, remain physical: cold sweat on the brow, upstanding hairs on the nape of the neck. . . ." "The entire nineteenth century failed to produce a single first-rate novelist who specialized in chills; the best the twentieth century can do in that line is Stephen King" (ignoring Peter Straub and Shirley Jackson among others). "The ingrained conservatism of scary entertainment, its characteristic habit of telling the same old story, using devices that were hackneyed 200 years ago, no doubt owes something to its confinement to a cultural ghetto." Aside from the fact that he might be talking about any bad fiction, horror or otherwise, he's wrong in his perception that horror fiction was always ghettoized. Only with the enormous popularity of Stephen King has horror become a "genre." Before that, horror novels such as *The Turn of the Screw, Dracula, We Have Always Lived in the Castle* and other novels of quality were not forced into such rigid classifications.

More: "For two centuries, horrid short stories have been one-note compositions, reducible to a gimmick apiece. Their length, of course, compels simplification, along with a narrow focus of emotional appeal . . . they seldom try anything radically new. . . ." Where has Kendrick been the last twenty years? Has he read any Shirley Jackson, Dennis Etchison, Karl Edward Wagner, Peter Straub or Joyce Carol Oates?

An awful lot of irrelevancies (his survey of theatre in the nineteenth century) and contradictions. He calls Poe and Hawthorne "two of the nation's finest writers," then pretty much trashes Poe and goes on to assert—I'm paraphrasing here—that Poe's unreliable narrators, who can call into question the nature of reality or of human knowledge, are an unintentional narrative device by Poe because he [Poe] obviously believes in rationality, proven by his detective M. Dupin stories. Hasn't Kendrick ever heard of using different narrative devices for different stories?

This is not to say he doesn't have some interesting points. He does. For example, he says "The effects of death are horrific, but immortality redeems them. We have forgotten the second half but preserved the first." For the most part, though, this book is a lot of glib nonsense.

Other nonfiction titles of note: *A Youth in Babylon: Confessions of a Trash-Film Movie King* by David F. Friedman (Prometheus); *The Charm of Evil: The Life and Films of Terrence Fisher* by Wheeler Dixon (McFarland); *The Cosmical*

Horror of H. P. Lovecraft: A Pictorial Anthology (Glittering Images–Italy [215] 374–7477 for information on ordering); *Science Fiction, Fantasy, & Horror: 1990* by Charles N. Brown and William G. Contento (Locus Press); *The Trial of Gilles de Rais* by George Bataille (Amok—first English translation of 1965 French); *So You Want to Make Movies* by Sidney Pink (Pineapple Press); *Science Fiction Stars and Horror Heroes* by Tom Weaver (McFarland); *The Modern Horror Film: 50 Contemporary Classics from "The Curse of Frankenstein" to "The Lair of the White Worm"* by John McCarty (Citadel); *Beauty and the Beast: Visions and Revisions of an Old Tale* by Betsy Hearne (University of Chicago); *The Annotated She: H. Rider Haggard's Victorian Romance,* introduction and notes by Norman Etherington (Indiana University Press); *Haunting the House of Fiction: Feminist Perspectives on Ghost Stories by American Woman* edited by Lynette Carpenter and Wendy K. Kolmar (University of Tennessee); *The Shape Under the Sheet: The Complete Stephen King Encyclopedia* by Stephen Spignesi (Popular Culture Ink); *Horror Comics: The Illustrated History* by Mike Benton (Taylor Publishing); *How to Write Tales of Horror, Fantasy, & Science Fiction* edited by J. N. Williamson (Writer's Digest Books); *True Stories from the Great Ghost Hunter* by Elliott O'Donnell (Avery); *Phantom of the Opera* by Philip J. Riley, includes script facsimile, complete pressbook, Lon Chaney's notes, art department sketches, and a reconstruction of the five versions of the 1925 production (Samuel French Trade); *The Nightmare Considered: Critical Essays on Nuclear War Literature* edited by Nancy Anisfield (Bowling Green State University Popular Press); *Mad Doctors, Monsters and Mummies!: Lobby Card Posters from Hollywood Horrors* and *Things, Its and Aliens! Lobby Card Posters from Sci-Fi Shockers!* by Denis Gifford are large format poster books (Green Wood–UK); *Boris Karloff* by Scott Allen Nollen (McFarland); *An Epicure in the Terrible: A Centennial Anthology of Essays in Honor of H. P. Lovecraft* by David E. Schultz and S. T. Joshi (Fairleigh Dickinson University Press); *Night Stalking: A 20th Anniversary Kolchak Companion* by Mark Dawidziak (Image Publishing); *H. R. Giger Art* by H. R. Giger—art book/autobiography (Taschen-Germany); *Edgar Allen Poe: Mournful and Never-Ending Remembrance* by Kenneth Silverman (HarperCollins); *Hoffman's Guide to SF, Horror and Fantasy Movies 1991–1992* (Corgi); *Images of Fear: How Horror Stories Helped Shape Modern Culture (1818–1918)* (McFarland); *The Cabinet of Dr. Caligari: Texts, Contexts, Histories* edited by Mike Budd (Rutgers University Press); *Invasion of the Body Snatchers* edited by Al LaValley—script of classic film plus reviews, essays, and commentary (Rutgers University Press); *The Dark Shadows Companion: 25th Anniversary Collection* by Kathryn Leigh Scott (Pomegranate Press); *Wandering Ghost: The Odyssey of Lafcadio Hearn* (Knopf); *How to Write Horror Fiction* by William F. Nolan (Writer's Digest); *Homicide: A Year on the Killing Streets* by David Simon (Houghton Mifflin); *The Stephen King Story: A Literary Profile* by George Beahm (Andrews & McMeel).

Odds and Ends:
   Words Without Pictures: A Collection of Short Stories from Some of the Most Popular Graphic Novelists of the Past Decade (Arcane/Eclipse trade paperback). It

isn't clear which, if any, of the stories are originals but the package, with amusing caricatures of each artist by John Bolton, is an impressive piece of work.

Jabberwocky: A Pop-Up Rhyme from Through the Looking Glass (Viking) by Nick Bantock, the creator of *There Was an Old Lady*, is charming but slight. Much better, by the same author/artist, is the best-selling *Griffin & Sabine* (Chronicle) mentioned in Terri Windling's Introduction.

The Year in Darkness Wall Calendar—1991 by Bucky Montgomery. Illustrations and one-page stories by small-press contributors Bentley Little, John Borkowski, Alfred Klosterman, Allen Koszowski, Janet Fox, John Rosenman and others. A good deal for the money. The 1992 calendar includes work by Jessica Amanda Salmonson, Mark Rainey, John Borkowski, Allen Koszowski and others. The cost is $12.88 for a copy signed by all contributors, $8.88 unsigned, from Montgomery Publishing Agency and Studio, Inc., 692 Calero Avenue, San Jose, CA 95123.

G. Michael Dobbs and Stephen R. Bissette's *The Year in Fear Calendar, Sixteen Month Calendar Portfolio—1992* (Tundra). Oversized and impressively grisly art, most painted exclusively for the calendar, with interesting horror tidbits throughout. Can be ordered through Tundra Publishing, Ltd., 320 Riverside Drive, Northampton, MA 01060 for $14.95 + $4 shipping and 5% sales tax for MA residents.

Scary Stories: More Tales to Chill Your Bones. Collected from folklore and retold by Alvin Schwartz. Drawings by Stephen Gammell (Harper Trophy). Young adult stories, only adequately told, are not the attraction of this book (except perhaps for the few young adults who have not yet heard these urban/suburban legends). The art, though, is something else. Keep a lookout for Gammell's black-and-white drawings, which are funny and horrific. I'd like to see them illustrating something a bit more original.

Now We Are Sick edited by Neil Gaiman and Stephen Jones (Dreamhaven Books) is the long-awaited sicko poetry anthology for kids with weird taste and their elders. The silver-on-black embossed cover by Clive Barker and interiors by Andrew Smith look elegant. Most of the poems, reprint and original, are quite a lot of fun and some of the originals are very good, particularly those by Neil Gaiman and Steve Jones, Richard Hill, Kim Newman, Galad Elflandsson, Colin Greenland and Storm Constantine. A lovely package.

Pandemonium: Further Explorations into the Worlds of Clive Barker conceived and edited by Michael Brown (Eclipse) makes an interesting companion volume to last year's *Clive Barker Illustrator*. Impressive essays by Barker on his own work, and others by Gary Hoppenstand and Douglas E. Winter; interviews with the cenobites and with friends who worked with Barker in the Dog Theatre company. Sometimes it's a bit hagiographic but for the most part there's genuinely insightful analyses of his work. Includes Barker-designed theater posters, photos and artwork and a complete unpublished play.

Clive Barker's Shadows in Eden edited by Stephen Jones (Underwood-Miller) would have had a far greater impact if it had been published when scheduled in 1989. Now it has competition—the two Eclipse volumes on Barker. There's some overlap in *Shadows* and *Pandemonium*, but *Shadows* is the more elegantly designed and better-looking of the two books (also pricier), with very funny and gruesome color-illustrated endpapers by Barker (a psychoanalyst would have a field day) and wonderful spot illustrations throughout by the author/artist. A conversation with J. G. Ballard I've never seen before, numerous quotes from magazine and news articles (some judicious pruning of overlapping material would have been useful) are scattered throughout the book. More than 450 pages with a full-color, six-page insert of photographs.

The True Story of the 3 Little Pigs! by A. Wolf, as told to Jon Scieszka and illustrated by Lane Smith (Viking Kestral–1989) is a very clever children's book amusingly told and beautifully illustrated. Smith has solo books out, including the following one. Highly recommended for those who like variations on fairy tales and for anyone who enjoys good children's illustration work.

Glasses Who Needs 'Em? by Lane Smith (Viking) is an illustrated book about a young boy who is told by his mad optometrist that he needs glasses. The boy thinks that only dorks wear glasses, but the good doctor proves otherwise in an amusing series of examples of who wears glasses.

A Witch by August Strindberg, translated by Mary Sandbach, (The Lapis Press) is the first English translation of this oddity by the Swedish playwright best-known for his bleak mysogynist plays *Dance of Death* and *Miss Julie.* Set in the period of history when witches were still "tested" and burned, this novella is about Tekla, a spoiled young woman desperate to rise above her station in life. Her shallowness, frustration, and envy congeal into active malice when she accuses a rich young woman who befriended her of witchcraft. The book itself is striking, with images of hellfire on the back and front covers. There are portraits of Strindberg and his daughter, and rare paintings by the author as illustrations. (The Lapis Press, 589 North Venice Blvd., Venice, CA 90291 for information).

The Castle of Argol by Julien Gracq, translated by Louise Varese, is also from The Lapis Press. Written in 1938, the author considered his first novel a "demoniac version" of the Grail legend. It tells of a quest for the essential that ends with the embrace of fatality and dissolution. Illustrations in color and black-and-white. (Not seen.)

Visions from the Twilight Zone by Arlen Schumer (Chronicle) is an homage to Rod Serling and his surrealistic creation, *The Twilight Zone.* Using actual images and words from the show, which ran from 1959–1964, Schumer lovingly recreates (as much as possible in two dimensions) the feel of the series. In addition, there are essays on the show and its impact on a generation of television viewers by Carol Serling, film critic Jonathan Hoberman, *TZ* producer Buck Houghton and Serling himself. A must for admirers.

A Social History of the American Alligator by Vaughn L. Glasgow (St. Martin's) is lavishly and amusingly illustrated. The natural history can be found in other books but the societal ramifications and accompanying illustrations are what make this book shine—for instance, a rundown of various Louisiana mascot gators' life histories. However, there are some minor annoyances that are very distracting from the text such as the use of "sic" every time some historical reference uses the word crocodile instead of alligator. A footnote would have been quite sufficient and less distracting. There are some odd errors peppering the section on popular culture: Captain Hook lost his hand to the croc, not his whole arm; V, A. C.

Crispin's novelization of the TV series is mentioned but the series itself is not. The mentions of movies with alligators in them are, mostly, a stretch and superficial— Glasgow doesn't even summarize the plots so why bother mentioning the films at all? Despite these minor flaws, the book is fun reading and terrific to look at.

The Carroll & Graf Colin Wilson series: paperback editions of nonfiction crime detection books previously published only in hardcover and only in Great Britain, including A *Criminal History of Mankind, The Mammoth Books of True Crime 1 & 2* and *The Mammoth Book of the Supernatural.*

Written in Blood: Detectives & Detection by Colin Wilson (Warner) is the first of three paperback volumes appearing for the first time in the U.S. This volume is an historic overview of the evolution of criminal detection, including the use of the microscope, the first informer, the use of forensic evidence and so forth. Fascinating book, which reads like a novel (I've been warned that Wilson is sometimes inaccurate, so beware).

Spring-Heeled Jack by Philip Pullman (Knopf) is described by *Locus* as "an extremely bizarre young adult combination of prose and cartoon, illustrated by David Mostyn, creating a superhero out of the 19th-century legend of the superhuman Spring-Heeled Jack—with Mack the Knife as the villain. Peculiar but fascinating." Sounds good to me.

Meat: A Natural Symbol by Nick Fiddes (Routledge) is a fascinating albeit biased study of humankind's relationship to "meat." The book started as a doctoral thesis presuming that the primary cultural importance of meat is founded on its vividly representing to us the domination we have sought over nature. It's quite readable, but only because of out-of-context interviews with unknown parties on their thoughts about meat-or-vegetable eating. For all the reader knows, Fiddes might have interviewed his own family. Some interesting points: According to Fiddes's sources, cannibalism has never been documented as a regular practice in any society but the accusation of it has always been used by one group in order to prove moral superiority over another. Excluded witnesses are missionaries and explorers (fairly or not) who have a vested interest in portraying the accused as in need of being "civilized." Pets are a "gray" area—they are given semihuman status—and Fiddes makes the intriguing point that we don't have canned mouse for cats to eat but rather, chicken, tuna, liver and so forth. An infuriating book if you're a meat eater and proud of it (as I am), but interesting.

The Faber Book of Madness edited by Roy Porter (Faber and Faber) is a nice large (over 500 pages) oddity through which to browse. An anthology mixing fact and fiction, serious and amusing, including writings by the mentally disturbed themselves, exploring consciousness in all its extremes and society's responses to the problems of psychic disorder. Includes quotations from the novels of Virginia Woolf, the plays of Shakespeare, treatises of Nietzsche and essays about asylum life.

Angry Woman, edited by Andrea Juno and V. Vale (Re/Search) is an important and fascinating document of some of the contemporary political artists who are putting themselves on the line (sometimes physically) in order to change society. Interviews with performance artists Karen Finley, Carolee Schneemann and Diamanda Galas, writers Kathy Acker and Bell Books and poets Lydia Lunch and

Wanda Coleman. This oversized book is about how men and women respond to female bodies; it's about political, economic and sexual power. A must for anyone interested in political art and sexual politics.

Witnesses from the Grave: The Stories Bones Tell by Christopher Joyce and Eric Stover (Little, Brown), ostensibly a profile of Clyde Snow, a prominent forensic anthropologist often called on by the police to identify victims of violent accidents or crime by their skeletal remains. But the book is actually much more than that. Although it begins with a brief history of forensics (overlapping somewhat with the Colin Wilson books) and a brief biography of Snow, a colorful Texan, those first chapters are only preparation for the good part—stories of how Snow and his colleagues used forensic anthropology to identify a mysterious outlaw whose mummified body ended up in a carnival; aircrash victims and some of John Wayne Gacy's victims; the alleged remains of Josef Mengele in Brazil; and opening mass graves in Argentina to help identify "the disappeared" of the late 1970s to help discourage human rights abuses. The best parts of the book read like detective stories, the step-by-step meticulous process of comparing skeleton and skull remains of the dead to antemortem x-rays and medical histories.

Permanent Londoners by Judi Culbertson and Tom Randall (Chelsea Green Press) details the lives and deaths of the rich and famous—and where they're buried (not seen).

Great White Shark: the Definitive Look at the Most Terrifying Creature of the Ocean by Richard Ellis and John E. McCosker with original photographs by Al Giddings and others (HarperCollins) is for anyone with an interest, fear, or obsession with the great white shark. It's a thorough and attractive combination of scientific information and popular lore on sharks, which covers everything from their taxonomy to man's hunt of them. There's a section covering reports of shark attacks in great detail, and one on the "Jaws" phenomenon, that is, the enormous popularity and aftermath of the film cycle. Copious paintings and photographs, and fascinating tidbits of information—the whale shark, which eats plankton, is actually the largest but the great white is the largest that attacks large prey. A $50 hardcover edition, which is worth every penny for shark aficionados.

The World of Charles Addams (Knopf) is a marvelous retrospective of the cartoonist's work from his first cartoon for *The New Yorker* at 20 years old to those appearing in 1990, after his death. His macabre sense of humor is evident throughout this coffee-table book. It's obvious that some of the actual cartoons were used as inspiration for the hit movie *The Addams Family*. The movie has most certainly brought renewed interest in Addams's work, perhaps seducing a new generation to look for and appreciate his cartoons. If you're a horror fan or reader and are not familiar with his work, shame on you.

More Haunted Houses by Joan Bingham and Dolores Riccio (Pocket Books) is the second guidebook to haunted houses, schooners, forts, cemeteries, and the like. (The authors, by the way, never claim to have seen a ghost themselves.) Well written and well researched, this looks like a fun book to take on a tour. Recommended.

—Ellen Datlow

Horror and Fantasy in the Media

I have mixed feelings about the fact that science fiction or fantasy films rarely trigger as much discussion among viewers as does, say, *Thelma and Louise*. Actually I got a big kick out of watching—and participating in—mixed-gender discussions of Ridley Scott's examination of women as aliens (I don't think it takes too large a sophist's shoehorn to slip the film in as a first cousin to *The Man Who Fell to Earth . . .*). Do *Bill and Ted* audiences exit the theatre with at least half the crowd mildly radicalized—and the other half either sobered or defensive? Is the end message of *Body Parts* as open to debate? Do viewers of *The Rocketeer* make observations like, "Huh, do you know *Thelma and Louise* is sort of a gender-turnaround of Richard Sarafian's classic (well, *I* think it is) *Vanishing Point* from twenty years ago?" Does the latest *Star Trek* installment or even *Terminator 2* catalyze the same level of activity in the head and the heart as *Jungle Fever* or *Boyz N the Hood*? Are all these unfair questions or just inappropriate ones?

Just asking, friends. As far as I'm concerned, *Thelma and Louise* doesn't hold a candle to the controversy of such past masters as *Do the Right Thing*. Before I talk myself out of writing this summary survey of the film of the fantastic for 1991, let me sip a slug of caffeinated diet cola, calm myself and admit there was plenty to talk about with last year's crop. But I think you see the point.

The Rapture is a film that could have been a contender. Much like a jet fighter, it screamed down the runway, started to lift off, then lost power and control toward the end and threatened to stall. *The Rapture* was director Michael Tolkin's second feature film. It is fantasy, though there are many who might consider it a prescient documentary. For others, the film would fall into no other category than horror. It's an unabashedly religious drama, though nothing like the cheapjack features you can catch for free at storefront tabernacles. *The Rapture* stars Mimi Rogers as a directory-assistance operator whose arid, empty life is filled only with the attentions of a kinky lover and group sex. She starts to sense the possibility of meaning after overhearing her co-workers talk around the water cooler about shared dreams of The Pearl. What occurs is a very literal playing out of the prophecies of Revelation, which is all done straight. Even though I don't think Tolkin's script really ever satisfactorily grappled with the material, it's a brash and sensational idea, and a genuinely ambitious film. More important, *The Rapture* may well turn out to be a bellwether, as the proximity of the century's end triggers more and more millennial pop art.

And now for some of my favorites, films that worked for me on a lot of levels. My two picks from the horror side are actually more dark—*very* dark—suspense—if you insist on sticky categories. A 1988 Dutch film, *The Vanishing*, finally was released in the U.S. last year. Directed by George Sluizer, this starts with one of everyone's favorite paranoid scenarios. A young Dutch couple who are in France to see the Tour de France stops at a bustling freeway service area. The woman disappears. Her boyfriend then spends three years obsessively trying to locate her. The viewers quickly find out who the kidnapper is, an otherwise dull French chemistry professor played by Bernard-Pierre Donnadieu. This villain is one of the screen's great psychos. Until the end, we do not understand his motives. He torments the disappeared woman's lover with teasing postcards. Eventually he works an act of evil that, for most beholders, is unforgettably disturbing. I found the surprise to be fairly planted, but still shocking in a way no film's done for me in years. One of the great achievements of *The Vanishing* is its total lack of blood. No graphic violence. No dismemberment. I didn't think this sort of horrific thriller could still be made.

The American film industry came through just fine with Jonathan Demme's film translation of Thomas Harris's *The Silence of the Lambs*. Minimally graphic, this bombshell way outclassed all the other new films of terror. I've got no problem with the aesthetic of carnography, but that makes me all the more admire film-makers who can create intensity in a movie with tools other than a simple violent bludgeon. Writing, acting, editing and cinematography can certainly help. *The Silence of the Lambs* made an instant shivery pop star of Anthony Hopkins as Hannibal Lecter, and deservedly so. But that shouldn't detract from Jodie Foster's strong performance as the smart, courageous, FBI rookie. Scott Glenn was almost invisible as her boss, which is too bad. Interestingly, both *The Vanishing* and *The Silence of the Lambs* are adaptations of novels. I haven't read the progenitor of the former, Tim Krabbe's *The Golden Egg*, but I am a great fan of Harris's novel. The script was a successful version of a very good book.

I also have a low-budget fondness in my heart for Wes Craven's *The People Under the Stairs*. This was an inexpensive horror comedy with no element of the occult, despite the rather misleading print campaign. The story's about a young black boy called Fool who attempts action when there's a landlord threat to raze the ghetto tenement in which his family lives, so that a new corporate tower can rise. Turns out, the greedy landlords are a psychotic couple who live in a sprawling old mansion, keep a lovely little blonde girl named Alice imprisoned in the attic, have a passel of Romero zombie look-alikes in the basement and are determined to replace the whole ghetto with pricey urban renewal projects. The humor's a little campy, but I was amused. When the police come to investigate neighborhood complaints of a shoot-out that would rival scenes in *The Wild Bunch*, the couple's spruced everything up. They're dressed just like Ward and June Cleaver, elevator Muzak is piped over the home's sound system, and they've reversed the growling, glowering painting of their Doberman pinscher to show a benign, cute-doggie portrait. The high-concept description of this movie's goal would be: What if John Sayles set out to create a modern, urban fairy tale in the mode of *Edward Scissorhands*? Wes Craven's reach exceeds his grasp, but it's a wonderful attempt and a great comeback.

For out-and-out fantasy, the champ is probably Disney's *Beauty and the Beast*. This animated feature has become an instant classic. The music's not terribly memorable, but everything else is. Robby Benson as the voice of the Beast? Yes, he's fine. Charges have been leveled that this movie is feminist propaganda. Strong, competent and altogether admirable, the heroine is a good role model for kids and an attractor for adults.

There were a couple of good romantic ghost fantasies, one very popular, the other rather more successful at what it set out to do. The popular one was *Dead Again*, directed by and starring Kenneth Branagh, along with his wife, Emma Thompson. The production values were lavish, the craft superb but the story was a bit wooden and all too predictable. Then there was *Truly, Madly, Deeply*, directed by Anthony Minghella, which featured a kinder, gentler Allan Rickman. If your only image of Rickman is as the cold, deadly villain in *Die Hard*, or the scenery-gobbling Sheriff in *Robin Hood: Prince of Thieves*, then rent a cassette of *Truly, Madly, Deeply*. You'll enjoy it.

There wasn't a whole lot of big-screen, unabashed science fiction in 1991. The one feature that most people in America saw was *Terminator 2: Judgment Day*. Director James Cameron followed up his own megahit *Terminator* almost as successfully as he did Ridley Scott's *Alien*. This was the highest grossing film of the year, to the tune of a fifth of a billion bucks. This adventure epic of a boy and his terminator succeeded not just because of the incredible effects (the shape-changing technology, which created the water creature in the *Abyss* and trans-muted Michael Jackson into a black kitty, has lately been selling Goodyear all-weather tires), but because the movie actually has heart. The relationships between mother, son and cyborg transcend the superficial. Linda Hamilton actually has the tougher acting role—her character is psychologically valid, but has to go through an incredible amount of change with only a limited opportunity afforded by the script. There's moxie here, and some brain and an awful lot of action.

The *other* science fiction film of the year was *Star Trek VI: The Undiscovered Country* directed by Nicholas Meyer. Neither the best nor the worst of the series, it was a fine grace note to sound as Gene Roddenberry transported from this plane. The plot was a nice reflection of contemporary realpolitik, the blood-globules-in-zero-gee effect was great, and Christian Slater stole a chunk of the show with a walk-on. No smart cookies are laying bets that there *won't* be a *Star Trek VII*.

Okay, let's look at a smorgasbord of what else was playing out there. This is certainly not all the cinema of the fantastic released during the year, but it's a sampling I think covers the spectrum.

Switch was the year's high-water mark for the rash of essentially dumb gender/life-and-death/age-switching movies. Although it wasn't Blake Edwards's greatest moment, this comedy of a swinish yuppy who is murdered and then transmigrates into the body of a woman (he's been very, very bad to females) works for one reason—Ellen Barkin. She plays the karma-cursed sexist with a keenly nasty edge.

Albert Brooks's *Defending Your Life* was an earnest and slightly plodding treat-ment of fate in that twilight zone between Heaven and Hell. The characters' backdrops—celestial cities composited from real and imaginary earthly build-ings—were masterfully realized. Their lines needed a bit more wit, more bite.

The surprise Christmas hit was *The Addams Family* (it has made about $100 million). The characters looked great, especially Anjelica Huston as Morticia. Some of the best jokes came from the original Addams cartoons. They were freighted, however, with the more banal feel of the TV series (that juxtaposition has led to a lawsuit filed by the creator of the TV show against the makers of the feature). This is a good kids movie for adults.

Perhaps the most obscure science fiction adventure of the year was *Harley Davidson and the Marlboro Man*. Starring Mickey Rourke and Don Johnson, this peculiar melodrama takes place a mere handful of years in the future. A manic (as ever) Rourke and a disheveled Johnson (actually quite good) become embroiled in corporate chicanery and have to deal with a squad of lethal goons who dress in black Kevlar dusters. No one seems to understand the value of head-shots in situations like this, nor that Kevlar only stops slugs—not the force behind them. The movie contains one enormous inside joke probably intelligible only to L.A. residents: in the future, Burbank Airport will become one of the great high-tech, big-money, international crossroads. . . .

The Rocketeer, a big-budget Disney production of Dave Stevens's comic was a very large disappointment. The heroine was watered down, the hero seemed to have had a lobotomy and only the villains handled themselves like champs. The zeppelin scenes notwithstanding, what this latter-day pulp adventure really needed was a healthy transfusion of intelligence.

And speaking of intelligence . . . *Bill and Ted's Bogus Journey*—which really should have stuck with the original title, *Bill and Ted Go to Hell* (changed when the marketing folks nervously glanced at the Bible Belt)—was still amusing, but not as laugh-provoking as the first film in the series. Death had all the good lines.

Terry Gilliam's *The Fisher King* should be seen, even though Robin Williams inexplicably didn't bring his title character to life as well as one would expect. This contemporary retelling and resetting of the English legend in New York City mostly works just fine until the ending wimps out.

Earnest: Scared Stupid? Earnest is, um, an acquired taste. This episode in his saga is about a malevolent troll set free in the rural South. It's funnier than you might think—at least it's funnier than the Ma and Pa Kettle movies. Then there was *Suburban Commando*, a lightweight adventure for kids of all ages and skewed IQs. As the star of this chase-adventure of alien bounty hunters stalking each other here on Earth, Hulk Hogan generates some real charm and a few funny lines and bits of business (though the *cat*-apult sequence is probably the topper).

Child's Play 3 was maybe a little better than *Child's Play 2*, but that's arguing extremely fine points of tedium. Rent the cassette of the first one—it's got more than a few good bits. But don't even buy a Chuckie doll with the suction cup limbs to stick on the inside of your car window. Garfield owners will laugh at you. *Highlander II: The Quickening?* Russell Mulcahy, who directed *Highlander*, somehow also directed this wretched follow-up. Watch it, if you must, for the twenty minutes or so of Sean Connery (the production company was doubtless holding his loved ones hostage). Try not to laugh at the bargain sub-basement *Bladerunner* sets lest you wake the other patrons.

The British time-travel horror thriller *Warlock*, directed by Steve Miner, was finally released in the U.S. Richard E. Grant and Julian Sands did well as the witch hunter and witch antagonists. An adequate horror movie, if not a good one. In *Body Parts*, writer-director Eric Red grappled with that old chestnut, Does a person's innate soul dwell in parts of the anatomy aside from the brain? Naturally the answer is "yes" or this wouldn't be a horror movie. Eric Red's scripts (*The*

Hitcher, Near Dark) are better produced when others direct than when he directs his own work (*Cohen and Tate*). This one had promise but ultimately foundered in silliness.

Teenage Mutant Ninja Turtles II's legacy of charm from its spectacularly successful predecessor wore a little thin this time around. The good will dissipated, partly because the quirkily endearing human love interest from the first film is gone. Perhaps another reason is that the filmmakers paid more attention to the "morality" and the nature of the role models in this sequel.

There's not much to say about *The Neverending Story II*. It's the same director, the same character, the same story. . . . I think maybe that says it all right there. Everything's the same. Ate de Jong's *Drop Dead Fred* is an incredibly irritating comedic fantasy. Phoebe Cates plays a young woman, jilted, who is aided by her childhood invisible friend now come back in adult form. Imagine Michael Keaton's character from *Beetlejuice* with absolutely no redeeming charm at all. None. Not funny, McGee.

Freddy's Dead: The Final Nightmare allegedly terminates the *Nightmare on Elm Street* series. Don't rest easy. This made a respectable amount of money. True, it did explain more of Freddy Krueger's history and had an amusing series of cameos by actors from the other films in the series. But, like its fellow sequels, it never equalled what Wes Craven's original accomplished. The final twenty minutes of *Freddy's Dead* is a 3-D sequence. When I saw this at a dollar cinema, the box office was out of polarized glasses. Nobody in the audience seemed to care.

And then there's *Hook*—Steven Spielberg's project that deals with a grown-up Peter Pan returning to Never-Never Land to help the Lost Boys and do battle with Captain Hook. This must have seemed like a great idea in development meetings. Robin Williams as Peter? Dustin Hoffman as Hook? Cool. And Bob Hoskins as Smee is great. This one tries very hard to be a children's classic for all ages. But it's just too self-conscious. The effect of absolute belief in the material and the effect of craft pushed to the limit are, alas, not guarantors of the same result.

Robin Hood: Prince of Thieves was another movie that wanted to be a classic. Oh, well. Kevin Costner's Robin never quite generates the passion this legend needs. Not that he needed to be an Errol Flynn, but Costner's character ended up a little too much a passive, sensitive male for the 1990s. The movie does take a genuine chance, though, when an unannounced Sean Connery turns up as King Richard in the last five minutes. The crowd murmurs. The viewing audience is amazed. And Kevin Costner might as well be invisible.

Gregory Hines starred in *Eve of Destruction*, yet another adventure about a robot jumping its programming tracks and causing consternation. Renee Soutendijk played Eve, the robot. Hines and Dutch actress Soutendijk both have immensely attractive presence. What this movie doesn't have is a good story.

Here are two gorgeously photographed and fairly interesting historical sagas with fantasy elements. *Shadow of the Raven*, directed by Hrafn Gunlaugsson, is a violent eleventh-century Icelandic saga about the onset of Christianity and the twilight of paganism, family blood feuds and political hardball. Bruce Beresford's *Black Robe*, from the novel by Brian Moore, takes us to a Canadian winter in

1634, where we see the French dealing with the Native Americans. Both are fascinating glimpses of cultures alien to our own, which make us all glad for modern central heating.

Luc Besson's *La Femme Nikita* starred Anne Parillaud as a beautiful young career criminal who is programmed by CIA-type folks into becoming an assassin. Less static and stylized than Besson's earlier efforts, but it's still not quite in a class with *The Manchurian Candidate* or *A Clockwork Orange*. Paul Schrader's *The Comfort of Strangers*, from Ian McEwan's novel, worked from a script by Harold Pinter. It's a drama of menace as young innocents are manipulated by the older and jaded; it looked great but stumbled badly at the end.

The *23rd International Tournee of Animation* wasn't the best in the series of showcase compilations, but such pieces as "Slow Bob in the Lower Dimensions" (the usual weirdly surreal suspects) and "The Potato Hunter" (prehistoric man stalking stop-action spuds) made it well worth watching. If you're a fan of endless beautiful tracking shots, find a copy of *Third Stone from the Sun*, Jan C. Nickman's desperately earnest paean to regaining humanity's empathy with Mother Earth. Filmed in a pristine, pre-Exxon Valdez Prince William Sound, this fantasy of a young boy on a quest benefits from Linda Hunt's voiceover as the soul of a magic ship. The sentiment is unimpeachable. But it does go on.

Krzysztof Kieslowski's *The Double Life of Veronique* stars Irene Jacob in a dual-role as two young women, one French, one Polish, who were born on the same day, share the same musical talent and who each have the same potentially fatal heart condition. They are linked tenuously, psychically, as doppelgängers. It's a beautiful, dreamlike production that, for most viewers, will lead to post-screening, semibewildered discussions over espresso.

And what was happening on the small screen this past year? Quite a lot, actually. David Lynch's and Mark Frost's "Twin Peaks" just seemed to run out of steam, out of punch and out of fuel altogether, and slid to an unceremonious stop. With a different tone, "Northern Exposure" took up some of the surreal slack. NBC's "Quantum Leap" stuck around successfully with Scott Bakula hopping from body to body. "Star Trek: The Next Generation" grew ever more successful, even as Paramount appears poised to shut the show down in favor of syndication, and to open the gate for "Star Trek: Deep Space Nine."

Matt Groening's "The Simpsons" continued to ornament Fox's schedule, although it got some hilarious competition from two new series. ABC's "Dinosaurs," retooled after an abortive trial run as "The Sinclairs," added some wonderful surrealism to what first appears to be standard sitcom fare, though populated with animated dinosaurs created by Jim Henson's company. I love the Sinclair family's running feud with the live leftovers in the fridge. The cable service Nickelodeon presented John Kricfalusi's "Ren and Stimpy," the cartoon series about the chihuahua on Prozac and the big silly-looking cat with the blue nose. The show's become a big underground hit on college campuses, and such venues as MTV have picked up on the characters. The big attraction is the manic pace, totally twisted humor and the makers' tendency to go beyond usual dramatic pacing by pushing scenes right over the top.

Other cable attractions include Lifetime's "The Hidden Room," a suspense series aimed particularly at women. It's much like "The Twilight Zone," with a budget and production values measurably higher than "Monsters" or "Tales from the Darkside." A wonderful short feature to catch on cable services is Jeff Barry's "The Secret of Easter Island." This live-action piece about a bored inhabitant of Easter Island (human body, large statue-type head) who makes his way to California, is priceless.

On Saturday mornings, try out Hanna-Barbera's "The Pirates of Dark Water." This is a reasonably adult science fantasy about adventurers on a distant planet. It's nicely textured. There's enough substance here for adult viewers.

NBC's new series, "Eerie, Indiana," is tenaciously clinging to life. It's about a kid's-eye view of *weird things happening* in a little midwestern hamlet. It's good. Then there's Fox, always eager to field a new high-concept potential success. "Hi Honey, I'm Home" (what if the Nielsens—as in the TV ratings—were a real family who were moved to a real neighborhood by the Sitcom Relocation Program) scored about what you'd guess. "Charlie Hoover" (an adult male nobody has a miniature alter ego who's trying to help him become a somebody) and "Herman's Head" (a young guy actually has four personified components of his personality—conscience, intelligence, sensitivity and lust—duking it out for control inside his mind) both have some substance going for them.

Stephen King's "Golden Years" had a lot going for it as an 8-hour miniseries on CBS. This melodrama about a man growing younger after an industrial snafu maintained some excitement and some interesting characters. Then there was the pilot for a Fox series, "Blood Ties," a multigenerational vampire saga, which just couldn't get it together.

The highwater mark of made-for-TV movies of the fantastic was probably HBO's *Cast a Deadly Spell* starring Fred Ward. This is a *noir*-style parallel-worlds period piece in which the wonderful, but all too frequently overlooked Ward plays a detective named Harry P. Lovecraft in a Los Angeles inhabited by magic-users. The low-water mark was probably ABC's *To Save a Child*, a movie-pilot aimed at introducing a series once called *The Craft*. The melodrama about a young woman whose child is kidnapped by southwestern witches was clearly designed to be a *Run for Your Life/Fugitive*-type chase series. Even Anthony Zerbe, as one of the villains, couldn't save it. Dumb, dumb, dumb. Wiccans lobbied to keep the show from being seen and picked up. Disastrous writing and production accomplished what political action could not.

Let's switch gears and look at some music. This is a truly patchwork area for me this time, but beyond that, I won't apologize. Expect some truly idiosyncratic choices. During the year I didn't encounter any albums that had the same conceptual impact as previous years' *Transverse City* by Warren Zevon or *Bloodletting* by Concrete Blonde. One nicely downbeat all-around compilation was the score from Wim Wenders' new feature, *Until the End of the World*, a film I'll be talking about next year. The soundtrack album was released in advance of the movie. The performers contributing to the film include Lou Reed, k.d. lang, R.E.M., U2, Peter Gabriel, Neneh Cherry, Talking Heads, Depeche Mode and a lot more. It's a solid catholic collection.

Warren Zevon's new album, *Mr. Bad Example* (Giant) isn't overtly science-fictional, but it sure feels right. It's got the dystopian, winding-down-to-the-end-of-the-millennium feel, the sensibility. And "Things to Do in Denver When You're Dead" is certainly dark fantasy.

I want to thank Kristine Kathryn Rusch for turning me on to Mark Germino's *Radartown* (Zoo). This is a nicely edgy and political album, rock in the Zevon/Hyatt/Prine style. The title song is a postindustrial dystopian/depression rocker that could become the anthem of the Rust Belt. John Wesley Harding's *Here Comes the Groom* (Sire) is much in the same vein. His "The Devil In Me" would make a terrific under-the-end-credits piece for the pending feature film of Dan Simmons's *Carrion Comfort*.

Contemporary folk artist Kristian Hoffman has an album out called, not surprisingly, *Kristian Hoffman* (52nd Street). This is solid, innovative, melodious material, boasting both social conscience and some witty playfulness. But then what else would you expect from the brother of fantasist Nina Kiriki Hoffman?

If you want to brighten your holiday season, slap a copy of *Lumps of Coal* (First Warning) in your player. This Christmas compilation ranges across "Little Drummer Boy" (Hoodoo Gurus) and "The First Noël" (Crash Test Dummies) to "Kings of Orient" (The Odds) and " 'Twas the Night Before Christmas" (Henry Rollins). Without lapsing into parody, it's fresh treatment given to tired material.

Live music? I hope you all went to see Queensryche's tour. Along with the new stuff, they performed—and extraordinarily effectively—the entirety of the Orwellian *Operation Mind Crime*.

And finally . . . live theatre. This is especially short, since I'm a long way from Broadway out here in Denver. Actually we *do* have a major thoroughfare named Broadway, but it's known much more for thousands of antique stores than for musicals and drama. So what can I say? I didn't fly to New York or London for *Return to the Forbidden Planet*. I'm afraid this reviewer's budget is a bit too limited. But I *did* catch the touring production of *Phantom of the Opera*. Kevin Gray played the Phantom very well indeed, as the production inaugurated the Denver Center for the Performing Arts' new, state-of-the-art, Temple Buell Theatre. Every aspect of the play was lavish. I spent the first act admiring the how and the look of *Phantom*. In the second half, I was a bit surprised to find myself caught up in the human story. So it worked. The best summary line comes from A. J. Moses, local cultural observer, who said of *Phantom*, "It's the *Terminator 2* of musical theatre."

I wish I'd said that.

—Edward Bryant

1991: Obituaries

As in any year, 1991 robbed us of a number of people whose talents brought us great edification and pleasure in the fields of fantasy and horror. Perhaps the most important figure to die last year was **Theodor Seuss Geisel**, 87, better known to children of all ages as Dr. Seuss. His whimsical and charming books were enormous best-sellers all around the world, and he taught generations of people how to have fun while learning important lessons of morality and ethics. His best-known works included *The Cat in the Hat*, *Green Eggs and Ham* and *How the Grinch Stole Christmas*. He worked as an illustrator before becoming a best-selling author, and he also wrote a novel for adults, *The Seven Lady Godivas* (1937), but it wasn't terribly successful. He wrote another book for adults, *You're Only Old Once*, in 1987, and it was understandably much more successful than his previous effort. He also made films, including the cartoon *Gerald McBoing-Boing*.

Frank Capra, 94, was a major motion-picture director, counting among his successes the now-beloved but initially neglected fantasy *It's a Wonderful Life*, along with *Lost Horizon* and a number of other fine films, most notably *It Happened One Night*, a romantic comedy that nearly killed the men's undershirt business when Clark Gable took his off. Also lost from the world of film was a much younger, but equally creative man, **Howard Ashman**, 40, who wrote the screenplay and lyrics for the musical adaptation of Roger Corman's horror film, *Little Shop of Horrors*. First a play and then a film, it took Ashman to Hollywood where he then proceeded to produce Disney's *The Little Mermaid*, and to write lyrics for the film's songs, one of which won him a Best Song Oscar for "Under the Sea." He and his collaborator Alan Mencken then wrote songs for another successful animated feature, *Beauty and the Beast*. Ashman was a playwright first, and had some of his plays, including *The Confirmation* and *Dreamstuff* (the latter an adaptation of Shakespeare's *The Tempest*) produced before his screen successes. His one Broadway show, *Smile*, for which Marvin Hamlisch wrote the music, closed quickly despite a talented cast and strong production values. Ashman was a singular talent, and his combination of wit and sensitivity brought new life to Disney's animated productions.

John Bellairs, 53, wrote a number of young adult fantasies, including *The House with a Clock in its Walls*, his most famous, and others. His first book was *The Face in the Frost* (1969), which, while ostensibly written for a young audience, was one of the landmark fantasies of the 1960s for adults as well. His work had deep feeling and a sense of the laughter and terror in life.

Several major literary authors whose work touched on the field died last year. **Graham Greene**, 86, was best known for his thrillers, including *The Third Man*, for which he also wrote the screenplay, and *The Honorary Consul*. **Isaac Bashevis Singer**, 87, winner of the Nobel Prize for literature, wrote stories that touched on moral and emotional issues of broad universality, in a style and context that were his own unique brand of philosophical fantasy. **Jerzy Kosinski**, 57, best known for

The Painted Bird, was a concentration camp victim during World War II. His work dealt with the survivor's experience in a uniquely charged way.

Authors firmly within the genre who died last year included **Thomas Tryon**, 65, an actor for many years who successfully began a career writing horror fiction later in life. His novel *The Other* put him on the map; *Harvest Home* was also successful. Both were filmed. **Chester Anderson**, 58, was a free spirit, best known for his fantasy novel of Greenwhich Village, *The Butterfly Kid*. He also collaborated with Michael Kurland on *Ten Years to Doomsday*, and wrote other fiction as well. Anderson was a figure of some cult interest because of his involvement with the beat life. He expanded the scope of *Crawdaddy* when he was the editor of that magazine. A mainstream novel, also about Greenwhich Village, *Fox and Hare*, was published in 1980. **Joyce Ballou Gregorian**, 44, was the author of the *Tredana* trilogy that consisted of *The Broken Citadel*, *Castledown*, and *The Great Wheel*. **Sharon Baker**, 53, was the author of *Quarreling, They Met the Dragon*, set on an exotic, richly detailed world, Naphar, on which her novels *Journey to Membliar* and *Burning Tears of Sassurum* were also set. Married and the mother of four children, she was a person who reached out to those around her, providing a home to exchange students and working with runaways in Seattle, where she and her family lived. Her deep social concerns were mirrored in all her work, enriching it considerably. In addition to other interests, she was active in academic circles within the field. **Jonathan Etra**, 38, was the author of the children's book *Aliens for Breakfast* and other fantastical works, including the outrageous trade paperback collaborative extravaganza *Junk Food*.

We lost editors as well. **Eleanor Sullivan**, 62, was an editor at *Ellery Queen's Mystery Magazine* for many years, serving as Managing Editor from 1970 to 1982, then as Editor-in-Chief. She was also Editor-in-Chief of *Alfred Hitchcock's Mystery Magazine*, from 1976 to 1982. Before her years with the mystery magazines where she became famous, she worked at Pocket Books and then Charles Scribner's Sons. She edited a number of anthologies as well, and wrote *Whodunit* (1984), a memoir about Frederick Dannay, one of the two cousins who together wrote as "Ellery Queen," and who was Editor-in-Chief of the magazine of the same name until his death in 1982. She also wrote fiction herself, and was nominated for an Edgar Award in 1989 for her story, "Ted Bundy's Father." In 1987 she was honored with the Mystery Writers of America's Ellery Queen Award for Excellence.

Thaddeus (Ted) Dikty, 71, was an editor and publisher of many small-press books, both academic and fiction. He was the cofounder of Shasta, one of the first hardcover publishers of science fiction and fantasy; he also edited a number of anthologies over the years. Years after the demise of Shasta, he cofounded Fax Collectors Editions, and after that, Starmont House. Dikty was married to author Julian May, and they worked together on many projects. **Clarence Paget**, 82, was first an agent, then an editor and publisher. He was Editor-in-Chief of Pan Books and founded their long-running series, *The Pan Book of Horror Stories*, edited by Herbert Van Thal for many years. After Van Thal's death, Paget edited the series alone for several years.

George T. Delacorte, 97, was a major publisher, founding Dell Books and Delacorte Press. Before publishing books, he distributed and published magazines. He was active in the company until its sale in 1976 to Doubleday. From the start, he was aided by the presence of Helen Meyer who, starting as his secretary, became the person most responsible for Dell's success for over a half century until her departure a year after Doubleday's acquisition. **W. Howard Baker**, 65, was a British publisher, writer and editor. He edited the Sexton Blake Library, directing the series of detective novels and writing some of them himself as Peter Saxon and others as William Arthur. He also edited and wrote a number of other books, principally horror and mystery novels, including *The Darkest Night* (1966) and *Drums of the Dark Gods*, the latter written as W. A. Ballinger. **Harry Shorten**, 76, was a publisher. He founded Tower Publications, a low-end publisher of magazines and mass-market paperbacks. Shorten also gained some fame for his syndicated newspaper feature, *There Oughta Be a Law*. **Henry Steeger III**, 87, was another pulp publisher, founding and running Popular Publications from its inception in 1930 until he sold it in 1970. Included in Popular's stable of pulp magazines in the thirties and forties were a number of SF and Fantasy titles.

Northrop Frye, 78, was an influential literary critic, one of the leading proponents of the symbolist movement in literary criticism. Among his major works were the 1947 study of William Blake's works, *Fearful Symmetry* and *Anatomy of Criticism*. **Chad Walsh**, 76, was a noted academic, a poet and a writer, justly respected for his C. S. Lewis scholarship in such works as *The Literary Legacy of C. S. Lewis* (1979). He wrote many book reviews and several volumes of children's fantasy.

Many actors associated in one way or another with the field died last year, including stars of stage, film and television. **Joan Bennett**, 80, starred in many films, and late in her career was a featured player in television's dark fantasy soap opera, *Dark Shadows*. **Gene Tierney**, 70, was a charming romantic comedienne in *Heaven Can Wait* (1943), *The Ghost and Mrs. Muir* (1947) and many other films. **Jean Rogers**, 74, was best known for playing Dale Arden to Buster Crabbe's Flash Gordon. **Michael Landon**, 54, was successful in a string of television series, and never escaped the notoriety of his early stint in the low-budget film *I Was a Teenage Werewolf*. **Keye Luke**, 86, played Charlie Chan's Number 1 Son in the film series; he was a fine character actor for decades on big screen and small, bringing dignity to the TV series *Kung Fu*.

A number of people involved in the creative process of film and television production left us last year. **Milton Subotsky**, 70, while never an award-caliber producer, was responsible for the production of a great number of horror films in the sixties and seventies. Starting as a screenwriter, he formed Amicus Productions, which made the very successful film *Tales from the Crypt* in 1971, among many other features. **David Lean**, 83, was a fine producer and director, best known for *Lawrence of Arabia* and *Bridge on the River Kwai*, both of which won him Oscars. **Don Siegel**, 78, is best remembered for his classic chiller, the original production of *Invasion of the Body Snatchers*. He also directed a number of adventure films and thrillers, including Clint Eastwood's *Dirty Harry* and *War of the Worlds*. **Irwin Allen**, 75, was a writer, producer and director who became famous in the

1970s for making big-scale disaster films such as *The Poseidon Adventure* and *The Towering Inferno*. In 1960 he produced *The Lost World*, based on the Conan Doyle novel. In 1961 he made a film, *Voyage to the Bottom of the Sea*, which he followed up with a television series of the same title. **William Dozier**, 83, produced the *Batman* television series as well as other shows.

French artist and author **Jean Bruller**, 89, wrote fiction under the name Vercors, starting when he wrote for the French resistance during World War II. His best-known work was *Les Animaux Denatures*, (1952), translated as *You Shall Know Them*. It was given the title *Borderline* in the U.K., then reprinted as *The Murder of the Missing Link* in the U.S. His works were sophisticated fantasies, including a novel about the transformation of a vixen into a human woman, *Sylva*, which was a 1963 nominee for the Hugo Award for best SF novel. **Roger Stine**, 39, was an artist who did a number of paintings for *Cinefantastique*, and for various science fiction and fantasy books and magazines. **Rick Griffin**, 47, was a noted artist whose work was famous in the underground comix of the sixties and seventies. He also did numerous psychedelic rock posters, and album covers for bands such as The Grateful Dead and Jefferson Airplane. British animator **Joy Batchelor**, 77, was best known for her collaboration with her husband, John Halas, on the 1954 feature, *Animal Farm*, based on the George Orwell novel.

Dan Henderson, 38, was nominated for the Compton Crook Award for his first novel, *Paradise* (1982). He had a number of short stories published, and was a journalist. **Dave Pedneau**, 47, was a writer of mystery and horror best known for his "initials" series of hardboiled novels, *D.O.A.*, *A.P.B.*, *B.O.L.O.*, *A.K.A.*, and *B. & E.*, all paperback originals. He wrote horror pseudonymously as Marc Eliot. He was the first editor of the Horror Writers of America's newsletter. Other writers who died in 1991 included the fantasy poet **Vera Bishop Konrick**, 90, **Ward Hawkins**, 77, a pulp writer whose career spanned many genres and six decades, and Lovecraftian poet **Walter Shedlofsky**, 71.

Many character actors died last year, including **John Hoyt**, 87, and **Fred MacMurray**, 83, who starred in *The Shaggy Dog*, and the TV series "My Three Sons." After years of playing heavies, **Berry Kroger**, 78, **Ronald Lacey**, 55, who like Kroger, was known for playing evil villains opposite many big stars in film and TV, **Coral Browne**, 77, a stage and screen actress who married Vincent Price after costarring with him in *Theater of Blood*, **Wilfred Hyde-White**, 87, **Gloria Holden**, 82, and the very tall **Kevin Peter Hall**, 35, whose face was never seen in his best-known roles, Harry in *Harry and the Hendersons*, and the alien in *Predator* also died. Other actors who died last year included **Nita Krebs**, 85, a 3 feet 8 inch actress who appeared in *The Wizard of Oz* and other films, **Glenn Langan**, 73, **Ralph Bates**, 50, who starred in many Hammer Films horror productions, **Thorley Walters**, 78, also a Hammer regular, English actress **Lillian Bond**, 83, French actress **Delphine Seyrig**, 58, **Jackie Moran**, 65, **Angelo Rossitto**, 83, a dwarf who starred in a number of major films and **Dwight Weist**, 81, an actor in many radio productions whose voice talents earned him the title, "the man of a thousand voices," in radio and later in films as well.

Others of the film industry's creative community who had fantasy credits and died last year were producer **Lester Cowan**, 83, best known for *One Touch of*

Venus, screenwriter **Warren Skaaren**, 44, who worked on many films, most notably *Beetlejuice*, art director **Robert E. Franklin**, 46, of HBO's *Tales of the Crypt* series, Oscar-winning art director **Gene Callahan**, 67, British film director **Don Chaffey**, 72, screenwriter **Howard Dimsdale**, 78, screenwriter/director **Andy Milligan**, 62, film director/art director **Eugene Lourie**, 89, director **Edward R. Blatt**, 88, sound effects engineer **James MacDonald**, 84, who also was the voice of Mickey Mouse for many years, screenwriter for film and television **Roger Swaybill**, 47, special effects technician **Roy Seawright**, 85, producer **George J. Morgan**, 77, and directors **George Sherman**, 82, **Richard Thorpe**, 95 and **Samuel G. Gallu**, 73. Not directly involved with fantasy or horror, but nonetheless heavily involved with works of fantastical imagination, was **Gene Roddenberry**, 70, who created *Star Trek* and was associated with the various incarnations and spin-offs of this vastly successful television series until his death. His show introduced hundreds of millions of viewers worldwide to science fiction and the realm of imagination upon which science fiction opens the door, and for that alone, Roddenberry deserves mention here. He, and all the other creative, talented people who died in 1991, will be missed, but their works and their vision will remain a part of all those who experienced their art. Through the works of those they influenced to create new art, their legacy grows, and will never die.

The *Year's Best*
Fantasy *and*
Horror

THE BEAUTIFUL UNCUT HAIR OF GRAVES

David Morrell

Morrell is best known for *First Blood,* the novel that became the first *Rambo* movie, and for the thriller trilogy *The Brotherhood of the Rose, The Fraternity of the Stone,* and *The League of Night and Fog.* His story "Orange Is for Anguish, Blue for Insanity" won the Horror Writers of America's Bram Stoker Award in 1989.

"The Beautiful Uncut Hair of Graves" is a mystery, a search for one's roots that takes the searcher on a long, tragic journey to the truth. The story is from the anthology *Final Shadows.*

—E.D.

Despite the rain, you've been to the cemetery yet again, ignoring the cold autumn gusts slanting under your bowed umbrella, the drenched drab leaves blowing against your soaked pant legs and shoes.

Two graves. You shiver, blinking through tears toward the freshly laid sod. There aren't any tombstones. There won't be for a year. But you imagine what the markers will look like, each birth date different, the death dates—God help you—the same. Simon and Esther Weinberg. Your parents. You silently mouth the kaddish prayers that Rabbi Goldstein recited at the funeral. Losing strength, you turn to trudge back to your rain-beaded car, to throw your umbrella on the passenger seat and jab the button marked Defroster, to try to control your trembling hands and somehow suppress your chest-swelling rage, your heart-numbing grief.

Eyes swollen from tears, you manage to drive back to your parents' home. An estate on Lake Michigan, north of Chicago, the mansion feels ghostly, hollow without its proper occupants. You cross the enormous vestibule and enter the oak-paneled study. One wall is lined with books, another with photographs of your precious father shaking hands with local and national dignitaries, even a president. As you sit at the massive desk to resume sorting through your father's papers, the last of them, the documents unsealed from your parents' safe-deposit box, your wife appears in the study's doorway, a coffee cup in her hand. She slumps against the wall and frowns as she did when you obeyed your repeated, so intense compulsion to go back—yet *again*—to the cemetery.

"Why?" she asks.

You squint up from the documents. "Isn't it obvious? I feel the need to be with them."

"That's not what I meant." Rebecca says. She's forty-nine, tall, with a narrow face and pensive eyes. "All the work you've been doing. All the documents and the meetings. All the phone calls. Can't you let yourself relax? You look terrible."

"How the hell should I look? My father's chest was crushed. My mother's head was . . . The asshole drunk who hit their car got away with just a few stitches."

"Not what I meant," Rebecca repeats. Using two hands, both of them shaky, she raises the coffee cup to her lips. "Don't make sympathy sound like an accusation. You've got *every* right to look terrible. It's bad enough to lose *one* parent, let alone *two at once*, and the way they died was"—she shakes her head—"obscene. But what you're doing, your compulsion to . . . I'm afraid you'll push yourself until you collapse. Don't torture yourself. Your father assigned an executor for his estate, a perfectly competent lawyer from his firm. Let the man do his job. I grant, you're a wonderful attorney, but right now it's time to let someone else take charge. For God's sake, Jacob—and if not for God, then for me—get some rest."

You sigh, knowing she means well and wants only what's best for you. But she doesn't understand: you *need* to keep busy, you *need* to distract yourself with minutiae so that your mind doesn't snap from confronting the full horror of losing your parents.

"I'm almost finished," you say. "Just a few more documents from the safe-deposit box. Then I promise I'll try to rest. A bath sounds . . . Lord, I still can't believe . . . How much I miss . . . Pour me a scotch. I think my nerves need numbing."

"I'll have one with you."

As Rebecca crosses the study toward the liquor cabinet, you glance down toward the next document: a faded copy of your birth certificate. You shake your head. "Dad kept *everything*. What a pack rat." Your tone is bittersweet, your throat tight with affection. "That's why his estate's so hard to sort through. It's so difficult to tell what's important, what's sentimental, and what's just . . ."

You glance at the next document, almost set it aside, take another look, frown, feel what seems to be a frozen fishhook in your stomach, and murmur, "God." Your breathing fails.

"Jacob?" Your wife turns from pouring the scotch and hurriedly puts the bottle down, rushing toward you. "What's wrong? Your face. You're as gray as—!"

You keep staring toward the document, feeling as if you've been punched in the ribs, the wind knocked out of you. Rebecca crouches beside you, touching your face. You swallow and manage to breathe. "I . . ."

"*What?* Jacob, tell me. What's the matter?"

"There has to be some mistake." You point toward the document.

Rebecca hurriedly reads it. "I don't understand. It's crammed with legal jargon. A woman's promising to give up two children for adoption, is that what this means?"

"Yes." You have trouble speaking. "Look at the date."

"August fifteen, nineteen thirty-eight."

"A week before my birthday. Same year." You sound hoarse.

"So what? That's just a coincidence. Your father did all kinds of legal work, probably including adoptions."

"But he wouldn't have kept a business affidavit with his personal papers in his private safe-deposit box. Here, at the bottom, look at the place where this was notarized."

"Redwood Point, California."

"Right," you say. "Now check this copy of my birth certificate. The place of birth is . . ."

"Redwood Point, California." Rebecca's voice drops.

"Still think it's just a coincidence?"

"It has to be. Jacob, you've been under a lot of strain, but this is *one* strain you don't have to deal with. You know you're not adopted."

"Do I? *How?*"

"Well, it's . . ."

You gesture impatiently.

"I mean, it's something a person takes for granted," Rebecca says.

"Why?"

"Because your parents would have told you."

"*Why?* If they didn't need to, why would they have taken the chance of shocking me? Wasn't it better for my parents to leave well enough alone?"

"Listen to me, Jacob. You're letting your imagination get control of you."

"Maybe." You stand, your legs unsteady, cross to the liquor cabinet, and finish pouring the drinks that Rebecca had started preparing. "*Maybe.*" You swallow an inch of the drink: made deliberately strong, it burns your throat. "But I won't know for sure, will I? Unless I find out why my father kept that woman's adoption agreement with his private papers, and how it happened that I was born one week later and in the same place that the woman signed and dated her consent form."

"So what?" Rebecca rubs her forehead. "Don't you see? It doesn't make a difference! Your parents loved you! *You* loved *them.* Suppose, despite Lord knows how many odds, suppose your suspicion turns out to be correct. What will it change? It won't make your grief any less. It won't affect a lifetime of love."

"It might affect a lot of things."

"Look, finish your drink. It's Friday. We still have time to go to temple. If ever you needed to focus your spirit, it's now."

In anguish, you swallow a third of your drink. "Take another look at that adoption consent. The woman agrees to give up *two* babies. If I *was* adopted, that means somewhere out there I've got a brother or a sister. A *twin.*"

"A stranger to you. Jacob, there's more to being a brother or a sister than just the biological connection."

Your stomach recoils as you gulp the last of the scotch. "Keep looking at the consent form. At the bottom. The woman's name."

"Mary Reilly."

"Irish."

"So?" Rebecca asks.

"Go to temple? Think about it. Have you ever heard of any Irish who . . . ? It could be I wasn't born Jewish."

*   *   *

Your uncle's normally slack-jowled features tighten in confusion. "Adopted? What on earth would make you think—?"

You sit beside him on the sofa in his living room and explain as you show him the documents.

His age-wrinkled brow contorts. He shakes his bald head. "Coincidence."

"That's what my wife claims."

"Then listen to her. And listen to *me*. Jacob, your father and I were as close as two brothers can possibly be. We kept no secrets from each other. Neither of us ever did anything important without first asking the other's opinion. When Simon—may he rest in peace—decided to marry your mother, he discussed it with *me* long before he talked to our parents. Believe me, trust me, if he and Esther had planned to adopt a child, *I'd have been told.*"

You exhale, wanting to believe but tortured by doubts. "Then why . . . ?" Your skull throbs.

"Tell me, Jacob."

"All right, let's pretend it *is* a coincidence that these documents were together in my parents' safe-deposit box. Let's pretend that they're unrelated matters. But why . . . ? As far as I know, Dad always lived here in Chicago. I never thought about it before, but why wasn't I born here instead of in California?"

Your uncle strains to concentrate. Weary, he shrugs. "That was so long ago. Nineteen"—he peers through his glasses toward your birth certificate—"thirty-eight. So many years. It's hard to remember." He pauses. "Your mother and father wanted children very much. *That* I remember. But no matter how hard they tried . . . Well, your father and mother were terribly discouraged. Then one afternoon, he came to my office, beaming. He told me to take the rest of the day off. We had something to celebrate. Your mother was pregnant."

Thinking of your parents and how much you miss them, you wince with grief. But restraining tears, you can't help saying, "That still doesn't explain why I was born in California."

"I'm coming to that." Your uncle rubs his wizened chin. "Yes, I'm starting to . . . Nineteen thirty-eight. The worst of the Depression was over, but times still weren't good. Your father said that with the baby coming, he needed to earn more money. He felt that California—Los Angeles—offered better opportunities. I tried to talk him out of it. In another year, I said, Chicago will have turned the corner. Besides, he'd have to go through the trouble of being certified to practice law in California. But he insisted. And of course, I was right. Chicago did soon turn the corner. What's more, as it happened, your father and mother didn't care for Los Angeles, so after six or seven months, they came back, right after you were born."

"That still doesn't . . ."

"What?"

"Los Angeles isn't Redwood Point. I never heard of the place. What were my parents doing there?"

"Oh, that." Your uncle raises his thin white eyebrows. "No mystery. Redwood Point was a resort up the coast. In August, L.A. was brutally hot. As your mother came close to giving birth, your father decided she ought to be someplace where she wouldn't feel the heat, close to the sea, where the breeze would make her comfortable. So they took a sort of vacation, and you were born there."

"Yes," you say. "Perfectly logical. Nothing mysterious. Except . . ." You gesture toward the coffee table. "Why did my father keep this woman's adoption agreement?"

Your uncle lifts his liver-spotted hands in exasperation. "*Oy vay.* For all we know, he found a chance to do some legal work while he was in Redwood Point. To help pay your mother's hospital and doctor bills. When he moved back to Chicago, it might be some business papers got mixed in with his personal ones. By accident, everything to do with Redwood Point got grouped together."

"And my father never noticed the mistake no matter how many times he must have gone to his safe-deposit box? I have trouble believing . . ."

"Jacob, Jacob. Last month, I went to my safe-deposit box and found a treasury bond that I didn't remember even buying, let alone putting in the box. Oversights happen."

"My father was the most organized person I ever knew."

"God knows I love him, and God knows I miss him." Your uncle bites his pale lower lip, then breathes with effort, seized with emotion. "But he wasn't perfect, and life isn't tidy. We'll probably never know for sure how this document came to be with his private papers. But this much I do know. You can count on it. You're Simon and Esther's natural child. You weren't adopted."

You stare at the floor and nod. "Thank you."

"No need to thank me. Just go home, get some rest, and stop thinking so much. What happened to Simon and Esther has been a shock to all of us. We'll be a long time missing them."

"Yes," you say, "a long time."

"Rebecca? How is . . . ?"

"The same as me. She still can't believe they're dead."

Your uncle's bony fingers clutch your hand. "I haven't seen either of you since the funeral. It's important for family to stick together. Why don't both of you come over for honey cake on Rosh Hashanah?"

"I'd like to, Uncle. But I'm sorry, I'll be out of town."

"Where are . . . ?"

"Redwood Point."

The major airport nearest your destination is at Salinas. There you rent a car and drive west to the coast, then south past Carmel and Big Sur. Preoccupied, you barely notice the dramatic scenery: the windblown cypresses, the rugged cliffs, the whitecaps hitting the shore. You ask yourself why you didn't merely phone the authorities at Redwood Point, explain that you were a lawyer in Chicago, and ask for information that you needed to settle an estate. Why did you feel compelled to come all this way to a town so small that it isn't listed in your Hammond atlas and could only be located in the Chicago library on its large map of California? For that matter, why do you feel compelled at all? Both your wife and your uncle have urged you to leave the matter alone. You're not adopted, you've been assured, and even if you were, what difference would it make?

The answers trouble you. One, you might have a brother or a sister, a twin, and now that you've lost your parents, you feel an anxious need to fill the vacuum of their loss by finding an unsuspected member of your family. Two, you suffer a form of midlife crisis, but not in the common sense of the term. To have lived these many years and possibly never have known your birth parents makes you uncertain of your identity. Yes, you loved the parents you knew, but your present limbo state of insecure uncertainty makes you desperate to discover the truth, one way or the other, so you can dismiss the possibility of your having been adopted or else adjust to the fact that you were. But this way, not being certain, is maddening, given the stress of double grief. And three, the most insistent reason, an identity crisis of frantic concern, you want to learn if after a lifetime—of having been circumcised, of Hebrew lessons, of your bar mitzvah, of Friday nights at temple, of scrupulous observance of sacred holidays—of being a Jew . . . if after all that, you might have been born a gentile. You tell yourself that being a Jew has nothing to do with race and genes, that it's a matter of culture and religion. But deep in your heart, you've always thought of yourself proudly as being *completely* a Jew, and your sense of self feels threatened. Who *am* I? you think.

You increase speed toward your destination and brood about your irrational stubborn refusal to let Rebecca travel here with you. Why did you insist on coming alone?

Because, you decide with grim determination.

Because I don't want anybody holding me back.

The Pacific Coast Highway pivots above a granite cliff. In crevasses, stunted misshapen fir trees cling to shallow soil and fight for survival. A weather-beaten sign abruptly says REDWOOD POINT. With equal abruptness, you see a town below you on the right, its buildings dismal even from a distance, their unpainted listing structures spread along an inwardly curving bay at the center of which a half-destroyed pier projects toward the ocean. The only beauty is the glint of the afternoon sun on the whitecapped waves.

Your stomach sinks. Redwood Point. A resort? Or at least that's what your uncle said. Maybe in 1938, you think. But not anymore. And as you steer off the highway, tapping your brakes, weaving down the bumpy narrow road past shorter, more twisted cypresses toward the dingy town where your birth certificate says you entered the world, you feel hollow. You pass a ramshackle boarded-up hotel. On a ridge that looks over the town, you notice the charred collapsed remnant of what seems to have been another hotel and decide, discouraged, that your wife and your uncle were right. This lengthy, fatiguing journey was needless. So many years. A ghost of a town that might have been famous once. You'll never find answers here.

The dusty road levels off and leads past dilapidated buildings toward the skeleton of the pier. You stop beside a shack, get out, and inhale the salty breeze from the ocean. An old man sits slumped on a chair on the few safe boards at the front of the pier. Obeying an impulse, you approach, your footsteps crunching on seashells and gravel.

"Excuse me," you say.

The old man has his back turned, staring toward the ocean.

The odor of decay—dead fish along the shore—pinches your nostrils.

"Excuse me," you repeat.

Slowly the old man turns. He cocks his shriveled head, either in curiosity or antagonism.

You ask the question that occurred to you driving down the slope. "Why is this town called Redwood Point? This far south, there *aren't* any redwoods."

"You're looking at it."

"I'm not sure what . . ."

The old man gestures toward the ruin of the pier. "The planks are made of redwood. In its heyday"—he sips from a beer can—"used to be lovely. The way it stuck out toward the bay, so proud." He sighs, nostalgic. "Redwood Point."

"Is there a hospital?"

"You sick?"

"Just curious."

The old man squints. "The nearest hospital's forty miles up the coast."

"What about a doctor?"

"Used to be. Say, how come you ask so many questions?"

"I told you I'm just curious. Is there a courthouse?"

"Does this look like a county seat? We used to be something. Now we're . . ."
The old man tosses his beer can toward a trash container. He misses. "Shit."

"Well, what about . . . Have you got a police force?"

"Sure. Chief Kitrick." The old man coughs. "For all the good he does. Not that we need him. Nothing happens here. That's why he doesn't have deputies."

"So where can I find him?"

"Easy. This time of day, the Redwood Bar."

"Can you tell me where . . . ?"

"Behind you." The old man opens another beer. "Take a left. It's the only place that looks decent."

The Redwood Bar, on a cracked concrete road above the beach, has fresh redwood siding that makes the adjacent buildings look even more dingy. You pass through a door that has an anchor painted on it and feel as if you've entered a tackle shop or boarded a trawler. Fishing poles stand in a corner. A net rimmed with buoys hangs on one wall. Various nautical instruments, a sextant, a compass, others you can't identify, all looking ancient despite their gleaming metal, sit on a shelf beside a polished weathered navigation wheel that hangs behind the bar. The sturdy rectangular tables all have captain's chairs.

Voices in the far right corner attract your attention. Five men sit playing cards. A haze of cigarette smoke dims the light above their table. One of the men—in his fifties, large chested, with short sandy hair and a ruddy complexion—wears a policeman's uniform. He studies his cards.

A companion calls to the bartender, "Ray, another beer, huh? How about you, Hank?"

"It's only ten to five. I'm not off duty yet," the policeman says and sets down his cards. "Full house."

"Damn. Beats me."

"It's sure as hell better than a straight."

The men throw in their cards.

The policeman scoops up quarters. "My deal. Seven-card stud." As he shuffles the cards, he squints in your direction.

The bartender sets a beer on the table and approaches you. "What'll it be?"

"Uh, club soda," you say. "What I . . . Actually I wanted to talk to Chief Kitrick."

Overhearing, the policeman squints even harder. "Something urgent?"

"No. Not exactly." You shrug, self-conscious. "This happened many years ago. I guess it can wait a little longer."

The policeman frowns. "Then we'll finish this hand if that's okay."

"Go right ahead."

At the bar, you pay for and sip your club soda. Turning toward the wall across from you, you notice photographs, dozens of them, the images yellowed, wrinkled, and faded. But even at a distance, you know what the photographs represent, and compelled, repressing a shiver, you walk toward them.

Redwood Point. The photographs depict the resort in its prime, fifty, sixty years ago. Vintage automobiles gleam with newness on what was once a smoothly paved, busy street outside. The beach is crowded with vacationers in old-fashioned bathing suits. The impressive long pier is lined with fishermen. Boats dot the bay. Pedestrians stroll the sidewalks, glancing at shops or pointing toward the ocean. Some eat hot dogs and cotton candy. All are well dressed, and the buildings look clean, their windows shiny. The Depression, you think. But not everyone was out of work, and here the financially advantaged sought refuge from the summer heat and the city squalor. A splendid hotel—guests holding frosted glasses or fanning themselves on the spacious porch—is unmistakably the ramshackle ruin you saw as you drove in. Another building, expansive, with peaks and gables of Victorian design, sits on a ridge above the town, presumably the charred wreckage you noticed earlier. Ghosts. You shake your head. Most of the people in these photographs have long since died, and the buildings have died as well but just haven't fallen down. What a waste, you think. What *happened* here? How could time have been so cruel to this place?

"It sure was pretty once," a husky voice says behind you.

You turn toward Chief Kitrick and notice he holds a glass of beer.

"After five. Off duty now," he says. "Thanks for letting me finish the game. What can I do for you? Something about years ago, you said?"

"Yes. About the time that these photographs were taken."

The chief's eyes change focus. "Oh?"

"Can we find a place to talk? It's kind of personal."

Chief Kitrick gestures. "My office is just next door."

It smells musty. A cobweb dangles from a corner of the ceiling. You pass a bench in the waiting area, go through a squeaky gate, and face three desks, two of which are dusty and bare, in a spacious administration area. A phone, but no two-way radio. A file cabinet. A calendar on one wall. An office this size—obviously at one time, several policemen had worked here. You sense a vacuum, the absence of the bustle of former years. You can almost hear the echoes of decades-old conversations.

Chief Kitrick points toward a wooden chair. "Years ago?"

You sit. "Nineteen thirty-eight."

"That *is* years ago."

"I was born here." You hesitate. "My parents both died three weeks ago, and . . ."

"I lost my own dad just a year ago. You have my sympathy."

You nod, exhale, and try to order your thoughts. "When I went through my father's papers, I found . . . There's a possibility I may have been adopted."

As in the bar, the chief's eyes change focus.

"And then again maybe not," you continue. "But if I *was* adopted, I think my mother's name was Mary Reilly. I came here because . . . Well, I thought there might be records I could check."

"What kind of records?"

"The birth certificate my father was sent lists the time and place where I was born, and my parents' names, Simon and Esther Weinberg."

"Jewish."

You tense. "Does that matter?"

"Just making a comment. Responding to what you said."

You debate, then resume. "But the type of birth certificate parents receive is a shortened version of the one that's filed at the county courthouse."

"Which in this case is forty miles north. Cape Verde."

"I didn't know that before I came here. But I did think there'd be a hospital. *It* would have a detailed record about my birth."

"No hospital. Never was," the chief says.

"So I learned. But a resort as popular as Redwood Point was in the thirties would have needed *some* kind of medical facility."

"A clinic," the chief says. "I once heard my father mention it. But it closed back in the forties."

"Do you know what happened to its records?"

Chief Kitrick raises his shoulders. "Packed up. Shipped somewhere. Put in storage. Not here, though. I know every speck of this town, and there aren't any medical records from the old days. I don't see how those records would help."

"My file would mention who my mother was. See, I'm a lawyer, and—"

The chief frowns.

"—the standard practice with adoptions is to amend the birth certificate at the courthouse so it lists the adopting parents as the birth parents. But the *original* birth certificate, naming the birth parents, isn't destroyed. It's sealed in a file and put in a separate section of the records."

"Then it seems to me you ought to go to the county courthouse and look for that file," Chief Kitrick says.

"The trouble is, even with whatever influence I have as a lawyer, it would take me months of petitions to get that sealed file opened—and maybe never. But hospital records are easier. All I need is a sympathetic doctor who . . ." A thought makes your heart beat faster. "Would you know the names of any doctors who used to practice here? Maybe *they'd* know who . . ."

"Nope, hasn't been a doctor here in quite a while. When we get sick, we have to drive up the coast. I don't want to sound discouraging, Mr. . . . ?"

"Weinberg."

"Yeah. Weinberg. Nineteen thirty-eight. We're talking ancient history. I suspect you're wasting your time. Who remembers that far back? If they're even still alive, that is. And God knows where the clinic's records are."

"Then I guess I'll have to do this the hard way." You stand. "The county courthouse. Thanks for your help."

"I don't think I helped at all. But Mr. Weinberg . . . ?"

"Yes?" You pause at the gate.

"Sometimes it's best to leave the past alone."

"How I wish I could," you tell him, leaving.

Cape Verde turns out to be a pleasant attractive town of twenty thousand people, its architecture predominantly Spanish: red-tiled roofs and clean bright adobe walls. After the blight of Redwood Point, you feel less depressed, but only until you hear a baby crying in the motel room next to yours. After a half-sleepless night during which you phone Rebecca to assure her that you're all right but ignore her pleas for you to come home, you ask directions from the desk clerk and drive to the courthouse, which looks like a hacienda, arriving there shortly after nine o'clock.

The office of the county recorder is on the second floor, at the rear, and the red-haired young man behind the counter doesn't think twice about your request. "Birth records? Nineteen thirty-eight? Sure." After all, those records are open to the public. You don't need to give a reason.

Ten minutes later, the clerk returns with a large dusty ledger. There isn't a desk, so you need to stand at the end of the counter. While the young man goes back to work, you flip the ledger's pages to August and study them.

The records are grouped according to districts in the county. When you get to the section for Redwood Point, you read carefully. What you're looking for is not just a record of *your* birth but a reference to Mary Reilly. Twenty children were born that August. For a moment that strikes you as unusual—so many for so small a community. But then you remember that in August the resort would have been at its busiest, and maybe other expecting parents had gone there to escape the summer's heat, to allow the mother a comfortable delivery, just as your own parents had, according to your uncle.

You note the names of various mothers and fathers. Miriam and David Meyer. Ruth and Henry Begelman. Gail and Jeffrey Markowitz. With a shock of recognition, you come upon your own birth record—parents, Esther and Simon Weinberg. But that proves nothing, you remind yourself. You glance toward the bottom of the form. Medical facility: Redwood Point Clinic. Certifier: Jonathan Adams, M.D. Attendant: June Engle, R.N. Adams was presumably the doctor who took care of your mother, you conclude. A quick glance through the other Redwood Point certificates shows that Adams and Engle signed every document.

But nowhere do you find a reference to Mary Reilly. You search ahead to September in case Mary Reilly was late giving birth. No mention of her. Still, you think, maybe she signed the adoption consent forms *early* in her pregnancy, so you check the records for the remaining months of 1938. Nothing.

You ask the clerk for the 1939 birth certificates. Again he complies. But after you reach the April records and go so far as to check those in May and still find no mention of Mary Reilly, you frown. Even if she impossibly knew during her first month that she was pregnant and even if her pregnancy lasted ten months instead of nine, she still ought to be in these records. *What happened?* Did she change her mind and leave town to hide somewhere and deliver the two children she'd promised to let others adopt? Might be, you think, and a competent lawyer could have told her that her consent form, no matter how official and complex it looked, wasn't legally binding. Or did she—?

"Death records, please," you ask the clerk, "for nineteen thirty-eight and 'thirty-nine."

This time, the young man looks somewhat annoyed as he trudges off to find those records. But when he returns and you tensely inspect the ledgers, you find no indication that Mary Reilly died during childbirth.

"Thanks," you tell the clerk as you put away your notes. "You've been very helpful."

The young man, grateful not to bring more ledgers, grins.

"There's just one other thing."

The young man's shoulders sag.

"This birth certificate for Jacob Weinberg." You point toward an open ledger. "What about it?"

"It lists Esther and Simon Weinberg as his parents. But it may be Jacob was adopted. If so, there'll be an alternative birth certificate that indicates the biological mother's name. I'd like to have a look at—"

"Original birth certificates in the case of adoptions aren't available to the public."

"But I'm an attorney, and—"

"They're not available to attorneys either, and if you're a lawyer, you should know that."

"Well, yes, I do, but—"

"See a judge. Bring a court order. I'll be glad to oblige. Otherwise, man, the rule is strict. Those records are sealed. I'd lose my job."

"Sure." Your voice cracks. "I understand."

The county's Department of Human Services is also in the Cape Verde courthouse. On the third floor, you wait in a lobby until the official in charge of adoptions returns from an appointment. Her name, you've learned, is Becky Hughes. She shakes your hand and escorts you into her office. She's in her thirties, blond, well dressed, but slightly overweight. Her intelligence and commitment to her work are evident.

"The clerk downstairs did exactly what he should have," Becky says.

But apparently you don't look convinced.

"The sealed-file rule on original birth certificates in the case of adoptions is a good one, Counselor."

"And when it's important, so is another rule: Nothing ventured, nothing gained."

"Important?" Becky taps her fingers on her desk. "In the case of adoptions, nothing's more important than preserving the anonymity of the biological mother." She glances toward a coffee pot on a counter. "You want some?"

You shake your head. "My nerves are on edge already."

"Decaffeinated."

"All right, then, sure, why not?"

She pours two cups, sets yours on the desk, and sits across from you. "When a woman gives her baby up, she often feels so guilty about it . . . Maybe she isn't married and comes from a strict religious background that makes her feel ashamed, or maybe she's seventeen and realizes she doesn't have the resources to take proper care of the child, or maybe she's got too many children already, or . . . For whatever reason, if a woman chooses to have a child instead of abort it and gives it up for adoption . . . she usually has such strong emotions that her mental health demands an absolute break from the past. She trains herself to believe that the child is on another planet. She struggles to go on with her life. And it's cruel for a lawyer or a son or a daughter to track her down many years later and remind her of . . ."

"I understand," you say. "But in *this* case, the mother is probably dead."

Becky's fingers stop tapping. "Keep talking, Counselor."

"I don't have a client. Or to put it another way, I do, but the client is . . ." You point toward your chest.

"*You?*"

"I think I . . ." You explain about the drunk driver, about the deaths of the man and woman that you lovingly thought of as your parents.

"And you want to know if they *were* your parents?" Becky asks.

"Yes, and if I've got a twin—a brother or a sister that I never knew about—and . . ." You almost add, if I was born a Jew.

"Counselor, I apologize, but you're a fool."

"That's what my wife and uncle say, not to mention a cop in Redwood Point."

"Redwood Point?"

"A small town forty miles south."

"Forty or four thousand miles. What difference does . . . ? Did Esther and Simon love you?"

"They *worshiped* me." Your eyes sting with grief.

"Then they *are* your parents. Counselor, I was adopted. And the man and woman who adopted me *abused* me. And that's why I'm in this office—to make sure that other adopted children don't go into homes where they suffer what I did. At the same time, I don't want to see a *mother* abused. If a woman's wise enough to know she can't properly raise a child, if she gives it up for adoption . . . in *my* opinion she deserves a medal . . . and *deserves* to be protected."

"I understand," you say. "But I don't want to meet my mother. She's probably dead. All I want is . . . I need to know if . . . The fact. *Was* I adopted?"

Becky studies you, nods, picks up the phone, and taps three numbers. "Records? Charley? How you doing, kid? Great. Listen, an attorney was down there a while ago, wanted a sealed adoption file. Yeah, you did the right thing. But here's what I want. It won't break the rules if you check to see if there *is* a sealed file." Becky tells him the date, place, and names that you earlier gave her. "I'll hold." Minutes seem like hours. She straightens. "Yeah, Charley, what have you got?" Becky sets down the phone. "Counselor, there's no sealed file. Relax. You're not adopted. Go back to your wife."

"Unless," you say.

"Unless?"

"The adoption wasn't arranged through an agency but instead was a private arrangement between the birth mother and the couple who wanted to adopt. The gray market."

"Yes, but even then, local officials have to sanction the adoption. There has to be a legal record of the transfer. In your case, there isn't." Becky looks uncomfortable. "Let me explain. These days, babies available for adoption are scarce. Because of birth control and legalized abortions. But even *today*, the babies in demand are WASPs. A black? A Hispanic? An Oriental? Forget it. Very few parents in those groups want to adopt, and even fewer Anglos want children from those groups. Fifty years ago, the situation was worse. There were so many WASPs who got pregnant by mistake and wanted to surrender their babies . . . Counselor, this might offend you, but I have to say it."

"I don't offend easily."

"Your last name is Weinberg," Becky says. "Jewish. Back in the thirties, the same as now, the majority of parents wanting to adopt were Protestants, and they wanted a child from a Protestant mother. If *you* were put up for adoption, even on the gray market, almost every couple looking to adopt would not have wanted a Jewish baby. The prospects would have been so slim that your mother's *final* option would have been . . ."

"The *black* market?" Your cheek muscles twitch.

"Baby selling. It's a violation of the antislavery law, paying money for a human being. But it happens, and lawyers and doctors who *arrange* for it to happen make a fortune from desperate couples who can't get a child any other way."

"But what if my mother was *Irish*?"

Becky blinks. "You're suggesting . . . ?"

"Jewish couples." You cringe, remembering the last names of parents you read in the ledgers. "Meyer. Begelman. Markowitz. Weinberg. Jews."

"So desperate for a baby that after looking everywhere for a Jewish mother willing to give up her child, they adopted . . . ?"

"WASPs. And arranged it so none of their relatives would know."

All speculation, you strain to remind yourself. There's no way to link Mary Reilly with you, except that you were born in the town where she signed the agreement and the agreement is dated a week before your birthday. Tenuous evidence, to say the least. Your legal training warns you that you'd never allow it to be used in court. Even the uniform presence of Jewish names on the birth certificates from Redwood Point that August so long ago has a possible, benign, and logical explanation: the resort might have catered to a Jewish clientele, providing kosher meals, for example. Perhaps there'd been a synagogue.

But logic is no match for your deepening unease. You can't account for the chill in the pit of your stomach, but you feel that something's terribly wrong. Back in your motel room, you pace, struggling to decide what to do next. Go back to Redwood Point and ask Chief Kitrick more questions? *What* questions? He'd react the same as Becky Hughes had. Assumptions, Mr. Weinberg. Inconclusive.

Then it strikes you. The name you found in the records. Dr. Jonathan Adams. The physician who certified not only *your* birth but *all* the births in Redwood Point. Your excitement abruptly falters. So long ago. The doctor would probably be dead by now. At once your pulse quickens. Dead? Not necessarily. Simon and Esther were still alive until three weeks ago. Grief squeezing your throat, you concentrate. Dr. Adams might have been as young as Simon and Esther. There's a chance he . . .

But how to find him? The Redwood Point Clinic went out of business in the forties. Dr. Adams might have gone anywhere. You reach for the phone. A year ago, you were hired to litigate a malpractice suit against a drug-addicted ophthalmologist whose carelessness blinded a patient. You spent many hours talking to the American Medical Association. Opening the phone-number booklet that you always keep in your briefcase, you call the AMA's national headquarters in Chicago. Dr. Jonathan Adams? The deep male voice on the end of the line sounds eager to show his efficiency. Even through the static of a long-distance line, you hear fingers tap a computer keyboard.

"Dr. Jonathan Adams? Sorry. There isn't a . . . Wait, there *is* a Jonathan Adams *Junior.* An obstetrician. In San Francisco. His office number is . . ."

You hurriedly write it down and with equal speed press the numbers on your phone. Just as lawyers often want their sons and daughters to be lawyers, so doctors encourage their children to be doctors, and on occasion they give a son their first name. This doctor might not be the son of the man who signed your birth certificate, but you have to find out. *Obstetrician?* Another common denominator. Like father, like . . . ?

A secretary answers.

"Dr. Adams, please," you say.

"The doctor is with a patient at the moment. May he call you back?"

"By all means, and this is my number. But I think he'll want to talk to me now. Just tell him it's about his father. Tell him it's about the clinic at Redwood Point."

The secretary sounds confused. "But I can't interrupt when the doctor's with . . ."

"Do it," you say. "I guarantee the doctor will understand the emergency."

"Well . . . If you're . . ."

"Certain? Yes. Absolutely."

"Just a moment, please."

Thirty seconds later, a tense male voice says, "Dr. Adams here. What's this all about?"

"I told your secretary. I assumed she told *you*. It's about your father. It's about nineteen thirty-eight. It's about the Redwood Point Clinic."

"I had nothing to do with . . . Oh, dear Jesus."

You hear a forceful click, then static. You set down the phone. And nod.

Throughout the stressful afternoon, you investigate your only other lead, trying to discover what happened to June Engle, the nurse whose name appears on the Redwood Point birth certificates. If not dead, she'd certainly have retired by now. Even so, many ex-nurses maintain ties with their former profession, continuing to belong to professional organizations and subscribing to journals devoted to nursing. But no matter how many calls you make to various associations, you can't find a trace of June Engle.

By then, it's evening. Between calls, you've ordered room service, but the poached salmon goes untasted, the bile in your mouth having taken away your appetite. You get the home phone number for Dr. Adams from San Francisco information.

A woman answers, weary. "He's still at . . . No, just a minute. I think I hear him coming in the door."

Your fingers cramp on the phone.

The now familiar taut male voice, slightly out of breath, says, "Yes, Dr. Adams speaking."

"It's me again. I called you at your office today. About the Redwood Point Clinic? About nineteen thirty-eight?"

"You son of a—!"

"Don't hang up this time, Doctor. All you have to do is answer my questions, and I'll leave you alone."

"There are laws against harassment."

"Believe me, I know all about the law. I practice it in Chicago. Doctor, why are you so defensive? Why would questions about that clinic make you nervous?"

"I don't have to talk to you."

"But you make it seem that you're hiding something if you don't."

You hear the doctor swallow. "Why do you . . . ? I had nothing to do with that clinic. My father died ten years ago. Can't you leave the past alone?"

"Not *my* past, I can't," you insist. "Your father signed my birth certificate at Redwood Point in nineteen thirty-eight. There are things I need to know."

The doctor hesitates. "All right. Such as?"

"Black market adoptions." Hearing the doctor inhale, you continue. "I think your father put the wrong information on my birth certificate. I think he never recorded my biological mother's name and instead put down the names of the couple who adopted me. That's why there isn't a sealed birth certificate listing my actual mother's name. The adoption was never legally sanctioned, so there wasn't any need to amend the erroneous birth certificate on file at the courthouse."

"Jesus," the doctor says.

"Am I right?"

"How the hell would *I* know? I was just a kid when my father closed the clinic and left Redwood Point in the early forties. If you *were* illegally adopted, it wouldn't have anything to do with *me*."

"Exactly. And your father's dead, so he can't be prosecuted. And anyway it happened so long ago, who would care? Except *me*. But, Doctor, you're nervous about my questions. That makes it obvious you know *something*. Certainly *you* can't be charged for something your father did. So what would it hurt if you tell me what you know?"

The doctor's throat sounds dry. "My father's memory."

"Ah," you say. "Yes, his reputation. Look, I'm not interested in spreading scandal and ruining anybody, dead or alive. All I want is the truth. *About me. Who* was my mother? *Do I have a brother or a sister somewhere?* Was I *adopted?*"

"So much money."

"What?" You clutch the phone harder.

"When my father closed the clinic and left Redwood Point, he had so much money. I was just a kid, but even *I* knew that he couldn't have earned a small fortune merely delivering babies at a resort. And there were always *so* many babies. I remember him walking up to the nursery every morning. And then it burned down. And the next thing, he closed the clinic and bought a mansion in San Francisco and never worked again."

"The nursery? You mean like a *plant* nursery?"

"No. The building on the ridge above town. Big, with all kinds of chimneys and gables."

"Victorian?"

"Yes. And that's where the pregnant women lived."

You shiver. Your chest feels encased with ice.

"My father always called it the nursery. I remember him smiling when he said it. *Why pick on him?*" the doctor asks. "All he did was deliver babies! And he did it well! And if someone paid him lots of money to put false information on birth certificates, which I don't even know if he did . . ."

"But you suspect."

"Yes. God damn it, that's what I suspect," Dr. Adams admits. "But I can't prove it, and I never asked. It's the Gunthers you should blame! *They* ran the nursery! Anyway if the babies got loving parents, and if the adopting couples finally got the children they desperately wanted, what's the harm? Who got hurt? Leave the past alone!"

For a moment, you have trouble speaking. "Thank you, Doctor. I appreciate your honesty. I have only one more question."

"Get on with it. I want to finish this."

"The Gunthers. The people who ran the nursery."

"A husband and wife. I don't recall their first names."

"Have you any idea what happened to them?"

"After the nursery burned down? God only knows," Dr. Adams says.

"And what about June Engle, the nurse who assisted your father?"

"You said you had only *one* more question." The doctor breathes sharply.

"Never mind, I'll answer if you promise to leave me alone. June Engle was born and raised in Redwood Point. When we moved away, she said she was staying behind. It could be she's still there."

"Could be. If she's still alive." Chilled again, you set down the phone.

The same as last night, a baby cries in the room next to yours. You pace and phone Rebecca. You're as good as can be expected, you say. You don't yet know when you'll be home. You try to sleep. Apprehension jerks you awake.

The morning is overcast, as gray as your thoughts. After checking out of the motel, you follow the desk clerk's directions to Cape Verde's public library. A disturbing hour later, under a thickening gloomy sky, you drive back to Redwood Point.

From the highway along the cliff, the town looks even bleaker. You steer down the bumpy road, reach the ramshackle boarded-up hotel, and park your rented car. Through weeds that cling to your pant legs, you walk beyond the hotel's once splendid porch, find eroded stone steps that angle up a slope, and climb to the barren ridge above the town.

Barren with one exception: the charred timbers and flame-scorched toppled walls of the peaked, gabled, Victorian structure that Dr. Adams Jr. had called the nursery. That word makes you feel as if an icy needle has pierced your heart. The clouds hang deeper, darker. A chill wind makes you hug your chest. The nursery. And in 1941 . . . you learned from old newspapers on microfilm at the Cape Verde library . . . thirteen women died here, burned to death, incinerated—their corpses grotesquely blackened and crisped—in a massive blaze, the cause of which the authorities were never able to determine.

Thirteen women. *Exclusively* women. You want to shout in outrage. And were they pregnant? *And were there also* . . . ? Sickened, imagining their screams of fright, their wails for help, their shrieks of indescribable agony, you sense so repressive an atmosphere about this ruin that you stumble back as if shoved. With wavering legs that you barely control, you manage your way down the unsteady stone slabs. Lurching through the clinging weeds below the slope, you stumble past the repulsive listing hotel to reach your car, where you lean against its hood and try not to vomit, sweating despite the increasingly bitter wind.

The nursery, you think.

Dear God.

The Redwood Bar is no different than when you left it. Chief Kitrick and his friends again play cards at the far right corner table. The haze of cigarette smoke again dims the light above them. The waiter stands behind the bar on your left, the antique nautical instruments gleaming on a shelf behind him. But your compulsion directs you toward the wrinkled, faded photographs on the wall to your right.

This time, you study them without innocence. You see a yellowed image of the peaked, gabled nursery. You narrow your gaze toward small details that you failed to give importance to the first time you saw these photographs. Several women, diminished because the cameraman took a long shot of the large Victorian building, sit on a lawn that's bordered by flower gardens, their backs to a windowed brick wall of the . . . your mind balks . . . the nursery.

Each of the women—young! so young!—holds an infant in her lap. The women smile so sweetly. Are they acting? Were they forced to smile?

Was one of those women your mother? Is one of those infants you? Mary Reilly, what desperation made you smile like that?

Behind you, Chief Kitrick's husky voice says, "These days, not many tourists pay us a second visit."

"Yeah, I can't get enough of Redwood Point." Turning, you notice that Chief Kitrick—it isn't yet five o'clock—holds a glass of beer. "You might say it haunts me."

Chief Kitrick sips his beer. "I gather you didn't find what you wanted at the courthouse."

"Actually I learned more than I expected." Your voice shakes. "Do you want to talk here or in your office?"

"It depends on what you want to talk about."

"The Gunthers."

You pass through the squeaky gate in the office.

Chief Kitrick sits behind his desk. His face looks more flushed than it did two days ago. "The Gunthers? My, my. I haven't heard that name in years. What about them?"

"That's the question, isn't it? What about them? Tell me."

Chief Kitrick shrugs. "There isn't much *to* tell. I don't remember them. I was just a toddler when they . . . All I know is what I heard when I was growing up, and that's not a lot. A husband and wife, they ran a boarding house."

"The nursery."

Chief Kitrick frowns. "I don't believe I ever heard it called the nursery. What's *that* supposed to mean?"

"The Gunthers took in young women. *Pregnant* women. And after the babies were born, the Gunthers arranged to sell them to desperate Jewish couples who couldn't have children of their own. Black market adoptions."

Chief Kitrick slowly straightens. "Black market . . . ? Where on earth did you get such a crazy . . . ?"

You press your hands on the desk and lean forward. "See, back then, adoption agencies didn't want to give babies to Jews instead of WASPs. So the Gunthers provided the service. They and the doctor who delivered the babies earned a fortune. But I don't think that's the whole story. I've got a terrible feeling that there's something more, something worse, though I'm not sure what it is. All I do know is that thirteen women—they were probably pregnant—died in the fire that destroyed the nursery in nineteen forty-one."

"Oh, sure, the fire," Chief Kitrick says. "I heard about *that*. Fact is, I even vaguely remember seeing the flames up there on the bluff that night, despite how little I was. The whole town was lit like day. A terrible thing, all those women dying like that."

"Yes." You swallow. "Terrible. And then the Gunthers left, and so did the doctor. *Why?*"

Chief Kitrick shrugs. "Your guess is as good as . . . Maybe the Gunthers didn't want to rebuild. Maybe they thought it was time for a change."

"No, I think they left because the fire happened in November and the authorities started asking questions about why all those women, and *only* women, were in that boarding house after the tourist season was over. I think the Gunthers and the doctor became so afraid that they left town to make it hard for the authorities to question them, to discourage an investigation that might have led to charges being filed."

"Think all you want. There's no way to prove it. But I *can* tell you *this*. As I grew up, I'd sometimes hear people talking about the Gunthers, and everything the townsfolk said was always about how nice the Gunthers were, how generous. Sure, Redwood Point was once a popular resort, but that was just during the tourist season. The rest of the year, the thirties, the Depression, this town would have starved if not for that boarding house. That place was always busy, year round, and the Gunthers always spent plenty of money here. So many guests. They ate a lot of food, and the Gunthers bought it locally, and they always hired local help. Cooks. Maids. Ladies in town to do washing and ironing. Caretakers to manage the grounds and make sure everything was repaired and looked good. This town owed a lot to the Gunthers, and after they left, well, that's when things started going to hell. Redwood Point couldn't support itself on the tourists alone. The merchants couldn't afford to maintain their shops as nice as before. The town began looking dingy. Not as many tourists came. Fewer and . . . Well, you can see where we ended. At *one* time, though, this town depended on the Gunthers, and you won't find anyone speaking ill about them."

"Exactly. That's what bothers me."

"I don't understand."

"All those pregnant women coming to that boarding house," you say. "All year round. All through the thirties into the early forties. Even if the Gunthers hadn't hired local servants, the town couldn't have helped but notice that something was wrong about that boarding house. The people here *knew* what was going on. Couples arriving childless but leaving with a baby. The whole town—even the chief of police—*had* to be aware that the Gunthers were selling babies."

"Now stop right there." Chief Kitrick stands, eyes glinting with fury. "The chief of police back then was my father, and I won't let you talk about him like that."

You raise your hands in disgust. "The scheme couldn't have worked unless the chief of police turned his back. The Gunthers probably bribed him. But then the fire ruined everything. Because it attracted outsiders. Fire investigators. The county coroner. Maybe the state police. And when they started asking questions about the nursery, the Gunthers and the doctor got out of town."

"I told you I won't listen to you insult my father! Bribes? Why, my father never—"

"Sure," you say. "A pillar of the community. Just like everybody else."

"Get out!"

"Right. As soon as you tell me one more thing. June Engle. Is she still alive? Is she still here in town?"

"I never heard of her," Chief Kitrick growls.

"Right."

Chief Kitrick glares from the open door to his office. You get in your car, drive up the bumpy street, turn, go into reverse, shift forward, and pass him. The chief glares harder. In your rearview mirror, you see his diminishing angry profile. You reduce speed and steer toward the left as if taking the upward jolting road out of town. But with a cautious glance toward the chief, you see him stride in nervous victory along the sidewalk. You see him open the door to the bar, and the moment you're out of sight around the corner, you stop.

The clouds are darker, thicker, lower. The wind increases, keening. Sporadic raindrops speckle your windshield. You step from the car, button your jacket, and squint through the biting wind toward the broken skeleton of the pier. The old man you met two days ago no longer slumps on his rickety chair, but just before you turned the corner, movement on your right—through a dusty window in a shack near the pier—attracted your attention. You approach the shack, the door to which faces the seething ocean, but you don't have a chance to knock before the wobbly door creaks open. The old man, wearing a frayed rumpled sweater, cocks his head, frowning, a homemade cigarette dangling from his lips.

You reach for your wallet. "I spoke to you the other day, remember?"

"Yep."

You take a hundred-dollar bill from your wallet. The old man's bloodshot eyes widen. Beyond him, on a table in the shack, you notice a half-dozen empty beer bottles. "Want to earn some quick easy money?"

"Depends."

"June Engle."

"So?"

"Ever heard of her?"

"Yep."

"Is she still alive?"

"Yep."

"Here in town?"

"Yep."

"Where can I find her?"

"This time of day?"

What the old man tells you makes your hand shake when you hand him the money. Shivering but not from the wind, you return to your car. You make sure to take an indirect route to where the old man sent you, lest the chief glance out the tavern window and see you driving past.

"At the synagogue," the old man told you. "Or what used to be the . . . Ain't that what they call it? A synagogue?"

The sporadic raindrops become a drizzle. A chilling dampness permeates the car, despite its blasting heater. At the far end of town, above the beach, you come to a dismal, single-story, flat-roofed structure. The redwood walls are cracked and warped. The windows are covered with peeling plywood. Waist-high weeds surround it. Heart pounding, you step from the car, ignore the wind that whips drizzle against you, and frown at a narrow path through the weeds that takes you to the front door. A slab of plywood, the door hangs by one hinge and almost falls as you enter.

You face a small vestibule. Sand has drifted in. An animal has made a nest in one corner. Cobwebs hang from the ceiling. The pungent odor of mold attacks your nostrils. Hebraic letters on a wall are so faded that you can't read them. But mostly what you notice is the path through the sand and dust on the floor toward the entrance to the temple.

The peak of your skull feels naked. Instinctively you look around in search of a yarmulke. But after so many years, there aren't any. Removing a handkerchief from your pocket, you place it on your head, open the door to the temple, and find yourself paralyzed, astonished by what you see.

The temple—or what used to be the temple—is barren of furniture. The back wall has an alcove where a curtain once concealed the torah. Before the alcove, an old woman kneels on bony knees, her hips withered, a handkerchief tied around her head. She murmurs, hands fidgeting as if she holds something before her.

At last you're able to move. Inching forward, pausing beside her, you see what she clutches: a rosary. Tears trickle down her cheeks. As close as you are, you still have to strain to distinguish what she murmurs.

". . . deliver us from evil. Amen."

"June Engle?"

She doesn't respond, just keeps fingering the beads and praying. "Hail, Mary . . . blessed is the fruit of thy womb . . ."

"June, my name is Jacob Weinberg."

"Pray for us sinners now and at the hour of our death . . ."

"June, I want to talk to you about Dr. Adams. About the clinic."

The old woman's fingers tighten on the rosary. Slowly she turns and blinks up through tear-brimmed eyes. "The clinic?"

"Yes. And about the Gunthers. About the nursery."

"God help me. God help *them.*" She wavers, her face pale.

"Come on, June, you'll faint if you kneel much longer. I'll help you up." You touch her appallingly fleshless arms and gently raise her to her feet. She wobbles. You hold her husk of a body against you. "The nursery. Is that why you're here, June? You're doing penance?"

"Thirty pieces of silver."

"Yes." Your voice echoes eerily. "I think I understand. Dr. Adams and the Gunthers made a lot of money. Did *you* make a lot of money, June? Did they pay you well?"

"Thirty pieces of silver."

"Tell me about the nursery, June. I promise you'll feel better."

"Ivy, rose, heather, iris."

You cringe, suspecting that she's gone insane. Just as you first thought that the expression "the nursery" referred to a *plant* nursery, so June Engle has made that same connection. But she knows better. She *knows* that the nursery had nothing to do with plants but instead with babies from unmarried pregnant women. Or at least she *ought* to know unless the consequence of age and what seems to be guilt has affected her mind and her memory. She appears to be free-associating.

"Violet, lily, daisy, fern," she babbles.

Your chest cramps as you realize that those words make perfect sense in the context of . . . They might be . . . "Are those names, June? You're telling me that the women in the nursery called themselves after plants and flowers?"

"Orval Gunther chose them. Anonymous." June weeps. "Nobody would know who they really were. They could hide their shame, protect their identities."

"But how did they learn about the nursery?"

"Advertisements." June's shriveled knuckles paw at her eyes. "In big-city papers. The personal columns."

"*Advertisements?* But that was taking an awful risk. The police might have . . ."

"No. Not Orval. He never took risks. He was clever. So clever. All he promised was a rest home for pregnant women. 'Feel alone?' the ad read. 'Need a caring trained staff to help you give birth in strictest privacy? No questions asked. We guarantee to relieve your insecurity. Let us help you with your burden.' Sweet Lord, those women came here by the *hundreds.*"

June trembles against you. Her tears soak through your jacket, as chilling as the wind-driven rain that trickles through the roof.

"Did those women get any money for the babies they gave to strangers?"

"*Get?* No, they paid!" June stiffens, her feeble arms gaining amazing strength as she pushes from your grasp. "Orval, that son of a . . . ! He charged them room and board! Five hundred dollars!"

Her knees sag.

You grasp her. "*Five hundred . . . ?* And the couples who took the babies? How much did the Gunthers get from *them?*"

"Sometimes as high as ten thousand dollars."

The arms with which you hold her shake. Ten thousand dollars? During the Depression? Hundreds of pregnant women? Dr. Adams Jr. hadn't exaggerated. The Gunthers had earned a fortune.

"And Orval's wife was worse than he was. Eve! She was a monster! All she cared about was . . . *Pregnant women* didn't matter! *Babies* didn't matter. *Money* mattered."

"But if you thought they were monsters . . . ? June, why did you help them?"

She clutches her rosary. "Thirty pieces of silver. Holy Mary, mother of . . . Ivy, Rose, Heather, Iris. Violet, Lily, Daisy, Fern."

You force her to look at you. "I told you my name was Jacob Weinberg. But I might not be . . . I think my mother's name was Mary Reilly. I think I was born here. In nineteen thirty-eight. Did you ever know a woman who . . . ?"

June sobs. "Mary Reilly? If she stayed with the Gunthers, she wouldn't have used her real name. So many women! She might have been Orchid or Pansy. There's no way to tell who . . ."

"She was pregnant with twins. She promised to give up both children. Do you remember a woman who . . . ?"

"Twins? *Several* women had twins. The Gunthers, damn them, were ecstatic. Two for the price of one, they said."

"But my parents"—the word sticks in your mouth—"took only *me*. Was it common for childless parents to separate twins?"

"Money!" June cringes. "It all depended on how much *money* the couples could afford. Sometimes twins were separated. There's no way to tell where the other child went."

"But weren't there records?"

"The Gunthers were smart. They *never* kept records. In case the police . . . And then the fire . . . Even if there *had* been records, *secret* records, the fire would have . . ."

Your stomach plummets. Despite your urgent need for answers, you realized you've reached a dead end.

Then June murmurs something that you barely hear, but the little you do hear chokes you. "What? I didn't . . . June, please say that again."

"Thirty pieces of silver. For that, I . . . Oh, how I paid. Seven stillborn children."

"*Yours?*"

"I thought, with the money the Gunthers paid me, my husband and I could raise our children in luxury, give them every advantage, send them to medical school or . . . God help me, what I did for the Gunthers cursed my womb. It made me worse than barren. It doomed me to carry lifeless children. My penance! It forced me to suffer! Just like . . . !"

"The mothers who gave up their children and possibly later regretted it?"

"No! Like the . . . !"

What you hear next makes you retch. *Black market adoptions*, you told Chief Kitrick. *But I don't think that's the whole story. I've got the terrible feeling that there's something more, something worse, though I'm not sure what it is.*

Now you *are* sure what that something worse is, and the revelation makes you weep in outrage. "Show me, June," you manage to say. "Take me. I promise it'll be your salvation." You try to remember what you know about Catholicism. "You need to confess, and after that, your conscience will be at peace."

"I'll *never* be at peace."

"You're wrong, June. You *will*. You've kept your secret too long. It festers inside you. You *have* to let out the poison. After all these years, your prayers here in the synagogue have been sufficient. You've suffered enough. What you need now is absolution."

"You think if I go there . . . ?" June shudders.

"And pray one last time. Yes. I beg you. Show me. Your torment will finally end."

"So long! I haven't been there since . . ."

"Nineteen forty-one? That's what I mean, June. It's time. It's finally time."

Through biting wind and chilling rain, you escort June from the ghost of the synagogue into the sheltering warmth of your car. You're so angry that you don't bother taking an indirect route. You don't care if . . . in fact, you almost *want* . . . Chief Kitrick to see you driving past the tavern. You steer left up the bumpy road out of town, its jolts diminished by the storm-soaked earth. When you reach the coastal highway, you assure June yet again and prompt her for further directions.

"It's been so long. I don't . . . Yes. Turn to the right," she says. A half mile later, she trembles, adding, "Now left here. Up that muddy road. Do you think you can . . . ?"

"Force this car through the mud to the top? If I have to, I'll get out and push. And if *that* doesn't work, we'll walk. God help me, I'll carry you. I'll sink to my knees and *crawl.*"

But the car's front-wheel drive defeats the mud. At once you gain traction, thrust over a hill, swivel to a stop, and scowl through the rain toward an unexpected meadow. Even in early October, the grass is lush. Amazingly, *horribly* so. Knowing its secret, you suddenly recall—from your innocent youth—lines from a poem you studied in college. Walt Whitman's "Song of Myself."

> A *child said* What is the grass? *fetching it to me with full hands.*
> *How could I answer the child? I do not know what it is any more than he.*
> *I guess it must be the flag of my disposition.*

You force your way out of the car. You struggle around its hood, ignore the mud, confront the stinging wind and rain, and help June waver from the passenger seat. The bullet-dark clouds roil above the meadow.

"Was it here?" you demand. "Tell me! Is *this* where . . . ?"

"Yes! Can't you hear them wail? Can't you hear them *suffer?*"

> . . . *the flag of my disposition, out of hopeful green stuff woven.*
> *Or I guess it is the handkerchief of the Lord.*
> *Or I guess the grass is itself a child, the produced babe of the vegetation.*

"June! In the name of God"—rain stings your face—"tell me!"

> . . . *a uniform hieroglyphic* . . .
> *Sprouting alike in broad zones and narrow zones,*
> *Growing among black folks as among white.*

"Tell me, June!"

"Can't you *sense?* Can't you *feel* the horror?"

"Yes, June." You sink to your knees. You caress the grass. "I can."

> *And now it seems to me the beautiful uncut hair of graves.*

"How many, June?" You lean forward, your face almost touching the grass.

"Two hundred. Maybe more. All those years. So many babies." June weeps behind you. "I finally couldn't count anymore."

"But *why?*" You raise your head toward the angry rain. "Why did they have to die?"

"Some were sickly. Some were deformed. If the Gunthers decided they couldn't sell them . . ."

"They murdered them? Smothered them? Strangled them?"

"Let them starve to death. The wails." June cringes. "Those poor, hungry, suffering babies. Some took as long as *three days* to die. In my nightmares, I heard them wailing. I *still* hear them wailing." June hobbles toward you. "At first, the Gunthers took the bodies in a boat and dumped them at sea. But one of the corpses washed up on the beach, and if it hadn't been for the chief of police they bribed . . ." June's voice breaks. "So the Gunthers decided they needed a safer way to dispose of the bodies. They brought them here and buried them in paper bags or potato sacks or butter boxes."

"Butter boxes?"

"Some of the babies were born prematurely." June sinks beside you, weeping. "They were small, so terribly small."

"*Two hundred?*" The frenzied wind thrusts your words down your throat. With a shudder, you realize that if your mother *was* Mary Reilly, *Irish,* there'd have been a chance of your having been born with red hair. The Gunthers might have decided that you looked too obviously gentile. They might have buried you here with . . .

Your brother or your sister? Your twin? Is your counterpart under the grass you clutch? You shriek. "Two hundred!"

Despite the howl of the storm, you hear a car, its engine roaring, its tires spinning, fighting for traction in the mud. You see a police car crest the rain-shrouded hill and skid to a stop.

Chief Kitrick shoves his door open, stalking toward you through the raging gloom. "God damn it, I told you to leave the past alone."

You stand, draw back a fist, and strike his mouth so hard he drops to the mushy ground. "You knew! You son of a bitch, you knew all along!"

The chief wipes blood from his mangled lips. In fury, he fumbles to draw his gun.

"That's right! Go ahead, kill me!" You spread out your arms, lashed by the rain. "But June'll be a witness, and you'll have to kill her as well! So what, though, huh? Two murders won't matter, will they? Not compared to a couple of hundred children!"

"I had nothing to do with—"

"Killing these babies? No, but your *father* did!"

"He wasn't involved!"

"He let it happen! He took the Gunthers' money and turned his back! That *makes* him involved! He's as much to blame as the Gunthers! The whole fucking town was involved!" You pivot toward the ridge, buffeted by the full strength of the storm. In the blinding gale, you can't see the town, but you shriek at it nonetheless. "You bastards! You sons of bitches! You knew! You all let it happen! You did nothing to stop it! You're responsible, as much as the Gunthers, for killing all these babies! That's why your town fell apart! God cursed you! Bastards! Sons of—!"

Abruptly you realize the terrible irony of your words. Bastards? *All* of these murdered children were bastards. You spin toward the grass, the beautiful uncut hair of graves, and lose control. Falling, you hug the rain-soaked earth, the drenched lush leaves of grass. "Poor babies! Poor sweet babies!"

"You can't prove anything, Weinberg," Chief Kitrick growls. "All you've got are suppositions. After fifty years, there won't be anything left of those babies. They've long since rotted and turned into—"

"Grass," you moan, tears scalding your face. "The beautiful grass."

"The doctor who delivered the babies is dead. The Gunthers—my father kept track of them—died as well. In agony, if that satisfies your need for justice. Orval got stomach cancer. Eve died from alcoholism."

"And now they burn in hell," June murmurs.

"I was raised to be . . . I'm a *Jew*," you moan and suddenly understand the significance of your pronouncement. No matter the circumstances of your birth, you *are* a Jew, totally, completely. "I don't believe in hell. But I wish . . . Oh God, how I wish . . ."

"The only proof you have," Chief Kitrick says, "is this old woman, a Catholic who goes every afternoon to pray in a ruined synagogue. She's nuts. You're a lawyer. You know her testimony wouldn't be accepted in court. It's over, Weinberg. It ended fifty years ago."

"No! It never ended! The grass keeps growing!" You sprawl on your stomach, feeling the chill wet earth, hugging the fertile grass. You try to embrace your brother or your sister and quiver with the understanding that *all* of these children are your brothers and sisters. "God help them! God have mercy!"

> *What do you think has become of the children?*
> *They are alive and well somewhere,*
> *The smallest sprout shows there is really no death,*
> *And if ever there was it led forward life, and does not wait at*
> *   the end to arrest it.*
> *All goes onward and outward, nothing collapses,*
> *And to die is different from what any one supposed, and luckier.*

"Luckier?" You embrace the grass, rubbing your face against it, wiping your tears. "*Luckier*? Whitman, you stupid—! The horror!" Through the rain-soaked earth, you think you hear babies crying and raise your face toward the furious storm. Swallowing rain, tasting the salt of your tears, you recite the kaddish prayers. You mourn Mary Reilly, Simon and Esther Weinberg, your brother or your sister, all these children.

And yourself.

"Deliver us from evil," June Engle murmurs. "Pray for us sinners. Now and at the hour of our death."

IN CARNATION
Nancy Springer

Pennsylvania writer Nancy Springer is the author of several popular High Fantasy novels including *The Sable Moon, The Silver Sun,* and *Wings of Gold;* her short fiction has been collected in *Chance and Other Gestures of the Hand of Fate.* Springer won the World Fantasy Award in 1987 for her tender story "The Boy Who Plaited Manes." Her excellent Pennsylvania Dutch novel *The Hex Witch of Seldom* is also particularly recommended.

"In Carnation" is a story as mysterious and sensual as the self-possessed cat who moves through its pages. It was written for Andre Norton and Martin H. Greenberg's theme anthology of magical cat stories, *Catfantastic II.*

—T.W.

She materialized, stood on her familiar padded paws and looked around at an utterly strange place. After every long sleep the world was more changed, and after every incarnation the next lifetime became more bizarre. The last time, a Norwegian peasant woman fleeing "holy" wars, she had come a long sea voyage to what was called the New World. Now she found it so new she scarcely recognized it as Earth at all. Under her paws lay a great slab of something like stone, but with a smell that was not stone's good ancient smell. Chariots of glass and metal whizzed by at untoward speeds, stinking of their own heat. Grotesque buildings towered everywhere, and in them she could sense the existence of people, more people than had ever burdened the world before, a new kind of people who jangled the air with their fears, their smallness, their suspicion of the gods and one another.

As always when she awoke from a long sleep she was very hungry, and not for food. But this was not a good place for her to go hunting. It terrified her. Running as only a cat can, like a golden streak, she fled from the chariots and their stench, from the buildings and the pettiness in their air until she found something that approximated countryside. Outside the town there was a place with trees and grass.

And on the grass were camped people whose thoughts and feelings did not hang on the air and make it heavy, but flitted and laughed like magpies. *We don't care what the world thinks,* the magpies sang. *Some of us are thieves and some of us are preachers, some are freaks and some are stars, some of us have three heads and*

27

some can't even get one together, and who cares? We all get along. We are the carnival people. Whether you are a pimp or a whore or a queer or a con artist, if you are one of us you belong, and the world can go blow itself.

A cat is one who walks by herself. Still, *A carnival! Yes,* thought she, the golden one. *This is better, I may find him here.* For she was very hungry, and the smells of the carnival were good. She was, after all, a meat eater, and a carnival is made of meat. The day was turning to silver dusk, the carnival glare was starting to light the sky and the carnival blare rose like magpie cries on the air. The cat trotted in through the gate, to the midway, where already the grass was trampled into dirt.

"Come see the petrified Pygmy," the barkers cried. "Come see the gun that killed Jesse James. Come see the Double-Jointed Woman, the Mule-Faced Girl, the Iron Man of Taipan."

High striker, Ferris wheel, motordrome, House of Mirrors—it was all new to her, yet the feel in the air was that of something venerable and familiar: greed. Carnival was carnival and had been since lust and feasting began. French fries, sausage ends, bits of cinnamon cake had fallen to the ground, but she did not gnaw at them. Instead, she traversed the midway, past Dunk Bozo and bumper cars, roulette wheel and ring toss, on the lookout for a man, any man so long as he was young and virile and not ugly. Once she had seduced him and satisfied herself, she would discard him. This was her holy custom, and she would be sure she upheld it. A few times in previous lives she had been false to herself, had married and found herself at the mercy of a man who attempted to command her; she had sworn this would not happen again. Eight of her lifetimes were gone. Only one remained to her, and she was determined to live this one with no regrets.

On the hunt, she found it difficult to sort out the people she saw crowding through the carnival. Men and women alike, they wore trousers, cotton shirts, and shapeless cloth shoes. And leather jackets, and hair that was short and spiky or long and in curls. She became confused and annoyed. True, some of the people she saw were identifiable as men, and some of the men she saw were young, but they walked like apes and had a strange chemical smell about them and were not attractive to her.

"Hey there, kitten! Guess your age, your weight, your birthdate?"

The cat flinched into a crouch. Though the words of this New World language meant nothing to her, she could usually comprehend the thoughts that underlay words, and for a moment she had unreasonably felt as if the guess-man's pitch had been directed at her. Narrow-eyed and coiled to run, she stared up at him.

"Yes, Mother! Congratulations." He was facing a pudding-cheeked woman with a pregnant belly. "What would you like me to guess? Name? Age? Date of your wedding day? Yes? Okay. Fifty cents, please. If I don't get it right, one of my fine china dolls is yours."

He was not talking to the cat after all. *Why would he?* she scolded herself. He offered his invitation to the dozens of people walking by. And many of them stopped for him, perhaps because there was a wry poetry in his voice, or perhaps because he was young and not ugly. Slim, dressed in denims and boots, he stood tall though he was in fact not very tall. In front of the booth that marked his place on the midway he took a stance like a bard in a courtyard. Something about him made her want to see his eyes, but because he wore dark glasses she could not. His face was quiet, unexceptional, yet he seemed like one who had something more to him than muscle and manhead.

Not that she needed anything more. It was enough that he was young and not ugly. He would suffice.

She trotted on, looking for a private place to make the change. It would take only a minute.

Within a few strides the familiar musky scent of lust touched her whiskers. Her delicate lip drew back from her tiny pointed teeth, and she slipped under a tent flap. She had reached the location of "Hinkleman's G-String Goddess Revue."

This will do.

Inside, all was heat, mosquitoes, dim light, and the smell of sweating men. Forty of them were crowded in there, watching a stripper at work on the small stage. The golden visitor leapt to a chair back and watched also. No one noticed her. She sat with her long tail curled around her slender haunches, and its softly furred tip twitched with scorn for what she was seeing.

Stupid, simpleminded cow. She uses her body like a club. She does not know how to walk, how to move, how to tease. Her breasts are huge, like melons, and that is all she knows.

The thoughts of everyone in the tent swarmed in its air thicker than the mosquitoes. Therefore the cat quickly knew that the stripper, called a kootch girl, was expected to more than mildly arouse the men, called marks. She knew that the kootch girl's repertory was limited by her meager talents, that the girl was planning to get out of her G-string in order to achieve maximum effect. She knew that several of the marks were thinking in terms of audience participation. She knew that in back of the tent was a trailer where those with fifty dollars might buy some private action later.

The men roared. The stripper was flashing her pudenda. Jumping down from her perch, the cat darted backstage, hot with scorn and anger.

Is that what they call a woman these days? Can no one show them how it should be done?

Backstage were two more strippers, spraying one another's semi-naked bodies with mosquito repellent. Mr. Hinkleman, the owner, was back there also, lounging in a tilted chair, bored, drinking gin between hot hoarse stints in the bally box. Off to one side was a booth with a flimsy curtain, a changing facility, not much used by women who were about to take off their clothes in front of an audience anyway. The golden cat walked into it. A moment later, a golden woman walked out.

"Carrumba!" Mr. Hinkleman, who had seen a lot over a career spanning twenty-three years in the carnival, nevertheless let his chair legs slam to the floor, jolting himself bolt upright. "Hoo! Where did you come from, honey?"

She answered only with a faint smile. There had been a time when she was more fully human, when she could talk. But that ability was a thousand years and four lifetimes gone. And she did not regret the loss. With each incarnation she found there were fewer to whom she wished to speak. Talking meant little but lies. Thoughts told her more truth.

"What's your name?"

The level look she gave him caused him to suddenly remember, without any resentment, the training his mother thought he had forgotten years before. He stood up to greet the naked visitor more properly.

"Hello, ma'am, welcome to—to wherever the heck this is. I'm Fred Hinkleman." His hand hovered in air, then went to his head as if to remove an invisible hat in her presence. "What can I do for you? Do you want to be in my show?"

"She don't got but little tits," one of the strippers put in scornfully. The girl from onstage had joined those backstage, and the three Hinkleman Goddesses stood huddled together like moose when the scent of panther is in the air.

"I know how she gets to look glowy like that all over," complained the dark kootch girl who was billed as the Wild Indian. "She just eats carrots, that's all. Any of us could do it. Eat carrots till they're coming out the kazoo."

Fred Hinkleman seemed not to hear them at all. His gaze was stuck on the newcomer. "Tell you what," he said to her. "You go onstage and show the yahoos what you can do. I'll go introduce you right now. What should I call you?"

Her mouth, smiling, opened into a soundless meow.

"Cat? Good. Suits you." He went out, and a moment later could be heard promising the marks "the hottest new talent in the adult entertainment business, the sleek, feline Miss Cat, uh, Miss Cat Pagan."

"Just another pussy," one of the strippers muttered.

She made her entrance onstage. Contrary to the logic of the word "stripper," it is not necessary for one actually to be wearing anything in order to perform. Cat was wearing nothing at all, but that was not what made the already-sated marks go wild and leap up and stand on their chairs in order to see her. It was the way she wore it.

She did not bump or grind or flash for them. All she did was walk, pose, hint at possibilities, and possess the stage as she had once possessed the known world. Dignity clothed her as if in robes of gold. No mark thought of touching her. Every mark knew that the price of going to her afterward would be more than he could afford.

Looking out over them, she knew she could have any one of them—and many of them were young and well built, far more showily muscled than the man in sunglasses on the midway. But no. It was him she wanted. There was something about the way he stood. He had dignity, too.

When she considered that the marks had seen enough, she went backstage and helped herself to clothing: a short strapless red dress with a flared skirt, a wisp of lace to throw around her shoulders, a picture hat. The other Hinkleman's G-String Goddess Revue girls watched her silently and did not try to stop her. Now that she had showed her stuff she was one of them. In the backstage air she could sense their stoical acceptance, and it surprised her. She had expected dislike, even enmity. But these women were carnies. They breakfasted with snake-eating geeks and sword swallowers, they bathed in buckets, camped in mud, and every day they were expected to perform magic, creating glamour out of dirt. So what was one more freak or freakish event to them? If the stranger wanted to show up out of nowhere, that was okay. They had weathered storms before.

"Honeycat, you're a walking advertisement," Hinkleman remarked when he saw her. "Go on, go do the midway. Have some fun."

The kootcher with the melon breasts went along with Cat—in order to be seen with her, Cat surmised, noticing the other woman's thoughts the way she noticed gnats in the air, with only a small portion of her attention. Melons wanted to make the best of a situation. Melons was not unwise.

"Been around the carousel a time or two, honey?" Melons chirped.

Married, she meant. Ignoring her, Cat headed straight toward the Guess Anything stand. Now that she was in her human form, she would make sure that the man there saw her. From her experience she knew this was all that would be necessary. She would smile just a little and look into his eyes, and when she walked away he would follow her as if she led him by an invisible chain of gold.

There was a crowd around the stand. The Guess Anything man was popular. Asked the standard questions concerning age and weight, he was often wrong, always on the side of flattery, and he gave away many prizes. But asked to guess far more difficult things—birthstones, marital status, number of children or grandchildren, home address, the place where a mark went to high school or nursing school or prison—he was often correct, uncannily so. And there was a quiet charisma about him. People stood listening to him in fascination, giving him their money again and again.

At the edge of the crowd Cat waited her turn with scant patience. She was not far away from him; he should see her. . . . Wishing to enjoy his reaction, she felt for his mind with hers and found it easily. In fact, it awaited her. And yes, there was an awareness of her presence in him, but it was unlike any awareness she had ever experienced in a man before. His cognition of her had no lust in it. Despite her lithe, barefoot, red-clad beauty, her appearance did not affect him in that way. Not at all.

"Who's next?" He took the mark's money and handed it to a boy in the stand, a good-looking youngster. His son, Cat knew from touching his mind at that moment. The mother was long dead but still very much missed. He was raising the boy himself.

As the boy made change, his father guessed the mark's age and weight, both incorrectly, then handed over the cheap ceramic prize with a smile. It was a warm, whimsical smile. Amusement in it: the "fine china dolls" were so worthless he made money even when he gave them away. But also something of heart: he liked to make people happy. Cat suddenly found that she liked his smile very much.

"Who's next?"

"Right here, Ollie," Melons said, nudging Cat forward. "Hey, Ollie, this here's Cat."

"I know. We met earlier." He faced her. His smile was wonderful, but he still wore the dark glasses, even though night had fallen. She could not see his eyes.

"Hello, Cat," he said. "Welcome."

Melons said, "She wants you to guess her age, I guess. I don't know. She don't seem to talk none. Cat got her tongue." Melons laughed at her own weak joke, chin angled skyward, breasts quaking. Ollie smiled but did not laugh.

"Some other time I'll guess for her if she wants," he said. "Not right now. I don't think that's what you really want right now anyway, is it, Cat?" His tone was mild, friendly. There was no flirtation in it.

Frustrated, she thought, *I want you to take off those barriers over your eyes. I want to see into them and make you follow me. I want to know you carnally, and I want to know what you are.*

No, his thought replied directly to her thought. *No, sorry, I can't do any of that. Not even for you, milady Cat.*

Back at the girl show tent, an hour later, she found herself still quivering in reaction. This man had made her feel naked, unshielded, exposed in a way that no lack of clothing could ever make her feel exposed. Whoever or whatever he was, he could touch her mind. Perhaps he could even tell what she was—or had been.

Partly, she felt outrage, humiliation, vexation. As much as she had ever wanted any man she wanted him, and he had not responded as he should have. It is no small matter when a fertility goddess is thwarted in lust.

And partly she felt great fear. The deities of the old religions are always the demons of the new. Once in her thrice-three lives Cat had been found out and put to death, while still in her feline form, by burning. She still remembered not so much the horrible pain as the helplessness of her clever cat body enslaved by rawhide bindings, the leaping, ravenous flames of the bonfire, the stench of her own consumed skin and fur. It was not a death she ever wanted to experience again.

Strutting and posing through her next kootch show, she picked out a broad-shouldered, handsome young mark and summoned him with her eyes. As she had wordlessly commanded, he was waiting for her in back of the tent afterward, not quite able to believe what was happening, his mouth moving uncertainly, soft as a baby's. She led him away into the darkness beyond the edge of the carnival, and he did what she wanted, everything she wanted, and he was good, very good. Afterward, she drove him away with her clawed hands. More punishment was not necessary. She knew he would go mad with thinking of her before many days had passed.

She should have been satisfied. Always before she had been satisfied by the simple, sacred act of lust. Yet she found that she was not.

She should have gone away on four speedy unbound paws from that dangerous place where someone had apprehended her truly. Yet she found that she would not.

Confusion take this Ollie person. He has shamed me and he has made me afraid, but he has not yet bested me utterly. We shall see whether he scorns me in the end.

Scorn was perhaps too strong a word, for when she came back to the carnival, walking alone, she found him waiting for her outside Hinkleman's trailer. "I just want to say I'm sorry if I offended you, Cat," he told her aloud. "I didn't mean to."

The words meant nothing to her. But the thought underlying them was clear as tears. *I didn't mean to stir up anger, and I don't want enemies. I just want to be let alone with my son and my sorrow.*

Sentiment annoyed her. She bared her teeth at him, nearly hissing, then passed him and went inside to sleep in the bunk Hinkleman's girls had cleared for her. When Hinkleman came, a few minutes later, to see if he could share it with her as was the kootch show owner's tacit right, she struck at him, leaving four long red scratches across his face. Then she listened in disgust as he comforted himself with the Indian instead. He was aging, potbellied, foul of breath, altogether repulsive. How could he be so goatishly eager while this man who attracted her, this Ollie, was so indifferent?

Men. Hell take them all. So Ollie wishes to be let alone? That will be no heartbreak for me.

Yet the next day when the carnival lights came on at sunset, she went first to the flower stand, and took a blossom—smiling, the old Italian woman gave it to her. Carnies give other carnies what they can. This was a flower like a woman's petticoat, frilled and fringed and fluted, white once but dipped in a stain that had spread from its petal tips along its veins and into its penetralia, blood red. It was very beautiful. Cat placed it in her golden hair. Then she walked the midway in her red dress again, and came to a certain booth, his booth, and stood there staring at him. It was her curiosity, she told herself, that drew her back to him this way. And she knew that partly this was true.

Hello, Cat, he greeted her without speaking and without looking at her.

Hello.

You are the only one I can talk to this way.

You are the only one I can talk to at all.

There was a pause. Then he thought to her very softly, *Yes. Yes, I see. It had not occurred to me, but there is such a thing as being too much alone.*

No, not really. I like being alone.

Still . . . if you wish to talk sometimes, it is no trouble for me to talk with you.

It would be a way, perhaps, of finding out how much he knew of her. As for the other thing she wanted of him . . . she still desired it badly, and still felt no response in him. And there was no way in cold frosty hell she was going to ask it of him again. The flower in her hair should have been invitation enough. That and the summons in her eyes.

She made mental conversation as casually as if she were hostessing a court function, chatting with the lesser vassals. *So you comprehend thoughts. When people come to you and ask you questions, then you can find the answers in their minds?*

Yes. And also many things they would not want me to know. Very beautiful things sometimes, and sometimes very ugly. She heard a poet's yearning in his tone of mind. He wanted to take what was in people and make a song, a saga great enough to hold all of it, everything he had heard and learned. But she did not wish to be in his song.

She could not ask him how much he knew of her. Why would he tell her the truth, anyway? He lied constantly.

So whatever questions the marks ask you, you could answer correctly every time.

Yes.

Then why do you so often give the wrong answer?

To please them. People like to win. So I let them win sometimes, and then they come back, you see, and try again.

She turned and walked away. Behind her she could hear him as he started ballying: "I can guess your age, your weight, your occupation! Challenge my skill, ladies and gentlemen! Ask me any question. See if I can answer."

Cat made sure she was well down the midway before she allowed herself to think it: *He keeps them coming back. He keeps me coming back.*

And then she thought, *If I win, will it be because he has let me?*

And she thought, *Who is he? What is he?*

But her sense of fear felt eased somewhat. If she did not know those things of him by touching his mind, there was little reason to think he knew more of her.

That night she lay with a mark again, and found that she despised him and what she did with him. "You should charge," Melons told her crossly after the man left. "It's stupid not to charge. You're making it bad for the rest of us." She glared at the kootcher, but she could not have loathed herself much more if she did indeed perform the holy act for pay. Even the thought of how insanity would punish the man for his daring did not comfort her.

The next morning she went to find Ollie in his trailer with his young son. For hours she sat in their kitchen, and conversed in her silent way with Ollie, and had fried trout, fresh caught, for breakfast with both of them. The boy tended to the breakfast, mostly, just as he tended the booth in the evenings, making change for his father, and for the same reason. The Guess Anything man could not do it for himself.

Ollie was blind.

Blind? But—I didn't know!

Hardly anybody does. Keep it to yourself, will you? His smile told her this was a small joke—he knew she could speak to no one. Yet it was no joke. A guess-man is supposed to see, to find clues with his eyes, to surmise, not to know. Anything else is too frightening. Ollie would be out of business if the marks knew the truth.

Of course.

Cat felt at the same time very foolish and strangely lighthearted. So he had never seen her in her red dress, he did not know how golden her hair glowed in the carnival lights, he had never seen the carnation softly bobbing at her temple, he could not see how beautiful she was at all. Yet he had been sorry to offend her. Yet he had greeted her the first time he felt her walk by.

Your eyes—how did it happen?

In the accident.

The fiery tragedy that had killed his wife. Afterward, he had sold his home, quit his job, and started traveling with the carnival. Built a life for himself the way he liked it. Letting people win. Giving them happiness.

Or—touching their minds, and learning all the truth about them, then telling them lies.

There was a pause. Then Cat asked gently, *May I see your eyes now?*

He hesitated only a moment, then reached up and removed the dark glasses. His eyes were not ugly. Really, she had known they could not be ugly. They were gray, misty, and seemed to stare far away, like the eyes of a seer. And his face, without its dark barrier in the way—how could she ever have thought his face was commonplace? It was exquisite, with arched aspiring cheekbones, brows that dreamed.

You are very beautiful.

You—they tell me you are also, Cat. I know—the feel of your mind—it is beautiful to me. It is proud, like a golden thing, a sunset thing.

You knew everything. Right from the start.

A silence. Then he admitted aloud, "Yes. I know."

I do not understand this strange barbaric language. I understand only what I feel in your mind. Which is now a great sadness. You know I want you. But you are still in love with your wife.

I think—I am now only in love with my memories of my wife.

You are afraid, then. You think I would punish you, as I did the others.

No, I am not afraid. Danger is part of the beauty of you. Everything that is beautiful is full of risk.

But when I came to summon you, you did not want me.

I do not know. . . . I am stubborn. Mostly I did not like the way you planned to take me.

You did not want me.

I want you now.

She had won. But perhaps he was letting her win?

The boy, who had finished scrubbing the dishes, smiled in the same winsome way as his father and went outside to wander the carnival grounds, to admire the motorcycle daredevil's new Harley, and watch the roughies play poker, and talk with the Bearded Lady, the Breasted Man, the Wild Woman of Borneo, the Amazing Alligator Girl.

Cat touched Ollie's fine-sculpted face. He leaned toward her, and let her touch guide him, and kissed her.

His body, she found within the next hour, was as beautiful as his face, and as ardent and clumsy as if he were a boy again. It truly had been years since he had given himself to a woman, a verity that made the gift all the more precious to her. She hugged him, she cradled his head in her arms and kissed him, she adored his awkwardness, she felt her heart burst open like a red, red flower into love of him.

Afterward, she was afraid. She was afraid. Love harrowed her with fear. She had sworn never to give her heart to a man again.

He said softly, "The carnival moves on tomorrow."

Yes.

"There is this about a carnival, it takes in all kinds of people. Criminals, whores, freaks, geeks, holy rollers, crap shooters, it doesn't matter, we're all carnies. We all belong. You, too."

Yes. She heard the wistfulness in herself. *I like that.*

"But there is also this, that we're like wild geese, we carnies. We move with the seasons, everything is always changing. We get used to leaving places behind, people behind, losing bits of ourselves. My problem is I look back too much. I've got to learn not to do that."

She no longer cared that he was letting her win. It was his gift to her, this offering of a choice. He knew what she was. He knew that a cat must walk by herself.

And perhaps he hoped to keep her coming back.

But she did not leave him yet. She put on her dress, but lay down again on his bed. A dying blossom fell from her hair. Her fingers interlaced with his. She thought to him quietly, *Guess my name and age?*

Why, Cat?

You said you would guess for me someday.

Okay. Because you want me to. He took a deep breath. Or perhaps he sighed. *Your name is Freyja. Or that is one of them, anyway. You were the great goddess of fruitfulness, you had many names in different places.*

Yes.

Your age? A lot older than I can comprehend. About four millennia?

Yes. Though for most of the time I have slept.

Catnaps. She felt his gentle smile in his tone of mind and knew he would never betray her.

Yes.

She lay silent awhile before she asked him, *Now tell me. What are you?*

Cat. He was both rueful and amused. *I must give you a prize, a little china doll. That is the one question that baffles me.*

Of course. Otherwise she would have been able to find the answer in his mind. *You do not know?*

Milady—I feel that there is a dream I have forgotten. I keep trying to find the words for the song, but they are gone. I truly do not know.

She lay with his head on her shoulder. Stroked his cheek and temple and the side of his neck. At her mercy and in her arms, he succumbed to her touch, he fell asleep, as she wished him to. When that had happened, very softly she withdrew herself and made the change. Her dress lay on the bed now. She, a golden cat, stood by her lover's pillow.

There is magic in the soft, twitching, fluffy end of the tail of a cat. Countryfolk know this and will sometimes cut off a cat's tail to use in their spells. This act is an abomination. The world that no longer remembers the holy ways of the golden goddess is full of danger for a cat.

Freyja curved the end of her tail so that it resembled the heavy head of a stalk of ripe wheat, her emblem. Softly she brushed it across the lidded eyes of the sleeping man.

Odin, my sweet faithless lover, when you awaken you will be able to see again. Give me no place in your song, do not remember me. And hang yourself no longer from the tree of sorrow, beautiful one. Be happy.

Not far away, the carousel calliope started to sound. The cat bounded to the floor, landing softly on padded paws.

There is still time to stay. Will I regret leaving him?

But perhaps there was no such thing as life without regrets. And a strange new world awaited her wanderings. She pushed her way through the loose screening of the kitchen window, thumped quietly to the ground, and trotted off.

The man would live long and bear her blessing. And it was an odd thing, now at last she felt satisfied.

She slipped away, a golden shadow quick as thought, into the silver dusk. But as she went, she felt the song of the carnival flitting on the air behind her, a fey and raucous magpie melody. *We don't care what the world thinks*, the minds of freaks and barkers and vendors sang. *We are old, we have been gypsying around this world for a long time. Come see a splinter of the true cross! Come see the pickled brains of the frost giant Ymir. Come see Napoleon's little finger. Come see a pressed flower from the Garden of Eden, from the Tree of Life.*

THE SOMEWHERE DOORS
Fred Chappell

Fred Chappell is one of the most intriguing voices on the contemporary American literary scene. The following story about an impoverished science fiction writer is a bittersweet cautionary tale that could be called science fiction and could be called fantasy, or magic realism . . . but what it is, in truth, is simply a damn fine piece of work.

Chappell is the author of six novels, two collections of stories, and twelve volumes of poetry. He has received the Award in Literature from the National Institute of Arts and Letters, the Best Foreign Novel prize from the French Academy, and the Bollingen Prize in Poetry. His short fiction has been cited five times in *Best American Short Stories*. His historical fantasy "Ancestors," published in the "Southern Writing" issue of *Chronicles: The Magazine of American Culture* (March 1991), is also recommended as one of the best of the year. "The Somewhere Doors" comes from Chappell's most recent collection, *More Shapes Than One*.

Chappell was born and reared in North Carolina, and currently teaches at the University of North Carolina.

—T.W.

No true light yet showed in the window, but he could feel the dawn coming on, the softness of it brushing his neck hair like a whisper, and heard the stir of trees outside the screen of his open window. He sat staring at the paper before him, the Blue Horse page he had so painstakingly covered with his light slant strokes, and held his pen poised above it, ready to write the final line of his story.

Here was his keenest pleasure, writing down at last the sentence he had aimed at from the beginning. It was like drawing the line beneath a column of numbers and setting in the sum, a feeling not only of winding up but of full completion. He waited, savoring the moment, then inscribed the words: "Lixor looked at the lights in the sky and wondered if one of them would begin to move toward him." And then, to prolong his satisfaction, he printed THE END below in tall, graceful capitals embellished with curls of flourish. Reverting to his careful script, he put down also his name: *Arthur Strakl, Cherry Cove, North Carolina, September 12, 1936.*

When he looked at his handiwork, his name seemed strange to him, out of place on this page full of exotic sights and notions, as homely alien as a worn tin thimble in a jeweler's fancy display case. So he set about inking the postscript out, producing a shiny black rectangle where each word had stood. The page looked better, he thought, without this reminder of our world of familiar impressions and of a dispiriting time in a place that was all too local. Anyhow, he would see his name enough times when "The Marooned Aldebaran" was published.

If it was published.

His luck was not good. Only about three of ten of the stories that he wrote ever saw print, and then in so mutilated a fashion, so mangled by editorial obtuseness, that he felt a sad weariness when they did appear.

He went to his one bookcase and took up a copy of a recent *Astounding Stories* from an unread stack of similar pulp magazines. It was the August issue, and commenced *The Incredible Invasion*, a serial novel by Murray Leinster. Names familiar to habitués of this kind of literature were displayed: Weinbaum, Fearn, Schachner, Gallun, and Williamson. The cover illustration showed grim hominoids in gleaming gray armor battling among themselves and menacing a brace of plucky young ladies in dapper short skirts. He supposed the armored men to be the Incredible Invaders. Arthur did not read invasion stories; he could not imagine that Earth, unfashionable and located far from its galactic center, would be a desirable prize.

We are, he reflected, a bunch of hicks. Why would anyone bother?

Opening the magazine, he flipped past the ads for self-education and self-medication, but his attention was drawn to the announcement for a new character pulp, *The Whisperer*. "The Whisperer!—NOT a Chinaman!—NOT a modern Robin Hood!—NOT a myth or a ghost!—But—HE IS———a good two-fisted, hard-hitting AMERICAN cop who gets his man!"

Arthur sighed, thinking how he could never write a story about The Whisperer, how in fact he probably could never bring himself to read one. He had tried to write some of those stories about two-fisted cops, two-fisted cowboys, two-fisted orphans of the jungle male and female, but that talent was not in him—nor for flying aces, nor scientific detectives, nor steel-armed quarterbacks or boxers. Again it was a question of belief. He did not believe that human beings came from so predictable a toy box and he could not engage himself in heroic fantasies. To him those daydreams lacked imagination and verged upon braggartry. But he did not wish to condemn. Hard times now, and writers needed to stock groceries, and readers wished to enjoy the brief glimpses of triumph the pulp stories afforded.

But his own stories were not fashioned in that mode. He could write only these melancholy twilight visions of things distant in time and space, stories that seemed not entirely his, but gifts or visitations from a source at which he could not guess. His most difficult task was to find words for them; he was a shy man, naturally taciturn, and he considered himself unhandy with language. But when the stories came to him, the impulse to write them down was too strong to resist. The stories compelled him to write, to struggle with phrases in a way that felt incongruous to his personality. And so he wrote, stealing the hours from his bed, the strength from his body. Each stroke of the pen, every noun and comma and period, brought him closer to the beautiful release that he always felt, as he did now, upon completion of a tale.

That was the main thing, to finish, to tell the stories through to the end. He got not much money for them and what he received was always late in arriving, and little acclaim came his way, for the readers who wrote to the letter columns preferred the loud, brawny stories of superscience, with their whirling rays and burning cities, colliding suns and flaming rocket ships, to his delicate accounts of loneliness under the stars, his elegies for dying worlds and soulful perishing species. Of course, his stories as they appeared were mutilated so that readers could not form fair opinions about them, but Arthur suspected that even if they were published just as they came in their final drafts from his typewriter, with every nuance and adverb complete, readers still would prefer the yarns about genius engineers and iron-thewed swordsmen.

He replaced the magazine on top of the stack and paced the narrow strip of floor between his desk and the foot of his lumpy bed. He was too elated to sleep and, anyway, the night was nearly gone. A dim gray began to show in the window. He would go to his job at the Red Man Café red-eyed and nervous and in the afternoon a dull lassitude would creep over him and he would drink cup after cup of acid coffee until closing time. He was "chief cook and bottle washer," as the owner, Farley Redmon, called him, and his hours were long and ill paid. But he earned his food and his rent for this little outbuilding that was formerly a tool shed—and he had a job and in this year of Our Lord 1936, he was grateful for it.

He would be grateful to light down anywhere he could find in order to write these stories that gave him no peace.

Arthur decided to walk out. The excitement of composition was still warm in him and the hour was inviting, cool and quiet. He pulled on his thinning blue wool sweater and peered out his window and, seeing no lights in any of the settlement windows, departed his room, taking care to turn off the little desk lamp with its green cardboard shade.

Cherry Cove was quiet, almost silent: no dogs barking, no radios in kitchens reporting farm prices, no clatter of breakfast cutlery. Everyone snug and warm and dreaming and, as he walked along the broad gravel road that led east, Arthur wondered whether any of their dreams might be as strange as the one he had just set down, in which the last survivor of a race of orchidaceous philosophers journeyed to the moon of its planet in order to send a signal to the cosmos, a message telling them that though the Kronori had died all but Lixor, he had one valuable secret to share with every other species everywhere.

Arthur smiled, assuring himself that the dreams of his neighbors would be stranger and more exciting and more urgent than his little tale. Then he set out at an easy walking pace for the Little Tennessee River two miles distant, the river that ran counter to all the others.

He was headed toward the peeling iron bridge. He had no particular purpose in mind, drawn only by that obscure impulse that leads us to the sound of running water as a source of comfort and refreshment. When he stood there at the railing, listening to the water twenty feet below rush away over the rocks—going the wrong way, for the Little Tennessee is a backwards river—his anxieties fell quiet and the utter lack of hope that characterized his days took on the aspect of courage rather than of fear. Arthur Strakl often felt that he stood on the abrupt edge of an ebony abyss, and that if he fell he would fall without crying out, without making a sound, and that no one on earth would remark his passing or remember that he had sojourned here. These considerations sometimes made him gloomy; at other times they strengthened his resolve, and did so now, with the completion of "The Marooned Aldebaran" fresh in his mind. He listened to the water and smelled its clean smell and watched where the river drew away into the forest of firs and oaks. On his right-hand side, just at the bridgehead, was a stand of slender trees with flowers beneath, and he glanced at it without really seeing it.

Then he became aware that he was not alone on the bridge. A woman stood beside him. He had not heard her approach, but he was not startled; her aspect was calm and easy. He was surprised to see that she was dressed in a white silk party frock with a wide square collar. She wore white pumps of patent leather and her dark hair was tied back with a broad ribbon of shiny white silk.

She was a beautiful woman, and when she spoke, it was with a quiet musical accent that was stranger than any other he had ever heard. "Are you Arthur Strakl?" she asked.

"Yes ma'am," he said, though she was not his elder. She looked rather younger than Arthur's thirty-five years.

"I'm glad," she said, and said no more for such a long moment that he began to think the conversation had ended. Then she added, "To meet you. I'm glad to meet you."

"I'm glad to meet you, too. You don't live in Cherry Cove, do you?"

"No," she said. "I've come a long way to find you."

"Me?" He laughed. "Well now, that's a little hard to believe."

"Why is it hard to believe?"

Arthur noted that she spoke slowly and hesitantly, as if these words were foreign to her. "There's no good reason for anyone to look for me. I don't have a family or any close friends. No one knows who I am."

"Are you not Arthur Strakl, the author?"

"I write a few odd stories. I never thought of calling myself an author."

"But didn't you write 'In the Titanic Deeps,' the story about sea dwellers in another galaxy?"

"Yes. My title was 'Blind Oceans,' but they changed it. That one was about the great worms that lived on the bottom of an ocean. They were suffering because they had the power to foresee centuries into the future and saw that nothing would change, that their destiny was fixed. Then one of their mathematicians devised a theory that admitted the possibility of the end of time, and this idea brought solace to them."

"And then what happened?"

"Nothing," he said. "That was it. . . . Well, their music changed."

She turned upon him a superbly friendly smile. Dawn brightened over the river below them. "Yes," she said. "Their music changed."

"I'm amazed," he said. "You can't imagine. This is the first time I ever met somebody who has read one of my stories."

"Oh, I've read many of your stories. I remember them all."

"Well, I actually haven't published all that many."

"I remember your story about the beings you called 'kindlers.' They were incandescent blue nervous systems that lived on the surface of a faraway sun. I remember the planet you called Zephlar, where the wind streaming over a continent of telepathic grasses produced an unending silent musical fugue. I remember your city Alphega, which was an enormous machine that was writing a book; each word of the book was a living human citizen. I remember your story about the language you named Spranza, which communicated so efficiently that listeners experienced directly the objects and actions it spoke of. And the sentient river Luvulio that had become a religious zealot, and the single amber eye named Ull, which lay in a primordial sea waiting for the remainder of its organism to evolve, and the parasite that reproduced itself by causing allergies in its hosts. At the magnetic pole of a tropical planet grew a tree whose leaves were mirrors; there was a world where humanlike people communicated by differences in skin temperature. There was a plague virus that heightened the sense of taste to a painful degree."

"Good Lord," Arthur said.

"So you see," she said sweetly, "I have read your stories. They have afforded me"—she paused, as if waiting for the correct phrase to present itself—"a fine pleasure. Many fine pleasures."

"Thank you for saying so," Arthur said. "But I didn't write all those stories. Somebody else must have written about the religious river and the alphabet city. And none of the magazines would take my story about the telepathic grasses. I don't see how you could have heard about that one."

"You have more admirers than you're aware of," she said. She smiled and turned away to watch the early light smear tree shadows on the river surface. "Sometimes the editors talk about your stories even when they don't buy them. Sometimes they want to buy them and are afraid to. But word gets around."

"Well, you obviously know a great deal about this," he said. "What do you do for a living? I mean, are you a literary agent?"

"I'm a representative for a group of people who are interested in new ideas," she said. "They have great faith in the power of ideas to make the future better for everyone."

"Who are they?"

She turned to meet his gaze directly. Her brown eyes were serious. "They prefer to remain anonymous."

"Are they Communists then?" he asked. "I met a Communist once who talked like that, sort of."

She laughed lightly. "I don't think they belong to any recognizable political group. . . . To tell the truth, I don't know all that much about them. They just pay me to deliver messages to people they think are important to their way of looking at things."

"And I'm important to them?"

"Oh yes," she said, and there was no mistaking the sincerity of her reply. "Extremely important. They're very pleased to discover you. That's why they sent me to trace you down."

"How did you find out where I live?"

"It wasn't hard. You are a publishing author, after all." She laughed again, and the light sound reminded Arthur of a child's laughter.

He found himself smiling. "Only a few people know about that."

"But it's not how many," she said. "It's who they are."

"And these are important people?"

"I don't know anything about them," she said, "but they seem to have decided that they're important."

"So now you know who I am, but I don't know who you are."

"I'm not supposed to tell my real name. I was supposed to choose any name that I took a fancy to. Do I look like a Francesca?"

"I don't know," he said. "I've never seen any Francescas."

"So this must be exciting for you." She offered her hand. "It's nice to meet you, Arthur."

He held it for a moment. "I'm pleased to meet you, too. May I ask about the way you're dressed? Or is that against the rules?"

"Oh, this," she said. "Of course. I came from a dinner party that went on till too late, so then I came straight here."

"Straight here to this bridge?"

"Yes."

Confused, he could not formulate the question he wanted to ask. "How did you get here?"

"My driver dropped me off," she said, and hurried on to add, "and the car will be returning for me very soon. So I'd better go ahead and deliver my message."

"From these unknown people?"

"Yes." She laughed again and now there was something teasing in the sound— teasing but not mocking. "Yes, my message that I don't understand from a group of people I don't know. . . . This doesn't really make sense, does it?"

"No," he said. "But I don't much care. A lot of things don't make sense to me."

"I'll bet you like it better that way."

"I do." His tone changed. "I sure do wish you lived around here. Are you married?"

She reached gently to touch his face with two fingers. "You're sweet. Truly. It's very sweet of you to say that. But I live far away and our time is short. I'd better tell you what I came to say."

"All right." He grinned. "Fire when ready."

She closed her eyes for a moment, then opened them. "Two doors will be brought to you. Don't be afraid. These doors open to other worlds, worlds different from our own. Behind the blue door is a world that has no people in it. The violet door is the entrance to a world of great cities. You can live in either world very pleasantly, but once you choose either door, you can never return. You will be gone from this planet forever."

"Wait. I don't understand."

"It's no good asking me," she said. "I don't understand, either. I can only tell you what I was told."

"Did they send a letter?" he asked. "I'd like to read it."

"It was a telephone message and the voice sounded like it came from a long way off. I couldn't even tell if it was a man or a woman speaking."

"Is that all then? Two doors?"

She closed her eyes once more, appearing to recollect, then went on: "The two doors will be brought to you at some future date. It may be soon, or it may be quite some time from now. And things may happen so that you think the doors never will arrive. But they will."

"Where will I find them?"

"I don't know," she said.

"All right. What else?"

"Nothing else."

"That's all?"

"As far as I can think, that's the end of the message. I hope I haven't forgotten anything. . . . Oh, don't look so alarmed. I'm sure I haven't."

"I honestly don't know what to make of all this."

"Neither do I," she replied, smiling her fine smile once more. "I'm just glad I don't have to make sense of it.—Wait. Now I remember. There was one other thing. You must keep writing your wonderful stories. That is the most important thing. You must keep on imagining the kinds of things that only you can imagine."

"All right. I wish I could sell more of them, though. I could use the money."

"I'm sorry. The person I talked to didn't say anything about that. But I'm sure you'll do well.—Oh, here comes my ride." She raised her right arm and waved.

He turned, to see that the car was at the end of the bridge, by the stand of birches there, rolling very slowly toward them, almost silent on the gravel. That was strange, and the car was strange, too, with its darkened windows and its smooth, almost featureless sedan shape and its deep oxblood color. There was something dreamlike about its appearance as it came on slowly.

When it drew abreast of them, it stopped and the passenger door opened—seemingly of its own accord—and the girl got in easily, showing neat ankles and pulling her skirt over her knees. He leaned down, trying to see the driver, but the car was in shadow on that side.

"Goodbye, Arthur," she said. Her tone was grave now and she didn't smile.

"I suppose I won't see you again."

"No," she said. "Never again."

"I hate it," he said. "I wish—"

"No. Say goodbye."

"All right. . . . Goodbye." He sighed.

And she closed the door and the strange smooth car pulled away, the sound of its motor no more than a warm hum and soon lost in the normal sounds of an autumn morning by the water: birdcalls and squirrels frolicking and the wash and gurgle of the river. He watched the car till it floated out of sight around the tall bank of the road all yellow and red with locust and sassafras bushes.

*   *   *

Two years passed and Arthur Strakl waited patiently. He had a serene confidence that the two doors, the doors that opened upon different Somewheres, would be brought to him. He did not know why he was so secure in his faith; he was not introspective in that particular way. The fancies that his mind produced entranced him, but the workings of his mind held no interest.

Not much changed. His employer, Farley Redmon, had undertaken to make his hut a little more comfortable, paying to have it plumbed and rewired. But he explained that he could not increase Arthur's wages and Arthur accepted the statement, his needs few. His heaviest expenses outside basic necessities were his pulp magazines and typewriter ribbons and now and again some small fees for the repair of the ancient Underwood. He was healthy and lucky.

For he kept on writing his stories, just as he had promised, and he was beginning to have a brighter success with them. He was still no great favorite with readers, but their letters now spoke of his work with intrigued bemusement rather than with irritated incomprehension. He appeared more regularly in the magazines and now and then his name would be featured on the cover, tucked away in the corner of the pictured insane laboratory where the flimsily clothed girl stared in horror at some loathsome transformation.

His better satisfaction, though, was that editors began to do less violence to his sentences. His style of writing was still hobbledehoy, he thought, but it was better left alone than improved. At least something of the intensity of his visions flamed through, even if sensual nuance was lost. The essential strangeness of the tales did not diminish. He wrote, for instance, a story based on the idea that the positions of the stars in our galaxy had been designed by the immensely powerful science of an ancient superrace as a kind of wallpaper. In another story the ghost of a dismantled robot visited its inventor and sat each night silent and reproachful at the foot of his bed. In "Black Receiver" an intelligent butterfly composed of a carbon gas picked up through its antennae the radio communications of a space fleet and thus formed a very surprising view of humankind.

So he was fairly content and hoped for better things to come, even though it was clear that the times were verging on catastrophe. Arthur was no great reader of newspapers, but no one could escape hearing about the events in Europe, and all the world was darkened by suspicion.

Arthur's own apprehensiveness deepened when he was visited by a man who claimed to be a government agent and asked whether he knew Sheila Weddell. "I don't think so," he said. "The name doesn't ring a bell."

The agent gave him a long stare. Then he said, "All right, sport. I'll have coffee."

When Arthur set the thick mug before him, the squat little man added cream and three spoons of sugar before saying, "You sure?"

"Sure of what?"

"About the woman. Sheila Weddell."

"I don't know her." He knew, however, that he didn't like this dumpy little man with his false smile that let the sneer show through and his slicked-back silver-blond hair. He had a firm impression of the fellow as one who took deep satisfaction in feeling contempt. His bored eyes and twisted mouth betrayed a jaded spirit.

"I got a picture." He reached into his inside jacket pocket and produced a crinkled photograph.

The picture, as Arthur had expected, was of the woman who called herself Francesca, and he already had decided to keep this agent—if that's what he was—at arm's length. "Pretty," he said, and handed it back.

The man laid it carefully on the Bakelite counter, then turned it around to face Arthur. "You've seen her before, haven't you? About two years ago?"

"Two years is a long time."

"It's longer inside the jailhouse than it is outside. Even in a fleabite place like this." He giggled. "What do you call it here? Cherry Cola?"

"Cherry Cove," Arthur said. "You're in Cherry Cove, North Carolina."

"And I want to know if you ain't seen this woman, Sheila Weddell, in Cherry Cove, North Carolina, about two years ago."

"You say you're some kind of an agent? I'd like to see your identification."

He drew a toothpick from an upper vest pocket and stuck it in the front of his mouth, so it bobbed up and down as he spoke. "You know, sport, I don't think you'd be asking for identification unless you were trying to hide something. I got me an idea you're hiding something."

"And I have an idea you're no government agent of any kind," Arthur said. "I have an idea you're a lawyer or a Pinkerton who is meddling in a lady's private affairs."

"I see. You kinda like her, do you? Well, let me tell you, you don't know what's going on. You don't know the least little thing. If you did, you wouldn't be calling Sheila Weddell no lady. I guess she must have been real nice to you, am I right?"

"You better leave now," Arthur said. "Your coffee is cold and we have just run fresh out."

"Sure, I understand," the oily blond man said. "She let you have a piece and you think you're Sir Galahad or somebody. But, brother, if you knew what I know . . ."

"Since you're a government agent, you'll be glad to talk to Robie Calkins. He is our sheriff here in Jackson County. Would you like to wait here for him? I'll give him a call right now."

"That's all right. I believe I've already found out what I needed to know. It's pretty clear she passed through here two years back." He laid a nickel on the counter and pushed it toward Arthur with one finger. "Here's what I owe."

Arthur pushed it back. "Keep it," he said. "I don't believe the coffee agreed with you."

The man smiled his twisted smile but did indeed rescue his nickel and make his surprisingly quick way to the door with an odd waddling stride. Arthur expected him to stop at the door and turn and make a last curdled remark, but he only pushed the screen open and stepped out into the late September sunlight that streamed saffron through the leaves of the big poplar there.

Arthur sighed tiredly and looked up and down the long room with its empty tables covered with red oilcloth and the big iron coal stove in the center of the aisle and the long counter with the five stools before it. When he emptied the remains of the coffee into the zinc sink behind him, he saw that his hands were shaking. He washed his hands and dried them on his apron and headed toward the storeroom in back to sit down and collect himself for a moment.

But Farley Redmon opened the kitchen door and called him back. "Arthur," he said, "could I talk to you just a minute?"

"Sure thing." He retraced his steps and when the older man held the door for him, he entered the kitchen.

"Sit down," Redmon said, indicating a tall wooden stool by the chop block. When Arthur sat, Redmon leaned back against the wall counter and folded his arms. "What was that all about with the little stout feller that come in?"

"I don't know," Arthur said. "He was asking questions about a woman I met one time."

"You got woman trouble, Arthur? Hard to believe."

"I've got an outstanding lack of woman trouble," he said. "It's hard for me to add up how much woman trouble I don't have."

"Ain't that kind of burdensome?"

"I just hope it's not fatal."

"Generally it ain't," Redmon said. "Not till some ornery husband stirs things up with a shotgun. You want to be careful now."

"I am careful," Arthur said. "I'm a careful man."

"Yes you are. That's the truth." Redmon produced a new package of Luckies from his shirt pocket, zipped it open, and tapped one out. He lit it with a kitchen match from a box on the counter. "I've been thinking about you," he said, "and how careful you are. I don't know what it was all about with that stout feller, but I thought you handled it okay."

"I don't usually drive away the customers."

"You did fine. You would've had your reasons." He looked into the cloud of smoke he exhaled toward the ceiling. "There's something I've been meaning to talk to you about. You know how it's been here at the café. Business is steady, what with the sawmill and the railroaders, but there ain't much profit. I've been trying to figure out how to do better by you, but I don't see no way I can come up with much more in terms of wages."

"That's all right," Arthur said. "I know how it is."

"Yeah. But you've been doing a good job. I don't know when I've seen a steadier man. I never could figure why you stuck."

"The arrangement suits me. I get time to write my stories."

"Your stories, yeah." Redmon tapped his ash into a soiled plate and smiled. "You know, I read one of your stories one time. I went down to the news store and bought one of them magazines and read it. Just to see. Beginning to end, I couldn't make head nor tail of it. It was about some animals on another world— that was all I understood. Do you believe there are other worlds with animals on them?"

"I don't know."

"The Bible don't say nothing about it. So it must be something you just make up in your mind, is that right?"

"The stories I write, I make up."

"You ever thought about writing a cowboy story, or something that people like more to read?"

"I'm not cut out for it," Arthur said. "I write the only kind of stories I'm able."

Redmon nodded. "Okay. The reason I ask, I always figured you were staying here till you made some big money with your writing and then you'd move on. If you did, I wouldn't know what to do. My boy Cletus ain't interested in this café and he ain't settled enough in mind to run it. I figure Cletus is just about ready to join the armed service, only he don't know it yet."

"Cletus is a good boy. He'll straighten out."

"I thought maybe if he got married, but then I got to studying on these women he's been running with. Ain't none of them would be any help. The trouble was losing his mother when he was little. I didn't have the furthest notion how to raise a youngun. So I reckon it's going to have to be Uncle Sam finishes the job."

"You're probably worrying about it too much."

"Well, I've worried myself gray-headed. Unless it's just natural age." He crushed his butt out in the littered plate. "Which was the other thing I was going to bring up. I don't want this business to go down the rathole. Someday Cletus might grow into it. Right now he don't want it, but later on he might. I want you to stay with me and help keep it going. Since I can't pay you better wage money, I thought I'd offer you an interest in the place. That don't mean much now, but when times lighten up it will. I can just about guarantee that."

"What do you have in mind?"

"Two percent to start with and then another percent every year till we get to ten. One of these days you'll find it was a good deal."

"But in order to get ten percent, I'd have to stay on another eight years."

"Yep."

"I'll have to think about it."

"That's all I want." Redmon offered Arthur his hand. "I just want your word you'll give it fair consideration."

"Sure I will. The offer means a lot to me." Arthur took Redmon's hard, dry hand and shook it twice gently. His own hand was soft and pulpy from washing dishes and he was beginning to grow flabby about the waist.

In fact, his health was none so sound as he had assumed. He learned from his army physical examination in 1942 that his teeth were in need of immediate repair and that one of the doctors thought he detected a heart murmur but wasn't sure. At any rate, Arthur Strakl was turned down for military service and rode in the bus back to Asheville with a group of other rejects who were rowdy and gloomy by turns. Then he took a westbound milk-stop bus to Cherry Cove, trudged through the lonesome hamlet dark at ten in the evening, went into his little hut, and fell asleep without undressing, only dropping his scuffed brown shoes by the bed.

When he woke next morning, he was still tired and all his skin felt grimy. He took off his shirt and pants and stumbled blindly to the tiny sink and ran water into a porcelain basin and bathed as quickly and thoroughly as he could. Then he placed a blue spatterware pot on his hot plate and set about making coffee.

It was only when he sat at his writing desk sipping at the strong unsugared coffee that he noticed how the big armoire standing against the opposite wall had changed. It was an ancient piece of work, this dim armoire, heavy oak boards stained dark. Inside were Arthur's other three white shirts and two pairs of pants and various socks and handkerchiefs—the respectable wardrobe of a penurious orphan bachelor. He always kept it neat and orderly, the way he kept all his few possessions, the way he kept his life. His life, like his little hut, was always prepared for visitation.

But now the visitation had occurred while he was absent. The doors of the armoire that had been stained almost chocolate were now blue on the right side and violet on the left. His Somewhere Doors had arrived. Arthur was so profoundly gratified that tears trickled down his cheeks and the back of his neck flushed red and warm.

They were not prepossessing. They were the same size and shape as the armoire doors always had been; only the color had changed. The surfaces were matte and cool to the touch when he placed his hand flat against them. But the texture of the surfaces was strange; the material didn't feel like wood or metal or plastic. More like glass with a subtle grain. He placed his ear directly against the blue door and waited a long time but could hear nothing. Still the old chest seemed to breathe silently and steadily, like a great distant creature asleep.

He began to take stock. The room seemed otherwise unchanged, except that his clothing and other belongings had been taken from the armoire and carefully folded and laid out on his one other chair and on his bookcase. But there was a sheet of paper in the typewriter with a sentence cleanly typed in capital letters.

THANK YOU FOR YOUR VALUABLE EFFORTS

It was unsigned.

"My valuable efforts," Arthur said. He rubbed his eyes, brushing away the wetness. "I wish I could see what was so valuable."

He knew already that the presence of the Somewhere Doors would make an enormous difference, but he could not foresee what different shapes his life might take.

Now, though, he would have to choose. Before the doors arrived he had thought only vaguely about their contrasting possibilities; today the choice had become serious. Would he like to inhabit the golden utopian world that philosophers and visionaries over the centuries had guessed at? To immerse himself in the grandest productions of religious thought, scientific ingenuity, governmental peace, and aesthetic achievement of which human beings were capable? Or would he not rather live on the Garden Planet, the world brimful of pristine creation, the way our own must have been before Adam appeared? There as nowhere else he would be living in the very throb of the heart of existence, in the closest proximity to truth that his organism could endure.

He had been assured that neither world was noxious or dangerous, and he relied upon Francesca's word.

He knew, though, that the choice would haunt him, sleeping and waking, until it was actually made, and he knew, too, that he would have to watch himself closely so that the balance of his daily existence was not disturbed. He would need to go on about his ordinary business as calmly and orderly as possible; only in this fashion could he make a wisely considered preference.

At this moment it came to him that there was a third choice. A third door, in effect: his own. He could choose to stay on the earth he knew and to go on with his life in Cherry Cove. Where before this obscure cranny of the universe had been a necessity, the haphazard lighting-down place of a kinless and disconnected man, now it assumed the dignity of election. He could choose to live here; he could choose to leave. He turned to look at the flimsy pine door of his little shack, warped and showing morning light at the jamb, and it seemed as strange to him and almost as inviting as the blue door and the violet.

When Cletus died at Anzio, the spirit of his father flickered violently and burned low. He was a man who rarely drank liquor, but during the months of February, March, and April of 1944, he was drunk almost every day. Arthur didn't mind that; he knew the frenzy would wear off. But he worried about what would happen when Redmon came to himself again. He couldn't think how the man might change.

After he stopped, it took another three weeks for him to dry out. He was sick the whole time, weak and shaking. Arthur ministered to him and gradually he began to eat normal meals and to drive his old Chevrolet pickup about and to tramp in the woods. One day he came into the café with a tinted photograph of Cletus under his arm, the one he'd gotten made with the boy in his uniform and overseas cap. When he climbed on a ladder to drive a nail and hang the picture on the wall behind the counter, Arthur knew that the old man had recovered and was going to make it.

For an old man was what he had become. His gray hair had whitened and his shirt hung loosely over his sunken chest; he had lost weight these last weeks. His eyes were watery behind his wire-rimmed bifocals and now and then Arthur detected a nervous tic new to him: Redmon's head would jerk suddenly to the left in response to some of the remarks he heard people make. But Arthur was unable to discern what kind of comment caused the reaction.

He took Arthur aside one evening in June when they had finished cleaning up after the supper trade. He spoke as plainly to his friend as he always did, telling him that he regretted his lapse from duty during the last months. "I hated to let go like that," he said. "But I knew it was either drink or die. And I figured you would either stand by me or you'd haul on down the line. My mind has got better now. It ain't never going to be well again, but it has got better. I probably wouldn't be here if you hadn't've helped me out. So I'm having the papers drawn up for you to take possession of one-third of the Red Man Café business. We have started to make a little money here now and if we can keep going for a while longer, there will be real money in it. Not millions, you know that. But comfortable—you can live comfortable."

"You must have known I'd stick with you in the hard time. You knew that, didn't you?"

Redmon nodded. "I figured you would, but I didn't know how bad it was going to be. To tell the truth, I still don't know. I don't remember it real clear. But I expect I was pretty far-gone."

"I was worried," Arthur said. "You came close to hurting yourself a couple of times."

"So I figured the best way to pay you back was to have these papers drawn up. And there's something else in the contract, too. It says that when I die, sole ownership of the business will come to you."

"Wait a minute," Arthur said. "Don't you have some relatives somewhere to take exception to that?"

"I got a sister I don't know where in California. I don't even know what her last name is these days. She'd have five or six of them by now, I reckon. I got three cousins and an aunt who will do fine on their own. You're about the closest thing to real family I got left."

"I'm afraid I make a mighty scrawny family."

"Times is hard," Redmon said, and he actually smiled a small sad smile. "What do you say to my offer?"

"It's just like you for being generous, and a man would be a pure fool not to take you up on it. But this time again I'm going to ask you to let me think about it for a while."

"Sure. I'd expect you to."

"I'll tell you right now that I've got an opportunity that few people get. Nobody that I ever heard of, in fact. And it's more than likely that one of these first days I'll be gone from here. I don't know when. It depends on some decisions I need to make."

"You let me know about any offers you get. I'll do my best to match them."

"This is the kind of opportunity that can't be matched. And I won't be able to let you know beforehand. Once I'm ready to go, I'll just leave. You won't know where and you won't be able to find out. Don't worry, I'll be all right. I'll be exactly where I want to be. But you won't be able to get in touch."

Redmon's face darkened and his shoulders slumped. "Are you going to be leaving real soon? You could tell me that much, at least."

"I don't know. I would tell you if I could."

"Listen," Redmon said. "Why don't we dress up that ratty little shack you live in? Or why don't you just move out of it for good? If you get set up nice and comfortable, you might change your mind about leaving."

"No." He spoke as calmly and firmly as he knew how. "I'm doing all right where I am. I've got everything fixed just the way I want."

It had been seven years since he had laid eyes on the man he had named in his mind Ugly Dick, but as soon as he pushed into the empty café at three in the afternoon, Arthur recognized him. Time had left the dumpy little man almost untouched. His silver-blond hair had thinned so that his mottled scalp showed through and contempt had made the lines of his lips and eyebrows more deeply crooked. When he spoke, he showed teeth small and brown and yellow.

"Hello, sport," he said. "You remember me?"

"Yes," said Arthur, and reached behind him for a soiled rag and wiped the clean counter in front of the man. "Last time you were in here, our coffee didn't suit you. I don't know that it's changed much."

"I believe I'll try me a cup anyhow. It couldn't've got no worse."

"Price went up," Arthur said. "Prices are up everywhere."

"Even in Cherry Cola, North Carolina, huh?"

"Even in Cherry Cove."

He poured in cream and added three precise spoons of sugar and stirred. Then he lifted his head to peer at Arthur and give him that wildly crooked smirk. "I bet you remember our mutual friend, too, don't you?"

"You say you've got a friend?"

"Oh sure, you remember. Sheila Weddell. You wouldn't be forgetting her." He gave Arthur a soiled, heavy wink.

"I recall you asking about a woman. But I figured that you must do a lot of that, considering."

"Considering what?"

"Considering what a low-down son of a bitch you are."

The man's smile only grew more saturnine. "Still playing Sir Galahad, ain't you? But I got to tell you, sport, that there ain't no use in it anymore. You might be interested to see this newspaper story." He took a white envelope from his shirt pocket and laid it on the counter. When Arthur stood unmoving, content to give the man a long stare, he tapped it with a pudgy finger. "Go ahead and read it. I guarantee you'll find it interesting."

He picked it up. The headline read: WOMAN IN SPY SCANDAL COMMITS SUICIDE. The story was short and vague. A group of New York people were suspected of gathering information for "a foreign power." Arthur supposed that the foreign power would be Russia, but the story was hazy in all its details. Sheila Weddell, thirty-four, had been found with her head in the gas oven of her apartment on Amsterdam Avenue. There was no evidence of foul play. The police investigation was continuing.

The clipping did not reveal which newspaper had printed the story. A photograph of the woman was placed above the headline and Arthur studied it intently. It was overexposed and the features were blurred. At first it looked a little like the woman he knew as Francesca and then it didn't. Then it did again.

"So what do you think of your sweetheart now, huh?"

"I never saw this woman in my life," Arthur said. He took care in replacing the clipping in the envelope, then laid it on the counter. "I hate to be such a big disappointment to you."

He produced a toothpick and put it between his front teeth. "We know she passed some information on to you. Something technical. We know you got brains. You don't fool us, hiding away in this little possum-turd settlement. We read them stories you write and I'll go ahead and tell you, sport—we're right on the edge of busting your code. We've just about got it figured out."

"My code?"

"Yeah. The hidden messages in that crazy horseshit you write in them weird magazines. You don't think your buddies overseas are the only ones that can read, do you?"

"I don't know what you're talking about."

"Yeah. I was just real positive you wouldn't know what I was talking about."

"I'm going to ask you again, just like last time, to show me some identification," Arthur said. "If you're a government agent, I want to see what kind."

"What for? I ain't asking you for nothing. I'm telling you about your girlfriend. That's all I came in for. I'll leave this newspaper story with you, to maybe give you something to think about." He stood up. "And a dime for the coffee, right?"

"Keep your damn dime. We don't want your money."

"Well now, that's mighty neighborly of you. So long, sport. Next time we meet it ain't going to be as pleasant as it has been."

"I'll bear that in mind," Arthur said. He watched the one enemy he ever knew he possessed waddle toward the door, his toothpick waggling up and down under his nose like a mechanical gadget. When he was gone, Arthur took fifteen cents from his pocket and rang the money into the cash register. He had just remembered that he still owed the café a nickel for the coffee Ugly Dick had ordered seven years before.

The next dawn found Arthur before his typewriter, struggling with a tale that was not progressing satisfactorily. He could not say why this particular story about visible creatures who inhabited an invisible planet was so difficult, but he had pottered with it two months now and it still didn't show signs of life. He sighed and stood up, arched his back and stretched his arms above his head. This mid-September morning, though still only pinkly lit by a pink sun, was full of life, cicadas and crickets sounding away and four roosters near and far voicing their victory over the nighttime.

He took up the envelope again for the dozenth time this morning and opened it and took out the clipping. Peering at it closely under the lamplight, he still couldn't tell. Was the woman in the photograph his Francesca? He would never be certain about the picture, he knew, and had decided simply to trust his instinct. He felt that the news story was about someone he didn't know.

The truth was, he didn't know anything. He didn't know who Francesca was or Ugly Dick, either. He would never understand what tangle of circumstance had bequeathed him the Somewhere Doors. He looked at them now, their colors still vivid, their surfaces still warmly and lightly pulsing with promise. One thing was certain: Ugly Dick with maybe some ugly help would have gotten into his hut and would have tried to open the doors and they had failed. Neither door would open even for Arthur until he made his fateful decision. Nor could they be damaged in any way.

He was forty-four years old now; he had grown middle-aged in this pleasure of indecision. They had hired a teenager to help wait tables and wash up at the café, so his work load had lightened, and his financial situation was secure, compared to the bone-scraping poverty he always had endured. His little hut was still brutally cold in winter and it was still an unhandy and often muddy trek to the outhouse at the edge of the field behind, but the Doors were here and their nearness supported him, comforted him, and never failed to entice with the dilemma they presented.

He slipped the clipping back into the envelope and laid it by his typewriter. Then he tugged on a light denim jacket and went out walking, stalking the dusty gravel road to the bridge and the river. The light was brightening now and a breeze came by as fresh as a cool hand across his forehead.

At the bridge he looked above the twisted waters into the swaying tops of the balsam trees and remembered meeting Francesca here in her white party frock and her white shoes. Maybe one of these days the smooth oxblood car would come darkly humming along again; maybe Francesca would step out. He turned to look, but the road was empty in both directions. Once more he sighed and began to retrace his steps to the hamlet.

On the bank by the bridgehead was a stand of six young silver-birch trees and beneath them a clump of knee-tall bright scarlet bee balm. He stopped for a moment to admire.

And then this scene—the lithe young trees with ragged bark fluttering, the brilliant red flowers nodding as the river purled—overwhelmed him. Almost every day he saw these things and did not see them, walking along absorbed. Anytime he liked he could remember this sight and yet he would always mostly forget. He burst into tears and went down in the road on the gritty gravel on his hands and knees, realizing that he had made his decision.

The sadness of utopia was the same sadness as that of paradise. Utopia and paradise could not remember. They were eternal and unaging and had no history to come to nor any to leave behind. They were dreams that Arthur for a long time had been experiencing with all his senses except those of his body. He had already opened both Doors and visited both Somewheres. He was ready to fling open wide the third door, the entrance to the world in which he already lived. Much had passed him by. Oh yes. Yet much awaited him still.

But right now and for five minutes longer he had no strength to rise. He remained on his hands and knees in the hard gray dirt of the road, weeping aloud like a child deceived or undeceived.

POE AT THE END

R. H. W. Dillard

Famous literary figures have often become themselves the subjects of others' creative art. In the poem that follows, R. H. W. Dillard uses many of the images Edgar Allan Poe invoked in his own work to express his despair at losing his dear wife, Virginia. Whereas such homages are frequently either self-indulgent or hagiographic, Dillard's poem is a powerful, poetically valid work. "Poe at the End" originally appeared in *Chronicles: A Magazine of American Culture*. Dillard is a professor of English at a southern university.

—E.D.

October. Poe in Baltimore. Poe
At the end, going North, away
From Virginia, keeping promises
Despite the black beak of despair,
Laid over, waiting for the train,
But just now, drunk, out of the coop,
Leaning in Lombard Street
Against the window of a store,
Making his pitched and stammered way
Toward Cooth & Sergeant's Tavern—
(Sergeant Major Poe, First Artillery,
Honorably discharged so many years ago)—
Slow way of starts and fits,
The drink and drugs sluing his heart
Into blind staggers and sways.

Away from Virginia and toward
Virginia in the grave. She played
The harp that January night and sang,
It was a good song, too,
But so soon, so quickly a tiny vessel
Popped in her throat like a New Year's squib

Just as she reached her last high note.
And for five years it broke and broke
Again, until she died, was laid away,
And Poe learned an awful truth:
Helter skelter or catcher in the rye,
Art kills as often as it saves.

On Lombard Street in Baltimore, memory
Twists him, presses his forehead against the glass,
His heart wheezing like wind through the cottage wall
In Fordham where Virginia lay. His heart lifts
In his chest, flaps clumsily aloft
Like a great white bird, then settles back,
And Poe is grounded, left in the lurch
As he was abandoned by his party friends
After voting all morning under a dozen names:
His own, Usher, Reynolds, Dupin, Pym,
Raising his hand again and again, taking the oath,
Swearing he was who he was and was not,
Swearing he was.

Hart Crane asked him
Nearly a century later whether he denied
The ticket, but how could he deny a thing,
He who was all things that day and none,
A multitude of beings and only one,
Leaning on a window, his forehead on the glass,
His eyes unfocused or focused deep within.

And yet he does see past Virginia
With blood on her blouse, past Elmira
Left behind in Richmond, jilted
Before she ever reached the altar,
Past even the bloated face of Edgar Poe
Reflected in the window, drawn and drawn out
In the wobbly glass, the sodden man
In a stranger's threadbare clothes
With only Dr. Carter's borrowed cane
Still clutched in that familiar hand,
Sees through the tortured glass
To a display of pewter and silver
Laid out within the shop, slick knives
With thin images of a singular man
Upon each blade, rounded shining cups
With a bulge-nosed alien face
In each curved surface, two large

Silver plates with his own desperate stare
Reflected plain in each, the brow,
The carved out cheeks, blue lips
Beneath the sad mustache.

        But he
Looks beyond this olio of images,
These hard lies and harder truths
Displayed before him, to find
A large silver coffee urn, beknobbed
And crusted with handles and thick
Vines, blossoms and twisted ribbons,
Its surface flat and curved and rounded,
Concave, convex, and convolute,
And in its turbulent reflections
He sees a young man's face,
A young man with dark hair
And uneven eyes, a young man
Leaning on a cane with promises
To keep, a face he recognizes
But cannot name, knows but cannot claim,
That looks him steadily eye to eye.

His heart will soon calm down enough
For him to stutter on, reach Cooth &
Sergeant's, fall onto a bench, he found,
Be carried to the hospital, lie there in fever,
Call Reynolds' name, ease out of delirium
Only to say, gently, "Lord help my poor soul,"
And die, having for one moment on Lombard Street
Learned still another awful truth:
Pell mell or waiting just to die,
Art saves as often as it kills.

ANGELS IN LOVE

Kathe Koja

In this story Kathe Koja perfectly captures the voice of a certain class of American—what many call "poor white trash." She also perfectly captures their dreams—and nightmares.

Koja has been writing attention-grabbing short fiction for a few years, but it was her first novel, *The Cipher*, that brought her work the critical acclaim it deserves. Both a science fiction novel and a horror novel, *The Cipher* boasts one of the meanest and most believable women I've ever read about. It was nominated for the Philip K. Dick Award. Her second novel, recently published, is *Bad Brains*.

"Angels in Love," which comes from *The Magazine of Fantasy & Science Fiction*, is both erotic and dangerous, concisely demonstrating the lure of the forbidden.

—E.D.

Like wings. Rapturous as the muted screams, lush the beating of air through chipboard walls, luscious like sex and, oh my, far more forbidden: whatever it was, Lurleen *knew* it was wrong.

Knew it from the shrieks, gagged and that was no pillow, no sir, no way—she herself was familiar with the gasp of muffled sex, and this was definitely not it. And not—really—kinky, or not in any way *she* knew of, and with a half-shy swagger, Lurleen could admit she had acquaintance of a few. Kiss me here. Let's see some teeth. Harder.

The sounds, arpeggio of groans, that basso almost-unheard thump, thump, rhythmic as a headboard or a set of baritone springs, but that wasn't it, either. Subsonic; felt by the bones. Lying there listening, her own bones tingled, skin rippled light with goose bumps, speculation: who made those strange, strange sounds? Someone with a taste for the rough stuff, maybe, someone who liked the doughy strop of flesh. Someone strong. An old boyfriend had used to say she fucked like an angel; she never understood the phrase till now. Her hands, deliberate stroll southward, shimmy of familiar fingers on as-familiar flesh; her own groans in counterpoint to the ones through the walls.

Waking heavy in the morning, green toothpaste spit and trying to brush her hair at the same time, late again. "You're late," Roger would say when she walked in, and she would flip fast through her catalog of excuses—which hadn't he heard lately?—and try to give him something to get her by, thinking all the while of last night's tingle, puzzling again its ultimate source. It was kind of a sexy game to Lurleen, that puzzling it gave her something to do at work.

Music store. No kind of music she liked, but sometimes it wasn't too bad, and the store itself had a kind of smell that she enjoyed, like a library smell, like something educational was going on. Sheet music, music stands, Roger fussy with customers, turning the stereo on loud and saying stuff like, "But have you heard Spivakov's Bach? Really quite good." Like he had probably heard Bach's Bach and could have suggested a few improvements. Right.

Today she felt dopey and sluggish, simple transactions done twice and twice wrong; Roger was pissed, glowered as she slumped through the day. At quitting time he made a point of pointedly disappearing, not saying good night; sighing, she had to find him, hide-and-seek through the racks. He was a stickler for what he called the pleasantries: Good night, Lurleen. Good night, Roger. Every day.

Finally: hunched behind the order counter, flipping through the day's mail like he hadn't read it nine times already. Lurleen leaned tippy-toe over, flat-handed on the cracking gray laminate: "Good night, Roger."

Chilly nod, like he'd just caught her trying to palm something: "Good night, Lurleen." Waited till she was almost out the door to say, "Lurleen?"

Stopped, impatient keys in hand. "What?"

"We open at ten o'clock. Every day."

Asshole. "See you tomorrow." Not banging the door, giving herself points for it. Outside, her skin warmed, like butter, spread velvet all over. He always kept the fucking store too cold. Like the music'd melt or something if he turned it up past freezing. Rolling all her windows down, singing to the Top 40 station. Stopped at the party store for cigarettes and to flirt with the clerk, old guy just about as ugly as Roger, but round where Roger was slack, furry where Roger was not.

"You headin' out tonight?" Sliding the cigarettes across the counter, grinning at her tits. "Have some fun?"

"Oh, I always manage to have fun." Over-shoulder smile as she headed for the door. Roger liked to stare at her tits, too, she was positive; she just hadn't caught him at it yet. Asshole probably went home and jerked off, dreaming about her bouncing around to Bach. And she laughed, a little: who'd been flying solo last night, huh?

But that was different.

In the dark, blind witness to the nightly ravishment, Lurleen, closed eyes, busy hands filling in the blanks, timing herself to the thump and stutter of the rapture beyond the walls. Longer tonight, ecstatic harmony of gulping cries, and after the crescendo wail, sound track to her own orgasm, she slept: to dream of flesh like iron, of rising whole, and drenched, and shiny-bright; shock-heavy with a pleasure poisonously rare. Woke just in time to see that she'd slept through the clock. Again.

In the hallway, pausing—already late, so what if she was later?—before the door next door. Identical in nondescription to every other down the grimy hall, there was no way to tell by looking just what kind of fun went on there every night. Lurleen, tapping ignition key to lips, thoughtful sideways stare. Imagining, all the reluctant way to work, what sort of exotica, what moist brutalities were practiced there, what kinds of kinks indulged. Wriggling a little, skirt riding up and the cracked vinyl edges of the too-hot seat pressing voluptuously sharp into the damp flesh of her thighs.

It came to her that she had never really seen that next-door neighbor of hers. Maybe they'd bumped into each other, exchanged laundry-room hellos, but for the life of her, Lurleen could not recall. She wasn't even sure if it was just one person or a couple. They sure were a couple at night, though, weren't they just?

The day spent avoiding Roger's gaze, colder than the store and just as constant, more than one smart remark about time clocks. Stopping for cigarettes, she picked up a six-pack, too, clandestine sips at red lights, rehearsing queenly answers she would never give. It was so hot it felt good, brought a warm, slow trickle of sweat down the plane of her temple, the hotter spot between her breasts.

She was going out tonight, that was for sure; she owed herself something for the just-past bitch of a day. Walking up the hot two flights, a thought nudged her, firm and brisk to get past the beer. She leaned to sight up the stairwell, heart a trifle nervous, quick and jangly in her chest. Well. No time like the present, was there, to scratch a little itch? I'll just say hi, she thought, walking quicker now. I'll say, Hi, I'm your next-door neighbor. I just stopped by to say hello.

Fourth can in hand, smart tattoo on the door before she could change her mind. Wondering who would open, what they would look like. What they would smell like—Lurleen was a great believer in smells. If they would ask her in, and what she might say, knowing she would say yes, and a smile past the thick spot in her throat, and she smiled at that, too; it wasn't that big a deal, was it?

Maybe it was.

Nothing. Silence inside, so she knocked again, louder, humming to herself and, oh boy, here we go: winded swing of the door and "Hi," before it was all the way open. "Hi, I'm Lurleen, your neighbor?"

Tall, her first thought. And skinny. Not model-skinny, just chicken bones, short blonde hair, Giants T-shirt over a flat chest. Anne, she said her name was, and past her curved shoulders, Lurleen could see a flat as cramped and dingy as her own, a little emptier, maybe, a little less ripe, but nothing special. Purely ordinary. Like Anne herself: no exotic bruising, no secret sheen. Just stood there in the doorway playing with the end of her baggy T-shirt, flipping it as she talked, and that thin-lipped smile that said, Are you ready to leave yet? Just one big disappointment, but Lurleen didn't show it, kept up her own smile through the strain of the stillborn chatter until she was back inside her own place, sucking up the last of her beer.

"Well," through a closed-mouth, ladylike burp. "Well."

How could someone so dull have such a wild sex life? Be better off meeting the boyfriend; he had to be the real show. Fucking angel. Lurleen's giggles lasted through the rest of the beer, her long, cool shower, and half hour's worth of mousse and primp. When she left for the bar, Anne's flat was silent still, not even the requisite TV drone. From the parking lot, the lifeless drift of her curtains, beige to Lurleen's red, was all there was to see.

At the bar she met a couple of guys, nice ones—she couldn't quite remember which was Jeff and which was Tony, but they kept her dancing, and drinking, and that was nice, too. After last call she swiveled off her seat, sweet, and smiled and said she was sorry, but she had an hour to make the airport to pick up her husband—and even as she said it, she had to wonder why; it was one of them she'd planned on picking up, and never mind that she couldn't remember who was who; names didn't exactly matter at that time of night; words didn't matter past Who's got the rubber. But still she left alone.

Coming home, off-center slew into her parking space, radio up way too loud, singing and her voice a bray in the cut-engine quiet; she almost slipped going up the stairs. Shushing herself as she poured a glass of milk, her invariable after-binge cure-all. Lifting the glass, she caught from the damp skin of her forearm an after-shave scent, mixed with the male smell of Tony. Jeff? It didn't matter, such a pretty boy.

But not as pretty as the boy next door.

And, her thought seeming eerily a signal, she heard the preliminary noises, shifting warm through the wall as if they stroked her: Anne's breathy, wordless voice, that rush of sound, half-sinister whirlwind pavane. Pressed against the wall itself, her bare-skinned sweat a warm adhesive, Lurleen stood, mouth open and eyes shut, working her thin imagination as Anne, presumably, worked her thin body, both—all three—ending in vortex, whirlpool, mouthing that dwindling symphony of screams, Lurleen herself louder than she'd ever been, with any man. Loud enough that they could, maybe, hear her through the walls.

Slumped, damp, she could not quite admit it, say to herself, You want them to hear you. You want *him* to hear you, whoever he is. You want what Anne's getting, better than any bar pickup, better than anything you ever had. Glamorous and dirty. And scary. And hot.

By the next night, she was ready, had turned her bed to lengthwise face the wall: willing herself, forcing herself like an unseen deliberate splinter in their shared and coupling flesh; she *would* be part of this. She had never had anything like what went on over there, never anything good. She would have this if she had to knock down the wall to get it. Fingers splayed against her flesh, heels digging hard into the sheets and letting go, crying out, Hear me. Hear me.

Exhausted at work, but on time, she couldn't take any of Roger's bitching now, not when she had to think. Make a plan. Anne, she was a sorry-looking bitch, no competition once the boyfriend got a good look at Lurleen. The trick was to get him to look. To see. See what he'd been hearing, night after night. Of course, it wouldn't be all that easy: if Anne had any brains at all, she would want to keep her boyfriend and Lurleen far, far apart. Lurleen decided she would have to take it slow and smart, *be* smart—not exactly her strong point, but she could be slick; she knew what she wanted.

She began to stalk Anne, never thinking of it in so many words, but as sure and surely cautious as any predator. Waiting, lingering in the hallway after work, for Anne to come home from whatever unfathomable job she did all day. Never stopping to talk, just a smile, pleasant make-believe. She made it her business to do her laundry when Anne did hers; at the first whoosh and stagger of the old machine, Lurleen was there, quarters in hand; her clothes had never been so clean; she had to see. Any jockey shorts, bikini underwear, jockstraps, what? She meant to take one if she could, steal it before, before it was clean. Smell it. You can tell a lot about a man. Lurleen believed, from the smell of his skin, not his aftershave or whatever, but the pure smell of his body. Until his body was beneath hers, it was the best she could do. She pawed through the laundry basket, poked around in the washer: nothing. Just Anne's Priss-Miss blouses, baggy slacks, cheap bras—and just about everything beige. Balked angry toss of the clothing, stepped on it to push it back into the basket. Maybe he liked Anne *because* she was so beige, so . . . nothing? *Could* a man want a woman to be nothing? Just a space to fill? Lurleen had known plenty of guys who liked their women dumb—it made them feel better—but anyway, Anne didn't seem dumb. Just empty.

And still, night after night the same, bed against the wall, Lurleen could be determined; Lurleen could work for what she wanted. Drained every morning, the sting of tender skin in the shower, even Roger noticed her red eyes.

"Not moonlighting, are you?" But she saw he knew it was no question, half-gaze through those tired eyes, and she even, for a moment, considered telling him, considered saying, I want the boy next door, Roger; I want him real bad. I want him so much I even jerk off so he can hear me, so he can know how he turns me on. I want him so much I don't know what to do.

She wasn't getting anywhere. Drumming slow one finger against the order counter, staring right past some guy bumbling on about some opera or something, she wasn't getting *anywhere*, and it was wearing her out. No time for anything else, bars, guys, whatever; there wasn't any other guy she wanted. Anne's smiles growing smaller, tighter, her gaze more pinched; was she catching on? Tired from sitting in the hallway—once or twice another neighbor had caught her at it, loitering tense and unseeing until the tap-tap-tap on her shoulder. Hey, are you O.K.? "Fine." Harsh involuntary blush. "Just looking for an earring." Right. Tired from staking out the parking lot, hot breeze through the window; she didn't even know what kind of car he drove. Tired to death and still no glimpse of him, proud author of the sounds; it was killing her to listen, but she couldn't stop. She didn't want to stop.

And then that night, mid-jerk, mid-groan, they stopped. The sounds. Ceased completely, but not to complete silence: a waiting sound, a whisper. Whispering through the walls, such a willing sound.

She yanked on a T-shirt, ends tickling her bare ass as she ran, hit on the door with small, quick fists. "Anne? Are you O.K.?" Never thinking how stupid she might look if the door opened, never considered what excuse she might give. I didn't hear anything, so I thought you might be in trouble. Right. So what. Bang bang on the door.

"Anne?"

The whisper, against the door itself. Hearing it, Lurleen shivered, convulsive twitch like a tic of the flesh, all down her body, and she pressed against the door, listening with all her might. "Anne." But quietly, feeling the heat from her body, the windy rush of her heart. Waiting. "Anne." More quietly still, less than a murmuring breath. "Let me in."

Abruptly, spooking her back a step: the sounds, *hot* intensity trebled, but wrong somehow, guttural, staggering where they should flow, a smell almost like garbage, but she didn't care; once the first scare had passed, she pressed harder into the door, as if by pure want she could break it down; she would get in, she would. T-shirt stuck, sweating like she'd run a mile. I'm sick of just listening. The hall was so hot. Sweat on her forehead, running into her eyes like leaking tears. The doorknob in her slick fingers.

It turned. Simple as that.

In the end, so quick and easy, and it seemed almost that she could not breathe, could not get enough air to move—but she moved, all right, oh yes, stepped right inside into the semidarkness, a fake hurricane lamp broken beside the bed, but there was light enough, enough to see by.

Like angels in love, mating in the cold, graceful rapture of thin air. Hovering above the bed, at least a yard or maybe more—no wonder she never heard springs—instead the groaned complaint of the walls itself as his thrusting brushed them, on his back the enormous strange construction that kept them airborne, as careless as if it had grown there amongst the pebbled bumps and tiny iridescent fins. His body beautiful, and huge, not like a man's, but so real it seemed to suck up all the space in the room, big elementary muscles, and he was using them all. Anne, bent like a coathanger—it hurt to see the angle of her back—her eyes wide and empty and some stuff coming out of her mouth like spoiled black jelly, but it was too late, Lurleen had sent the door swinging backward to close with a final catch, and in its sound his gaze swiveling to touch hers: the cold regard of a nova, the summoning glance of a star.

Her mouth as open as Anne's as she approached the vast brutality of his embrace, room enough for two there, oh my, yes. Fierce, relentless encroachment promising no pleasure but the pleasure of pain. Not an angel, never had been. Or maybe once, long, a long, long time ago.

VIVIAN
Midori Snyder

The daughter of a French poet and an American scholar of Asian culture, Midori Snyder grew up in the United States and Africa and studied African myth and languages at the University of Wisconsin. She currently lives with her husband and two children in Milwaukee, where she plays Irish music in addition to writing.

Snyder's multicultural background has given the author rich and unique storytelling skills, as showcased in her High Fantasy novels *Soul-String, New Moon, Sadar's Keep*, and *Belden's Fire*. She has also published short fiction for both adults and children in several magazines and anthologies, and is at work on a book in collaboration with British illustrator Brian Froud.

"Vivian" is a magical tale set within the canon of British "Robin Hood" folk ballads and stories. It was written for *The Fantastic Adventures of Robin Hood*, edited by Martin H. Greenberg.

—T.W.

> "Give me my bent bow in my hand,
> And a broad arrow I'll let flee.
> And where this arrow is taken up,
> There shall my grave digge'd be."
>
> —From the "Song of Robin Hood"

In the early dawn Robin stalked the woods, a small cloud of steam forming in the cold air as he exhaled. He heard the quiet crack of a branch, the rustle of dry leaves and he stopped, his body tense. Slowly he looked around, searching the origin of the noise. A doe edged into his sight, her dun flanks thinned from the long winter, but her belly rounded with pregnancy. She browsed hungrily on a low shrub, her long neck stretching out as she tugged loose the frail spring buds nestled between the dried leaves.

Robin gritted his teeth and raised the longbow. He nocked his arrow, the grey goose fletch drawn back beside his ear. His gaze followed the curve of the animal's chest, imagining the shaft penetrating to the heart. The doe snorted as a breeze stirred the branches of the tree above and water droplets sprinkled her head. She shook, startled and then caught Robin's scent. The two knuckles that held the bowstring back dug deeper into Robin's cheek as he willed himself to remain steady. The doe withdrew behind the bush, seeking cover. Robin stepped forward to keep his target in view. Beneath his foot a twig snapped a loud warning in the wood. Within a heartbeat the doe leapt from her hiding place and fled.

Cursing, Robin swerved his body, trying to track the rump of the fleeing doe as he let loose his arrow. The hopeful twang was silenced abruptly as the arrow thudded harmlessly into a tree.

Robin hung his head and groaned. Sweat chilled his temples, darkening the curly hair. Damn the greenwood! he swore in frustrated rage. It had turned against him, willing that he should starve from lack of game and freeze with the cold damp of a harsh winter. He looked up angrily and stared out at the black and grey trunks of the wintery trees. The leather-brown leaves of the oaks shivered dryly in response.

He had been a fair shot once. Life in the greenwood the last two years had been good, or at least possible. With twenty men he had formed a band of free-foresters, claiming no allegiance to the King's command, or the Sheriff's taxes. They had survived on their skill with the bow, their bravery in the contests against the Sheriff's men and the goodwill of the people they protected from the worst of the Sheriff's abuses. But the winter had proved hard. Game alluded them, arrows that seemed so sure of their targets suddenly careened wildly as if batted by unseen hands. Wood refused to burn and their camps were cold and wet. Robin pulled his cloak tighter around his shoulders, feeling the winter's damp penetrate beneath the worn wool.

Among the cottages they found a guarded welcome. Grain was scarce and for people who worked hard on the land, it was hard to part with the little they owned to the outlaws that haunted the greenwood. Robin scowled, thinking how in their hunger the cottagers forgot the small gifts of money, or the haunch of venison that had appeared at other times from those same outlaws.

Robin retrieved his arrow and began walking again, moving angrily through the woods. He climbed the brow of a small hill where the trees of the greenwood gave way to the fields. At the edge of the forest, he stared down across the fields of Lincolnshire. In the distance, smoke rose in a thin grey curl from a cottage chimney. The long road that scarred the landscape was empty. Of late, even the rich had found no reason to pass through the greenwood. Robin and his men had not been able to take even the coin that would have bought them food and shelter for the winter.

Robin's stomach grumbled. He scratched his cheek, feeling how thin the winter had made it. His men were growing discontent. The lack of meat, the lack of a warm fire had scattered companionship. Petty quarrels broke out frequently, his men choosing to fight each other rather than succumb to desperation. That morning he and Little John had crossed words, and only Friar Tuck coming between them had stayed their fists. Robin had left the camp, determined that he would not return without fresh game.

He sighed, his squared shoulders hunched with cold. The muscles of his thighs trembled, having grown weary from the long morning search for game. The sword at his side felt heavy and useless. "Spring," he whispered, thinking of the rounded belly of the doe. Daily they watched for signs of its coming, bringing with it the promise of warmth and the living green. "Spring," he repeated more loudly, his cold breath clouding around his head.

His eyes followed the rounded hills as the sun lifted from the edge of the horizon. Gold rays slanted across the fields, brightening the dull pewter land to a burnished copper. Robin stepped forward, away from the shelter of the trees to touch the advancing light. The bright rays of the sun reached him, climbing up his legs, his torso and his chest. Warmth spread across him, and the light of the sun blinded him as it caressed his face.

Bathed in brilliance, Robin's plea was answered. In the muffled damp air, Robin heard the soft trickle of water melting, the quiet sigh of snow settling into the muddy earth. Birdsong sounded from the trees and a gentle moist wind shook the remnants of last year's leaves. Robin opened his eyes and turned to face the greenwood.

For the first time in many months, Robin smiled, his dry lips cracking.

The dull bark of trees shimmered with wetness in the dawn's light. Mist gathered between the black branches and formed a veil of the palest green. When still a boy at Lockesley, his mother had called it the "greenmist": the slow waking breath of the greenwood's spirit world, rousing after the winter. The creature Tidy Munn would soon be churning the water of the streams and the fens, driving it over the fields to melt the remaining snow. The Greencoaties, small beings well hidden in the greenwood, would begin unwrapping the brown leaves of their wintery beds. And the tall, stately Oakmen would step forth from the trunks of their ancient trees to hunt in the spring morning.

A child's story perhaps, but standing here at the ragged end of a Lincolnshire winter, watching the greenwood misting to life with the breath of spring, Robin could almost believe in its magic. He shook himself, the warm sun on his back freeing the cramped muscles of his shoulders. All would be well, he told himself.

With a sudden resolve he plunged into the woods again to hunt for game. He walked firmly, eagerness driving his step, the longbow slung tightly over one shoulder, the quiver of arrows bouncing lightly across his back. He passed a fallen oak, the leathered leaves of its branches reaching skyward. Robin stopped, seeing the chips of wood that lay scattered about the base of the huge tree. Someone had chopped it down and then left without claiming the wood. New shoots had sprung from the old stump as the oak refused to die. Robin kicked the trunk questioningly. The wood was still hard, dried out from the cold winter air. Robin rejoiced, for once split, the wood would burn quick and hot, unlike the wood they had saved which had gone soggy and produced sputtering fires that gave off more smoke than warmth.

He'd no axe about him to chop the wood then but decided to mark a trail that would lead him back to this site, later in the day when he had finished his hunting. For now, he decided he would give himself the gift of a fine staff that he could set in a friendly challenge against Little John. He reached up and pulled at a straight branch, one foot braced against the trunk of the fallen tree. He heard the wood groan and then snap as the branch tore away from the flesh of the trunk.

"And what manner of man are you who robs from me?" spoke an angry voice.

Startled, Robin wheeled around, drawing his sword. The torn branch he kept in his other fist like a ready club.

Standing near the base of a tree was a tall man, his face filled with hatred. He wore a cloak of green, the high collar framing a narrow face of deep brown. Broad shoulders arrowed down into a neat waist, and around his waist, Robin saw the well-tempered blade that stretched down along the length of a heavily muscled thigh. A huge hand with long, gnarled fingers wrapped around the hilt.

Robin's eyes darted through the bush, wondering how the man came to be here with no sound, no warning of his advance. Behind the man waited a horse, the silver bridle ornate with carved acorns about the cheek strap and the reigns hung with the likeness of rusted oak leaves. The horse stood silent as if waiting the word of its master.

"I asked you a question," the man spoke coldly. "Who are you that you would dare rob from me?"

"Rob from you?" Robin answered more boldly than he felt. "You are not the King's forester. And even if you were, it would make no difference to me. I take what I please from the greenwood."

The horse neighed shrilly as the man in the green cloak lunged towards Robin. Robin raised his sword, anticipating the clash of weapons. But the man stopped and drew himself up solemnly. The mist steamed from the man's shoulders like the heat of his anger. Robin stared back uneasily at green eyes that flashed in the morning light.

"There is no mortal man that owns the greenwood. Neither king nor commoner has claims to these words. What you take, you steal."

Robin gave a harsh laugh. "If you think to shame me with such words you are mistaken. You are not from here or you would know that I am Robin Hood. I am a lord of thievery. I steal from the King, from the Sheriff and even you, strange lord, for I can see now by the fat purse hanging from your belt that you have not yet paid to Robin Hood his due." Robin gripped his sword more firmly. He had lost the doe this morning by being over-cautious and waiting too long. He would not lose this second chance for profit.

The man in the green cloak smiled coldly. "My purse is a small bounty for a lord of thieves," he answered. "If you would agree, I would make a contest for a more worthy prize."

"And what prize is that?" Robin asked, curious, but wary. In the trees above a flock of crows had settled on the branches. They stopped their preening to stare at him with interest, cocking their heads to one side as they glimpsed him through their black-beaded eyes.

"I would give that which I prize most from my estate. A treasure that has no greater value." He took the fat purse and emptied its contents on the ground. Robin held his breath as gold coins and three emeralds tumbled to the forest floor. "These are nothing compared to that which I offer from my estate at Kirkley Hall."

Robin knew the name of the estate. It was an old stone house deep in the heart of the greenwood. He had not known that a lord lived there for the look of it was a tumbled ruin. Still, his eyes could not deny the wealth that now lay scattered carelessly on the wet leaves.

"And how can I be certain of such a contest?"

The man laughed coldly again and he withdrew from his cloak a small gold horn. He blew three sharp blasts. The crows lifted noisily from the branches in alarm, their wings flapping frantically.

Robin stared up at their harsh cawing and their wild flight. As he lowered his gaze again to the man, he gasped. Sitting astride chestnut stallions, two men waited. Like the man, they dressed in cloaks of green, even their trousers were of green wool. Their faces were rugged, their features resembling roughly hewn wood. The horses were still, and only the steam rising from their flanks suggested they were creatures of flesh. Where had they come from? How had they answered the horn so quickly? Robin's mind crackled with questions and a warning bell clanged in his thoughts.

"I will make these two witness to this contest. And if you win, they are charged with giving you my treasure," the man was saying.

"And if I lose?" Robin asked. "What do I forfeit?"

"If you lose, you must ride the hunt with me as my servant man."

"Is that all?"

The man shook his head. "No. I must know first before we seal the bargain whether you have honor. For a man without honor has blood that runs thinner than water and carries no power to the hunt."

Robin's face flushed angrily. "I may be a thief, but even thieves have honor. I do not steal from the poor, only take from the rich. And I will not permit any woman who travels in the greenwood to be harmed or molested."

"It is enough," replied the man and with a sudden movement freed his sword from his belt. He slashed the blade upward towards Robin's head, the sword leaving a trail of silvery light.

Robin grunted in surprise and stumbled back, avoiding the rising sword. He lifted his own weapon to meet the attack and the two blades clashed with a grinding screech. Sparks ignited from the sword's point.

Robin scrambled back another step, seeking an even footing. Roots from the fallen oak snaked unexpectedly from the ground and he stumbled again as the man's sword drove him down. Crouching, Robin tried to face his attacker. The man's sword landed a heavy blow on Robin's weapon. Robin screamed as he felt his shoulder wrenched with the force of the blow, his sword arm shoved from the socket with an explosion of pain. Stars lit up in his eyes and he heard the roaring of blood in his ears. Robin collapsed on the ground and rolled, sensing the fierce rush of air as the man's sword chased him. He still gripped his sword but his injured arm refused to lift the weapon. He saw through eyes dazed with fear the bright arc of the sword above him once more. He rolled, instinct rather than courage pushing him away from certain death. The sword came down and the tip sliced neatly through his side. Pain bloomed again in his body and he cried out as his shirt grew wet with blood.

Through the wild pounding of his own heart, Robin heard the man's triumphant laugh and saw the silvery flash of his sword. Without hope, Robin raised the staff of oak he still clutched in his left hand. The hard wood took the edge of the man's sword. Robin's body shook violently as the oaken staff split, splinters raking his face.

And at once the man's laughter turned to howls. Numbed with pain, Robin gazed up and saw the man stagger backward, the sword dangling from one hand, his face hidden in the crook of his other arm. Robin dropped the shattered staff and, using both hands, raised his sword from the ground. His shoulder throbbed but he ignored it as he forced his sword upright. Only one chance.

Already the man had lowered his arm, tightening his grip anew on his sword. Robin saw the green flash of rage in the man's eyes as he turned once more to Robin's prostrate figure.

Robin heaved his body upward, thrusting the point of his sword into man's chest. The man shouted with outrage, his arms flailing the air. But he could not stop his body from falling onto Robin's sword.

Robin held the sword steady, feeling the strangeness of the man dying on his blade. The sword drove deep, not finding bone, nor the soft parting of muscled flesh, but something different. It cleaved through the man's chest like an ax separating layers of wood, splitting apart the grainy fibers. There was no blood, but a greenmist that boiled in the air around him. Robin gagged as the mist clung to his face, burning cold and wet. It was rank with the odor of rotten wood, of mould and decaying bone. His mind reeled with images of a grave, newly opened in the earth, and himself cast into its depths. He reached out a hand, scrabbling at the dead leaves of the forest floor. He choked in terror as the gold morning light dimmed and a darkness as thick as spring mud was cast over him.

"Robin?" a soft voice called.

Robin stirred, feeling a small hand gently shake his shoulder. He smiled, thinking of Marion. He could see the curve of her cheek, the tilt of her chin when she teased him. Then he frowned, knowing that there was something else to be remembered. Something ominous. Dangerous.

Robin's eyes snapped open with panic. He gasped at the air and tried to raise himself up from the ground.

"Stay," the voice urged. "Stay yourself and be at peace." Two small hands rested on his chest, gently pushing him down again.

Robin stared up into a woman's face, her smile sad, but kind. Her skin was a pale gold and he blinked, thinking it the light of the morning sun he saw reflected there. But as he lay back he saw her arms, naked to the shoulders, the same golden color. He stared again at her face and with a start recognized the bright green gaze of her eyes.

He inhaled, releasing the air slowly as he looked around him. He spied first the grey, lichen-covered stones of Kirkley Hall. He was not inside the Hall, but rather lying on a pallet outside the courtyard. He was covered with dark green blankets and he grew gradually aware that his body was dry and warm. Cautiously he pulled aside the blankets and looked at himself.

His brown cloak and white shirt were gone. In their place he had been dressed in the same green wool as the man who had attacked him in the forest. Robin raised himself on his elbow, astonished to discover that his swordarm was healed and that his side no longer bled. He started to lift the shirt when the woman stopped him, urging him to lie down again.

"You are well enough," she said, covering him with the blankets.

"Who are you?" Robin asked.

"You may call me Vivian."

"Do you know what has happened to me? How I came to be here?" He stared confused at Vivian. She wore a simple shift of pale green linen but no cloak. Her arms were bare and yet she seemed not in the least bit bothered by the cold morning air. She moved slowly, as if awakened too early from sleep. Her tousled brown hair had rust-colored streaks and hung around her shoulders in a knotted tangle.

"I know that my father's men brought you here. I know that I am to serve you."

"I fought a man dressed in green in the forest," Robin said, trying to remember clearly. "We held a contest. If I won, I was to gain the most valued treasure of his estate, here at Kirkley Hall."

"Is that what he called me?" Vivian said sharply. "His treasure, that he bargained away for the hunt. Arrogant fool." She began to cry, tears flowing down her gold-colored cheeks.

Robin lifted his hand to her, and wiped away the tears. "Stop now. I would ask nothing of you. I've no need of a servant." As he brought his hand back to his chest, he caught the woody scent of tree sap. It came from the dampness of her tears on his hand.

"I have no choice, Robin. My father's words have bound me, just as surely as he meant to bind you to him for the hunt had he won instead."

"I am no man's servant," Robin retorted sharply.

"My father was not a man," Vivian said and stood. "He would have used you as all Oakmen use mortals. Blood is important to a good hunt. You would have run for him, like a fox before the hounds."

Beneath the warm green blankets Robin shivered, hearing the truth spoken in her words, seeing again the hatred in the Oakman's eyes.

He stood weakly and Vivian held his arm until he gained a steady stance. She took one blanket from the ground and wrapped it around his shoulders like a cloak. She took a second blanket for herself.

"Wrapped in the greencloth, you will never be seen either by your enemies, or by the game you seek. Come, let us go into the forest and I will show you the deer."

Vivian hoisted his longbow on her shoulder and carried the quiver of arrows at her side. Robin followed, his steps uncertain at first and then growing more confident as he felt the blood flow in his cheeks and his heart beat strongly.

It was still morning when they entered the forest again, and Robin marveled that in so short a time the greenmist had flowed through the woods and brought them to life. The branches of trees were still black and leafless, but the air smelled sweet and pungent with new growth. Snow gave way to the mud and Vivian pointed out to him the bright orange blooms of the lichen set like goblets to catch the spring mist. Mosses along the trunks of trees turned dark green and yellowed fruiting stems bowed their heads with beads of dew. The sun slanted through the trees, chasing away the cold breath of winter.

They had not gone far into the woods when Vivian stopped him with a hand just touching his shoulder. She nodded toward a break in the trees. A young stag, his horns still a winter red, entered the clearing. Vivian handed Robin his longbow and arrows.

Robin smiled broadly, excitement threading his pulse as he nocked the arrow. He wouldn't miss this time. He pulled the bowstring back and let loose the arrow. It wobbled slightly in its flight and Robin held his breath fearing failure. And then it landed unerringly in the stag's chest.

The stag reared back his hooves in angry surprise. The tines of his horns crashed against the low-lying branches and his bellows filled the forest. He tried to run, but Robin shot a second arrow that landed close to the first. The stag leapt into the air and then landed heavily, the long slender legs collapsing beneath the huge body.

Robin cheered, raising the longbow high into the air. There would be game for the fire. And there would be dry wood with which to cook it, he thought, remembering the fallen tree where he had met the Oakman. He turned to thank Vivian and then stopped seeing the stricken expression on her face.

She lowered her eyes and he saw the beads of sweat on her upper lip. "Forgive me," she said softly and Robin thought she meant it for him.

He smiled understandingly at her and clasped her by the shoulder. "The hunt is hard to see the first time. It gets easier." Beneath his hand she trembled.

"The problem now is how to get the stag back to camp quickly," he mused aloud. "I'll dress it here, but there are others in these woods as hungry as my men. I don't want to lose the meat to the scavengers."

Vivian untied a small gold horn from her waist and handed it to Robin. He recognized it as the horn her father had used to call his men. "Use this whenever you need the assistance of your men. They will answer it, if they can hear it."

Robin took the horn and placed it to his lips. He blew into it, hearing the long shrill notes of the horn soar above the forest. He stopped and was aware of the silence. He blew again and this time when he stopped he heard voices calling to him from the greenwood.

"Robin? Is that you?" cried a loud voice.

Robin smiled widely. "Little John, over here!"

"I told you it would be him," said another voice triumphantly and Robin recognized Will Stutely.

"It was *I* told you," grumbled a third voice, a little out of breath. Robin searched the trees and saw the black habit of Friar Tuck, his belly breaking first through the bushes.

"In God's name, will you look at the stag!" Little John shouted, rushing to examine the fallen beast. He looked around, puzzlement on his broad face.

"Robin?" he called. "Are you still here?"

"Aye, I'm here," Robin laughed. "Can you not see me standing next to you?"

Little John jumped at the sound of Robin's voice so close to him in the woods. Robin let slip the cloak and moved closer, to stand by the stag.

"I would never have seen you had you not shown yourself." Little John smiled with amazement. "You've a new game afoot, Robin. To wear such a green in the wood. We will all disappear."

"That's why he remains the leader of our band," answered Will with pride.

"Wait, there is more," Robin started to say, turning to look for Vivian. But she was gone. Robin frowned, searching the trees for sight of her.

"Well, then?" Little John said, already bending over the stag with his knife. He had opened its belly and begun the job of gutting it. Steam rose from the stag's belly as the viscera, glistening like wet jewels, spilled out on to the leaves.

"Don't hold back good fortune man," encouraged Will, helping Little John to turn the stag's body.

Robin hesitated. For an unknown reason he changed his mind about telling them of Vivian. He looked down at his belt and saw the pouch of money that had once belonged to the Oakman. Seizing it, he lifted it up to show them. "I've money here which I took in taxes off a man not used to paying them," he said with a grin.

"Is that where you got the horn, too?" asked Friar Tuck.

"Indeed. I'll use it from now on to call you, whether for trouble or good news."

Friar Tuck approached Robin. The normally round face had become slack over the unforgiving winter. The skin of his shaven pate was spattered with freckles. He gazed at Robin worriedly and one hand grasped him firmly around the wrist. "The green of your cloak, Robin, concerns me," he said in a low voice.

"It is a good practice in the woods," Robin answered defensively. "Here, take this money and go into Barnsdale. There purchase bolts of Lincoln green wool. We shall all wear it. The better to fox the Sheriff's men."

"There is something in this that is not right, Robin," the Friar whispered. "Tell me so that your soul will not be in danger. For I feel it in my bones that there is something wrong in this."

Robin gave a short, barking laugh. "What you feel, my good Tuck, is your own hunger. I have done nothing wrong," Robin answered with a smile. "I have taken wealth from a man in a fair contest."

"A man dressed in green?" Friar Tuck asked.

Robin's smile remained but he refused to say more.

"Come on, good Friar," Little John yelled, "let us see how well you can cook this. It will be a feast in which to welcome the Spring!"

Friar Tuck turned away from Robin to help Little John and Will to bind the stag's hooves to a long staff. They hoisted it on their shoulders and carried it away to camp. Behind them Robin fingered the horn and looked once more for signs of Vivian. Finding none, he followed his men to camp.

Throughout the Spring and into the long summer Robin and his men found a new life in the greenwood. The game that had once alluded them now scampered passed their waiting arrows. Friar Tuck had claimed to Robin that he had never in all his years of hunting the greenwood found so many wild morels and strawberries. The Elderberry trees were thick with wide heads of white blossoms and the good Friar watched them daily, waiting for the heads to turn and become studded with the small purple berries.

Robin's spirits soared in the greenwood. The sunlight shone only for him, he thought, drowsing in a shady thicket with the soft buzzing of summer bees. He glanced up sleepily at the trees, their canopy of green leaves sheltering him. His face had filled out during the prosperous summer. His cheeks were squared and strong, his eyes bright with good humor. He had closed his eyes to sleep again when a blade of grass tickled his nose.

He woke with a snort and found Vivian sitting beside him. He smiled at her, startled as always by her strange beauty. The summer sun had lightened the crown of her hair from rust to light brown. Her eyes were a soft green and her skin the color of honey.

"Is it well with you Robin?" she asked.

"Aye, very well, Vivian," he answered.

"They say the Sheriff of Nottingham rides the greenwood today, near the road to Kirkley Hall. I would bid you have a care."

Robin grinned and sat up. "More than a care, I think. Perhaps a bit of sport."

And before long, Robin with the sounding of his horn, had assembled his band together. He had grown accustomed to Vivian's unexpected visits, and equally sudden disappearances. But acting on her advice, he led his men through the woods to Kirkley Hall. It was as she said. Robin saw the gloomy visage of the Sheriff of Nottingham, riding through the greenwood, his foresters dressed in bright livery beside him. Robin laughed quietly to note how close they passed him by without seeing him, despite the searching looks of the foresters.

That night Robin and his men feasted the Sheriff of Nottingham, after first depriving his foresters of their lives and then the Sheriff of his purse. They fed him a meal of venison from the King's own deer and to add insult to the injury, they served him on the silver plates they had stolen from him earlier. At the next daylight, they tied the Sheriff's hands and legs and hoisted him over the back of a horse. A farmer, making his way to Nottingham market, found the Sheriff cursing Robin's name as he lay facedown tied to his horse, while the lazy creature cropped the grass growing by the side of the road. Before the end of market day, the word had scattered from one mouth to another of Robin's daring attack on the Sheriff of Nottingham. And from that night on, in many cottages, the outlaws found a renewed welcome.

The winter came, but still the game followed the camp. The green Lincoln wool of their cloaks kept Robin and his men dry and in the worst of weather, there were many inns willing to hide them for a night or two. Robin often looked for Vivian in the woods when he rambled alone. Sometimes she appeared, wearing a green dress bordered with the seed down of milkweeds, and other times she wore cape of snow-white wool, owl feathers stitched about the hem. She stayed with him briefly, telling him news of the greenwood that would be of use to him and his men. She showed him where different animals wintered over, their dens covered by mounded snow. And even when she wasn't there, Robin always felt her presence in the snapping of twigs underfoot, or the tired creak of the oaks, and he knew that had he need of her, she would be there.

When the spring came again, Vivian met him in the woods. She had gathered wild garlic in her apron and gave it to him.

"They say the Sheriff of Nottingham intends to have an archery contest," she told him. "The prize is a golden arrow."

Robin grinned at her. "Then I mean to go and win that arrow."

"I thought you might." She reached into the pocket of her apron and withdrew a small pot of brown cream. "It will stain your skin brown and give you a good disguise."

Robin laughed and snatching up the pot tossed it lightly into the air. "I shall go as a poor wanderer. And I shall win beneath the very noses of the Sheriff and his men."

"You will succeed, Robin, as always," Vivian said quietly.

Despite the warnings of his men, Robin went to the archery contest. He had it in his mind to win the golden arrow and give it to Vivian. He smiled to himself, standing unrecognized amid the Sheriff's men. Only one other contestant had given him cause to worry. A man with a patch over one eye whose shooting was confident and straight-arrowed. Robin's palms sweat with anticipation. He would have to be better than the stranger.

His eyes glanced up at the stand where the Sheriff and his daughter awaited the outcome of the contest. Robin froze suddenly, recognizing the woman sitting farther back from the Sheriff's daughter. It was Marion, returned at long last from France. Robin's heart soared with delight to see her, her face changed from a coltish girl into an elegant young woman. But there was still a spark of mischief in her, for he saw in the blue eyes that stared back at him that she alone had penetrated his disguise. He tipped his hat to her as he took his place in line. She nodded back and then looked away, but not before he had seen her smile.

Robin raised his longbow for the final match. The stranger had shot well. Very well, and for a moment Robin doubted the worth of his own skill to beat the man. There was a fitful breeze. It fluttered the flags of the tents and worried the fletch of his arrow. It would be hard to shoot straight in such a wind. Robin tried to slow the rapid beating of his heart, and take careful aim. The target seemed so vague and distant.

In the corner of his eye he glimpsed a face peering at him from the crowds that eagerly lined the edges of the contest grounds. Rust-colored hair billowed in the breeze around a face with honey-colored skin. At once the wind calmed. The target that had seemed so distant became sharp and clear in Robin's mind. He released his arrow and watched it soar, upward at first and then glide down unerringly to split the shaft of his opponent's arrow as the head buried itself in the center of the target.

The roar of the crowd's approval was not half as loud as Robin's own joy.

He looked again to the crowd but the face he sought was not there.

Later, after his return and the celebration that followed in the camp, Robin walked out by himself through the greenwood. The moon shone brilliantly above the trees, the silvery light dappling the bushes. He walked to Kirkley Hall and in the bright moonlight the stones of the old manor gleamed.

"Well met, Robin," said Vivian stepping from the shadows of the trees to meet him. "And did you win today?"

"Aye," he answered. "I did." And then he bowed his head sheepishly. "I had meant to bring you the golden arrow as a gift. But in the heat of my victory, I forgot and gave it to another."

Vivian laughed and Robin stared astonished, for he had never heard her laugh before. It was a bittersweet sound, without joy. "It were better given to Marion, Robin. I have no need for golden arrows." As she approached him, Robin saw an expression of longing on her face. "I have served you faithfully for a year, Robin. There is no one in the greenwood who does not speak well of you. You are a man others will follow, will love. You no longer need me."

Robin frowned at her words. They made him uncomfortable.

"I would ask one boon of you, Robin."

"Name it."

"It takes courage."

"I am Robin Hood," he answered, as if that were enough.

"I wish to be released from my service to you. I wish to return to my own life," she said.

"You have always been free to go, Vivian."

"To release me, you must kill me," she said. She stepped back from him, her arms opened wide. "Shoot me, Robin, that I may be returned to my life."

Robin's hands chilled. His heart thudded in his chest. "I will not," he stammered. "No Vivian, I will not. I rob the rich to give to the poor and I am protector of women in the greenwood. I can not go against my own word and kill you."

"I am not a mortal woman. I beg of you, Robin, release me."

Robin spun angrily on his heel and began to run. He didn't want to be convinced into so shameful an act by the look of pleading on her face. "No," he told himself as he ran, "I will not kill a woman," reminding himself of his own vows as he tore through the woods, branches snapping underfoot. But beneath his resolve Robin felt the scratch of doubt. It festered in his heart like a thorn lodged too deep to be pulled free. Until then, he had not questioned his good fortune. Now he asked himself, How much of his skill did he owe to Vivian? How much of his name, of his success was her doing? Robin hacked at a bush with his sword seeing again the glimpse of her face at the archery contest. And he knew he battled the rising fear that in losing Vivian, he might lose his own future.

"No!" he shouted aloud. "I am my own man. No servant to any. I will not kill Vivian because on my word as a man, as Robin Hood, I will not harm any woman."

As he neared the camp, he heard Allan-a-Dale singing. The smooth tenor voice eased away the sting of Robin's doubt. Allan-a-Dale was singing of Robin's victory at the archery contest. And when he entered the camp again, Robin smiled at the shouts of praise that greeted him. He belonged here. However it had happened, he had made a name for himself and nothing would change that.

*   *   *

The years followed and so did Robin's fame, spreading wide from Nottingham and Barnsdale, throughout the county of Lincolnshire and to the King himself. There was no act too daring, or too dangerous, for Robin and his men. They had made a great sport of the Sheriff of Nottingham, frustrating his every attempt to bring them to the gallows. And always and without fail, Robin's arrows with the grey-goose fletch found their mark in the Sheriff's men.

Robin walked the greenwood as if it were his own estate, the deer his deer and the purses of the wealthy his own private tax. There was only one change in him, hardly discernible by the closest of his own men. He almost never walked the woods alone. Once it had been his pleasure, but now he avoided it. For it was in those private moments that Vivian would come to him. Every time he saw her, she would beg again for her release.

"Kill me, Robin, that I may return to my life."

"Kill yourself," he replied once cruelly, enraged by her persistence.

Her face stilled to a wooden mask, her eyes dulled like stone. "I cannot. My father bound me to you. Only you can release me. I will stand here before you. It will take no skill of the bow to free me."

"Damn you!" Robin cursed, turning his back to her.

"You already have," she answered bitterly.

It was summer when the word was cried through Nottingham's markets that King Henry was dead and his son Richard the Lionhearted was crowned King. And before the summer was over, Richard himself had come to the greenwood, curious to see if the tales of Robin Hood were true.

They met in the greenwood and after a night of feasting on the King's own deer, Richard was impressed enough in Robin's skill as a leader to award Robin clemency and the return of his noble rank. To the men that had followed Robin loyally, Richard offered the positions of foresters. They accepted, since no other life but one in the forest held any interest to them.

Robin married Marion in a quiet ceremony, ringed by the trees of Kirkley Hall that had since been turned into a small abbey. He kissed her beneath the spreading oaks, and pledged his heart to her. He promised her a life of peace and happiness.

And they were happy, for a while. But the calm, sedate life of a lord bored Robin and he soon became restless. He missed the challenge of living in the greenwood, the hard ground for his bed and the openness of the night sky. And deep within his heart, there stirred another pain as the thorn pushed deeper and he knew he missed Vivian as well.

"The life of a lord does not suit you, my love," Marion said to him on his return from seeing the King. He had ridden hard in the rain and his cloak was soaked and mud-spattered.

He smiled at her. "Is it that easy to see?"

She nodded, her hands on her hips, waiting for him to speak.

He placed his hands on her shoulders and gazed into her troubled eyes. "I have spoken to the King. I want to go to Palestine. To see more of the world."

Her eyes sparkled with determination. "Then I will go with you."

Robin clasped her tightly until Marion laughed, gaily protesting his wet cloak and dripping hair.

He left her to make the necessary arrangements and walked out into the night toward the greenwood. Out of habit, he slung his longbow over his shoulder and carried his quiver of arrows. The rain had abated and overhead only a few lingering clouds scudded across the clearing night sky. The half moon shone brightly.

In the shifting play of shadows, Robin saw Vivian, waiting for him in the garden beside a bush of drenched roses. White petals had scattered on the walk around her feet.

"You go to Palestine," she said, her face downturned.

"Aye," he answered.

She looked up at him and in the moonlight her eyes glowed green. "Robin, if you leave the greenwood I cannot serve you. I cannot protect you as in the past."

He had been prepared to offer some words of kindness to her, perhaps even reconciliation. But the words she spoke now angered him.

"I have no need of your help," he snapped.

"But I have need of yours," she replied evenly. "If you should die without releasing me, I am doomed forever in this form. Forever. As you say, you do not need me anymore. Then kill me that I might go free at last."

"I am Robin Hood," he said, drawing his cloak tighter around his shoulders against the sudden chilly wind that blew between them. More petals scattered in the air like new snow. "I robbed from the rich to give to the poor and I never harmed a woman in the greenwood."

Vivian raised her hands to her face and cried out one long piercing wail. She fled into the woods, her bare arms flickering in the moonlight like the wings of a moth.

Robin stared after her, pride warring with doubt. He clutched his longbow, his gaze following the ghostly white shadow of her form. He could kill her now, if he chose. But he hesitated and she disappeared into the darkened forest. When Marion's voice called out to him, he turned slowly and left the garden to join her.

Five years later Robin returned from Palestine much aged. The world there had been hot, dry and full of dust. The color of the landscape a sun-faded brown mingled with the red blood of the dying. The battles had been too many and without reason. He had done well, though not any better than any other man. He had received a wound in the side that had taken months to heal. And even now he felt it throb with a cold ache. His hands trembled with fever and his mouth was always parched. But worst of all, Marion was dead. The fever that lingered in him had taken her quickly. He had buried her far from the cool green of Lincolnshire in a grave guarded by rocks and Cedar trees. There was nothing left of his life that gave him joy.

Robin had returned to the greenwood in order to recover something of the past, a purpose in his life that he could comprehend amidst his grief. But the greenwood had changed in his absence as well. King John held the throne now and once again Robin found himself out of favor with the King's court.

He had wandered the greenwood alone for two days, until he came to Kirkley Hall. He saw the grey stones of the old manor and something stirred in his heart. Robin nodded over his horse, feeling dizzy and faint. He slipped clumsily from the saddle and sat in the cool grass beneath the trees, his back to an oak.

A sharp pain in his side caused him to glance down. His white shirt was stained with fresh blood. The wound in his side had opened and begun to bleed. Robin tried to drag himself upright. At once, he felt a hand on his arm, pulling him, helping him to stand.

A nun in a brown habit tucked an arm around him and half supporting him, helped him into Kirkley Hall. Robin's heels fairly dragged across the stone flagons as she led him toward a small cell where a single bed faced a window. She laid him down gently on the bed.

Robin sighed with relief, his tired body sinking into the softness of the bed.

"I am bleeding," he said.

The nun straightened up and pulled back the cowl of her habit. Rust-colored hair spilled from the hood and framed her face. Vivian's green eyes were wet with tears.

Robin gasped, startled at seeing her and reached his hand to touch her cheek. His hand returned to his chest and he smiled at the familiar woody scent on his fingers.

"You have returned," she said.

"Just," he answered with a weak smile. "I have a wound that has begun to bleed. Please help me."

Vivian shook her head. "I cannot. There is nothing more I can do. The years you were gone have weakened my power. The wound you now have is the one my father gave you so long ago by his fallen oak. I can no longer stop its bleeding."

Robin closed his eyes and turned his head toward the wall.

"Robin," Vivian whispered and he knew what she wanted to say.

He shook his head, bitterness rising in his throat like gall.

"The pain you feel now is the same that I have lived with since our first meeting." She spoke gently and without rancor.

He refused to look at her. Then he felt her stand, heard her bare feet begin to pace the floor.

"How I despise my life. How my limbs burn in this shape, the soles of my feet cut by the rocks. I long for the peace of the earth, for the sleep of winter, for the sweet silence of the new spring. Robin, do not let me remain thus."

Her pleading stabbed at Robin's heart. The thorn of doubt twisted, causing him to cry out. In desperation, he reached for the gold horn at his side and blew three shrill blasts on it.

"No," Vivian sobbed and fled.

Alone in the room Robin stared hopelessly at the ceiling. If any of his men were near, they would come to him. He would not die alone, nor die tormented by Vivian's pleading.

The steady beat of Robin's heart slowed. The sheets were soaked with blood. On the ceiling of the quiet cell Robin thought he saw his life drawn in the faint etchings of its cracks and seams. He followed the patterns, seeing the tiny flecks of green that resembled Vivian at every turn of the lines.

If he had killed her and she was mortal flesh, he would have dishonored his own vow. He would have failed in his own eyes.

The pattern of the ceiling twisted around the line of a tree, its branches tipped with the buds of new leaves. And if he did kill her, and she was not mortal, but an Oakman's daughter, a greenfairy, then he must accept that his accomplishments had been a lie. A lie shaped for the eyes of other men by Vivian's hand.

Would that he had died that spring, he thought angrily, suddenly resentful of Vivian. At least he would have died his own man.

No, his mind retaliated, not your own man. But cursed to be the Oakman's servant, just as Vivian was his servant now. And Robin knew remembering the look of hatred in those green eyes, that had he begged for mercy, pleaded for release from bondage, the Oakman would have served Robin no better than he now served Vivian.

He felt overcome with anguish, terrified to look into his heart and pluck out the thorn of doubt. Without the illusion of his deeds, what was he?

"God's mercy, it is Robin!" boomed a voice from the door of his cell.

Robin turned his head slowly and saw Little John.

"I heard the horn. I knew it was you!" he cried and rushed to Robin's side. "But you are wounded!"

"I am dying," Robin answered softly.

"No," Little John groaned and lifted Robin from the bed by the shoulders. He wept, big tears streaming down the sides of his face into his beard.

Robin stared at him, and an easiness settled over the wound in his heart. Love and loyalty. However false his deeds may have been, he had found truth in his companionships. He had loved them without duplicity and in that, he had gained strength.

"Give me my bow and an arrow," Robin said weakly.

Little John propped Robin up in the bed, and held the bow up for him.

Robin stared out the window and saw Vivian standing amid the trees. She was facing him, smiling, her arms opened wide to receive the arrow. His hand shook but he willed it steady. Sweat trickled down the side of his face. This shot must be his own; its aim true.

"Where the arrow lands," he said to Little John, "bury me."

Robin let loose the arrow, hearing its hard twang echo in his ear. The shaft buried itself cleanly in the center of Vivian's chest.

As her arms flung skyward, she changed. The nun's habit spiraled around her legs, darkening into the rough hue of bark. Her arms sprouted branches and then leaves. Her head of tousled hair rounded into a burl at the base of two lifting branches. Before Robin was lain back on the bed again, he had seen his arrow fall harmlessly from its target to rest at the base of a young sapling oak.

His breathing was shallow, death brushing the dust of his final thoughts. He closed his eyes wearily. He was aware of Little John holding him, but his mind turned elsewhere. He imagined Vivian, her long roots deep in the earth tangled around his skeleton, clinging protectively to his bones. His eyes snapped open in surprise as he smelled the sweet fragrance of fresh sap in the air. Then he smiled, and closing his eyes once more, relinquished himself to the mercy of the greenwood.

TRUE LOVE
K. W. Jeter

K. W. Jeter has been prolific in both the science fiction and the horror genres since the 1975 publication of his novel *Seeklight*. At the time he was twenty-four. Since then he has published, among other novels, the notorious protocyberpunk *Dr. Adder, In the Land of the Dead, Madlands,* and most recently, *Wolf Flow.* He only began to publish short fiction in 1988, and his stories are about archetypical relationships (a young man's first sexual experience with a prostitute in "The First Time," the daughter-father relationship in "True Love") with horrific twists. "The First Time," Jeter's third published story, earned a great deal of critical attention and was chosen for two year's-best anthologies.

"True Love," from A *Whisper of Blood,* is a story of filial devotion and responsibility. The monstrous manifestation of this responsibility is only one part of the horror inherent in this shocker.

—E.D.

The brown leaves covered the sidewalk, but hadn't yet been trodden into thin leather. She held the boy's hand to keep him from slipping and falling. He tugged at her grip, wanting to race ahead and kick the damp stacks drifting over the curbs. The leaves smelled of wet and dirt, and left skeleton prints on the cement.

"Now—be careful," she told the boy. What was his name? She couldn't remember. There were so many things she couldn't forget. . . . Maybe her head had filled up, and there was no more room for anything else. The mounded leaves, slick with the drizzling rain. Her father scratching at the door, the word when there had been words in his mouth, the little word that used to be her name. . . . The boy's name; what was it? She couldn't remember.

The boy had tugged her arm around to the side, not trying to run now, but stopping to press his other hand against one of the trees whose empty branches tangled the sky.

"You don't want to do that." She pulled but he dug in, gripping the tree trunk. "It's all dirty." His red mitten was speckled with crumbling bark. A red strand of unraveled wool dangled from his wrist.

You do want to . . . That was her father's voice inside her head. The old voice, the long-ago one with words. She could have, if she'd wanted to—she'd done it before—she could've recited a list of sentences, like a poem, all the things her father had ever said to her with the word *want* in them.

"There's something up there."

She looked where the boy pointed, his arm jutting up straight, the mitten a red flag at the end. On one of the wet branches, a squirrel gazed down at her, then darted off, its tail spiked with drops of rain.

The boy stared openmouthed where the squirrel had disappeared. The boy's upper lip was shiny with snot, and there was a glaze of it on the back of one mitten, and the sleeve of the cheap nylon snow jacket. She shuddered, looking at the wet on the boy's pug face. He wasn't beautiful, not like the one before, the one with the angel lashes and the china and peach skin.

"Come on." She had to bite her lip to fight the shudder, to make it go away, before she could take the boy's hand again. "It's gone now. See? It's all gone." She squeezed the mitten's damp wool in her own gloved hand. "We have to go, too. Aren't you hungry?" She smiled at him, the cold stiffening her face, as though the skin might crack.

The boy looked up at her, distrust in the small eyes. "Where's my mother?"

She knelt down in front of the boy and zipped the jacket under his chin. "Well, that's where we're going, isn't it?" There were people across the street, just people walking, a man and a woman she'd seen from the corner of her eye. But she couldn't tell if they were looking over here, watching her and the boy. She brushed a dead leaf off the boy's shoulder. "We're going to find your mother. We're going to where she is."

She hated lying, even the lies she had told before. All the things she told the boy, and the ones before him, were lies. Everything her father had ever told her had been the truth, and that was no good, either.

Her knees ached when she stood up. The cold and damp had seeped into her bones. She squeezed the boy's hand. "Don't you want to go to where your mother is?"

Now his face was all confused. He looked away from her, down the long street, and she was afraid that he would cry out to the people who were walking there. But they were already gone—she hadn't seen where. Maybe they had turned and gone up the steps into one of the narrow-fronted houses that were jammed so tight against each other.

"And you're hungry, aren't you? Your mother has cake there for you. I know she does. You want that, don't you?"

How old was he? *His name, his name . . .* How big, how small was what she really meant. If he wouldn't move, tugging out of her grasp, wouldn't come with her . . . She wanted to pick him up, to be done with saying stupid things to his stupid little face, its smear of snot and its red pig nose. Just pick him up and carry him like a wet sack, the arms with the red-mittened hands caught tight against her breast. Carry him home and not have to say anything, not have to tell lies and smile . . .

She had tried that once and it hadn't worked. Once when there hadn't been any other little boy that she could find, and the one she had found wouldn't come with her, wouldn't come and it had been getting dark, yet it had been all light around her, she had been trapped in the bright blue-white circle from a street lamp overhead. And the boy had started crying, because she had been shouting at him, shouting for him to shut up and stop crying and come with her. She had picked him up, but he'd been too big and heavy for her, his weight squirming in her arms, the little hard fists striking her neck, the bawling mouth right up against one ear. Until she'd had to let him go and he'd fallen to the ground, scrambled to his feet and run off, crying and screaming so loud that other people—she had known they were there, she'd felt them even if she couldn't see them—had turned and looked at her. She'd scurried away and then started running herself, her heart pounding in her throat. Even on the bus she'd caught, she'd known the others were looking at her, even pointing at her and whispering to each other. How could they have known? Until she'd felt a chill kiss under the collar of her blouse, and she'd touched the side of her face and her fingers had come away touched with red. The boy's little fist, or a low branch clawing at her as she'd run by . . . The tissue in her purse had been a wet bright rag by the time she'd reached home.

That had been a bad time. The little boy had run away, and she'd been too frightened to try again, scared of people watching when it had gotten so dark, so dark that she couldn't see them looking at her. She'd had to go home to where her father was waiting. And even though he couldn't say the words anymore, to say what he wanted, she knew. One or the other, and the little boy had run away.

She'd stood naked in her bathroom, the tiny one at the back of the house, her face wet with the splashed cold water. She'd raised her arm high over her head, standing on tiptoe so she could see in the clouded mirror over the sink. A bruise under one breast—the little boy had kicked her; that must've been where she'd got it, though she couldn't remember feeling it. Her father couldn't have done that, though her ribs beneath the discolored skin ached with a familiar pain. He wasn't strong enough, not anymore. . . .

"Where are we?"

The boy's voice—this one, the little boy whose mittened hand she held in her own—brought her back. They were both walking, his hand reaching up to hers, and the streetlights had come on in the growing dark.

"This isn't my street. I don't live here."

"I know. It's okay." She didn't know where they were. She was lost. The narrow, brick-fronted houses came up so close to the street, the bare trees making spider shadows on the sidewalk. Light spilled from the windows above them. She looked up and saw a human shape moving behind a steam-misted glass, someone making dinner in her kitchen. Or taking a shower, the hot water sluicing around the bare feet on white porcelain. The houses would be all warm inside, heated and sealed against the black winter. The people—maybe the couple she had seen walking before, on the other side of another street—they could go naked if they wanted. They were taking a shower together, the man standing behind her, nuzzling her wet neck, hands cupped under her breasts, the smell of soap and wet towels. The steaming water would still be raining on them when he'd lay her down, they'd curl together in the hard nest of the tub, she'd have to bring her knees up against her breasts, or he'd sit her on the edge, the shower curtain clinging wet to her back, and he'd stand in front of her, the way her father did but it wouldn't be her father. She'd fill her mouth with him and he'd smell like soap and not that other sour smell of sweat and old dirt that scraped grey in her fingernails from his skin . . .

The boy pressed close to her side, and she squeezed his hand to tell him that it was all right. He was afraid of the dark and the street he'd never been on before. She was the grown-up, like his mother, and he clung to her now. The fist around her heart unclenched a little. Everything would be easier; she'd find their way home. To where her father was waiting, and she'd have the boy with her this time.

Bright and color rippled on the damp sidewalk ahead of them. The noise of traffic—they'd come out of the houses and dark lanes. She even knew where they were. She recognized the signs, a laundromat with free dry, an Italian restaurant with its menu taped to the window. She'd seen them from the bus she rode sometimes.

Over the heads of the people on the crowded street, she saw the big shape coming, even brighter inside, and heard the hissing of its brakes. Tugging the boy behind her, she hurried to the corner. He trotted obediently to keep up.

The house was as warm inside as other people's houses were. She left the heat on all the time so her father wouldn't get cold. She'd found him once curled up on the floor of the kitchen—the pilot light on the basement furnace had gone out, and ice had already formed on the inside of the windows. There'd been a pool of cold urine beneath him, and his skin felt loose and clammy. He'd stared over his shoulder, his mouth sagging open, while she'd rubbed him beneath the blankets of his bed, to warm him with her own palms.

Warm . . . He had kissed her once—it was one of the things she couldn't forget—when she had been a little girl and he had been as big as the night. His eyes had burned with the wild rigor of his hunt, the world's dark he'd held in his iron hands. The kiss had tasted of salt, a warm thing. Long ago, and she still remembered.

She took off the boy's jacket in the hallway. Her shoes and his small rubber boots made muddy stains on the thin carpet runner. Her knees were so stiff now that she couldn't bend down; she had the boy stand up on the wooden bench against the wall, so she could work the jacket's zipper and snaps.

"Where's my mother?" Coming in to the house's warmth from the cold street had made his nose run again. He sniffed wetly.

"She'll be here in a minute." She pushed the open jacket back from the boy's shoulders. "Let's get all ready for her, and then we can have that cake."

The boy had just a T-shirt on underneath the jacket, and it was torn and dirty, with a yellow stain over some cartoon character's face. The boy's unwashed smell blossomed in the close hallway air, a smell of forgotten laundry and milk gone off. She wanted that to make her feel better. The boy's mother was a bad mother. Not like that other boy's mother, the one three or four times ago. She remembered standing by the greasy fire in the backyard, turning that boy's clothing over in her hands, all of it clean-smelling, freshly washed. Inside the collar of the boy's shirt, and in the waistband of the corduroy trousers, little initials had been hand-stitched, his initials. That was what she'd do if she'd had a child of her own; she would love him that much. Not like this poor ragged thing. Nobody loved this little boy, not really, and that made it all right. She'd told herself that before.

"What's that?" He looked up toward the hallway's ceiling.

She pulled his T-shirt up, exposing his pink round belly. His hair stood up— it was dirty, too—when she pulled the shirt off over his head.

"Nothing." She smoothed his hair down with her palm. "It's nothing." She didn't know if she'd heard anything or not. She'd heard all the house's sounds for so long—they were all her father—that they were the same as silence to her. Or a great roaring hurricane that battered her into a corner, her arms over her head to try to protect herself. It was the same.

She dropped the T-shirt on top of the rubber boots, then unbuttoned the boy's trousers and pulled them down. Dirty grey underwear, the elastic sagging loose. The little boys things (*little . . . not like . . .*) made the shape of a tiny fist inside the stained cotton. (*Great roaring hurricane*) (*Arms over her head*) She slipped the underpants down.

The boy wiggled. He rubbed his mouth and nose with the back of his hand, smearing the shiny snot around. "What're you doing?"

"Oh, you're so cold." She looked into his dull eyes, away from the little naked parts. "You're freezing. Wouldn't a nice hot bath . . . wouldn't that be nice? Yes. Then you'd be all toasty warm, and I'd wrap you up in a great big fluffy towel. That'd be lovely. You don't want to catch cold, do you?"

He sniffled. "Cake."

"Then you'd have your cake. All you want."

His face screwed up red and ugly. "No. I want it now!" His shout bounced against the walls. The underpants were a grey rag around his ankles, and his hand a fist now, squeezing against the corner of his mouth.

She slapped him. There was no one to see them. The boy's eyes went round, and he made a gulping, swallowing noise inside his throat. But he stopped crying. The fist around her heart tightened, because she knew this was something he was already used to.

"Come on." She could hear her own voice, tight and angry, the way her father's had been when it still had words. She tugged the underpants away from the boy's feet. "Stop being stupid."

She led him, his hand locked inside hers, up the stairs. Suddenly, halfway up, he started tugging, trying to pull his hand away.

"Stop it!" She knelt down and grabbed his bare shoulders, clenching them tight. "Stop it!" She shook him, so that his head snapped back and forth.

His face was wet with tears, and his eyes looked up. He cringed away from something up there, rather than from her. Between her own panting breaths, she heard her father moving around.

"It's nothing!" Her voice screamed raw from her throat. "Don't be stupid!"

She jerked at his arm, but he wouldn't move; he cowered into the angle of the stairs. He howled when she slapped him, then cried openmouthed as she kept on hitting him, the marks of her hand jumping up red on his shoulder blades and ribs.

She stopped, straightening up and gasping to catch her breath. The naked little boy curled at her feet, his legs drawn up, face hidden in the crook of his arm. The blood rushing in her head roared, the sound of a battering wind. The saliva under her tongue tasted thick with salt.

For a moment she thought he was still crying, little soft animal sounds, then she knew it was coming from up above. From her father's room. She stood for a moment, head tilted back, looking up toward the sounds. Her hair had come loose from its knot, and hung down the side of her face and along her back.

"Come on . . ." She kept her voice softer. She reached down and took the boy's hand. But he wouldn't stand up. He hung limp, sniffling and shaking his head.

She had to pick him up. She cradled him in her arms—he didn't feel heavy at all—and carried him the rest of the way up the stairs.

Her father was a huddled shape under the blankets. He'd heard them coming, and had gotten back into the bed before she'd opened the door.

She knew that was what he'd done. A long time ago, when he'd first become this way—when she'd first made herself realize that he was old—she had tried tying him to the bed, knotting a soft cord around his bone-thin ankle and then to one of the heavy carved lion's paws underneath. But he'd fretted and tugged so at the cord, picking at the knot with his yellow fingernails until they'd cracked and bled, and the ankle's skin had chafed raw. She'd untied him, and taken to nailing his door shut, the nails bent so she just had to turn them to go in and out. At night, she had lain awake in her room and listened to him scratching at the inside of his door.

Then that had stopped. He'd learned that she was taking care of him. The scratching had stopped, and she'd even left the nails turned back, and he didn't try to get out.

She sat the little boy at the edge of the bed. The boy was silent now, sucking his thumb, his face smeared wet with tears.

"Daddy?" She pulled the blanket down a few inches, exposing the brown-spotted pink of his skull, the few strands of hair, tarnished silver.

"Daddy—I brought somebody to see you."

In the nest of the blanket and sour-smelling sheets, her father's head turned. His yellow-tinged eyes looked up at her. His face was parchment that had been crumpled into a ball and then smoothed out again. Parchment so thin that the bone and the shape of his teeth—the ones he had left, in back—could be seen through it.

"Look." She tugged, lifted the little boy farther up onto the bed. So her father could see.

The eyes under the dark hood of the blanket shifted, darting a sudden eager gaze from her face to the pink softness of the little boy.

"Come here." She spoke to the boy now. His legs and bottom slid on the blanket as she pulled him, her hands under his arms, until he sat on the middle of the bed, against the lanky, muffled shape of her father. "See, there's nothing to be afraid of. It's just nice and warm."

The shape under the blanket moved, crawling a few inches up to the turned-back edge.

The boy was broken, he had been this way a long time, it was why she'd picked him out and he'd come with her. Nobody loved him, not really, and that made it all right. He didn't fight as she laid him down, his head on the crumpled pillow, face close to her father's.

A thing of twigs and paper, her father's hand, slid from beneath the blanket. It cupped the back of the boy's head, tightening and drawing the boy close, as though for a kiss.

The boy struggled then, a sudden fluttering panic. His small hands pushed against her father's shoulders, and he cried, a whimpering noise that made her father's face darken with his wordless anger. That made her father strong, and he reared up from the bed, his mouth stretching open, tendons of clouded spit thinning to string. He wrapped his arms around the little boy, his grey flesh squeezing the pink bundle tight.

The boy's whimpering became the sound of his gasping breath. Her father pressed his open mouth against the side of the boy's neck. The jaws under the translucent skin worked, wetting the boy's throat with white-specked saliva.

Another cry broke out, tearing at her ears. She wanted to cover them with her hands and run from the room. And keep running, into all the dark streets around the house. Never stopping, until her breath was fire that burned away her heart. The cry was her father's; it sobbed with rage and frustration, a thing bigger than hunger, desire, bigger than the battering wind that shouted her name. He rolled his face away from the boy's wet neck, the ancient face like a child's now, mouth curved in an upside-down U, tongue thrusting against the toothless gums in front. His tears broke, wetting the ravines of his face.

He couldn't do it, he couldn't feed himself. She knew, it had been that way the last time, and before. But every time, hope made her forget, at least enough to try the old way. The way it had been years ago.

She couldn't bear the sound of her father's crying, and the little boy's fearful whimper. She knew how to stop it. On the table beside the bed was the knife she'd brought up from the kitchen—that had also been a long time ago—and had left there. Her hand reached out and curled around the smooth-worn wood. Her thumb slid across the sharp metal edge.

She brought her lips to the boy's ear, whispering to him. "Don't be afraid, it's all right . . ." The boy squirmed away from her, but she caught him fast, hugging his unclothed body against her breast. "It's all right, it's all right . . ." He saw the knife blade, and started to cry out. But she already had its point at his pink throat, and the cry leaked red, a drop, then a smearing line as the metal sank and cut.

The red bloomed on the sheets, the grey flooded to shiny wet. The boy's small hands beat against her, then fluttered, trembled, fell back, fists opening to stained flowers.

He didn't fight her now, he was a limp form in her embrace, but suddenly he weighed so much and her hands slipped on the soft skin that had been pink before and now shone darker and brighter. She gripped the boy tighter, her fingers parallel to his ribs, and lifted him. She brought the bubbling mouth, the red one that she had pulled the knife from, up to her father's parted lips.

The blood spilled over her father's gums and trickled out the corners of his mouth. The tendons in his neck stretched and tightened, as though they might tear his paper flesh. His throat worked, trying to swallow, but nothing happened. His eyes opened wider, spiderwebs of red traced around the yellow. He whimpered, the anger turning to fear. Trapped in the thing of sticks his body had become, he scrabbled his spotted hands at her face, reaching past the boy between them.

She knew what had to be done. The same as she'd done before. Her father's bent, ragged nails scraped across her cheek as she turned away from him. She nuzzled her face down close to the little boy's neck. She closed her eyes so there was only the wet and heat pulsing against her lips. She opened her mouth and drank, her tongue weighted with the dancing, coiling salt.

She didn't swallow, though her mouth had become full. Her breath halted, she raised her face from the boy's neck and the wound surging less with every shared motion of their hearts. A trickle of the warmth caught in her mouth leaked to her chin.

A baby bird in its nest . . . a naked thing of skin and fragile bone . . . She had found one once, on the sidewalk in front of the house, a tiny creature fallen from one of the branches above. Even as she had reached down, the tip of her finger an inch away from the wobbling, blue-veined head, the beak had opened, demanding to be fed . . .

The creature's hunger had frightened her, and she'd kicked it out into the gutter, where she wouldn't have to see it anymore. That had been a baby bird.

This was her father. She kept her eyes closed as she brought herself down to him, but she could still see the mouth opening wide, the pink gums, the tongue in its socket of bubbled spit. She lowered her face to his, and let the lips seal upon her own. She opened her mouth, and let the warmth uncoil, an infinitely soft creature moving over her own tongue, falling into his hunger.

The little boy's blood welled in her father's mouth. For a moment it was in both their mouths, a wet place shared by their tongues, his breath turning with hers. She felt the trembling, a shiver against the hinges of her jaw as his throat clenched, trying to swallow. She had to help even more, it had been this way the last time as well; she pressed her lips harder against her father's mouth, as her tongue rolled against the narrow arch of her teeth. The warmth in their mouths broke and pushed past the knot in her father's throat. He managed to swallow, and she felt the last of the blood flow out of her mouth, into his and then gone.

She fed him twice more, each mouthful easier. Between them, the little boy lay still, beautiful in his quiet.

The boy's throat had paled, and she had to draw deep for more. The sheets were cold against her hands as she pushed herself away from him.

Her father was still hungry, but stronger now. His face rose to meet hers, and the force of his kiss pressed against her open lips.

The blood uncoiled in that dark space again, and something else. She felt his tongue thrust forward to touch hers, a warm thing cradled in warmth and the sliding wet. Her throat clenched now. She couldn't breathe, and the smell of his sweat and hunger pressed in the tight space behind her eyes.

His hands had grown strong now, too. The weak flutter had died, the palms reddening as the little boy had become white and empty. One of her father's hands tugged her blouse loose from the waistband of her skirt, and she felt the thing of bone and yellowed paper smear the sheet's wet on her skin. Her father's hand stroked across her ribs and fastened on her breast, a red print on the white cotton bra. He squeezed and it hurt, her breath was inside his hand and blood and the taste of his mouth, the dark swallowing that pulled her into him, beat a pulsing fist inside her forehead.

She pushed both her hands against him, but he was big now and she was a little girl again, she was that pale unmoving thing rocking in his arms, playing at being dead. She was already falling, she could raise her knees in the dark wet embrace of the bed, she could wrap herself around the little blind thing at the center of her breasts, that just breathed and stayed quiet, and that even he couldn't touch, had never been able to touch . . . the little boy was there, his angel face bright and singing, her ears deafened, battered by that song that light that falling upward into clouds of glory where her mother in Sunday robes reached for her, her mother smiling though she had no face she couldn't remember her mother's face—

She shoved against her father, hard enough to break away from him, his ragged fingernails drawing three red lines that stung and wept under her bra. She fell backward off the bed, her elbow hard against the floor, sending numb electricity to her wrist.

Another shape slid from the edge of the bed and sprawled over her lap. The little boy, naked and red wet, made a soft, flopping doll. She pushed it away from herself and scrambled to her feet.

The bed shone. From its dark center, the depth of the blanket's hood, her father looked out at her.

She found the doorknob in her hands behind her back. Her blouse clung to her ribs, and had started to turn cold in the room's shuttered air. The door scraped her spine as she stepped backward into the hallway. Then she turned and ran for the bathroom at the far end, an old sour taste swelling in her throat.

In the dark, between the streetlights' blue islands, she could feel the leaves under her feet. They slid away, damp things, silent; she had to walk carefully to keep from falling.

There was work to be done back at the house. She'd do it later. She would have to change the sheets, as she always did afterward, and wash the stained ones. She used the old claw-footed bathtub, kneeling by its side, the smell of soap and bleach stinging her nose, her fingers working in the pink water. He let her come in and make the bed, and never tried to say anything to her, just watching her with his blank and wordless eyes, his hungers, all of them, over for a while.

And there were the other jobs to be done, the messier ones. Getting rid of things. She'd have to take the car, the old Plymouth with the rusting fenders, out of the garage. And drive to that far place she knew, where these things were never found. She would come back as the sun was rising, and there would be mud on the hem of her skirt. She'd be tired, and ready to sleep.

She could do all that later. She'd been brave and strong, and had already done the hardest jobs; she could allow herself this small indulgence.

The cold night wrapped around her. She pressed her chin down into the knot of the scarf she'd tied over her hair. The collar of her coat had patches where the fur had worn away. The coat had been her mother's, and had been old the first time she'd worn it. A scent of powder, lavender and tea roses, still clung to the heavy cloth.

At the end of the block ahead of her, the Presbyterian church hid the stars at the bottom of the sky. She could see the big stained-glass window, Jesus with one hand on his staff and the other cupped to the muzzle of a lamb, even though there were no lights on in the church itself. The light spilling over the sidewalk came from the meeting room in the basement.

She went down the bare concrete steps, hand gripping the iron rail. And into the light and warmth, the collective sense of people in a room, their soft breathing, the damp-wool smell of their winter coats.

Where she hung her coat up, with the others near the door, a mimeographed paper on the bulletin board held the names for the altar flowers rotation. Sign-ups to chaperone the youth group's Christmas party. A glossy leaflet, unfolded and tacked, with pledges for a mission in Belize. Her name wasn't anywhere on the different pieces of paper. She didn't belong to the church. They probably wouldn't have wanted her, if they'd known. Known everything. She only came here for the weekly support group.

There was a speaker tonight, a woman up at the front of the room, talking, one hand gesturing while the other touched the music stand the church gave them to use as a podium.

She let the speaker's words flutter past as she sat down in one of the metal folding chairs at the side of the room; halfway down the rows, so she only had to turn her head a bit to see who else had come tonight. She had already counted close to twenty-four. There were the usuals, the faces she saw every week. A couple, a man and a woman who always held hands while they sat and listened, who she assumed were married; they nodded and smiled at her, a fellow regular. At the end of the row was somebody she hadn't seen before, a young man who sat hunched forward, the steam from a Styrofoam cup of coffee rising into his face. She could tell that he was just starting, that this was a new world for him; he didn't look happy.

None of them ever did, even when they smiled and spoke in their bright loud voices, when they said hello and hugged each other near the table with the coffee urn and the cookies on the paper plates.

They had another word for why they were here, a word that made it sound like a disease, just a disease, something you could catch like a cold or even a broken arm. Instead of it being time itself, and old age, and the grey things their parents had become. Time curled outside the church, like a black dog waiting where the steps became the sidewalk, waiting to go home with them again. Where the ones who had known their names looked at them now with empty eyes and did not remember.

She sat back in the folding chair, her hands folded in her lap. The woman at the front of the room had the same bright, relentless voice. She closed her eyes and listened to it.

The woman had a message. There was always a message, it was why people came here. The woman told the people in the room that they had been chosen to receive a great blessing, one that most people weren't strong enough for. A chance to show what love is. A few years of grief and pain and sadness and trouble, of diapering and spoon-feeding and talking cheerily to something that had your father or your mother's face, but wasn't them at all, not anymore. And then it would be over.

That was a small price to pay, a small burden to carry. The woman told them that, the same thing they'd been told before. A few years to show their love. For these things that had been their parents. They'd be transfigured by the experience. Made into saints, the ones who'd shown their courage and steadfastness on that sad battlefield.

She sat and listened to the woman talking. The woman didn't know—none of them ever did—but she knew. What none of them ever would.

She looked around at the others in the room, the couple holding hands, the young man staring into the dregs of his coffee. Her burden, her blessing, was greater than theirs. and so was her love. Even now, she felt sorry for them. They would be released someday. But not her. For them, there would be a few tears, and then their love, their small love, would be over.

She kept her eyes closed, and let herself walk near the edge of sleep, of dreaming, in this warm place bound by winter. She smiled.

She knew that love wasn't over in a few sad years. Or in centuries. She knew that love never died. She knew that her love—real love, true love—was forever.

THE SECOND MOST BEAUTIFUL WOMAN IN THE WORLD

A. R. Morlan

A. R. Morlan published two horror novels in 1991, *The Amulet* and *Dark Journey*. Over the past years she has been making a name for herself with short stories that have appeared in *Night Cry*, *The Horror Show*, and numerous small-press publications.

"The Second Most Beautiful Woman in the World," from the anthology *Obsessions*, is a beautiful evocation of the southwest of artist Georgia O'Keeffe and a chilling depiction of—appropriately enough—an obsession.

—E.D.

"Where I was born and where and how I have lived is unimportant. It is what I have done with where I have been that should be of interest."

—Georgia O'Keeffe

Blasted porous white bone arcs to join pitted terra cotta against blue, blue ever-changing sky, and the small bones join with the windhoned stones flecking the shifting sand below . . . framed against the distant Pedernal, she has become one with Art . . .

Like Georgia O'Keeffe before me, I too grew disenchanted with my native Wisconsin. Taking a cue from my spiritual mentor, I too professed disdain for the gently rolling, ever-unsure contours of the land, and for the indecisive blur of green and brown below me. *Paint* such landscapes? *Me?* One look at O'Keeffe's "Red Hill and White Shell" or "Pelvis With Pedernal" had this boy hooked; never mind those glossy fliers the New Mexico Tourist Bureau sent to me.

So, I left home, suitcase of art supplies and dufflebag of old clothes in hand, in search of the land which had inspired the most beautiful woman in the world to create the most exquisite artwork I'd ever seen—as she herself once proclaimed, "God told me that if I painted that mountain enough, I could have it."

O'Keeffe was speaking about her beloved Pedernal, that flat-topped mountain not far off from Ghost Ranch, but in my case, "that mountain" was *all* of what I'd long dubbed "Georgia's land." The sun-whitened cow skulls and striated pale cliffs. The pink hills fuzzed with clumps of piñon trees. The hills, cliffs, and runneled dark mesas Georgia (later, Georgia and her companion Juan) had stared at, in search of what Art lay there. O'Keeffe had found that elusive Muse in this warm, dry place of singing color and clean colorless air, and I was determined to find Art there too.

As things turned out, I not only missed the opportunity to meet my mentor (the grand lady died five months before I arrived in the state), but, as I ruefully had to admit six months into my new New Mexico life, somehow I missed my meeting with Art, too.

For me, burnt umber and ocher only looked like . . . globs of brush-smeared burnt umber and ocher on poorly stretched canvas. What I had envisioned as a fresh view of Georgia's land was only worth viewing when hung above the grease-dotted surface of a diner range-top. And those paintings were only hung there because *I* had put them there. My boss, the man who put fresh grease spatters on the chipped white enamel of the range with every flip of a burger, he didn't mind my efforts to sell my work. As long as the dishes were washed, Duke didn't care if I hung my paintings in the restrooms next to the machine that sold rubbers.

I came to Duke's Burgers with a stack of paintings in the trunk of my rust-fringed Volvo (bought in Taos, the rust filagree attested to a previous owner in a more northern clime than barely-humid and certainly road-salt free Taos); aside from the vague hope that the owner would let me hawk my paintings there, I wanted nothing more than a cup of coffee and a place to relieve myself. I was wary of using the wayside between Talpa and Pilar; even the mere possibility of rattlers spooked me.

But after my second cup of watery java, Duke—I never have learned whether that dog-like name was given or adopted—shyly hinted that his top-of-the-building sign needed freshening. For a second I wanted to sputter, "Sir, I am an *artist*," but my trunk full of semi-motel art made me reconsider.

Duke's sign only needed so much touch-up work; after that, he found real work for me. And I never added any more paintings to my series, hell, there isn't any more room above the range anyway. But I had the whole of the desert outside my above-the-washer window, and nothing—not lack of real talent, not missed opportunities, not even the loss of something so intangible that its loss was more of an inner sigh of relief (*rest easy, Georgia-girl, this Wisconsin wanna-be won't steal your desert thunder*)—could take the beauty of the desert away from me. True, nothing could make that same desert, that distant Pedernal give up its secrets to my now paint-stiffened brush, or to my now paint-free fingers, but I had resigned myself to what couldn't be.

Another Wisconsinite had beat me to this place, the most beautiful woman God ever created to puzzle and delight man (if I were to say that back home, people would look at me funny-like; in Wisconsin a woman has to be hung on the back of a door wearing a suede bikini to be considered "beautiful" . . . diner-job or not, I'm glad I left).

Georgia had painted "that mountain" enough times that God gave the whole damned *desert* to her. But she earned every grain of sand, every sun-glinting chip of bone, seemingly forever.

Until her rival, her only *real* competition, arrived at Duke's.

Indentations, the dark places in the skull catch the darkness and hold onto it, greedily, and the places where the moonlight caresses gleam all the brighter against the contrasted darkness, in a moment of purest, most unconscious Beauty . . .

Duke waved the newspaper in front of my nose, asking, "West Salem, in Wisconsin—you come from 'round there, no?"

I dried my hands before taking the paper from him. The article under the header "Hands Down Victory" was from the AP; I frowned slightly as I read it, while Duke watched me read with dancing, moist eyes.

When Duke's eyes were all shiny and jiggling, I knew it was time to get nervous. That old "this-promotion-will-nab-the-tourists" look. Lately of the "Free Friers for Flyers" give away (kids from neighboring towns took to fishing airline tickets out of dumpers to cash in on the offer) and the Mother's Day corsage debacle. Not that I blamed him for wanting to make it big. Tucked slightly out of the way as his diner was, just out of reach of the tourists heading to or from Taos Ski Valley, Kit Carson Memorial State Park and other draws, Duke missed the *really* big crowds. And as I read the article, I sensed another promotion in the works.

A Chevrolet dealer and a radio station gave away a car to a man who had stood—not counting short breaks every few hours—with both hands touching a Sprint for more hours than any other contestant. Oh, true, the contestants started out only attached to the car with a rope that got shorter as the contest progressed, but the ending of it all was pure 1930's "they shoot horses, don't they?" marathon stuff. No sitting, no leaning on the car, just stand upright next to that car, with both hands laid on it, evangelist-healing-the-dying style. With only five minutes of rest every three hours.

I folded the paper into thirds before tossing it on the faintly damp counter, and snorted dryly through my nose.

"Forget it, Duke. AP's spread that story all over the country. Old hat. Pole-sitting's passé. Even that girl in the midwest gave up after she broke the record her mom set. It won't draw anyone—"

"A camper. Big one. Lots of people could lean against it, no? Lots of room out back, you could paint the sign. Put it up against the front, next to the door. Real bright, you can paint it. Red, lots of red. And yellow, customers, they like yellow—"

I turned my back to Duke, tried to lose myself in the subtle shift of the top layer of sand in the wind (it reminded me of the way powdery snow would snake across the highways when the Wisconsin winter winds blew, and I silently cussed those people in West Salem), but minutes later something round bumped up against my back.

A paint can. Duke had found a big can of red in the back shed. Plus a huge brush.

*   *   *

Two weeks in the sun and occasionally blowing sand had scoured my freshly painted sign to a deep fuchsia by the day the contest was to begin rolled around. Duke had all but left the running of the diner to me; he scooted around Taos, Talpa, Pilar and Dixon, not to mention La Medera and Santa Fe, with photocopied and hand-colored (thanks to me) fliers advertising the "Put Up Yer Dukes Camper Give-Away." I had to hand it to Duke; he shook butt and got the word out. Newspaper ads, fliers stapled to telephone poles and thumbtacked to bulletin boards in supermarkets, even a radio spot. And, God help the man, he *bought* a camper.

Huge thing. White as a cow skull, all banded in gleaming chrome, and the windows sparkled, like old bottles thrown to shatter in a ditch. A massive, insane, beautiful, *impossible* hulk of a camper. Once, I tried to tell Duke that the Chevy dealer in West Salem only gave away an auto worth less than $7,000 dollars— and the guy went in with a radio station. Duke only gave me a sad, blissful smile, and I said no more.

The camper *was* a wonderous thing; Duke parked it out back, where there would be plenty of room for the would-be winners of it, and come sunset, the camper was a thing of shell-like purity against the raw intense colors of the hills beyond. It was almost enough to make me want to dig out my box of scrunched and flattened oils and try once more to . . . to be what only a sunburned and slat thin woman already *was*, for now and forever. No matter how much I painted the mountain, the desert, the stones—even the damned *camper*—they would never be mine. The box of paint tubes stayed under my cot in the back room.

But nothing could keep me from *looking* at it, parked under a cloudless and swelling blue sky, like a pebble of white near a still ocean. Others looked at the camper, too, but I don't think they saw it in the same way I did. O'Keeffe, *she* might have understood it, but the other people who came to gawk at it, *they* saw only gas mileage, something to win and then sell, or a thing to impress their friends with the winning of it.

Except for the woman in the faded denim, the one who . . . who *claimed* it.

Spaces between the bone say the most about the bone, the spaces define what is all around them, accentuate the white purity of line, of sweeping form, and when sunlight or moonlight hit the bone, the spots free of bone complement the clean bareness, in perfect Symmetry . . .

Duke wasn't *quite* as crazy as I had thought him. He pulled me aside minutes before we opened the doors of the diner to admit the fifty or so people waiting outside, and whispered, "See the big guy, bandana on his head, mustache?"

"You gonna tell me something I really don't want to hear?"

"That guy, he's the winner. From Santa Fe. Trucker. Used to holding it, y'know? Used to going thirsty. Riding in that rig, they get used to things like that. Found him last week. He wins, I get the camper, and it goes back to the dealer."

"And if he doesn't?"

"He'll win. He's a good boy. He don't want to see Duke lose the diner, no?" Duke's eyes were doing their soggy jig, and I just shrugged. I still had the Volvo; no rope was tying me to the diner.

Duke was playing Mr. Bountiful before the contest was to begin; every contestant was treated to a free meal. From the way Duke laid on the salt earlier that morning, I knew that more than one entrant would spend more than the limit of two minutes in the porta-potty come the first three-hour break. And naturally, the water jugs were free, and plentiful. And the menu that morning was loaded with fish, salty scrambled eggs and hash browns.

There wasn't enough room for every contestant to sit and eat, so plates were passed amid the nervous laughter, and most people had to lean against walls or put their plates on the narrow windowsills. As I circulated with a carafe of coffee, I noticed that some folks were wise to Duke; they avoided the sodium rich stuff and stuck to sips of water and nibbles of dry toast.

The woman in the distressed denim (as in bleached naturally by the sun, her shoulders were almost white) forked her fish filet into delicate chevrons of cooked flesh; when I offered her some coffee she slowly shook her head. She was so sun-browned and leathery it was hard to tell if she came by her dark complexion naturally or had worked at it; her cheeks were worthy of O'Keeffe, though. High flaring wings of bone under spare taut skin. Her eyes were dark, almost dry stones set in sullen clouds. Thin, cracked lips (striated, with moist valleys of pink between) moved into a rictus of a smile before I left her for the next entrant.

I hadn't seen the woman among the crowds who had come in the days before the contest. Her, I would have remembered. She was easily the second most beautiful woman I'd ever seen; Art embodied in worn denim and a work shirt with frayed cuffs. Whether she was twenty or fifty was impossible to tell, her black hair signified nothing. Some reservation women kept black hair, or near enough, into their dotage. But no jewelry, turquoise or otherwise, adorned her neck, wrists, or fingers, and I'm of the opinion that most Indian women are *born* with silver and blue jewelry on their bodies.

She had stationed herself near the back of the diner, close by "my" above-the-dishwasher window. Every few seconds, when she wasn't toying with her uneaten breakfast, she'd look at the camper. Not in a *greedy* way. Appreciative, the way you or I would look at a piece of art in a museum. Yet, there was this aching-to-buy pull to her mouth, and furrowing of her brow . . .

"Good crowd, no?"

Reluctantly, I turned to Duke. He shook the cash box full of entrant's money, two bucks per person, all for a "free" breakfast and the privilege of standing out in the hot desert sun with an umbilical cord of rope between the entrant and the camper. Judging from the way the box rattled, a lot of people had paid in change. I swallowed so hard I felt my adam's apple rub against my buttoned collar.

Behind me, I could all but *feel* the dark woman stare at that camper, the waves of longing wavering hot and invisible, like heat devils on a highway at noon.

"Hundred bucks ain't much, Duke."

"That's jus' the *start*," he bubbled, rattling the box in time with his words. "People, they'll come to *watch*, and they gotta eat, no? Be like a circus, you see.

Radio station, papers, they'll come. They got to eat, no? AP, they come. Free advertising—"

Duke didn't notice when I turned away to watch the woman. Her flayed breakfast rested on the plate balanced on her extended arm, as if she had already endured the initial rounds of the contest and was in the home stretch. Her palm was held sideways, outspread, and by moving my head, I could see that her hand was in perfect alignment with the camper beyond the window. Those pebble eyes were closed, and those parched lips formed a word I couldn't make out.

"—then, after the others drop out, when it's down to one, two 'sides—" Duke's voice dropped here "—my *pal*, maybe TV stations come, and they gotta eat, no?"

"Yeah, Duke, yeah," I mumbled, as I watched the woman in denim devour the camper with her fixed, staring eyes.

Dry winds play soft tunes through the bone, a muted whistle, and the gentle sussuration of shifting sand provides the gentle harmony, and far, far off, the piñon trees move slowly in time to the eternal music of Time . . .

As I expected, few people made it past the first bathroom break. Some of the men didn't make it to the porta-potties at all, just dashed around the back of the shed, but all that running there and back ate up their two minutes of freedom from the long ropes. Soon there were only thirty, thirty-five people standing six feet away from the camper. As the day progressed, Duke's expected crowd of on-lookers did arrive . . . and by the next biffy-break, the crowd was augmented by former entrants.

After the second break, the ropes were shortened to five feet. With fewer people attached to the camper, I was able to pick out the dark woman. She hadn't used either opportunity to relieve herself, which was as I'd expected. Her breakfast of fish didn't need any water to swim in, and I saw that she hadn't touched her jug of water.

The third break freed a handful of entrants, but the woman stood her ground, only moving when Duke shortened her tether to the camper.

I couldn't believe the woman's perseverance. Nine hours without a break; hell, she didn't even sit on the *ground*. No water, no food come evening (Duke offered cold-cut sandwiches, or fried chicken wings), and once it got cold, she didn't so much as draw her worn jacket tighter across her shoulders.

When the moon came up, shone down cold on the camper and the ring of people around it, Duke whispered, "I thought they'd give up come night, no?"

It had finally dawned on Duke that he had made no provisions for watching his entrants come night time; he had no one to spell him in the diner come morning after a sleepless night. The hordes of radio, newspaper and television reporters hadn't shown, yet he was honorbound to at least make a *show* of fair play . . . until his buddy the trucker was the only person standing by the camper.

"That article, how many days it say the contest was running?" Moonlight turned the deep furrow between his eyes into a mooncrater, all high pale ridges and black shadow.

"Five and a half days," I said as evenly as I could. It was hard not to smile.

"Five and a . . . *sheesh*. I thought the sun . . . or the *cold*—"

Before me, the woman in denim was a piece of umber sculpture, softened only by the dark fall of her hair and the white-worn clothes she wore. I thought again of O'Keeffe, the earth-nun in black and white, posed before a bare wall and a hanging cow skull. Spare, but lush at once. Shadows pooled in her eye sockets as the woman stood there, bound to the camper with faintly luminous rope, and all the scene needed was a white rose, suspended in space.

Around her, the other entrants settled down for the easy part. Many, including the trucker from Santa Fe, slept, curled like dark shells on the sand. Duke offered me a ten spot if I sat out there and stayed awake while the entrants slept. I took it, not telling him I would have watched the woman for free.

I *swear* that I didn't sleep at all that night; I had to have been awake to call out the break times twice that night. I *know* that I was awake; I docked the stragglers and untied their ropes. I *had* to be alert, awake; I told the people that once the ropes were a foot away (come morning) Duke would take them off and everyone would have to keep at least one hand on the camper, for starters.

I did, I *did* stay awake through it all, but yet . . . the woman didn't move, save for a sideways shuffle of her worn cowboy boots when I drew her rope in. Oh, yeah, she *blinked*, and she *breathed*, she wasn't *dead*, but . . . God, she was still. And she hadn't peed, I mean *nobody* can hold it like that. *Can* they?

She didn't eat, she didn't drink. Her water jug rested obscenely full, sloshing when Duke or I kicked it along after her with each foot-long pulling-in of the rope. I've heard about how starving people get to a point where they can't eat; the body forgets or something. But not to take water? Lizards, some desert mice pull that shtick, not *people*.

Come sun-up, she was still *standing there*, conserving strength, I supposed. Her camper-mates numbered around twenty or so. I was too rattled to count.

Duke spelled me, watching through the back window he kept track of his people while fixing food, while I napped. But my dreams were full of stark white and oily black hair above denim, and I went back out come ten, ten-thirty. Before I stepped outside, Duke said, "That woman, she don't take breaks, no?"

"No."

The reporters were there, and so were the crowds. And the woman was still standing, one hand pressed against the hot skin of the camper. Yes, she stood on the *hot* side, even though she was now free to move to the cooler side of the camper.

"Hey, you work here?" The moist-faced man in the madras plaid shirt held a notebook and pen in his hand. Second-string flunky from the local news, I supposed.

"No, I wash the dishes for my health—sorry, didn't sleep—"

"That's okay. You been here from the start, right? See that woman, in the jeans jacket? She some kind of nutcase?"

I marveled at the fellow's lack of verbal skills. I scraped my hand against my cheek; the beard stubble was faintly audible as I replied, "Just determined, I guess. Maybe she likes the heat," I added defensively. The reporter probably wouldn't think she was beautiful, either.

"I tried to talk to her, but no go. Can she talk?"

"Beats me." I wished the man would leave; his cologne was offensive, all fussy woody notes and overlaid thickly with musk. He shaded his eyes, and blathered on, "I been asking around, and nobody knows who she is, where she comes from, nothing. Think she's from the reservation?"

I repeated my theory about Indians being born wearing jewelry; when he asked if he could use it in his story, I told him to blow. The gods were smiling down on me; the guy actually left to go bother people in the crowd.

If the woman noticed the man pointing at her before, she either didn't care or cared too much to let it show. Her plastic water jug was sweating, a dark ring circled it on the sand. She didn't so much as swallow down spit.

I was swallowing for her as Duke called out the next break. She stayed in place, and when the break was over, she calmly put both hands on the white skin of the camper. The sun was shining full on the metal; against it, her hands looked brittle black.

I caught myself looking at her, even as I helped the waitresses who came in at midday to dish up the food. Duke's till swelled. Duke bit his lips until blood came and dried red-black—the woman still hadn't had a bite to eat, let alone a sip of water, or so he told me in a bile-scented whisper.

"Not that I got to worry, my boy, he's doin' fine. Pisses in a bucket so he don't go over the breaks. Sunburned, but that's not much, no?"

The woman didn't sweat, that was the hard part for me. No water goes in, none can come out. I told myself that she'd *have* to keel over sometime, no *body* can live like that.

When the film crew approached her, tried to distract her, I bolted from the diner and told them to fuck off, knowing full well that they'd have to scrape their tape or erase the sound.

That was around four o'clock; there were only nine people left, including the woman. And one guy was swaying in place, his face cheesy pale under a dotting of black dead pores. Thinking, *Let him fall*, I looked away from the guy and took a good, close look at the woman. With a stillness which reminded me of a jackrabbit before it leaps away from a sudden intruder, she focused on the glaring surface of the camper, ignoring me.

She was so beautiful. Up close, under the harsh sun, I saw that she was past middle age. Thin lines creased her skin, dozens of them. Her nose was big at the tip, and her ears were just beginning to get that "big" look associated with old age. But she was so *pure*, so utterly, *simply* perfect. Her colors were so true, against the brightness of the land and sky around her. I could draw her face, describe her veined hands with their chipped, striated nails in detail, but O'Keeffe had painted her. Oh, not a *portrait*, Georgia didn't stoop to such foolishness, bless her artist's soul.

"Cow's Skull: Red, White and Blue." From 1931, when O'Keeffe was still earning her flat-topped mountain with her brush. Simple cow's skull, and bands of color behind. I can't describe the denim woman any better. No human can.

A faint breeze ruffled her dark hair, and I wanted to cry. Her eyes were *dry*. The cracks in her lips were furrows. She was past sweating, past ever drinking again. I knew it. She was old jerky on million year old bones, and she had both hands pressed on that great stupid beast of a camper so flat even the wind couldn't squeeze itself in there, between her dry palms and the blistering hot paint.

I kicked the water jug, made it slosh. Clearing my throat, I asked, "Ma'am, you sure you don't want any water? It's allowed," I added, thinking that perhaps there had been a ghastly misunderstanding and the woman thought she *couldn't* drink.

She shook her head *no* and the earth moved under me. She was *aware*, of everything. Beyond us, people were laughing, eating, slurping down cold pop. Obscene.

I hunkered down near her, stared at her dusty worn boots with the frayed stitching. Those boots had walked many a mile of Georgia's land, and beyond. Her legs weren't even shaking, nor had she taken a secret pee while standing out there for over a day. Her jeans were worn, but clean. I smelled no sweat.

Sick at heart, I asked, "Lady, it isn't any of my business, but why are you doing this? Shit, you have no *chance.*" I cupped a hand around my mouth, to shield it from Duke, and whispered, "It's fixed, lady. *Fixed.* That slob in the bandana is the winner. It's his camper, until he gives it to Duke. And Duke's giving it to the dealer. You've proved your point . . . hell, lady, if it were my camper I'd *give* it to you."

I noticed that she didn't have a purse. Probably didn't have a driver's license, either. Not the way those boots were scuffed.

It was hard for her to blink. Not much fluid to ease the eyelids. So . . . I blinked for her. I swallowed, and spit, and cried. I *had* to. She was past doing it for herself.

Duke yelled, "Hey, lover-boy, we got customers." The crowd loved that, but the woman didn't seem to notice. Dusting off my pants, I got up and said, "It's true. You've got no chance. Don't let the whole thing turn into a freak show, 'kay? They don't deserve your dignity." I started to walk away, but after only three feet I couldn't resist a look back. I almost jumped when I saw that she'd turned her head my way.

The denim woman said but one word, and God bless her she said it to me. Spreading her fingers against the flesh of that metal beast, she said in a quiet, even voice, "*Mine.*"

Sunrise brings out the last metallic gleam of what had once been the bumpers, against the rusted terra cotta of the once-white sides the silvery gleam is all the brighter, all the more shiny, a compliment to the statue of white beside it, together they form Art . . .

Another night came and went, and still the woman did not move, did not eat, did not drink, did not eliminate. Only two men remained to stand alongside her camper, and Duke's trucker's knees shook under soggy denim. As if sensing that what was happening was no longer the stuff of pleasant news, the reporters crept away. By the third dawn, the crowd had thinned.

Duke didn't shave, didn't bathe. His eyes were dead marbles. He couldn't watch the woman, not after his trucker flopped over as the first rays of the sun hit him that last morning. The other man standing, a wiry Indian from the Taos reservation, was wild-eyed and sweating even before the sun grew hot.

The woman . . . What can I say? That someone should have pulled her away? That the reporters should have called the authorities, pulled the plug on the first and last "Stick Up Yer Dukes" contest? It was just too *late* for that, or for anything.

Her head was tilted forward, crown touching the camper. Her hair hid her face, and her already oversized jacket hid any motion her body may have been making under it. But she stood, God bless her, she stood straight and proud, hands pressed firmly on that damned, gorgeous, asinine camper. Cool night dew had washed the camper each evening, and the sides were pristine, spotless. And she stood on and on, with no break for three days and then some; nothing had detracted her from her goal. It was hers, *all* hers.

Maybe she scared the people. I know she spooked me. By the evening of the third day, the third day of hot July sun and cold desert night, she still stood, straight except for her bent head. And, looking back on it, maybe that alone should have told us, should have *warned* us.

But the Indian was so tough, he ran on cramping legs to make his pit stops, and ran back as if his life depended on it when his two minutes were almost up. And his partner in stubbornness was silent and still.

Oh Jesus we should have *known* . . . but Duke and I kept up the pretense, even though we only had a spare handful of onlookers who were perhaps too scared and awed to leave after witnessing what had to be a miracle.

On the fourth day, the Indian began to sway in place, a stalk straining against a killing wind. Duke was already ruined; the dealer had agreed to hold back payment until after the contest or three days, whichever came first. Duke admitted that to me on the fourth day, the day when he actually cried.

I mumbled something assuring, I can't remember what.

The Indian fell at six-thirty; I have to hand it to him, he kept both palms against the camper as he slid down. The virgin white paint bore two streaks of pus and blood.

The crowd—all five of them—made no sound, save for a simultaneous taking-in and letting-out of breath that blended in with the fitful wind, and the sounds of morning birdcalls.

And still the woman stood.

Duke, ever the after-the-fact gentleman, walked up to her and began to say, "Congratulations—" when he stopped, bent down low enough to see under her waving hair . . . and dropped in a faint on the sand. I ran over to him, checked to make sure he was still alive, then approached the woman.

Under that gently shifting curtain of hair, she wore a smile on her face—and then I noticed that her eyes were all white, whiter than bone, but just as dead . . .

I made a tiny, strained noise in the back of my throat when I saw that silent, eternal smile, and as I tried to get to my feet I knocked into her—but she didn't fall over.

She was cold and she was warm where the sun hit her, but she didn't move, not at all. She defied gravity, she defied a rigged contest, and she defied death . . . after a fashion. But her prize, that camper she had died for, it was hers. And

as the people standing near the diner figured out what had happened, and some woman screamed, I heard over and over in my head the woman's lone word:
    "*Mine.*"

Duke was right; he was ruined. He lost the diner, because no one wanted the camper. Not because there was anything wrong with it. There wasn't. Still, it just wasn't *right*, taking away a person's hard-won property.

And, besides, the denim woman wouldn't *let* anyone take it away. *She never fell down.* People were afraid to move her; after Duke lost the diner a couple of weeks later (our previously meager share of customers quit coming in), people chose to ignore the denim woman. People didn't even care when I moved back into the diner after it had been closed three months; if anyone owned the building, or if any bank had repossessed it, no one came to check.

And she was still standing there. Her denim was tattered, and her skin leather hard. The paint was starting to blister on the sides of the camper, but it was all right by me. By her too, for all I knew. The wind still blew her hair, and the sun shone down on it each morning, just as it had.

With the passing of the days, the weeks, the months and years, she and her camper have changed. The denim, the flesh, the hair are gone, and the sides of her camper no longer gleam in the sun. Yet, the changes are good, and they are beautiful, as beautiful as she and it were in life.

They change, and I watch, and I have never demeaned her with name, or a fabricated history. Enough that there was a mountain that work of art called woman wanted, and enough that she used the only medium available to her to earn that mountain.

A good many years ago another woman who earned a mountain drove through and walked these deserts, and when she died her ashes were scattered in the dust of a place called Ghost Ranch. The beauty that she once was has become part of a beauty that endures. Dust unto dust beauty unto beauty . . . but oh, Georgia girl, you have company now . . .

Originless, like the sun, the sand, the scattered stones, the shifting wind the two skeletal shapes are joined on the desert; one metal, one a small frame of bone, and the winds which blow through the joined ribs of steel and chalky bone whisper something, a word of earning, a word of eternal possession—a word for the few times when God grants mortals their mountain.

THE SWORDSMAN WHOSE NAME WAS NOT DEATH

Ellen Kushner

Ellen Kushner is the author of two highly acclaimed novels, *Swordspoint: A Melodrama of Manners* and *Thomas the Rhymer* (winner of the 1991 World Fantasy Award). She has also published adventure books for children, short fiction and poetry in numerous anthologies and magazines, and edited the anthology *Basilisk*. To music fans Kushner is best known as the host (and script writer) for the International Music Series of classical music concerts broadcast across the country on American Public Radio, as well as the host of a weekly worldbeat music show on WGBH Radio in Boston. Also a performer of tradional folk music, she is currently working in collaboration with British folk singer June Tabor. Kushner lives in Somerville, Massachusetts.

Fans of Kushner's dark and witty first novel, *Swordspoint*, will be glad to see Alec and his swordsman lover Richard St. Vier reappear in the following pages. Readers new to Kushner's imaginary city of Riverside are in for a treat. "The Swordsman Whose Name Was Not Death" comes from the September issue of *The Magazine of Fantasy and Science Fiction*.

—T.W.

After the fight, Richard was thirsty. He decided to leave the parrots alone for now. Parrots were supposed to be unlucky for swordsmen. In this case the curse seemed to have fallen on his opponent. Curious, he had asked the wounded man, "Did you slam into me on purpose?" People did sometimes, to provoke a fight with Richard St. Vier, the master swordsman who wouldn't take challenges from just anyone. But the wounded man only pressed his white lips together. The rest of him looked green. Some people just couldn't take the sight of their own blood.

Richard realized he'd seen him before, in a Riverside bar. He was a tough named Jim—or Tim—Something. Not much of a swordsman; the sort of man who made his way in the lawless Riverside district on bravado, and earned his living in the city doing cheapjack sword jobs for merchants aping the nobility in their hiring of swordsmen.

A man with a wreath of fresias hanging precariously over one ear came stumbling up. "Oh Tim," he said mournfully. "Oh Tim, I told you that fancy claret was too much for you." He caught hold of the wounded man's arm, began hauling him to his feet. As a matched set, Richard recognized them: they'd been the ritual guards in the wedding procession he'd seen passing through the market square earlier that afternoon.

"Sorry," the flower-decked drunk said to St. Vier. "Tim didn't mean to give you trouble, you understand?" Tim groaned. "He's not used to claret, see."

"Don't worry about it," Richard said charitably. No wonder Tim's swordplay had been less than linear.

Over their heads the caged parrots started squawking again. The parrot lady climbed down from the box where she'd escaped to get a better view of the fight. With St. Vier there to back her up, she shook her apron at the two ruffians to shoo them as if they were chickens escaped from the yard. The children who'd surrounded them, first to see if the quiet man was going to buy a parrot so they could see one taken down, and then to watch the fight, laughed and shrieked and made chicken noises after the disappearing toughs.

But people made way for Richard St. Vier as he headed in the direction of a stall selling drinks. The parrot lady collared one of the street kids, saying, "See that? You can tell your grandchildren you saw St. Vier fight right here." Oh, honestly, Richard thought, it hadn't been much of a fight; more like bumping into someone on the street.

He leaned on the wooden counter, trying to decide what he wanted.

"Hey," said a young voice at his elbow. "I'll buy you a drink."

He thought it was a woman, from the voice. Women sometimes tried to pick him up after fights. But he glanced down and saw a pug-faced boy looking at him through slitted eyes, the way kids do when they're trying to look older than they are. This one wasn't very old. "That was real good, the way you did that," the boy said. "I mean the quick double feint and all."

"Thank you," the swordsman answered courteously. His mother had raised him with good manners, and some old habits cling, even in the big city. Sometimes he could almost hear her say, *Just because you can kill people whenever you want to doesn't mean you have a license to be rude to anyone.* He let the boy buy them both some fancy drink made with raspberries. They drank silently, the boy peering over the rim of his cup. It was good; Richard ordered them both another.

"Yeah," the kid said. "I think you're the best there is, you know?"

"Thanks," said the swordsman. He put some coins on the counter.

"Yeah." The kid self-consciously fingered the sword at his own side. "I fight too. I had this idea, see—if you needed a servant or something."

"I don't," the swordsman said.

"Well, you know," the boy went on anyway. "I could, like, make up the fire in the morning. Carry water. Cook you stuff. Maybe when you practice, I could be—if you need somebody to help you out a little—"

"No," said St. Vier. "Thank you. There are plenty of schools for you to learn in."

"Yeah, but they're not . . ."

"I know. But that's the way it is."

He walked away from the bar, not wanting to hear any more argument. Behind him the kid started to follow, then fell back.

Across the square he met his friend Alec. "You've been in a fight," Alec said. "I missed it," he added, faintly accusing.

"Someone slammed into me by the parrot cages. It was funny." Richard smiled now at the memory. "I didn't see him coming, and for a moment I thought it was an earthquake! Swords were out before he could apologize—if he meant to apologize. He was drunk."

"You didn't kill him," Alec said, as if he'd heard the story already.

"Not in this part of town. That doesn't go down too well with the Watch here."

"I hope you weren't thinking of getting a parrot again."

Richard grinned, falling into step beside his tall friend. It was a familiar argument. "They're so decorative, Alec. And you could teach it to talk."

"Let some bird steal all my best lines? Anyhow, they eat worms. *I'm* not getting up to catch worms."

"They eat bread and fruit. I asked this time."

"Too expensive."

They were passing through the nice section of the city, headed down to the wharves. On the other side of the river was the district called Riverside, where the swordsman lived with sharpsters and criminals, beyond reach of the law. It would not have been a safe place for a man like Alec, who barely knew one end of a knife from another; but the swordsman St. Vier had made it clear what would happen to anyone who touched his friend. Riverside tolerated eccentrics. The tall scholar, with his student slouch and aristocratic accent, was becoming a known quantity along with the master swordsman.

"If you're feeling like throwing your money around," Alec persisted, "why don't you get us a servant? You need someone to polish your boots."

"I take good care of my boots," Richard said, stung in an area of competence. "*You're* the one who needs it."

"Yes," Alec happily agreed. "I do. Someone to go to the market for us, and keep visitors away, and start the fire in winter, and bring us breakfast in bed . . ."

"Decadent," St. Vier said. "You can go to the market yourself. And I keep 'visitors' away just fine. I don't understand why you think it would be fun to have some stranger living with us. If you wanted that sort of life, you should have—" He stopped before he could say the unforgivable. But Alec, in one of his sudden shifts of attitude, which veered like the wind over a small pond, finished cheerfully for him, "I should have stayed on the Hill with my rich relatives. But they never kill people—not out in the open where we can all enjoy it, anyway. You're so much more entertaining. . . ."

Richard's lips quirked downward, unsuccessfully hiding a smile. "Loved only for my sword," he said.

Alec said carefully, "If I were the sort of person who makes crude jokes, you would be very embarrassed now."

Richard, who was never embarrassed, said, "What a good thing you're not. What do you want for dinner?"

*   *   *

They went to Rosalie's, where they ate stew in the cool underground tavern and talked business with their friends. It was the usual hodgepodge of fact and rumor: A new swordsman had appeared across town claiming to be a foreign champion, but someone's cousin in service had recognized him as Lord Averil's old valet, with fencing lessons and a dyed mustache. . . . Hugo Seville had finally gotten so low as to take a job offing some noble's wife . . . or maybe he'd only been offered it, or someone wished he had.

Nobles with jobs for St. Vier sent their messages to Rosalie's. But today there was nothing. "Just some nervous jerk looking for an heiress."

"Aren't we all!"

"Sorry, Reg, this one's taken; run off with some swordsman."

"Anyone we know?"

"Naw . . . fairy-tale swordsman—they say all girls have run off with one, when it's really their father's clerk."

Big Missy, who worked the mattress trade at Glinley's, put her arm around Richard. "I could run off with a swordsman." Seated, he came up only to her bosom, which he leaned back into, smiling across to Alec, eyebrows raised a little provocatively.

Alec took the bait: "Careful," the tall scholar told her; "he bites."

"Oh?" Missy leered becomingly at him. "Don't *you*, pretty baby?"

Alec tried to hide a flush of pure delight. No one had ever called him "pretty baby" before, especially not women other people paid to get into.

"Of course I do," he said with all the brittle superciliousness he was master of. "Hard."

Missy released St. Vier, advancing on his tall young friend. "Oh *good* . . . ," she breathed huskily. "I like 'em rough." Her huge arms pointed like weather vanes into the rising wind. "Come to me lover."

The old-time crowd at Rosalie's was ecstatic. "Missy, don't leave me for that bag of bones!" "So long, then, Alec; let us know how it comes out!" "Try it, boy; you just might like it!"

Alec looked like he wanted to sink into the floor. He held his ground, but his hauteur, already badly applied, was slipping treacherously.

At the last minute, Richard took pity on him. "I saw a wedding today," he said to the room at large.

"Oh yeah," said Lucie; "we heard you killed one of the guards. Finally made them earn their pay, huh?"

"Thought you didn't *do* weddings, Master St. Vier." Sam Bonner looked around for approval of his wit. Everyone knew that St. Vier disdained guard work.

"I don't," Richard said. "This was after. And I didn't kill him. Tim somebody."

"No lie! Tim Porker? Half-grown mustache, big ears? Said he hurt himself falling down some stairs. Dirty liar."

"No weddings for Richard," Alec said. He'd regained his aplomb, but was still eyeing Missy warily from across the room. "He is morally opposed to the buying and selling of heiresses."

"No, I'm not. It's just not interesting work, being a wedding guard. It doesn't mean anything anymore, just rich people showing they can afford swordsmen to make their procession look pretty. It's no—"

"Challenge," Alec finished for him. "You know, we could set that to music, you say it so often, and hawk it on the street as a ballad. What a good thing for the rich that other swordsmen aren't too proud to take their money, or we'd never see an heiress safely bedded down. What's the reward offered for the runaway? Is there one? Or is she damaged goods already?"

"There's a reward for information. But you have to go Uptown to get it."

"I'm not above going Uptown," said Lucie haughtily; "I've been there before. But I don't know as I'd turn in a girl that's run away for love. . . ."

"Ohh," bawled Rosalie across the tavern; "is that what you call it?"

"Speaking of money," Alec said, rattling the dicebox, "is anyone interested in a small bet on whether I can roll multiples of three three times running?"

Richard got up to go. When Alec had drunk enough to become interested in mathematical odds, the evening's entertainment was over for him. St. Vier was not a gambling man.

The Riverside streets were dark, but St. Vier knew his way between the close-set houses, past the place where the broken gutter overflowed, around the potholes of pried-up cobbles, through the back alleys and home. His own lodgings were in a cul-de-sac off the main street; part of an old townhouse, a discarded veteran of grander days. Richard lived on the second story, in what had once been the music rooms.

On the ground floor, Marie's rooms were dark. He stopped before the front door: in the recessed entryway, there was a flash of white. Cautiously St. Vier drew his sword and advanced.

A small woman practically flung herself onto his blade. "Oh help!" she cried shrilly. "You must help me!"

"Back off," said St. Vier. It was too dark to see much but her shape. She was wearing a heavy cloak, and something about her was very young. "What's the matter?"

"I am desperate," she gasped. "I am in terrible danger. Only you can help me! My enemies are everywhere. You must hide me."

"You're drunk," said Richard, although her accent wasn't Riverside. "Go away before you get hurt."

The woman fell back against the door. "No, please. It means my life."

"You had better go home," Richard said. To speed her on her way, he said, "Do you need me to escort you somewhere? Or shall I hire you a torch?"

"No!" It sounded more annoyed than desperate, but quickly turned back to pleading: "I dare not go home. Please listen to me. I am—a Lady of Quality. My parents want to marry me to a man I hate—an old miser with bad breath and groping hands."

"That's too bad," Richard said politely, amused in spite of the inconvenience. "What do you want me to do about it? Do you want him killed?"

"Oh! Oh. No. Thank you. That is, I just need a place to stay. Until they stop looking for me."

Richard said, "Did you know there's a reward out for you?"

"There *is*?" she squeaked. "But—oh. How gratifying. How . . . like them."

"Come upstairs." St. Vier held the door open. "Mind the third step; it's broken. When Marie gets back, you can stay with her. She's a, she takes in customers, but I think propriety says you're better off with her than with me."

"But I'd *rather* stay with you, sir!"

In the pitch-black of the stairs, Richard halted. The girl almost stumbled into him. "No," St. Vier said. "If you're going to start that, you're not coming any farther."

"I didn't—" she squeaked, and began again: "That's not what I meant at all. Honestly."

Upstairs, he pushed open the door and lit a few candles. "Oh!" the girl gasped. "Is this—is this where you—"

"I practice in this room," he said. "The walls are wrecked. You can sit on that chaise, if you want—it's not as rickety as it looks." But the girl went over to the wall, touching the pockmarks where his practice sword had chipped holes in the old plaster. Her fingertips were gentle, almost reverent.

It was an old room, with traces of its former grandeur clinging about the edges in the form of gilded laurel-leaf molding and occasional pieces of cherub. The person who had last seen fresh paint there had long since turned to dust. The only efforts that its present occupants had made to decorate it were an expensive tapestry hung over the fireplace, and a couple of very detailed silver candlesticks, a few leather-bound books, and an enamel vase, scattered about the room in no discernible order.

"I'd offer you the bed," said Richard, "but it would annoy Alec. Just make yourself comfortable in here."

With the pleasantly light feeling of well-earned tiredness, the swordsman drifted into the room that held his big carven bed and his chests for clothes and swords, undoing the accoutrements of his trade: unbuckling the straps of his sword belt, slipping the knife sheath out of his vest. He paced the room, laying them down, unlacing and unpeeling his clothes, and got into bed. He was just falling asleep when he heard Alec's voice in the other room:

"Richard! You've found us a servant after all—how enterprising of you!"

"No—" he started to explain, and then thought he'd better get up to do it.

The girl was hunched up at the back of the chaise longue, looking awed and defenseless, her cloak still wrapped tight around her. Alec loomed over her, his usual untoward clutter of unruly limbs. Sometimes drinking made him graceful, but not tonight.

"Well," the girl was offering hopefully, "I can cook. Make up the fire. Carry water."

Richard thought, That's the second time I've heard that today. He started to say, "We couldn't ask a Lady of Quality—"

"Can you do boots?" Alec asked with interest.

"No," Richard stated firmly before she could say yes. "No servants."

"Well," Alec asked peevishly, "then what's she doing here? Not the obvious, I hope."

"Alec. Since when am I obvious?"

"Oh, never mind." Alec turned clumsily on his heel. "I'm going to bed. Have fun. See that there's hot shaving water in the morning."

Richard shrugged apologetically at the girl, who was staring after them in fascination. It was a shrug meaning, *Don't pay any attention to him*; but he couldn't help wondering if there would be hot water to shave with. Meanwhile, he meant to pay attention to Alec himself.

Alec woke up unable to tell where his limbs left off and Richard's began. He heard Richard say, "This is embarrassing. Don't move, Alec, all right?"

A third person was in the room with them, standing over the bed with a drawn sword. "How did you get in here?" Richard asked.

The pug-faced boy said, "It was easy. Don't you recognize me? My enemies are everywhere. I think I should, you know, get some kind of prize for that, don't you? I mean, I tricked you, didn't I?"

St. Vier eased himself onto his elbows. "Which are you, an heiress disguised as a snotty brat, or a brat disguised as an heiress?"

"Or," Alec couldn't resist adding, "a boy disguised as a girl disguised as a boy?"

"It doesn't matter," St. Vier said. "Your grip is too tight."

"Oh—sorry." Still keeping the sword's point on target, the kid eased his grip. "Sorry—I'll work on it. I knew I'd never get in like this. And girls are safe with you; everyone knows you don't like girls."

"Oh no," Richard protested, surprised. "I like girls very much."

"Richard," drawled Alec, whose left leg was beginning to cramp, "you're breaking my heart."

"But you like *him* better."

"Well, yes, I do."

"Jealous?" Alec snarled sweetly. "Please die and go away. I'm going to have the world's worst hangover if I don't get back to sleep soon."

Richard said, "I don't teach. I can't explain how I do what I do."

"Please," said the boy with the sword. "Can't you just take a look at me? Tell me if I'm any good. If you say I'm good, I'll know."

"What if I say you're not?"

"I'm good," the kid said stiffly. "I've got to be."

Richard slid out of bed, in one fluid motion regathering his limbs to himself. Alec admired that—like watching a chess expert solve a check in one simple move. Richard was naked, polished as a sculpture in the moonlight. In his hand was the sword that had been there from the start.

"Defend yourself," St. Vier said, and the boy fell back in cautious *garde*.

"If you kill him," said Alec, hands comfortably behind his head, "try not to make it one of the messy ones."

"I'm *not*—going to *kill*—him." With what was, for him, atypical flashiness, Richard punctuated each word with a blow of steel on steel. At his words the boy rallied, and returned the strokes. "Again," snapped the swordsman, still attacking. There was no kindness in his voice. "We're going to repeat the whole sequence, if you can remember it. Parry all my thrusts this time."

Sometimes the boy caught the quick-darting strokes, and sometimes his eye or his memory failed, and the blade stopped an inch from his heart, death suspended by the swordsman's will.

"New sequence," Richard rapped out. "Learn it."

They repeated the moves. Alec thought the boy was getting better, more assured. Then the swordsman struck hard on the boy's blade, and the sword flew out of his pupil's hand, clanging on the floor, rolled into a corner. "I told you your grip was too tight. Go get it."

The boy retrieved his sword, and the lesson resumed. Alec began to be bored by the endless repetition. "Your arm's getting tired," St. Vier observed. "Don't you practice with weights?"

"Don't have—any weights."

"Get some. No, don't stop. In a real fight, you can't stop."

"A real fight—wouldn't go on this long."

"How do you know? Been in any?"

"Yes. One.—*Two*."

"You won both," Richard said coldly, his arm never resting, his feet never still. "Makes you think you're a hero of the field. *Pay attention*." He rapped sharply on the blade. "Keep going." The boy countered with a fancy double riposte, changing the line of attack with the lightest pressure of his fingers. Richard St. Vier deflected the other's point, and brought his own clean past the boy's defenses.

The boy cried out at the light kiss of steel. But the swordsman did not stop the movements of the play. "It's a nick," he said. "Never mind the blood."

"Oh. But—"

"You wanted a lesson. Take it. All right, fine, you're scared now. You can't let it make a difference."

But it did make a difference. The boy's defense turned fierce, began to take on the air of desperate attack. Richard let it. They were fighting silently now, and really fighting, although the swordsman kept himself always from doing real damage. He began to play with the boy, leaving tiny openings just long enough to see if he would take advantage of them. The boy took about half—either his eye missed the others, or his body was too slow to act on them. Whatever he did, Richard parried his attacks, and kept him on the defensive.

"Now—" the swordsman said harshly—"Do you want to kill me, or just take me out?"

"I—don't know—"

"For death"—Richard's blade flew in—"straight to the heart. Always the heart."

The boy froze. His death was cold against his burning skin. Richard St. Vier dropped the point, raised it to resume the fight. The boy was sweating, panting, from fear as much as exertion. "A good touch—can be anywhere. As light as you like—or as deep."

The pug-nosed boy stood still. His nose was running. He still held his sword, while blood welled onto his skin and clothing from five different places.

"You're good," Richard St. Vier said, "but you can be better. Now get out of here."

"Richard, he's bleeding," Alec said quietly.

"I know he's bleeding. People do when they fight."

"It's night," Alec said, "in Riverside. People are out. You said you didn't want to kill him."

"Hand me that sheet." Sweat was cooling on Richard's body; he wrapped the linen around himself.

"There's brandy," Alec said. "I'll get it."

"I'm sorry I'm bleeding on your floor," the boy said. He wiped his nose with his sleeve. "I'm crying from shock, that's all. Not really crying."

He did not examine his own wounds. Alec did it for him, dabbing them with brandy. "You're remarkable," he told the boy. "I've been trying to get Richard to lose his temper forever." He handed the flask to St. Vier. "You can drink the rest."

Alec undid what the sword had left of the boy's jacket, and began pulling out the shirt. "It's a girl," he said abruptly, unsuspecting midwife to unnatural birth.

The girl said something rude. She'd stopped crying.

"So are you," Alec retorted. His hand darted into her breast pocket, pulled out the small book that had rested there, its soft leather cover warm and sweaty. He flipped it open, snapped it shut.

"Don't you know how to read?" the girl asked nastily.

"I don't read this kind of trash. *The Swordsman Whose Name Was Not Death*. My sister had it; they all do. It's about some Noble girl who comes home from a ball and finds a swordsman waiting in her room for her. He doesn't kill her; he fucks her instead. She loves it. The End."

"No—" she said, her face flushed—"You've got it wrong. You're stupid. You don't know anything about it."

"Hey," said Alec, "you're cute with your nose running, sweetheart—you know that?"

"You're stupid!" she said again fiercely. "*Stupid bastard.*" Harsh and precise, as though the words were new in her mouth. "What do you know about anything?"

"I know more than you think. I may not have your exceptional skill with steel, but I know about your other tricks. I know what works for you."

"Oh," she flared, "so it's come down to *that*." Furious, she was starting to cry again, against her will, furious about that, too. "The sword doesn't matter to you; the book doesn't matter—*that's* all you can understand. You don't know anything—anything at all!"

"Oh, don't I?" Alec breathed. His eyes were bright, a spot of color high on each cheek. "You think I don't know all about it? With my sister, it was horses—both real and imaginary." He mastered himself enough to assume his usual sneer, passionless and obnoxious. "Mares in the stable, golden stallions in the orchard. She told me their names. I used to eat the apples she picked for them, to make it seem more real. I know about it," he said bitterly. "My sister's magic horses were powerful; she rode them across sea and land; she loved them and gave them names. But in the end they failed her, didn't they? In the end they took her nowhere, brought her nothing at all."

Richard sat on the edge of the bed, brandy forgotten in his hand. Alec never spoke of his family. Richard didn't know he had a sister. He listened.

"My sister was married—to a man chosen for her, a man she didn't like, a man she was afraid of. Those goddamned horses waited for her in the orchard, waited all night for her to come to them. They would have borne her anywhere, for love of her—but she never came . . . and then it was her wedding day." Alec lifted the book high, slammed it against the far wall. "I know all about it."

The girl was looking at Alec, not at her broken book. "And where were you?" she said. "Where were you when this forced marriage took place—waiting in the orchard with them? Oh, I know, too—You took them and you escaped." Holding herself stiffly against her cuts, she bent over, picked up the book, smoothed it back into shape. "You don't know. You don't know at all. And you don't want to. Either of you."

"Alec," Richard said, "come to bed."

"Thank you for the lesson," she said to the swordsman. "I'll remember."

"It wouldn't have made a difference," he told her. "You'll have to find someone else. That's the way it is. Be careful, though."

"Thank you," she said again. "I will be careful, now that there's something to be careful for. You meant what you said, didn't you?"

"Yes," Richard said. "I don't usually get that angry. I meant it."

"Good." She turned in the doorway, asked in the same flat, cold tone, "What's your sister's name?"

Alec was still where he'd been when he threw the book, standing stiff and pale. Richard knew that his reaction, when it hit, would be violent.

"I said, what's her name?"

Alec told her.

"Good. I'm going to find her. I'll give her this"—the book, now fingerprinted with dried blood—"and your love."

She stopped again, opened the book, and read: " 'I was a girl until tonight. I am a woman now.' That's how it ends. But you never read it, so you'll never know what comes in between." She smiled a steel-biting smile. "I have, and I do. I'll be all right out there, won't I?"

"Come to bed, Alec," Richard said again; "you're shaking."

THE RAGTHORN

Robert Holdstock and Garry Kilworth

Two of England's finest writers have collaborated on the following dark and splendid tale, which is inspired by the original Anglo-Saxon text of the Old English poem "The Dream of the Rood."

Garry Kilworth has published thirteen novels for adults, four for children, and numerous excellent stories collected in *The Songbirds of Pain, In the Hollow of the Deep-Sea Wave*, and most recently, *In the Country of Tattooed Men*. Kilworth's semipermanent home is in rural Essex, but he has traveled and lived abroad for much of his life and currently resides in Hong Kong.

Robert Holdstock is the author of several novels and collections, including *The Bone People, Lavondyss*, and *Mythago Wood*, which received the World Fantasy Award in 1988 and was aptly hailed by Alan Garner as "a new expression of the British genius for true fantasy." Holdstock was born in rural Kent and now makes his home in London.

"The Ragthorn" is reprinted from the pages of my co-editor's anthology, *A Whisper of Blood*.

—T.W.

Quhen thow art ded and laid in layme
And Raggtre rut thi ribbis ar
Thow art than brocht to thi lang hayme
Than grett agayn warldis dignite

Unknown (c. A.D. 1360)

September 11, 1978

I am placing this entry at the beginning of my edited journal for reasons that will become apparent. Time is very short for me now, and there are matters that must be briefly explained. I am back at the cottage in Scarfell, the stone house in which I was born and which has always been at the centre of my life. I have been here for some years and am finally ready to do what must be done. Edward Pottifer is with me—good God-fearing man that he is—and it will be he who closes this journal and he alone who will decide upon its fate.

The moment is *very* close. I have acquired a set of dental pincers with which to perform the final part of the ritual. Pottifer has seen into my mouth—an experience that clearly disturbed him, no doubt because of its intimacy—and he knows which teeth to pull and which to leave. After the inspection he muttered that he is more used to pulling rose thorns from fingers than molars from jaws. He asked me if he might keep the teeth as souvenirs and I said he could, but he should look after them carefully.

I cannot pretend that I am not frightened. I have edited my life's journal severely. I have taken out all that does not relate forcefully to my discovery. Many journeys to foreign parts have gone, and many accounts of irrelevant discovery and strange encounters. Not even Pottifer will know where they are. I leave for immediate posterity only this bare account in Pottifer's creased and soil-engrimed hands.

Judge my work by this account, or judge my sanity. When this deed is done I shall be certain of one thing: that in whatever form I shall have become, I will be beyond judgement. I shall walk away, leaving all behind, and not look back.

Time had been kinder to Scarfell Cottage than perhaps it deserves. It has been, for much of its existence, an abandoned place, a neglected shrine. When I finally came back to it, years after my mother's death, its wood had rotted, its interior decoration had decayed, but thick cob walls—two feet of good Yorkshire stone—had proved too strong for the ferocious northern winters. The house had been renovated with difficulty, but the precious stone lintel over the doorway—the beginning of my quest—was thankfully intact and undamaged. The house of my childhood became habitable again, twenty years after I left it.

From the tiny study where I write, the view into Scardale is as eerie and entrancing as it ever was. The valley is a sinuous, silent place, its steep slopes broken by monolithic black rocks and stunted trees that grow from the green at sharp, wind-shaped angles. There are no inhabited dwellings here, no fields. The only movement is the grey flow of cloud shadow and the flash of sunlight on the thin stream. In the far distance, remote at the end of the valley, the tower of a church: a place for which I have no use.

And of course—all this is seen through the branches of the tree. The *ragthorn*. The terrible tree.

It grows fast. Each day it seems to strain from the earth, stretching an inch or two into the storm skies, struggling for life. Its roots have spread farther across the grounds around the cottage and taken a firmer grip upon the dry stone wall at the garden's end; to this it seems to clasp as it teeters over the steep drop to the dale. There is such menace in its aspect, as if it is stretching its hard knotty form, ready to snatch at any passing life.

It guards the entrance to the valley. It is a rare tree, neither hawthorn nor blackthorn, but some ancient form of plant life, with a history more exotic than the Glastonbury thorn. Even its roots have thorns upon them. The roots themselves spread below the ground like those of a wild rose, throwing out suckers in a circle about the twisted bole: a thousand spikes forming a palisade around the trunk and thrusting inches above the earth. I have seen no bird try to feed upon the tiny berries that it produces in mid-winter. In the summer its bark has a terrible smell. To go close to the tree induces dizziness. Its thorns when broken curl up after a few minutes, like tiny live creatures.

How I hated that tree as a child. How my mother hated it! We were only stopped from destroying it by the enormity of the task, since such had been tried before and it was found that every single piece of root had to be removed from the ground to prevent it growing again. And soon after leaving Scarfell Cottage as a young man, I became glad of the tree's defensive nature—I began to long to see the thorn again.

To begin with however, it was the stone lintel that fascinated me: the strange slab over the doorway, with its faint alien markings. I first traced those markings when I was ten years old and imagined that I could discern letters among the symbols. When I was seventeen and returned to the cottage from boarding school for a holiday, I realised for the first time that they were cuneiform, the wedge-shaped characters that depict the ancient languages of Sumeria and Babylon.

I tried to translate them, but of course failed. It certainly occurred to me to approach the British Museum—after all my great-uncle Alexander had worked at that noble institution for many years—but those were full days and I was an impatient youth. My study was demanding. I was to be an archaeologist, following in the family tradition, and no doubt I imagined that there would be time enough in the future to discover the meaning of the Sumerian script.

At that time all I knew of my ancestor William Alexander was that he was a great-uncle, on my father's side, who had built the cottage in the dales in 1880, immediately on his return from the Middle East. Although the details of what he had been doing in the Bible lands were obscure, I knew he had spent many years there, and also that he had been shot in the back during an Arab uprising: a wound he survived.

There is a story that my mother told me, handed down through the generations. The details are smudged by the retelling, but it relates how William Alexander came to Scarfell, leading a great black-and-white Shire horse hauling a brewer's dray. On the dray were the stones with which he would begin to build Scarfell Cottage, on land he had acquired. He walked straight through the village with not a word to a soul, led the horse and cart slowly up the steep hill to the valley edge, took a spade, dug a pit, and filled it with dry wood. He set light to the wood and kept the fire going for four days. In all that time he remained in the open, either staring out across the valley or tending the fire. He didn't eat. He didn't drink. There was no tree there at the time. When at last the fire died down he paid every man in the village a few shillings to help with the building of a small stone cottage. And one of the stones to be set—he told them—was a family tombstone whose faded letters could still be seen on its faces. This was placed as the lintel to the door.

Tombstone indeed! The letters on that grey-faced obelisk had been marked there four thousand years before, and it had a value beyond measure. Lashed to the deck of a cargo vessel, carried across the Mediterranean, through the Straits of Gibraltar, the Bay of Biscay, the obelisk had arrived in England (coincidentally) at the time Cleopatra's Needle was expected. The confused Customs officers had waved it through, believing it to be a companion piece to the much larger Egyptian obelisk.

This then is all I need to say, save to add that three years after the building of the cottage the locals noticed a tree of unfamiliar shape growing from the pit where the fire had burned that night. The growth of the tree had been phenomenally fast; it had appeared in the few short months of one winter.

The rest of the account is extracted from my journal. Judge me upon it. Judge my sanity. There are many questions to which there seem no answers. Who, or what, guided me to previously hidden information during the years? My uncle's ghost perhaps? The ghost of something considerably more ancient? Or even the spirit of the tree itself, though what would be its motive? There are too many coincidences for there *not* to have been some divine, some spiritual presence at work. But who? And perhaps the answer is: *no person at all,* rather a force of destiny for which we have no words in our language.

August 7, 1958

I have been at Tel Enkish for four days now, frustrated by Professor Legmeshu's refusal to allow me onto the site of the excavation. It is clear, however, that a truly astonishing discovery is emerging.

Tel Enkish seems to be the site of an early Sumerian temple to a four-part god, or man-god, with many of the attributes of Gilgamesh. From the small town of Miktah, a mile away, little can be seen but a permanent dust cloud over the low, dry hills, and the steady stream of battered trucks and carts that plough back and forth between the dump site and the excavation itself. All the signs are that there is something very big going on. Iraqi officials are here in number. Also the children of the region have flocked to Tel Enkish from miles around the site. They beg, they pester, they demand work on what is now known as "The Great Tomb." They are unaware that as a visitor I have no authority myself.

August 9, 1958

I have at last been to the site. I have seen the shrine that William Alexander uncovered eighty years ago. I have never in my life been so affected by the presence of the monumental past in the corroded ruins of the present.

My frantic messages were at last acknowledged, this morning at eight. Leg-meshu, it seems, has only just made the connection between me and William Alexander. At midday, a dust-covered British Wolesley came for me. The middle-aged woman who drove it turned out to be Legmeshu's American wife. She asked me, "Have you brought the stone?" and looked around my small room as if I might have been hiding it below the wardrobe or something. She was angry when I explained that I had brought only my transcription of the glyphs on the weathered rock. She quizzed as to where the stone was now located, and I refused to answer.

"Come with me," she snapped, and led the way to the car. We drove through the jostling crowds in silence. Over the nearest rise we passed through barbed-wire fencing and checkpoints not unlike those to be found in army camps. Iraqi guards peered into the vehicle, but on seeing Dr. Legmeshu waved us on. There was a sense of great agitation in the air. Everyone seemed tense and excited.

The site itself is in a crater of the tel, the mound on which the temple had been built and over which later generations of buildings in mud had been added. In the fashion of the notorious archaeologist Woolley, the top layer of the tel had been blasted away to expose the remains of the civilisation that had flourished there in the third millennium B.C. It had not been Legmeshu who had been so destructive, but my ancestor, Alexander.

As I feasted my eyes on the beautifully preserved building, she waited impatiently. She told me that the temple was from the period associated with Gilgamesh the King. It was made of refined mud-brick, and had been covered with a weatherproof skin of burnt brick set in bitumen.

"Where had the Alexander stone been set?" I asked, and she pointed to the centre of the ruins. "They had created a megalith structure at the very heart of the temple. The stone that your relative stole was the keystone. This is why you *must* return it. We cannot allow . . ." She broke off and looked at me angrily. If she had been about to make a threat, she had thought better of it.

Her attitude led me to expect the worst from the male Dr. Legmeshu, but I am delighted to say that he could not have been more charming. I found him in the tent, poring over a set of inscriptions that had been traced out on paper. He was leaning on a large slab of rock and when I looked more closely I saw that it was identical to the lintel at Scarfell Cottage.

He was fascinated by the route I had taken in discovering him. The Iraqi government had made formal representation to the British government, five years before, for the return of the "Tel Enkish Stone" to its natural site. Unlike Elgin Marbles, which the British Museum regarded as their right to keep safe, no official in London had ever heard of the Tel Enkish Stone.

The argument had waged within those same "scenes" for years, and had finally been taken up by the press. A picture of one of the other Tel Enkish stones had caught my attention, along with the headline: WHERE IS THE ALEXANDER STONE? some keen reporter had obviously done his research to the point where he had made the connection.

The museum by that time had established that the stone had been removed by Professor Alexander, who they understood had retired to an unknown location after returning from the Middle East in the late 1890s. The Iraqi government believed none of this of course, thinking that the British Museum had the stone hidden, and relations were soured between the two countries for some years afterwards.

I have told Legmeshu that the stone lies in a quarry, the location of which I shall make known to the museum on my return to the United Kingdom. He has accepted this.

The story of those events, eighty years before, is difficult to ascertain. Alexander had worked on the site with Legmeshu's own great-grandfather. The two men had been close friends, and had made the astonishing discovery of the megaliths at the heart of the mud-brick temple together. There had been eight stones arranged in a circle, standing vertically. Four stones had lain across their tops. A mini Stonehenge. And in the centre, four altars, three to known gods, one . . . one that defied explanation.

"No trace of those altars remain," Legmeshu told me over tea. "But my great-grandfather's notes are quite clear. There were three altars to the three phases of the Hunter God: the youth, the king, the wise ancient. But to whom the fourth altar was dedicated . . . ?" He shrugged. "A goddess perhaps? Or the king reborn? My relative left only speculation."

There had been a difference of opinion during that first excavation; a fight; and a death. Apart from what I have written here, the record is blank, save for a folk memory from the inhabitants of Scarfell concerning a tree that grew one winter— a black and evil-looking thorn.

Legmeshu snatched my copy of the Scarfell inscription. He ran his eyes over the signs, the cuneiform script that seemed as familiar to him as was my own alphabet to me. "This is not all of it," he said after a long while. I had realised some time before that the fourth surface of the stone, flush with the brickwork between door and ceiling, had characters on it like the other three. They could not be read of course without demolishing the cottage, which I had not been prepared to do at the time. I told Legmeshu that the fourth side had been exposed over a long period to the toxic air of a northern English factory town and the characters had been all but erased.

He seemed beside himself with fury for a moment. "What a destructive and stupid thing to do, to leave the stone in such a place. It *must* be returned! It *must* be rescued!"

"Of course," I said. "I intend to do so on my return to England. I have only just located the stone myself, after years of studying my great-uncle's notes . . ."

He seemed mollified by this. I have no intention of giving up the whereabouts of the stone however. I lie without shame. I feel obsessively protective towards the stone . . . towards the cottage, and yes, in my adulthood, towards the tree. Somehow they are linked through my great-uncle and to remove or destroy any one of them would be like smashing the Rosetta Stone with a sledge hammer.

Legmeshu seemed to come to a sudden decision, saying, "Follow me," and led me down to the site itself. We came at last to the wide tarpaulin that covered the centre of the temple.

It was an area of mystical energy. I could sense the presence of invisible power. It had an immediate and lasting effect on me. I began to shake. Even as I write— hours after the experience—my hand is unsteady. As I stood there I was in the far past. Fingers of time brushed through my hair; the breath of the dead blew gently against my face. Sounds, smells, touches . . . and an overwhelming, awe-inspiring *presence*—silently watching me.

Legmeshu seemed entirely unaware of these things.

His voice brought me back to the present. He was pointing to the small concrete markers that now showed where the stones had stood, in a circle about twenty feet in diameter. On the floor, clearly outlined in the dry mud, were the twisting impressions of roots.

"It was open to the sky," Legmeshu said. "In the centre of the stones a tree had been grown, quite a large tree by the looks of it. The four altars were oriented east–west. We think there may have been a mud-filled pit below the trunk of the tree, to support its growth."

"And the purpose of the place?" I asked. Legmeshu smiled at me and passed me a small book. I opened it and saw that he had written out the translations from each stone. The particle content of the Alexander stone had just been added and I studied the stilted English. Almost immediately I was aware of what I was reading.

Legmeshu's breathless, "It includes much of the original epic that has been lost, and earlier forms of the rest. It is a momentous find!" was quite unnecessary. I was lost in words:

> And behold the waters of the Flood were gone. The mud covered the land as a cloak which stifles. Gilgamesh waited on a hill and saw Utnapishtim, Boatman of the Flood, rise from the plain of mud and beckon. "Gilgamesh I shall reveal to you a secret thing, a mystery of the gods. Hark my words. There is a tree that grows from fire under the water, under the mud. It has a thorn prick, a rose blade on every twig. It will wound your hands, but if you can grasp it, then you will be holding that which can restore youth to a man. Its name is Old Man Who Would Be Young."
> "How deep is the mud?" Lord Gilgamesh asked. "Seven days and seven nights," answered the Boatman, and Gilgamesh drew breath and swam into the blackness.
> When he had cut Old Man Who Would Be Young he swam again to the surface of the mud. Utnapishtim sent a woman with golden tresses to clean and annoint the body of the kingly man. And Gilgamesh possessed her for seven days and seven nights in a fury of triumph, and not for one moment did he let go of Old Man Who Would Be Young. And when the child was born, Utnapishtim gave it at once to Old Man Who Would Be Young, so that the first berry appeared on the branches. "Now it will grow," the Boatman said. "And I have told you of the temple you must build and the manner of annointing the flesh."
> Now Gilgamesh departed for high-walled Uruk, and when the thorns of Old Man Who Would Be Young pricked his thumbs he was increased of power. And he denied all the old men their touch of the tree, so that their youth was denied them. But when the time came, Gilgamesh alone would place Old Man Who Would Be Young in the proper way, and lie with it in an embrace of seven days and seven nights.

Here then, carved in stone, was a version of the immortality tale of The Epic of Gilgamesh that was quite unlike the story from the clay tablets. And it was an *earlier* version, Legmeshu was quite adamant, a cruder form, with hints of the magic ritual that the later version appears to have lost.

"The stone came from Egypt," Legmeshu said. "This place functioned as a ritual site of enormous importance for perhaps two hundred years. The secret plant seems to have been a thorn, which would account for the pattern of roots on the mud there. I believe this place celebrated immortality. And the fourth altar may be representational: the risen life. So we have Youth, King, Magus, and again Youth."

Legmeshu spoke, but his words became just sounds. He seemed more interested in archaeology than in the astonishing *literary* discovery. To him, legends are only part of the story of the people; they are one more tool, or one more part of the machine that is archaeology. He wants the words intact, as much as he wants the stone intact, but I realise now that he has not been affected by the *meaning* of the words, neither their literal interpretation nor what they imply about culture and ritual in the earliest of civilised times.

Quite clearly my great-uncle was! What other reason could there have been for his dragging away one of the stones—the key stone—and raising, too, a strange and gloomy tree. Did he find the seed of a familiar thorn that in the time of Babylon was known as Old Man Who Would Be Young?

The key! It tells of the growth from fire of a tree. It tells of the child who must be given to the growing sapling. And what other salient information lies on the hidden face of the lintel, awaiting discovery?

August 10, 1958

I can stay here no longer. I wish to return to the site at Tel Enkish but I have received word that the Iraqis are unhappy that I "own" the stone. The time has come to slip away from this country. For a while, anyway. I leave so much unfinished; I leave so many questions unanswered.

June 14, 1965

I had almost come to believe that my supernatural encounter at Tel Enkish was no more than imagination; whimsy. The intervening years have been very barren and very frustrating. (Legmeshu has finally ceased to hound me for the stone, but I still watch my back whenever I am in the Near or Middle East.) Now, something has turned up and I have flown to Cairo from Jerusalem (via Cyprus).

It began two months ago. I was in Jerusalem, initiating the project for which Cambridge has at last agreed to fund me: namely, to identify and discover that true symbolic and mythological meaning of the type of tree that provided the Crown of Thorns at Christ's execution. (A briar wreath, a coif of knotted thistles, a halo of thorn tree twigs? From what species of shrub or tree?) The reference to the "resurrecting thorn" in the work of the unknown writer of Gilgamesh has haunted me for years. Of all the world's great resurrections, Christ's is the most famous. I am increasingly obsessed with the true manner of that raising, and the Crown of Thorns is a teasing symbol, a provocative invitation that came to me while staring at the ragthorn through the window of Scarfell Cottage.

One afternoon, in the university library canteen, a noisy crowded place, I overheard a conversation.

The two men were behind me, speaking in awkward English, obviously a second language to them both. One of them was an Israeli diplomat I recognised; the other was an Arab. I guessed from the dialect of his occasional exclamations in his first language, that he was Egyptian. Their conversation was hushed, but I could hear it quite clearly, and soon became intrigued.

The Egyptian said, "Some diving men, with the tanks on the back—not professional men—tourist. They are swim near Pharos Island, where sunk the old light warnings for ships . . ."

The Israeli took a moment to work out what was being said.

"Light warnings? Lighthouse. The Pharos lighthouse?"

The Egyptian said excitedly, "Yes, yes! By ancient city Alexandria. Yes. Find some very old jar. Very old. Thousands years. No sea get into jar. Papers inside. Old papers. Old before coming of Roman peoples. Many more jars in sea, so I am told."

Their voices dropped even lower and I found it was hard to catch what was being said. All I could determine was that the Israeli government are interested in any scroll that relates to its own culture. Naturally, they are prepared to pay a great deal of money and the Egyptian was busy lining his own pockets by bringing this information to the attention of the Israeli Ministry of Culture.

The thought occurred to me immediately: Might there be something in the jars that relates to the *thorn?*

It has been years since Tel Enkish, but once again I have a feeling of fate unfolding: of being watched by the silent past. I am convinced there is something in Cairo for *me.*

June 19, 1965

My contact here is Abdullah Rashid. He is well known to the professors at the University in Jerusalem and has "supplied" objects and information to them for some years.

Professor Berenstein in Jerusalem is a friend of mine and kindly arranged the surreptitious meeting with this man who is in a position to inspect and copy the contents of the jars. This morning, after "checking my credentials," Abdullah came to my hotel. Over breakfast he explained that five of the ancient jars had already been taken from the water and two of them opened in controlled conditions. He is cagey about this knowledge of the contents, but has remarked, cryptically, that he believes there *is* a reference to some thorn tree amongst the first papers to be removed and examined.

The discovery is, as I knew, being kept under tight wraps, and Abdullah was surprised and impressed that I managed to hear about the parchments. It is the intention of the Egyptians to translate the documents and plays themselves, and take full credit before releasing the finds to the world at large. Hence, people like Abdullah are making a great deal of money leaking facsimilies of the parchments.

This is what Abdullah has told me: The discovery so far is of several documents that survived the fire in the Library of Alexandria two thousand years ago. The belief is that before the rioting crowd managed to penetrate the library, strip its shelves, and set the place alight, a number of soldiers loaded saddlebags with whatever the librarians could select to save, and rode from the city to a galley, which pulled offshore. Here, forty glazed amphorae were filled with manuscripts and sealed with wax, linen, more wax, and finally corked with clay. For some reason the jars were thrown overboard near the lighthouse. Perhaps the crew suddenly found themselves in danger and unable to set sail? Nothing more is known of this. Certainly the intention would have been to recover the vessels, once the danger was past, but it must be surmised that there were no survivors who knew of the whereabouts of the jars, or even that they existed. Seawater rotted the rope nets holding them together and then currents carried some of the jars out into the Mediterranean, and stretched them in a line towards Cyprus.

June 20, 1965

Today we saw the recovery operation at work. The shores of Alexandria are always bustling with small craft, mostly feluccas similar to that in which we serenely approached the island. We blended well, since I had dressed in local fashion. It was calm on the blue waters, but the sun bore down on us with unrelenting pressure and its effects have made me quite dizzy. We sailed to Pharos Island, to the northern point, and watched a large rusty dredger assist a team of divers in bringing up the precious artifacts.

Eventually we received our reward. We saw one of the amphorae winched from the water. It was long and slender, encrusted with limpets and barnacles, and dripped a particularly silky, dark green weed, which hung from the bullet-blunt jar like a beard. A crab of gigantic size dangled from this furze by one claw, as if reluctant to release the treasure that had for so long been the property of the ocean.

I asked Abdullah where the amphora would now be taken. He told me, "To the museum." There it would be opened in controlled conditions.

"Is there no chance I could witness the opening?"

He shook his head and laughed. He told me that only certain government ministers and professors would be there. And some technical assistants, who were highly trusted.

Again the laughter as he prodded his chest.

"People like me," he said.

Abdullah's work would be to photograph the opening of the jars, at each stage, then any contents, page by page. Facsimilies would be made from the photographs.

"These facsimilies would be for sale?"

"Not officially of course"—he smiled—"but all things are negotiable, yes?"

June 23, 1965

Abdullah was here, but the news is not good. He has been unable to obtain copies yet, not just for me but for others, as he must not be caught compromising his position at the museum. He has photographed several manuscripts so far.

It is a mixed bag, apparently, and includes two pieces by Plato, a play by Platus called *Servius Pompus*, and twenty pages of a manuscript by Julius Caesar, entitled *His Secret Dialogues with the Priests of Gaul on the Nature of their Magic and Rituals*.

The final piece of parchment contains an even more exquisite original hand: that (it is believed) of Homer himself. It is a fragment of his *Iliad*, and consists of half of the Death of Hector, all the Funeral of Patroclus, and a third or so of the Funeral Games. It is a manifestly ancient hand, and the Egyptians are quite convinced that it *is* the writings of Homer, adding weight to the argument that Homer was one man, and not a collective of writers.

All of this would be enough to excite me beyond tolerance, but Abdullah, aware of the nature of my search, has now told me something that holds me breathless in anticipation: that the *Iliad* fragment contains reference to a "blood thorn."

That is the facsimile I want. I have told him that no matter what else he obtains, he *must* get that fragment of unknown Homer. My enthusiasm has no doubt put up the price of those lines of verse, but I am sure I am being skillfully teased into such a state by Abdullah. He could probably produce the goods now, but is jigging the price up with his procrastination, pretending he is being watched too closely. I can play the game too, and have let him see me packing my suitcase, and looking anxiously at my diary.

October 1, 1965
I am back at the cottage in Scarfell, the place of my birth. I have come here because I *feel* I have been summoned home. I have been at Cambridge for most of the summer, but the voice of something dark, something omnipresent, has called me here . . . home to the cottage, to the wild valley, to the tree.

I have translated much that Abdullah was able to sell me. And indeed, the documents make fascinating reading.

The "new" play by Titus Maccius Plautus (200 B.C.) is hilarious. *Servius Pompus* is completely typical, dealing with a common legionary in Fabius' army who is convinced he is of noble birth, and treats his comrades like dirt. His ultimate discovery that he is slave-born earns him a permanent position: on a cart, collecting the dung left behind by Hannibal's elephants.

The fragment of Caesar is most atypical however and very strange, detailing as it does the legendary and magic matter of the Celtic inhabitants of Europe, and there is a fascinating revelation concerning the coded language that existed within the arrangement of the stones on the landscape.

All that is for another paper. For the moment, it is the Homeric verse that excites me, for in this fragment of the epic cycle of the Greeks on the shores of Asia Minor there is a reference to the resurrection that confirms me in two beliefs: that there has been a deliberate effort to obliterate this knowledge from the world, and that someone—or some *thing*—is guiding my search to build again that knowledge from the clues I am gradually discovering.

The autumn day is dark as I write this, with huge columns of thunderous cloud drifting over Scarfell from the west. I am working by lamplight. I am chilled to the bone. The great rugged face of the fell surrounds me, and the solitary thorn— black against the darkness—seems to lean towards me through the small leaded windows that show its sinister form. That tree has known eternity. I sense now that it has seen me learn of Achilles, and *his* unsure use of the ancient magic.

Here then is my crude translation of the passage of the *Iliad* that is relevant. It is from the "Funeral of Patroclus," Achilles' great friend. While Achilles sulked in his tent, during the siege of Troy, Patroclus donned the man's armour and fought in his place, only to be killed by the Trojan hero Hector. After Patroclus's body had been burned on the funeral pyre . . .

. . . then they gathered the noble dust of their comrade
And with ashes from the fire filled a golden vase.
And the vase was double-sealed with fat
Then placed reverently in the hut of the gallant Patroclus,
And those who saw it there laid soft linens
Over the gold tomb, as a mark of respect.
Now the divine Achilles fashioned the barrow for his friend.
A ring of stone was laid upon the earth of the shore
And clear spring water was sprinkled amongst the stones.
Then rich dark soil was carried from the fields and piled upon the stones.
Until it was higher than the storm-soaked cedar.
Prince Achilles walked about the barrow of Patroclus
And wept upon the fertile ground which held his friend
While Nestor, son of Neleus, was sent a Dream from Heaven.
The Dream Messenger came from Zeus, the Cloud-compeller
Whose words reached the ears of the excellent Achilles
Who pulled the blood thorn from the wall of Troy
And placed the thorn tree on the tear-soaked mound.
In its branches he placed the sword and shield of Patroclus
And in so doing pierced his own flesh with the thorn,
Offering lifeblood as his blood for life.

Here, the fragment returns to the story content as we know it: the funeral games for Patroclus and the final reckoning between Achilles and the Trojan champion, Hector. My translation leaves a great deal to be desired. The *metre* of Homer's verse in the original seems very crude, not at all as we have become used to it, and perhaps later generations than Homer have "cleaned up" the old man's act, as it were. But there is power in the words, and an odd obsession with "earth." When Homer wrote them, I am sure he was powered by the magic of Zeus, a magic that Achilles had attempted to invoke.

Poor Achilles. I believe I understand his error. The whole ritual of the burial, of course, was intended to *bring Patroclus back to life!*

His mistake was in following the normal Mycenaean custom of burning the body of his friend upon the pyre. Patroclus never rose again. He couldn't. It is apparent to me that Zeus tried to warn him *not* to follow custom, *not* to place the body of his friend upon the burning faggots, because several lines previously (as the body of Patroclus was laid upon the pyre), Homer had written:

Now in the honouring of Patroclus there was unkind delay,
No fire would take upon the wood below the hero.
Then the excellent Achilles walked about the pyre and mourned anew
But through his grief-eyes he saw the answer to the fire
And raised his arms and prayed to all the winds
And offered splendid sacrifice to the two gods
Boreas from the North and Zephyr of the Western Gale.
He made them rich libations from a golden cup

And implored them blow among the kindling
So that the honouring fire might grow in strength and honoured ash be
   made of brave Patroclus.

No fire would take and Achilles failed to see the chance that his god was offering him. Zeus was keeping the wind from the flames, but seeing his warnings go unheeded, he turned away from Achilles in a passing pique.

Nothing else in this fragment seems to relate to the subject of the thorn, or its means of operation. Abdullah has promised to send me more material when and if he can, but since nothing has arrived for several months, already I suspect that the knowledge of the lost amphorae and their precious contents is being suppressed.

What can I learn from Homer? That there was a genuine belief in the power of the *thorn* to raise the dead? That some "pricking of the flesh" is important? Achilles pricks his arm: his blood for life. But this is not the only life hinted at in the two references I have so far found: a child was given to the tree, according to the Gilgamesh fragment.

I feel the darkness closing in.

March 11, 1970

The stone lintel is *bound* to the tree! Bonded to it. Tied! It is a frightening thought. This morning I tried to dislodge the stone from its position, scraping at the cement that binds it to the rest of the coarse stone of the cottage. I discovered that the ragthorn's roots are *in the house itself!* It is clear to me now that my great-uncle had a far better understanding of the importance of the tree and stone than I have so far imagined. Why did he drag back the Gilgamesh stone to England? Why did he embed it in the way he did: as part of a door, part of a house? Is the "doorway" symbolic? A divide through which one passes from one world to another? Obviously the hidden side of the lintel contains words of great importance, words that he decided had to be concealed from the curious eyes of his contemporaries.

The stone is not a tomb's marker, it is the tomb itself: the tomb of lost knowledge!

All this has occurred to me recently and this morning I began to extract the lintel from its resting place. I used proper tools and a great deal of brute strength. Imagine my surprise when I discovered that I was scraping through *plant tissue!* A thorny root stabbed out at me, then hung there, quivering and slowly curling. It has frightened me deeply. The whole lintel is covered and protected—on its hidden face—by an extension from the ragthorn that grows at the end of the garden, a menacing and evil presence. I could sever the root to the cottage, but I feel a chill of fear on each occasion that I ponder this possibility. Even now, as I write, I feel I am drawing a terrible darkness closer.

The tree has come to inhabit the house itself. There is a thick tendril of dark root running along the wall in the kitchen.

The chimney stack is webbed with tree roots. I lifted a floorboard and a thin tendril of the ragthorn jerked away from the sudden light. The floor is covered with tiny feelers.

Webbed in tree. And all centering on the stone lintel, the ancient monolith.

No wonder I feel watched. Was it my uncle's doing? Or was he merely obeying the instructions of a more sinister authority?

September 22, 1970

I have received a message from the British Museum, forwarded from my rooms in Cambridge by my research assistant, David Wilkins. He alone knows where I live. He is an able student, a keen researcher, and I have confided in him to a considerable degree. On my behalf he is searching the dusty archives of Cambridge for other references to the "ragthorn" or to resurrection. I am convinced that many such references must exist, and that it is a part of my new purpose to elicit them, and to use them.

"Has the museum any record of William Alexander, or any knowledge of the whereabouts of his papers?" I had asked in 1967, without result.

The new letter reads quite simply thus: "We have remembered your earlier enquiry concerning the effects, records, papers, and letters of William Alexander and are pleased to inform you that a small string-bound, wax-sealed file has been discovered, a fragment of his known effects that has clearly been overlooked during the process of reinstatement of said effects to the rightful owner. We would be most pleased to offer you the opportunity to break the seal on this file, and to review the contents, prior to discussing a mutually suitable arrangement for their final disposal."

September 25, 1970

I wonder now whether or not William Alexander *intended* this file to be discovered. I would like to think that in his aging bones, he felt someone coming behind, a soul-mate, a follower, who would become as entranced with his work as he was himself. Considering what I believe now, however, I think it more likely that he intended at some time to recover the file in person, and perhaps *after* most people believed him gone.

Today I have spoken to my great-uncle. Or rather . . . he has spoken to me. He is as close to me now, as I sit here in my room in the Bonnington Hotel writing these notes, as close to me as if he were here in person. He has left a fragment of his work, a teasing, thrilling fragment.

What did he do with the rest of his papers? I wonder.

The man was born in 1832. There is no record of his death. The year is 1970. It is autumn. I tremble to think of this, but I wonder if a man, born before the reign of Victoria had begun, is still walking abroad, still soaking up the rain and the wind and the sun of the England that birthed him, or of the Bible lands that so captured his heart.

This is a summary, then, of the day's events and discoveries:

This morning I entered the labyrinthine heart of the British Museum: those deep dark corridors and rooms that have been burrowed into the bruised London clay below the building. I was conducted to a small book-lined room, heavy with history, heady with the smell of parchment and manuscript. A man of sober demeanor and middle age received us. He had been working under a single pool of desk lamplight, imprisoned by it like some frugal monk. On my arrival he favoured me with room lighting, so that his desk was no longer a captive of the lamp. He was, despite his dour looks, a cheerful soul, and was as delighted by his discovery of William Alexander as I would become of my discovery of his remaining notes. Alexander, it seems, was an old rogue. He had a formidable reputation. He was known as an eccentric man, of extravagant tastes, and frontiersman's manners. He had shocked the denizens of the nineteenth-century archaeological establishment with his rough Yorkshire speech, his outlandish manners. If it were not for the fact that he produced priceless historical artifacts from lands closed to most Europeans, he might have been ostracized by society from the outset.

He had, it seemed, collected his papers and belongings from his private offices in the deep recesses of the museum, on the 15th March, 1878. His departure had been quite typical of the man. He had placed his files and books upon a handcart and hauled it, clattering, up the levels, dragging it through the reading room disturbing everyone present, through the wide foyer, and out into the day, having caused more than one jowl in the establishment to quiver with indignation. He used to tell my mother, with a hearty chuckle, that if the Victorians were good at one thing, it was displaying indignation.

On passing the Chief Curator on the steps outside, he reached into a bag, drew out a vase of exquisite Egyptian design, and passed it over. When opened, within the neck of the previously sealed vase was a perfectly preserved red rose, its scent a fleeting moment of an ancient summer day, instantly lost as the flower became dust.

Not on the cart that day, however, were thirty sheets of paper, loosely bound between two stiff pieces of cardboard (marked with his initials) and tied with string. He had placed a red wax seal across each of the round edges of the sheaf. On being handed the package, I slit the seals and cut through the formidable string knot with my penknife: shades of an Alexander who lived long before William.

Most of the sheets in the folio are blank. I shall summarise the puzzling contents of the rest.

> *Sheet 21.* This consists of the single word: REVELATION!
> *Sheet 22.* This is written in a more precise hand, but clearly William Alexander's. It reads: "The Bard too! The knowledge passed down as far as ELZBTH 1st. Who censored it? Who changed the text? Two references are clear, but there must be more. There *must* be. Too sweet a myth for WAS to ignore. P———has discovered lost folio, but spirited it away." (Two sheets covered with numbers and letters: a code of some sort?)
> *Sheet 25.* This is headed "The Dream of the Rood." It is one of two sheets that clearly relates to the "thorn" and "resurrection." The margin of this sheet is peppered with words from the Anglo-Saxon language, but the main body of Alexander's text reads like this: "*Sigebeam.*" This means Victory tree? The runic character "thorn" is used more prolifically in the alliterative half-lines than seems usual around this point in the poem's body. Then the word *swefna*: "of dreams." Then there are the words *syllicre treow*: "wonderful tree." This phrase is enclosed by the rune

"thorn." A dream tree, a tree of victory (victory over death?) *surrounded and protected by thorns.*

"Yes." *The tree of everlasting life.* The tree is the *rood*, of course, the symbol of Christ's cross. But surely "tree" is meant in another sense too? A literal sense. Then, to confirm this, the phrase in the poem "adorned with coverings." Perhaps this means more than it says? Perhaps strips of material? *Rags?*

"I am certain that the message here is the *ragthorn tree.*"

This is the only note on *The Dream of the Rood* in my great-uncle's file, but it proves that *some* albeit cryptic references to the ragthorn remain extant, since this text can be read in any school edition of the poem.

It is clear that an abiding and darker myth concerning the return to life of a soul "buried beneath a tree" has been imposed upon the Christianity of the author (who probably wrote the "Rood" in the eighth century). But was the ragthorn at that time a tangible shrub that could be plucked, planted, and left to resurrect the corpse of the thane or lord buried below? Or was it already a myth by that time in Old England?

The last sheet contains two fascinating pieces of Middle English poetry, dating from the late 1300's, I would think, as one of them is the last stanza of Chaucer's famous poem *The House of Fame*, believed to be unfinished. It is clear that the poem *was* completed, but the last few lines removed, either by Chaucer himself, or by orders of his patron:

Alexander, who must have discovered the parchment, though it is not part of his file, had this to say:

"It is Chaucer's script, no doubt about it. The parchment page is faded, the ink has spread, but I am certain this is the original. Other editions omit the final four lines. Here they are, following the *known* ending:

> *Atte laste y saugh a man,*
> *Which that y (nevene) nat ne kan*
> *But he seemed for to be*
> *A man of great auctorite* . . . (here the known MS ends)
> *Loo! how straungely spak thys wyght*
> *How* ragethorn *trees sal sithe the night,*
> *How deeth sal fro the body slynke*
> *When doun besyde the rote it synke.*

To put those last few lines into more familiar language: Lo, this man spoke of strange things, of ragthorn trees scything away the darkness and how death will creep away from the body if it is buried beneath the ragthorn's roots.

Finally, a single stanza from an English religious lyric, which my uncle found at the same time:

> *Upon thys mount I fand a tree*
> *Wat gif agayne my soule to me!*

Wen erthe toc erthe of mortual note
And ssulen wormes feste in thi throte
My nayle-stanged soule will sterte upriss
On ssulen wormes and erthe to piss.

(On this hill I found a tree
which gave me back my (soul)—
While the world might take note of mortality
And sullen worms feast on *your* throat,
My thorn-pierced body will rise up
To treat the worms and the world with contempt.

This, then, concludes my listing of the sheets bound into what I shall call "The Alexander Folio." How much further in his quest my great-uncle managed to journey is hard to know, but he certainly discovered more than have I. What fire must have burned within him. What a fever of discovery!

How death shall from the body slink when down beside the root it sinks . . . .

That tree. That terrifying tree. It is the route to and from the Underworld for a man who is reluctant to die, who wishes to remain . . . *immortal.*

October 13, 1971

I am being directed, or drawn, towards new discoveries. It is my great-uncle? Or the tree? If it is William Alexander, then he must be dead, for the spirit of a living man would not work this way. It is only spirits that have been freed from mortality that can guide the living.

This leaves me wondering about whether Alexander attempted immortality—and *failed.*

I suspect that if I searched the grounds of Scarfell Cottage carefully, or dug below the walls, into the space below the tree, I believe I would find his bones. Is he here, urging me to finish what he could not, whispering to me: Do it right, do it right? Or . . . am I influenced by something else, some other spiritual presence?

I can only conclude that if not he, then the ragthorn is my guide. This would beg the question: Why? Why would the thorn wish me to find the clues to its secret power over life and death, its unnatural, no, *supernatural,* force? Unless—and my heart races at the thought—*unless I am its chosen disciple!* Gilgamesh was chosen. No doubt others after him, with Alexander the last. It is possible to fail. Of course it is possible to fail. But I intend to understand, thoroughly, what is expected of me, and succeed where Alexander did not.

A low mist, thick and blunt-nosed, winds through the valley like a soft sentient beast, sniffing amongst the mosses and rocks and leaving damp crags and stunted hawthorns dripping with moisture. Its restlessness finds its way into my spirit. I find writing difficult. There is a feeling on the land of permanent, mist-ridden dusk. I pace the house, constantly going outside to stare at the ragthorn, perched like some black-armoured mythical bird upon the crumbling drystone wall.

Even inside the house, my eyes continually stray to the lintel, to the evidence of the tree that has it in its tendrilous grasp. My work lies scattered around the house. I am possessed by a desire to leave the place. But I cannot. I have not heard from Wilkins for months. It is a year since I have opened the Alexander folio. Something *must* happen soon. Something must happen.

April 10, 1972

The tree has grown. For the first time in years the ragthorn shows signs of growth, twig tips extending, roots inching farther across the garden, extending below the house itself. It is coming into bud, and it seems to shake, even when there are no winds.

September 17, 1972

An odd fragment has come to light as I worked in Cambridge, searching for the Shakespearean folio owned and hidden by Lionel Pervis (the P———of the Alexander folio), who I have discovered was my uncle's contemporary. The fragment is a further piece of Middle English, perhaps once part of a collection of Sacred Songs. This fragment, a faded vellum sheet pressed between the pages of a copy of the second edition of *Paradise Lost*, may once have belonged to Milton himself. Certainly, this edition of his book has annotations in his own hand, still clear despite his blindness. One is tempted to wonder whether the dying man was clutching at a truth whose greatness had only been hinted at. He had perhaps discovered this obscure and frightening stanza from a hymn and kept it as an odd symbol of hope and resurrection.

> *Quben thow art ded and laid in layme*
> *And Raggtre rut this ribbis ar*
> *Thow art than brocht to thi lang hayme*
> *Than grett agayn warldis dignite.*

> When you are dead and buried in lime
> And the roots of the Ragthorn form your ribs
> You will then be brought back to your home
> To greet the world again with dignity.

November 22, 1974

I have at last found a fragment of the lost folio of *Hamlet*, but not from my searches at Cambridge! It was here all the time, in the Alexander papers. One of the apparently blank sheets is not blank at all. I would not have discovered the fact but for a coincidence of dropping the sheets onto the floor and gathering them by the dim light of the hurricane lamp. The shadowy signs of word-impressions caught my attention immediately. The marks were shallow, the merest denting of the heavy paper from the rapidly scrawled writing on the now-lost top sheet. But the impressions were enough for me to use a fine powder of lead, and a wash of light oil, to bring out the words fully.

Clearly, Alexander was privileged to hear the relevant passage from *Hamlet*, from the original prompt copy of the play, and wrote them down. Lionel Pervis would not part with the whole folio itself, and perhaps it is now destroyed.

(Even as I write these words I feel apprehensive. I am certain, those years ago, that I carefully examined these blank sheets and found nothing. I know I tested for secret ink. I *know* that. I would surely have noticed signs of overwriting.)

The fragment of *Hamlet* makes fascinating reading, and tells me much about the method: the actual means by which the process of burial and rebirth must be achieved.

Here is Alexander's account of the discovery, and his copy of the scene that some hand, later, had eliminated from the versions of Shakespeare's play that have come down to us:

> Pervis is a difficult man to talk to. His career is in ruins and he is an embittered man. He has confirmed certain thoughts, however. Added valuable insight. In summary: The most reliable text of *Hamlet* is to be found in the Second Quarto. However, no editor would dismiss entirely the text that appears in the First Folio, though scholars have proved that the First Folio was derived from a corrupt copy of the prompt-book, used at the Globe Theatre.
>
> Pervis' brother is a barrister of repute, in Lincoln's Inn Fields. Was present during the discovery of a hidden room in the cellars of his firm's building, which had been walled up and forgotten. A mountain of documents was discovered in that room, among them several pages of a manuscript of great interest to Shakespearean scholars. Pervis (the barrister) sent these to his brother, in order for the Shakespearean actor to assess their worth in academic terms and asked what monetary value they might have. Pervis (the actor) claimed never to have received the papers and was taken to court by his brother and, though he could not be convicted on the evidence, was widely believed to have stolen the manuscript. It ruined his life and his career.
>
> Pervis later claimed to have been "given" a copy of the manuscript, though it is fairly certain he sold the original to a private collector who will have it now, in some safe in Zurich. Pervis would not release the copy to anyone, but insisted that the new version must first be heard from him, playing Hamlet's ghost at the Old Vic. Victorian society was scandalised and he was refused and demands were made upon him, which sent him into retreat, somewhere in Wales. It was there I managed to track him down. He was by that time a bitter old man. He knew of me, of my reputation for scandalising the society that he believed had dealt him meanly, and with a certain amount of gold was persuaded to part with lines of the text, including reference to the burial place of Hamlet's father, beneath the roots of an *exotic thorn tree*.

(*From Act I, Scene V*)
Ghost: *Thus was I sleeping by a brother's hand,*
  Of life, of crown, of queen at once dispatched,

Cut off even in the blossoms of my sin,
Unhouseled, disappointed, unaneled,
No reck'ning made, but sent to my account
With all my imperfections on my head.
Aye, quarters to the four winds pointed right
Below the 'bracing ragthorne's needled limbs,
Yet by ironic touch my flesh immured,
Base metal traitoring this but perfect tomb.
O, horrible! O, horrible! Most horrible!
If thou has nature in thee bear it not,
Let not the royal bed of Denmark be
A couch for luxury and damned incest . . .
But howsoever thou pursues this act,
Taint not thy mind, nor let thy soul contrive
Against thy mother aught—leave her to heaven,
And to those thorns that in her bosom lodge
To prick and sting her.

Fare thee well at once,

The glow-worm shows the matin to be near
And 'gins to pale his uneffectual fire,
To where my bones lie compassed.

Thus to thee

Adieu, adieu, adieu, remember me.

(The ghost vanishes)

I have read this speech fifty times now, and still the words thrill me. Since William Alexander had seen this verse, he must surely have seen the clear indications of *method*, the method of burial beneath the ragthorn's "root vault."

"*Quarters to the four winds pointed right . . .*" The body positioned so that it formed a star, confirmed by that later line: "*where my bones lie compassed.*" Obviously not a *set* of compasses, because the angles on such instruments are variable. It has to be the four main points of the magnetic compass: north, south, east, and west.

Then also that warning, not to take metal into the grave.

Yet by ironic *touch my flesh immured,*
Base metal *traitoring this but perfect tomb . . .*"

But for the metal, the tomb would have been perfect. (For the raising of the dead?) *Ironic touch.* That play on *irony* and the metal *iron.* Perhaps he had been buried in full armour, or an amulet, whatever, the metal touched his body and imprisoned it within the roots of the ragthorn. The miracle could not take place. Metal had negated the power of wood, a living substance.

I am this much closer to an understanding.

March 18, 1976

My great-uncle is buried beneath the ragthorn. I say this without evidence of bones, or even a final letter from the strange man himself, but I sense it as surely as I feel the tree feeds from the stone.

This afternoon, with a trusted local man called Edward Pottifer, I excavated into the hillside beyond the drystone wall, where the valley slope begins to drop away steeply towards the stream. The ragthorn's roots have reached here too, but it soon became clear where Alexander himself had dug below the tree to make his tomb. We cleared the turf and found that he had blocked the passage with rubble, capping it with two slabs of slate. He must have had help, someone like Pottifer perhaps, because he could not have back-filled the passage himself. I suppose there is no record of his death because he knew it had to be that way. If a man took his body and buried it beneath that tree, it would have been done in the dead of night, in the utmost secrecy, for the church, the locals, and the authorities would surely have forbidden such a burial.

He knew the method, and yet I feel that he failed.

He is still there. I'm afraid to dig into the ragthorn root mass. I am afraid of what I shall find. If he failed, what did he do wrong? The question has enormous importance for me, since I have no wish to repeat his failure.

I am ill. The illness will worsen.

April 12, 1976

I have been studying the evidence, and the manner and nature of the burial is becoming clearer. At Cambridge, Wilkins has sought out all the different meanings of the various key words and I am increasingly convinced that I have a firm knowledge of just *how* the body must be placed in the encompassing, protective cage of roots. The orientation of the body must be north–south, with the arms raised as in a cross to the east and west. There must be no metal upon or within it. The armour is stripped away, the weapons are removed. Metal is counter to the notion of resurrection, and thus I have left instructions that my back teeth are to be removed when I am dead.

May 1, 1976

In preparation for that *time* when it comes, I have now—with the help of Pottifer—dug a passage several feet long into the side of the hill, below the ragthorn. I have finally taken the same route as that followed by William Alexander, but a hundred years has compacted the earth well, and it is no easy task. That we are on the right track is confirmed only by the mixture of slate that appears in the soil, and the fact that the thorn *allows* our excavation to continue in this direction. We press on, striking up, away from the bedrock. We did attempt other passages at first, but with every foot in the *wrong* direction there was a battle to be made with the protecting thorny roots. They snagged at our flesh and pulled at our hair, until we had to abandon those first diggings. The tree knows where it wants to put me.

May 3, 1976

I have found the remains of an infant! Thank God Pottifer was not with me at the time, for it would have shaken him badly. There is a reference in the passage from Gilgamesh: *"and when the child was born, Utnapishtim gave it at once to Old Man Who Would Be Young, and the first berry appeared on the branches."* William Alexander planted this particular shoot or cutting of the tree and would have needed a similar offering. The thought horrifies me, that some mother in a nearby village, or some passing gypsy family, lost their newborn child one Victorian night.

May 10, 1976

Pottifer has made the breakthrough. He came scuttling out of the hole, his face black with earth, his fingers bloody from his encounters with sharp slate and wild thorns.

"Bones!" he cried. "Bones, Professor. I've found bones. Dear God in heaven, I touched one."

He stared at his hand as if it might have been tainted. I crawled into the passage and edged along to the place where he had found my great-uncle. The earth here was looser. The cage of roots was behind me and I could feel into what seemed to be a soft soil. It was possible to work my hands through and touch the dismembered bones and the ribs of the man who lay there. Every bone was wrapped around with the fibrous wormlike rootlets of the tree.

I became very disturbed. I was invading a place that should have been inviolate, and felt that I was an unwelcome intruder into this earthy domain.

My great-uncle had failed to attain resurrection. He had done something wrong and now, I swear, the tree has his soul. It had sucked his spirit from his body to strengthen itself, perhaps to extend its root system, its power over the surrounding landscape? Was this the price of failure, to become the spiritual slave of the tree? Or am I just full of wild imaginings?

Whatever, the embrace of those roots is not a loving one, but one of possession. It is a cruel grip. The tree had hung on to the ash urn of Patroclus because the bones must not be burned. It had not released the flesh of Hamlet's father because there was metal on the body. But *I* am determined to triumph.

When I touched my ancestor's skull, I drew back sharply, then probed again. There were no teeth in the jaws. The skeleton was also oriented correctly, north, south, east, and west.

It was as I withdrew my probing hand from the soft-filled earth chamber that my fingers touched something cold and hard. I noted where it lay, that it was at the top of the leg, close to the spine, and clutched it and drew it out.

Edward Pottifer stared at the iron ball in my hand. "That's from an old gun," he said, and at once I remembered the story of my great-uncle's skirmish in the Middle East. Yes. He had been shot and close to death. They had operated on him in the field, but then transported him, delirious, to a hospital in Cyprus, where he recovered. He must have been under the impression that the bullet was removed from his body at that first operation. Of course, his back would have pained him at times, but old wounds do that, without iron in them. That must have been it, for he surely wouldn't have taken the chance, not after finding the method in *Hamlet*.

I did not mean to laugh. It was not disrespect, but relief. He had carried that iron ball into the grave with him. He had removed his teeth, perhaps gold-filled, but not the bullet.

I spoke carefully and succinctly to Edward Pottifer. I told him my teeth were to be removed at death. That my body was to be stripped and *no* metal, not even a cross around my neck, was to be buried with me. My body would be a cross. I marked clearly where my head was to be placed, and how my arms should be raised to the sides. "I will give you a compass. There must not be the slightest deviation."

He stared at me for a long time, his young face showing the anguish he felt. "When do you expect that might be, sir?" he asked me. I assured him that it would not be immediately, but that I was in my fifties now, and a very ill man. I told him to come every day to the house, to make sure I was still alive, and to become familiar with me, and less afraid of me. And of course, I would pay him well for his services. Work was not easy to find in the dale, and the temptations of this offer were too strong for him: I have my gravedigger, and I know he can be trusted.

December 24, 1976

As I write this I am experiencing a sense of profound awe. Young Wilkins is here, and he is frightened and shocked. He arrived at the cottage last night, an hour or so before I was ready to retire. I had not expected him. He had travelled from London that afternoon, and had decided not to telephone me from the station. I understand his reasons for coming without forewarning.

I wonder what it must have felt like for him to be picking through the decaying fragments of several old parchments—brought to Cambridge by Abdullah Rashid, who subsequently vanished!—separating by tweezers and pallet knife those shards of some ancient writer's records that showed any legible writing at all; how it must have felt to be sorting and searching, eyes feasting upon the forgotten words . . . and then to find John the Divine himself!

The writing is fragmentary. The state of ruination of the scrolls is appalling. The Arab traders had already cut each precious document into forty pieces, thinking that by so doing they would increase forty-fold the value of their find. And they were struck by the Hand of Calamity as surely, as certainly, as if Jehovah himself had taken control of their fate. All of them are now imprisoned. Abdullah Rashid is now an exile (perhaps even dead?). Yet he was compelled to come to England, to seek me out . . . to bring his last "gift" (he asked for nothing in return) before disappearing into the night.

I was fated to discover these parchments.

It is the last reference of the ragthorn that I shall discover. No more is needed. It is a fragment that has given me *courage*.

At last I understand my great-uncle's reference to REVELATION! He had heard of the lost passage from Revelations of St. John the Divine. Perhaps he saw them? It was enough for him too. Revelation! Triumph!

Oddly, the references to resurrection are not what has frightened Wilkins. If he is afraid it is because he feels that too many of his beliefs are being threatened. He has been sobered by the encounter. But he saw the words "thorn" and "rag" and has brought to me my final, most conclusive proof that there is indeed a lost and forgotten mechanism for the resurrection of the dead, nature's alchemy, nature's embrace, a technique that defies science. No scientist will accept the revivification of the flesh under the influence of thorn, and root, and cold clammy earth. Why should they? But it happened! It has been recorded throughout history; it had begun, perhaps, in ancient Sumeria. There have been deliberate attempts to lose, to deny the fact . . . folios have been scratched out, poems obliterated, classics rewritten . . . the words of the ancients have been edited dutifully, perhaps by frightened servants not of God, but of *dogma* that preaches only the resurrection of the *soul* . . .

Oh, the irony! Oh, the pleasure at what St. John the Divine has told me.

It was all there for us to see, all the symbols, all the truths. The wooden cross, which He himself fashioned in His carpenter's shop, ready for the moment of His thricefold death, drowned, stabbed, and hanged on the tree.

The Crown of Thorns, His mastery over the forest.

The immortal wood, the tree of life, the regenerating forest—of course it can shelter and protect the moral flesh. There is in the tree a symbol, a reality too powerful for monks with quill pens to dare to fight, to challenge. So they cut it out, they *excised* it. In this way cutting out the soul of John, they cut out the heart from the past.

"He that dies by the wood shall live by the wood."

Perhaps I have the original copy of the parchment, the *only* copy remaining? It was found in a jar, in the hills of Turkestan, and had come into the possession of Abdullah . . . and had done so because it was *meant* to find its way into my hands.

For now I shall record in the journal only part of what St. John said. It is from Chapter 10 of the Revelations. It might have preceded verse 3. It is my great hope. It has confirmed my faith in the rightness of what I shall achieve. A miracle occurred in the house of Lazarus.

> *And I looked into the Light, and Lo, I saw Him command a thorn tree to spring from the roof of the house of Lazarus. And the tree had seven branches and on each branch there were seven times seven thorns. And below the house seven roots formed a cradle around the dead man, and raised him up so that again his face was in the light.*
>
> *So cometh the power of the Lord into all living things.*
>
> *And again He cried: That ye might rise anew and laugh in the face of Death, and blow the dust from thy lungs in the eyes of Death,* so that ye can look on Hell's face *and scorn the fires and rage upon the flames and* rise thee up.
>
> *And Lo, I saw how the thorn withered and died and the Angel of the Lord flew from its dust.*
>
> *And He cried out in the voice of the Immortal King:*

The Lord is in all things and He is in the One Tree.
He that dies by the wood shall live by the wood.
He that dies by the thorn shall live again by the thorn.

April 15, 1978
Pottifer was here. I sent him to the tree, to begin to clear the chamber. The pain in my chest is greater than I can bear sometimes. I must refuse the sensible remedy of moving to London, to be closer to the hospital that can relieve such things, and extend my life, even though they cannot cure me.

Pottifer is very calm. We have kept the secret from the village and not even his family knows. He has managed to clear the root chamber whilst keeping the failed bones of my ancestor undisturbed below a thin layer of soil. As long as I am within that quivering cage of thorns I shall succeed. I shall live again.

There is a great danger, however. I believe now that the tree took William Alexander, body and soul, for its own. Perhaps that is its exacted compensation for the failure of its disciples, to possess *all* that remains, not just the flesh, but the spirit also?

I *know* I have it right, and I can depend on Pottifer, completely, just as my great-uncle must have depended on such a man. Pottifer is devoted to me, and obeys me implicitly.

September 11, 1978 (extract)
The moment is very close. I have now acquired a set of dental pincers with which to perform the final part of the ritual. Pottifer has seen into my mouth and knows which teeth to pull.

September 20, 1978
Pottifer is with me. I am certainly going. How vigorously the body clings to life, even when the mind is urging it to relax in peace. There is no longer any pain. Perhaps the closeness of death banishes such mortal agonies. I can hardly move, and writing is now an effort of will. This will be the final entry in my journal. Pottifer is very sad. I admire him. I have come to like him very much. His great concern is to get my body into the chamber before the *rigor* of death stiffens my limbs. I have told him to relax. He has plenty of time. Even so, he need wait only a few hours for the rigor to pass. I have thought of everything. I have missed no point, no subtlety. When I am gone, Pottifer will end this journal and wait for one year and one day before returning to Scarfell Cottage. These papers, I am sure, will not be there. They will be in my own hands. If they *are* still in evidence, Pottifer is to send them to young Wilkins, but I am absolutely certain that I will be here to decide their fate, just as I have decided my own.

Adieu, or rather *au revoir.*

September 21
This is Pottifer. The docter told me to rite this when he was gone. I berried him as he told me to, and no dificulties. He said there must be no mistakes and spoke on the tree saying it sucked men dry of there souls who make mistakes. His

last words to me were Pottifer I must face Hell and look on its face like Saint John tells. He seemed very fearfull. I give him a kiss and said a prayre. He shouted out in pain. You do not understand I must first look on Hells face he shouted you must berry me face down.

I said to him, you are a good man docter, and you shall *not* face Hell. You shall face Heaven as you diserve. Saint John does not need your penance. Do not be fearful of Hell. You are to good and if you come back I shall be your good friend and welcome you straight.

Then he died. His fists were clenched

He is in the earth now and all that I have is his teeth, God bless him. I wanted to put a cross but the thorns have grown to much and there is green on tree and I do not like to medle to much since there is more growth and very fast. No one has seen the tree so green and florished for a long wile not since that time in the last centry so the tales go.

P.S.

This is Pottifer agen. I have got some thing more to say. Some thing odd has hapened. It is more that one year and one day. The docter is still in the ground. I was in the pub and a man came in and asked for a drink. He said he was the royal poet. I think he said his name was John Betcherman. He had been walking near Scarfell and had seen the tree. He had felt some thing very strange about the place he said. A strong vision of death. Someone screaming. He was upset. He asked about the cottage but I said nothing. He wrote a poem down and left it on the table. He said there I have exercised this terrible place and you have this and be done with it. Then he left. Here is the poem. It makes me feel sad to read it.

> *On a hill in highland regions*
> *Stands an aged, thorny tree*
> *Roots that riot, run in legions*
> *Through the scattered scrub and scree:*
> *Boughs that lap and lock and lace*
> *Choke the sunlight from that place.*
>
> *Deep below its tangled traces*
> *Rots the corpse of one unknown*
> *Gripped by roots whose gnarled embraces*
> *Crush the skull and crack the bone.*
> *Needled fingers clutch the crown*
> *Late, too late to turn facedown.*

THE SMELL
Patrick McGrath

McGrath (pronounced McGraw) was born in England but lives in New York City. He is the author of two novels, *The Grotesque* and *Spider,* and of a collection of short stories, *Blood and Water and Other Tales.* He co-edited, with Bradford Morrow, the anthology *The New Gothic,* from which this story comes.

McGrath writes baroque, usually (but not always) nonsupernatural tales of horror. His writing is often witty and nasty, his narrators are frequently unreliable—such as in "The Smell."

—E.D.

There is a room in my house that for reasons of my own I have always kept locked. It is a downstairs room and was once, I imagine, a dining room, though I use it now to store boxes containing items pertaining to my work. It has a large fireplace and windows facing the wall that surrounds my property. These windows are kept shuttered, and the few pieces of furniture in the room are covered with sheets. Every few months I light a fire in the grate, but not this year, for the winter was mild. We observed Christmas with the solemnity appropriate to the holiday, and my wife prepared a festive meal. I do not permit decorations as they tend in my opinion to trivialize the occasion, though I do allow the exchanging of gifts as this nurtures selflessness, provided of course that the gifts are either useful or educational, good books for example.

For I have a family, I have a wife and children. There's also my wife's younger sister living in the house, rather a disorganized young woman I'm afraid. I support these people through my work at the museum, work that demands my utter concentration, and this is why I insist on silence in the house during the early hours of the evening (five to seven). The children are permitted to make conversation at the dinner table provided that it's of a serious nature, and the same applies to my wife (and her sister). A stern regime, you may think, but I point out to you that such was the climate of my father's house, and I have not suffered as a result, the reverse in fact. You will understand my recent consternation, then, when having refused to allow the children to keep a stray dog they'd found and begun to care for, several of them expressed feelings of resentment. What's more, my wife supported them, and so, apparently, did her sister!

I punished them of course. And having punished them I explained to them why I had punished them, though whether they appreciated this I cannot say. And it was a few days after this that I first detected the smell.

Now what is so curious about all this is that the work I do is the sort that appeals to scholarly, even pedantic minds, and requires little in the way of imagination. In my field an inexhaustible passion for small detail is of much greater value than imagination per se, for it is with fragments that I work, incomplete pieces of ancient figures that must be identified and catalogued. Given, then, that this is the type of mind I have, does it not strike you as peculiar that I and I alone should have detected the odor?

Actually it began less as a smell, more a sort of ineffable vague suggestion of sweetness in the air. I suspected at first some uncleanness in the kitchen, and had my wife's sister thoroughly scour the floors, ovens, cupboards, and pantry with carbolic. To no avail. It grew stronger. I had my wife's sister then scrub out all of the downstairs rooms, with the exception of course of the one I keep locked at all times (for reasons of my own), for who could have entered that room, shuttered as it is and I in sole possession of the key? I began, when this scouring failed to eliminate the corruption, to suspect that she herself might be responsible for the smell, in retaliation, perhaps, for what she perceived as the injustice of my position regarding the stray dog; and I interviewed her in my room. She did not respond to my inquiries with candor, and I punished her again. *And the smell grew worse!*

The smell grew worse. It made me think of fruit, ripe fruit—a bowl of plums all gone soft and rotten and turning to slime. Was it any wonder that I began to spend so much time at the museum? Of course I did, I couldn't be in the house with that smell, though what really disturbed me was this: the rest of them pretended it wasn't there. They stared at me blankly when I referred to it. They affected concern, or perplexity, or impatience or boredom or fear, but they pretended it wasn't there. And refer to it I certainly did, how could I not, how could I ignore it, and here's something else that disturbed me, that it came and went, and how do you explain that, its coming and going like that?

My authority began to crumble. The children were not openly insubordinate, rather there was a subtle hesitation in their manner that I found deeply impertinent. One night I heard them on the roof, and they know they're not allowed on the roof, though when I went out into the garden I couldn't see anyone up there. With my wife it was the same, and with her sister: in fact, my wife's sister grew so bold, one day I discovered her rattling the doorknob of the room I keep locked! If you think the smell's coming from in there, I told her tartly, you're wrong. She gave me a saucy look and walked off.

She would have to be punished. I would have to make an example of her. Behavior like this could not be tolerated, not in a man's own house, not from her, not from any of them. You do see that, don't you? You do see that I had to do it, even though they were my own family and I loved them? You see that love must at times be cruel if it is to rise above the merely sentimental? Is it a loving father who fails to guide and instruct his family, who fails to teach them self-control, who permits them to flaunt his authority with impunity?

I decided to begin with my wife's sister. I asked her to join me in that certain room after dinner. This gave me ample opportunity to prepare for her visit. The day passed with excruciating slowness. I could not concentrate on my work, and left the museum earlier than usual. After dinner, as I rose from my chair, I glanced at her, meaningfully, and went out of the room. A moment later she followed me. I crossed the hall, extracting from my trouser pocket the key. I unlocked the door and ushered her in, and at that moment, to my unutterable horror, I discovered that the foulness that had been so tormenting my senses did originate in the locked room after all: it *stank* in there, my God it stank, such a sick, sweet stink that I felt my gorge rise and a wave of nausea almost overwhelmed me. I mastered myself, with some difficulty—and then became aware of something else in the room, some new abomination. It was liquid, dripping liquid, there was a sweet and viscous liquid dripping into the fireplace.

Oh, viscosity! She turned to me and asked why I'd brought her here. She appeared *not to smell the smell*. A light, cold prickle of sweat broke out on my skin and I was barely able to control the impulse to retch though I did control it, I did. She asked me again why I'd brought her here, and again I could not answer, for I'd clapped my hands to my mouth to keep from vomiting.

I stared wildly about me. Boxes of fragments, sheeted chairs, shuttered windows, all swam before my eyes. I told her to go, and as she left the room she barely troubled to conceal her contempt. I managed to lock the door from the inside, and then with no little trepidation I approached the fireplace. I was trembling I remember, and damp with perspiration. I knelt down on the hearth, and careful to avoid the puddle of sticky liquid in the grate leaned forward into the fireplace, turning my head so as to gaze up the chimney. I found only blackness, but the smell was bad, oh, it was very bad indeed, and there was little doubt in my mind that I had discovered the source: somewhere up this chimney, somewhere not far above my head, was the thing that dripped and stank.

In a sudden frenzy of rage and frustration I seized up a broomhandle, intending to dislodge the foulness. But broom-handles are stiff, and as the flue sloped backward at an angle just above the fireplace I was unable to get it to go up. I introduced instead a length of wire, and with this succeeded in negotiating the slope, and then thrust upward forcefully a number of times. All that came down was a shower of dead leaves and soot. I waited a few moments and then tried again. I inserted the wire and pushed and thrust with great violence, but again my efforts availed me nothing but chimney rubbish and coal dust.

I spent the next hours in the room. I paced the floor, pondering the events of the evening. And what I couldn't get out of my mind was the way my wife's sister had looked at me, the way she'd spoken to me—it infuriated me, the picture of her flouncing out like that, with a sneer on her lips. That sneer—! But it wasn't only her, they were all in on it, every single one of them, and I knew that I couldn't delay it much longer, for the situation was rapidly getting out of hand.

They were alarmed now. They knew they'd gone too far. My wife was most agitated when I sent for her, she stood before me fidgeting with great unease and was completely unable to meet my eye. I was not easy on her, I was not easy on any of them, why should I be, after what they'd put me through? But despite my anger I didn't raise a finger, I didn't even raise my voice. I spoke, rather, in cool, quiet tones, I told them what I knew, and saw them grow shifty and afraid, for they had thought me a fool, this was clear now, they'd taken me for a fool.

Dead of night, punishment time. I left my room. I listened to the house. Silence. I am a small-boned, agile man, slightly built, simian in fact. I padded quickly and quietly up the stairs, two at a time, and came to the door of my wife's sister's bedroom. I put my ear to the door. I could hear nothing. I crossed the landing and entered another bedroom. A sleeping child sprawled on the bed with sheet and blanket tangled about its limbs. Then I heard coughing, and I went down the passage to a room where two of the younger children slept. I would start here. I went in and closed the door behind me. I was feeling an immense sadness: oh, that it should come to this—two sleeping children—little fragments, delicate, unfinished things, but no less guilty for that. Then the anger came and I experienced the familiar sensation, the *milky* feeling—how else to describe it?—the sudden loss of clarity, the rapid shift into a sort of pale sunless liquid mist, the numbness, watching the horror from somewhere outside one's own body, and when it had passed, when it was over, finding myself once more out in the passage and *again* the sadness, again the intense, almost overwhelming sense of sorrow, though something had changed, for now there was something that was stronger even than the sorrow.

Even from upstairs I could tell it had grown worse, much, much worse. I knew then I *had* to have done with it, that I could wait no longer: more punishment later, I thought, though in an odd way it was no longer me thinking, no longer me in control, for I was drawn to the smell like a moth to a flame, it was *pulling me in*. Rapidly I descended the stairs and unlocked the room—and almost gagged, it was so strong, the wave of foulness that hit me, but in I came, and covering nose and mouth with my arm stumbled to the fireplace and this time ducked my head under the mantelpiece and stood upright in the foul sooty blackness, *I couldn't help myself!* Above my head bricks projected every three feet, it was stepped, so grasping a brick I began blindly to clamber up the inside of the fireplace to the sloping section. There it became more difficult, for the opening was narrow, but I managed to squeeze myself up and along on my front until I reached the passage of the chimney proper, where I somehow turned myself over in the foetid blackness so I could press my back against the one wall of the chimney, get the soles of my shoes hard against the other, legs bent double, and wedged tight like this start poking upward with the wire. But to my horror I'd wedged myself so tight I couldn't move!

I couldn't move. Slowly the blind hysterical compulsion that had seized me faded, slowly I began to understand where I was, and what I'd done. The effort, then, to suppress panic, and terror, and the nausea born of an almost overwhelming stench of putrefying flesh, as a voice inside my own brain whispered, You're suffocating, you're going to die. You're going to die. You're going to die in this putrid chimney. And *then* the thought, So is it *me?* Is it me who makes the smell? Am I the thing that drips and stinks?

Suddenly in my mind's eye I saw my wife's sister, I saw her as she flounced out of my presence, flung out of the room with her eyes flashing and her little chin lifted, like a little white vessel buoyed and swept forward on the current of her own indignation. And then did I hear her laughing? She was outside the door, laughing at me, and at last I saw it, at last I saw the ghastly gallows humor of it all. For I was indeed the source, I the smell, I the thing that dripped and stank. Behind the locked door I could still hear her laughing, while I slowly suffocated, stuffed up my chimney like a dirty cork in a bottle of rancid milk.

THE TENTH SCHOLAR
Steve Rasnic Tem and Melanie Tem

Between the two of them, the Tems have almost twenty stories recommended by me this year, which shows they are as talented as they are prolific. Melanie Tem's first novel, *Prodigal*, was published early in 1991 and I recommend you read it. "The Tenth Scholar" is their twelfth collaboration. It is about the will to power that can cause a person to do *anything* to achieve it. Unfortunately, there is always someone smarter, stronger, and more corrupt. . . . The story is from *The Ultimate Dracula*.

—E.D.

He answered the door himself. I was disappointed that it wasn't his aide-de-camp; the term had always made me think of tents and marshmallows and songs around a fire and two weeks in the country, where I'd never been. "A woman," he said.

"Yeah," I said. "So?"

We looked at each other. I knew I couldn't let him stare me down; I had experience on the streets, and I'd thought about this a lot before I'd come here, practiced looking tougher than I really am. You had to keep a balance. I'd always had to do that. Out on the streets it was important to look tougher than you were, and talk dumber than you were. If you talked too smart, then people got it into their heads that you were all head and weak everywhere else. But with *him*, I knew I just had to look tough, but I couldn't let him think I was dumb. His eyes were green and he had really long white eyelashes. "A very *young* woman," he said.

"Not as young as you think," I shot back, but that wasn't true. I was sixteen and pregnant, and I looked like a twelve-year-old who hadn't lost her baby fat.

His thick white eyebrows rose a little, and he said, "Interesting." During the next months I would hear that comment from him countless times. It was the only compliment he ever paid any of us, and it always surprised me how often he used it, how many things he still genuinely found interesting, after all the years he'd lived and all the years he knew he still had coming.

"I saw your ad," I told him.

He nodded and stepped back, bowing slightly and making a welcoming gesture with one hand. I remember thinking that his hands were elegant, long and pale and thin, except that they were so hairy. "Come in, my dear."

" 'My dear'?" I laughed. I'd figured he would talk like that, and I wanted him to know right away that it didn't impress me.

Except, of course, that it did. Not so much his fancy accent or old-fashioned language, but the way he *noticed* me, the fact that he really did seem to think it was interesting that I was there. That was new for me, and as soon as I got a little of it I wanted more. I went in, noticing the gold dragon under the gold cross on the door.

Against the bright, trendy pastels of this penthouse office suite, he looked like something out of a black-and-white movie. The only colors on him were his green eyes and the red of his mouth, so red I thought he might be wearing lipstick. He was dressed in crisp, creased black, although he wasn't wearing a cloak; I'd been expecting a cloak, and that threw me a little. His face and hands were so white that I wouldn't have thought anything could be whiter, but then I saw the tips of his teeth pushing out over the edge of his lower lip. His curly hair went past his shoulders—black, when I'd imagined it would be white—and his moustache was as white as his eyebrows, so that I could hardly see them across his skin.

"Sit down, my dear." When he soundlessly shut the door, it was as if we were the only two creatures in the world. "What can I do for you?"

"I'm answering your ad," I repeated stubbornly. I didn't like it when people made fun of me, and I heard mockery everywhere. I'd punched people out, scratched their green eyes, for less. "I'm applying for the school. The ad didn't say you needed an appointment."

I wished I could think of things to say that sounded more intelligent. People on the street were easy to impress; even Oliver didn't take much. Though at first I'd thought he would. But this guy would be a real challenge; I'd known that before I came. He'd be like my grandmother, only more so—able to see who you really were and what you really wanted when even you didn't know. I sat down on the gigantic couch that took up one whole wall of the room. The couch was that peculiar yellow-green color they call chartreuse, and the walls and carpet were mauve. Who'd have thought that mauve and chartreuse would go together? Who'd have expected this guy to be an interior decorator? But then, he'd already lived long enough to be anything he wanted.

The guy had *power*. Once you had power, nobody could hurt you. I'd learned that much on the streets. And before. Power might have kept my grandmother alive. It didn't really matter how you got it, because once you had it nobody much cared about the how. I'd been around the powerful people in my life—my mother, a social worker or two, PD's and DA's and juvenile court judges, Oliver. But they were little fish. They had power only in relation to utterly powerless people like me. This guy had real power, and he could teach me how to have it, too. So I could pass it on to my baby.

I shivered in appreciation, then stiffened my body to still it and hoped he hadn't noticed. He had, of course; I saw the amusement in his eyes.

My jeans were dirty and smelled of the streets. It pleased me to think I might be soiling the fancy upholstery. I squirmed on the couch, moved my butt around a lot, just to make sure.

"Pregnant," he observed. He was standing too close to me, and he was really tall. I hated it when people, especially men, towered over me like that; too many times, at home and in juvie and in foster homes and on the street, some guy had stood too close to me like that and had ended up fucking me over.

I wasn't about to let him know he was making me nervous; you didn't dare let them know. I yawned, hoping my breath smelled as bad as it tasted, and put my filthy tennis shoes up on the arm of his elegant sofa. "So," I demanded, looking up at him as insolently as I could, "what do I have to do?"

He sat down in the enormous armchair that faced the couch. He crossed his legs, meticulously adjusted his pantleg. He wasn't a very big man; he was as thin as anybody I'd ever met under a bridge or in a shelter, as if, like them, he was always hungry—though I doubted it was because he couldn't afford food. For some reason, I'd thought he'd be bigger. I wondered what Oliver, who thought he knew everything there was to know about him, would think of him in person. "I ain't smart enough to go to some hot-shit yuppie school," Oliver had sneered. "You're the schoolgirl. You go, and then you come back and tell us." But I was never going back. I hadn't loved Oliver; I just let him think I did. He wasn't very powerful; for a while he could keep me safer than I could keep myself, but now I was ready for more.

There was a long silence. I noticed that I couldn't hear anything from the street or from the rest of the building, only his breathing and mine. Wondering about that, I pressed the back of my fist against the wall over my head; the wall was spongy and gave a little, like living tissue, and before I could stop myself I'd gasped and jerked my hand away.

He saw me do that, too, of course, and I knew he was keeping score. This was some creepy kind of exam. He sat there quietly with his thin white hands looking very thin and white against the wide chartreuse arms of the chair, and he looked at me calmly without saying anything. I was used to that. There was this chick in a doorway up across from Columbia who looked at you that way; you knew she saw everything about you and kept a list in her head, but I'd never heard her say anything, even the night she came after me with her nails and teeth and stole my sandwich—whole, still wrapped in wax paper—that I'd found on a table in a sidewalk cafe that lunchtime and been saving all day. The next day I went to her doorway and just sat on the stoop beside her and stared at her, to see what she'd do. She didn't do anything, so finally I gave up.

I didn't give up this time. I sat as quietly as he did and stared back at him. I didn't exactly look him in the eye; his eyes were too much for me. But I did stare at his face, and all of a sudden I was seeing a tiny drop of bright red—blood, I supposed—on the point of one of his teeth.

He spoke first, but not because I'd won anything. "What is your name?"

I couldn't think of any reason not to tell him. "Marie."

"And your surname?"

That was none of his business, and I wasn't part of that family anymore anyway. So I said, "Bathory," just to see what his reaction would be, sort of the way I'd sometimes shit on the sidewalk in front of some snooty restaurant.

He chuckled. He was laughing at me. "And why do you wish to attend the *scholomance*, Marie Bathory?"

I was ready for that one. I said what Oliver had told me to say, although I didn't always follow his orders no matter what he did to me. "Hey," I shrugged, "beats living on a heat grate, y'know?"

His face sharpened like a blade, and in one swift sharp motion he had stood up. "You are wasting my time."

I panicked. I'd overplayed the tough and ended up sounding stupid. As usual, Oliver didn't know what he was talking about. I told him, too soon and too eagerly, "When my grandmother died they drove a nail through her forehead."

"Interesting," he said, and I relaxed a little. "Why?"

I was confused by that, and my temper flared. I put my feet down on the thick carpet, leaned forward, even raised my voice. "What do you mean, why? Why do you think? They thought she was a vampire."

He nodded. "And was she?"

I started to give him some smart-ass answer, but then I was remembering my grandmother and having to fight back tears. She'd loved me. I remembered a lot of whippings, a few times locked in a dark rustling closet, but I'd deserved that. I also remembered feeling safe with her, and noticed, and understanding that my grandma was the most powerful person in the whole world and that if I was good and did what she told me I could grow up to be just like her.

But she died. She hadn't been powerful enough. Some lady in a shawl came and hammered a nail through her forehead. I remembered the shiny nailhead among the soft wrinkles between her eyes. My father had pulled her yellow-white hair down low, trying to hide the nail, but he'd made no move to pull it out. That's how I knew she was really dead, and no one would ever love me again.

Sometimes, though, I looked at the New York City buildings I'd lived among all my life, and saw them the way she must have seen them when her own grandmother brought her here from Rumania. Mountains, they became, and the alleys crevasses, and lightning could be made to strike from the lake in Central Park or from the crowded ocean beaches as powerfully as from any isolated Carpathian pool deeper than a dream.

"Yeah, she was." I'd never said it out loud before, though I'd always secretly believed it. Foolishly, I added, "I miss her."

"Interesting. And your grandmother the vampire told you about the *scholomance*, did she?"

"No. Oliver did." That was a lie, partly. She'd told me a little—about the *scholomance*, about the tenth scholar, but when I kept asking her about them she'd shut up, as if she was sorry she'd told me anything at all. Then Oliver came along, and he told me more, and I wanted to be that tenth scholar, and *would* be, because I *had* to be for me and my baby.

He didn't ask who Oliver was. It wasn't as if he already knew; he just didn't care. So much for Oliver's power; I smiled to myself. When Oliver died, I wondered, would there be a shooting star? And would anybody notice it among all the city lights?

"Who is the father of your child?"

"I don't know." That was the truth, but I wouldn't have told him if I had known. On an impulse, watching his face, I added, "You can be if you want."

His face changed. Not much, but enough that I knew I'd scored a point. He smiled, showing more of his teeth under the moustache.

"Nobody gave my grandmother a candle while she was dying," I heard myself say. "So she died without light. She always said that was the worst thing that could happen to anybody, to die without light."

He understood what I meant better than I did. "And that is why you want to study at our school."

"I guess." The tenth scholar wouldn't die without a light, I was pretty sure of that. It was hard to believe, but maybe the tenth scholar wouldn't die at all.

He was moving around the room. Gliding, really; I half-expected him to vaporize at any second. I wondered if he really could do that, and if he could teach me; I wondered what I'd do if he left me, too. "Not a bad reason to apply," he said. "But you must understand that you will be expected to study diligently. To apply yourself."

"I'm not stupid," I said, feeling stupid.

"Only ten scholars are accepted into each class."

"I know. And one stays. As payment."

"Correct. So far, I see, you have done your homework."

"I'll be the one to stay," I said boldly.

"Ah, my dear, but *I* make that choice."

"You'll choose me."

He came too close to me again and peered down from his great height. The drop of blood was gone; his teeth gleamed. "Marie Bathary, do you know who I am?"

"Vlad Tepes," I said, giving the first name Oliver's broad Brooklyn "a" and pronouncing the last name "Teeps," the way Oliver did.

He exploded into laughter and I was mortified. "Tsepesh!" he exclaimed. "It is pronounced 'Tsepesh'!" I tried and failed to say it right. He bent like a huge shiny insect and took my face in his cold hands. "Marie. Say it. V*lad Tepes*, the Impaler."

I could hardly breathe, but I managed to say, "Tepesh."

"Very good. Now say *nosferatu*."

That was easier. "Nosferatu," I gasped. His nails were digging into the soft flesh behind my ears.

Then his sharp cold face was only inches away from mine, and I thought he was going to kiss me or to sink his teeth into my neck. I would have been glad for either. He whispered "*Dracule*," and I repeated "*Dracule*," and then he let me go. My face was numb where he'd held me.

"Classes begin tomorrow," he said. "You will stay with me tonight, and you will be prepared."

Later that night he sent me down to the alley with his garbage, as he would so many other nights during my stay. I suppose this was meant to be part of my payment to him. He didn't trust the service the building provided, he said. They were lax and inefficient, he said. He said he wanted something more private.

That first night when I reached the alley I couldn't resist the temptation to peer into the thick, black plastic bag. The bag had been so heavy, I couldn't imagine what he'd thrown away.

It was a Rottweiler, its throat torn open sloppily, the edges of the wound frayed as if the killer had been starving, hadn't been able to wait to do it right.

Somehow, I would have thought him above all that. It embarrassed me. I closed the bag up quickly, and tried not to think about it after that. And I never told anyone.

I never thought I had much competition. Although Dracula would comment once in a while that he found us "interesting," individually or as a group, it didn't seem to me that we were an especially strong class, compared to those who must have gone before.

I was the only female, the only student under twenty-five, of course the only one pregnant, the only one who lived at the school. The others all came and went, and they actually seemed to have lives outside. I couldn't imagine any of them staying. I was so sure I had a lock on Tenth Scholar that I didn't worry much about what I'd do if he sent me away, where I'd go, how I'd ever live.

Some of my classmates I scarcely remember now, and wouldn't recognize on the street. Some of them, though, I remember. Andy, for instance, was an accomplished serial killer before classes ever started, and I'm sure he's still going strong. Although Dracula never made distinctions based on how we'd come to the school, we all guessed that Andy had been recruited, and he never did quite grasp what he was doing there, what was expected of him, what opportunities there were. I lost count of how many whores and street people he killed and dismembered; for one thing, it was more every time he talked about it. I used to sit in class and stare at him, sometimes losing track of the lesson; I'd try to figure out what Dracula saw in him, and whether I'd have pegged him as dangerous if I'd just met him on the street. I doubted it, not because he looked innocent—nobody has looked innocent to me in a long time—but because he looked so *dumb*.

Conrad preyed on kids. I remember him. The official *scholomance* policy was that child-molestation and -murder were inherently no more or less praiseworthy than any other approach, but I couldn't help taking special note of Conrad. He was old, maybe fifty, and he participated a lot in class. He stared at me a lot, too, at my belly as I started to show.

Then there was Harlequin. Actually, Harlequin might have been a woman. He might also have been an animal—a lizard, say, or a bat—or some alien thing nobody'd ever heard of. I had no idea, either, how old he was, or what race. He was an exotic dancer, a hooker, a performance artist, a beggar. By turns he was fey and crude, heavy-handed as a rapist in a reeking alley and light-footed as the eternally restless spirits my grandmother had called *strigoi* (restless, I remembered, either because of some great sin or because of some great unclaimed treasure). I never knew exactly what he'd done to be admitted or how he got such spectacularly high grades—except that, rather than stalking and terrifying his victims, he dazzled and seduced them, and they died not out of fear of him but out of passion.

What I remember most vividly about Harlequin, though, are thunderbolts and blood.

We were having our regular early-morning nature class in Central Park. The sun was probably just rising over a horizon we couldn't see; the bowl of the park, inside our horizon of mountainous buildings, was still pretty dark, the charcoal-rose sky like a lid.

Andy, as usual, was already half-asleep; he should have been in his element here. Conrad, as usual, was sulky because there were so few children in the park at this time of the night, and those who were out were already taken.

Harlequin was even more spectacular than usual. He'd been studying, I could tell. I always hated brown-noses. The first of us to master vaporization, he kept disappearing and reappearing all over the place, leaping in the fountain like waterdrops himself, slithering through the dewy grass to coil himself adoringly around Dracula's ankles.

Dracula always put up with more from Harlequin than he should have. But finally that morning he observed sternly, "All this is most entertaining, but you are only distracting yourself and the others from serious application to the matters at hand."

Harlequin laughed like the cry of a gull, made himself very tall and thin, and swept both cupped palms across the paling sky. A shower of stars fell into the city, stars I didn't think had been ready to fall yet. Souls leaving this world, my grandmother would have said. Souls pulled from this world before their time, I thought, and grudgingly I acknowledged to myself Harlequin's skill and style.

The baby kicked. I could feel it drinking my blood through the umbilical cord, and I knew it was transforming me into something I didn't want to be. I imagined sinking my teeth into its not-yet-developed little neck, through the layers of my own flesh and blood.

Harlequin raced to the lake, the rest of us following. He found a rock the size of a baby, raised it above his glittering bald head, and threw it in. The splash wasn't very impressive in the noisy city dawn, and the surface of the water had already been deeply rippled, but there was a dragon in there and it awoke. Two, three, four long thunderbolts leaped out of the lake and crackled through the air to the sky, where they lit up the craggy top floors of the buildings. There was the immediate odor of burned hair and flesh, and from the shadows on the other side of the lake somebody screamed.

Beside me, always beside me, Dracula murmured, "Interesting," and jealousy licked like a fetus at the bottom of my heart. But Harlequin got on everybody's nerves, and just before the end of class, with the sun about to show above the buildings and Andy all but snoring, Dracula finally lost his patience. "Harlequin, enough. I have had enough. This morning, right now, you must prove yourself or leave the *scholomance*."

I was shocked. I hadn't known you could be expelled. Scared, I tried to move close to Dracula, yearning to touch him openly, to claim him in front of the others and put an end to the pointless competition for Tenth Scholar. But Dracula was watching Harlequin and took no notice of me.

Harlequin stood absolutely still among the moving shadows of the sunrise, looking small and frail. I hadn't realized until then how sick he was, and always would be. Immortal now, of course, like the rest of us, and eternally wasting away. The disease was his curse and his power; his kisses brought to his victims, who were his lovers, immortal sickness, too.

From behind the bushes that separated us from the path, we heard voices. We all sat up straight, even Conrad, who I knew was hoping for the sweet voice of a child unattended. Even Andy tried to rouse himself, but the sun was too high for him.

I started to move but Dracula held me back, his cold hand across my belly. Harlequin paused for maybe five seconds, centering himself as Dracula had taught us to do before an approach, and then stepped through the bushes. Conrad and a few of the other students repositioned themselves quietly to watch, but Dracula stayed where he was and kept me there, too.

There was almost no noise. Harlequin made none, of course, and his victims never knew what happened. That was the way it should be; Dracula loathed noise. I remembered how quiet my grandmother had been, too: how peaceful. We waited. Daylight had started to seep into the park and class was almost over when Harlequin stepped like a dancer back into the clearing among us.

His face and clothes were scarlet with blood. His teeth dripped. He looked stronger than he had in a long time, more substantial. His movements were more fluid and directed, less flighty.

In outstretched hands he carried two tall ridged silver thermos bottles, apparently taken from the victims. He dropped to his knees, bowed his head as if in offering, and passed one of the bottles in each direction around the circle. Dracula drank first, his eyes closed in pleasure and his long throat working. At last, without opening his eyes, he passed the thermos to me.

The blood was warm and sweet. Obviously the victims had been virgins, barely so, a young man and a young woman on the verge of becoming lovers when Harlequin had intervened. The mouth of the thermos was wide enough that the blood spilled over my nose and chin, bathing me in its vitality. I knew some of it was reaching the baby and I was glad, then I wished it wouldn't because maybe there wouldn't be enough left for me, but there was nothing I could do about that. I drank until I felt renewed, and then, reluctantly, passed the bottle on.

When Dracula said, "Prove yourself" to me, we were making love on his red silk sheets. The others had gone home for the day, or had gone wherever it was they went when they weren't at school; I couldn't imagine. City daylight came through the high window gray and pale blue, and it was exciting to be awake.

He was straddling me on all fours, and under the huge mound of my belly his penis entered me easily. It thrilled me to think of his penis pushing back and forth past the fetus like a fang.

I would turn seventeen soon. The baby would be born soon. Soon we would be graduated.

"Prove yourself," he said, and I thought he was talking about something sexual.

Although I couldn't guess what there was left that I hadn't already done, I gasped, "Tell me what you want."

He buried his face in my shoulder. His teeth grazed my neck and found a spot, but they didn't go in yet; he was playing with me. "Prove yourself," he murmured again, "or leave the *scholomance*. Now."

I stiffened with fear and outrage and frantic desire. I tried to wrap my arms and legs around him, but my stomach was too big, the baby was between us, and Dracula was moving down my body. I spread my legs and waited for his sharp tongue, but he stopped at my navel and I felt his teeth.

"You are not the Tenth Scholar," I heard him say.

"Why not? Who is? Harlequin? Shit, I thought you were smart enough to see through him—"

"The baby is the Tenth Scholar."

A fang went into my belly button and withdrew again. There was the suggestion of pain.

I struggled weakly to get out from under him. Of course I couldn't, and, anyway, I didn't know where I'd go if I got free. "You mean I can't stay?"

"I have taught you as much as it is possible for you to learn."

Betrayal made me light-headed, as though he'd already bitten through. "No," I cried foolishly. "Please."

His voice came up to me singsong, seductive, and cold as immortal blood. "If you give me the baby now, you may stay to raise it until it can take its place at my side. Twelve years, perhaps, or ten years, or fourteen, depending on its nature and inclinations. If you do not give me the baby, you will leave. Tonight. I have lost interest in you."

"Take it," I said.

A vision of the dog with the butchered throat came into my head. A vision of my grandmother, dying when I'd been sure she'd never die, leaving me. I bit my lower lip hard to drive the visions away.

At first there was no more pain, really, than during any normal bite, except that the nerves in my abdomen were exquisitely sensitive. He sucked and drank a lot of blood. Before he was done I was so dizzy I could barely see, and he, obviously, was stoned.

His hands went all over my body—cold skin, sharp nails. His tongue went all over my body. He had started to sing as if to himself, to croon, and his laughter was sweet and smooth. Unable to fathom what I'd be like in fourteen years, what the city would be like when I had to go back into it alone, I paid attention only to him, only to the perforations his teeth were making from my navel to my pubic hair, only to his promise that if I did this he would let me stay.

Now pain and blood gushed. I lost and regained consciousness and lost it again; stars fell. When I awoke, the light was the same blue-gray it had been, but I was sure time had passed. There was a terrible, wonderful emptiness in my abdomen, and the wound had already started to close.

I heard Dracula's odd crooning and the gurgling of an infant, but for a while I couldn't find them. The colors in the room—chartreuse, mauve, blood-red—

gave around me like living tissue. Then I saw the tall thin form by the window, blackened by my blood and the baby's and the rich nourishing blood of the placenta and afterbirth.

"It's a girl," he told me.

I was dizzied by a peculiar kind of pride: I'd borne a healthy daughter who would be the Tenth Scholar, even if I could not be. I'd carried on my grandmother's line. I'd given Dracula something he'd wanted, something that, apparently, no one else had ever given him. And fourteen years was a long time.

It was, of course, a trick. "Go now," he said, almost casually, staring at the baby in his arms.

"What?"

"Leave. The *scholomance* is filled."

"You said I could stay. You said—"

"I saw no point in exerting myself to take my daughter by force when you would give her to me out of love."

"She's *my* daughter!"

The baby in his arms curled and stretched. Somehow, she was feeding. "I am her father," he said, and I understood that it was true. He looked at me then, green gaze forking like lightning, and said, "Go. You have no place here."

My daughter is fourteen now. I look for her everywhere and see her nowhere. Probably I wouldn't know who she was, anyway, except for her resemblance to him.

I kill for sustenance; there is no pleasure in it. I infect some of my victims with immortality in hopes that they will be my companions, but they always leave.

I know that my classmates are out here, and they've been taught by the Master; I try not to forget that. I try to protect myself against them, but it's unclear to me what danger there is, what pain there could be left. The city seems full of *scholomance* graduates and wannabes, and it's hard for me to believe these days that Dracula accepts only ten students at a time.

FISHER DEATH
WALK IN SABLE

Jessica Amanda Salmonson

Salmonson has written or edited more than twenty books of fantasy and the supernatural including the anthology *Amazons!*, which won the World Fantasy Award in 1980. She is also a prolific poet.

These two short poems, from *Weird Tales* and *Haunts* respectively, are imbued with longing and sensuous images of death.

—E.D.

FISHER DEATH

Stricken by favors of a darkened place
Falling through limbo
      upon fractured wings
Greeted in deserts by scorpion stings
Glaring at Love without eyes in its face.
Sifting through dust
      that was once a great God
Laughing in echoes
      that fade without trace
Twined in our graveclothes
      of gossamer lace
Peering in chasms
      where light is outlawed.

Tears fall like knives into the fearful pit,
Spirits glint like moonbows in jet cascade
Sought by Fisher Death
      for his waiting spit.
Fear not. Even this indignity will fade.
Trampled beneath our impossible dreams,
Vanished in rips in reality's seams.

WALK IN SABLE

"I and this Love are one, and I am Death."

—Dante Gabriel Rossetti

Death came walking in my garden
of pale white lilies and blood-red roses.

A stone angel crumbles in her pool,
her broken lips spouting silent prayers.
Nestlings cease their hungry song,
moveless midst the branches.

I alone rushed to Death's embrace,
my heart quickened with desire—
"Who fears me not," said Death
"comes to me no sooner,"
and coldly I was cast aside.

Death came walking in my house
where shadows shroud the rooms;
grief resounds; sadness looms
because a child from me was taken.

"Take me as well; take me!"
was my prayer,
yet Death spurned me anew.

Years have passed;
the world has passed me by;
and I lay gasping on a lonesome bed.

"Turn from me a while," I begged
of the skeletal presence,
who proclaimed,
"The sad, the elderly, the maimed,
or the quick and strong—
to me, all are the same."

Then with Death I went walking
and I looked behind to see my life
with so much left undone.
"No," I whispered. "No," and "No."
But Death said softly, "Yes."

THE CUT MAN
Norman Partridge

I first noticed Norman Partridge's work in 1989 in the small-press magazine *Noctulpa: Guignoir and Other Furies,* and included his story "Cosmos" in my annual recommendations. Since then he has published stories in *Iniquities, Pulphouse,* and *Final Shadows,* among other places. For this year's collection I was torn between two stories of his published in 1991: the excellent "Guignoir," from the anthology of the same name, and "The Cut Man," which appeared in *Copper Star,* the World Fantasy Convention anthology. I decided to take "The Cut Man" for *The Year's Best* because of the fascinating milieu in which it takes place—the world of boxing. Norman Mailer and Joyce Carol Oates are both aficionados of the sport and have written articles and books on the subject, but boxing is not usually associated with the horror field. Partridge asserts that his story was inspired by Jess Willard, the Pottawatomie Giant who, even after being trounced by Jack Dempsey in nine minutes in 1919, came back to box again and again.

—E.D.

I'd forgotten that the knocker on Torito's front door was shaped like a boxing glove. I tapped a flurry of jabs on the brass face-plate and waited, my heart thumping a staccato speed-bag rhythm, the desert emptiness swelling at my back. Why Torito lived in the middle of the desert instead of in Vegas was a mystery to me. The sleeping black sky stretching forever, dry sandpaper breezes scudding this way and that like indecisive ghosts, heat waves radiating from the highway in the middle of the night—it was creepy.

I knocked again and listened at the narrow stained-glass window to the right of the door. Just then a zombie opened up, the kind of zombie you see nearly everywhere these days—empty eyes, gray skin, skinny as a bantamweight. He stood there smiling at nothing, his teeth yellow-green from neglect or the weird glow of the halogen porch-light. Finally his eyes did a little focusing trick and he saw me.

"You ain't Willie," he rasped. "You bring Willie's heroin?"

I shook my head, thankful for the succinct way the zombie had explained the situation. "I guess Willie's gonna be a little late," I said, checking my disgust, hoping to keep the junkie calm. "I'm here to see Rosie."

A sharp click echoed in the entryway as a glinting blade disappeared into the hollow of the zombie's palm. He shrugged, turned, and shuffled to the base of a wrought-iron circular staircase. "Rosie!" he called, his raspy voice straining for volume. "It's for you!"

No answer from above. The zombie shot me another tired shrug and wandered away, into the shadows.

I stepped into the entryway, brushing past a withered fern that stood guard just inside the doorway. A chill rose from the marble floor that Torito had had installed after the Kalambay fight in Naples. Carrara marble. Michelangelo's favorite. TV sounds bounced through the house and lingered over the smooth white rock. *Pung pung pung.*

I guessed tennis. Then I heard the familiar voice of an ESPN announcer and knew that I was right. It was a safe bet that Torito wasn't watching TV—he hated tennis. Football, basketball, and baseball, too. He said they were kid games, games that you played, and Torito never played at anything. Fact is, you never hear about anyone "playing" boxing.

Someone whispered from above, "Willie? Is that you?"

A bronze foot appeared on the circular staircase, and then a shapely ankle, a gold bracelet shimmering around its delicate circumference. A perfect calf followed, and then a perfect thigh. Rosie's wispy lavender negligee came into view midthigh, but it hid nothing.

I swallowed hard.

Slivers of shadow melted across Rosie's face. Her strong Navajo features had shriveled on the bone. Her empty eyes blinked through a private haze, her eyelids too small and dark in deeply hollowed sockets. She smiled, leered really. A zombie smile.

"Richeeee," she said. "Thank God you came!"

"All the way from A.C.," I said, sounding like a happy uncle who'd come to visit. "I came as soon as I got your letter. My mail's not so good, you know. I move around too much. But it finally caught up to me at Caesars. The concierge from Trump Plaza sent it over. And I tried to call first, but no one's been answering your phone . . ."

She wasn't listening. We hugged. I felt too many bones, smelled greasy hair and too much Anne Klein II.

I followed her upstairs and down a long hallway. My shoes sank into thick mint-green carpet and I worried that I hadn't wiped them. Rosie was very proud of her carpets and her Italian marble. After growing up in a New Mexico hogan with nothing but dirt under her heels, I guess she had a thing about floors. In happier times, she'd sent her decorator after carpets that would match those at Caesars Tahoe. Drove the guy nuts. Torito told me that the decorator finally bribed some maintenance guys at Caesars into stealing a couple hundred square yards of the stuff.

Better days, better ways, I thought.

I caught up to Rosie at the bedroom door. A framed poster from the Barkley fight hung to my left; blank wall stared at me from the right. While Rosie fumbled with the doorknob, I prayed that Torito wasn't saving that space for another poster. A comeback was the last thing I wanted to see. Two years ago he'd had nothing left, now he'd be worse.

Gus's voice: "They always come back. You know that, Richie. They say they won't, but they always do."

Rosie flipped on the light. Torito was sitting up in bed, staring at a big screen Mitsubishi that stood to the right of the door.

Dried blood on the padded leather headboard.

Spots of fresh blood on Torito's silk pajama top.

The stink of sweat and blood hit me as I stepped into the room. Heavy, worse than the stench of a slaughterhouse. Reflexively, my eyes darted from Torito to the spinach-green wallpaper above his bed; the flocked pattern squirmed like a tangle of snakes and I wiped my eyes and looked again. This time I saw a wooden crucifix nestled in the mossy velvet above Torito's head, the figure of Jesus red with paint or Torito's blood. A rusty nail had been hammered through Jesus' chest, pinning the crucifix to the wall, splitting the icon from breastbone to head, but the old wood scissored tightly around it as if clinging there.

Rosie took my hand. "Richie, you gotta make it okay again . . . I need you . . . Toro needs you . . ."

She kept talking, but I couldn't hear her over the blaring Mitsubishi. It shouted, "BARK-LEY, BARK-LEY, BARKLEY!"

Torito looked at me through swollen eyes. "Help me, Richie," he said, his voice barely audible. "You gotta help me . . . I can't see the punches."

The ice in the bucket had melted in the Vegas heat, but the Enswell iron was still cold. Gus pressed it against Torito's swollen cheek and begged him to follow his jab with a double-hook to the body. "You can't stop Barkley unless you take his legs," he said.

I was working on the cuts. Torito was a mess. I've saved fights for lots of guys who had tender faces—Saad Muhammad and Antuofermo included—but Torito made those two look like they had skin of iron. After four rounds, he had deep slices over both eyes and the bridge of his nose. I mopped off the blood, pressed a Q-tip soaked with adrenaline chloride 1-1000 into the cuts, and glopped Vaseline over Torito's brow.

The ring doctor tried to elbow past Gus. "He's fine," Gus assured the man, not giving an inch. "If you want to look at cuts, go check Barkley."

Gus was right. Iran "The Blade" Barkley's face was a mess, too.

The warning whistle sounded. Gus ducked between the ropes. I followed, pulling the stool as Torito rose. "Remember, Barkley's trying to take your title!" Gus yelled, as if Torito needed reminding.

Round five. Torito came out jabbing, driving his fist into Barkley's bloody nose. Barkley bent at the middle, but he was only ducking under the jabs, not going down, and then Torito pivoted and threw the money punch—a big left hook to the ribs. Again. The Blade spit blood and gasped, then came back with a two-handed body-attack that sent Torito into the ropes. Jabbing his way to the center of the ring, Torito bent and delivered another left hook, but Barkley's right was already on its way and it caught Torito high on the head. Blood geysered from Torito's brow and spattered the referee's white shirt, and as Torito stumbled backward, Barkley nailed him with another chopping right that shattered his jaw and sent him to the canvas.

The referee didn't bother to count.

"You see why I asked you to come," Rosie said innocently. "I can't call anyone else. Not with him around . . . not the way I am."

That last part came in a whisper, like a confession. Turning away, I opened my snakeskin bag and set my gear on the walnut nightstand. Then I turned off the TV, my hands shaking.

"How can you let Torito watch that?" I asked.

"He makes Toro watch it all the time, because just watching it makes Toro bleed now. He says it's the only way he can find Toro's weak spots."

Junkie logic. I couldn't follow it, no more than I could imagine the zombie I'd met downstairs making Torito do anything. I asked Rosie if that's who she was talking about, but she ignored my question.

"You got to hurry," she said. "You got to fix Toro and then we got to get out of here before he comes back. He went looking for wood a couple hours ago. He probably won't be back 'til morning. That'll give us a head start. If we can get to New Mexico, to the reservation, my family will hide us."

"Rosie, who the hell are you talking about?"

"Ask Toro," she said, slipping through the doorway.

Torito's hand closed over mine. "I don't want to go to New Mexico," he whispered.

"Jesus, Torito, how could you get mixed up with this shit? Who did this to you? Do you owe money or—"

"It ain't like that. The horse, that's Rosie's thrill. I don't mess with it."

I stared at his swollen brow, trying to see his eyes, trying to see if he was lying.

Torito's grip tightened. "He wants to help me, Richie. Just like he said he would. You remember. A long time ago he told Gus that he'd help me when I was through . . . Gus told you about that, didn't he?"

I cleaned Torito's cuts and stitched his face together. I couldn't get a straight answer out of him, but I couldn't get him to shut up, either.

"You should have seen Gus the first time he met him," Torito laughed, his swollen lips twisting into a lumpy grin. "You know Gus, by the book and everything. Well, he had to get the devil to sign some papers—"

"The devil? Cut the bullshit, Torito. Tell me who did this to you."

Torito's voice was impatient: "That's what I'm doing."

I shook my head. "Whatever you say, Toro."

"Okay. I can't tell it like Gus, but let me try. See, when I was a boy, the devil lived in a little adobe behind our house. Even when my mother died and we moved away, he still lived there. He liked to carve; he could put the Santeros to shame. Of course, the devil didn't make holy things. He made statues of demons, the death cart, coyotes . . . even La Llorona. He gave them to my brothers and me, but we didn't like to play with them, and we locked them in a footlocker at night.

"Anyway, Gus didn't want to make the trip because we had to drive all the way up to the Sangre de Cristos, but there was nothing else that he could do because he had to have the devil's signature before he could enter me in the Junior Olympics at Colorado Springs. You know Gus, he complained every inch of the way.

"It's early afternoon when we get to the old adobe, but the devil's already awake. He's sitting outside with a bucket at his feet and he's whittling away with a carving knife that he stole off a Penitente man. Anyway, I know better than to bother the devil while he's busy, but Gus up and asks him 'Whatcha makin'?' You know Gus, can't keep his mouth shut. So the devil holds out his hand, palm up. It's empty. Then he rolls it over and Gus can see how he'd carved his fingernails down to nothing.

"The devil shoves his bloody fingertips under Gus's nose. 'I'm making me,' he says.

"Gus almost threw up. He looked green enough. Then the devil pointed down at the bucket, at the little bits of fingernail floating in the pink water. Richie, you should have heard the devil laugh. And then he said, 'When you're done with my boy, bring him back and I'll fix him, too.' "

I was sweating. I didn't want to hear this kind of talk, and Torito could see that I thought he was crazy.

His eyes cut at me from beneath swollen brows. "You don't believe me, huh? You just look at that first contract, Richie. You'll see the bloodstains there."

Torito fell asleep at that point. I checked his arms for tracks but didn't find any. There were three cherry-red scars in the hollow of his right elbow and another bunch on his left forearm, but they were about the size of thumbtacks—much too large for needle scars.

I packed my gear, trying to figure who'd done this to Torito. Maybe Rosie's heroin connection had gone sour; maybe Torito didn't want to admit that he'd been busted up by an ordinary fingerbreaker. Then I remembered that the zombie was expecting a guy named Willie. And Rosie had mentioned Willie, too, so I doubted that there was a connection problem. That left the promoter and the cable TV people. Both had lost big dinero when Torito pulled out of the Barkley rematch. And they'd both made threats, admittedly the kind of tidy threats that you'd expect from incorporated organizations. But even tidy threats have a way of turning nasty in this business.

I stepped into Torito's bathroom to wash my hands and almost slipped on the wet floor before I could turn on the lights. Blood was everywhere, smeared on the green tile, the mirror, and the counter. Antuofermo and Saad Muhammad could have gone a few rounds in the tiny room and it wouldn't have looked any worse.

But the mirror wasn't broken. And the bath towels hung neatly on lacquered teak racks. No sign of a struggle at all.

The pea-green basin was splattered with scarlet gore—thick, sticky blood dotted with little tan flecks. I pushed at the flecks with a toothbrush, not wanting to touch something that I couldn't identify. I remembered Torito's story about the devil and suddenly knew what I was looking at. Bits of wood, splinters and curls. And tiny chunks of flesh.

I tried to rinse the horror away, but the bloody water drained too slowly and the flecks of skin stuck to the green porcelain as if glued there. I wiped the faucet clean. My throat was gritty-dry but the thought of drinking from the tap revolted me.

I poked around the room. The bathtub was filled with wood, kindling really: broken survey stakes, greasewood twigs, stunted Joshua tree branches, and stubby bits of mesquite. On the floor behind the toilet, I found a claw hammer smeared with blood. Next to it was a tin can filled with rusty nails.

Suddenly I thought of Jesus on the bedroom wall, split down the middle.

I hefted the hammer. Had the blood spattered it? Or had Torito stood before the mirror, looking at himself like I was looking at myself now, hefting the tool, wondering what it would feel like crashing against his skull again and again?

The cuts healed, at least the ones that you could see. Torito looked fine, a hell of a lot better than Barkley. Even I'll admit that.

In training camp for the rematch, everybody else ignored the warning signs. When Torito refused to wear headgear in sparring, they said he wanted to be macho. Same story when he started hitting the heavy bag without handwraps. And when he ran eight miles instead of his usual four, everyone said that Torito only wanted to improve his endurance.

Early one morning, I learned the truth. Torito came limping back from a run, couldn't even make it past my cabin, which was on the edge of camp. He sat on the front steps and pulled off his shoes, not knowing that I was watching. His sockless feet were wet with blood. He upended his shoes and tapped the heels. Something red sprinkled over the dirt, and then Torito rose and limped away.

I stepped outside. Little red flecks, like bugs, dotted the ground. I scooped up a handful and blew away the dirt. The hard, bloodstained slivers of pine that remained felt warm in the palm of my hand.

I realized then that after a while pain is just pain, and there's nothing you can do to make it into glory ever again. I told Torito what I thought, and even though he denied trying to hurt himself, he decided to pull out of the rematch. Gus and the promoter and the TV people gave him a hell of an argument. But with Rosie's help, Torito held firm.

My heart thundered. I looked at my reflection in the blood-streaked mirror and saw a sweaty old guy who was about to have a heart attack. I'd done that once already, and it hadn't been fun.

I sucked a deep breath. Okay, hot shot. You're out in the desert, surrounded by nothing but miles and miles of cactus and nasty reptiles. Maybe there's a sadistic mob-enforcer out there, too. And a candyman named Willie. Hell, maybe they're one and the same. For company you've got a couple of junkies and a masochistic former middleweight champion who's in presently undefinable deep-shit trouble.

What next?

Number one: Torito needed help, but he needed help that knew how to keep things quiet. Number two: Vegas wasn't my turf. In this case, one plus two equaled Gus. He'd spent lots of time in Vegas over the years. He wasn't a saint, but Torito was always "his boy." I fished through the business cards in my wallet and found his number in L.A.

It was quiet downstairs. No sign of Rosie or the zombie. I flipped on a light in the kitchen, lit a smoke to mask the stink of old grease and moldy Spanish rice, and dialed Gus's number.

"Whoever the hell this is had better be makin' me money, callin' at this time of the night."

"No money, Gus," I said. "It's me, Richie."

"The crazy Italian cut man! What's up, Paisan?"

I sucked on my cigarette. Briefly, I explained what I'd found.

"Doesn't sound good."

"No shit. And it isn't over. Rosie says that someone's coming back to finish the job. She wants me to take Torito to New Mexico."

"What does Toro say?"

"Not much. At least, nothing that makes any sense."

Gus broke in with a few choice words. "Jesus, this is perfect fucking timing. Can you believe that I was talking to Barkley's people today? The crazy S.O.B.s want to go pay-per-view. They're offering two mil for Toro on marquee value alone. I haven't even put the screws to 'em yet. I mean, if Duran and Hearns and Leonard can make five-ten mil, why not my boy?"

"Gus, there's no way. The kid is drowning. Something is very wrong out here, and the last thing we can worry about is Toro climbing into the ring again. That's crazy. If you could see him—"

"Christ, it's that bad?" For the first time, he sounded truly worried.

"Yeah . . . can you get someone over here?"

"I'll see what I can do. I know some Italian boys over on the Strip. I'll give them a call, tell them a fellow spaghetti-bender is in trouble."

"Thanks," I said. "Gotta go."

"Richie?"

"Yeah?"

"Don't get all weepy on me. I need you strong, pal. I'm counting on you to protect my investment."

I started to curse him, but Rosie screamed, and I dropped the phone and headed into the dark hallway.

Bleached-out halogen light spilled through the open door, silhouetting Rosie and the zombie. A man came over the threshold, his moccasined feet silent on the Italian marble. He grabbed a handful of the zombie's hair and kicked his legs out from under him. The zombie went down hard.

"I told you not to come back," the man said, kicking the zombie's stiletto across the floor.

The knife hit the wall and snicked open.

"You don't know nothing about blades," the man said. "You don't know nothing about my family, either." He drove the zombie's face against the cold Italian marble, shattering his front teeth. "You get out now, or I'm gonna teach you about blades."

Whimpering, the zombie crawled outside. The man slammed the door and scooped up the stiletto. "Sorry I'm late," he said, frowning at Rosie. "I met a guy named Willie down the road, and I had to straighten him out on a few things."

He stared at me then, and my chest tightened.

"Rosie," he whispered, "is this the man you told me about?"

Her eyes brimmed with tears. She looked at me. "I . . . I didn't tell."

"Just because you didn't say anything doesn't mean that you didn't tell." He closed the blade and pocketed it. "Aren't you going to introduce us, then?"

"Richie, this is Toro's father."

I looked into the old man's eyes, and something exploded in my chest.

I came to in a chair in Torito's bedroom. At first I thought the old man had shoved the stiletto into my heart. But the pain was familiar, something I'd felt before, and I tried to sneak careful breaths around it, tried to keep alive.

The old man bent over me. His hair was as white as the marble floor downstairs and his eyes were a polished, sparkling brown. "I think you're gonna make it," he pronounced, the cool scent of piñon on his breath. "I think you're gonna be fine."

He sat down on the foot of the bed, a carving knife in one hand, a fist-shaped piece of mesquite in the other. Torito watched him from behind, saying nothing. The old man whittled away, his blade whispering over the wood. Every now and then he looked up at me or stared over at the big Mitsubishi, which was still showing Torito's fight with Iran Barkley.

"It's a funny thing," the old man said as Barkley trapped Torito against the ropes. "When wood is alive, it's strong. You can drive a nail into it . . . doesn't matter, it'll keep growing. But dead wood, wood that's seen too many seasons, that's different. Drive a nail too hard, dead wood splinters on you." He flicked shavings over my lap. "After a while, you don't even have to use a nail. You just put that wood out under the sun, the sun that it's seen a million times before, and it rots and falls apart." He glanced at Torito, and then at me. "You understand."

The bell rang. Torito dropped onto his stool, his eyes closed, his cuts swelling. I watched myself working with adrenaline chloride 1-1000, with Vaseline, blood smeared on my fingers.

"You understand."

I looked at the TV. Torito taking punches. I glanced at Torito, helpless in bed. A line of stitches split open on his brow and his cheek turned the color of a rotten plum.

The old man smiled. "You understand. The TV, it's like the sun."

The fist was taking shape. Thick at one end. Almost pointed at the other. The old man worked the knife like a gouge, carving a network of veins over the top.

The bell rang again. Torito rose from his stool. His face was lumpy, smooth, slick with Vaseline.

In bed, Torito grunted and spat blood.

"You did good work," the old man said. "You know, you could have learned to carve."

I sucked a shallow breath. "Torito says that you're the devil."

Flick flick flick. The old man worked the knife like a sixth finger.

"Rosie says that you want to hurt your son."

He grinned. "She's wrong. She doesn't want me to help her . . . she doesn't want me to help my boy. She doesn't even know what he is."

The veins were finished now. The old man started on the fingers. But they were bent and arthritic, turning back on the hand, and they ended at the first joint.

The crowd screamed, "BARK-LEY, BARK-LEY, BARK-LEY!"

"Rosie just wants the drugs," the old man said. "She's afraid of the things I can do for her . . . and for Torito." He looked at his son and smiled proudly. "Torito's not afraid, though. He's brave. He wants me here."

"BARK-LEY, BARK-LEY, BARK-LEY!" A left hook from Torito. "BARK-LEY, BARK-LEY, BARK-LEY!" Barkley's punch already on the way . . . "BARK-LEY, BARK-LEY, BARK-LEY!" Torito's blood geysering through the air . . .

Blood spattered the padded leather headboard.

Torito screamed.

A bitter metallic taste washed over my tongue. I clenched my teeth against the sour pain.

The old man watched his son go down. "He was beautiful when he was young. One day I took a burro and a cart, went up into the mountains. I found a big old tree up there with roots that ran so deep you wouldn't believe it. I burned it down, dug a trench around the stump, peeled it back and hauled the green core down the mountain. Let it season for five summers." He smiled, "Then I went to work. In another year I had my son."

I doubled over. My face came near the mesquite fist, and I saw that it wasn't a fist at all. It was covered with veins, but what I had taken for fingers were actually arteries.

The old man patted my shoulder. "You're lucky that I found this piece today. I don't think that anything else I have would've worked."

He passed a strong hand over the smooth wood, and the mesquite heart began to beat.

I awoke in another room. The old man stood over Rosie, who lay unconscious on a low couch. Soft light filtered through a heavy green lampshade to her right, bathing her sharp features in a liquid glow.

He moved away, wiping his bloody blade on a white handkerchief. Rosie's right arm was laid open to the bone. Blood dripped from what remained of her fingers and splattered on the heavy carpet, the Caesars Tahoe carpet, and on the smooth wooden arm that lay in the green shadows.

The old man saw that I was awake. "She'll be fine," he said. "I had to cut the poison out first, but soon she'll be ready to be whole again."

I looked away.

He ignored my disgust. "Feeling better now?" he asked.

I glared at him.

"Good. You can help me with Torito."

I climbed the stairs on my own. My chest still ached, but the pain had reduced to a dull throbbing and my heartbeat felt even and strong. I had no idea how long I'd been unconscious. I hoped it had been a very long time, because I figured the longer I'd been out, the sooner Gus's Vegas buddies would come to my rescue.

I didn't know what kind of trick the old man had pulled with the mesquite heart, but I was certain that what he'd done to Rosie wasn't an illusion. I followed him down the hall, my left hand sweaty on the grip of my snakeskin bag. Inside was a straight razor. It was too late to help Rosie, but I was going to make damn sure that the old man didn't try the same thing on Torito. I dipped into the bag with my right hand and came out with the razor. One quick slice across the jugular and it would be over. I followed the old man into the bedroom.

A pistol came down hard on my wrist and I dropped the razor.

Another pistol poked under my chin, prodding my gaze to the ceiling.

Footsteps whispered across the carpet. I smelled expensive cologne.

"Well, well, this must be Richie." A deep voice, with just the slightest hint of an Italian accent. "Gus has told me all about you."

He was a thickset man with a fresh haircut and fashionably graying temples. He introduced himself as Jimmy Gemignani.

"So my friend Gus calls me," Gemignani said. " 'Jimmy,' he says, 'we've got trouble out at Torito's. A good friend of mine is over there, and he's got the wrong idea. I'm afraid that someone might get hurt.' "

I started to rise from my seat, but Gemignani's two toughs dropped big hands on my shoulders and stopped me. "Look," I said. "I don't know what you know, but if you go downstairs and take a look at Torito's wife you'll see that you're roughing up the wrong guy." I pointed at the old man, who was examining Torito's swollen brow. "Get him away from Torito. Please."

Torito's father seemed amused by my concern. "Don't listen to him. He doesn't understand yet."

Gemignani nodded. "Then make him understand. I don't have a lot of time, and neither does Gus. He needs Torito for a press conference next week." Gemignani's lips curled in disgust. "And we can't use Toro like this."

The old man shook his head. "That wasn't the deal. I got a contract. It's very specific. Besides, nobody's paid me yet."

"You'll get your money," Gemignani said shortly. "Now, make him understand. If this thing's going to work, we're going to need his full cooperation."

Torito's father put the straight razor in my right hand, and then he raised my left and placed it over my heart. I felt it beating . . .

. . . pounding a staccato speed-bag rhythm. I felt the sleeping black sky stretching forever, dry sandpaper breezes scudding this way and that like indecisive ghosts, heat waves radiating from the highway in the middle of the night. The old man in the desert picking up a piece of mesquite, me knocking at Torito's door. The old man grinning. Me closing Torito's wounds. The old man carving, *flick flick flick*.

I concentrated on the sound of the knife. In a few moments, my heartbeat was even, steady.

I looked at Torito's ruined face. He tried to grin. "C'mon, Richie," he said. "It's the only way. You got to help me." He stared at the TV, watched himself fall under Barkley's fists. "I can't go out like that."

Gemignani's toughs moved away. Gemignani himself handed me my snakeskin bag.

"I guess everybody wants it," I said, as if I'd forgotten all about Rosie.

"He understands now." The old man winked at me. "We got a deal, you and me. We're in this together. That's the way it's got to be."

"Okay," Gemignani said. "Let's do what needs to be done."

A smirking bellboy opened the limo door and Gemignani handed him my bag and a ten-dollar bill. The bellboy scurried away, whistling, his polished black shoes silent on red carpet. He slapped the marble knee of a statue of Hercules and disappeared through a revolving door. For a moment I heard the jingling music of slot machines, but then the door's rubber seals caught and I heard nothing.

Vegas. When it was quiet, it was nothing more than a piece of the desert.

Gemignani patted my knee. I could feel his wedding ring through my thin slacks. I wanted to shove his hand away, but I knew that would be a mistake.

"I never saw anything like that before," he said, a tinge of admiration in his voice. "I never did."

I got a cigarette out of my jacket pocket and planted it between my lips.

"We don't have a reservation in your name," Gemignani said. "Just tell the desk clerk that Jimmy G sent you. Torito's press conference is gonna be on Wednesday at noon—that'll give you three days to rest up. Check with the concierge on Wednesday morning and he'll give you the details."

Another pat, and then Gemignani's hand slipped away. "You do good work, Richie. I'm glad you're part of the team."

I climbed out of the limo and closed the door too hard; the slam sounded like a hammer blow. My lips quivered and I almost lost my cigarette. I waited for a scream of pain, but it didn't come.

I patted my pockets, searching for a match. Gemignani's driver offered a lighter, but I was shaking so badly that I could barely catch the flame.

The driver flicked his fingers against my chest. "Don't get to close. A man in your condition shouldn't play with fire."

I blew smoke in his face.

He looked hurt. "Just a piece of friendly advice," he said, handing me a thick envelope. "Here's some more: stay away from the roulette wheel, and never hit when the dealer is showing a six, no matter what you've got in your hand."

I took the envelope and started up the red carpeted stairs. Hercules stared down at me, a hunk of dead marble.

I thought about wood, dead and seasoned, smelling of muscle and blood. Claw hammers and carving knives stolen from Penitente men, adrenaline chloride

1-1000 and Enswell irons and Vaseline. All the rotten pieces of Torito that the old man cut away and flushed down the toilet. All the surgical thread and bloodstained sandpaper and rusty nails. Rusty nailheads fading to cherry-red scars. Avitene and thrombin, whittled survey-stake ankles and knuckles made of ironwood. Slivers and shavings that writhed and died like worms on the green tiled floor, my cramping fingers fighting to grip a surgical needle slick with blood. I thought about wood that splits, and men with knives, and men who never see the punches coming.

And then I didn't want to think anymore.

My heartbeat was strong and even—mesquite is a damn tough wood—and I knew how to keep it that way.

The desert whispered behind me, but inside the hotel there'd be noise. I ditched the cigarette. Opened the envelope. I had three days of nothing, money to burn, and a new ticker that could keep the pace.

The rest I'd learn to live with.

I wasn't going to worry about the scars.

THE KIND MEN LIKE
Karl Edward Wagner

Karl Edward Wagner, a former psychiatrist, has been a full-time writer since 1975. He has written or edited more than thirty-five horror and science fiction books, including his collections *In a Lonely Place* and *Why Not You and I?* and the annual *Year's Best Horror Stories* anthology published by DAW Books.

What is it about the pin-up? The fantasy woman has always played an important part in American pop culture, and probably always will. The Vargas girl, the Playboy bunny, and the Penthouse pet all provide something to generations of males. But there is a darker side to the pin-ups that can be seen in the bondage magazines and the kinkier leather magazines. In this story from the anthology *Hotter Blood*, Wagner uses the career of Betty Page, a ubiquitous girlie model in the fifties whose spirit permeates this story, as the foundation for a multilayered portrait of a protagonist both erotically alluring and ultimately terrifying.

—E.D.

"She was better than Betty Page," said Steinman. "We used to call her *Better Page!*"

He laughed mechanically at his own tired joke, then started to choke on his beer. Steinman coughed and spluttered, foam oozing down his white-goateed chin. Chelsea Gayle reached across the table and patted him ungently on his back.

"Thanks, miss. It's these cigarettes." Morrie Steinman dabbed at his face with a bar napkin, blinking his rheumy eyes. He gulped another mouthful of beer and continued: "Of course, that always made her mad. Kristi Lane didn't like to be compared to any other model—didn't matter if you told her she was ten times better. Kristi'd just pout her lips that way she'd do and tell you in a voice that'd freeze Scotch in your mouth that there was *no one* like her."

"And there wasn't," Chelsea agreed. "How long did you work with her?"

"Let's see." Steinman finished his beer and set down the empty glass with a deep sigh. Chelsea signaled to the barmaid, who was already pouring another. She guessed Steinman was a regular here. It was an autumn afternoon, and the tired SoHo bar was stagnant and deserted. Maybe soon new management would convert it into something trendy; maybe they'd just knock it down with the rest of the aging block.

"I was working freelance, mostly. Shooting photo sessions sometimes for the magazines, sometimes for the mail-order pin-up markets, sometimes for the private photo clubs where you could get away with a lot more. Of course, 'a lot more' back in the fifties meant 'a lot less' than you can see on TV these days.

"Thank you, miss." Steinman sipped his fresh beer, watching the barmaid walk away from their booth. "I remember doing a few pin-up spreads of Kristi for Harmony Publishing back about '52 or '53—stuff for girlie magazines like *Wink* and *Eyeful* and *Titter*. They'd seem tame and corny now, but back then . . ."

The paunchy photographer rolled his eyes and made a smacking sound with his lips. Chelsea thought of a love-stricken geriatric Lou Costello.

"After that I shot several of her first few cover spots—magazines like *Gaze* and *Satan* and *Modern Sunbathing*. That must have been the mid '50s. Of course, she was also doing a lot of work for the old bondage-and-fetish photo sets, same as Betty Page. I heard once that Kristi and Betty did a few sessions together, but if that's true no one I know's ever seen them."

"Did Kristi Lane do any work for Irving Klaw?"

"Not a lot that I can recall. I remember introducing them sometime about 1954, or was it 1953? I think they may have shot a few sessions—high heels and black lingerie, pin-up stuff. No bondage."

"Why not?"

"Word was that Kristi Lane was a little too wild for Klaw, who was really pretty straightlaced." Steinman wheezed at his joke. "People said that Kristi could get a little too rough on the submissive model when she had the dominant role. I know some of the girls wouldn't work with her unless they played the mistress."

"Where did she get all her work, then?"

"Mostly from the private photo clubs. And from the mail-order agencies who'd change their drop-box number every few months. You know, the ones with the ads in the back of the girlie mags for comics and photos—'the kind men like.' They could get away with murder, and poor Irving got busted and never showed so much as a bare tit in his photo sets."

While Steinman sucked down his fresh beer, Chelsea opened her attaché case and withdrew several manila envelopes. She handed them to Steinman. "What can you tell me about these?"

Each envelope contained half a dozen black-and-white four-by-fives. Steinman shuffled the photo sets. "That's Kristi Lane, all right."

The first set showed the model in various pin-up poses. The white bikini would have been too daring for its day, and Kristi Lane's statuesque figure seemed about to burst its straps. Her hair was done in her characteristic short blond pageboy, her face held her familiar pout (Bardot's was a careful copy), and her wide blue eyes were those of a fallen angel.

In the next set Kristi was shown dressed as a French maid. Her short costume exposed ruffled panties and lots of cleavage, as she bent over to go about her dusting.

"I shot this one," Steinman said, licking his lips. "About 1954. She said she was twenty. Anyway, they ran it in *Beauty Parade*, I think."

Kristi was tied to a chair in the next set. She was wearing high heels, black stockings and garter belt, black satin panties and bra. A black scarf was knotted around her mouth, and her eyes begged for mercy. She was similarly clad in the next set, but this time she was lying hog-tied upon a rug. In the next, she was tied spread-eagled across a bed.

"All shot the same afternoon," Steinman judged. "Do a few costume changes, give the girl a chance to stretch between poses, and you could come up with maybe a hundred or so good stills."

The next series had Kristi wearing thigh-high patent leather boots and a matching black corset. Her maid, attired in heels, hose, and the inevitable skimpy uniform, was having trouble lacing up Kristi's boots. Over the subsequent poses, the maid was gagged and bound facedown across a table by Kristi, who then applied a hairbrush to the girl's lace-clad bottom.

"Could have been done for Klaw," said Steinman, "but none of these were. The numbers at the bottom aren't his numbering system. There were a lot of guys doing these back then. Most, you never heard of. It wasn't my thing, you gotta understand, but a buck was a buck, then same as now."

Chelsea pulled out another folder. "What about these?"

Steinman flipped through a selection of stills, color and black-and-white, four-by-fives and eight-by-tens. In most of them, Kristi Lane was completely nude, and she was obviously a natural blonde.

"Private stock. You couldn't do that over the counter back then. Even the nudist magazines had to use an airbrush."

"Here's some more."

Kristi Lane was wearing jackboots, a Nazi armband, an SS hat, and nothing else. The other girl was suspended by her wrists above the floor and wore only a ball gag. Kristi wielded her whip with joyous zeal, the victim's contorted face hinted at the screams stifled by the rubber ball, and the blood that oozed from the welts across her twisting body looked all too real.

"No. I never did any of this sort of stuff." Steinman seemed affronted as he handed her back the folder.

"Who did?"

"Lot of guys. Lot of it amateur. Like I say, it wasn't sold openly. Hey, I'm surprised a girl like you'd even want to know about this kind of stuff, Miss . . . uh . . ." He'd forgotten her name since her phone call yesterday.

"Ms. Gayle. Chelsea Gayle."

"Miss Gayle. I thought all modern girls were feminists. Burning their bras and dressing up like men. I guess you're not one of them." His stare was suddenly professional, and somewhere in his beer-soaked brain he was once again focusing his 4 × 5 Speed Graphic camera.

Chelsea tasted her rum and flat cola and tried not to look flustered. After all, she was wearing her wide-shouldered power suit with a silk blouse primly gathered at the neck by a loose bow, and there was no nonsense about her taupe panty hose or low-heeled pumps. Beneath the *New Woman* exterior, she was confident that her body could as easily slither into a *Cosmopolitan* party dress. Her face took good close-ups, her blond hair was stylishly tousled, and she wore glasses more for fashion than necessity. Let the old fart stare.

"It's for an article on yesterday's pin-up queens," she said, repeating the lie she had told him over the phone. "Sort of a nostalgic look back as we enter the nineties: The women men dreamed of, and where are they now?"

"Well, I can't help you there on Kristi Lane." Steinman waved to the barmaid. "I don't know of anyone who can."

"When did you last work with her?"

"Hard to say. She was all over the place for those few years, then she moved out of my league. I'd guess the last time I shot her would have been about 1958. I know it was a cover for one of those *Playboy* imitations, but I forget the title. Didn't see much of her after that."

"When did you last see her?"

"Probably about 1960. Seem to recall that's about when she dropped out of sight. A guy told me once he'd run into her at a hippie party in the Village late in the sixties, but he was too strung out to know what he was seeing."

"Any ideas?"

"Nothing you haven't heard already. Some said she got religion and entered a convent somewhere. There was some talk that she got pregnant; maybe she married some Joe from Chillico and settled down. There was one story that she was climbing in bed with JFK, and the CIA snuffed her like they did Marilyn Monroe."

"But what do *you* think happened to her?"

Steinman chugged his beer. "I think maybe she got a little too wild."

"Too wild?"

"You know what I mean. Maybe got in too deep. Had to drop out of sight. Or somebody made sure she did."

Chelsea frowned and dug into her case. "This one is pretty wild."

It was a magazine, and on the front it said, *Her Satanic Majesty Requests*, and below that, *For Sale to Adults Only*. The nude woman on the cover was wearing a sort of harness about her hips with a red pointed tail in back and a monstrous red dildo in front. Her face was Kristi Lane's blond pageboy and all.

Steinman flipped to the centerfold. A writhing victim was tied to a sacrificial altar. Kristi Lane was astride her spread-eagled body, vigorously screwing her with the dildo.

Steinman slapped the magazine shut, shoved it back to Chelsea. "Not my bag, baby. I never shot any porno."

Chelsea replaced the magazine. "Was that Kristi Lane?"

"Maybe. It sure looked like her."

"But the magazine has a 1988 copyright. Kristi Lane would have looked a lot older—she'd be in her fifties."

"You can't tell about that sort of smut. Maybe it was bootleg stuff shot years before. You don't worry about copyrights here."

"The publisher is given as Nightseed X-Press, but their post office box now belongs to some New Age outfit. They weren't helpful."

"The old fly-by-night. Been gone for years."

"Who was shooting stuff like this back then? This looks fresh from the racks on 42nd Street."

"So it's a Kristi Lane lookalike. Hey, I saw Elvis singing at a bar just yesterday. Only, he was Jewish."

Steinman reached again for his empty glass, gave it a befuddled scrowl. "Look. It's all Mob stuff now. The porno racket. Don't ask. Forget it. But—you *really* interested in the old stuff, the pin-up stuff? I got all my work filed away at my studio. No porno. Want to come up and see it?"

"Come up and see your etchings?"

"Hey, on the level. I could be your grandfather."

"Do you have any shots of Kristi Lane?"

"Hundreds of them. Say, have you ever posed professionally? Not pin-ups, I mean—but you have a wonderful face."

Chelsea smiled briskly and closed her case. "Tell you what, Morrie. Here's my business card. See what you've got on Kristi Lane, and then phone me at work. Could be I'll come by and take off my glasses for you."

She gathered up her things and the bar tab, and because he looked so much like a gone-to-seed gnome, she kissed him on top of his balding head.

"Hey, Miss Gayle!" he called after her. "I'll ask around. Look, doll, I'll be in touch!"

Chelsea played back the messages on her answering machine, found nothing of interest, and decided on a long, hot bath. Afterward, she slipped into a loose T-shirt and cotton boxer shorts, and she microwaved the first Lean Cuisine dinner she found in her freezer. A dish of ice cream seemed called for, and she curled up with her cat to consider her day.

The old geek at the used books and magazines dump off Times Square had given her Morrie Steinman's name after she had purchased an armload of Kristi Lane material from him. Apart from adding to her collection, she had really gained nothing from it at all—although it was a thrill to talk with someone who had actually photographed Kristi Lane back at the start of her career.

Chelsea gave her cat the last of the ice cream and hauled the heavy coffee-table book on Kristi Lane onto her lap. It had recently been published by Academy Editions, and she had lugged it back to New York from the shop in Holland Street, Kensington, certain that there was not likely to be a U.S. edition. Its title was *Kristi Lane: The Girl of Men's Dreams*, but Chelsea had already been dreaming of her for years.

She turned through the pages, studying photo after photo of Kristi Lane. Kristi Lane in stripper's costumes, Kristi Lane in high heels and seamed tights and pointed bras and lacy panties and bulky girdles and all the clumsy undergarments of the fifties. Kristi Lane decked out in full fetish gear—boots and corsets and leather gloves and latex dresses and braided whips. Kristi Lane tied to chairs, lashed to tables, spread-eagled over wooden frames, chained and gagged, encased in leather hoods and body sheaths. Kristi Lane tying other women into stringent bondage positions, gagging them with tape and scarves and improbable devices, spanking them with hairbrushes and leather straps.

Chelsea already had many of the photos in her own collection. However familiar, she kept paging through the book. Perhaps this time she might find a clue.

Of course, there was nothing new to be learned: Kristi Lane. Real name unknown. Birthplace and date of birth unknown. Said to be from Ohio. Said to be a teenager when she began her modeling career in New York. Much in demand as pin-up and bondage model during the 1950s. Dropped out of sight about 1962. End of text. Nothing left to do but look at the pictures.

Chelsea shoved the book aside and plopped her cat onto her vacated warmth on the couch. It was bedtime for the Chelsea girl.

Her dream was not unexpected. Nor surprising.

She was wearing one of those funny conical bras that made her breasts stick out like Dagmars on a fish-tail Cadillac—that was her first impression. After that came the discomfort of the boned white corset that pinched her waist, and the tight girdle that squeezed her hips and gartered her seamed hose. She tottered on six-inch-high heels, as her mistress scolded her for some imagined offense. Her mistress looked very stern in her black corselet and spike-heeled boots, and it was only the flip of a page before she was punishing her clumsy maid.

There was a wall-length mirror, so Kristi could watch herself being tied across a coffee table. Her ankles were tied to the table legs at one end, her wrists bound to the legs at the other end, forcing her to support her weight with her flexed legs and arms. Another rope secured her waist to the tabletop, and a leather gag stifled her pleas. Kristi wriggled in helpless pain in her cramped position, rolling her eyes and whimpering through the leather strap. Her thighs were spread wide by her bondage, and she flushed as she saw her mistress smiling at the dampening crotch of her girdle. Her cunt was growing hotter and wetter the harder she struggled . . .

Chelsea awoke with the pulse of her orgasm. After a moment she decided that, in the morning, she would try to search out the photo set and make a notation. She had made hundreds of such notations.

Her secretary told her: "Your grandfather phoned while you were at lunch."

"What?" Chelsea studied the memo. "Oh, that has to be Morrie."

"Said he has some new etchings to show you. Your grandfather is quite the kidder."

"He's a randy old goat. I'll see what he wants."

Chelsea returned the call from her office. Morrie's answering machine said that Mr. Steinman was at work in the darkroom just now and to please leave a message and number at the tone. Chelsea started to speak, and Steinman picked up the phone.

"Hey, doll! Got something for you."

"Like what?"

"Nightseed X-Press. The porno mag you showed me."

"Yes?"

"Most of them aren't really models. Just hookers doing a trick in front of a camera. I had a friend ask around. Discreetly. Found a girl who says she did some work for Nightseed about a year ago, gave me the address."

"Did she say anything about Kristi Lane?"

"The bimbo's maybe eighteen. She wouldn't know Kristi Lane from Harpo Marx. No phone number, but it's a loft not far from here. Want I should check it out?"

"I can do that."

"I don't think so. Not a job for a lady. Why don't you come by here sometime after five, and I'll make a full report. I got some photos you might like to see as well."

"All right. I'll come by after work."

Chelsea hung up and opened her shoulder bag. Yes, the can of Mace was right on top.

Steinman's studio was a second-floor walk-up above a closed-down artists' supply shop a few blocks from the bar where they'd met. The stencil on the frosted glass read *Morris Steinman Photography*, and Chelsea tried to imagine what sort of business he might attract.

The door was unlocked, and the secretary's desk had probably been vacant since Kennedy's inauguration. It was going on six, so Chelsea rapped on the glass and walked inside. The place was surprisingly neat, if a bit faded, and the wastebasket contained only a beer can. A row of filing cabinets had been recently dusted.

Chelsea let herself into the studio beyond the front office. She smelled coffee. There was a green davenport, a refrigerator, a hot plate, and an electric percolator, which was steaming slightly. There was a large empty room with a lot of backdrops and lighting stands and camera tripods. In the back there was a darkroom with a red light glowing above the DO NOT ENTER sign on the door. As she watched, the light winked out.

"Morrie?" Chelsea crossed to the darkroom. "It's Chelsea Gayle."

The door of the darkroom slowly opened. Morrie Steinman shuffled out into the studio. He was holding a still-damp print, but he wasn't looking at it or at Chelsea. His face was a pasty mask, his eyes staring and unfocused. Steinman stumbled past Chelsea, moving dreamily toward the couch. He was a puppet whose strings were breaking, one by one. By the time he collapsed onto the davenport, there were no more strings to break.

Chelsea pried the photograph from his stiff fingers. Blood was trickling from beneath the frayed sleeve of his shirt, staining the four-by-five print as she tore it free. The photo was smeared, but it was a good pose of Kristi Lane in a tight sweater with a bit of stocking-top laid bare by her hiked-up skirt. She was seated with her knees crossed on the green davenport.

"Morrie always did good work," Kristi Lane said, stepping out of the darkroom. "I thought I owed him one last pose."

She closed her switchblade and pouted—teenage bad girl from the 1950s B-movies. In face and figure, Kristi Lane hadn't changed by so much as a gray hair from the pin-up queen of 1954. Chelsea reflected that her pageboy hairstyle was once again high fashion.

"Why kill him?"

Kristi slowly walked toward her. "Not too many left from the old days who could recognize me. Now there's one less. You shouldn't have prodded him into looking for me."

"There's thousands of photographs. You're a cult figure."

"Honey, if you passed Marilyn Monroe jogging in Central Park, you'd know she was just another lookalike."

Chelsea reached for the can of Mace as Kristi stepped close to her. Kristi's hand closed like steel over her wrist before she could work the spray. The can flew from her grasp, as Kristi effortlessly flung her across the studio. She crashed heavily against the wall opposite and slid down against it to her knees.

Kristi reached down for her throat, and the switchblade clicked. "We can make this as rough as you want, honey."

Chelsea lunged to her feet and caught Kristi beneath her arms, lifting the other woman and hurling her through a backdrop. Kristi lost her switchblade as she crashed down amidst a tangle of splintering wood.

Struggling free, she swung a heavy light-stand at Chelsea's head. Chelsea caught the blow with her forearms and wrenched the bent metal stand away from her. Diving forward as Kristi stumbled back, she tackled the other woman—pinning her as the two smashed through the wreckage of another backdrop.

Kristi Lane suddenly stopped struggling. She stared in wonder at the woman crouched on top of her.

"Who are you?"

"I'm your daughter," Chelsea panted. "Now tell me what I am!"

Kristi Lane laughed and pushed Chelsea off her. "Like mother, like daughter. You're a succubus."

"A succubus!"

"Dictionary time? A demon in female form—a temptress who haunts men's dreams, who draws youth and strength from their lust. Surely by now you've begun to wonder about yourself."

"I'd found out from agency records that you were my mother. I thought that if I could find you, you might explain things—like why I'm unnaturally strong, and why I look like I'm still twenty, and why I keep having dreams about being you."

"I think it's time we had our mother-daughter chat," Kristi said, helping her to her feet. "Let's go home."

"Chelsea Gayle," Kristi murmured. "I gave you the name, Chelsea."

"Why did you give me up?"

"No place for a baby in my life. The social agency had no problems with that, although they hardly could have guessed the full reasons. Most offspring never survive infancy. You've been feeding off my energy all these years—and you turned out very well."

Chelsea tugged off the remains of her blouse and slipped into a kimono. She couldn't decide whether her mother's gaze held tenderness or desire.

"Who was my father?"

"All men. The thousands who fucked me in their wet-dream fantasies, who jacked off over my pictures. Their seed is our strength. Sometimes the combined energy of their lust is strong enough to create a child. It happens only rarely. Perhaps someday you'll bear another of us."

"I work in advertising."

"Selling false dreams. Already you were becoming one of us."

Kristi took away Chelsea's kimono and unhooked her bra. Chelsea did not resist.

"You shouldn't hide your beauty," Kristi told her. "We *need* to feed from their secret lusts. Both of us. Now it's time you were weaned. Get rid of those clothes, and I'll find you something better to wear."

Chelsea was naked when Kristi returned from another corner of the loft. Her mother had changed into spike-heeled boots and a studded leather bikini. Her arms were loaded with leather gear.

"I'll teach you," she said. "They need stronger stimulation now than they did when I began. I almost waited too long; I'd become nostalgia to them, no longer their sexual fantasy. My comeback will also be your coming out."

Kristi Lane led her over to a small stage area. Lights were coming on, and Chelsea sensed cameras and presences behind them in the encircling darkness, but she couldn't see beyond the lights.

"Now then, dear." Kristi set down her bondage paraphernalia and picked up a riding crop. "I am mistress here, and you must obey me in every way. Do you promise?"

"Yes, mistress. I promise."

"After all," her mother said softly, "this is what you've always known you wanted."

Then, sharply: "Now then! Let's get you into these!"

Meekly Chelsea put on the leather corselet and thigh-high boots, then submitted to having her arms laced tightly behind her back in a leather single-glove. By then it was pointless to struggle when Kristi strapped a phallus-shaped gag deep into her mouth, then brought out what at first glance had looked like a leather chastity belt. Choking on the gag, Chelsea moaned as the twin dildos penetrated her vagina and rectum, stretching her as they pushed inward to rub together against the thin wall that separated their bulbous heads.

Her mother leaned forward to kiss her face as she padlocked the belt securely into place. "You'll stay like me, Chelsea—forever young and beautiful."

Kristi helped her lie down on top of a long leather sheath. As Chelsea writhed on her belly, Kristi began to lace together the two edges of the leather sleeve, tightly encasing her daughter within a leather tube from her ankles to her neck.

Kristi kissed her face again, just as she fitted the leather hood over Chelsea's head and laced it across the back of her neck. "Their lust is our strength. I'll help you."

Chelsea lay helpless, blinded and gagged, barely able to wriggle so much as her fingers. She felt her ankles being strapped together. Then, slowly, she was lifted into the air by her ankles until she was completely suspended above the stage.

Hanging upside down, tightly wrapped in her leather sheath, Chelsea could sense the gloating touch of the cameras. She writhed helplessly, beginning to experience the warmth that flowed into her from the hard rubber penises swollen inside her mouth and cunt and ass. She did not feel violated. Instead she felt the strength that she was drawing from an unseen prey.

Suspended and satisfied, Chelsea Gayle waited to be released from her cocoon, and wondered what she had become.

THE COON SUIT
Terry Bisson

Terry Bisson had published several acclaimed novels, including *Talking Man* and *Fire on the Mountain*, before he or anyone else realized that he could also write terrific short stories. Then he began to write excellent short pieces, including the recent "Over Flat Mountain," "Bears Discover Fire," and "They're Made Out of Meat." His outpouring of fine stories has created a sensation. "Bears . . ." is his best-known story to date, having won the Nebula, Hugo, and Sturgeon Awards. A collection of his short fiction, titled *Bears Discover Fire and Other Stories*, will be published in 1993.

"The Coon Suit," originally published in *The Magazine of Fantasy & Science Fiction*, is short, folksy, and ultimately terrifying.

—E.D.

I'm not much of a hunter and I don't care for dogs. I was driving out Taylorsville Road in Oldham County one Sunday, when I saw this bunch of pickups down in a hollow by a pond. My own yellow-and-white '77 Ford half-ton was bought from a coon hunter, and it could have been the truck as much as me that slowed down to take a look. Men were standing around the pickups, most of which had dog boxes in the beds. I saw a xeroxed sign stapled to a telephone pole, and realized I had been seeing the same sign for a couple of miles along the road.

COON RUN, SUNDAY, CARPENTERS LAKE.

If this was Carpenters Lake, it was not much more than a pond. I could hear dogs barking. I pulled over to watch.

There was a cable running across the water. It ran from a pole where the trucks were parked, into the trees on the other side of the pond. Hanging under it, like a cable car, was a wire cage. While I watched, two men took six or eight hounds out of the back of a half-ton Ford and down to the bank. The dogs were going wild and I could see why.

There was a coon in the cage. From where I was parked, up on the road, it was just a little black shape. It looked like a skunk or a big house cat. It was probably just my imagination, but I thought I could see the black eyes, panicky under the white mask, and the handlike feet plucking at the wire mesh.

A rope ran from the cage, through a pulley on a tree at the far end of the cable, and back. A man pulled at the rope, and the cage started across the cable, only three or four feet off the water. The men on the bank let the dogs go, and they threw themselves in the pond. They were barking louder than ever, swimming under the cage as it was pulled in long, slow jerks toward the woods on the other side.

My wife Katie tells me I'm a watcher, and it's true I'd generally rather watch than do. I wasn't even tempted to join the men by the pond, even though I probably knew one or two of them from the plant. I had a better view from up on the road. There was something fascinating and terrifying at the same time about the dogs splashing clumsily through the water (they don't call it dog-paddling for nothing), looking up hungrily at the dark shape in the wire cage.

Once the cage was moving, the coon sat dead still. He probably figured he had the situation under control. I could almost see the smirk on his face as he looked down at the dogs in the water, a sort of aviator look.

On the bank, the men leaned against their trucks, drinking beer and watching. They all wore versions of the same hat, drove versions of the same truck, and looked like versions of the same guy. Not that I think I'm better than them; I'm just not much of a hunter and don't care for dogs. From the boxes in the truck beds, the other hounds waiting their turn set up a howl, a background harmony to the wild barking from the pond.

The situation wasn't fair, though, because whenever the dogs fell behind, the man pulling the rope would stop pulling and let them catch up. While the cage was moving, the coon was O.K.; but as soon as it stopped, he would go crazy. He would jump from side to side, trying to get it going again, while the hounds paddled closer and closer. Dogs when they're swimming are all jaws. Then the man would pull on the rope, and the cage would take off again toward the trees on the other side, and I could almost see the coon get that smirk on his face again. That aviator look.

The second act of the drama began when the cage reached the tree at the end of the cable. The tree tripped the door, and the coon dove out and hit the ground. In a flash he was gone, into the woods that ran up over the hill alongside the road. A few seconds later, and the dogs were out of the water after him, the whole pack running like a yellow blur up the bank, shaking themselves as they ran, the water rising off their backs like a cloud of steam. Then they were gone into the trees, too.

One of the pickups was already on its way up the road, presumably to follow. The guys in it looked at me kind of funny as they drove by, but I ignored them. Down by the pond, the cage was being pulled back, six more dogs were being taken out of the trucks, and a man held a squirming gunnysack at arm's length.

Another coon.

They put him into the cage, and I should have left, since I was expected somewhere. But there was something interesting—or I guess fascinating is the word—about the whole business, and I had to see more. I drove a hundred yards up the road and stopped by the edge of the woods.

I got out of the truck.

The brush by the roadside was thick, but after I got into the woods, things opened up a little. It was mostly oak, gum, and hickory. I made my way down the slope toward the pond, walking quietly so I could listen. I could tell by the barking when the dogs hit the water. I could tell when the cage stopped, and when it started up again. It was in the dogs' voices. Through them, I could almost feel the coon's terror when the cage stopped, and his foolish annoyance when it started moving again.

Halfway down the hill, I stopped in a little clearing at the foot of a big, hollow beech. All around me were thick bushes, tangles of fallen limbs, and brush. The barking got louder and wilder, and I knew the cage was reaching the cable's end. There was a howl of rage, and I knew the coon was in the woods. I stood perfectly still. Soon I heard a sharp slithering sound, and, without a warning, without stirring a leaf, the coon ran out of the bushes and straight at me. I was too startled to move. He ran almost right across my feet—a black-and-white blur—and was gone up the hill, into the bushes again. For a second I almost felt sorry for the dogs: how could they ever hope to catch such a creature?

Then I heard the dogs again. Pitiless is the word for them. If they had looked all jaws in the water, they sounded all claws and slobber in the woods. Their barking got louder and wilder as they got closer, at least six of them, hot on the coon's trail. Then I heard a crashing in the brush down the hill. Then I saw the bushes shaking, like a storm coming up low to the ground. Then I heard the rattle of claws on dry leaves, getting closer and closer. Then I saw a yellow blur as the dogs bolted from the bushes and across the clearing straight at me. I stepped back in horror.

That's when I realized—or I guess remembered is the word—that I had my coon suit on.

QUEEN CHRISTINA AND THE WINDSURFER

Alison Fell

Alison Fell is a Scottish poet and novelist who lives in London. Her novels include *Every Move You Make*, *The Bad Box*, and *Mer de Glace*; her poetry collections are *Kisses for Mayakovsky* and *The Crystal Owl*. She also edited and contributed to the women's collections *The Seven Deadly Sins* and *The Seven Cardinal Virtues*.

"Queen Christina and the Windsurfer" is a fresh and contemporary re-working of the European "Undine" folk legends—the same legends that inspired Hans Christian Andersen's tragic "Little Mermaid" (bearing slight resemblance to the cheery Disney movie version) and Charles de Lint's urban mermaid story elsewhere in this volume. Fell's sparkling fantasy tale comes from the *Winter's Tales* annual, edited by Robin Baird-Smith.

—T.W.

The big ferry steamed past the mouth of the bay, stately, discoing, lit up like a castle. In the broad white wake Poseidon's daughter lurked unseen, as one by one coke cans plopped into the waves around her. She watched a pretty German girl stretch out her long brown neck to be kissed; watched how the German boy lifted the glossy sheet of hair and twisted it up on to the crown of her head while he touched his lips to her nape. The hair was toffee-dark with the wheaty sheen of sun, and straight as the farthest horizon.

Swamped with envy, Poseidon's daughter rolled on to her back, and sighed, and sank. Down in the green deeps of the palace nothing was straight, and everything was uncertain and wavered: or so thought Poseidon's daughter as she combed out her tough black curls in the mirror, and glowered her thick brows, and blew small rainbow bubbles of disgust.

Presently she swam up to her mother and circled hopefully, waiting for an opening.

'Am I pretty, Mother?' she demanded at last, with as much petulance as she dared, for Amphitrite was harassed and crusty and had little patience with such energetic despairs.

Amphitrite glanced up from her housework and frowned. It was the holiday season again: six million tourists to shit and piss in the sea. From strayed missiles

181

to ham sandwiches, everything fell from the air and the water rotted it, and try as she might to sweep and sort, to recycle and dispose, the Mediterranean was fast becoming a garbage bin. Amphitrite hurled three thonged sandals and a Daytona Beach T-shirt into a large cockle-shell, and for a moment thought rancorously of Aphrodite—she who rose from the foam and never did a day's work thereafter.

'Any young girl with clean hair is pretty,' she said testily, thrusting a broom at her daughter, and her daughter, silenced, took it and the two women set to work in concert, sighing, as women do.

On the beach of Plati Yialos, in Nicos' Taverna, Hanni the windsurfer was watching television. Hanni the windsurfer was salt-streaked and golden; his jeans were cut off at the knee and the snakelets of his hair were crystalline blond. At night Hanni camped on the beach and ate water-melons filled with rum, and each morning early he would run to the shore and mount his surfboard in one bold bound, and the sail would take the wind and the light board leave the surface and skip from wave-crest to wave-crest until it was virtually flying.

Poseidon's daughter had watched all this, daily, from the first flush of summer to the harsh height of it, had watched Hanni's mouth taste the wind and the wind trickle through his hair, watched also the slim girls with cigarettes in their mouths who on the sunburned beach shielded their eyes with their hands and gazed out to sea, waiting for his return . . . had slipped, finally—in love and frustration— under the keel of his board where, clinging on by the tips of her fingers, she had flown beneath him for mile upon ardent mile, all green and unseen in the dappled shadow of the sail.

Down in the deeps Poseidon's daughter swept and swept and the white sand flew in clouds and the startled inkfish scuttled off to safety.

'Am I as pretty as . . . ?' she brooded, frowning so fiercely that she was no longer pretty at all. 'Am I as pretty as . . . ?'

At last the question weighed so heavily that she threw down her broom and entered the throne-room and asked without preamble, 'Who is the most perfect woman in the world, Father?'

From the uncomfortable heights of his throne Poseidon listened unwillingly, tapping his foot on a ramp of seaweed. Above the waves a new moon was rising and at the palace gates his golden sea-horses pranced and whinnied, eager to be off.

'Why, Aphrodite,' he said absently, and then, with a guilty glance over his shoulder, he corrected himself. 'I mean Amphitrite, of course.'

'But apart from her?' said his daughter crossly.

Poseidon stroked his long beard for a moment, considering. 'Helen?' he pondered, but in truth he had hardly given the matter a thought for the last few centuries. 'Why don't you ask your uncle,' he suggested at last. 'Zeus always did have an eye for the ladies.' Then, relieved to have discharged his fatherly duty, he bade his daughter a quick good night and, jumping into his waiting chariot, drove at full speed around the curve of the coast. At the flat rock of Krissopigi Poseidon slithered out of the sea and trained his telescope on the farthest moons of Uranus: Miranda, where blue snows of nitrogen arched and plumed from furious geysers; Triton, with its sheer cliffs of ice more than twenty miles high. As his eye strained to pick out the lovely details, his thoughts strayed to his brother, and he let out an involuntary sigh which stirred the waves to a tumult and spattered the lens of his telescope with spray. For, try as he might to accept his destiny, he could not help feeling that his own inheritance was in every way inferior. However you looked at it, water was simply not as virile an element as earth or time, as fire or air. Down in the green gloom it was easy to become dispirited, whereas out here the air was sharp and the stars so still and clear you could have cut them out with scissors and pinned them to your breast for all eternity.

Back at the palace there was the habitual fuss and bother as Amphitrite made ready for the night. Libations had to be offered up; potions had to be ground and bound and mixed with ambergris and applied to her face and hands; silver hairpins fell from her hair and had to be retrieved from the soft white sand. Restraining her vast impatience, Poseidon's daughter did her duty, combing and soothing, until at last her mother's head drooped on the pillow. Then with a flick of her tail she fled the bedroom and swam fast towards the shore.

With her nose just above the wooden landing-stage of Nicos' Taverna, she could easily spy on Hanni in the lit interior. A television blared from a high shelf above the bar. The film was black and white and old, and accompanied by the scratchings of an invisible orchestra, but Hanni's full brooding attention was fixed on it. From her secret vantage-point Poseidon's daughter watched two ringleted young men make merry swordplay in more snow than she had ever seen, even on the highest summit of Mount Olympus. Later, one of the two young men was revealed as a woman, and then the old men in the café slapped their thighs and all the small ouzo bottles romped and rolled on the café tables, and when Poseidon's daughter whispered Hanni's name to the lapping waves it was a small sound, quite drowned in the uproar of wolf-whistles.

Before the sun rose next morning Poseidon's daughter was arrowing towards the high cliff of Kastro, where her uncle Zeus received minor deities and petitioning mortals in the first light of dawn. But as the sun rose red over the eastern seas she scanned the high rock and the lemon groves and saw only the silent cocoons of several sleeping-bags, and a stray goat rooting hopefully among the scattered rucksacks.

Back at Plati Yialos, the sand was brazen yellow and the first tourists were stumbling on to the terrace of the taverna, calling for foreign breakfasts. A small snort from the mouth of the bay signalled the arrival of the first boat-load of day-trippers, who presently clambered out on to the jetty by the church and marched in a straggling crocodile along the curving sands, past the few Greeks at their fishing nets, towards the small blue tent where Hanni, patient and cross-legged, awaited prospective pupils.

'*Kalamares!*' cried the English, conscious of the need for politeness in foreign lands, and if the Greeks were surprised to be thus greeted with the word for octopus, with the great tact of their nation they gave no sign of it. '*Guten Morgen!*'

cried the Germans with Goethe in their knapsacks. '*Ciao!*' bubbled the Italians in their slight and slippery swimsuits.

At last, scanning the throng, Poseidon's daughter caught sight of her uncle exercising on a stone jetty at the far end of the beach, where the Germans congregated. His biceps glistened with oil, his stomach was pulled in tautly, and his grey-black hair was gelled straight back from his noble forehead. All around him the Germans threw down their rucksacks, cast off their clothes and thundered mother-naked into the surf.

'Uncle Zeus,' cried Poseidon's daughter from the waves. 'Who is the most perfect woman in the world?'

'Don't "Uncle" me,' hissed Zeus, swivelling his pectorals towards a naked Nordic girl who stood knee-deep in the surf with her face turned up to the sun. 'The name's Stavros.'

Poseidon's daughter was undaunted, however, and, tugging at his ankle, repeated her question.

'Well, Greta Garbo, of course,' said Zeus, with a jealous glance at Hanni's tent, which was by now quite surrounded by Euro-beauties, so that nothing could be glimpsed of Hanni but the topmost tuft of his blond hair and a faint blue curl of cigarette smoke. He had been lobbied, recently, to make Garbo an immortal, although just at that moment he could see little advantage in immortality and indeed would gladly have exchanged the entire inheritance of Kronos and Ouranos for one sole afternoon inside the sleek hide of that taciturn youth.

Disconsolate, Poseidon's daughter swam ever-widening circles in the broad bay. Under the surface ripples of light wavered over the rocks, and the anemones opened sleepy brilliant eyes to watch her pass. By now it was almost lunchtime; the caiques with their ballast of water-melons rode at anchor by the quay, and charcoal flared under the griddle on the taverna terrace.

On a promontory near the entrance to the bay she spied her aunt, Athena the owl-eyed, battering squid against a rock to tenderize it. Filled with that urge to confess which love inspires in us, and eager to indulge in the compensatory thrills of chatter, Poseidon's daughter swam up strongly and surfaced in the hot noon air. Besides—although she herself had no spinsterly aspirations—she genuinely did admire her aunt, who, unlike her mother Amphitrite, had proved that she would be a doormat to no man on earth or in heaven.

'Aunt Athena,' she murmured languorously, lying along a wave and all prepared for confidences.

'Don't tell me,' said Athena in a voice that knew everything and tolerated much of it. 'You're in love with that beach-bum.' Raising her eyes to heaven, she slapped the squid hard against the rock and pronounced, 'For youthful folly it is the most hopeless thing to entangle itself in empty imaginings. The more obstinately it clings to such unreal fantasies, the more certainly will humiliation overtake it.' And then she patted Poseidon's daughter kindly enough and saw her off with a firm admonition to look to her studies and develop herself.

That night, when he had drunk too well and was dreamy with retsina, Hanni the windsurfer wandered down to the shore and stretched his fine frame out on his surfboard. Flat on his back he watched the moon rise: his mouth was open, his hands dangled in the wavelets. Presently, lulled by the soft sound of the wind in the tamarisk trees, he fell into a deep sleep. Hidden by a wreath of sea-wrack, Poseidon's daughter gazed on him longingly, until at last, astonished by her own temerity, she tugged lightly at the prow and drew the board down from the sand until it floated entire in the shallows.

Now, of all the talents that the gods had apportioned to Poseidon's daughter, the only one she had taken pains to nurture was the capacity to see into dreams. And so she lay below the board, watching, nibbling at Hanni's fingertips like a hungry minnow. Meanwhile, Hanni dreamt on, oblivious: dreamt of a full sail, of waves like white stallions. Stealthily, so as not to wake him, Poseidon's daughter pressed her wet lips to his dry ones, and hoisted herself on to the board, mouthing words of love. But in the dream she saw that the words blew like froth or spume from her lips, and seaweed streaked her white face, and Hanni shrank back from this apparition from the deeps and shuddered piteously in his sleep. Fearful that he would fall splashing into the shallows, Poseidon's daughter steadied the board with her hand, until the dreamer sighed and settled again. The wind of the dream recovered and blew breath into the quickening sail, and now there was a woman with her straight back braced against the mast, but it was not she, not Poseidon's daughter, not a thick-browed girl with stormy curls, but a woman of cool bones and superior deep eyes, and she knew then, most certainly, that this was the most perfect woman in the world. And as the dreamer stretched out his arms to the lovely paragon, Poseidon's daughter dived ever deeper into the bitter waters of her jealousy, and she would have given all the world to wrap her own form around the woman like a cloak, so that it would be her face Hanni sought and her body his arms reached out to with such speechless longing.

Of all the skills the gods possessed, it was Zeus alone who knew the trick of snipping the rope that holds the dream to the dreamer. Once—or so her aunt Athena had told her—incensed by the intrusion of aeroplanes into the peaceful Attic skies, Zeus had made fearful mischief. Looking above him, he saw that each plane towed the dreams of its passengers behind it, like a trawler tows its netted catch. Inside the blond fuselage the travellers, having kicked off their shoes and bound velvet masks over their eyes, had slept their way across the troubled Gulf, across Syria and Turkey, so that when the plane turned north-west and struck out across the Ionian Sea their dreams were in full flight—or rather in full dive; for although it is commonly believed that dreams rise up from the dreamer like word-balloons in a cartoon strip, the truth of the matter is that by their very nature they seek out those slower watery elements which blur boundaries and mix one thing up with another, and although, in these rapid times, few are the dreams that find their way there, those that do so live and leap most happily, like dolphins, in the shifting seas. So it happened that when Zeus took his silver scissors and snipped at the cords, the dreams were cast out across the sea and drifted there, higgledy-piggledy, like waterskiers who have lost hold of their tow-rope, and the plane flew on with its perfectly straight jet-trail and its perfectly empty-headed passengers. And some of the dreams Zeus seized by their tails and flung like thunderbolts, so that they fell into the orange groves of Lebanon or shrivelled unnoticed on the salt strands of the Red Sea. Only much later, when the passengers had scattered to their various destinations and slept several nights of empty sleep, did the dreams which survived swim blindly back towards their owners. But as fortune or Zeus would have it, there was no way of telling which dream belonged to a Catholic mission-nurse *en route* from Calcutta, and which to an investment analyst from Kyoto, so that the dreams were forced to seek parents quite at random, like orphaned penguin chicks on the rocky shelves of Patagonia. And Zeus, seeing the broker fall on his knees to ask forgiveness, and the angel-faced Sister take out options on holy relics, laughed so loud in his lemon grove that the rock of Kastro shivered, and cracks appeared in the stepped white streets of the village, and memorial urns fell marvellously asunder in the chapel. Or so her aunt Athena had told her; Athena who had no patience with capriciousness and who made no secret of her opinion that in all respects she was better suited than Zeus to command the company of the gods.

But although Zeus was both boastful and unpredictable, he could also be generous, and it was with this hope in her heart that Poseidon's daughter swam for the second time to the white rock of Kastro to throw herself upon her uncle's magnanimity and beg from him the trick of dream-conjuring.

Under the lemon trees Zeus opened his eyes; beside him the lovely German girl stirred in her sleeping-bag, and her lovely mouth murmured the name 'Stavros'. Zeus stroked the silky pelt on his chest and was well pleased with the night's work. When he saw the rough head of his ragamuffin niece break the surface of the bay he laughed indulgently.

'What now?' he cried, throwing a handful of figs at her. For a daughter of the meek and myopic Poseidon she was certainly demanding.

Affecting not to notice the sleeping girl, Poseidon's daughter drew herself up and made her request with as much dignity as she could muster.

'Stop wanting, start having,' said Zeus, flicking the silver scissors casually up into the air, where they hung suspended. Poseidon's daughter leapt like a porpoise to catch them, but not until she had made a solemn promise to return them after seven nights did the scissors fall into her eager hand.

And so every night for seven nights Poseidon's daughter waited and watched by the jetty, and each time the foreign woman flickered into Hanni's dreams she took the silver scissors and cut her out completely. And Hanni snorted with distress in his sleep, and in the mornings was fretful and clumsy, like a woman at her monthly time, and took to sitting crouched under the tamarisk trees, surly and unspeaking. But if the beauties who had clustered around him so admiringly were disgruntled and drifted off in search of more responseful men, so too was Poseidon's daughter farther from her goal than ever. For although she could cut the Nordic woman out of Hanni's dreams and scatter her images as far as Africa, try as she might she could find no way of filling the gaps that the woman's face had left. For her own dream was not clear enough, was boundaryless and wavered, and would not be fitted in.

* * *

From her rock promontory Athena saw her niece swim asymmetrical and distraught towards the high rock of Kastro, saw also the dangerous flash of the silver scissors in the light of the setting sun; and from her erratic path in the sea Poseidon's daughter saw the clean-cut limbs of her aunt Athena, who knew how to develop herself. Athena set down her weighing-scales and stopped bargaining with the fishermen, and called her niece to her. But as she listened to the girl's unhappy tale, and as she stroked the stormy curls on the unhappy head, all the time her eyes rested with longing on the silver scissors, and despite itself her mind filled with plans to steal them from Zeus, although—or so she persuaded herself—her only desire in so doing would be to put an end to his ungodly nonsense. In her mind's eye all Attica lay before her, just and fair as her own daughter-city of Athens, and the vision glittered as her voice spoke comfort and resolution to Poseidon's daughter. She spoke of the power of the will, and how it must be tended like the melon seed in its earthy bed or the speckled egg in the belly of the heron, and she waxed long and lyrical in this vein until she had quite forgotten her less honourable intentions.

Finally, remembering herself, she said, 'But you are young yet and only learning. So I will pit the power of my own will behind yours and, believe me, we will send Hanni the dream that he deserves. Only you must give the silver scissors to me now, for safe-keeping.'

At first Poseidon's daughter demurred, saying that she had made her uncle a solemn promise, but the fireflies winking at her from the juniper bushes said that indeed she was young and weren't promises for adults to keep, and finally she was persuaded and handed over the silver scissors.

That night Poseidon's daughter did not go to the jetty but slept soundly in her palace bed, and in her dream her aunt Athena was a wise and whiskered fish which plied peacefully in and out of the windows.

Athena, meanwhile, took up her knapsack and hiked through the spinifex under the whitest of moons until she looked down upon the silvered rock of Kastro and the sleeping form of Zeus. Zeus lay outstretched on a marble boulder, his arms flung above his head like a child who has never known fear. Under cover of a cloud which shadowed the moon. Athena crept up on the sleeping figure and knelt beside him. She gazed at his right hand, at the soft palm upturned, at the squat thumb, and lastly at the elongated pointing forefinger, the finger of pride, the finger which stabbed out such arbitrary commands. Then, full of resolve to separate the finger from its knuckle and the god from his pride, she took the silver scissors from her knapsack.

But before the blade encountered the golden skin, Zeus, without opening an eye, let out a great snort of triumph and seized Athena's wrist, so that her ambitions were quite confounded.

Athena, however, was above all a stateswoman, and possessed at all times an understanding of the political weaknesses of her opponents; understood, for instance, that Zeus could ill afford to see the citizens of Athens roused against him.

And so she folded her hands in her lap and bowed her head with all appearance of meekness while Zeus paced the lemon grove till the red dust rose, and in his heart wrath struggled with expediency.

But what of Poseidon's daughter, then, with the night over and the butterfly-blue morning just beginning, the morning when Athena would pit wits and will behind her quest for Hanni? She stretched out her limbs in her cockle-shell bed, imagining how Hanni too would be waking now, stretching his lissom brown form, rubbing sleep from eyes slaty-green as a lizard's back; in luxurious superstition she mimicked every move he might make, down to the tiniest moue of the mouth and the most exquisite twitch of the toe.

When the conch shell sounded at the palace gate Poseidon's daughter could hardly contain her excitement. However, it was not her aunt Athena who was ushered in but—with much pomp and ceremony and pawing of horses—her eminent uncle Zeus. Zeus waved aside the deferences that were due to him and fixed a ferocious eye on his unruly niece, who, seeing the silver scissors safe once again in his belt, threw herself at his feet and was much afraid.

'Forgive me, Uncle,' she cried piteously.

Grasping her thick curls, Zeus gave vent to his temper.

'So you're discontented with your lot?' he bellowed, jerking her head this way and that. 'For a dream of mortality you would make fools of us all?'

'Forgive me, Uncle,' cried Poseidon's daughter, 'but I am young and foolish and in love.' And she sobbed and sobbed until her hot tears poured over her uncle's sandalled feet.

Somewhat mollified, Zeus slapped her lightly on the cheek. 'To live for such a brief time and float up like a dry leaf? Is this what you wanted?'

'Yes, Uncle, forgive me for my foolishness,' she sobbed.

At last Zeus picked her up and, stroking the tears from her reddened cheeks, said, 'Indeed you are young and foolish, my dear. But'—and now his lids drooped and his smile, if she had but noticed, was the smile of the panther before the pounce—'unlike Poseidon and Amphitrite, you are at least ardent in your discontent. And this moves me to grant your wishes.'

Hearing this, Poseidon's daughter threw herself once more at Zeus's feet, but this time the tears she wept were tears of gratitude for his generosity.

'So up, my dear, and away to your Hanni,' purred Zeus. And taking his silver scissors he cut meticulously around her edges, leaving a mermaid-shaped gap in the sea for her hapless parents to mourn over.

Like an arrow Poseidon's daughter sped to the beach of Plati Yialos, where Hanni the windsurfer breakfasted moodily and alone. Up came her head from the tossing waves; her sharp eyes saw, and her sharp nose scented. On the shore the sand was smooth and yellow and stretched a mile on either side, and there was a dog-rose hedge which lilted pink in the wind and smelled of heaven.

Out of the foam came her tail, shaking off the last salty drops. Then she lay down on the sand to dry, as she had seen mortals do. Her tail, being the thinnest part of her, dried first, and the wind tickled it up and played with it. Then her belly and breasts dried and narrowed and the wind, having more purchase, blew her body straight up until she stood, as it were, on her narrow wet head, until finally, all dry and thin as paper, she floated up entirely.

Poseidon's daughter felt loose and tumbled and free, soaring in arcs as the wind willed her, and so happy was she with this fine flight that she did not hear the rumble of Zeus's laughter in the wind that tossed her. Presently, however, when she turned her will against the wind and sought to swoop low over Hanni's tent, she found that there was no weight in her, and although three seals in their half-sleep saw her flutter in the air helplessly, like a rag, later each remembered it as a dream and told nobody.

Meanwhile on the bright beach Hanni the windsurfer noticed nothing but the freshening of the air and the quickening of the wind, noticed not at all, as he ran down the shelf of the sand and sprang on to his surfboard, the sliver of celluloid which lay drying on the shore, glossy and transparent as a stranded jellyfish.

Only Athena on her rock promontory saw the trick that Zeus had played, and wrung her hands at the cruel fate of Poseidon's daughter. And turning her gaze vengefully on the belling sail of the surfboard and the mortal man who was the source of so much trouble, she sent up from the deeps in a great turmoil of waters a galleon fit for an emissary from Spain, and on the deck with her back to the mast was a grave-eyed dream of a woman with her face coolly empty and her fine straight hair adrift on the wind.

Hanni, seeing this vision erupt before him, spurred his surfboard until his sails filled and his board scudded, and with a soaring heart he set off in fleet pursuit across the blue Ionian sea. And for weeks afterwards the old men in the taverna, knowing nothing of Poseidon's daughter or the self-shaped gap she had left in the sea, speculated on the melancholy of the Nordic races and the madness the sun makes in them, and how poor Hanni with the heat in his head sped like a white stallion towards Turkey and was never seen again.

CHUI CHAI

S. P. Somtow

S. P. Somtow has authored many science fiction, fantasy, and horror novels, including *The Shattered Horse*, *Vampire Junction*, and *Moon Dance*. He is also a highly regarded post-serialist composer and a movie maker, having directed, produced, scored, and acted in the obscure horror film *The Laughing Dead*. Thai by birth, Somtow has lived in Japan, Holland, and England and now resides in Los Angeles as an American citizen.

The following story took me by surprise because I've never associated Somtow's writing with eroticism. "Chui Chai," which appeared in *The Ultimate Frankenstein*, is set in the red light district of Bangkok in the 1980s. The title is a dance of transformation.

—E.D.

The living dead are not as you imagine them. There are no dangling innards, no dripping slime. They carry their guts and gore inside them, as do you and I. In the right light they can be beautiful, as when they stand in a doorway caught between cross-shafts of contrasting neon. Fueled by the right fantasy, they become indistinguishable from us. Listen. I know. I've touched them.

In the 80s I used to go to Bangkok a lot. The brokerage I worked for had a lot of business there, some of it shady, some not. The flight of money from Hong Kong had begun and our company, vulture that it was, was staking out its share of the loot. Bangkok was booming like there was no tomorrow. It made Los Angeles seem like Peoria. It was wild and fast and frantic and frustrating. It had temples and buildings shaped like giant robots. Its skyline was a cross between Shangri-La and Manhattan. For a dapper yuppie executive like me there were always meetings to be taken, faxes to fax, traffic to be sat in, credit cards to burn. There was also sex.

There was Patpong.

I was addicted. Days, after hours of high-level talks and poring over papers and banquets that lasted from the close of business until midnight, I stalked the crammed alleys of Patpong. The night smelled of sewage and jasmine. The heat seeped into everything. Each step I took was colored by a different neon sign. From half-open nightclub doorways buttocks bounced to jaunty soulless synthrock.

Everything was for sale; the women, the boys, the pirated software, the fake Rolexes. Everything sweated. I stalked the streets and sometimes at random took an entrance, took in a live show, women propelling ping-pong balls from their pussies, boys buttfucking on motorbikes. I was addicted. There were other entrances where I sat in waiting rooms, watched women with numbers around their necks through the one-way glass, soft, slender brown women. Picked a number. Fingered the American-made condoms in my pocket. Never buy the local ones, brother, they leak like a sieve.

I was addicted. I didn't know what I was looking for. But I knew it wasn't something you could find in Encino. I was a knight on a quest, but I didn't know that to find the holy grail is the worst thing that can possibly happen.

I first got a glimpse of the grail at Club Pagoda, which was near my hotel and which is where we often liked to take our clients. The club was on the very edge of Patpong, but it was respectable—the kind of place that serves up a plastic imitation of *The King and I*, which is, of course, a plastic imitation of life in ancient Siam . . . artifice imitating artifice, you see. Waiters crawled around in mediaeval uniforms, the guests sat on the floor, except there was a well under the table to accommodate the dangling legs of lumbering white people. The floor show was eminently sober . . . it was all classical Thai dances, women wearing those pagoda-shaped hats moving with painstaking grace and slowness to a tinkling, alien music. A good place to interview prospective grant recipients, because it tended to make them very nervous.

Dr. Frances Stone wasn't at all nervous, though. She was already there when I arrived. She was preoccupied with picking the peanuts out of her *gaeng massaman* and arranging them over her rice plate in such a way that they looked like little eyes, a nose, and a mouth.

"You like to play with your food?" I said, taking my shoes off at the edge of our private booth and sliding my legs under the table across from her.

"No," she said, "I just prefer them crushed rather than whole. The peanuts I mean. You must be Mr. Leibowitz."

"Russell."

"The man I'm supposed to charm out of a few million dollars." She was doing a sort of coquettish pout, not really the sort of thing I expected from someone in medical research. Her face was ravaged, but the way she smiled kindled the memory of youthful beauty. I wondered what had happened to change her so much; according to her dossier, she was only in her mid-forties.

"Mostly we're in town to take," I said, "not to give. R&D is not one of our strengths. You might want to go to Hoechst or Berli Jucker, Frances."

"But Russell . . ." She had not touched her curry, but the peanuts on the rice were now formed into a perfect human face, with a few strands of sauce for hair. "This is not exactly R&D. This is a discovery that's been around for almost a century and a half. My great-grandfather's paper—"

"For which he was booted out of the Austrian Academy? Yes, my dossier is pretty thorough, Dr. Stone; I know all about how he fled to America and changed his name."

She smiled. "And my dossier on you, Mr. Leibowitz, is pretty thorough too," she said, as she began removing a number of compromising photographs from her purse.

A gong sounded to announce the next dance. It was a solo. Fog roiled across the stage, and from it a woman emerged. Her clothes glittered with crystal bead-work, but her eyes outshone the yards of cubic zirconia. She looked at me and I felt the pangs of the addiction. She smiled and her lips seemed to glisten with lubricious moisture.

"You like what you see," Frances said softly.

"I—"

"The dance is called *Chui Chai*, the dance of transformation. In every Thai classical drama, there are transformations—a woman transforming herself into a rose, a spirit transforming itself into a human. After the character's metamorphosis, he performs a *Chui Chai* dance, exulting in the completeness and beauty of his transformed self."

I wasn't interested, but for some reason she insisted on giving me the entire story behind the dance. "This particular *Chui Chai* is called *Chui Chai Benjakai* . . . the demoness Banjakai has been despatched by the demon king, Thotsakanth, to seduce the hero Rama . . . disguised as the beautiful Sita, she will float down the river toward Rama's camp, trying to convince him that his beloved has died . . . only when she is placed on a funeral pyre, woken from her deathtrance by the flames, will she take on her demonic shape once more and fly away toward the dark kingdom of Lanka. But you're not listening."

How could I listen? She was the kind of woman that existed only in dreams, in poems. Slowly she moved against the tawdry backdrop, a faded painting of a palace with pointed eaves. Her feet barely touched the floor. Her arms undulated. And always her eyes held me. As though she were looking at me alone. Thai women can do things with their eyes that no other women can do. Their eyes have a secret language.

"Why are you looking at her so much?" said Frances. "She's just a Patpong bar girl . . . she moonlights here . . . classics in the evening, pussy after midnight."

"You know her?" I said.

"I have had some . . . dealings with her."

"Just what is it that you're doing research into, Dr. Stone?"

"The boundary between life and death," she said. She pointed to the photo-graphs. Next to them was a contract, an R&D grant agreement of some kind. The print was blurry. "Oh, don't worry, it's only a couple of million dollars . . . your company won't even miss it . . . and you'll own the greatest secret of all . . . the tree of life and death . . . the apples of Eve. Besides, I know your price and I can meet it." And she looked at the dancing girl. "Her name is Keo. I don't mind procuring if it's in the name of science."

Suddenly I realized that Dr. Stone and I were the only customers in the Club Pagoda. Somehow I had been set up.

The woman continued to dance, faster now, her hands sweeping through the air in mysterious gestures. She never stopped looking at me. She *was* the character she was playing, seductive and diabolical. There was darkness in every look, every hand-movement. I downed the rest of my Kloster lager and beckoned for another. An erection strained against my pants.

The dance ended and she prostrated herself before the audience of two, pressing her palms together in a graceful *wai*. Her eyes downcast, she left the stage. I had signed the grant papers without even knowing it.

Dr. Stone said, "On your way to the upstairs toilet . . . take the second door on the left. She'll be waiting for you."

I drank another beer, and when I looked up she was gone. She hadn't eaten one bite. But the food on her plate had been sculpted into the face of a beautiful woman. It was so lifelike that . . . but no. It wasn't alive. It wasn't breathing.

She was still in her dancing clothes when I went in. A little girl was carefully taking out the stitches with a seamripper. There was a pile of garments on the floor. In the glare of a naked bulb, the vestments of the goddess had little glamor. "They no have buttons on classical dance clothes," she said. "They just sew us into them. Cannot go pipi!" She giggled.

The little girl scooped up the pile and slipped away.

"You're . . . very beautiful," I said. "I don't understand why . . . I mean, why you *need* to . . ."

"I have problem," she said. "Expensive problem. Dr. Stone no tell you?"

"No." Her hands were coyly clasped across her bosom. Gently I pried them away.

"You want I dance for you?"

"Dance," I said. She was naked. The way she smelled was different from other women. It was like crushed flowers. Maybe a hint of decay in them. She shook her hair and it coiled across her breasts like a nest of black serpents. When I'd seen her on stage I'd been entertaining some kind of rape fantasy about her, but now I wanted to string it out for as long as I could. God, she was driving me mad.

"I see big emptiness inside you. Come to me. I fill you. We both empty people. Need filling up."

I started to protest. But I knew she had seen me for what I was. I had money coming out my ass, but I was one fucked-up yuppie. That was the root of my addiction.

Again she danced the dance of transforming, this time for me alone. Really for me alone. I mean, all the girls in Patpong have this way of making you think they love you. It's what gets you addicted. It's the only street in the world where you *can* buy love. But that's not how she was. When she touched me it was as though she reached out to me across an invisible barrier, an unbreachable gulf. Even when I entered her she was untouchable. We were from different worlds and neither of us ever left our private hells.

Not that there wasn't passion. She knew every position in the book. She knew them backwards and forwards. She kept me there all night and each act seemed as though it been freshly invented for the two of us. It was the last time I came that I felt I had glimpsed the grail. Her eyes, staring up into the naked bulb, brimmed with some remembered sadness. I loved her with all my might. Then I was seized with terror. She was a demon. Yellow-eyed, dragon-clawed. She was me, she was my insatiable hunger. I was fucking my own addiction. I think I sobbed. I accused her of lacing my drink with hallucinogens. I cried myself to sleep and then she left me.

I didn't notice the lumpy mattress or the peeling walls or the way the light bulb jiggled to the music from downstairs. I didn't notice the cockroaches.

I didn't notice until morning that I had forgotten to use my condoms.

It was a productive trip but I didn't go back to Thailand for another two years. I was promoted off the traveling circuit, moved from Encino to Beverly Hills, got myself a newer, late-model wife, packed my kids off to a Swiss boarding school. I also found a new therapist and a new support group. I smothered the addiction in new addictions. My old therapist had been a strict Freudian. He'd tried to root out the cause from some childhood trauma—molestation, potty training, Oedipal games—he'd never been able to find anything. I'm good at blocking out memories. To the best of my knowledge, I popped into being around age eight or nine. My parents were dead but I had a trust fund.

My best friends in the support group were Janine, who'd had eight husbands, and Mike, a transvestite with a spectacular fro. The clinic was in Malibu so we could do the beach in between bouts of tearing ourselves apart. One day Thailand came up.

Mike said, "I knew this woman in Thailand. I had fun in Thailand, you know? R&R. Lot of transvestites there, hon. I'm not a fag, I just like lingerie. I met this girl." He rarely stuck to the point because he was always stoned. Our therapist, Glenda, had passed out in the redwood tub. The beach was deserted. "I knew this girl in Thailand, a dancer. She would change when she danced. I mean *change*. You shoulda seen her skin. Translucent. And she smelled different. Smelled of strange drugs."

You know I started shaking when he said that because I'd tried not to think of her all this time even though she came to me in dreams. Even before I'd start to dream, when I'd just closed my eyes, I'd hear the hollow tinkle of marimbas and see her eyes floating in the darkness.

"Sounds familiar," I said.

"Nah. There was nobody like this girl, hon, nobody. She danced in a classical dance show *and* she worked the whorehouses . . . had a day job too, working for a nutty professor woman . . . honky woman, withered face, glasses. Some kind of doctor, I think. Sleazy office in Patpong, gave the girls free V.D. drugs."

"Dr. Frances Stone." Was the company paying for a free V.D. clinic? What about the research into the secrets of the universe?

"Hey, how'd you know her name?"

"Did you have sex with her?" Suddenly I was trembling with rage. I don't know why. I mean, I knew what she did for a living.

"Did you?" Mike said. He was all nervous. He inched away from me, rolling a joint with one hand and scootching along the redwood deck with the other.

"I asked first," I shouted, thinking, Jesus, I sound like a ten-year-old kid.

"Of *course* not! She had problems, all right? Expensive problems. But she was beautiful, mm-mm, good enough to eat."

I looked wildly around. Mr. Therapist was still dozing—fabulous way to earn a thousand bucks an hour—and the others had broken up into little groups. Janine was sort of listening, but she was more interested in getting her suntan lotion on evenly.

"I want to go back," I said. "I want to see Keo again."

"Totally, like, bullshit," she said, sidling up to me. "You're just, like, externalizing the interior hurt onto a fantasy-object. Like, you need to be in touch with your child, know what I mean?"

"You're getting your support groups muddled up, hon," Mike said edgily.

"Hey, Russ, instead of, like, projecting on some past-forgettable female two years back and ten thousand miles away, why don't you, like, fixate on someone a little closer to home? I mean, I've been *looking* at you. I only joined this support group cause like, support groups are the only place you can find like *sensitive* guys."

"Janine, I'm married."

"So let's have an affair."

I liked the idea. My marriage to Trisha had mostly been a joke: I'd needed a fresh ornament for cocktail parties and openings; she needed security. We hadn't had much sex; how could we? I was hooked on memory. Perhaps this woman would cure me. And I wanted to be cured so badly because Mike's story had jolted me out of the fantasy that Keo had existed only for me.

By now it was the 90s, so Janine insisted on a blood test before we did anything. I tested positive. I was scared shitless. Because the only time I'd ever been so careless as to forget to use a condom was . . . that night. And we'd done everything. Plumbed every orifice. Shared every fluid.

It had been a dance of transformation all right.

I had nothing to lose. I divorced my wife and sent my kids to an even more expensive school in Connecticut. I was feeling fine. Maybe I'd never come down with anything. I read all the books and articles about it. I didn't tell anyone. I packed a couple of suits and some casual clothes and a supply of bootleg AZT. I was feeling fine. Fine, I told myself. Fine.

I took the next flight to Bangkok.

The company was surprised to see me, but I was such a big executive by now they assumed I was doing some kind of internal troubleshooting. They put me up at the Oriental. They gave me a 10,000 baht per diem. In Bangkok you can buy a lot for four hundred bucks. I told them to leave me alone. The investigation didn't concern them. They didn't know what I was investigating, so they feared the worst.

I went to Silom Road, where Club Pagoda had stood. It was gone. In its stead stood a brand new McDonald's and an airline ticket office. Perhaps Keo was already dead. Wasn't that what I had smelled on her? The odor of crushed flowers, wilting . . . the smell of coming death? And the passion with which she made love. I understood it now. It was the passion of the damned. She had reached out to me from a place between life and death. She had sucked the life from me and given me the virus as a gift of love.

I strolled through Patpong. Hustlers tugged at my elbows. Fake Rolexes were flashed in my face. It was useless to ask for Keo. There are a million women named Keo. Keo means jewel. It also means glass. In Thai there are many words that are used indiscriminately for reality and artifice. I didn't have a photograph and Keo's beauty was hard to describe. And every girl in Patpong is beautiful. Every night, parading before me in the neon labyrinth, a thousand pairs of lips and eyes, sensuous and infinitely giving. The wrong lips, the wrong eyes.

There are only a few city blocks in Patpong, but to trudge up and down them in the searing heat, questioning, observing every face for a trace of the remembered grail . . . it can age you. I stopped shaving and took recreational drugs. What did it matter anyway?

But I was still fine, I wasn't coming down with anything.

I was fine. Fine!

And then, one day, while paying for a Big Mac, I saw her hands. I was looking down at the counter counting out the money. I heard the computer beep of the cash register and then I saw them: proffering the hamburger in both hands, palms up, like an offering to the gods. The fingers arched upwards, just so, with delicacy and hidden strength. God, I knew those hands. Their delicacy as they skimmed my shoulder blades, as they glided across my testicles just a hair's breadth away from touching. Their strength when she balled up her fist and shoved it into my rectum. Jesus, we'd done everything that night. I dropped my wallet on the counter, I seized those hands and gripped them, burger and all, and I felt the familiar response. Oh, God, I ached.

"Mister, you want a blowjob?"

It wasn't her voice. I looked up. It wasn't even a woman.

I looked back down at the hands. I looked up at the face. They didn't even belong together. It was a pockmarked boy and when he talked to me he stared off into space. There was no relation between the vacuity of his expression and the passion with which those hands caressed my hands.

"I don't like to do such thing," he said, "but I'm a poor college student and I needing money. So you can come back after 5 p.m. You not be disappointed."

The fingers kneaded my wrists with the familiarity of one who has touched every part of your body, who has memorized the varicose veins in your left leg and the mole on your right testicle.

It was obscene. I wrenched my own hands free. I barely remembered to retrieve my wallet before I ran out into the street.

I had been trying to find Dr. Frances Stone since I arrived, looking through the files at the corporate headquarters, screaming at secretaries. Although the corporation had funded Dr. Stone's project, the records seemed to have been spirited away.

At last I realized that that was the wrong way to go about it. I remembered what

Mike had told me, so the day after the encounter with Keo's hands, I was back in Patpong, asking around for a good V.D. clinic. The most highly regarded one of all turned out to be at the corner of Patpong and Soi Cowboy, above a store that sold pirated software and videotapes.

I walked up a steep staircase into a tiny room without windows, with a ceiling fan moving the same sweaty air around and around. A receptionist smiled at me. Her eyes had the same vacuity that the boy at McDonald's had possessed. I sat in an unraveling rattan chair and waited, and Dr. Stone summoned me into her office.

"You've done something with her," I said.

"Yes." She was shuffling a stack of papers. She had a window; she had an airconditioner blasting away in the direction of all the computers. I was still drenched with sweat.

The phone rang and she had a brief conversation in Thai that I couldn't catch. "You're angry, of course," she said, putting down the phone. "But it was better than nothing. Better than the cold emptiness of the earth. And she had nothing to lose."

"She was dying of AIDS! And now I have it!" It was the first time I'd allowed the words to cross my lips. "You *killed* me!"

Frances laughed. "My," she said, "aren't we being a little melodramatic? You have the virus, but you haven't actually come down with anything."

"I'm fine. Fine."

"Well, why don't you sit down. I'll order up some food. We'll talk."

She had really gone native. In Thailand it's rude to talk business without ordering up food. Sullenly I sat down while she opened a window and yelled out an order to one of the street vendors.

"To be honest, Mr. Leibowitz," she said, "we really could use another grant. We had to spend *so* much of the last one on cloak-and-dagger nonsense, security, bribes, and so on; so little could be spared for research itself . . . I mean, look around you . . . I'm not exactly wasting money on luxurious office space, am I?"

"I saw her hands."

"Very effective, wasn't it?" The food arrived. It was some kind of noodle thing wrapped in banana leaves and groaning from the weight of chili peppers. She did not eat; instead, she amused herself by rearranging the peppers in the shape of . . . "The hands, I mean. Beautiful as ever. Vibrant. Sensual. My first breakthrough."

I started shaking again. I'd read about Dr. Stone's great-grandfather and his graverobbing experiments. Jigsaw corpses brought to life with bolts of lightning. Not life. A simulacrum of life. Could this have happened to Keo? But she was dying. Perhaps it was better than nothing. Perhaps . . .

"Anyhow. I was hoping you'd arrive soon, Mr. Leibowitz. Because we've made up another grant proposal. I have the papers here. I know that you've become so important now that your signature alone will suffice to bring us ten times the amount you authorized two years ago."

"I want to see her."

"Would you like to dance with her? Would you like to see her in the *Chui Chai* one more time?"

*   *   *

She led me down a different stairwell. Many flights. I was sure we were below ground level. I knew we were getting nearer to Keo because there was a hint of that rotting flower fragrance in the air. We descended. There was an unnatural chill.

And then, at last, we reached the laboratory. No shambling Igors or bubbling retorts. Just a clean, well-lit basement room. Cold, like the vault of a morgue. Walls of white tile; ceiling of stucco; fluorescent lamps; the pervasive smell of the not-quite-dead.

Perspex tanks lined the walls. They were full of fluid and body parts. Arms and legs floating past me. Torsos twirled. A woman's breast peered from between a child's thighs. In another tank, human hearts swirled, each neatly severed at the aorta. There was a tank of eyes. Another of genitalia. A necklace of tongues hung suspended in a third. A mass of intestines writhed in a fourth. Computers drew intricate charts on a bank of monitors. Oscilloscopes beeped. A pet gibbon was chained to a post topped by a human skull. There was something so outlandishly antiseptic about this spectacle that I couldn't feel the horror.

"I'm sorry about the décor, Russell, but you see, we've had to forgo the usual decoration allowance." The one attempt at dressing up the place was a frayed poster of *Young Frankenstein* tacked to the far wall. "Please don't be upset at all the body parts," she added. "It's all very macabre, but one gets inured to it in med school; if you feel like losing your lunch, there's a small restroom on your left . . . yes, between the eyes and the tongues." I did not feel sick. I was feeling . . . excited. It was the odor. I knew I was getting closer to Keo.

She unlocked another door. We stepped into an inner room.

Keo was there. A cloth was draped over her, but seeing her face after all these years made my heart almost stop beating. The eyes. The parted lips. The hair, streaming upward toward a source of blue light . . . although I felt no wind in the room. "It is an electron wind," said Dr. Stone. "No more waiting for the monsoon lightning. We can get more power from a wall socket than great-grandfather Victor could ever dream of stealing from the sky."

And she laughed the laughter of mad scientists.

I saw the boy from McDonald's sitting in a chair. The hands reached out towards me. There were electrodes fastened to his temples. He was naked now, and I saw the scars where the hands had been joined at the wrists to someone else's arms. I saw a woman with Keo's breasts, wired to a pillar of glass, straining, heaving while jags of blue lightning danced about her bonds. I saw her vagina stitched onto the pubis of a dwarf, who lay twitching at the foot of the pillar. Her feet were fastened to the body of a five-year-old boy, transforming their grace to ungainliness as he stomped in circles around the pillar.

"Jigsaw people!" I said.

"Of course!" said Dr. Stone. "Do you think I would be so foolish as to bring back people whole? Do you not realize what the consequences would be? The legal redefinition of life and death . . . wills declared void, humans made subservient to walking corpses . . . I'm a scientist, not a philosopher."

"But who are they now?"

"They were nobody before. Street kids. Prostitutes. They were dying, Mr. Leibowitz, dying! They were glad to will their bodies to me. And now they're more than human. They're many persons in many bodies. A gestalt. I can shuffle them and put them back together, oh, so many different ways . . . and the beautiful Keo. Oh, she wept when she came to me. When she found out she had given you the virus. She loved you. You were the last person she ever loved. I saved her for you. She's been sleeping here, waiting to dance for you, since the day she died. Oh, let us not say *died*. The day she . . . she . . . I am no poet, Mr. Leibowitz. Just a scientist."

I didn't want to listen to her. All I could see was Keo's face. It all came back to me. Everything we had done. I wanted to relive it. I didn't care if she was dead or undead. I wanted to seize the grail and clutch it in my hands and own it.

Frances threw a switch. The music started, the shrilling of the *pinai*, the pounding of the *taphon*, the tinkling of marimbas and xylophones rang in the *Chui Chai* music. Then she slipped away unobtrusively. I heard a key turn in a lock. She had left the grant contract lying on the floor. I was alone with all the parts of the woman I'd loved. Slowly I walked toward the draped head. The electron wind surged; the cold blue light intensified. Her eyes opened. Her lips moved as though discovering speech for the first time. . . .

"Rus . . . sell."

On the pizzafaced boy, the hands stirred of their own accord. He turned his head from side to side and the hands groped the air, straining to touch my face. Keo's lips were dry. I put my arms around the drape-shrouded body and kissed the dead mouth. I could feel my hair stand on end.

"I see big emptiness inside you. Come to me. I fill you. We both empty people. Need filling up."

"Yes. Jesus, yes."

I hugged her to me. What I embraced was cold and prickly. I whisked away the drape. There was no body. Only a framework of wires and transistors and circuit boards and tubes that fed flasks of flaming reagents.

"I dance for you now."

I turned. The hands of the McDonald's boy twisted into graceful patterns. The feet of the child moved in syncopation to the music, dragging the rest of the body with them. The breasts of the chained woman stood firm, waiting for my touch. The music welled up. A contralto voice spun plaintive melismas over the inter-locking rhythms of wood and metal. I kissed her. I kissed that severed head and lent my warmth to the cold tongue, awakened passion in her. I kissed her. I could hear chains breaking and wires slithering along the floortiles. There were hands pressed into my spine, rubbing my neck, unfastening my belt. A breast touched my left buttock and a foot trod lightly on my right. I didn't care that these parts were attached to other bodies. They were hers. She was loving me all over. The dwarf that wore her pudenda was climbing up my leg. Every part of her was in love with me. Oh, she danced. We danced together. I was the epicenter of their passion. We were empty people but now we drank our fill. Oh, God, we danced. Oh, it was a grave music, but it contented us.

And I signed everything, even the codicil.

*   *   *

Today I am in the AIDS ward of a Beverly Hills hospital. I don't have long to wait. Soon the codicil will come into effect, and my body will be preserved in liquid nitrogen and shipped to Patpong.

The nurses hate to look at me. They come at me with rubber gloves on so I won't contaminate them, even though they should know better. My insurance policy has disowned me. My children no longer write me letters, though I've paid for them to go to Ivy League colleges. Trisha comes by sometimes. She is happy that we rarely made love.

One day I will close my eyes and wake up in a dozen other bodies. I will be closer to her than I could ever be in life. In life we are all islands. Only in Dr. Stone's laboratory can we know true intimacy, the mind of one commanding the muscles of another and causing the nerves of a third to tingle with unnamable desires. I hope I shall die soon.

The living dead are not as you imagine them. There are no dangling innards, no dripping slime. They carry their guts and gore inside them, as do you and I. In the right light they can be beautiful, as when they stand in the cold luminescence of a basement laboratory, waiting for an electron stream to lend them the illusion of life. Fueled by the right fantasy, they become indistinguishable from us.

Listen. I know. I've loved them.

MAMA GONE
Jane Yolen

Jane Yolen has published more than one hundred books for children and adults and has been called "the Hans Christian Andersen of America" for her many original fairy tales. Her books have won the Caldecott Medal, the Christopher Award, the World Fantasy Award, the Golden Kite Award, and the Kerlan Awards. Her fantasy works for adult readers include *Sister Light, Sister Dark*; *White Jenna*; *Halls of Grief*; *Merlin's Booke*; and *Tales of Wonder*. Her latest adult work, *Briar Rose*, retells the Sleeping Beauty legend against the backdrop of World War II.

"Mama Gone," like much of Yolen's best work, was first published in *Vampires*, a collection of children's stories. It is a chilling little tale, and we are pleased to offer it here for the enjoyment of adult readers.

—T.W.

Mama died four nights ago, giving birth to my baby sister Ann. Bubba cried and cried, "Mama gone," in his little-boy voice, but I never let out a single tear.

There was blood red as any sunset all over the bed from that birthing, and when Papa saw it he rubbed his head against the cabin wall over and over and over and made little animal sounds. Sukey washed Mama down and placed the baby on her breast for a moment. "Remember," she whispered.

"Mama gone," Bubba wailed again.

But I never cried.

By all rights we should have buried her with garlic in her mouth and her hands and feet cut off, what with her being vampire kin and all. But Papa absolutely refused.

"Your Mama couldn't stand garlic," he said when the sounds stopped rushing out of his mouth and his eyes had cleared. "It made her come all over with rashes. She had the sweetest mouth and hands."

And that was that. Not a one of us could make him change his mind, not even Granddad Stokes or Pop Wilber or any other of the men who come to pay their last respects. And as Papa is a preacher, and a brimstone man, they let it be. The onliest thing he would allow was for us to tie red ribbons round her ankles and wrists, a kind of sign like a line of blood. Everybody hoped that would do.

But on the next day, she rose from out her grave and commenced to prey upon the good folk of Taunton.

Of course she came to our house first, that being the dearest place she knew. I saw her outside my window, gray as a gravestone, her dark eyes like the holes in a shroud. When she stared in, she didn't know me, though I had always been her favorite.

"Mama, be gone," I said and waved my little cross at her, the one she had given me the very day I'd been born. "Avaunt." The old Bible word sat heavy in my mouth.

She put her hand up on the window frame, and as I watched, the gray fingers turned splotchy pink from all the garlic I had rubbed into the wood.

Black tears dropped from her black eyes, then. But I never cried.

She tried each window in turn and not a person awake in the house but me. But I had done my work well and the garlic held her out. She even tried the door, but it was no use. By the time she left, I was so sleepy, I dropped down right by the door. Papa found me there at cockcrow. He never did ask what I was doing, and if he guessed, he never said.

Little Joshua Greenough was found dead in his crib. The doctor took two days to come over the mountains to pronounce it. By then the garlic around his little bed to keep him from walking, too, had mixed with death smells. Everybody knew. Even the doctor, and him a city man. It hurt his mama and papa sore to do the cutting. But it had to be done.

The men came to our house that very noon to talk about what had to be. Papa kept shaking his head all through their talking. But even his being preacher didn't stop them. Once a vampire walks these mountain hollars, there's nary a house or barn that's safe. Nighttime is lost time. And no one can afford to lose much stock.

So they made their sharp sticks out of green wood, the curling shavings littering our cabin floor. Bubba played in them, not understanding. Sukey was busy with the baby, nursing it with a bottle and a sugar teat. It was my job to sweep up the wood curls. They felt slick on one side, bumpy on the other. Like my heart.

Papa said, "I was the one let her turn into a night walker. It's my business to stake her out."

No one argued. Specially not the Greenoughs, their eyes still red from weeping.

"Just take my children," Papa said. "And if anything goes wrong, cut off my hands and feet and bury me at Mill's Cross, under the stone. There's garlic hanging in the pantry. Mandy Jane will string me some."

So Sukey took the baby and Bubba off to the Greenoughs' house, that seeming the right thing to do, and I stayed the rest of the afternoon with Papa, stringing garlic and pressing more into the windows. But the strand over the door he took down.

"I have to let her in somewhere," he said. "And this is where I'll make my stand." He touched me on the cheek, the first time ever. Papa never has been much for show.

"Now you run along to the Greenoughs', Mandy Jane," he said. "And remember how much your mama loved you. This isn't her, child. Mama's gone. Something else has come to take her place. I should have remembered that the Good Book says, 'The living know that they shall die; but the dead know not anything.' "

I wanted to ask him how the vampire knew to come first to our house, then, but I was silent, for Papa had been asleep and hadn't seen her.

I left without giving him a daughter's kiss, for his mind was well set on the night's doing. But I didn't go down the lane to the Greenoughs' at all. Wearing my triple strand of garlic, with my cross about my neck, I went to the burying ground, to Mama's grave.

It looked so raw against the greening hillside. The dirt was red clay, but all it looked like to me was blood. There was no cross on it yet, no stone. That would come in a year. Just a humping, a heaping of red dirt over her coffin, the plain pinewood box hastily made.

I lay facedown in that dirt, my arms opened wide. "Oh, Mama," I said, "the Good Book says you are not dead but sleepeth. Sleep quietly, Mama, sleep well." And I sang to her the lullaby she had always sung to me and then to Bubba and would have sung to Baby Ann had she lived to hold her.

> "Blacks and bays,
> Dapples and grays,
> All the pretty little horses."

And as I sang I remembered Papa thundering at prayer meeting once, "Behold, a pale horse: and his name that sat on him was Death." The rest of the song just stuck in my throat then, so I turned over on the grave and stared up at the setting sun.

It had been a long and wearying day, and I fell asleep right there in the burying ground. Any other time fear might have overcome sleep. But I just closed my eyes and slept.

When I woke, it was dead night. The moon was full and sitting between the horns of two hills. There was a sprinkling of stars overhead. And Mama began to move the ground beneath me, trying to rise.

The garlic strands must have worried her, for she did not come out of the earth all at once. It was the scrabbling of her long nails at my back that woke me. I leaped off that grave and was wide awake.

Standing aside the grave, I watched as first her long gray arms reached out of the earth. Then her head, with its hair that was once so gold now gray and streaked with black and its shroud eyes, emerged. And then her body in its winding sheet, stained with dirt and torn from walking to and fro upon the land. Then her bare feet with blackened nails, though alive Mama used to paint those nails, her one vanity and Papa allowed it seeing she was so pretty and otherwise not vain.

She turned toward me as a hummingbird toward a flower, and she raised her face up and it was gray and bony. Her mouth peeled back from her teeth and I saw that they were pointed and her tongue was barbed.

"Mama gone," I whispered in Bubba's voice, but so low I could hardly hear it myself.

She stepped toward me off that grave, lurching down the hump of dirt. But when she got close, the garlic strands and the cross stayed her.

"Mama."

She turned her head back and forth. It was clear she could not see with those black shroud eyes. She only sensed me there, something warm, something alive, something with the blood running like satisfying streams through the blue veins.

"Mama," I said again. "Try and remember."

That searching awful face turned toward me again, and the pointy teeth were bared once more. Her hands reached out to grab me, then pulled back.

"Remember how Bubba always sucks his thumb with that funny little noise you always said was like a little chuck in its hole. And how Sukey hums through her nose when she's baking bread. And how I listened to your belly to hear the baby. And how Papa always starts each meal with the blessing on things that grow fresh in the field."

The gray face turned for a moment toward the hills, and I wasn't even sure she could hear me. But I had to keep trying.

"And remember when we picked the blueberries and Bubba fell down the hill, tumbling head-end over. And we laughed until we heard him, and he was saying the same six things over and over till long past bed."

The gray face turned back toward me and I thought I saw a bit of light in the eyes. But it was just reflected moonlight.

"And the day Papa came home with the new ewe lamb and we fed her on a sugar teat. You stayed up all the night and I slept in the straw by your side."

It was as if stars were twinkling in those dead eyes. I couldn't stop staring, but I didn't dare stop talking either.

"And remember the day the bluebird stunned itself on the kitchen window and you held it in your hands. You warmed it to life, you said. To life, Mama."

Those stars began to run down the gray cheeks.

"There's living, Mama, and there's dead. You've given so much life. Don't be bringing death to these hills now." I could see that the stars were gone from the sky over her head; the moon was setting.

"Papa loved you too much to cut your hands and feet. You gotta return that love, Mama. You gotta."

Veins of red ran along the hills, outlining the rocks. As the sun began to rise, I took off one strand of garlic. Then the second. Then the last. I opened my arms. "Have you come back, Mama, or are you gone?"

The gray woman leaned over and clasped me tight in her arms. Her head bent down toward mine, her mouth on my forehead, my neck, the outline of my little gold cross burning across her lips.

She whispered, "Here and gone, child, here and gone," in a voice like wind in the coppice, like the shaking of willow leaves. I felt her kiss on my cheek, a brand.

Then the sun came between the hills and hit her full in the face, burning her as red as earth. She smiled at me and then there was only dust motes in the air, dancing. When I looked down at my feet, the grave dirt was hardly disturbed but Mama's gold wedding band gleamed atop it.

I knelt down and picked it up, and unhooked the chain holding my cross. I slid the ring into the chain, and the two nestled together right in the hollow of my throat. I sang:

> *"Blacks and bays,*
> *Dapples and grays . . ."*

and from the earth itself, the final words sang out,

> *"All the pretty little horses."*

That was when I cried, long and loud, a sound I hope never to make again as long as I live.

Then I went back down the hill and home, where Papa still waited by the open door.

PETER

Pat Murphy

Bay Area writer Pat Murphy is the author of novels that defy publishers' categorizations, crossing the boundaries between science fiction, fantasy, and mainstream literature. Murphy won the Nebula Award in 1987 for her novel *The Falling Woman* and the World Fantasy Award in 1991 for her novella "Bones." Her other works include *The City, Not Long After* and *Points of Departure*.

"Peter" is a dark look at J. M. Barrie's fantasy classic, *Peter Pan*—a book which, for those who have not read the original, is itself more dark and droll than the various screen versions would have you believe. Murphy asks us to consider Wendy and the Lost Boys long after Barrie's novel closes, sent away from Never-never Land and into the land of adulthood.

—T.W.

I went to see Wendy when I was in London. For old times' sake. It's a drag, but she expects it, and what can I do.

"Oh, Slightly, you really are a sight," she says, and smiles as if she expects me to share the joke. "You look so silly in that black leather jacket. And why do you have a hoop in your ear? Do you think you're a pirate?" She laughs girlishly, even though she's over thirty, saddled with a kid, and afflicted with a husband who's never home.

I don't even know why I go to see her. She always insists I stay to tea and serves sweet biscuits and fusses over her kid the whole time. She gets to me. We have what passes for conversation in her household.

"Slightly writes for the newspaper, Jane. What do you think of that?" Wendy asks the kid. Jane looks at me owlishly and says nothing.

"He just got back from somewhere very far away and exotic. Where was it this time, Slightly?"

"Nicaragua," I say. "I was a stringer for the *Times*. Covering the war. You may have heard about it?"

*   *   *

Can't get under her skin. She smiles sweetly and I just can't bear it. "I suppose. It's so far from our little world here."

"Could you please call me Hank," I say, a little testily. "I really prefer it."

"Very well, dear," she says. She looks hurt but covers by busying herself with cleaning up a spot of tea that has dripped from the teapot spout onto the oilcloth table cover. "I will."

She won't. She never remembers.

Finally, the kid goes out to play, dressed in a little pink frock trimmed with lace. Wendy herself is wearing a housedress that looks a bit worse for wear, but the kid has to have the best. "She's such a dear," Wendy says, and then settles in her chair to reminisce. "I was just her age when I first flew off with Peter."

I don't want to hear about it, but she's off and running. "Remember the lovely little house you boys made for me? Oh, I was so happy there." And then she goes on and on, about the sweet little room under the trees and the fun we had chasing the pirates. In her memories, she even likes Tiger Lily, the Indian princess, though I recall at the time Wendy was quite put out by Tiger Lily's obvious interest in Peter.

Wendy's memories are all quite tidy. She remembers the sweet room beneath the trees and doesn't remember that it stank like wood smoke half the time because the chimney didn't draw. She remembers the jolly pirate ship and forgets the death cries of the dying pirates. The deck was slick with blood when we were done. I remember it, even if she doesn't.

They died horribly—two in the cabin at Peter's blade. The rest on deck, mobbed by the lost boys, harried by Peter. I didn't kill any myself, but that doesn't mean I was innocent. I carried the lantern and called to the other boys to follow. I remember flashing the lantern in one man's face—Bill Mullins, I think his name was—and he ran out half blinded, to be cut down by three boys. Fair play didn't enter into it—we were just kids. Kids with death in our hands and a song in our hearts. The air reeked of blood and we watched Hook leap overboard into the jaws of the crocodile.

Wendy seems to have forgotten all this. She remembers a tidy Neverland. Perhaps she believes the Disney version, where people died neatly, never soiling their pants.

I look around the room as she talks, chattering about fairy dust and Tinker Bell. The arms of the chairs are covered with off-white doilies that are a little lumpy and don't lie flat. Wendy's work, no doubt. The windows are covered with a thin layer of dust, the kind of dirt that hangs in the air of industrial towns, settling on everything. By the door, the carpet is worn; the underlying threads show through. Wendy herself looks worn—tired around the eyes. Her hands are a little chapped; she hasn't been taking care of herself.

Her husband is an actor, or so Wendy says. He gets work now and then—minor parts in minor productions. Never anything big. He's a good-looking man, in a callow, beardless way. I've met him once or twice, and I didn't much care for him. When Wendy's reminiscences slow down, I ask about him. "How's your husband? Getting any work?"

She looks worried. "Oh, he has hopes. He's being considered for a part."

"I see." I see all too well. His sort is always being considered for a part. Always having lunch with a producer. Always chasing after the dream and never catching it, leaving his wife to grow worn and tired alone.

"And what about you, Slightly? Are you seeing anyone?"

I've been married three times. And divorced three times. It never takes. The third one was the worst. "I don't mind that you're gone half the time," my wife told me. "I knew that when we got married. But you're not looking for a wife. You're looking for a mother to rock you to sleep."

"I've sworn off marriage," I say. "I'm always gallivanting off to some adventure or other."

"You sound so much like him," Wendy says wistfully.

"No. Don't say that. It's not so." But even as I deny her words, I know she's right. He left his mark on me, just as he left it on her. When all the lost boys came home, I was the one who never fit in. At school, I told the other kids about our adventures with the pirates, the battles with the redskins, the long afternoons by the mermaids' lagoon. When kids called me a liar, I fought back with my fists and got a reputation as a troublemaker, a bad boy. When the other lost boys were promoted to the next grade, I was kept back. But by that time, it didn't really matter to me. I couldn't talk to them anymore. They were busy forgetting the island, forgetting Peter, adjusting to the real world.

Wendy is staring into the fire, ignoring me. I care about Wendy, you know. For all the nasty things I say, I care about her. Though she was just a little girl herself, she tried to be a mother to us all. She tucked us in; she told us stories. And Peter treated her worse than he treated any of the boys.

When he left us here, he promised to come back each spring and take her to Neverland for a week. She was supposed to go help with his spring cleaning.

I found her sitting by the open window the year that he forgot her. She wore a frock that looked too young for her. Though she was only eleven, she was growing up fast.

"What do you think has happened to him, Slightly?" she asked, peering out the window. "Do you think he's sick?"

"He's never sick," I told her. "The bastard just forgot." She slipped his mind. She didn't matter, any more than the rest of us mattered. I put my arms out to comfort her, but she ran away crying. And after that, she grew up quickly.

She looks up from the fire and meets my eyes. "It's almost spring," she says. "I wonder if he'll come this year. I think he will. I have a feeling that he'll come soon. Maybe tonight."

"Forget it, Wendy. Just forget it. Lock the window, for Christ's sake. He's gone."

Though she nods as if she agrees, her gaze returns to the fire. I stay for a little longer, then excuse myself. She smiles and hugs me when I go, but her thoughts are elsewhere.

When I leave Wendy's house, I go to my motorcycle and then hestitate, considering what Wendy said earlier. She's right—there's a feeling in the air, a sense of anticipation.

I wait in the darkness by the window to Jane's bedroom. Wendy's left it open, of course. I knew she would. It's dark, but her husband hasn't come home yet. He'll be home late and drunk, if I know the type. Through the window, I listen to Wendy read a Disneyfied version of Snow White to her daughter and bid her goodnight.

The blind at the kitchen window is up. I watch Wendy take a whiskey bottle from the cupboard and pour herself a glass. I wait in the darkness, watching Wendy drink.

My second wife once asked me about my family. I told her as close to the truth as I could manage: "My father left me and my mother when I was just a kid." She asked me if I had ever thought about trying to find my father. I said that if I ever found him, I would kill him for what he did to me.

He didn't mean to do it. He didn't know what he was doing. He was cocky, thoughtless, and innocently heroic. And he blighted my life. All my life, I have wanted to be like him. I run from continent to continent, from war to war, writing stories and books and searching for the great adventure that he always promised us. I look for a leader who laughs in the heart of the battle, sublimely confident in the way that only a boy can be.

I don't belong in this place, any more than Wendy does. But he left me here. And there's nowhere else to go.

He'll come tonight. I know he will. And I know that I would fly away with him if I could.

If he took me by the hand and told me I could fly, I would go back to the island with all its joys and terrors. I would follow him and join the lost boys once again.

But I can't go back. I lost my innocence long ago; now I have lost my youth as well.

Though I am only thirty years old, I feel ancient, worn-out, used up. The butterfly knife that I bought in the Philippines fits comfortably in my hand. I have learned a thing or two about fighting in my visits to various war zones. If I take him by surprise, I'll have a chance, I think.

Tonight, it's either Peter or me. And if he wins, he won't think twice. He'll slit my throat without hesitation, never recognizing his old companion. He'll laugh of childhood and fly off on the evening wind, eternally proud, eternally careless, eternally young.

OUR LADY OF THE HARBOUR

Charles de Lint

Canadian author Charles de Lint is both prolific and versatile; his long list of publications includes works of adult fantasy fiction, horror (under the pseudonym Samuel M. Key), children's fiction, poetry, and critical nonfiction. He is best known, however, as a pioneer of Urban Fantasy, bringing myth and folklore motifs into a modern-day urban context. *The Little Country*, *The Dreaming Place*, and *Spiritwalk* are among his most recent books.

De Lint is also a musician specializing in traditional folk material; he and his wife, MaryAnn Harris, perform with the Celtic band Jump at the Sun in their home city of Ottawa. "Our Lady of the Harbour" tells the story of a folk musician in the imaginary Canadian city of Newford. The story fits into de Lint's excellent "Newford" cycle, and is an homage to the classic Hans Christian Andersen fairy tale, *The Little Mermaid*.

—T.W.

People don't behave the way they should; they behave the way they do.

—Jim Beaubien & Karen Caesar

She sat on her rock, looking out over the lake, her back to the city that reared up behind her in a bewildering array of towers and lights. A half mile of water separated her island from Newford, but on a night such as this, with the moon high and the water still as glass, the city might as well have been on the other side of the planet.

Tonight, an essence of *märchen* prevailed in the darkened groves and on the moonlit lawns of the island.

For uncounted years before Diederick van Yoors first settled the area in the early part of the nineteenth century, the native Kickaha called the island Myeengun. By the turn of the century, it had become the playground of Newford's wealthy, its bright facade first beginning to lose its luster with the Great Depression when wealthy land owners could no longer keep up their summer homes; by the end of the Second World War it was an eyesore. It wasn't turned into a park until the late 1950s. Today most people knew it only by the anglicized translation of its Kickaha name: Wolf Island.

Matt Casey always thought of it as *her* island.

The cast bronze statue he regarded had originally stood in the garden of an expatriate Danish businessman's summer home, a faithful reproduction of the well known figure that haunted the waterfront of the Dane's native Copenhagen. When the city expropriated the man's land for the park, he was generous enough to donate the statue, and so she sat now on the island, as she had for fifty years, looking out over the lake, motionless, always looking, the moonlight gleaming on her bronze features and slender form.

The sharp blast of a warning horn signaling the last ferry back to the city cut through the night's contemplative mood. Matt turned to look to the far side of the island where the ferry was docked. As he watched, the lights on the park's winding paths winked out, followed by those in the island's restaurant and the other buildings near the dock. The horn gave one last blast. Five minutes later, the ferry lurched away from the dock and began the final journey of the day back to Newford's harbour.

Now, except for a pair of security guards who, Matt knew, would spend the night watching TV and sleeping in the park's offices above the souvenir store, he had the island to himself. He turned back to look at the statue. It was still silent, still motionless, still watching the unfathomable waters of the lake.

He'd been here one afternoon and watched a baglady feeding gulls with bits of bread that she probably should have kept for herself. The gulls here were all overfed. When the bread was all gone, she'd walked up to the statue.

"Our lady of the harbour," she'd said. "Bless me."

Then she'd made the sign of the cross, as though she was a Catholic stepping forward into the nave of her church. From one of her bulging shopping bags, she took out a small plastic flower and laid it on the stone by the statue's feet, then turned and walked away.

The flower was long gone, plucked by one of the cleaning crews no doubt, but the memory remained.

Matt moved closer to the statue, so close that he could have laid his palm against the cool metal of her flesh.

"Lady," he began, but he couldn't go on.

Matt Casey wasn't an easy man to like. He lived for one thing, and that was his music. About the only social intercourse he had was with the members of the various bands he had played in over the years, and even that was spotty. Nobody he ever played with seemed willing to just concentrate on the music; they always wanted to hang out together as though they were all friends, as though they were in some kind of social club.

Music took the place of people in his life. It was his friend and his lover, his confidant and his voice, his gossip and his comfort.

It was almost always so.

From his earliest years he suffered from an acute sense of xenophobia: everyone was a stranger to him. All were foreigners to the observer captured in the flesh, blood and bone of his body. It was not something he understood, in the sense that one might be aware of a problem one had; it was just the way he was. He could trust no one—perhaps because he had never learned to trust himself.

His fellow musicians thought of him as cold, aloof, cynical—descriptions that were completely at odds with the sensitivity of his singing and the warmth that lay at the heart of his music. The men he played with sometimes thought that all he needed was a friend, but his rebuffs to even the most casual overtures of friendship always cured such notions. The women he played with sometimes thought that all he needed was a lover, but though he slept with a few, the distance he maintained eventually cooled the ardor of even the most persistent.

Always, in the end, there was only the music. To all else, he was an outsider.

He grew up in the suburbs north of the city's center, part of a caring family. He had an older brother and two younger sisters, each of them outgoing and popular in their own way. Standing out in such contrast to them, even at an early age, his parents had sent him to a seemingly endless series of child specialists and psychologists, but no one could get through except for his music teachers—first in the school orchestra, then the private tutors that his parents were only too happy to provide for him.

They saw a future in music for him, but not the one he chose. They saw him studying music at a university, taken under the wing of some master whenever he finally settled on a chosen instrument, eventually playing concert halls, touring the world with famous orchestras. Instead he left home at sixteen. He turned his back on formal studies, but not on learning, and played in the streets. He traveled all over North America, then to Europe and the Middle East, finally returning home to busk on Newford's streets and play in her clubs.

Still the outsider; more so, perhaps, rather than less.

It wasn't that he was unfriendly; he simply remained uninvolved, animated only in the presence of other musicians and then only to discuss the esoterics of obscure lyrics and tunes and instruments, or to play. He never thought of himself as lonely, just as alone; never considered himself to be a social misfit or an outcast from the company of his fellow men, just an observer of the social dance to which most men and women knew the steps rather than one who would join them on the dance floor.

An outsider.

A gifted genius, undoubtedly, as any who heard him play would affirm, but an outsider all the same.

It was almost always so.

In the late seventies, the current band was Marrowbones and they had a weekend gig at a folk club in Lower Crowsea called Feeney's Kitchen—a popular hangout for those Butler University students who shunned disco and punk as well as the New Wave. The line-up was Matt on his usual bouzouki and guitar and handling the vocals, Nicky Doyle on fiddle, Johnny Ryan on tenor banjo, doubling on his classic Gibson mando-cello for song accompaniments, and Matt's long-time musical associate Amy Scallan on Uillean pipes and whistles.

They'd been playing together for a year and a half now and the band had developed a big, tight sound that had recently brought in offers for them to tour the college and festival circuits right across the country.

But it'd never happen, Amy thought as she buckled on her pipes in preparation for the selection of reels with which they were going to end the first set of the evening.

The same thing was going to happen that always happened. It was already starting. She'd had to listen to Nicky and Johnny going on about Matt earlier this afternoon when the three of them had gotten together to jam with a couple of other friends at The Harp. They couldn't deal with the dichotomy of Matt off-stage and on. Fronting the band, Matt projected the charming image of a friendly and out-going man that you couldn't help but want to get to know; off-stage, he was taciturn and withdrawn, uninterested in anything that didn't deal with the music.

But that was Matt, she'd tried to explain. You couldn't find a better singer or musician to play with and he had a knack for giving even the simplest piece a knockout arrangement. Nobody said you had to like him.

But Nicky had only shaken his head, brown curls bobbing. "Your man's taking all the *craic* from playing in a band."

Johnny nodded in agreement. "It's just not fun anymore. He'll barely pass the time of day with you, but on stage he's all bloody smiles and jokes. I don't know how you put up with him."

Amy hadn't been able to come up with an explanation then and looking across the stage now to where Matt was raising his eyebrows to ask if she was ready, then winking when she nodded back that she was, she couldn't explain it any better. She'd just learned over the years that what they shared was the music—and the music was very good; if she wanted more, she had to look for it elsewhere.

She'd come to terms with it where most people wouldn't, or couldn't, but then there was very little in the world that ever fazed her.

Matt started a G-drone on his bouzouki. He leaned close to the mike, just a touch of a welcoming smile tugging the corner of his mouth as a handful of dancers, anticipating what was to come, stepped onto the tiny wooden dance floor in front of the stage. Amy gave him a handful of bars to lock in the tempo, then launched into the first high popping notes of "The Road West," the opening salvo in this set of reels.

She and Matt played the tune through twice on their own and room on the dance floor grew to such a premium that the dancers could do little more than jig in one spot. Their elbows and knees could barely jostle against one another.

It wasn't quite a sea of bobbing heads, Amy thought, looking down from the stage. More like a small lake, or even a puddle.

The analogy made her smile. She kicked in her pipe drones as the fiddle and tenor banjo joined in on "The Glen Allen." It was halfway through that second tune that she became aware of the young woman dancing directly in front of Matt's microphone.

She was small and slender, with hair that seemed to be made of spun gold and eyes such a deep blue that they glittered like sapphires in the light spilling from the stage. Her features reminded Amy of a fox—pointed and tight like a Rackham sprite, but no less attractive for all that.

The other dancers gave way like reeds before a wind, drawing back to allow her the room to swirl the skirt of her unbelted flowered dress, her tiny feet scissoring intricate steps in their black Chinese slippers. Her movements were at once sensual and innocent. Amy's first impression was that the young woman was a professional dancer, but as she watched more closely, she realized that the girl's fluidity and grace were more an inherent talent than a studied skill.

The dancer's gaze caught and held on Matt, no matter how her steps turned her about, her attention fixed and steady as though he had bewitched her, while Matt, to Amy's surprise, seemed just as entranced. When they kicked into "Sheehan's Reel," the third and final tune of the set, she almost thought Matt was going to leave the stage to dance with the girl.

"Again!" Matt cried out as they neared the usual end of the tune.

Amy didn't mind. She pumped the bellows of her pipes, long fingers dancing on the chanter, more than happy to play the piece all night if the dancer could keep up. But the tune unwound to its end, they ended with a flourish, and suddenly it was all over. The dance floor cleared, the girl was swallowed by the crowd.

When the applause died down, an odd sort of hush fell over the club. Amy unbuckled her pipes and looked over to see that Matt had already left the stage. She hadn't even seen him go. She tugged her chanter mike up to mouth level.

"We're, uh, going to take a short break, folks," she said into the mike. Her voice seemed to boom in the quiet. "Then," she added, "we'll be right back with some more music, so don't go away."

The patter bookending the tunes and songs was Matt's usual job. Since Amy didn't feel she had his natural stage charm, she just kept it simple.

There was another smatter of applause that she acknowledged with a smile. The house system came on, playing a Jackson Browne tune, and she turned to Nicky who was putting his fiddle in its case.

"Where'd Matt go?" she asked.

He gave her a "who cares?" shrug. "Probably chasing that bird who was shaking her tush at him all through the last piece."

"I don't envy her," Johnny added.

Amy knew exactly what he meant. Over the past few months they'd all seen the fallout of casualties who gathered like moths around the bright flame of Matt's stage presence only to have their wings burnt with his indifference. He'd charm them in a club, sometimes sleep with them, but in the end, the only lover he kept was the music.

Amy knew all too well. There was a time. . . .

She pushed the past away with a shake of her head. Putting a hand above her eyes to shade them from the lights, she scanned the crowd as the other two went to get themselves a beer but she couldn't spot either Matt or the girl. Her gaze settled on a black-haired Chinese woman sitting alone at a small table near the door and she smiled as the woman raised her hand in a wave. She'd forgotten that Lucia had arrived halfway through their first set—fashionably late, as always— and now that she thought about it, hadn't she seen the dancer come in about the same time? They might even have come in together.

Lucia Han was a performance artist based in Upper Foxville and an old friend of Amy's. When they'd first met, Amy had been told by too many people to be careful because Lucia was gay and would probably make a pass at her. Amy just ignored them. She had nothing against gays to begin with and she soon learned that the gossips' reasoning for their false assumption was just that Lucia only liked to work with other women. But as Lucia had explained to Amy once, "There's just not enough women involved in the arts and I want to support those who do make the plunge—at least if they're any good."

Amy understood perfectly. She often wished there were more women players in traditional music. She was sick to death of going to a music session where she wasn't known. All too often she'd be the only woman in a gathering of men and have to play rings around them on her pipes just to prove that she was as good as them. Irish men weren't exactly noted for their liberated standards.

Which didn't mean that either she or Lucia weren't fond of the right sort of a man. "Au contraire," as Lucia would say in the phony Parisian accent she liked to affect, "I am liking them too much."

Amy made her way to the bar where she ordered a beer on her tab, then took the brimming draught glass through the crowd to Lucia's table, trying to slosh as little of the foam as she could on her new jeans.

"Bet you thought I wouldn't come," Lucia said as Amy sat down with her stein relatively full. The only spillage had joined the stickiness of other people's spills that lay underfoot.

Lucia was older than Amy by at least six or seven years, putting her in her mid-thirties. She had her hair in a wild spiky do tonight—to match the torn white T-shirt and leather jeans, no doubt. The punk movement had barely begun to trickle across the Atlantic as yet, but it was obvious that Lucia was already an eager proponent. A strand of safety pins dangled from one earlobe; others held the tears of her T-shirt closed in strategic places.

"I don't even remember telling you about the gig," Amy said.

Lucia waved a negligent hand towards the small poster on the wall behind her that advertised the band's appearance at Feeney's Kitchen this weekend.

"But you are famous now, ma chérie," she said. "How could I not know?" She dropped the accent to add, "You guys sound great."

"Thanks."

Amy looked at the tabletop. She set her stein down beside a glass of white wine, Lucia's cigarettes and matches and a half-filled ashtray. There was also an empty teacup with a small bright steel teapot on one side of it and a used tea bag on the lip of its saucer.

"Did you come alone?" she asked.

Lucia shook her head. "I brought a foundling—fresh from who really knows where. You probably noticed her and Matt making goo-goo eyes at each other all through the last piece you did." She brought a hand to her lips as soon as she'd made the last comment. "Sorry. I forgot about the thing you used to have going with him."

"Old history," Amy said. "I've long since dealt with it. I don't know that Matt ever even knew anything existed between us, but I'm cool now."

"It's for the better."

"Definitely," Amy agreed.

"I should probably warn my little friend about him," Lucia said, "but you know what they're like at that age—it'd just egg her on."

"Who *is* your little friend? She moves like all she was born to do was dance."

"She's something, isn't she? I met her on Wolf Island about a week ago, just before the last ferry—all wet and bedraggled like she'd fallen off a boat and been washed to shore. She wasn't wearing a stitch of clothing and I thought the worst, you know? Some asshole brought her out for a quick wham, bam, and then just dumped her."

Lucia paused to light a cigarette.

"And?" Amy asked.

Lucia shrugged, blowing out a wreath of blue-gray smoke. "Seems she fell off a boat and took off her clothes so that they wouldn't drag her down while she swam to shore. Course, I got that from her later."

Just then the door to the club opened behind Lucia and a gust of cool air caught the smoke from Lucia's cigarette, giving it a slow dervishing whirl. On the heels of the wind, Amy saw Matt and the girl walk in. They seemed to be in the middle of an animated discussion—or at least Matt was, so they had to be talking about music.

Amy felt the same slight twinge of jealousy watching him with the dancer as she did in the first few moments of every one of the short relationships that came about from some girl basically flinging herself at him halfway through a gig. Though perhaps "relationship" was too strong a word, since any sense of responsibility to a partner was inevitably one-sided.

The girl laughed at what he was saying—but it was a silent laugh. Her mouth was open, her eyes sparkled with a humored appreciation, but there was no sound. She began to move her hands in an intricate pattern that, Amy realized, was the American Sign Language used by deaf-mutes.

"Her problem right then," Lucia was saying, "was finding something to wear so that she could get into town. Luckily I was wearing my duster—you know, from when I was into my Sergio Leone phase—so she could cover herself up."

"She took off everything while she was in the water?" Amy asked, her gaze returning to her friend. "Even her underwear?"

"I guess. Unless she wasn't wearing any in the first place."

"Weird."

"I don't see you wearing a bra."

"You know what I meant," Amy said with a laugh.

Lucia nodded. "So anyway, she came on the ferry with me—I paid her fare— and then I brought her back to my place because it turned out she didn't have anywhere else to go. Doesn't know a soul in town. To be honest, I wasn't even sure she spoke English at first."

Amy looked over Lucia's shoulder to where Matt was answering whatever it was that the girl's hands had told him. Where had he learned sign language? she wondered. He'd never said anything about it before, but then she realized that for all the years she'd known him, she really didn't *know* much about him at all except that he was a brilliant musician and good in bed, related actions, perhaps, since she didn't doubt that they both were something he'd regard as a performance.

Meow, she thought.

"She's deaf-mute, isn't she?" she added aloud.

Lucia looked surprised. "Mute, but not deaf. How you'd know?"

"I'm watching her talk to Matt with her hands right now."

"She couldn't even do that when I first met her," Lucia said.

Amy returned her attention to Lucia once more. "What do you mean?"

"Well, I know sign language—I learned it when I worked at the Institute for the Deaf up on Gracie Street when I first got out of college—so when I realized she was mute, it was the first thing I tried. But she's not deaf—she just can't talk. She didn't even try to communicate at first. I thought she was in shock. She just sat beside me, looking out over the water, her eyes getting bigger and bigger as we approached the docks.

"When we caught a bus back to my place, it was like she'd never been in a city before. She just sat beside me all wide-eyed and then took my hand—not like she was scared, it was more like she just wanted to share the wonder of it all with me. It wasn't until we got back to my place that she asked for pen and paper." Lucia mimed the action as she spoke.

"It's all kind of mysterious, isn't it?" Amy said.

"I'll say. Anyway, her name's Katrina Ludvigsen and she's from one of those little towns on the Islands further down the lake—the ones just past the mouth of the Dulfer River, you know?"

Amy nodded.

"Her family came over from Norway originally," Lucia went on. "They were Lapps—as in Lapland—except she doesn't like to be called that. Her people call themselves Sami."

"I've heard about that," Amy said. "Referring to them as Lapps is a kind of insult."

"Exactly." Lucia took a final drag from her cigarette and butted it out in the ashtray. "Once she introduced herself, she asked me to teach her sign language. Would you believe she picked it up in *two* days?"

"I don't know," Amy said. "Is that fast?"

"Try *fantastique, ma chérie.*"

"So what's she doing here?"

Lucia shrugged. "She told me she was looking for a man—like, aren't we all, ha ha—only she didn't know his name, just that he lived in Newford. She just about had a fit when she spotted the picture of Matt in the poster for this gig."

"So she knows him from before."

"You tell me," Lucia said.

Amy shook her head. "Only Matt knows whatever it is that Matt knows."

"Katrina says she's twenty-two," Lucia went on, "but if you ask me, I think she's a lot younger. I'll bet she ran away from home—maybe even stowed away on some tourist's powerboat and jumped ship just outside the harbour because they were about to catch her and maybe take her back home."

"So what are you going to do about it?"

"Not a damn thing. She's a nice kid and besides," she added as Katrina and Matt walked by their table, heading for the bar, "I've got the feeling she's not even going to be my responsibility for much longer."

"Don't count on it," Amy said. "She'll be lucky if she lasts the night."

Although maybe not. Katrina *was* pretty, and she certainly could dance, so there was the musical connection, just as there had been with her.

Amy sighed. She didn't know why she got to feeling the way she did at times like this. She wouldn't even *want* to make a go at it with Matt again.

Lucia reached across the table and put her hand on Amy's, giving it a squeeze. "How're you handling this, Amy? I remember you were pretty messed up about him at one point."

"I can deal with it."

"Well—what's that line of yours? More power to your elbow then if you can, though I still can't figure out how you got past it enough to still be able to play with him."

Amy looked over to the bar where Matt was getting the girl a cup of tea. She wished the twinge of not so much jealousy, as hurt, would go away.

Patience, she told herself. She'd seen Matt with who knew how many women over the years, all of them crazy over him. The twinge only lasted for a little while—a reminder of a bad time, not the bad time itself. She was past that now.

Well, mostly.

"You just change your way of thinking about a person," she said after a few moments, trying to convince herself as much as Lucia. "You change what you need from them, your expectations. That's all."

"You make it sound easy."

Amy turned back to her friend. "It's not," she said in a quiet voice.

Lucia gave her hand a squeeze.

The girl was drunk on Matt, Amy realized. There was no other explanation for the way she was carrying on.

For the rest of the night, Amy could see Katrina sitting with Lucia at the back of the club, chin cupped in her hands as she listened to Matt sing. No, not just listening. She drank in the songs, swallowed them whole. And with every dance set they played, she was up on her feet at the front of the stage, the sinuous grace of her movement, the swirl and the lift and the rapid fire step of her small feet capturing each tune to perfection.

Matt was obviously complimented by her attention—or at least whatever it was that he'd feel that would be close to flattered—and why not? Next to Lucia, she was the best looking woman in the club, and Lucia wasn't exactly sending out "available" signals, not dressed the way she was.

Matt and the girl talked between each set, filling up the twenty minutes or so of canned music and patron conversation with a forest of words, his spoken, hers signed, each of them oblivious to their surroundings, to everything except for each other.

Maybe Katrina will be the one, Amy thought.

Once she got past her own feelings, that was what she usually found herself hoping. Although Matt could be insensitive once he stepped off the stage, she still believed that all he really needed was someone to care about to turn him around. Nobody who put such heart into his music could be completely empty inside. She was sure that he just needed someone—the right someone. It hadn't been her, fine. But somewhere there had to be a woman for him—a catalyst to take down the walls though which only his music dared forth to touch the world.

The way he'd been so attentive towards Katrina all night, Amy was sure he was going to take her home with him, but all he did was ask her out tomorrow.

Okay, she thought standing beside Lucia while Matt and Katrina "talked." That's a start and maybe a good one.

Katrina's hands moved in response to Matt's question.

"What's she saying?" Amy asked, leaning close to whisper to Lucia.

"Yes," Lucia translated. "Now she's asking him if they can ride the ferry."

"The one to Wolf Island?" Amy said. "That's where you found her."

"Whisht," Lucia told her.

"We'll do whatever you want," Matt was saying.

And then Katrina was gone, trailing after Lucia with a last lingering wave before the world outside the club swallowed her and the door closed behind the pair of them.

Matt and Amy returned to the stage to pack up their instruments.

"I was thinking of heading up to The Harp to see if there's a session on," Matt said. He looked around at the other three. "Anyone feel like coming?"

If there were enough musicians up for the music, Joe Breen, the proprietor of The Harp, would lock the doors to the public after closing hours and just let the music flow until the last musician packed it in, acting no different on this side of the Atlantic than he had with the pub he'd run back home in Ireland.

Johnny shook his head. "I'm beat. It's straight to bed for me tonight."

"It's been a long night," Nicky agreed.

Nicky looked a little sullen, but Amy doubted that Matt even noticed. He just shrugged, then looked to her.

Well, and why not? she thought.

"I'll give it a go," she told him.

Saying their good-byes to the other two outside the club, she and Matt walked north to the Rosses where The Harp stood in the shadow of the Kelly Street Bridge.

"Katrina seemed nice," Amy said after a few blocks.

"I suppose," he said. "A little intense, maybe."

"I think she's a little taken with you."

Matt nodded unselfconsciously. "Maybe too much. But she sure can dance, can't she?"

"Like an angel," Amy agreed.

Conversation fell flat then, just as it always did.

"I got a new tune from Geordie this afternoon," Amy said finally. "He doesn't remember where he picked it up, but it fits onto the end of 'The Kilavel Jig' like it was born to it."

Matt's eyes brightened with interest. "What's it called?"

"He didn't know. It had some Gaelic title that he'd forgotten, but it's a lovely piece. In G-major, but the first part has a kind of a modal flavor so that it almost feels as though it's being played out of C. It'd be just lovely on the bouzouki."

The talk stayed on tunes the rest of the way to The Harp—safe ground. At one point Amy found herself remembering a gig they'd played a few months ago and the story that Matt had used to introduce a song called "Sure, All He Did Was Go" that they'd played that night.

"He couldn't help himself," Matt had said, speaking of the fiddler in the song who gave up everything he had to follow a tune. "Music can be a severe mistress, demanding and jealous, and don't you doubt it. Do her bidding and isn't it just like royalty that she'll be treating you, but turn your back on her and she can take back her gift as easily as it was given. Your man could find himself holding only the tattered ribbons of a tune and song ashes and that's the God's own truth. I've seen it happen."

And then he'd laughed, as though he'd been having the audience on, and they'd launched into the song, but Amy had seen more than laughter in Matt's eyes as he started to sing. She wondered then, as she wondered now, if he didn't half believe that little bit of superstition, picked up somewhere on his travels, God knew where.

Maybe that was the answer to the riddle that was Matt Casey: he thought he'd lose his gift of music if he gave his heart to another. Maybe he'd even written that song himself, for she'd surely never heard it before. Picked it up in Morocco, he'd told her once, from one of the Wild Geese, the many Irish-in-exile, but she wasn't so sure.

Did you write it? she was ready to ask him right now, but then they were at The Harp and there was old Joe Breen flinging open the door to welcome them in and the opportunity was gone.

Lucia put on a pot of tea when she and Katrina returned to the apartment. While they waited for it to steep, they sat on the legless sofa pushed up against one wall of the long open loft that took up the majority of the apartment's floor space.

There was a small bedroom and a smaller bathroom off this main room. The kitchen area was in one corner—a battered fridge, its paint peeling, a sink and a counter with a hot plate on it and storage cupboards underneath and a small wooden kitchen table with five mismatching chairs set around it.

A low coffee table made of a plank of wood set on two apple crates crouched before the couch, laden with magazines and ashtrays. Along a far wall, three tall old mirrors had been fastened to the wall with a twelve-foot-long support bar set out in front of them. The other walls were adorned with posters of the various shows in which Lucia had performed. In two she had headlined—one a traditional ballet, while the other had been a very outré multimedia event written and choreographed by a friend of hers.

When the tea was ready, Lucia brought the pot and two cups over to the sofa and set them on a stack of magazines. She poured Katrina a cup, then another for herself.

"So you found him," Lucia said as she returned to her seat on the sofa.

Katrina nodded happily.

He's just the way I remember him, she signed.

"Where did you meet him?" Lucia asked.

Katrina gave a shy smile in response, then added, *Near my home. He was playing music.*

The bright blue fire of her eyes grew unfocused as she looked across the room, seeing not plaster walls and the dance posters upon them, but the rough rocky shore of a coastline that lay east of the city by the mouth of the Dulfer River. She went into the past, and the past was like a dream.

She'd been underlake when the sound of his voice drew her up from the cold and the dark, neither of which she felt except as a kind of malaise in her spirit; up into the moonlight, bobbing in the white-capped waves; listening, *swallowing* that golden sound of strings and voice, and he so handsome and all alone on the shore. And sad. She could hear it in his song, feel the timbre of his loneliness in his voice.

Always intrigued with the strange folk who moved on the shore with their odd stumpy legs, this time she was utterly smitten. She swam closer and laid her arms on a stone by the shore, her head on her arms, to watch and listen.

It was his music that initially won her, for music had been her first love. Each of her four sisters was prettier than the next, and each had a voice that could charm moonlight from a stone, milk from a virgin, a ghost from the cold dark depths below, but her voice was better still, as golden as her hair and as rich and pure as the first larksong at dawn.

But if it was his music that first enchanted her, then he himself completed the spell. She longed to join her voice to his, to hold him and be held, but she never moved from her hiding place. One look at her, and he would be driven away, for he'd see only that which was scaled, and she had no soul, not as did those who walked ashore.

No soul, no soul. A heart that broke for want of him, but no immortal soul. That was the curse of the lake-born.

When he finally put away his instrument and walked further inland, up under the pines where she couldn't follow, she let the waves close over her head and returned to her home underlake.

For three nights she returned to the shore and for two of them he was there, his voice like honey against the beat of the waves that the wind pushed shoreward and she only loved him more. But on the fourth night, he didn't come, nor on the fifth night, nor the sixth, and she despaired, knowing he was gone, away in the wide world, lost to her forever.

Her family couldn't help her; there was no one to help her. She yearned to be rid of scales, to walk on shore, no matter the cost, just so that she could be with him, but as well ask the sun not rise, or the wind to cease its endless motion.

"No matter the cost," she whispered. Tears trailed down her cheek, a sorrowful tide that would not ebb.

"Maraghreen," the lake replied as the wind lifted one of its waves to break upon the land.

She lifted her head, looked over the white caps, to where the lake grew darker still as it crept under the cliffs into the hidden cave where the lake witch lived.

She was afraid, but she went. To Maraghreen. Who took her scales and gave her legs with a bitter potion that tasted of witch blood; satisfied her impossible need, but took Katrina's voice in payment.

"A week and a day," the lake witch told her before she took Katrina's voice. "You have only so long to win him and your immortal soul, or to foam you will return."

"But without my voice. . . ." It was through song she'd thought to win him, voices joined in a harmony so pure how could he help but love her? "Without it. . . ."

"He must speak of his love first, or your soul will be forfeit."

"But without my voice. . . ."

"You will have your body; that will need be enough."

So she drank the blood, bitter on her tongue; gained legs, and each step she took was fiery pain and would be so until she'd gained a soul; went in search of him who held her love, for whose love she had paid such a dear price. Surely he would speak the words to her before the seven days were past and gone?

"Penny for your thoughts," Lucia said.

Katrina only smiled and shook her head. She could tell no one. The words must come unbidden from him or all would be undone.

Matt was late picking Katrina up on Sunday. It was partly his own fault—he'd gotten caught up with a new song that he was learning from a tape a friend had sent him from County Cork and lost track of the time—and partly from trying to follow the Byzantine directions that Lucia had used to describe the route to her Upper Foxville apartment.

Katrina didn't seem to mind at all; she was just happy to see him, her hands said, moving as graceful in speech as the whole of her did when she danced.

You didn't bring your guitar, she signed.

"I've been playing it all day. I thought I'd leave it at home."

Your voice . . . your music. They are a gift.

"Yeah, well. . . ."

He looked around the loft, recognizing a couple of the posters from having seen them around town before, pasted on subway walls or stuck in amongst the clutter of dozens of other ads in the front of restaurants and record stores. He'd never gone to any of the shows. Dance wasn't his thing, especially not modern dance or the performance art that Lucia was into. He'd seen a show of hers once. She'd spent fifteen minutes rolling back and forth across the stage, wrapped head to toe in old brown paper shopping bags to a soundtrack that consisted of water dripping for its rhythm, the hypnotic drone only occasionally broken by the sound of footsteps walking through broken glass.

Definitely not his thing.

Lucia was not his idea of what being creative was all about. In his head, he filed her type of artist under the general heading of lunatic fringe. Happily, she was out for the day.

"So," he said, "do you want to head out to the island?"

Katrina nodded. *But not just yet,* her hands added.

She smiled at him, long hair clouding down her back. She was wearing clothes borrowed from Lucia—cotton pants a touch too big and tied closed with a scarf through the belt loops, a T-shirt advertising a band that he'd never heard of and the same black Chinese slippers she'd been wearing last night.

"So what do you want—" he began.

Katrina took his hands before he could finish and placed them on her breasts. They were small and firm against his palms, her heartbeat echoing through the thin fabric, fluttering against his skin. Her own hands dropped to his groin, one gently cupping him through his jeans, the other pulling down the zipper.

She was gentle and loving, each motion innocent of artifice and certainly welcome, but she'd caught Matt off-guard.

"Look," he said, "are you sure you . . . ?"

She raised a hand, laying a finger against his lips. No words. Just touch. He grew hard, his penis uncomfortably bent in the confines of his jeans until she popped the top button and pulled it out. She put her small hand around it, fingers tight, hand moving slowly up and down. Speaking without words, her emotions were laid bare before him.

Matt took his hands from her breasts and lifted the T-shirt over her head. He let it drop behind her as he enfolded her in an embrace. She was like liquid against him, a shimmer of movement and soft touches.

No words, he thought.

She was right. There was no need for words.

He let her lead him into Lucia's bedroom.

Afterward, he felt so still inside it was though the world had stopped moving, time stalled, no one left but the two of them, wrapped up together, here in the dusky shadows that licked across the bed. He raised himself up on one elbow and looked down at her.

She seemed to be made of light. An unearthly radiance lay upon her pale skin like an angelic nimbus, except he doubted that any angel in heaven knew how to give and accept pleasure as she did. Not unless heaven was a very different place from the one he'd heard about in Sunday School.

There was a look in her eyes that promised him everything—not just bodily pleasures, but heart and soul—and for a moment he wanted to open up to her, to give to her what he gave his music, but then he felt something close up thick inside him. He found himself remembering a parting conversation he'd had with another woman. Darlene Flatt, born Darlene Johnston. Belying her stage name, she was an extraordinarily well-endowed singer in one of the local country bands.

Partial to slow-dancing on sawdusted floors, bolo ties, fringed jackets and, for the longest time, to him.

"You're just a hollow man," she told him finally. "A sham. The only place you're alive is on stage, but let me tell you something, Matt, the whole world's a stage if you'd just open your eyes and see."

Maybe in Shakespeare's day, he thought, but not now, not here, not in this world. Here you only get hurt.

"If you gave a fraction of your commitment to music to another person, you'd be. . . ."

He didn't know what Darlene thought he'd be because he tuned her out. Stepped behind the wall and followed the intricate turns of a song he was working on at the time until she finally got up and left his apartment.

Got up and left.

He swung his feet to the floor and looked for his clothes. Katrina caught his arm.

What's wrong? she signed. *What have I done?*

"Nothing," he said. "It's not you. It's not anything. It's just . . . I've just got to go, okay?"

Please, she signed. *Just tell me. . . .*

But he turned away so that he couldn't see her words. Got dressed. Paused in the doorway of the bedroom, choking on words that tried to slip through the wall. Turned finally, and left. The room. The apartment. Her, crying.

Lucia found Katrina when she came home later, red-eyed and sitting on the sofa in just a T-shirt, staring out the window, unable or unwilling to explain what was wrong. So Lucia thought the worst.

"That sonuvabitch," she started. "He never even showed up, did he? I should have warned you about what a prick he can be."

But Katrina's hands said, *No. It wasn't his fault. I want too much.*

"He was here?" Lucia asked.

She nodded.

"And you had a fight?"

The shrug that came in response said, sort of, and then Katrina began to cry again. Lucia enfolded her in her arms. It was small, cold comfort, she knew, for she'd had her own time in that lonely place in which Katrina now found herself, but it was all Lucia had to offer.

Matt found himself on the ferry, crossing from the city over to Wolf Island, as though, by doing so, he was completing some unfinished ritual to which neither he nor Katrina had quite set the parameters. He stood at the rail on the upper deck with the wind in his face and let the words to long-dead ballads run through his mind so that he wouldn't have to think about people, about relationships, about complications, about Katrina.

But in the dusking sky and in the wake that trailed behind the ferry, and later on the island, in the shadows that crept across the lawn and in the tangle that branches made against the sky, he could see only her face. Not all the words to all the songs he knew could free him from the burden of guilt that clung to him like burrs gathered on a sweater while crossing an autumn field.

He stopped at the statue of the little mermaid, and of course even she had Katrina's face.

"I didn't ask to start anything," he told the statue, saying now what he should have said in Lucia's bedroom. "So why the hell do I have to feel so guilty?"

It was the old story, he realized. Everything, everybody wanted to lay claim to a piece of your soul. And if they couldn't have it, they made you pay for it in guilt.

"I'm not a hollow man," he told the statue, saying what he should have said to Darlene. "I just don't have what you want me to give."

The statue just looked out across the lake. The dusk stretched for long impossible moments, then the sun dropped completely behind the horizon and the lamps lit up along the island's pathways. Matt turned and walked back to where the ferry waited to return him to Newford.

He didn't see Katrina again for two days.

I'm sorry was the first thing she said to him, her hands moving quickly before he could speak.

He stood in the hallway leading into Lucia's apartment, late on a Wednesday afternoon, not even sure what he was doing here. Apologizing. Explaining. Maybe just trying to understand.

"It wasn't your fault," he said. "It's just . . . everything happened too fast."

She nodded. *Do you want to come in?*

Matt regarded her. She was barefoot, framed by the doorway. The light behind her turned the flowered dress she was wearing into gossamer, highlighting the shape of her body under it. Her hair was the color of soft gold. He remembered her lying on the bed, radiant in the afterglow of their love-making.

"Could we go out instead?" he said. "Just for a walk or something?"

Let me get my shoes.

He took her to the lakefront and they walked the length of the boardwalk and the Pier, and then, when the jostle of the crowds became too much, they made their way down to the sand and sat near the shoreline. For the most part, his voice, her hands, were still. When they did talk, it was to make up stories about the more colorful characters with whom they shared the beach, both using their hands to speak so that they wouldn't be overheard, laughing as each tried to outdo the other with an outrageous background for one person or another.

Where did you learn sign language? she asked him at one point.

My cousin's deaf, he replied, his hands growing more deft, remembering old patterns, the longer they spoke. *Our parents were pretty close and we all saw a lot of each other, so everybody in the family learned.*

They had dinner at Kathryn's Cafe. Afterward, they went to the Owlnight, another of Newford's folk clubs, but this one was on the Butler University campus itself, in the Student Center. Garve MacCauley was doing a solo act, just guitar and gravelly voice, mostly his own material.

You're much better, Katrina signed to Matt after the first few songs.

"Just different," he said.

Katrina only smiled and shook her head.

After the last set, he took her back to Upper Foxville and left her at Lucia's door with a chaste kiss.

Thursday evening they took in a play at the Standish, a small concert hall that divided its evenings between repertory theater and music concerts. Katrina was entranced. She'd never seen live actors before, but then there was so much she didn't know about this new world in which she found herself and still more that she hadn't experienced in his company.

It was just past eleven by the time they got back to the apartment. Lucia had gone out so they could have the place to themselves but when Katrina invited Matt in, he begged off. His confused mumble of an explanation made little sense. All Katrina knew was that the days were slipping away. Saturday night, the lake witch's deadline, was blurring all too close, all too fast.

When he bent to kiss her on the forehead as he had the night before, she lifted her head so that their lips met. The kiss lasted a long time, a tangle of tongues. She pressed in close to him, hands stroking his back, but he pulled away with a confused panic fluttering in his eyes.

Why do I frighten you? she wanted to ask, but she had already guessed that it wasn't just her. It was any close relationship. Responsibility frightened him and perhaps more to the point, he just didn't love her. Maybe he would, given time, but by then it would be too late. Days went by quickly; hours were simply a rush, one tumbling into the other.

She gave him a sad smile and let him go, listened to his footsteps in the stairwell, then slowly went into the apartment and closed the door behind her. Each step she took, as it always did since she stepped onto the land, was like small knives cutting through her feet. She remembered the freedom of the waves, of movement without pain, but she had turned her back on scales and water. For better or worse, she belonged on the land now.

But that night her dreams were of foam. It gathered against the craggy shore near her home as the wind drove the lake water onto the rocks. Her sisters swam nearby, weeping.

Late Friday afternoon, Amy and Lucia were sitting on a bench in Fitzhenry Park, watching the traffic go by on Palm Street. They'd been to the Y to swim laps and they each nursed a coffee now, bought from one of the vendors in the little parade of carts that set up along the sidewalk first thing every morning. The sky was overcast, with the scent of rain in the air, but for all the weather report's warnings, it had held off all day.

"So how's Katrina doing?" Amy asked.

An expression that was more puzzlement than a frown touched Lucia's features. She took a sip of her coffee then set it down on the bench between them and took out her cigarettes.

"Well, they started off rocky on Sunday," she said. "He left her crying."

"God, so soon?"

"It's not as bad as it sounds," Lucia said.

She got her cigarette lit and blew out a wreath of smoke. Amy coughed.

"Sorry," Lucia said. She moved the cigarette away.

"It's not the smoke," Amy told her, lifting a hand to rub her throat. "I've had a tickle in my throat all day. I just hope I'm not coming down with something." She took a sip of her coffee and wished she had a throat lozenge. "So what did happen?" she asked.

"He didn't show up for a couple of days, didn't call—well, I guess he wouldn't want to speak to me, would he?—but then he's been real nice ever since he did show up on Wednesday. Took her to see your friend MacCauley over at the Owlnight, the next night they went to that production of Lizzie's play that's running at the Standish and earlier today they were out just mooching around town, I guess."

"He really needs someone," Amy said.

"I suppose. But knowing your history with him, I don't know if I wish him on Katrina."

"But at least they're doing things. He's *talking* to her."

"Yeah, but then he told her today that he's going to be away this weekend."

"That's right. He canceled Saturday morning band practice because he's got a gig at that little bar in Hartnett's Point. What's the problem with that? That's his job. She must know that."

Lucia shrugged. "I just think he should've taken her with him when he left this afternoon."

Amy sighed in sympathy. "Matt's not big on bringing his current belle to a gig. I remember how it used to really piss me off when we were going together."

"Well, she's heartbroken that he didn't ask her to come along. I told her she should just go anyway—show up and meet him there; I even offered to lend her the money for the bus—but she thinks he'd get mad."

"I don't know. He seemed to like her dancing when we played at Feeney's last weekend." Amy paused. "Of course he'll just be doing songs on his own. There won't be anything for her to dance to."

"She likes his songs, too," Lucia said.

Amy thought of the intensity with which Katrina had listened to Matt's singing that night at Feeney's and she knew exactly why Matt hadn't asked Katrina along to the gig.

"Maybe she likes them too much," she said. "Matt puts a lot into his music, and you know how bloody brilliant he is, but he's pretty humble about it all at the same time. He probably thinks it'd freak him too much having her sitting there just kind of—" her shoulders lifted and fell "—I don't know, swallowing the songs."

"Well, I wish he'd given it a try all the same. I've got to help Sharon with some set decorations, so Katrina's going to be on her own all night, just moping about the apartment. I asked her to come along, but she didn't want to go out."

"I could drop by your place," Amy said.

Lucia grinned. "I thought you'd never offer."

Amy punched her lightly on the arm. "You set me up!"

"Has she still got it or what?" Lucia asked, blowing on her fingernails.

Amy laughed and they went through a quick little flurry of slapping at each other's hands until they were too giddy to continue. They both leaned back on the park bench.

"I bet I'll have a better time," Amy said after a moment. "I've helped Sharon before. If she's got anything organized at all, it'll only be because someone else did it."

Lucia nodded glumly. "Don't I know it."

Amy went home to change and have a bite to eat before she took the subway north to Upper Foxville. Looking in the mirror as she put on her makeup, she saw that she was looking awfully pale. Thinking about feeling sick made her throat tickle again and she coughed. She stopped for some lozenges at a drug store that was on her way. They helped her throat, but she felt a little light-headed now.

She should just go home, she thought, but she'd promised Lucia and she couldn't help but be sympathetic towards Katrina. She'd just stay a little while, that was all.

It was just going on nightfall when she reached Lucia's street. She paused at the corner, as she saw a small familiar figure step from the stoop of Lucia's building and head off the other way down the street. She almost called Katrina by name, but something stopped her. Curiosity got the better of her and she kept still, following along behind instead.

It was easy to keep track of her—Katrina's cloud of gold hair caught the light of every streetlamp she passed under and seemed to reflect a burnished glow up into the night. She led Amy down to MacNeil Street, turning west once she reached it. Her stride was both purposeful and wearied, but always graceful.

Poor kid, Amy thought.

More than once she started to hurry to catch up with Katrina, but then her curiosity would rise to the fore and she'd tell herself to be patient just a little longer. Since Katrina didn't know anyone in Newford—according to Lucia she didn't even know the city—Amy couldn't couldn't figure out where Katrina might be going.

Where MacNeil ended at Lee Street, Katrina crossed over and went down to the bank of the Kickaha River. She followed the riverbank southward, pausing only when she came near the Gracie Street Bridge. There the fenced-off ruins of the old L & N sawmill reared up in the darkness, ill-lit, drowning the riverbank with its shadow. It took up enough room that a person walking along the river by its chain-link fence would be almost invisible from any of the more peopled areas roundabout. Even across the river there were only empty warehouses.

Amy started to hurry again, struck by the sudden fear that Katrina meant to do herself harm. The river ran quicker here, rapiding over a descending shelf of broken stone slabs from where an old railway bridge had collapsed a few years ago. The city had cleared a channel through the debris, but that just made the river run more quickly through the narrower course. More than one person had drowned on this stretch of water—and not always by accident.

Matt's not worth it, she wanted to tell Katrina. Nobody's worth it.

Before she could reach Katrina, she came to an abrupt halt again. She stifled a cough that reared up in her throat and leaned against a fence post, suddenly dizzy. But it wasn't the escalating onset of a flu bug that had made her stop. Rather it was what she had spied, bobbing in the swift-moving water.

The light was bad, just a diffused glow from the streets a block or so over, but it was enough for her to make out four white shapes in the dark water. They each seemed as slender and graceful as Katrina, with the same spun gold hair, except theirs was cut short to their skulls, highlighting the fox-like shape of their features. They probably had, Amy thought, the same blue eyes, too.

What were they *doing* there?

Another wave of dizziness came over her. She slid down the side of the fence pole until she was crouched on the ground. She remembered thinking that this way she wouldn't have as far to fall if she fainted. Clutching the pole for support, she looked back to the river.

Katrina had moved closer to the shore and was holding her arms out to the women. As their shapes moved closer, Amy's heartbeat drummed into overtime for she realized that they had no legs. They were propelling themselves through the water with scaled fish tails. There was no mistaking the shape of them as the long tail fins broke the surface of the water.

Mermaids, Amy thought, no longer able to breathe. They were mermaids.

It wasn't possible. *How* could it be possible?

And what did it make Katrina?

The sight of them blurred. For a moment she was looking through a veil, then it was like looking through a double-paned window at an angle, images all duplicated and laid over each other.

She blinked hard. She started to lift her hand to rub at her eyes, but she was suddenly so weak it was all she could do to just crouch beside the pole and not tumble over into the weeds.

The women in the river drew closer as Katrina stepped to the very edge of the water. Katrina lifted her hair, then let it drop in a clouding fall. She pointed at the women.

"Cut away and gone," one of the women said.

"All gone."

"We gave it to Maraghreen."

"For you, sister."

"We traded, gold for silver."

Amy pressed her face against the pole as the mermaids spoke. Through her dizziness, their voices seemed preternaturally enhanced. They chorused, one beginning where another ended, words molten, bell-like, sweet as honey, and so very, very pure.

"She gave us this."

The foremost of the women in the river reached up out of the water. Something glimmered silver and bright in her hand. A knife.

"Pierce his heart."

"Bathe in his blood."

"Your legs will grow together once more."

"You'll come back to us."

"Oh, sister."

Katrina went down on her knees at the water's edge. She took the knife from the mermaid's hand and laid it gingerly on her lap.

"He doesn't love you."

"He will never love you."

The women all drew close. They reached out of the water, stroking Katrina's arms and her face with gentling hands.

"You must do it—before the first dawn light follows tomorrow night."

"Or foam you'll be."

"Sister, please."

"Return to those who love you."

Katrina bowed her head, making no response. One by one the women dove into the river deeps and were gone. From her hiding place, Amy tried to rise— she knew Katrina would be coming back soon, coming back this way, and she didn't want to be caught—but she couldn't manage it, even with the help of the pole beside her. Then Katrina stepped away from the river and walked towards her, the knife held gingerly in one hand.

As their gazes met, another wave of dizziness rose in Amy, this one a tsunami, and in its wake she felt the ground tremble underfoot, but it was only herself, tumbling into the dirt and weeds. She closed her eyes and let the darkness take her away.

It was late afternoon when Amy awoke on the sofa in Lucia's loft. Her surroundings and the wrong angle of the afternoon light left her disoriented and confused, but no longer feeling sick. It must have been one of those 24-hour viruses, she thought as she swung her legs to the floor, then leaned back against the sofa's cushions.

Lucia looked up from the magazine she was reading at the kitchen table. Laying it down she walked over and joined Amy on the sofa.

"I was *très* surprised to find you sleeping here when I got in last night," she said. "Katrina said you got sick, so she put you to bed on the sofa and slept on the floor herself. How're you feeling now, *ma chérie?*"

Amy worked through what Lucia had just said. None of it quite jibed with her own muddled memory of the previous evening.

"Okay . . . I guess," she said finally. She looked around the loft. "Where's Katrina?"

"She borrowed the bus money from me and went to Hartnett's Point after all. True love wins over all, *n'est-ce pas?*"

Amy thought of mermaids swimming in the Kickaha River, of Katrina kneeling by the water, of the silver knife.

"Oh, shit," she said.

"What's the matter?"

"I. . . ."

Amy didn't know what to say. What she'd seen hadn't made any sense. She'd been sick, dizzy, probably delirious. But it had seemed so real.

Pierce his heart . . . bathe in his blood. . . .

She shook her head. None of it could have happened. There were no such things as mermaids. But what if there were? What if Katrina was carrying that silver knife as she made her way to Matt's gig? What if she did just what those . . . mermaids had told her. . . .

You must do it—before the first dawn light that follows tomorrow night. . . .

What if—

Or foam you'll be. . . .

—it was real?

She bent down and looked for her shoes, found them pressed up against one of the coffee table's crate supports. She put them on and rose from the sofa.

"I've got to go," she told Lucia.

"Go where? What's going on?"

"I don't know. I don't have time to explain. I'll tell you later."

Lucia followed her across the loft to the door. "Amy, you're acting really weird."

"I'm fine," Amy said. "Honest."

Though she still didn't feel quite normal. She was weak and didn't want to look in a mirror for fear of seeing the white ghost of her own face looking back at her. But she didn't feel that she had any choice.

If what she'd seen last night *had* been real. . . .

Lucia shook her head uncertainly. "Are you sure you're—"

Amy paused long enough to give her friend a quick peck on the cheek, then she was out the door.

Borrowing a car was easy. Her brother Pete had two and was used to her sudden requests for transportational needs, relieved that he wasn't required to provide a chauffeur service along with it. She was on the road by seven, tooling west along the old lakeside highway in a gas-guzzling Chevy, stopping for a meal at a truck stop that marked the half-way point and arriving at Hartnett's Point just as Matt would be starting his first set.

She pulled in beside his VW van—a positive antique by now, she liked to tease him—and parked. The building that housed Murphy's Bar where Matt had his gig was a ramshackle affair, log walls here in back, plaster on cement walls in front. The bar sat on the edge of the point from which the village got its name, with a long pier out behind the building, running into the lake. The water around the pier was thick with moored boats.

She went around front to where the neon sign spelling the name of the bar crackled and spat an orange glow and stepped inside to the familiar sound of Matt singing Leon Rosselson's "World Turned Upside Down." The audience, surprisingly enough for a backwoods establishment such as this, was actually paying attention to the music. Amy thought that only a third of them were probably even aware of the socialist message the song espoused.

The patrons were evenly divided between the back-to-the-earth hippies who tended organic farms west of the village, all jeans and unbleached cotton, long hair and flower-print dresses; the locals who'd grown up in the area and would probably die here, heavier drinkers, also in jeans, but tending towards flannel shirts and baseball caps, T-shirts and workboots; and then those cottagers who hadn't yet closed their places up for the year, a hodge-podge of golf shirts and cotton blends, short skirts and, yes, even one dark blue captain's cap, complete with braided rope trim.

She shaded her eyes and looked for Katrina, but didn't spot her. After a few moments, she got herself a beer from the bar and found a corner table to sit at that she shared with a pair of earth-mothers and a tall skinny man with drooping eyes and hair longer than that of either of his companions, pulled back into a pony-tail that fell to his waist. They made introductions all around, then settled back into their chairs to listen to the music.

As Matt's set wound on, Amy began to wonder just exactly what it was that she was doing here. Even closing her eyes and concentrating, she could barely call up last night's fantastic images with any sort of clarity. What if the whole thing *had* just been a delirium? What if she'd made her way to Lucia's apartment only to pass out on the sofa and have dreamt it all?

Matt stopped by the table when he ended his set.

"What brings you up here, Scallan?" he asked.

She shrugged. "Just thought I'd check out how you do without the rest of us to keep you honest."

A touch of humor crinkled around his eyes. "So what's the verdict?"

"You're doing good." She introduced him to her companions, then asked, "Do you want to get a little air?"

He nodded and let her lead the way outside. They leaned against the back of somebody's Bronco and looked down the length of one of the village's two streets. This one cut north and south, from the bush down to the lake. The other was merely the highway as it cut through the village.

"So have you seen Katrina?" Amy asked.

Matt nodded. "Yeah, we walked around the Market for awhile yesterday afternoon."

"You mean, she's not up here?"

"Not so's I know."

Amy sighed. So much for her worries. But if Katrina hadn't borrowed the money from Lucia to come up here, then where *had* she gone?

"Why are you so concerned about Katrina?" Matt asked.

Amy started to make up some excuse, but then thought, screw it. One of them might as well be up front.

"I'm just worried about her."

Matt nodded. He kicked at the gravel underfoot, but didn't say anything.

"I know it's none of my business," Amy said.

"You're right. It's not." There was no rancor in Matt's voice. Just a kind of weariness.

"It's just that—"

"Look," he said, turning to Amy, "she seems nice, that's all. I think maybe we started out on the wrong foot, but I'm trying to fix that. For now, I just want to be her friend. If something else comes up later, okay. But I want to take it as it comes. Slowly. Is that so wrong?"

Amy shook her head. And then it struck her. For the first time that they weren't on stage together, or working out an arrangement, Matt actually seemed to focus on her. To listen to what she was saying, and answer honestly. Protective walls maybe not completely down, but there *was* a little breach in them.

"I think she loves you," Amy said.

Matt sighed. "It's kind of early for that—don't you think? I think it's more a kind of infatuation. She'll probably grow out of it just as fast as she fell into it."

"I don't know about that. Seems to me that if you're going to be at all fair, you'd be just a little bit more—"

"Don't talk to me about responsibility," Matt said, breaking in. "Just because someone falls in love with you, it doesn't mean you owe them anything. I've got no control over how other people feel about me—"

That's where you're wrong, Amy thought. If you'd just act more human, more like this. . . .

"—and I'm sure not going to run my life by their feelings and schedules. I'm not trying to sound self-centered, I'm just trying to . . . I don't know. Protect my privacy."

"But if you don't give a little, how will you ever know what you might be missing?"

"Giving too much, too fast—that just leaves you open to being hurt."

"But—"

"Oh, shit," Matt said, glancing at his watch. "I've got another set to do." He pushed away from the Bronco. "Look, I'm sorry if I don't measure up to how people want me to be, but this is just the way I am."

Why didn't you open yourself up even this much while we were going out together? Amy wanted to ask. But all she did was nod and say, "I know."

"Are you coming in?"

She shook her head. "Not right away."

"Well, I've got—"

"I know." She waved him off. "Break a leg or whatever."

She moved away from the Bronco once he'd gone inside and crossed the parking lot, gravel crunching underfoot until she reached the grass verge. She followed it around to the lawn by the side of the building and down to the lakefront. There she stood, listening to the vague sound of Matt's voice and guitar as it carried through an open window. She looked at all the boats clustered around the pier. A splash drew her attention to the far end of the wooden walkway where a figure sat with its back to the shore having just thrown something into the lake.

Amy had one of those moments of utter clarity. She knew immediately that it was Katrina sitting there, feet dangling in the water, long hair clouding down her back, knew as well that it was the silver knife she'd thrown into the lake. Amy could almost see it, turning end on slow end as it sank in the water.

She hesitated for the space of a few long breaths, gaze tracking the surface of the lake for Katrina's sisters, then she slowly made her way down to the pier. Katrina turned at the sound of Amy's shoes on the wooden slats of the walkway. She nodded once, then looked back out over the lake.

Amy sat beside her. She hesitated again, then put her arm comfortingly around Katrina's small shoulders. They sat like that for a long time. The water lapped against the pilings below them. An owl called out from the woods to their left, a long mournful sound. A truck pulled into the bar's parking lot. Car doors slammed, voices rose in laughter, then disappeared into the bar.

Katrina stirred beside Amy. She began to move her hands, but Amy shook her head.

"I'm sorry," she said. "I can't understand what you're saying."

Katrina mimed steering, both hands raised up in front of her, fingers closed around an invisible steering wheel.

Amy nodded. "I drove up in my brother's car."

Katrina pointed to herself then to Amy and again mimed turning a steering wheel.

"You want me to drive you somewhere?"

Katrina nodded.

Amy looked back towards the bar. "What about Matt?"

Katrina shook her head. She put her hands together, eyes eloquent where her voice was silent. Please.

Amy looked at her for a long moment, then she slowly nodded. "Sure. I can give you a lift. Is there someplace specific you want to go?"

Katrina merely rose to her feet and started back down the pier towards shore. Once they were in the Chev, she pointed to the glove compartment.

"Go ahead," Amy said.

As she started the car, Katrina pulled out a handful of roadmaps. She sorted through them until she came to one that showed the whole north shore of the lake. She unfolded it and laid it on the dashboard between them and pointed to a spot west of Newford. Amy looked more closely. The place where Katrina had her finger was where the Dulfer River emptied into the lake. The tip of her small finger was placed directly on the lakeside campgrounds of the State Park there.

"Jesus," Amy said. "It'll take us all night to get there. We'll be lucky to make it before dawn."

As Katrina shrugged, Amy remembered what Katrina's sisters had said last night. *Before the first dawn light follows tomorrow night.*

That was tonight. *This* morning.

Or foam you'll be.

She shivered and looked at Katrina.

"Tell me what's going on," she said. "Please, Katrina. Maybe I can help you."

Katrina just shook her head sadly. She mimed driving, hands around the invisible steering wheel again.

Amy sighed. She put the car in gear and pulled out of the parking lot. Katrina reached towards the radio, eyebrows raised quizzically. When Amy nodded, she turned it on and slowly wound through the stations until she got Newford's WKPN-FM. It was too early for Zoe B.'s "Nightnoise" show, so they listened to Mariah Carey, the Vaughan Brothers and the like as they followed the highway east.

Neither of them spoke as they drove; Katrina couldn't and Amy was just too depressed. She didn't know what was going on. She just felt as though she'd become trapped in a Greek tragedy. The storyline was already written, everything was predestined to a certain outcome and there was nothing she could do about it. Only Matt could have, if he'd loved Katrina, but she couldn't even blame him. You couldn't force a person to love somebody.

She didn't agree with his need to protect his privacy. Maybe it stopped him from being hurt, but it also stopped him from being alive. But he was right about one thing: he couldn't be held responsible for who chose to love him.

They crossed over the Dulfer River just as dawn was starting to pink the eastern horizon. When Amy pulled into the campgrounds, Katrina directed her down a narrow dirt road that led to the park's boat launch.

They had the place to themselves. Amy pulled up by the water and killed the engine. The pines stood silent around them when they got out of the car. There was birdsong, but it seemed strangely muted. Distant. As though heard through gauze.

Katrina lifted a hand and touched Amy's cheek, then walked towards the water. She headed to the left of the launching area where a series of broad flat rocks staircased down into the water. After a moment's hesitation, Amy followed after. She sat down beside Katrina who was right by the edge of the water, arms wrapped around her knees.

"Katrina," she began. "Please tell me what's going on. I—"

She fussed in her purse, looking for pen and paper. She found the former, and pulled out her checkbook to use the back of a check as a writing surface.

"I want to help," she said, holding the pen and checkbook out to her companion.

Katrina regarded her for a long moment, a helpless look in her eyes, but finally she took the proffered items. She began to write on the back of one of the checks, but before she could hand it back to Amy, a wind rose up. The pine trees shivered, needles whispering against each other.

An electric tingle sparked across every inch of Amy's skin. The hairs at the nape of her neck prickled and goosebumps traveled up her arms. It was like that moment before a storm broke, when the air is so charged with ions that it seems anything might happen.

"What . . . ?" she began.

Her voice died in her throat as the air around them thickened. Shapes formed in the air, pale diffused airy shapes, slender and transparent. Their voices were like the sound of the wind in the pines.

"Come with us," they said, beckoning to Katrina.

"Be one with us."

"We can give you what you lack."

Katrina stared at the misty apparitions for the longest time. Then she let pen and checkbook fall to the rock and stood up, stretching her arms towards the airy figures. Her own body began to lose its definition. She was a spiderweb in the shape of a woman, gossamer, smoke and mist. Her clothing fell from her transparent form to fall into a tangle beside Amy.

And then she was gone. The wind died. The whisper stilled in the pines.

Amy stared open-mouthed at where Katrina had disappeared. All that lay on the rock were Katrina's clothes, the pen and the checkbook. Amy reached out towards the clothes. They were damp to the touch.

Or foam you'll be.

Amy looked up into the lightning sky. But Katrina hadn't just turned to foam, had she? Something had come and taken her away before that happened. If any of this had even been real at all. If she hadn't just lost it completely.

She heard weeping and lowered her gaze to the surface of the lake. There were four women's heads there, bobbing in the unruly water. Their hair was short, cropped close to their heads, untidily, as though cut with garden shears or a knife. Their eyes were red with tears. Each could have been Katrina's twin.

Seeing her gaze upon them, they sank beneath the waves, one by one, and then Amy was alone again. She swallowed thickly, then picked up her checkbook to read what Katrina had written before what could only have been angels came to take her away:

"Is this what having a soul means, to know such bittersweet pain? But still, I cherish the time I had. Those who live forever, who have no stake in the dance of death's inevitable approach, can never understand the sanctity of life."

It sounded stiff, like a quote, but then Amy realized she'd never heard how Katrina would speak, not the cadence of her voice, nor its timbre, nor her diction.

And now she never would.

The next day, Matt found Amy where her brother Pete said she was going. She was by the statue of the little mermaid on Wolf Island, just sitting on a bench and staring out at the lake. She looked haggard from a lack of sleep.

"What happened to you last night?" he asked.

She shrugged. "I decided to go for a drive."

Matt nodded as though he understood, though he didn't pretend to have a clue. The complexities that made up people's personalities were forever a mystery to him.

He sat down beside her.

"Have you seen Katrina?" he asked. "I went by Lucia's place looking for her, but she was acting all weird—" not unusual for Lucia, he added to himself "—and told me I should ask you."

"She's gone," Amy said. "Maybe back into the lake, maybe into the sky. I'm not really sure."

Matt just looked at her. "Come again?" he said finally.

So Amy told him about it all, of what she'd seen two nights ago by the old L & N sawmill, of what had happened last night.

"It's like in that legend about the little mermaid," she said as she finished up. She glanced at the statue beside them. "The real legend—not what the Disney studios used for their movie."

Matt shook his head. " 'The Little Mermaid' isn't a legend," he said. "It's just a story, made up by Hans Christian Andersen, like 'The Emperor's New Clothes' and 'The Ugly Duckling.' They sure as hell aren't real."

"I'm just telling you what I saw."

"Jesus, Amy. Will you listen to yourself?"

When she turned to face him, he saw real anguish in her features.

"I can't help it," she said. "It really happened."

Matt started to argue, but then he shook his head. He didn't know what had gotten into Amy to go on like this. He expected this kind of thing from Geordie's brother who made his living gussying up fantastical stories from nothing, but Amy?

"It looks like her, doesn't it?" Amy said.

Matt followed her gaze to the statue. He remembered the last time he'd been on the island, the night when he'd walked out on Katrina, when everything had looked like her. He got up from the bench and stepped closer. The statue's bronze features gleamed in the sunlight.

"Yeah," he said. "I guess it does."

Then he walked away.

He was pissed off with Amy for going on the way she had and brooded about her stupid story all the way back to the city. He had a copy of the Andersen Fairy Tales at home. When he got back to his apartment, he took it down from the shelf and read the story again.

"Aw, shit," he said as he closed the book.

It was just a story. Katrina would turn up. They'd all share a laugh at how Amy was having him on.

But Katrina didn't turn up. Not that day, nor the next, nor by the end of the week. She'd vanished from his life as mysteriously as she'd come into it.

That's why I don't want to get involved with people, he wanted to tell Amy. Because they just walk out of your life if you don't do what they want you to do.

No way it had happened as Amy had said it did. But he found himself wondering about what it would be like to be without a soul, wondering if he even had one.

Friday of that week, he found himself back on the island, standing by the statue once again. There were a couple of tattered silk flowers on the stone at its base. He stared at the mermaid's features for a long time, then he went home and started to phone the members of Marrowbones.

"Well, I kind of thought this was coming," Amy said when he called to tell her that he was breaking up the band, "except I thought it'd be Johnny or Nicky quitting."

She was sitting in the windowseat of her apartment's bay window, back against one side, feet propped up against the other. She was feeling better than she had when she'd seen him on Sunday, but there was still a strangeness inside her. A lost feeling, a sense of the world having shifted underfoot and the rules being all changed.

"So what're you going to do?" she added when he didn't respond.

"Hit the road for awhile."

"Gigging, or just traveling?"

"Little of both, I guess."

There was another long pause and Amy wondered if he was waiting for her to ask if she could come. But she was really over him now. Had been for a long time. She wasn't looking to be anybody's psychiatrist, or mother. Or matchmaker.

"Well, see you then," he said.

"Bon voyage," Amy said.

She cradled the phone. She thought of how he talked with her the other night up at Hartnett's Point, opening up, actually *relating* to her. And now. . . . She realized that the whole business with Katrina had just wound him up tighter than ever before.

Well, somebody else was going to have to work on those walls and she knew who it had to be. A guy named Matt Casey.

She looked out the window again.

"Good luck," she said.

Matt was gone for a year. When he came back, the first place he went to was Wolf Island. He stood out by the statue for a long time, not saying anything, just trying to sort out why he was here. He didn't have much luck, not that year, nor each subsequent year that he came. Finally, almost a decade after Katrina was gone—walked out of his life, turned into a puddle of lake water, went sailing through the air with angels, whatever—he decided to stay overnight, as though being alone in the dark would reveal something that was hidden from the day.

"Lady," he said, standing in front of the statue, drowned in the thick silence of the night.

He hadn't brought an offering for the statue—Our Lady of the Harbour, as the baglady had called her. He was just here, looking for something that remained forever out of reach. He wasn't trying to understand Katrina or the story that Amy had told of her. Not anymore.

"Why am I so empty inside?" he asked.

"I can't believe you're going to play with him again," Lucia said when Amy told her about her new band, Johnny Jump Up.

Amy shrugged. "It'll just be the three of us—Geordie's going to be playing fiddle."

"But he hasn't changed at all. He's still so—cold."

"Not on stage."

"I suppose not," Lucia said. "I guess all he's got going for him is his music."

Amy nodded sadly.

"I know," she said.

THE VISITORS' BOOK

Stephen Gallagher

Gallagher is the author of more than twenty short stories and ten novels, including *Chimera*, *Valley of Lights*, *Oktober*, and most recently, *Nightmare, with Angel*. He has also worked extensively in radio and television in England, where he was born and lives.

Nothing overtly frightening or even bad occurs in "The Visitors' Book," but despite this I found it quietly terrifying. It first appeared in *Darklands*.

—E.D.

"Someone's torn a page out of this," she said, turning the book toward me. "Look, you can see."

She was almost right. The page hadn't been torn, it had been cut; taken out with a blade that had been run down the middle of the book as close to the centre as it was possible to get. It was the kind of cut you make when you don't want your handiwork to be noticed. The only thing that gave it away was that when the book was closed, a slight gap appeared as if a bookmark had been lost in there somewhere. It made me faintly curious, but no more than that. I really didn't think that it was any big deal.

"So it has," I said, and tried to look more interested than I was.

Some time later, I remember getting it out of the drawer to look at it again. It was a big book, album-sized, and it was two-thirds filled with handwritten entries by many of the families who'd stayed in the summerhouse before us. Only one or two of them were in a language I could understand, and they gave a few hints about the place—how to puzzle out how the circuit breakers worked, where to get English newspapers two days out of date—as well as the standard, had-a-lovely-time kinds of sentiments. There were some people from Newcastle, others who'd come over from Dorset. Many of the others were Germans, a few French. Sally hadn't come across the book until we'd been in the place for three days already, and then she'd found it while rummaging around in the sitting-room furniture for maps and brochures. When I eventually went back and brought it out again, I turned to the place where the missing page had been and looked at the entries before and after. I couldn't remember anything of what had been written, but by

239

then I was only interested in the dates. The gap seemed to correspond to a two-week period exactly one year before.

No, I remember thinking. *It can't have any significance.* All that it probably meant was that someone had messed up their entry and had taken the leaf out to try it again. The paper-cutter they'd used was still there at the back of the drawer, a little plastic block with just the corner of a razor blade showing.

When I turned the paper to the light, I could see that some of the missing writing had pressed through onto the next page. Not to the extent that I could make out any words, but enough to get an idea of the overall style. It was neat, it was rounded. A feminine hand.

And it didn't match with any of the entries that came before or after.

But that was later. Back on that third day, there was no reason for the Visitors' Book to bother me at all. I left Sally looking through the remaining pages, and went out onto the covered terrace on the front of the summerhouse.

"Watcha doing, Minx?" I said.

The Minx looked up at me from the table. On her birth certificate and by her grandparents she was called Victoria, but to us she'd been the Minx for so long that we had to make an effort to remember that she had any other name. She was four years old that autumn, and was due to start at school the following spring. She'd have her own books, nametabs, a uniform, everything. We'd always told ourselves that we could look forward to this—like all children she'd hit our lives like a hurricane, leaving us dazed and off-kilter and somehow feeling that we'd never quite be able to make up the ground again to become the people we'd once been—but I found that I wasn't quite anticipating the event in the way that I'd imagined. I suppose I was just beginning to realise how closely the growing and the going away were entwined, and would ever be so.

"I'm colouring," she said.

She was, too. She'd coloured the page in her book and a good piece of the old vinyl tablecloth around it. She'd coloured a cow blue, and the sky behind it black.

I said, "That looks really good. Are you going to do another?"

"I'll do another next Tuesday," she said, Next Tuesday being her way of indicating some undetermined time in the future. "Let's go and look for froggies."

"Clear your lunch away first," I said, "or you'll bring in all kinds of creepy-crawlies."

She climbed down from the bench to the wooden planking of the terrace, and surprised me by doing what I'd asked of her. Then we set off down the steps and into the grounds to find some froggies.

It was a pretty good house. I'd felt a twinge of disappointment when we'd first rolled up the grassy drive after a long haul by road and ferry, but within a few hours of unpacking and beginning to unwind it had started to grow on me. It was bigger than we needed, but I liked the sense of space. So what if it was a little shabby round the edges and the shower arrangements were kind of spartan and the beds were dropped in the middle in a way that would have suited a hunchback perfectly and nobody else at all; after a while this only seemed to add to the atmosphere.

It was late, a quiet time of the year. Almost all of the other summerhouses, including the newer one that shared this grassy clearing in a thicket just a little way back from the beach, appeared to be unoccupied. When the road gate at the end of the driveway was closed, it was almost as if we were shutting ourselves into a private world. When the Minx had spotted the horde of tiny frogs that seemed to migrate across the drive at around four o'clock every afternoon, that more or less confirmed it. It seemed that we were going to be okay.

"Have you found any?" she asked brightly, but I had to tell her that I hadn't. She liked to hold them on her hand. By now they probably just sat there toughing it out and thinking, *Oh, shit, not again* and *Why me, God, why me?*

"No," I said. "It's the wrong time of day. Look, I saw a bike in the garage yesterday. Why don't you ride it around the garden?"

"A big bike?" she said warily.

"No, just a little bike."

So we spent the afternoon playing with the house's rusty old tricycle and a football that we'd picked up from Willi's Market about a half-mile down the shore road, and after we'd eaten picnic-style out on the terrace we all took a walk along the beach until it was too cold for everybody but the Minx, who had to be picked up out of the sandhole that she'd dug and carried home squalling.

And as we were tracing our way back through the upturned boats and then across the strip of coarse grassland that divided the shoreline from the shore road, I found myself thinking: *Maybe the people who wrote the page weren't the ones who took it out. Maybe it was something that the owners didn't want the rest of us to see.*

The owners.

Those shadowy people who weren't actually present but whose mark was everywhere, so that they seemed to stand just out of sight like a bunch of watchful ghosts. Their pictures, their ornaments, their old castoff furniture—their house. Maybe they came in after each new tenant and read the book, and there was something here that they'd censored.

Maybe.

Exactly what I had in mind, I couldn't have said. Something uncomplimentary, some insult even; written by someone who perhaps didn't have a good time and blamed the place and not themselves for it. Or worse. It could have been something worse. I was surprised to find that the possibility had been playing on my mind. I said nothing to Sally, but I decided there and then that I'd think about it no further. I mean, you worry at something to which you know you can never find the answer, and where does it get you?

Nowhere. So I thought I'd better stop.

That night, after the Minx had been installed in her room and had exhausted every avenue for stories and drinks and had eventually exhausted herself as well, we got a couple of the local beers out of the fridge and turned on the sitting-room lights. Sally flicked through some of the magazines that she'd picked up on the boat coming over, and I hunted around for the paperback I'd been reading. I'm not much of a reader, and thinking of the two weeks that lay ahead I'd bought the book for its size and weight as much as for any other reason. Every other page was dotted with CIA and MI5 and KGB, and the plot went on and on and had about as much grip as a wet handshake; after a while I gave up looking for it, and went over to the shelves instead.

There had to be something here I could read. There was a cabinet full of books and overseas editions of the *Reader's Digest*, most of them probably abandoned and accumulated from visitors over the years, but there wasn't much that was in the English language. There was a fat book by Leon Uris that I put back because it looked such heavy going and, besides, I'd already seen the movie, and an old and brittle Agatha Christie which, on a quick check, appeared to have lost its last ten pages. The only decent bet seemed to be a two-fisted private eye story titled *Dames Die First*.

When I pulled it out, a photograph dropped to the floor. It had been between the books. I picked it up and looked at it, and saw that there was the sign of a crease across the middle. At a guess, it had been slipped in between the volumes for the pressure to flatten it out, and then it had been forgotten. It was of a blonde girl of about six or seven, and if it had been taken anywhere around here I didn't recognise the spot. I carried the picture over to the chest of drawers and then started to go through them, much as Sally had earlier in the day. After a while I became aware of her watching me.

"What's the matter?" she said.

"Just checking on something."

She didn't seem to think much of my answer, but it was the best one I had. As she was laying down her magazine to come over, I found what I was looking for; another, different photograph that lay in one of the drawers underneath some boxed games and out-of-date timetables.

It was a family group. Nothing formal, just a snapshot. The house was recognisable in the background, although they'd added to it since. These, I'd been guessing, were the people who actually owned the place and who let it out through an agency for the times when they didn't need it themselves.

I laid the two photographs side by side on top of the dresser. The girl who appeared in one didn't appear in the other.

Sally picked up the portrait shot and said, "She doesn't look local," before dropping it again and going on through the kitchen toward the bathroom.

Yeah, fine.

That's probably what I'd been thinking, too.

Saturday came around.

I didn't actually realise that it was Saturday until I saw a strange car coming up the driveway that morning. At first I thought that it was somebody on their way to speak to us, but the car turned off and pulled in by the other of the two houses that shared the driveway and the private clearing at its end. Suddenly it didn't seem so private any more.

The family got out and we nodded to each other. They didn't seem to have brought much in the way of luggage and they went straight into the house as if they already knew their way around. My guess was that they were another set of owners, just up for the weekend. I went back into our own place and warned Sally and the Minx, just in case either of them happened to be wandering around after a shower in less than their underwear. There was just a stretch of open ground between the two buildings, nothing screening them at all. The other house was newer, neater. I know it was theirs, but I couldn't help thinking of them as intruders.

I looked at the two children. Neither of them was anything like the girl in the photograph.

So then I wondered if they might be able to tell me what had happened here, in this same week exactly one year before.

But I never asked.

On Sunday we took the Minx on a long drive to the zoo, where she acted up so much that we had to threaten to leave her there and halfway meant it. When we got back late in the afternoon, our short-term neighbours were apparently loading up to go. We nodded as we passed just as before, and then they went.

I gave it a few minutes after their departure and then I took a walk down the driveway to check that the gate was secure; the driveway curved and was lined with dense bushes, so the gate couldn't be seen directly from the house. The Minx came after me, on the prospect of froggies. She squatted down looking hopefully at the ground while I rattled the wide gate, but the bolt was secure.

"Why are you doing that?" she said.

"So that we can let you wander around without worrying about you getting onto the road where the cars are," I told her. "Haven't you noticed how one of us checks on it every morning?"

"I check on it too," she said.

"Really."

"Yes," she said. "Someone keeps coming in and leaving it open."

Either the frogs had already been and gone, or else they were getting wiser and waiting. We walked back up to the house. The day was dying and the shadows were long and deep, and the houselights glowed yellow-on-blue like a twilit jack-o'-lantern. The Minx took hold of my hand as we climbed the wooden steps. Only a couple of hours before, she'd been winding me up to bursting point outside the monkey house and she'd known it. Now this. I couldn't help thinking, and not for the first time, that the worst thing in the world for me would be to lose her.

And, of course, eventually to lose her was one of the few things in my life that could fairly be called inevitable.

With only a few days left of our stay, we found ourselves less inclined toward loading up the car and going looking for late-season amusements and so instead we just stayed around the place. I'm not exactly sure what we did, but the time carried on leaking away from us anyway. Anything we needed, we could usually get it from Willi's Market. The only problem was that we couldn't mention the name of the place when the Minx was in earshot without her latching onto it and getting us helpless with laughter.

Sometimes the Minx walked down with me. Thursday was one of the days when she didn't.

It was a rambling, one-storey building set back from the road with space for about half a dozen cars in front of it, and although it wasn't big it sold just about everything from fresh bread to padlocks. It was clean and it was bright and it was modern, and the only note that jarred when I compared it to similar places back home was the sales rack of shrink-wrapped pornography stuck in there by the checkout between the Disney comics and the chewing gum. One man seemed to run the place on his own, at least at this quiet time of year when there were only the few locals and late visitors like ourselves to keep it ticking over. He wore a sports shirt and glasses and combed his thinning hair straight back, and whenever I went in we communicated entirely by nods and signs and smiles.

As he was punching up my stuff on the till, I brought out the little girl's picture and showed it to him.

He paused in his work and looked at the picture. He wasn't certain of why I was doing this, and so he looked closely without any reaction other than mild puzzlement for a few moments. Then he glanced up at me.

He shook his head. There was sadness and sympathy in his eyes.

And he said something, and right there and then I'd have given almost anything to know what it was; but I just took the picture from him and stowed it away again, and I nodded my head as if I understood. The words meant nothing to me, but I thought I knew the tone of them.

It was the tone, I believed then, that one would use when speaking of someone else's tragedy.

As I was walking back along the side of the shore road, I felt as if the formless apprehensions of the past few days had suddenly come together and made a creature with a name. Its name was dread, and it sat in me like an angry prisoner with no sight of daylight. A few cars zipped by me, one with a windsurfing board on its rack. I knew I'd closed and bolted the gate behind me, I *knew* it, and yet . . .

In my mind's eye I could see the Minx running hell-for-leather down the drive, giggling in mischief the way she often did, with Sally screaming a warning and falling behind and the Minx too giddy to realise what she was being told . . . *Someone keeps coming in and leaving it open*, she'd said, and I'd paid her no attention . . .

But who? Apart from our weekend neighbours, we were the only ones to be using the gateway at all. *Was* there someone who'd been prowling around the place, and I'd overlooked the evidence because it was the Minx who was telling me and I was so used to the workings of her imagination that I was dismissing the truth along with the usual dose of unreality?

Come to think of it, the garage door had been standing open when we'd gone to get the bike a few days before.

And I still hadn't found that damned paperback, even though I was pretty sure of where I'd left it.

And there was the Visitors' Book, which had planted the seed of my unease.

And the reaction of the checkout man in Willi's Market, that had brought it into flower . . .

Pretty thin fabric, I know.

But by the time I reached the house I was running.

* * *

Sally saw me coming up the drive. I must have been a sight. Breathless, my shirt half-out, the bag of groceries crushed up against my side. She was out on a sun lounger in front of the house, and she raised her head and squinted at me. I slowed. Everything seemed normal, and I was a dope. But I wasn't sorry.

"Where's the Minx?" I said.

"She's set herself up with a picnic on the porch," she said. "What's the matter with *you*?"

"Nothing," I said, almost sharply, and I walked past her and up the steps to the covered entrance. As my eyes adjusted to the shade, I could see the Minx; in a world of her own as she so often was, with plates and crockery from the kitchen set out on the outdoor dining table and her all-time favourite doll, clothes long gone and the rest of her distinctly frayed around the edges, propped up outside. She'd hijacked the big tub of margarine and a packet of biscuits, and Sally must have a opened a bottle of cola for her to round off the feast. She was just raising it to her lips and tilting it as I came into sight.

Nothing amiss here.

And then, in an instant, I saw that I was wrong.

I don't know exactly what happens when you're in a situation like that. You can see the most minor detail with the utmost clarity, and it burns itself deep into your awareness; but it's almost as if the sheer volume of information suddenly slows the speed of processing, so that you don't seem to act or react in any positive way at all. You see your own failure, even before it's had the chance to happen. Disaster's heading straight for you like a rocket, and your responses are moving like letters in the mail.

If I had any talent with a paintbrush, I could probably reproduce the scene exactly. The well-worn sheen on the checkered vinyl cloth. The sunlight, back-lighting the Minx's hair as she raised the bottle. The mismatched china and the scattering of crumbs. The open margarine tub, its contents churned like an angry sea. The last inch of flat cola.

And the live wasp in the bottle, floating toward the neck as the bottle was tilted.

She screamed and dropped the bottle, and clapped both her hands to her face. The wasp was on the deckboards now, buzzing furiously but too wet or too damaged to rise; she'd squeezed it between her mouth and the rim of the bottle as it had tried to escape, and it had reacted the only way it knew how. Which got no sympathy out of me at all. I stepped on it quickly, and it popped like a grape.

The Minx was still screaming as I hauled her up and onto my knee. Sally was already on her way up the steps. I tried to pull the Minx's hands away, but she was hysterical. Sally was saying "What is it, what's happened?" and I remember thinking, completely unfairly but in the lash-out, bite-anything manner of a run-over dog, that she should have been right there and this should never have been allowed to happen. Which makes no sense, of course, but that's the way I was thinking. I don't think it showed on the outside, but I was in a panic. I didn't know what to do. We were in the middle of nowhere in a place where we didn't speak the language, and there was a crisis here and I *didn't know what to do*.

The stinger was still in the Minx's lip, like a tiny yellow thumbtack. I managed to pick it out carefully with my thumbnail. And what then? I tried to have a go at sucking out the poison, but the Minx beat me away. Sally ran to the kitchen and brought back half an onion to rub the wound, but the Minx batted that away too. She was screaming for a plaster, the little-kids' answer to every hurt. I handed her over and went for the first-aid kit in the car.

There were Band-aids, there were bandages, there was a folded-up sling for a broken arm. I'd bought the kit as a ready-made box and I don't think I'd even looked into it since I'd taken a curious glance over the contents and then stowed it away in the car at least three years before. I fumbled it, and the contents went everywhere. I saw some antiseptic wipes and grabbed one up and went back to the covered terrace.

The Minx, still tearful, was quieter. Sally was rocking her and whispering *Sshh, sshh*, and the Minx was sobbing. I tore open the sachet and crouched down before them both and managed to get a few dabs in with the wipe. Her lip was already beginning to swell.

I was scared.

When the swelling grew steadily worse over the next half-hour, we loaded her into the car and went out looking for a hospital. I had no idea. We were already on the road and moving when I thought that I should have checked through the old brochures and guides for an area map which might have some indication on it. I had a terrific sense of desperation, as if there were a bomb ticking in the back of the car. I hardly knew what I was doing. In the end it was the cashier at a big Shell service area who marked the nearest hospital on a tourist map and then waved me away when I tried to pay for it.

Carrying the Minx into the Emergency Room, I felt like a wrecked sailor reaching the shore. I mean, for all I knew, she could have *died*—she could have been dying right then, and I'd have been no more useful. As it was they checked her over, gave her a couple of shots, painted the sting site with something, and then sent us away. The Minx stayed quiet in the back with Sally as I drove us all home. It was dusk when we got there, and it was to find that we'd gone off leaving every door and window of the place wide open. Even the gate at the end of the drive was swinging to and fro, and I knew that I'd stopped and jumped out of the car to close it behind us.

I knew that I'd never feel quite the same again, about anything. I'd crossed a line. I'd peeped into the abyss.

Nothing much more happened those last couple of days. I put the child's photograph back on the shelf where I'd found it, and I made no further enquiries. The Minx looked like a defeated boxer, five rounds and then out for the count, but by the next morning we were even able to make jokes about it. They were morale-boosters, not the real thing, and I suppose they must have sounded pretty hollow to both of us. The camera stayed in its case for the rest of the trip. Nothing was said or agreed, but I think that this was something that none of us would ever want to be reminded of.

So, no more photographs.

We'd probably have gone home early if we could, but the boat ticket couldn't be transferred. And, besides, there was so little time remaining. The weather held good, but we stuck around the house killing time as if on the rainiest of rainy days.

On the last day we packed almost in silence, and the Minx went for one last froggie-hunt while I loaded up the car. Sally stayed in the house. When I went inside to bring out the last few items—the boots, the overcoats, the radio . . . all the stuff that didn't belong in any particular box or bag—I found her at the big table in the sitting room. The Visitors' Book was open on the table before her. She looked up, and she seemed almost defensive.

"We've got to write something," she said. "It's not the house's fault. Not to put anything at all would be rude."

I shrugged, and didn't say anything. We hadn't been saying much of anything to each other since the accident, at least not directly. I picked up the stuff that I'd come for and went out to the car.

Half an hour later, with everything loaded away and the house locked up for the last time behind us, we rolled down the driveway and out through the open gate.

"Say Goodbye, house," Sally told the Minx, and the Minx turned and waved through the back window and said, "Bye!"

I stopped the car.

"I just realised, I left my sunglasses," I said.

"I checked everywhere before we locked up," Sally said. "Are you sure?"

"I only meant to put them down for a second," I said. "I know where they are. Let me have the keys."

The keys were to be dropped off at the agents' office in the nearest town as we drove on by to the ferry. Sally got them out of the big envelope and passed them forward to me, and I got out of the car and walked back up the drive. I left the engine running. This wasn't going to take very long.

Already the house seemed different. No longer ours, it was a place of strangers again. I felt out-of-place, almost observed, as I walked up the steps with the door key in my hand. I could hear the car's engine running at the end of the driveway, over on the far side of the bushes.

I entered the newly regained silence of the place. There was no sign of my sunglasses but then, I'd known there wouldn't be; they were in their case, safe inside my jacket.

I didn't have much time. I crossed the room to the chest of drawers and crouched, pulling open the one which I knew held the Visitors' Book. It was uppermost on all the brochures, and I took it out and laid it on top of the chest before feeling around at the back of the drawer. Then I straightened, and opened the book to the latest entry.

I didn't want to read it. In fact I'd turned the book around so that all of the entries were upside-down to me, on purpose. I didn't know whether Sally had mentioned anything about how the visit had ended, and I didn't want to. I spread the pages flat and I took a grip on the little cutter and I ran it, firmly and neatly, down the final page as close to the spine as I could get.

A firm tug, and it came out cleanly. I screwed it up and stuffed it into my pocket, for quiet disposal at a stopover point somewhere on the journey ahead.

And then I closed the book, returned it to the drawer, locked up the house, and walked away.

Forever.

AT THE END OF THE DAY
Steve Rasnic Tem

Steve Rasnic Tem is a prolific and talented short story writer living in Colorado. His short story "Firestorm" was a World Fantasy Award finalist and his "Leaks" received the British Fantasy Award in 1988. Five traditional ghost stories of his have been collected by England's Haunted Library as *Absences: Charlie Goode's Ghosts*.

"At the End of the Day" is a beautiful, haunting piece of urban malaise from the anthology *Dead End: City Limits*.

—E.D.

Tem's evocative story falls in the shadowed border country between fantasy and horror. Tem's prose has the rhythm of poetry and dreams; the tale lingers in memory long after it is done.

—T.W.

At the end of the day Sam has one final package to deliver, a perfect cube a foot on a side wrapped so tightly in its heavy brown paper that not even a stray microbe could get in, and thinking this increases his sense of urgency more even than the bright red envelope marked URGENT affixed to the top of this package and containing the day's final, imperative and unequivocal message.

For hours Sam has searched his maps of the metropolitan area—maps so complete, complex, and expensive they remain unavailable to the average commuter—but he is still unable to find the address. Earlier calls to the dispatcher have confirmed that the address is a true address although the dispatcher herself—a voice soft, yet utterly convincing—cannot help him with its exact location. A thorough perusal of the twelve volumes of executed and planned revisions to the city's constantly changing street nomenclature and arrangement—stacked in order within his delivery van's oversized glove compartment—provides no significant clues, although there are sixteen similarly named streets, avenues, drives, places, courts, ways, and circles. Despite its apparent futility he has hunted down each one in the seemingly unlikely event that a mistake in address has been made.

By the end of the day all urgent packages and messages within the city limits (including extended suburbs) must be delivered. At the end of the day who can know what disaster might follow if such a delivery has failed to go through?

At the end of the day Sam wonders if there will ever be a time when his job ends at the end of the day. At the end of the day Sam is still driving his van up and down the same streets, endlessly circling the same routes where every day he delivers packages wrapped in plain brown paper to people who are rarely at home to accept them. Sam wonders, briefly, if any of these absent recipients might imagine that magic played a part in these timely, mysterious deliveries, but he admits to some difficulty crediting the average person with such imagination.

At the end of the day Sam tries to remember if his job has ever been any different than it was today. He began the job when he was eighteen, right out of high school, intent on earning a few dollars while he decided what his heart's work might be. Delivering the packages had been a game, and an opportunity to learn the routes which might some day lead into his future. His father had once told him that sometimes what you like to do has little relation to what you can get paid to do. Sam discovered times had changed—now it had almost no relation.

At the end of the day Sam dreams about an early-morning ambition he once had to be a poet. Now the dispatcher's soft but unerring patter is the poetry that fills him like alcohol: "Four thirty-two, four thirty-two, Park Avenue, Trader Bill's, four forty-four, Wilmott Square, three-two, three-two." But the dispatcher's voice faded out hours ago, and he is lost with his delivery, packing his lost message through the late afternoon, the message itself no doubt a longed-for poem, and his quest fit subject matter for poetry.

At the end of the day fatigue is a shadow-self just beginning to separate from his skin, adhering stubbornly to his body, waiting for the dying sun to change its color. Sam wonders what a sun the blue-gray color of death would do to the shape and texture of the human shadow. He suspects that it would do nothing, for the combination of polluted air and skyscrapers filtering the sun has already resulted in many blue-gray sunny days. And he has simply become used to these shadows whose tone and color remind him of the face of his grandmother a few hours after her death.

Those shadows with legs stagger out of alleyways as if intent on stealing his package and plagiarizing his message, but he is highly skilled at the wheel, sailing around them so closely they spin so quickly that blood flies from their mouths like song.

At the end of the day shadows form with little resemblance to the objects casting them. Behind a street sign looms a giant, upraised fist. Bus benches front a broad torso broken in half. Corner streetlights hang below huge, shadowed eye sockets. The spaces between tall buildings are filled with gray, unfocused limbs attempting to crawl their way back into the roar of evening traffic. Now and then Sam vaguely recognizes a profile or a stance. Over the years he has known some of the men and women who built, formed, and poured these inhuman monuments. But as the pace of the day wears to its end, his sense of recognition fades, the transition into night making him an alien plying his vessel through the narrow lanes of fragmented landscape.

Out on the main streets there are few pedestrians, for this is rush hour and most have retreated to their cars for the long, anxious ride home. But he knows that there are those who cannot afford cars, who take to the sidewalks and the buses. There are those who cannot afford homes, who cannot afford even a shadow, and who look exactly the way their missing shadows would look. Gray and smudged as if they had struggled against erasure. These people live in the alleys and doorways and under the bridges, where countless shadows collect. There they blend together and blend with the night. Sometimes streetlights send them running, but few of the streetlights work downtown. The city does not pay its bills.

Someone else is unable to return home at the end of the day, he knows, someone trapped in an office positioned awkwardly between dead streetlights, anxiously awaiting the arrival of the urgent package Sam has been ferrying through every section of the city. His client is late. Sam is even later. But far later still, he suspects, is the city itself, changing its names and hiding from its tired messengers.

At the end of the day he thinks about his children, and how they must anticipate his arrival. How the three of them will line up at the base of the stairs as he enters the front door, each with a question, a request, or the gift of today's story. It is the stories he likes best, and he will devote the most time to these, the daily retellings of how the world is both the same and constantly changing, perspectives he misses on his repetitive routes delivering messages and packages across the city. The questions are sometimes almost as interesting, inquiries as to the nature of life, the world, and the end of the day. He seldom has answers—his life as deliveryman having limited his insights—but the questions make all of them think, and it is his children thinking that he prizes above all else. The requests are seldom true requests but merely excuses for talking; having been filled by the endless chatter of hot exhaust expanding and contracting metal all day, he is more than happy to listen to his children's aimless talk.

Awaiting a change of light he stares down at the package also waiting, resting solidly across his right front seat. At the end of the day he again wonders why he never looks inside the packages he delivers, why he never reads the messages. There is always ample time for such surreptitious activity. With the current volume of traffic no one really expects him to deliver either packages or messages on time. And yet so many are marked URGENT. So many, he is told, must be delivered by the end of the day.

In fact, he has long suspected that the messages he delivers are never very urgent, for if they were his clients would use the telephone or the fax machine. He has wondered if, rather, what he delivers are scattered moments of contact, simple statements of existence from random citizens to other random citizens, with the unpredictability of his delivery times an essential part of the message. During holiday seasons there are always many more such messages to deliver. He sometimes considers inserting his own messages into his deliveries for random distribution, but thus far has not had the courage.

But at the end of the day the particular package in question seems much more than this. At the end of the day his final message seems an essential delivery. At the end of the day it seems the job he took on after high school has all come down to this. He can feel his van deteriorating, bolts and washers and scattered bits of metal dropping off from the stress of his final delivery.

At the end of end of at the end of the rat a tat tat tat . . .

At the end of the day he wonders what his wife is cooking for dinner. The traditional role she has taken in their lives has always made him feel guilty, but although he has attempted to convince her many times to continue her career, she has adamantly declined, preferring the company of their children with their endless supplies of questions, requests, and stories. In recent years his attempts to get her out of the house have been rare. At the end of the day he envies her place in their home.

He suspects his wife could have done his job better. He suspects his wife would have delivered this package by the end of the day. She has always been far more controlled than he, far more organized.

He maneuvers his van through city divisions which seem to vary greatly in climate. The poorer sections of the urban sprawl always seem colder. At times he switches on his heater. After a few blocks a quick change to the air conditioner engenders a whine of stress in the engine compartment behind the thin metal wall in front of his knees.

At the end of the day various city walls are coming down, some at the express instructions of the city fathers, instructions he himself had delivered on earlier days when he managed to get all messages and packages out before the end of the day. But there are always those which crumble unexpectedly, leaving piles of rubble with which his van must dance.

At the end of the day the various models of automobile seem to regress, as if the day's passage has taken years off the streetscape. The foreign cars are the first to disappear. Ancient Fords and Studebakers fill the poorly paved roads. The bordering buildings warp their architectures in the twilight, as if shifting in earthquake trauma or melting beneath the last rays of a thermonuclear sun. A rain of darkness pours down across his windows. A layer of memory disappears each time the blades wipe across the windshield. Half-forgotten faces fold and gather in the gutter line. The streets along the edge of darkness become a litany of all that has been lost and that he is likely to lose.

At the end of the day the pavement begins releasing its heat and the air loses its color a small portion at a time. Darkness fills all empty spaces and someone remembers to turn the stars on. He sometimes wonders if that someone can go home now, his or her job completed. For himself, he still has this one more delivery, one more package and message he cannot make himself forget, perched patiently on the front seat of his van.

In the darkness, familiar directions become untrustworthy dreams. New street signs appear, providing a fresh supply of obstacles. Shadows spread and ignore their loyalties. He sticks his head out the driver's-side window and attempts to find his way by smell. In the past he has been good at smelling despair and hunger and the locations of those waiting long hours to receive a delivery.

When the light dims at the end of the day it always seems a sudden event, even though the sun may have been sinking or the clouds rolling in for hours. But beyond his consideration the day is suddenly gray or amber, depending upon the time of the year, and he feels a strain in his eyes as they attempt to see all the details they are used to seeing. He feels dangerous driving a vehicle at such times, and is surprised at the end of the day to find that he has failed to run over any of the shadows.

The deepening night is like black snowfall, a mass of dark flakes carved from the giant ball waiting at the end of the day, the flakes gathering first in the corners and hiding places of the world, finally filling up the very air he breathes. Every morning he has breathed it out again, but a sooty residue of the previous night always remains inside him, in his heart and blood, in his thoughts and the words he uses.

He does not believe anyone would mind his peeking inside the package. He cannot believe anyone would deny him his right to know the final message. But he must hurry, he thinks, and decide what he must do, for the address scrawled on the bright red envelope might suddenly appear at any time.

But at the end of the day time passes slowly. Each block is longer and the intervals between lights stretch out lazily. He remembers all the dead ones, the ones who were former lovers, family members, even the dead strangers named by the newspapers. He can almost see them fleeing the headlights. At the end of the day he speculates about what their lives have become. At the end of the day he can feel the shadow of their fatigue in his hands clutching the steering wheel.

At the end of the day the lines of the streets disappear and he follows the final sparks of head- and tail-lights into the night. Static fills all positions on his radio. He drives through a landscape of black birds, thousands of birds gathered under his wheels, no light to reflect their colors or everyday shapes, wings overlapping until they are one solid, mobile mass rocking his van with their movements. He drives through a landscape of broken trees, their ragged ends scratching at the night. He drives through a landscape of window frames and door frames, their buildings transparent and filled with black.

At the end of the day he imagines that somewhere else, beyond the limited vision his windshield provides, events of terrible beauty are taking place. Faces are melting and hair is burning. Somewhere beyond his vision his children's lives are turning to smoke. In his undelivered package he believes there must be revelations about the causes of such events. In his unopened message there may be instructions concerning what to do at the end of the day. At the end of the day he will have no one to tell him stories, no one to make requests, no one to speak the orders.

Sam opens a window to feel the dark air, and his fingers come away so raw and blistered at the end of the day that he can barely grasp the steering wheel.

And yet there is still this one more delivery to make, one more service to perform. As his route stretches out into darkness the lights in the houses dim to amber, then fade to black. Body heat escapes through open windows and chimneys, causing the neon signs to burn noticeably brighter. At the end of the day the city burns its citizens for the fuel that keeps the buildings tall, the concrete rigid, that prevents the asphalt melting into a viscous sea. Sometimes there are power failures. Sometimes the tires on his van adhere to the road, making this final delivery more difficult at the end of the day.

At the end of the day all the customers have forgotten their orders. At the end of the day there is no one left to receive his package. His message is written in a forgotten language. There are no more tongues wrapped around difficult communications. In the empty streets there are no more tongues. The windows of the stores are grimed. Abandoned cars join together into metallic reefs to block his passage. At the end of the day all the vessels lie empty. At the end of the day torn scraps of paper, discarded messages, litter the plazas and lawns. At the end of the day everything sleeps. There is nothing else to do at the end of the day.

In the dark faraway he hears his wife and children calling him. His shift should be over by now, they tell him. He should be coming home. But at the end of the day there are very few roads fit for travel. At the end of the day he has lost his name. At the end of the day he cannot find his way home.

But at least he knows he still has his unopened package. At least at the end of the day he can imagine its contents. He can recite the poetry of its unopened message. Because it is urgent. Because it is essential. And because it is all that he has.

THE MONSTER
Nina Katerli

"The Monster" is a charming and offbeat little tale of domestic life by Russian author Nina Katerli. Originally published in Russian as "Chudovishche" in *Tsvetnye otkrytki*, 1987, the English translation (by Bernard Meares) comes from the pages of *Soviet Women Writing*, published by Abbeville Press, with delightful illustrations by Russian artist Leonid Tishcov.

Katerli lives in St. Petersburg, where she was born. Trained as an engineer, her first story was published in the journal *Kostyor* in 1973. She is the author of four collections of stories, including *The Window* and *Colored Postcards*. Her work has been translated into English, German, Hungarian, Polish, and other languages.

—T.W.

"If only things were the way they used to be," said Aunt Angelina, and wiped her eyes.

"The way they used to be? Thanks very much! That's all I need. 'The way they used to be.' " Anna Lvovna could be seen choking back her tears and sniffling. "All my life I've lived in this apartment and cooked soup on a single burner in my own room, and I scarcely use any gas at all. And until very recently I had to go to the public baths, even though we have a bathtub right here. I was afraid to go to the toilet too often, not to mention the way my personal life . . ."

"No, if only things were the way they used to be," Aunt Angelina repeated obstinately. "I simply can't look at him the way he is now."

I myself had gotten used to the Monster, and even as a child had not been very much afraid of him. I was born after he moved into our apartment, so for me there was nothing unusual about coming across a shaggy creature with a single crimson eye in the middle of its forehead and a long scaly tail, whether in the hall near the bathroom or in the kitchen. But why go in for descriptions? One monster's very much like another, and ours was no more monstrous than the next.

They say that before I was born the other tenants in our apartment had filed an application with some agency, requesting that the Monster be evicted and housed someplace else, even that he be given an apartment all to himself. But the application was rejected on the grounds that if all monsters were given individual housing, there would be nothing left for large families. The argument ran that there were too many monsters and too few apartments, and when our application was turned down, the reason given was: "Yours is not the most serious case: There has not been a single fatality or instance of grievous bodily harm."

The fact that Anna Lvovna's husband had been turned into an aluminum saucepan for a whole month did not constitute grievous bodily harm, apparently. They say that as soon as her husband had returned to normal after having had borscht boiled in him and meat stewed in him for a month, he immediately abandoned her for another woman. Anna Lvovna was left on her own and since then has never forgiven the Monster for ruining her life. But the Monster claimed, on his honor, that he had turned Anna Lvovna's husband into a saucepan only because the man had been sweet-talking his mistress every evening from the phone in the hall, and he would have left home in any case. That way, at least he stayed home one more month, even if he spent the time as a saucepan.

I don't know how the story would have ended—Anna Lvovna, they say, was threatening to drop a burned-out light bulb in the Monster's feeding dish—but at that very time the Monster set off to work as an exhibit in a long traveling exposition organized by the museum of ethnography and anthropology.

In time, the tale about Anna Lvovna's husband came to be forgotten, but as the Monster grew older, he began to turn nasty, and gave us no peace at all.

You'd go into the bathroom and the sink and bathtub would be full of frogs and newts; or suddenly all the refrigerators would begin to howl horribly and heat up, the milk inside them would boil and the meat would roast; or else poor Anna Lvovna's nose would erupt in a boil of amazing size that changed color with each passing day: One day it would be blue, the next day lilac, and the day after that a poisonous green color.

It should be mentioned that Aunt Angelina and the Monster were on somewhat more equable terms. If she found a tortoise in her cupboard instead of bread, she would exclaim with pleasure, "Look, a reptile! I'll take it straight to the kindergarten for their pet corner!"

I now realize that when I was little the Monster simply couldn't stand me because I annoyed him so much. Everything I did annoyed him: I clattered up and down the hall and I laughed too loudly and I loved peeking into his room at him. So he kept giving me tonsillitis. Not serious cases, but the kind that if you so much as laugh you lose your voice, and if you run you get sent to bed.

When I grew up, the Monster did me great harm for a time; whenever anyone called me up, he would always get to the phone before the others and hiss, "She's not in. She's gone out with someone else."

I live alone now. My parents are no longer alive, I have never had a family of my own, and Aunt Angelina, with whom I share the apartment, takes care of me after a fashion, but as for the Monster . . . At least he's stopped tormenting me. Of course, if I come back late from the theater or from visiting friends, I'm bound to trip over the cat in the hall even though we've never had a cat. Or I'll tear my new dress on barbed wire. But that's nothing—mere trivialities. And recently even that kind of thing has stopped happening. Something's gone wrong with the Monster. You wouldn't recognize him: his eye has turned from red to a kind of dirty ginger color and his fur has gone gray; to put it in a nutshell, our Monster is getting old. He's stopped going to work and sits for days on end in his room, just hissing occasionally and sometimes sighing. And it was only today that Aunt Angelina said she'd prefer things the way they used to be because it broke her heart to look at the Monster, and she didn't have the energy to sweep up his scales after him.

"About those dreadful scales I totally agree with you, Angelina Nikolayevna," declared Anna Lvovna. "It's disgraceful! He must be made to do an additional week of cleaning duty. Nobody should have to wipe his dirt up after him!"

At this point the conversation came to a sudden halt because the Monster's door squeaked loudly, and a minute later there he was in the kitchen.

"Picking on me behind my back, eh?" he asked, and his eye reddened slightly. "Well, now I'm going to make you all freeze. You've never felt such cold!"

And the Monster began to blow so hard that his cheeks turned blue and his head started to tremble.

He blew and blew and suddenly I noticed Aunt Angelina shivering and jumping in place and knocking her legs against each other and rubbing her nose as if it had been frostbitten.

"It's so cold, oh, it's freezing!" she moaned dolefully, for some reason winking at me. Then she suddenly screeched, "What are you standing around like that for? Keep moving! Keep moving! Or else you'll catch your death of cold! Hands on your waist! Bend your knees! One, two, three!"

I wasn't that cold; in fact, I was even rather warm, all the more so because we were in the kitchen and all the gas burners were lit. But Aunt Angelina was winking and shouting so that I, too, put my hands on my hips and started doing knee bends.

"There you go! There you go!" shouted the Monster gleefully. "Now you're going to dance for me!"

I scarcely had time to think before Aunt Angelina grabbed me by the hand and began leaping about in a frenzied dance. I followed her lead.

"This is a nuthouse!" declared Anna Lvovna angrily and left the kitchen.

The Monster stared after her with a frightened look, then turned to Aunt Angelina as she danced and asked quietly, "Why isn't she dancing? Why did she go away?"

"She's stiff with cold!" shouted Aunt Angelina, gasping for breath but continuing to dance. "Can't you see?"

But the Monster had already forgotten what he had been asking. Dragging his tail and leaving a trail of scales across the floor, he went over to his refrigerator and opened the door.

"Where's my bone?" he said in perplexity, "I remember it was here yesterday, I bought it at the store!"

"Your bone? There it is, you made soup out of it this morning, don't you remember?" shouted Aunt Angelina, stamping away, but at the same time managing to pass the Monster her own white enamel saucepan with soup in it.

"I did? Oh . . ." and the Monster looked uncertainly into the saucepan, "I never had a pot like this."

"But it really is your pot, I just cleaned it up a bit, that's all."

"Aaargh!" he roared, "You dare touch my pot?! I forbid you to! For that both of you will . . . you will both . . . turn to stone for thirty-five minutes!"

Aunt Angelina suddenly froze the way children do when they play Statues. As fate would have it, my nose started itching and I was about to rub it with my hand when she inconspicuously but painfully jabbed me in the side, so I froze, too.

The Monster glared at us triumphantly, then grabbed the boiled chicken out of Aunt Angelina's saucepan and ate it whole.

"A delicious bone!" he rumbled, licking his lips, and then took pity on us.

"You can go now," he said dismissively, and strode imperiously out of the kitchen, slurping soup from the top of the saucepan.

"Why did you give him your entire dinner?" I asked, when the door closed behind the Monster. "And where is his bone, anyway?"

"He didn't have a bone!" said Aunt Angelina, "He hasn't been to the store for a week."

"Then what's he looking for?"

"God knows! Maybe he forgot. Or maybe he's just being that way to show us that everything's all right. But he doesn't have any money, not a single kopeck, and he's going hungry."

"What about his pension?"

"He doesn't have a pension! He's an exhibition object, and . . . he's been written off, dropped from the show." Aunt Angelina lowered her voice. "It's as if he doesn't exist. And now I'm afraid about his room. I'm afraid he'll be evicted. Just make sure you don't tell Anna Lvovna."

"I won't breathe a word," I said, also in a whisper.

Aunt Angelina and I began taking turns buying bones and chopped meat from the butcher and leaving them in the Monster's refrigerator. On one occasion she left two apples and a small carton of kefir.

"All this meat's very bad for him! It can ruin his digestion," she said. "I wanted to buy him a big bottle of kefir but he always immediately bolts any food he has, so I bought a carton instead."

"He's bound to throw out the apples," I said.

"We'll see. Maybe he won't realize. Lately his eyesight's been getting poor," and at that moment Aunt Angelina looked around at the door; Anna Lvovna was just coming into the kitchen.

"It makes me laugh just to look at the two of you," she declared. "All this undercover charity—do you think I'm blind? Such pretense—what a show! And for whom! If he was human, it would be one thing, but he's not, he's just vermin."

"You should feel sorry for him; after all, he's old," I said.

"My dear, pity's not a feeling you should brag about, pity's humiliating. And in this case," she said as she put her coffeepot on the stove, "in this case, pity doesn't enter into it. It was one thing when he was making himself useful in his

. . . in his freak show; we could put up with him then, but not now. Animals should live in the wild."

The Monster had crept into the kitchen so softly that we didn't even know he was there. He now stood in the doorway and his eye was as ruddy as it had been in the first flush of youth.

"So, I'm an animal, am I?" he said slowly and slumped onto a stool. "I'll show you."

His breathing was heavy and irregular, the sparse gray fur on his head and neck stood on end.

"I'll show you. . . . Your . . . legs . . . will . . . give way . . . beneath you! . . . Yeah! . . . You will . . . all . . . fall . . . on the floor . . . and then . . . One, two, three . . . All fall down!"

Aunt Angelina and I collapsed simultaneously. Anna Lvovna remained standing, leaning against the edge of the stove, and grinned, staring the Monster straight in the eye.

"And you?" said the Monster. "What about you? This doesn't mean you, I suppose? Fall down, I tell you!"

"Give me one good reason why I should," she said, scowling.

"Because I've put a spell on you, that's why."

"Oh, you slay me," said Anna Lvovna, going right up to him. "What have we here, a magician? All you know how to do is leave your scales all over the floor and help yourself to everyone else's food! You're just trash and you're due for the dump! Just garbage. You've been written off!"

"Written off?" repeated the Monster in a whisper. "Who's been written off? Me? Written off? Not true, not true! I can do anything! Look at them! They fell down!"

"Ha! Ha! Ha!" Anna Lvovna burst out laughing. "They're just pretending. They're sorry for you, see. You've been written off. You've lost your job. I've been to the museum myself and I've seen the directive with my own eyes."

"No!" The Monster leapt up from the stool and rushed from the door to the stove, thrashing his mangy tail across the floor. "I'll show you. I'll turn you into a rat! A rat! Now!"

"Ha! Ha! Ha!" was Anna Lvovna's only reply, and suddenly she stamped on the Monster's tail with all her might.

The Monster screamed. One after another great tears streamed from his eye, which immediately turned pale blue and dimmed. Aunt Angelina and I jumped up from the floor.

"You ought to be ashamed of yourself! Let him go! An old man. Don't be so cruel to him!"

"A rat! a rat!" hissed the Monster, forgetting himself, and he poked Anna Lvovna in the shoulder with a dark and crooked finger. "One! Two! Three!"

"Ha! Ha! Ha!" sniggered Anna Lvovna.

But now Aunt Angelina and I began to shout. "A rat! A rat!" we screamed. "You're a rotten rat! Vermin! One! Two! Three!"

Suddenly Anna Lvovna was gone.

She had just been laughing in our faces, her shoulders shaking in her white blouse, when suddenly she was no more. She had totally disappeared, as if she had never existed.

The kitchen suddenly fell silent. Something live jabbed against my foot and immediately leapt away to the wall. I screeched and jumped onto the stool.

A large gray rat shot across the kitchen and scuttled under Anna Lvovna's table. The Monster was whimpering softly, his face turned toward the wall.

"See," said Aunt Angelina, "you did it. Don't cry. Now let's go and have some soup."

"It's you who did it, not me. And it's true, you know; I have been written off. There has been a directive."

"What do we care about directives," said Aunt Angelina, carefully stroking the Monster's fur. "Don't you be afraid of anybody. And if anybody touches you I'll give him . . . I'll give him ants."

"And so will I," I said. "Okay?"

The Monster didn't reply. Slumped against the wall, he dozed off, shutting his eye and wrapping his thin hairless tail around his legs.

HUMMERS
Lisa Mason

Ursula Le Guin has described fantasy as "a different approach to reality, an alternate technique for apprehending and coping with existence."

Fantasy, like myth and legend, provides a means of storytelling that at its best goes beyond mere entertainment to travel the inner roads of the human soul. The following story does this beautifully, using the form of fantasy fiction and the symbols of Egyptian mythology to enter one of the most mysterious lands of all: the one that lies at the threshold of death. Readers who have experienced the loss of loved ones to cancer or AIDS will find this story cuts particularly close to the bone, but the fear of death is universal, and Mason's exploration of this fear is both unsentimental and compassionate.

Lisa Mason has published short fiction in *Omni* and *Asimov's* magazines, and her first novel, *Arachne*, was published in 1991. "Hummers" comes from the February '91 issue of *Asimov's*.

—T.W.

Laurel is having a bad morning when Jerry brings her the gift. The pain is so bad she loses her shredded wheat within an hour after breakfast, but not bad enough to numb her completely, sweep her off into that suspended, solitary state of soul-annihilation.

This really pisses her off. And she dreamed again of the great ox, the sacrifice and the pipe and drums, the awful blood.

Plus she is bleeding again, staining her clothes and bedding like a teenager who doesn't understand her changing body. Laurel's body is changing, too, and at this late date more mysteriously, irretrievably, than she or the doctors can understand.

What a weird shitty world this is, she's thinking, when Jerry knocks on her door. So she lets ol' Jere have it, and she doesn't give a damn when his big brown eyes mist over and his womanly lips twitch.

"What the fuck is this?" she says, chucking the box he's brought on top of the litter of death books strewn on the coffee table. The box is small, oblong, neatly wrapped in bright red, flowery paper. The box looks like a birthday present, a holiday offering, a lipsticked smile, and she hates it, she doesn't give a damn what's inside.

"A gift, Laurel." He quietly goes about his business, but she can tell he's appalled at how awful she looks.

"A *gift?* A gift implies tomorrow. A gift suggests hope. You're not supposed to encourage my hope, now are you, Jerry? Kübler-Ross, Chapter 12. It's cruel to encourage hope, when there is no goddamn hope."

He flinches at her anger. "Everyone needs hope. Even you, Laurel. Even now."

"Oh, especially fucking *now.*"

"Want your shot?" He turns away with his so-be-a-bitch patience. What a saint this guy is, and his own lover mysteriously, irretrievably dying of AIDS.

He trots out his little black bag; actually, Jerry's is sky blue. He's not a doctor. She wouldn't let him in her house if he were. Fucking doctors, with their six-figure lifestyles and their dreadful incompetence, their absurd impotence in the face of diseases they ought to have cured by now. No, the hospice authorizes homecare nurses to dispense all sorts of fun drugs to people who won't live long enough to become dope-crazed menaces to society.

Want your shot, your hit, your high, Laurel baby? Hey, sounds like her days in Haight-Ashbury when she was a twenty-year-old old-lady painting psychedelic posters for rock bands. Day-glo pink hearts, electric-blue tears. Damn, she was cool. She tied a leather headband around her hair. She laced Greek sandals up to her knees.

"Hell, I guess so," Laurel says.

Morphine is Dolly Dagger, Lady Dreamknife, junkie stuff. Oh, her wild days in Haight-Ashbury when they'd pop a pill because it was a pretty color. Now she is afraid of such soul-annihilation. She is afraid of Dolly Dagger.

Afraid of the dream that sometimes comes when she yields to morphine: a great ox heavy with dumb life brought before a fevered assembly. Drums and pipes and chants, crazed eyes rimmed with blue and black. A shining scythe brought down on the captive neck, bellows of rage and pain, and blood, and the great head rolling, falling, how this disgusts and terrifies her, a head wild-eyed with fear and pain and horror . . .

He preps her.

"You really should go up to San Rafael," Jerry says. "I'm only thinking of you, it would be easier for you."

"I want to die at home," she says. He nods, does not want to meet her eyes. "I don't want to be trapped in some sanitized bed in a sanitized clinic. I don't want some nameless night nurse to find me. After so much indignity, I must finally claim my own dignity."

"Then you're going to have to learn how to shoot it up yourself," Jerry says flatly. "Learn soon. Because I can't be here every time you need it. And you're going to need it more and more, Laurel."

"What if the goddamn champagne-sipping doctors, what if they find a cure tomorrow, Jere, a new radiation therapy, a DNA mutation like the AIDS cure they're working on in Europe. *Something.* It could happen; it could happen! Couldn't it?"

"What if? Sure. What if could always happen. But never does." Then he plunges her arm with the tenderness of the angels, like shooting up hard drugs is an act of grace.

Laurel sits on her deck and watches the world slide by. Mr. Oake jogs past her vista; he even has the nerve to wave. Mr. Oake must be eighty-two years old and he jogs like a cartoon in slow motion: his skinny-flabby arms swing back and forth, his skinny-bony legs pump up and down, sweat rolls into his red terry cloth headband. But he hardly gets anywhere, he practically jogs in place. He moves down East Blithedale at an absurd snail's pace.

Laurel doesn't wave back. Mr. Oake is useless to society. He is probably living off the public dole. He will never do anything else with his mediocre old life except jog by her deck and drive her crazy with the uselessness of it all.

Why her? Why not a useless old man nearly double her age? She is talented, she is forty-five, she has so much left to give. She has a whole life left. Why *her*?

She sees the Collins girl stride by, too. The girl doesn't wave. If she sees Laurel sitting there, she doesn't give a damn, but Laurel suspects she doesn't notice her at all. The girl must be sixteen or seventeen, a lean little oblivious bitch oozing with hormones and hostility. She has the kind of thick, wavy, below-the-shoulder hair Laurel had before chemo stripped that from her, too.

Only forty-five. Not young; but not *old*, either, damn it. Until six months ago, she was doing okay. Packaging, ad agency work, shit work really, hustle hustle hustle. But she was waiting, saving up a bit, dreaming of the day she could chuck it all and do what *she* wanted to do. Go back to her art. Electric-blue tears were only the beginning. Why did she never go past the tears?

It is her own damn fault, her own procrastination.

They told her she had ovarian cancer.

So stupid. She'd smoked for twenty, twenty-five years. The lungs ought to be the first to go, but no. There is this stupid statistic about women who smoke. The lungs go, certainly, but these women also have a high incidence of cervical and ovarian cancer. Something about concentration of nicotine on the fingers, touching, for one purpose or another, there.

Humiliating. She'd started to bleed off and on; yes, she denied it. She'd been bleeding for two months straight and aching with the worst cramps she'd ever felt when she broke down and went to the doctors.

Fucking doctors. They couldn't tell that her father had a blockage until a heart attack killed him while he was driving to the office on a sunny Monday morning. They couldn't save her mother when a stroke knifed her brain. They couldn't help her make a baby with Christopher before he bailed out of their marriage.

She has had enough grief in the last five, six years.

So she could not believe it. So she smoked; take her at seventy-five when she's a crazy old Nevelson or an O'Keeffe stashed away in her Mill Valley chalet. A Lillian Hellman type with withered scarlet lipstick and mascaraed crow's-feet, a full life of drinking and smoking and man-chasing behind her, and a masterpiece or two to her credit.

Would you believe there is nothing more they can do for you, and you're only forty-five?

When her father died, she cried because she never really knew him. When her mother died, she cried because she knew her only too well. When her fetuses miscarried, she cried because she would never have the chance to know or not know them.

Her past, her present, her future; she can't cry for them anymore. There are no tears left for Laurel.

She feels better after Jerry leaves the way lifting therapeutic pressure off a throbbing nerve calms the trauma. She'll have to remember to tell him next time. An emotional tourniquet, ol' Jere, that's what you are, man. She hardly ever has something even halfway good to tell him.

Next time. Does she have the right to think about next time? Jerry comes to see her, administers her morphine like a real gentleman, *plus* gives her a gift, and she acts like an asshole. That's just great. "To Laurel," he'll say at her funeral. He'll be crying. "We all loved her very much, but God, she could be a bitch."

She picks up the merry red box from the coffee table. The Egyptian Book of the Dead lies beneath it. She tears open the thick wrapping paper.

Jerry's gift is a hummingbird feeder. A Droll Yankee. It is a pale green plastic flying saucer with bright red plastic flower decals mounted over the feeding holes, a bright red plastic circle on top, an elegant brass rod with a curved hook top. You boil three parts water to one part white granulated sugar and let cool. You pour the cooled nectar up to the metal band. You hang the feeder from a tree branch or, in Laurel's case, with great and painful effort, you slide open your screen door, you take down the browning spider plant, you hang the feeder from the macramé planter-holder nailed to the roof over the deck.

Jerry's gift box also contains a tiny, hand-printed book on care and maintenance of the feeder, lore on birds in general and hummingbirds in particular. Jewels of the air, the book calls them. Hummers.

Hummers? Laurel has seen hummingbirds on TV, in National Geographic videos, as illustrations on greeting cards, wrought in crystal as Christmas ornaments. Maybe once or twice for real, but only from afar. Quick magical creatures hovering around fuchsia, disappearing into the foliage before her eyes could focus. Look! What was that?

According to the book, hummingbirds are plentiful in northern California. They're everywhere, in downtown Oakland, on San Francisco's Telegraph Hill, in Mill Valley arbors. They've been around her all this time, and she's never really *seen* them!

Such a simple pleasure of life, coming at this late date. Oh, to see a hummer from her deck, so close. Please!

She scans her view with new eyes. Across East Blithedale stand ancient California date palms, fragrant eucalyptus, sturdy pine trees, weeping willows, brilliant fuchsia, strange cacti with fleshy, alien fingers. That glorious northern California arbor; she's sketched it many times. How she cursed the arbor yesterday, raged at its exuberance; damn palms would witness her death, fucking cacti would outlive her.

But now, as she waits and she watches, something strange and disturbing and wonderful happens: the fringes of the palm fronds fall away, and disembodied arms reach to the sky. The gray-barked eucalyptus turn translucent; within stand decapitated torsos of men, their purple-blue hearts beating brown blood into the branches. Green-haired maidens bow and bob among the willows, sweep elegant fingers in obeisance to the earth. Fuchsia blossoms form voluptuous lips that whisper vermilion secrets to the wind. The cacti impatiently await some signal to pull up their knobby feet and hop away.

She waits and she watches, first fears replaced by fascination, and hours tick by. The arbor darkens. But no hummer comes. The little pale green plastic flying saucer sways in the Pacific breeze, lonely and alone, like a broken promise. The tiny book says she may have to wait a month before hummingbirds will discover her feeder.

Hummers, I may not have a month. God damn you, hummers. Don't be one more disappointment to me.

Laurel goes inside, surrenders to exhaustion. Sleep; after the hell of chemotherapy failed, she was afraid to sleep. Now more and more she welcomes it, the little brother of death.

On principle she should curse all hummingbirds. But you know what? She cannot curse them. Jewels of the air, she promises as she sinks into sleep, I will wait for you as long as I can.

This decision to wait without anger or bitterness gives her a strange sense of peace. She slides into dreams of beating wings.

Beating wings shooting rainbows off their fringes and a presence: huge calm eyes rimmed with blue and black, a fan of dark hair, breasts, a spangled body arching . . .

Laurel wakes, and a woman wearing a dress like the night sky bends over her. She always has been terrified of intruders, especially since she has become so physically helpless, and she should be terrified now, but she isn't, though she realizes that the woman is not bending over her, she is floating. The floating woman looks at her, eye to eye, before she disappears into the ceiling.

It is four in the morning. This hour has got to be the loneliest and most profound of the twenty-four. No one in their right mind is up at four in the morning, not even the birds.

Disturbed, disoriented, she rises. She isn't bleeding, but pain socks her in the gut the moment she stands up. A sudden wallop like nothing she's felt before. Now she is terrified. Laurel, this is It.

But this isn't It. She doesn't even pass out or fall back on the bed. She stands there in the night, clutching her stomach. Morphine? She finds the kit Jerry left her. She is shaky and clumsy and rips the hell out of her arm, but she finally manages to do it. Then, repulsed but not beaten by her own cowardice, she grips the walls like a blind woman, goes into the moonlit living room, and sits down with her death books.

Laurel never thought much about death before. She never knew her grandparents; death hadn't touched her. Oh, she philosophized about it with her freaky friends when they were twenty and smoking doo in Golden Gate Park. Initiation, man; wow, the Trip of All. She read an interview with Rod Serling that took place two months before the man died. The interviewer had asked the fantasist what he thought happened, and he said: nothing. You just go off into nothing. No Willoughby, no Owl Creek, no next reality in a dark alley with jazz in the air. Then his heart gave out at age fifty. Mr. Serling smoked twenty, twenty-five years, Laurel recalls.

Twilight Zonish speculations always appealed to her; Mr. Serling's bleakness did not. And then her father and her mother and the children she could never have; death caught up with her.

It was sometime after her mother's death that she began to collect Madame Blavatsky and the works of the Golden Dawn, the Theosophists, the Rosicrucians. Carl Jung, Edinger, and their various disciples of metapsychology. Elisabeth Kübler-Ross for clinical details. Out-of-the-body experiences, near-death experiences; many modern works of varying quality on these topics. And an ancient text: The Egyptian Book of the Dead.

The modern philosophers and psychologists and therapists are as enlightened and humane and cool as they can be. But they are too clinical for Laurel, too willing to concede the finiteness of human existence. She likes *Fate* magazine, the column, "My Proof of Survival." The column is comprised of anecdotes from humble readers: "Dad Knocked On The Wall"; "Mama's Last Kiss"; "Boodles Said Goodbye." Boodles was a poodle. Laurel is amazed at how many people's pets visit them from the grave and reassure them the soul survives. Even Boodles's soul.

She wants to see the long tunnel, the white light. Maybe her mother will greet her there, ready with a scolding for her latest mistake. She wants details. She wants instructions, damn it.

Maybe that's why that strange ancient text, the Egyptian Book of the Dead, is so perversely thrilling to her.

She plays the book oracle with it more than any other death book. Book oracle: you close your eyes, turn the book over and under, around and around, then flip the pages, plunge your index finger down.

This is how she finds elegant hieroglyphs and sloe-eyed god-animals, ceremonies and strictures, prescriptions and proscriptions. There is a weird ring of truth to these. As though death is just another reality. So when you emerge from the other side, you've got to roll up your sleeves and master it. She likes the idea; that it's possible to master the inevitable.

Survival of the soul flies in the face of all known science. But Laurel can't help but wonder if there could be something to the great journey. Whether the ancients could have understood life and death more completely than their confused and frightened progeny five thousand years later.

*   *   *

Dawn shifts through a leaden mist, and Laurel sees her first hummer.

She feels okay, not sick, not great, just *compressed*. Like she's squeezed more tightly into herself; like how a trash compactor crunches down garbage. This image cracks her up; isn't that the truth, this body such a piece of crap? She is laughing to herself when she sees a tiny presence flitting around the feeder.

It is the tiniest bird she has ever seen. It cannot be more than three inches from head to tail. In the dim morning light, she can see a glint of scarlet wreathing its throat, a gleam of green sliding down its back. Its long, slim beak dips into the hole at the center of one red plastic flower atop the feeder. She is so close she can see the tendril of its tongue extruding from the tip of its beak, lapping up the sugar water. It dips, sips, levitates and hovers, beady bird eyes casting quick glances about. It darts down and around to the next plastic flower, hovers, dips, and samples the same sugar water from a different hole. She can see the blurred upbeat of its wings simultaneously with an image of their downstroke, so that the hummer appears to be transported by four ghostly wings. The tiny tail beats furiously up and down, forming a fan of optical illusions.

She is still catching her breath when the hummer darts away, disappearing like magic into the morning mist.

She scrambles through the pile of death books, finds her tiny, hand-printed book. No, he could not have been a ruby-throated hummingbird; they live only east of the Mississippi. He must have been a male Allen's hummingbird; the scarlet gorget, the green back, the neat fan tail. A California coastal hummer, all right.

Laurel goes out on her deck and sits, despite the chill. Mr. Oake jogs by, waves. God, he jogs at six in the morning *and* six in the evening? The creaky old bastard, what did he ever do to deserve . . . but she finds herself swallowing her bitterness. She doesn't exactly return his wave, but she nods, and he nods back. A gonzo jogger at eighty-two, with twenty-twenty vision, too.

She sits there for hours, shivering in the morning mist, and no more hummers come. But she is not distressed. They will. More hummers will come.

Jerry gets all concerned about the sudden wallop of pain. Laurel realizes right away that her big mouth and her bitching have gone too far this time, and she tries to soft soap it. No big deal, Jere, she tells him; so what else do you want to hear from me? I'm fine, I'm okay, just leave me *alone*.

But he doesn't leave her alone. He drags her off in an ambulance and throws her to the doctors at San Rafael Cancer Clinic.

As usual, the doctors strap her down and peer into her and intrude on her dignity. No, her bowels have not been irregular; her bowels have not been functioning at all, why the hell should they? She hardly eats.

It turns out the cancer has metastasized into her colon. She asks, does this mean I can smoke again? The poor young doctor, some kid she's never seen before, looks at her with such pity that she laughs out loud. No, I'm not kidding, she says. I loved to smoke; can I smoke now?

And believe it or not, she forgives the poor young doctor. She forgives all the fucking doctors. Yes, she really does. What percentage of doctors will wind up with shit for guts some day? The bastards have no special guarantee, now do they? Radon gas could infiltrate your house for years, the electric blanket could tear apart your white blood cells, electromagnetic radiation from a PC could devour your mucous membranes.

Or you could smoke and drink and be merry until you're eighty-two years old.

On the way home—Laurel demanded they let her go home—the only thing she can do to make Jerry smile is tell him about hummers.

"The Portuguese call them flower-kissers. The color at the gorget—the throat area—is due not just to actual pigmentation of the feather, but to structural color, iridescence reflecting off facets of the feather itself. Like a gemstone, Jere. Hummer homes in zoos worldwide are called jewel rooms. Isn't that wonderful?"

"I know you don't like the clinic, Laurel . . ."

"I *hate* the fucking clinic. Did you know hummingbirds strip abandoned spider webs for nest material?"

"You refuse another try at surgery, refuse another try at chemo. That's your choice. I respect your choice. But there is more they could do for you, and I've got to say it: you're wrong to reject help, Laurel."

"They eat half their weight in sugar a day. When they get excited, their heartbeat doubles to over a thousand beats per minute!"

"Laurel, please. You're very sick. Much sicker than before. Do you know that?"

"Jerry, I know. Don't make me say more than that, because I can't. I'll deal with being sicker. Okay?"

"Not okay. I worry. You're so alone in this place."

"I'm not alone, Jere. I've got hummers."

She gets to know them.

There is the gorgeous male Allen's hummer. His mate is plainer, but no less thrilling in her aerial acrobatics, her negotiation of the feeder, her sheer delicacy and verve. As days go by, Laurel notices she carries two jelly bean–sized eggs in her lower abdomen. This gives Laurel such irrational joy that she gets out her sketchpad and pastels and starts to draw for the first time in months.

There is an aggressive Anna's hummer with a brilliant rosy-red head. He goes *chup-chup-chup!* when he sees other hummers at the feeder, the tiniest, tinny chirp she's ever heard, but unmistakably macho, territorial. If the other hummers don't dart away, he swoops down and chases them in frenetic loop-the-loops back to the arbor.

There is a laid-back black-chinned hummer who perches atop the brass ring from which the feeder is hung or lazily sits on the rim of the feeder itself and sups on sugar water.

The Egyptian Book of the Dead is replete with elegant hieroglyphs of birds. The solar hawk of Horus, Thoth's sacred ibis, vultures, and buzzards signifying the terrible aspect of divine power that purifies putrefactions of the world.

Laurel shivers, riffles the strange pages. Other fragments of myth, other images: Isis, that enigmatic goddess who is the mother and the sister *and* the lover of God, loses her husband Osiris to a spectacularly painful death, seeks him through the world and underworld, and finds—in a peculiar twist of mythic plot—his dismembered corpse embedded inside a living tree.

The eucalyptus with their translucent trunks; whose heart beats there, sends brown blood into the branches? Whose arms reach to the sky within the fronds of palms?

And more: the ceremony of Opening the Mouth and the Eyes during which oxen or fowl were beheaded, their sacrificial blood daubed upon the mouth and eyes of the body of the deceased, signifying renewed wholeness, magical restoration. Restoration in the Land of the Dead.

But this too is shocking, reminiscent. Of what? Laurel recalls the recurring morphine dream, the great sacrifice. Her own horror; why?

Why: because the death is not the poor dumb ox's; it's hers. Because the sacrifice is hers. Can she accept that?

Evening: rose gold shafts of sunset, scents of eucalyptus and fireplaces. Laurel goes out on her deck, with sketchpad and pastels and a bottle of good fumé blanc. Cars careen over Highway 101 from San Francisco, seeking solace in Mill Valley, if they can find solace without a fatal crash. They are like ants, all these cars, scurrying to some blind instinct of survival.

As Mr. Oake jogs his comical way up the avenue, something even more hilarious happens: the concrete turns into a ribbon of rippling silver water. But Mr. Oake doesn't sink; no, he stands on a flatbed barge slowly forging its way upstream. From his terry cloth headband extrude scarlet serpentine heads. His jogging shorts become a gilt loincloth, his sweaty T-shirt an embroidered breastplate. Instead of his silly standing-in-place jogging, Mr. Oake floats majestically up East Blithedale. The pumping of his skinny-flabby arms mimics priestly exhortations to the setting sun.

Fear flutters up Laurel's spine; she has been dancing with Dolly Dagger, after all. But she is an artist, isn't she? That destiny must bring some small ecstasies, along with the agonies. Could she be tapping into an archetypal pool, the mythos within the Egyptian Book of the Dead?

All right! At once she accepts the silver waves lapping at the lip of her deck. She feverishly tries to capture Mr. Oake's majestic journey with her pastels. All right; East Blithedale is the great river, she the maker of hieroglyphs.

But the waves grow quiet, the concrete firms, the magic flees. Or so it seems.

As she watches and sketches, a hummer zooms up to the feeder above her deck. The aggressive male Anna's, with his flashy hood of red. She flips the page, tries to sketch him, too, when another hummer comes.

He startles her.

Chup-chup-chup! and the Anna's spirals away. The new hummer; he is a dusky charcoal gray, strangely dark even in the evening light. She can see at once that his head is pale, round, oblong. She keeps blinking her eyes, straining to see.

This hummer doesn't have a beak!

He hovers there, not sipping sugar water. He's got a tiny, round, flat pale face, eyes that are not bird eyes, and wrinkles, she is quite sure she can see wrinkles around his eyes and mouth, streaks of pale gray over his crown. He looks directly at her and nods his tiny head, then darts away into the twilight arbor.

She is stunned. The archetypal pool; is she drowning in its delusions? No! She *saw* him, saw the hummer only too clearly, not more than two feet away from where she sits. She slaps her sketchpad shut and staggers inside.

She collapses on the couch, sinks into the exhausted sleep morphine permits. Hypnogogics: she sees the ox and the ax, his helpless head, how his rage imbues the sacrificial blood with the dumb will to survive.

And dreams of flashing red lights. She flutters, blinded, beating furiously, before them. She keeps hearing over and over the sound of sirens wailing in the night.

Jerry is red-eyed and puffy-faced. For once Laurel is the one remarking on how awful he looks.

"David died last night," Jerry says.

David is Jere's lover of fifteen years. Two dapper gents with a spectacular townhouse in Diamond Heights, trips abroad, good taste and success, perhaps an extra-relationship affair or two like any other long-term couple. Until David, a forty-seven-year-old stockbroker, tested positive and started down that slow cruel road of no return.

"We loved each other very much," Jerry says.

But Laurel doesn't know how she can comfort him. In a weird way, she envies the Jerrys and Davids of the world. They got what they wanted. She and Christopher, they coupled blindly, with expectations that could not be fulfilled, and they failed.

"I bet David is pissed." This is all she can say in a brittle voice. "I bet he and the others will be waiting to beat the crap out of the first doctor who comes over to the other side and didn't have the balls to try the DNA mutation, FDA testing be damned."

He looks at her with those big brown eyes, like, gee, Laurel, a bitch to the very end and fucking crazy, too. Then a deep-down look like yeah, this makes sense to him. Or maybe nothing makes sense to him anymore.

"Hey," he says. "You know that old guy up the street from you? The one you call The Ancient Jogger?"

"Mr. Oake?"

"He died last night. Heart failure. Eighty-four years old, isn't that something? While we're on the Big D, thought I'd better tell you since you knew him."

"Oh hell, I didn't know him. God; I guessed eighty-two. Well, at least you're holding down the fort, Jere."

"I tested positive last week," he says.

Laurel uncorks chenin blanc at ten in the morning. Jerry declines a cigarette; Laurel chainsmokes four. They talk about their wild youths and their almost-as-wild middle years. Is living to old age such a great idea after all? they joke.

Jerry leaves at noon. Laurel lies down on the couch. She is dizzy from the wine. Her mouth tastes like ashes. She keeps seeing a tiny, wrinkled face, eyes that are not bird eyes.

Dark, beating wings fill her dreams.

✳   ✳   ✳

Birds throughout antiquity symbolize the human soul, Laurel reads in the tiny, hand-printed book. Playing the book oracle, she finds significant passages. The Latin *aves* means both bird and ancestral spirit. In the Rig-Veda, the bird of Savitri is the Higher Self that struggles for expression, seeking freedom from the cage of mundane life. Birds, like angels, are emissaries between heaven and earth. Birds are symbols of thought, imagination, aspiration, spiritual longing, the swiftness of cosmic creativity. Birds are possessors of occult secrets. Birds are givers of omens.

Laurel smokes a cigarette with great pleasure out on her deck. It is five o'clock on a Saturday night, and she's got a bottle of cabernet sauvignon sitting next to her chair. She took morphine earlier. She's started coughing like when she smoked three packs a day, that deep-chested hack that usually tells the average moron to quit. Laurel, she tells herself, you are not the average moron anymore, hell no, so she lights another and picks up a beautiful pastel called dusty rose.

The Collins girl strides by in her usual adolescent huff, bound for her family's house on East Blithedale. Oh, those angry dark eyes, the pinched face that would be pretty if she didn't scowl so much.

But instead of envying the girl's youth and rebel vitality, Laurel decides to transform her on the sketchpad. Now goes earnest young royalty, crowned with her long and lovely hair, off to quest among the eucalyptus and date palms.

Laurel has seen twenty-five hummers today. She keeps a separate page in her sketchpad where she ticks off each sighting in groups of four short lines slashed by a fifth. Tick! Five groups of five.

This gives her focus, keeps her alert, lets her forget herself from time to time: keeping track of hummingbird sightings.

Despite the morphine and the wine and the cigarettes, she can feel a heavy dull pain in this body of hers. Not just in the gut, but all over, everywhere. She is not pissed off anymore. She is not entirely without the bitterness, no, and not entirely resigned. But she is aware of a turning away from the world. She unplugged the phone jack. She turned off the thermostat. She dumped old food, rotting alfalfa sprouts, from the refrigerator. She made her bed for the first time in months, sheets and blankets tucked in neatly at the corners, turned down at the top, as though for guests.

What a glory to sip wine and smoke and sketch just like the independent, eccentric, successful artist she once fantasized she would be one day. In a weird way, she feels this is it: she has made it. Here is Laurel, working on sketches for a major new fantasy triptych; "Princess of the Arbor," she decides to call it. Now sits the Mill Valley artist, observing hummingbirds from her deck.

The light changes and changes again. The black-chin is sitting on his perch, the flamboyant Allen's is flitting nearby. The two commence squabbling—*chup-chup-chup!*—being belligerent little bastards . . .

. . . when she sights another strange dark hummer, its gorget sparkling black the way obsidian gleams. Like any hummer, it zooms up to the feeder, scaring away the others, and hovers there.

Her heart beats at the sight of the dark bird. Dusk again, although she immediately intuits that dusk has nothing to do with the hummer's appearance.

She stares until her eyes tear; fear clouds her vision. She blinks, stares again, and this is what she sees: a tiny dark bird body hovering; the fantastic wings, the illusion of simultaneous upbeat and downbeat, a black lace fan so fast is the movement; an ebony wedge of tail bobbing like a frenetic ballast.

And a delicate, rounded, flat-sided head with a face: the face of a sulky adolescent girl. And more: the illusion of long and lovely hair spilling down around sloping bird shoulders.

So tiny. So fantastic! Charming in the way all hummers are infinitely charming.

But ominous: The sparkling black feathers, the tiny, pale face, its soft dark eyes almost wistful. No, impossible! Laurel wishes she could deny her perception like she's denied so many other things.

The hummer disappears into the arbor from which sunset flees in shafts of dusty rose.

A long, cold shudder makes her drop the sketchpad and pastels, reach for the woolen shawl draped over the back of her chair. The heavy, dull gut-pain throbs, but she does not move. She sits on her deck, snuggles into the shawl, and smokes and drinks and smokes some more. And waits.

There is something Laurel must witness here tonight. She dozes and wakes, shivers as the fog rolls in, and dreams of a river like a shining silver ribbon.

The sirens come at last after midnight. So close and shrill and jarring that Laurel wakes up at once, painfully knocking her left knuckles against the side of the chair. The Collins house. A green and white ambulance, two squad cars. Crackle of static, the bland, doom-filled voice of police radio garbled in the night. "One five zero, one five zero; we uh have a *shsh* at *shsh* East Blithedale; uh confirmed; attempted suicide, female, seventeen years old . . ."

The mother is sobbing, the father paces hopelessly, and they bring her out on a stretcher with a tube up her nose, tubes in her arm. They shove her into the ambulance, slam the doors, race off, sirens wailing.

But Laurel can tell from how the paleness of her sulky face surrenders to the paleness of the sheets that she will fly away tonight.

Becoming a bird in visionary trance is a widespread symbol of initiatory death and rebirth into eternal consciousness. Shamans and prophets in the South Pacific, Indonesia, Central Asia, the Americas, Siberia, as well as ancient Egypt, have claimed transformation into birds. Aztec priests wore ceremonial robes made entirely of hummingbird feathers. Voodoo mam'bo use the carcasses of hummingbirds to entice the presence of the mystère Simbi, the mercurial, aerial loa who conducts the souls of the dead past the crossroads of eternity. Yogis say ecstatic soul-flight is the first magical power to be developed on the path of deathlessness.

Laurel turns on the radio exactly at four in the morning. Is there any news of a young woman's attempted suicide, is she stable, critical, DOA? But the late-breaking news is the usual thing: soldiers are invading a mud hut village somewhere; a multimillionaire actress is divorcing her gigolo husband amid much scandal; the mayor of a local municipality is caught with his hand in the public cookie jar. No one gives a fuck about a seventeen-year-old girl disturbed enough to take her life or, for that matter, a forty-seven-year-old stockbroker breaking the heart of a brown-eyed homecare nurse who loved him for fifteen years.

How can anyone care? Death is everywhere: smashed animals on the freeway, rain forests crashing down, mothers crushed beneath collapsed freeways, young men gunned down for a rock of crack or a political philosophy.

The living should care; the young should attend to the old; families should look beyond insular cares to the community; political activists should pause from self-righteous panoramas to see their own beloveds.

Oh hell, *should*. Laurel does not care, either. No, she really doesn't, and why *should* she? She is not among the living. The cares of the world do not concern her. She cannot protest or even remark upon the death in everyday existence. She is a yin to the yang of life. Denial, anger, bitterness, resignation; even this evolution of emotions presents itself as life-bound categories that make no sense anymore. She can feel how she is inexorably slipping into the dark.

And it's okay. Yes. Her concerns have shifted: To the life in death. The flip-side. The metaphysical balance: If death pervades life, then surely life must permeate death. Surely; beyond her fear, her horror, beyond her comprehension.

She turns off the radio, plays the book oracle, and contemplates images of birds in the Egyptian Book of the Dead.

When the questing Isis discovered her dead husband Osiris at last, he who in ceremony symbolizes all the Dead, she hovered over his body in the form of a bird, sending forth the light of everlasting life from the sheen of her feathers.

The floating woman, her eyes rimmed in blue and black; there were arcs of shimmering color sprouting from her arms and shoulders. In the moment split between dreams and wakefulness the woman was, Laurel recalls, comforting, like a blanket or firelight, heat reaching into her cold, sick bones.

But that was right before the sudden pain, the metastasis. What does your comfort signify, Lady Isis?

Most charming of the avian hieroglyphs in the Egyptian Book of the Dead is the *ba*: depiction of the human soul as a delicate, human-headed bird. Plate Twenty-three of the book reads: Opened is the way of the souls (a tiny, human-headed bird), and my soul (the tiny bird again) does see it.

Chapter Nineteen is entirely devoted to the free, unfettered flying of, and feeding of nectar to, the *ba*. The *ba* has a corporeal, yet ethereal, existence. It converses with the gods and goddesses even while the humble earthly body still exists and is charged with taking the soul to the otherworld when the body dies. The *ba* is depicted as a territorial, inquisitive, hungry, sometimes belligerent, always frenetic being with a luminous presence and bright beating wings.

Dawn comes with a spectacular show of rose and gold. The eucalyptus and weeping willow sway and rustle, and Laurel wakes to their ancient presence, their sturdiness, their mute witness.

A sharp pain came again in the night. She took morphine, but Dolly Dagger does less and less for her. How can she explain what this pain is like? After the visceral torment, a disengagement. This is the personal grief at last, she knows; the final irrevocable coming apart of the vessel that once was the only carrier of her consciousness. However crappy it may have been, this body is all she knows. Of all goodbyes, this is the last.

Laurel goes to the bathroom. Another morphine shot in this awful skinny arm of hers. She washes her face. She combs what is left of her hair, wraps a purple silk scarf around her skull like a turban. Next makeup; thick, black eyeliner, dusty rose blush over too-prominent cheekbones; scarlet gloss smeared liberally on withered lips, make them flower-kissers.

Laurel, she tells herself, you look outtasight, baby.

She goes out to the living room, to the coffee table, and straightens the death books littered there. But her hand strays again to the Egyptian Book of the Dead, the elegant hieroglyphs, the weird imagery.

Close eyes, flip the heft of paperbound wisdom, index finger seeking prophecy. And here: Chapter Nine, Plate Eighteen, at random and for the first time, the editor's preface and notation:

> The title of these works as a whole is a misnomer. In fact, if one must call this compilation of scrolls by a single name, one should refer to the title of this particular plate: *The Book of Coming Forth Into Day To Live After Death.*

Ah; and she smiles despite everything. *Not* a book of the Dead. A weird sensation rises up in her like a gulp of air turned inside out. Coming Forth Into Day: a book of Life! A book of instruction!

All the beautiful girls on Haight-Ashbury twenty years ago claimed to be Egyptian princesses in a previous lifetime. How she remembers their sandalwood incense and their sloe-eyes and their young breasts naked under Egyptian cotton. But Laurel knows better now. Who would want to return to this world of shadows after coming forth into day?

She takes her sketchpad, the pastels, her cigarettes, the last of the good cabernet out on her deck. She slides the glass door shut behind her and sits. The little pale green plastic flying saucer with the bright red plastic flower decals sways gently in the Pacific breeze.

She doesn't wait long before her dependable Allen's hummer comes. What a hungry guy he is, visiting her morning 'til night. Wouldn't she love a guy like that, couldn't stay away from her all day long?

Then a Calliope comes, candy-cane striped gorget, gleaming gold-green back, cinnamon belly. A Calliope, she's never seen a Calliope before!

And a Costa's, with his violet-purple crown and his dark leaf-green feathers, and a Lucifer, with his violet-red gorget and his distinctive forked emerald tail.

The air all around her is filled with flitting, winged jewels.

Her lazy little black-chinned hummer perches and sips for a while, but then a tiny, tinny belligerent *chup-chup-chup!* pierces the morning blaze, and the black-chin and the Lucifer spiral away.

She sees a magnificent hummer.

Hovering over her. A tiny, exquisite golden body, levitating on gleaming fans of silver and vermilion and chrysolite, chupping excitedly. And looking down at her, a pale, round, flat face. A sad and lovely face.

Of course she knows that face, has rendered it in countless self-portraits, idealized it, corrupted it, broken it into planes and angles, rendered it fantastic with electric-blue tears sliding from the eyes. She's always been proud of the eyes. Not so proud of the mouth that has uttered meanness and nasty words, but she cannot do anything about that now.

The hummer darts away.

There is a sort of *click*, a huge compression in her chest, and she screams, the pain is terrifying, and she screams again, eyes wide open, every nerve snapping, and then she swoons.

There is a clanging noise that almost disturbs her from the task at hand. Go away, go away. If that's Jerry banging at her front door, he'll have to let himself in.

She looks down and sees the body crumpled there, so much baggage that must be left behind. The grief passes quickly now.

She soars up into the turquoise sky. The sun is dazzling. Bright beating wings take her.

SANTA'S WAY

James Powell

From James Powell, author of the offbeat police procedural "A Dirge for Clowntown" (winner of the *Ellery Queen's Mystery Magazine* Reader's Poll and reprinted in our *Third Annual Collection*), comes a hard-boiled Christmas tale.

James Powell is a popular mystery writer whose work appears regularly in *Ellery Queen's Mystery Magazine*. "Santa's Way" comes from their mid-December, 1991 issue.

—T.W.

Lieutenant Field parked behind the Animal Protective League van. The night was cold, the stars so bright he could almost taste them. Warmer constellations of tree lights decorated the dark living rooms on both sides of the street. Field turned up his coat collar. Then he followed the footprints in the snow across the lawn and up to the front door of the house where a uniformed officer stood shuffling his feet against the weather.

Captain Fountain was on the telephone in the front hallway and listening so hard he didn't notice Field come in. "Yes, Commissioner," he said. "Yes, sir, Commissioner." Then he laid a hand over the mouthpiece, looked up at a light fixture on the ceiling, and demanded, "Why me, Lord? Why me?" (The department took a dim view of men talking to themselves on duty. So Fountain always addressed furniture or fixtures. He confided much to urinals. They all knew how hard-done-by Fountain was.) Turning to repeat his question to the hatrack he saw Field. "Sorry to bring you out on this of all nights, Roy," he said. He pointed into the living room and added cryptically, "Check out the fireplace, why don't you?" Then he went back to listening.

Field crossed to the cold hearth. There were runs of blood down the sides of the flue. Large, red, star-shaped spatters decorated the ashes.

A woman's muffled voice said, "I heard somebody coming down the chimney." A blonde in her late thirties sitting in a wing chair in the corner, her face buried in a handkerchief. She looked up at Field with red-rimmed eyes. "After I called you people I even shouted up and told him you were on your way. But he kept on coming."

Captain Fountain was off the telephone. From the doorway he said, "So Miss Doreen Moore here stuck her pistol up the flue and fired away."

"Ka-pow, ka-pow, ka-pow," said the woman, making her hand into a pistol and, in Field's opinion, mimicking the recoil quite well. But he didn't quite grasp the situation until men emerged from the darkness on the other side of the picture window and reached up to steady eight tiny reindeer being lowered down from the roof in a large sling.

"Oh, no!" said Field.

"Oh, yes," said Fountain. "Come see for yourself."

Field followed him upstairs to the third-floor attic where the grim-faced Animal Protective League people, their job done, were backing down the ladder from the trap door in the roof.

Field and Fountain stood out on the sloping shingles under the stars. Christmas music came from the radio in the dashboard of the pickle-dish sleigh straddling the ridge of the roof. Close at hand was Santa, both elbows on the lip of the chimney, his body below the armpits and most of his beard out of sight down the hole. He was quite dead. The apples in his cheeks were Granny Smiths, green and hard.

Only the week before Field had watched the PBS documentary "Santa's Way." Its final minutes were still fresh in his mind. Santa in an old tweed jacket sat at his desk at the Toy Works backed by a window that looked right down onto the factory floor busy with elves. Mrs. Claus, her eyes on her knitting, smiled and nodded at his words and rocked nearby. "Starting out all we could afford to leave was a candy cane and an orange," Santa had said. "The elves made the candy canes and it was up to me to beg or borrow the oranges. Well, one day the United Fruit people said, 'Old timer, you make it a Chiquita banana and we'll supply them free and make a sizable donation to the elf scholarship fund.' But commercializing Christmas wasn't Santa's way. So we made do with the orange. And look at us now." He lowered his hairy white head modestly. "The Toy Works is running three shifts making sleds and dolls and your paint boxes with your yellows, blues, and reds. The new cargo dirigible lets us restock the sleigh in flight." Santa gave the camera a sadder look. "Mind you, there's a down side," he acknowledged. "We've strip-mined and deforested the hell out of the North Pole for the sticks and lumps of coal we give our naughty little clients. And our bond rating isn't as good as it used to be. Still, when the bankers say, 'Why not charge a little something, a token payment for each toy?' I always answer, 'That isn't Santa's way.' "

An urgent voice from the sleigh radio intruded on Field's remembering. "We interrupt this program for a news bulletin," it said. "Santa is dead. We repeat, Santa is dead. The jolly old gentleman was shot several times in the chimney earlier this evening. More details when they are available." At that late hour all good little boys and girls were in bed. Otherwise, Field knew, the announcer would've said, "Antasay is eadday," and continued in pig Latin.

Field stood there glumly watching the street below where the A.P.L. people were chasing after a tiny reindeer which had escaped while being loaded into the van. Lights had come on all over the neighborhood and faces were appearing in windows. After a moment, he turned his attention to the corpse.

But Fountain was feeling the cold. "Roy," he said impatiently, "Santa came down the wrong chimney. The woman panicked. Ka-pow, ka-pow, ka-pow! Cut and dried."

Field shook his head. "Rooftops are like fingerprints," he reminded the Captain. "No two are alike. Santa wouldn't make a mistake like—" He frowned, leaned forward, and put his face close to the corpse's.

"It wasn't just the smell of whiskey on his lips, Miss Moore," said Field. "You see, if Santa'd been going down the chimney his beard would've been pushed up over his face. But it was stuck down inside. Miss Moore, when you shot Santa he was on his way up that chimney."

The woman twisted the handkerchief between her fingers. "All right," she snapped. Then in a quieter voice she said, "All right, Nicky and I go back a long way. Right around here is end of the line for his Christmas deliveries. I'll bet you didn't know that."

Field had guessed as much. Last year when his kids wondered why the treat they left on a tray under the tree was never touched he had suggested maybe Santa was milk-and-cookied out by the time he got to their house.

"Anyway," continued Miss Moore, "Nicky'd always drop by afterwards for a drink and some laughs and one thing would lead to another. But I'm not talking one-night stands," she insisted. "We took trips. We spent time together whenever he could get away. He said he loved Mrs. Claus but she was a saint. And I wasn't a saint, he said, and he loved me for that. And I was crazy about him. But tonight he tried to walk out on me. So I shot him."

In the distance Field heard the police helicopter come to take the sleigh on the roof to Impound.

Fountain said, "Better get Miss Moore down to the station before this place is crawling with reporters. I'll wait for the boys with the flue-extractor rig."

Field turned on his car radio to catch any late-breaking developments. "O Tannenbaum, O Tannenbaum, how beautiful your branches!" sang a small choir. They drove without speaking for a while. Then out of nowhere the woman said, "You know that business about Nicky having a belly that shook like a bowl full of jelly? Well, that was just the poet going for a cheap rhyme. Nicky took care of himself. He exercised. He jogged. And he had this twinkle in his eye that'd just knock my socks off."

"I heard about the twinkle," Field admitted.

"But underneath it all there was this deep sadness," she said. "It wasn't just the fund-raising, the making the rounds every year, hat in hand, for money to keep the North Pole going. And it wasn't the elves, although they weren't always that easy to deal with. 'They can be real short, Doreen,' he told me once. 'Hey, I know elves are short, Nicky. Give me credit for some brains,' I said. He said, 'No, Doreen, I mean abrupt.'

"One time I asked him why he got so low and he said, 'Doreen, when I look all those politicians, bankers, lawyers, and captains of industry in the eye do you know who I see staring back at me? Those same naughty little boys and girls I gave the sticks and lumps of coal to. Where did I go wrong, Doreen? How did they end up running the show?'

"Well, a while back Nicky got this great idea how he could walk away from the whole business. Mr. Santa franchises. He'd auction the whole operation off country by country. Mr. Santa U.S.A. gets exclusive rights to give free toys to American kids and so on, country by country. 'And the elves'd take care of Mrs. Claus,' he said. 'They love her. She's a saint. And with the money I'll raise you and me'll buy a boat and sail away. We'll live off my patented Mr. Santa accessories. You know, my wide belt and the metered tape recorder of my laugh at a buck a 'ho!' "

Suddenly a voice on the radio said, "We now take you to New York where Leviathan Cribbage, elf observer to the United Nations, is about to hold a press conference." After the squeal of a microphone being adjusted downward a considerable distance, a high-pitched little voice said, "The High Council of Elves has asked me to issue the following statement: 'Cast down as we are by the murder of our great leader, Santa Claus, we are prepared, as a memorial to the man and his work, to continue to manufacture and distribute toys on the night before Christmas. In return we ask that our leader's murderer, whom we know to be in police custody, be turned over to elf justice. If the murderer is not in our hands within twenty-four hours the Toy Works at the North Pole will be shut down permanently.' " The room erupted into a hubbub of voices.

"Turn me over to elf justice?" said Miss Moore with a shudder. "That doesn't sound so hot."

"It won't happen," Field assured her as he parked the car. "Even a politician couldn't get away with a stunt like that."

Four detectives were crowded around the squad room television set. Field took Miss Moore into his office. Gesturing her into a chair, he sat down at his desk and said, "Now where were we?"

"With a buck a 'ho!' and me waiting there tonight with my bags packed," she said. "And here comes Nicky down the chimney. 'Doreen,' he says, 'I've only got a minute. I've still deliveries to make. Honey, I told Mrs. Claus about us. She's forgiven me, as I knew she would. But I can't see you again.'

" 'What about the Mr. Santa auction?' said I.

" 'Some auction,' he said. 'Everybody wanted America or Germany. Nobody wanted to be the Bangladeshi or the Ethiopian Mr. Santa. Crazy, isn't it? Everybody wants to load up the kids who've already got everything when giving to kids with nothing is the real fun.' Then he looked at me and said, 'It got me thinking about where I went wrong, Doreen. Maybe I should have given my naughty little clients toys, too. Maybe then they wouldn't have grown up into the kinds of people they did. Anyway, I'm going to give it a try. From now on I'll be Santa of all the children, naughty or nice. Goodbye, Doreen,' he said and turned to go.

"That's when I pulled out the revolver I keep around because I'm alone so much. I was tired of men who put their careers ahead of their women. I swore I'd kill him if he tried to leave. He went 'ho-ho-ho!' and took the gun out of my hand. He knew I couldn't shoot. I burst into tears. He gathered me in his arms and gave me a good-bye kiss. Emptying the bullets onto the rug, he tossed the pistol aside and walked over to the fireplace. 'You're a nice girl, Doreen,' he said with a twinkle in his eye. 'Don't let anybody ever tell you different.' But just before he ducked his head under the mantel I saw the twinkle flicker."

"Flicker?" asked Field.

"Like he was thinking maybe he'd figured me wrong," she explained. "Like maybe I'd reload the gun. Well, up the chimney he went, hauling ass real fast. And suddenly I was down on my knees pushing those bullets back into that pistol, furious that I'd wasted my whole life just to be there any time that old geezer in his red wool suit with that unfashionably wide belt could slip his collar and be with me, furious that he was dumping me just so he could give toys to naughty little boys and girls. I was trembling with rage. But every bullet I dropped I picked up again. When I'd gotten them all I went over and emptied the pistol up the chimney. Then I called you people."

Field's telephone rang. "Roy," said his wife, "I just heard the news about Santa. Roy, there aren't any presents under our tree. What are we going to do?"

"Lois, I can't talk now," said Field. "Don't worry. I'll think of something." He hung up the phone. Maybe if he worked all night he could cobble together some toys out of that scrap lumber in the basement.

Fountain was signaling from the doorway. He had an efficient-looking young woman with him. Field stepped outside. "Roy, this is Agent Mountain, Federal Witness Protection Program," he said. "I just got off the phone with the Commissioner. We're not bringing charges."

"Captain, we could be talking premeditated murder here," insisted Field, telling the part about her putting the bullets back into the pistol.

Fountain shrugged. "You want a trial? You want all the nice little boys and girls finding out that Santa was murdered and why? No way, Roy. She walks. But we can't let those damn knee-highs get her."

"You mean elves?" asked Field, who had never heard elves referred to in that derogatory way before.

"You got it," said Fountain. "So Agent Mountain's here to relocate her, give her a whole new identity."

Agent Mountain waved through the door at Doreen Moore. "Hi, honey," she said cheerily. "It looks like it's back to being a brunette."

Field put on his overcoat and closed his office door behind him. He stopped for a moment in front of the squad room television set. Somebody from the State Department was saying, "Peter, let's clear up one misconception right now. Elves are not short genetically. Their growth has been stunted by smoking and other acts of depravity associated with a perverse lifestyle. Can we let such twisted creatures hold our children's happiness hostage? I think not. I refer the second part of your question to General Frost."

A large man in white camouflage placed a plan of the Toy Works at the North Pole on an easel. "In case of a military strike against them, the elves intend to destroy the Toy Works with explosive charges set here, here, and here," he said, tapping with a pointer. "As I speak, our airborne forces, combined with crack RCMP dogsled units, have moved to neutralize—"

Field's phone was ringing. He hurried back to his office. "Hey, Lieutenant," said Impound. "We found presents in Santa's sleigh, some with your kids' names on them. Want to come by and pick them up?"

Field came in with the presents trapped between his chin and his forearm, closing the door quietly behind him. His wife was rattling around in the kitchen. He didn't call out to her, not wanting to wake the children. The light from the kitchen would be enough to put the presents under the tree. He was halfway across the living room when the lights came on. His children were staring down at him from the top of the stairs. Zack and Lesley, the eldest, exchanged wise glances. Charlotte was seven. She'd lost her first baby tooth that afternoon and her astonished mouth had a gap in it.

Field smiled up at them. "Santa got held up in traffic," he lied. "So he deputized a bunch of us as Santa's little helpers to deliver his presents." Charlotte received this flimsy nonsense with large, perplexed eyes. It was the first time he had ever told her anything she didn't believe instantly.

Ordering the children back to bed, Field went into the kitchen. Lois was watching a round-table discussion called "Life After Santa" on the little television set. When he told her about the presents from Impound she said, "Thank God." He didn't tell her what had just happened with the kids. Maybe one of these days he'd be able to sit down and give them the straight scoop, how there really had been this nice guy called Santa Claus who went around in a sleigh pulled by reindeer giving kids presents because he loved them, so, of course, we had to shoot him.

He turned on the kettle to make himself a cup of instant coffee and sat down beside his wife. On the screen a celebrated economist was saying, "Of course, we'll have to find an alternate energy source. Our entire industrial base has always depended on Santa's sticks and lumps of coal."

"But what a golden opportunity to end our kids' dependence on free toys," observed a former National Security advisor. "That's always smelled like socialism to me. Kids have to learn there's no free lunch. We should hand the Toy Works over to private enterprise. I hear Von Clausewitz Industries are interested in getting into toys."

"What about distribution?" asked someone else.

"Maybe we could talk the department stores into selling toys for a week or two before Christmas."

"Selling toys?" asked someone in disbelief.

The National Security advisor smiled. "We can hardly expect the Von Clausewitz people to pick up the tab. No, the toys'll have to be sold. But the play of the marketplace will hold prices—"

Field heard a sound. Someone had raised an upstairs window. Footsteps headed down the hall toward the children's rooms. He took the stairs two at a time, reaching the top with his service revolver drawn. Someone was standing in the dark corner by Charlotte's door. Crouching, pistol at the ready, Field snapped on the hall light. "Freeze!" he shouted.

The woman turned and gave him a questioning look. She had immense rose-gossamer wings of a swallow-tail cut sprouting from her shoulder-blades and a gown like white enamel shimmering with jewels. He didn't recognize who it was behind the surgical mask until she tugged at the wrists of her latex gloves, took a shiny quarter from the coin dispenser at her waist and stepped into Charlotte's room.

Field came out of his crouch slowly. Returning his weapon to its holster he went back down to the kitchen. He turned off the kettle, found the whiskey bottle in the cupboard and poured himself a drink with a trembling hand. "Lois," he said, "I almost shot the Tooth Fairy."

"Oh, Roy," she scolded in a tired voice.

On the television screen someone said, "Of course, we'll need a fund to provide toys for the children of the deserving poor."

"Don't you mean 'the deserving children of the poor'?" someone asked.

" 'Deserving children of the deserving poor,' " suggested another.

Lois shook her head. "Store-bought toys, Roy?" she asked. "We've got mortgage payments, car payments, Lesley's orthodontist, and saving for the kids' college. How can we afford store-bought toys?"

It'd been a hard day. He didn't want to talk about next year's toys. "Lois, please—" he started to say a bit snappishly. But here the program broke for a commercial and a voice said, "Hey, Mom, hey, kids, is Dad getting a little short? (And we don't mean abrupt). Why not send him along to see the folks at Tannenbaum Savings and Loan. All our offices have been tastefully decorated for the season. And there's one near you. So remember—" here a choir chimed in "—Owe Tannenbaum, Owe Tannenbaum, how beautiful their branches!"

CALL HOME

Dennis Etchison

Etchison is a consummate stylist who has unfortunately been seduced away from writing short stories by the film industry. He is the author of three remarkable collections, *The Dark Country*, *Red Dreams*, and *The Blood Kiss*. He has edited three Masters of Darkness anthologies and *Cutting Edge*, one of the most provocative and interesting original anthologies of the eighties. A follow-up anthology, *Meta-Horror*, has just been published.

What are little girls made of? Sugar and spice and everything nice—that's what little girls are made of. Say that little rhyme again after you read "Call Home," from the anthology *Psycho-Paths*.

—E.D.

When he walked in, the red light on the answering machine was blinking.

He dropped the mail on the coffee table and sat down. He ran a hand through his hair and leaned into the sofa, his ears still ringing from the rush-hour traffic.

He was in no hurry to replay his messages. It was easy to guess what they wanted: time, money, answers. He had none to spare. He reached out and stirred the pile of letters.

More of the same.

He got up, went to the bedroom and changed his clothes. Then he came back and sank deeper into the cushions. He propped his feet up and closed his eyes.

When the phone rang again, he let the machine take over.

"I'm not home right now," he heard his own recorded voice say, *"but if you care to leave a message, please begin speaking when you hear the tone. Thank you for calling. . . ."*

Beep.

A pause, and the incoming tape started rolling.

He waited to monitor the call.

Static. A rush of white noise. Like traffic.

No one there. Or someone who did not like talking to a machine.

A few more seconds and it would hang up automatically.

"Daddy? Is t-that you?"

He opened his eyes.

"Please, c-can you come get me? I don't know how to get home . . . and I'm scared!"

What?

"It's getting cold . . . and dark . . ."

He sat forward.

"There's a man here . . . and he's bothering me! I think he's crazy! And it's going to rain and . . . and . . . Daddy, tell me what to do!"

He got to his feet.

"I don't like this place! There's a rooster . . . it's burning . . . and a gas station . . . and a sign. It says, um, it starts with a p. P-I-C-O . . ."

He crossed the living room.

"Daddy, please come quick . . . !"

He snatched up the receiver.

"Hello?" he said.

The child's voice began to sing brokenly.

"Ladybird, ladybird, fly away home . . . your house is on fire . . . and your children will burn. . . ."

Her voice trailed off as she started to cry.

"Hello? Hello?"

Click.

He stood there holding the phone, wondering what to do.

He was sure of only one thing.

He had no daughter.

So what if it was a wrong number? She was in trouble. A child, a little girl. What if something happened to her?

He couldn't let it go.

She had spelled out a word. P-I-C-O. The sign. A rooster, a gas station . . . yes, it sounded familiar.

The chicken restaurant. Next to the 76 station. On Pico Boulevard.

It wasn't far.

The traffic was still gridlocked. He crossed Wilshire in low gear, then Santa Monica, and turned west. A stream of cars growled past him, ragged music and demanding voices leaking from beneath shimmering hoods. He made a left on Westwood and kept to the right as he passed Olympic, slowing to a crawl as he came to the next corner.

She was huddled in the doorway of El Pollo Muerto, a school book bag at her feet. Her legs were dirty and her hair was in her eyes. A few yards away, at the gas station, was the phone booth. She did not look up as he braked by a loading zone.

He leaned over and rolled down the window.

"Hey!"

The people at the bus stop glanced his way blankly, then stared past him down the street.

She lowered her head, resting her forehead on her arms.

He cleared his throat and shouted above the din. "Hey, little girl!"

She raised her head.

A woman eyed him suspiciously.

"Hi!" he called. "Hello, there! Do you need any help?"

The woman glared at him.

He ignored her and spoke to the girl.

"Are you the one who—?" Suddenly he felt foolish. "Did you call me?"

The little girl's face brightened.

"Daddy?"

The crowd moved closer. Then there was a rumbling and a pumping of brakes. He saw in his rearview mirror that an RTD bus had pulled up behind him.

"Come on," he said. "And your books—"

He opened the door for her as the bus sounded its horn.

"Daddy, it *is* you!"

The crowd surged past. The woman took notice of his license plate. The bus tapped his bumper.

"Get in."

He slipped into gear and got away from the curb. The pressure of traffic carried him across the intersection.

"Where do you want to go?" he asked. He passed another corner before it was possible to turn. "What's the address?"

"I don't know," said the little girl.

"You don't remember?"

She did not answer.

"Well, you'll have to tell me. Which way?"

"Want to go home," she said. She was now sitting straight in her seat, watching the lights with wide eyes.

"Are you all right?"

"I guess so."

At least it hasn't started to rain, he thought. "Did anyone hurt you?"

"I'm kind of hungry," she said.

He idled at a red light and got a good look at her. Seven, maybe eight years old and skinny as a rail. The bones in her wrists showed like white knuckles through the thin skin.

"When was the last time you had anything to eat?"

"I don't know."

She crossed her legs, angling a bruised ankle on a knobby knee, and he saw that her legs were streaked and smudged all the way up. My God, he thought, how long since she's had a bath? Has she been living on the streets?

"Well then," he said, "the first thing we'll do is get you some food." And then he would figure out what to do with her. "Okay?"

He took her to a deli. She gulped down a hot dog, leaving the bun on the plate, and watched him as he chewed his sandwich. He started to order her another, and realized something. He touched his hip pocket. Empty. He had forgotten his wallet when he changed his clothes.

"Take half of mine," he told her, trying to think.

"I don't like that kind."

She continued to watch him.

Finally he said, "Do you want another hot dog?"

"Yes, please!"

He ordered one more and saw to it that she drank her milk.

Afterward, while the waitress was in another part of the restaurant, he said abruptly, "Let's go."

They drove away as the waitress came out onto the sidewalk.

"That was good," said the little girl.

"Glad you liked it. Now—"

"The way you did that. You didn't even leave a tip. You did it for me, didn't you?"

"Yes." *What was I supposed to do?* he thought. *I'll come back tomorrow and take care of it.* "Now where are we going?"

"Home," she said. "Oh, Daddy, you're so silly! Where did you think?"

"You've got to tell me," he said in the driveway.

"Tell you what?"

She got out and skipped to the front door, dragging her book bag. She waited for him on the porch.

He shook his head.

"Well," he said once they were inside, "are you going to tell me?"

"Um, where's the bathroom?"

"In there." He went to the phone. "But first—"

He heard water running.

He stood outside the bathroom door and listened. The shower was hissing, and presently she began to sing a song.

In the living room, the phone rang.

"*I'm not home right now—*"

"*Jack, would you pick it up, please? I know you're there. . . .*"

"Hello, Chrissie. Sorry. I just got in."

"*So late? Poor baby . . .*"

"Listen, Chrissie, can I call you back? There's something I have to—"

"*Are Ruth and Will there yet?*"

"What?"

"*Don't tell me you forgot! Well, I guess I can pick up something on the way over. You know, maybe we can get rid of them early. Would you like that?*"

"Yeah, sure. But—"

"*See you in a few minutes, love. And Jack? I've missed you . . . !*"

Click.

"Daddy," called the little girl, "can you come here?"

He entered the darkened bedroom.

The bathroom door was open and steaming. She wrapped herself in a big towel and jumped up on the bed. She opened the towel.

"Dry me?"

"Listen," he said, "who told you to do this? I don't think it's such a good idea to—"

" 'S okay. I can do it myself." She made a few swipes with the towel and dropped it on the bed. Even in the faint light he could see how pink, how clean she was. And how small, and how vulnerable. She lay down and wriggled under the sheet.

"Sleepy," she said.

He sat next to her, on the edge of the mattress.

"Kiss me good-night," she said. Her pale arms stretched out. He started to push her away, but she clung to him with all her might. He felt her tears as sobs wracked her body.

"There," he told her, patting her between sharp shoulder blades. "Shh, now . . ."

"Don't go," she said.

"I'm not going anywhere."

"Promise?"

"I promise."

He lay down next to her till her breathing became slow and regular. After a while he covered her with the blanket, and planted a kiss on her cool forehead before he left the room.

Ruth and Will parked behind Chrissie. He watched from the porch as they helped her carry the take-out food into the house.

He cleared his throat. "There's something I have to tell you."

"We already know," said Ruth.

"How?"

"They didn't hear it from me, I swear," said Chrissie.

"A little bird told me," Ruth said. "And all I can say is, it's about time."

Will plopped down on the sofa. "Well, I think it's great. No point in paying rent on two places."

"*This* place sure isn't big enough," said Ruth. She stopped on the way to the kitchen and scanned the dining room. "Even if you got rid of these bookcases, it wouldn't work. You need more space."

"You know, Jack," said Will, "I have a friend in the real estate business. If you need any advice. Where's the Scotch?"

"Hold on . . ."

Chrissie winked at him as she passed. "They want to know if we've set the date. What do you think? Should we tell them everything?"

"Yes," he said.

"Wait a minute," said Will, rising and navigating for the bedroom door. "I want to hear this."

His stomach clenched. "Where are you going?"

Will grinned. "To take a leak. That all right with you?"

"Uh, would you mind using the other bathroom? This one's—stopped up."

Chrissie said, "It is? You didn't tell me that."

"I was going to. I was going to tell you all."

"Tell us what?" asked Ruth, coming out of the kitchen.

They looked at him expectantly. There was a long pause. His hands were shaking.

"I don't know where to start," he said. He tried a laugh but it came out wrong.

"Take your time," said Ruth. "We've got all evening."

Chrissie squeezed his arm. "Who needs a drink?" she said.

"Yes," he said. "Maybe we could have a drink first."

"What's this?" said Chrissie. She kicked the book bag on the floor, where the little girl had left it.

"Nothing," he said. "Here. Let me give you a hand."

He walked her to the kitchen.

"I can explain," he said.

"Explain what? You look tired, Jack. Was it an awful week?"

He took a deep breath. "Just this. I know it sounds crazy, but—"

On his way out of the small bathroom, Will stuck his head in the kitchen.

"Am I interrupting anything?"

"Of course not," said Chrissie.

"If this is a bad night for you two—"

There was a piercing scream from another part of the house.

He knew what it was before he got there.

The little girl was in the bedroom doorway, rubbing her eyes. She had on one of his shirts.

"Daddy?"

Ruth and Will looked at her. So did Chrissie. Then they looked at him.

"Oh, Daddy, there you are! I had a nightmare. There were people. Are they going now?"

"*Daddy?*" Chrissie stared at him as though she had never seen him before.

He focused on the little girl as his stomach clenched tighter.

"Tell them," he said.

"What?"

"Everything."

"I don't know what you mean, Daddy."

"All right," he said, "that's it. You're leaving—right now. I'll tell them the whole story myself. Come on. Let's go."

"No! I'll tell. How you picked me up at the bus stop and got me in the car in front of all those people? Or how you cheated and stole for me? Or the part where you gave me a bath and dried me and kissed me and we took a nap together?"

"I think we'd better be leaving," Ruth said.

"Yes," said Chrissie. "That might be a good idea. A very, very good idea."

"Wait." He followed her out. "Chris, I—"

"Don't," she said. "I have to think. And don't call me."

He watched numbly as the cars drove off. It started to rain softly, a misting drizzle in the trees above the mercury-vapor lamps. He watched until their red taillights turned the corner, like the reflection of a fire passing and moving on, leaving the street darker than ever.

"No," he said, hunching his shoulders. "No. No. No . . ."

He went back into the house.

"Where are you?" he shouted.

She was in the kitchen, helping herself to the food.

"Hi, Daddy," she said. "You got dinner for us. Just you and me. Thank you!"

"Who the hell do you think you are?"

He shook her violently.

"Daddy, you're hurting me!"

"I'm not your daddy and you know it, you little wretch."

"You're scaring me!"

"Don't bother to turn on the tears this time," he said. "It won't work."

She broke free and ran.

He braced himself against the table to stop shaking while he reached for the bottle of scotch and poured a double shot.

Then he walked slowly, deliberately to the living room.

"Out," he said. "I don't care if it's raining. You've done enough. Get your things and—"

She had the phone in her hand.

"Daddy?" she said into the mouthpiece. "C-can you come get me? I don't know how to get home . . . and I'm scared!"

He tried to take the phone away, but she dodged him and kept on talking.

"It's cold . . . and dark . . . and there's a man here . . . I think he's crazy! Daddy, tell me what to do! I don't like this place!"

She gave a description of his street.

"Daddy, please come quick!"

Then she began to sing sweetly, a high, plaintive keening like the wind outside, and the rain that blew with it, settling so coldly over the house.

"*Ladybird, ladybird, fly away home . . . your house is on fire . . . and your children will burn. . . .*"

Her voice trailed off as she started to cry.

She hung up. She stopped crying. Then she went about her business, collecting her clothing and her book bag as though he no longer existed.

He stood there, wondering what it was that was supposed to happen next.

THE BRAILLE ENCYCLOPAEDIA
Grant Morrison

Grant Morrison, like Alan Moore (author of the acclaimed story "A Hypothetical Lizard," which appeared in our *First Annual Collection*), is a prominent graphic novelist. And like Moore, he makes an auspicious debut in this medium; "The Braille Encyclopaedia" is his first published short story. Morrison is known best for the Batman graphic novel *Arkham Asylum* but I suspect this story from the anthology *Hotter Blood* will bring him an even greater audience.

Although quite different in some ways, this story shares certain elements with the classic John Varley novella "The Persistence of Vision." "The Braille Encyclopaedia" is elegant in language, erotic, terrifying, and horrifying—and compulsively readable. You don't want to go on, but you must.

—E.D.

Blind in the City of Light, Patricia walked carefully back through the Cimitière Père-Lachaise.

"Are you all right?" Mrs. Becque said again. "Now be careful here, the steps are a little slippery . . ."

Patricia nodded and placed her foot tentatively on the first step. Through the soles of her shoes she could feel the edge of a slick patch of moss.

"Are you all right?" Mrs. Becque said again.

"I'll be fine," Patricia said. "Really."

All around, she could feel the shapes of sepulchers and headstones. The echoes they returned, the space they displaced, the subtle patterns of cold air they radiated; all these things gave the funeral monuments of Père-Lachaise a weight and solidity that lay beyond sight. From the locked and chambered earth, a fragrance arose. The elaborate alchemy of decay released a damp perfume which combined with the scent of spoiled wreaths and hung like a mist around the stones. Rain drummed on the stretched skin of Patricia's umbrella.

"So what did you think?" said Mrs. Becque. "Of Wilde's monument, that is? Did you like it?"

"Lovely," Patricia said.

"Of course, the vandals have made a terrible mess, writing all over the statue, but it's still very impressive, don't you think?"

Mrs. Becque's voice receded into a rainy drone. Patricia could hardly mention how amused she'd been when she'd run her hands over Epstein's stone angel, only to discover that the balls of the statue had been chopped off by some zealous souvenir fiend. Mrs. Becque would most certainly disapprove of so ironic a defacement, but Patricia felt sure that Oscar Wilde would have found the whole thing thoroughly entertaining. Mrs. Becque, in fact, seemed to disapprove of almost everything and Patricia was growing desperately tired of the woman's constant presence.

"We must get in out of this awful rain," Mrs. Becque was saying. They crossed the street, found a café and sat down.

"What would you like, dear?" asked Mrs. Becque. "Coffee?"

"Yes," Patricia said. "Espresso. And a croissant. Thanks."

Mrs. Becque ordered, then eased herself up out of her seat and set off in search of a telephone. Patricia took her book from her bag and began to read with her fingertips. She found no comfort there. More and more often these days, books did nothing but increase her own sense of isolation and disaffection. They taunted and teased with their promise of a better world but in the end they had nothing to offer but empty words and closed covers. She had grown tired of experiencing life at second hand. She wanted something that she had never been able to put into words.

A waiter brought the coffee.

"Something else for you, sir?" he said.

Patricia started up from her book. Someone was sitting at her table, directly opposite. A man.

"I'm fine with this," the man said. His voice was rich and resonant, classically trained. Every syllable seemed to melt in the air.

"I hope you don't mind," the man said. He was talking to Patricia now, using English. "I saw you sitting all alone."

"No. Actually, I'm with someone," Patricia said. She stumbled over the words, as she might stumble over the furniture in some unfamiliar room. "She's over there. Over there." She gestured vaguely.

"I don't think you're with anyone at all," the man said. "You seem to me to be alone. It's not right that a pretty girl should be alone in Paris."

"I'm not," Patricia said flatly. The man was beginning to disturb and irritate her.

"Believe me," the man said. "I know what you want. It's written all over your face. I *know* what you want."

"What are you talking about?" Patricia said. "You don't know me. You don't know anything about me."

"I can read you like a book," he said. "I'll be here at the same time tomorrow, if you wish to hear more about the Braille Encyclopaedia."

"I beg your pardon?" Patricia's face flushed. "I really don't . . ."

"Everything all right, dear?"

Patricia turned her head. The voice belonged to Mrs. Becque. Foreign coins chinked into a cheap purse.

"It's just this man . . ." Patricia began.

Mrs. Becque sat down. "What man?" she said. "The waiter?"

"No. That man. There." Patricia pointed across the table.

"There's no one there, Patricia," Mrs. Becque said, using the voice she reserved for babies and dogs. "Drink up your coffee. Michel said he'd pick us up here in twenty minutes."

Patricia lifted her cup in numbed fingers. Somewhere the espresso machine sputtered and choked. Rain fell on the silent dead of Père-Lachaise, on the streets and the houses of Paris, covering the whole city like a veil, like a winding sheet . . .

Patricia raised her head. "What time is it?" she said.

In her room, in the tall and narrow hotel on the Boulevard St. Germain, Patricia sat listening to traffic. Outside, wheels sluiced through rain.

Rain sieving down through darkness. Rain spattering on the balcony. Rain dripping, slow and melancholy, from the wrought-iron railing.

She sat on the edge of the bed, in the dark. Always in the dark. No need for light. The money she saved on electricity bills! She sat in the dark of the afternoon, ate another slab of chocolate and tried to read. It was hopeless; her fingers skated across the braille dots, making no sense of their complex arrangements. Unable to concentrate, she set her book down and paced to the window again. Soon it would be evening. Outside, in the dark and the rain, Paris would put on its suit of lights. Students would gather to argue over black coffee, lovers would fall into one another's arms. Out there, in the breathless dark and the flashing neon, people would live and be alive; and here, in this room, Patricia would sit and Patricia would read.

She sat down heavily and, unutterably miserable, slotted a cassette into her Walkman. Then she lay back on the bed, staring wide-eyed into her private darkness.

Debussy's "La Mer" began to play—the first wash of strings and woodwind conjured a vast and empty shore. White sand, desolate under a big sky. White waves smashed on the rocks. Patricia was writing something on the sand. Lines drawn on a great blank page of sand. She could not read what she was writing but she knew it was important.

Patricia licked dry lips, tasting chocolate.

What did he look like? The man in the café. The man with the voice. What would he look like if she could see him?

She unzipped her skirt and eased her hand down between her legs. The bed began to creak faintly, synchronizing itself with Patricia's harsh, chopped breathing . . .

She was stretched out on watered silk in a scented room of flowers and old wine and he was there with his voice and his breath on her body his breath circulating

*in the grottoes of her ear and in her mouth and his skin and the mesh of muscles
as he went into her*

. . . Debussy's surf broke against the walls of her skull. White wave noise drowning
out the traffic and the rain, turning the darkness into incendiary light.

The music had come to an end. The room was too hot. An airless box. Patricia
was suffocating in the dark. She rose, unsteadily, and faced the mirror's cold eye.
She knew how she must look: a fat, plain girl, playing with herself on a hotel bed.

"Stop it or you'll go blind," she said quietly. She felt suddenly sick and stupid.
She would never meet anyone, never do or be anything. It all came down to this
stifling room. No matter where she went, she found herself in this room. Reading.
Always reading. Nothing would ever happen.

The dark closed in.

"I knew you'd be here," the man said. "I knew it."

"I don't see how you could just know," said Patricia and felt stupid. She was
saying all the wrong things.

"Oh, I know," he said. "I'm trained to recognize certain things in people.
Certain possibilities. Certain . . . inclinations." His hand alighted on hers and
she jumped. "I can tell we're going to be friends, Patricia."

"I don't even know your name," she said. She was becoming frightened now.
She felt somehow that she was being *circled*. His voice was drawing a line around
her. Sweat gathered between her breasts.

"My name?" He smiled. She could hear him smile. "Just call me L'Index."

"Sorry?" Patricia felt sure she must have misheard him. She tried not to be
afraid. Being afraid was what had made her lonely.

"L'Index," the man repeated. "Like a book. L'Index."

"I can't call you that," Patricia said.

"You can. You must." He reached out and took her hand. It was like a soft
trap, fastening around her wrist. "Dear Patricia. You must. You will. I will show
you such things . . ." The fear was almost unbearable. She wanted to run. She
wanted to go back. Back to that room, that book, like the coward she was. The
man was holding open a door. Beyond lay darkness, it was true, but then again,
Patricia was no stranger to the dark.

"L'Index," she said.

When Mrs. Becque returned to the café to collect Patricia, Patricia had gone.
One of the waiters had seen her leave with someone but found it impossible to
describe the man. No one could describe the man. He had come and he had
gone: a gray man in the rain. Invisible. The police were alerted. Half-heartedly
they scoured the city, then gave up. Patricia's parents mounted their own futile
search. The newspapers printed photographs of a rather plump, blind girl, smiling
at a camera she could not see. Her eyes were pale blue, their color diluted to
invisibility. Eyes full of rain, like puddles in a face. Very soon the papers and the
public lost interest. Patricia's room lay untenanted. A stopped clock. The girl was
never found and the police file stayed open, like a door leading nowhere.

* * *

The Chateau might have seemed like a prison were it not for the fact that it appeared to perpetually renew its own architecture. No door ever led twice to the same room, no corridor could ever be followed to the same conclusion, no stair could be made to repeat its steps.

Additionally, the variety of experiences offered by life in the Chateau was of such diversity that life outside could only be timid and pale by comparison. Here, there was no sin which could not be indulged to exhaustion. Here, the search for fresh sensation had long ago led to the practice of continually more refined atrocities. Here, finally, there were no laws, no boundaries, no limits, no judgment.

And the motto above the door read simply "Hell is more beautiful than Heaven."

Tonight was to be a special night. In the red room, in the room of the Sign of Seven, whose walls beat like a heart, Patricia lay in a tumble of silk cushions. She found a vein in her thigh and slowly inserted the needle. After the first rush, her head seemed to unlock and divide like a puzzle box. Her nervous system suffered a series of delicious shocks and smoke spilled into her brain. She licked red lips and began to shake. The tiny bells pinned to her skin reacted to her shudders. Her body became a tambourine. She drew a long breath. The room was hot and sweat ran on her oiled skin, trickling from the tongues of the lewd tattoos which now adorned her belly.

Above the pulse of the room, Patricia could hear the boy spitting, still spitting. L'Index had allowed her to touch the boy—to run her nails through his soft hair, to pluck feathers from the clipped and ragged wings he wore on his back and to finger the scars of his castration.

"What's he doing?" she said dreamily. "Why is he spitting?"

L'Index had come back into the room. He closed the door and waited for the boy to finish.

"He's been spitting into this glass," L'Index said. "Here."

Patricia took from him a beautiful crystal wineglass. L'Index knelt down beside her. Heat radiated off his body and he smelled faintly of blood and spiced sweat.

"The boy is an angel," L'Index said. "We summoned him here from Heaven and then we crippled and debauched him."

Patricia giggled.

"Our own little soiled angel," L'Index continued. "Come here, angel."

The boy shuffled across the room, slow as a sleepwalker. His wings rustled like dry paper.

"What shall I do with this?" Patricia asked, weighing the glass in her hand.

"I want you to drink it," L'Index said. "Drink."

Patricia dipped her tongue into the warm froth of saliva.

"He has AIDS, of course," L'Index said casually. "The poor creature has been the plaything of god knows how many filthy old whores and catamites. As you might expect, his spit is a reservoir of disease." He paused, smiling his almost-audible smile. "Nevertheless, I do insist that you drink it."

Patricia heard the boy whimpering as he was forced onto his hands and knees. She swirled the liquid round in the glass.

"Drink it *slowly*."

She heard the chink and creak of a leather harness. A match was struck. Was there no limit to what he would ask of her?

"All right," she said, nosing the glass like a connoisseur. It smelled of nothing. "I told you. I'll do anything."

And she drank, slowly, savoring the bland, flat taste of the boy's saliva. The whole glass, to the dregs. As she drank, she could hear the boy gasp—sodomized. Patricia licked the rim of her glass.

"You were lying," she said. "AIDS. I knew you were lying."

The boy cried out, with the voice of a bird. L'Index had done something new to him. Patricia waited for L'Index to undo the harness and sit down beside her.

"I knew I was right about you, when I saw you all those months ago," L'Index said. He tugged on the ring that was threaded through her nipple, pulling her toward him. Automatically, she opened her mouth and allowed him to place an unclean treat on her tongue.

"I knew you were worthy of admission."

"Admission?" said Patricia. "Admission into what?" The sound of her own voice seemed to recede and return. She was beginning to feel strange.

"Do you remember when I mentioned to you the Braille Encyclopaedia?" L'Index asked.

"Yes." Fragments of music flared in Patricia's head. Choral detonations. She felt that she was falling through some terrible space. "The Braille Encyclopaedia. Yes. What is it?"

"Not a thing," L'Index said. "A society. Here. On your knees. Touch me."

He took her hand.

"But you've never let me . . ." she began, growing excited. White noise blasted through her, like a stereo pan, from ear to ear.

"I'm letting you now," he said. "You've shown a rare appetite for all the sweet and rotting fruits of corruption. Sometimes, I'm almost frightened by your dedication. Now, I think it's time you were allowed to taste the most exquisite delicacy." He set her hand to his bare chest. Her fingers brushed his skin and she started.

"What is it?" Patricia lightly traced her fingertips across tiny raised scars. Alarm returned as she realized that his entire body, from neck to feet, was similarly disfigured. She ran along a row of dots, suddenly unable to catch a breath.

"It's braille," she said. "Oh, God, it's braille . . . I feel so strange . . ." He filled her mouth and stopped her speech. Like a nursing child, she sucked and swallowed and allowed her hands to crawl across his skin.

"You drank angel spit," L'Index said. His voice was full of echoes and ambiguous reverberations. "You drank the rarest of narcotics. Now it's time to read me, Patricia. Read me!"

She read.

Entry 103   THE DEFORMATION OF BABY SOULS
Entry 45   THE HORN OF DECAY
Entry 217   THE MIRACLE OF THE SEVERED FACE
Entry 14   THE ATROCIOUS BRIDE
Entry 191   THE REGIMENTAL SIN
Entry 204   BLEEDING WINDO . . .

Patricia snatched back her hand and pulled away, terrified. L'Index came into her face, spattering her useless eyes.

"What are you?" she whispered. She blinked and sperm tears ran down her cheeks. Somewhere, the fallen angel whimpered in the darkness.

"There are several hundred of us," L'Index explained. "And together we form the most comprehensive collection of impure knowledge that has ever been assembled. Monstrous books, long thought destroyed, have survived as marks on our flesh. Through us, an unholy tradition is preserved."

"And what about me," Patricia said.

"One of our number died recently," L'Index said. "It happens, of course, in the due process of time. Usually, we initiate a relative, often a child. My grandfather, for instance, was the Index before me. In this case, however, that was not possible. Part of my job is to find a suitable successor . . ."

Gripped by an extraordinary fear, Patricia dropped to the floor.

"Don't be afraid, Patricia," L'Index said. "Not you."

As she lay there, he pissed on her hair. She lifted her face into the hot stream, grateful for an act of degradation she could still understand. It helped her to know he still cared.

"Will you abandon your last claim to self? Will you embrace the final release, Patricia? That is what I'm asking of you. Will you step over the threshold into a new world?"

"You sound like an evangelist," she said. His urine steamed in her hair. Patricia breathed deeply, inhaling a mineral fragrance. Slowly her heart rate came to match the pulsing of the room. She thought of what she had been and of what he had helped her become.

She held her breath for a moment. Counted to ten.

"Yes," she said hoarsely. "Yes."

They came singly, they came in twos and in groups: the Braille Encyclopaedia. Some were driven in black limousines with mirrored windows and no registration plates. Others walked, haltingly. Men, women, hollow-eyed children. They came from all directions, traveling on roads known only to a few mad or debased souls. They came and the doors of the Chateau opened to receive them. There was an almost electrical excitement in the air. The current ran through enchanted flesh, conjuring static in the darkness. Blue sparks played on fingertips as the Braille Encyclopaedia made its way into the Chateau. They were, each of them, blind, even the youngest. Silent and blind, blue ghosts, they entered the darkness. And the doors closed behind them.

*   *   *

Patricia did not hear them enter, nor did she hear L'Index welcome his guests. She sat in her chamber, listening to the fall of surf on an interior beach. On the bedside cabinets were vibrators, clamps, unguents, suction devices, whips: all the ludicrous paraphernalia of arousal. She was familiar with each and every item and she had endured or perpetrated every possible permutation of indecency that the body could endure.

Or so she had thought.

She touched her own smooth skin. She had removed the bells and the rings and toweled the oil away. Her skin was blank, like a parchment upon which L'Index wished to write unspeakable things. The music of Debussy crashed through her confusion.

We are all of us, she thought, written upon by time. Our skin is pitted and eroded by the passage of years. No one escapes. Why not then defy time by becoming part of something eternal? Why not give up all claims to individual identity and become little more than a page in a book which renews itself endlessly? It was, as L'Index had said, the final surrender.

Patricia removed her headphones and made her way downstairs.

L'Index was waiting for her and he introduced her to the members of the Braille Encyclopaedia. Blind hands stroked her naked body and, finding it unmarred, lost interest. She trembled as, one by one, they approached and examined her with a shocking frankness. Shameless fingers probed and penetrated her: the dry-twig scrapings of old men and women, the thin furtive strokes of wicked children. By the end of their examination, Patricia teetered on the brink of delirium. Her darkness filled with inarticulate flashes and fireworks displays of grotesque color and grossly ambiguous forms.

"They don't speak," she said. It seemed terribly important.

"No," said L'Index simply.

She felt them crowd around her in a circle, felt the pressure and the heat of unclothed flesh. No sound. They made no sound.

"Are you ready?" L'Index asked, touching Patricia's shoulder gently. She nodded and let him lead her into a tiny room at the back of the Chateau. Soundproofed walls. A single unshaded bulb, radiating a light she could not see. L'Index kissed her neck and instructed her not to move under any circumstances. She wanted to say something, but she was too afraid to speak. The words jammed at the back of her throat.

And then the door opened. Someone she did not know came into the room. Patricia suddenly wanted to run. The light was switched off and candles were lit, filling the room with a sickly sweet narcotic scent.

Patricia heard then a thin metallic ring. A sharp-edged sound. The brief conversation of scalpels and needles and blue-edged razors.

"L'Index?" she said nervously. "L'Index, are you there? I'm afraid . . ."

No one answered. Patricia rocked on the balls of her feet. The air was too hot, the candlesmoke too bitter. She gulped lungfuls of oily, shifting smoke.

Someone came toward her, breathing harshly, sometimes mewing.

"L'Index?" she whispered again, so quietly that it was no more than the ghost of a name. In her head, the noise and the colors mounted toward an intensity she felt she could not possibly bear.

The first cut caused her to spontaneously orgasm. Her brain lit up like a pinball machine. She swayed and she cried out but she did not fall as hooks and needles were teased beneath her skin.

Moaning, coming again and again, Patricia was delicately scarred and cicatrized. Alone on a private beach, she realized what word it was that she had scrawled in the sand. And in that moment of understanding, the surf surged in and obliterated every trace of what she had written. Her identity was finally erased in the white glare of a pain so perfect and so pure that it could only be ecstasy. Fat, awkward Patricia was at last, at last, written out of existence by articulate needles.

She came to her senses and found that she was still standing. Thin spills of blood streamed down her body, pooling on the floor. She touched her stomach. The raw wounds stung but she could not help but run her fingertip along the lines of braille. She read one sentence and could hardly believe that such abomination could possibly exist let alone be described. Her whole body was a record of atrocities so rare and so refined that the mind revolted from the truth of them. How could things like this be permitted to exist in the world? She felt dizzy and could read no more.

"I'm still alive. I'm still alive," was all she could say. At last, she fell but L'Index was there to catch her.

"Welcome to the Encyclopaedia," he said, salting her wounds so that they burned exquisitely. "Now you are Entry 207—The Meat Chamber."

She nodded, recognizing herself, and he led her out of the room and down an unfamiliar corridor. She could feel herself losing consciousness. There was something she had to ask him. That was all she could remember.

"The Chateau," she said, slurring her words. "Who owns the Chateau?"

"Can't you guess?" L'Index said.

He brought her into the ballroom, where they were all waiting for her. Hundreds of people were waiting for her. She smiled weakly and said, "What now? Can I please sit down?"

"These gatherings happen only rarely," L'Index said. "The entire Encyclopaedia is not often assembled together in one place and so our lives take on true meaning only at these moments. I can assure you that what is about to follow will transcend all your previous experiences of physical gratification. For you, this will be the ultimate, most beautiful defilement. I promise."

He sat her down in a heavy wooden chair.

"I envy you so much," he said. "I'm only the Index, you see. The mysteries and abominations of the flesh are denied to me."

He pulled a strap across her arms, tugged it tight and buckled it.

"What are you doing?" she said. "Is this the Punishment Chair? It's not, is it?" She began to panic now as he clamped her ankles to the legs of the chair. The

Encyclopaedia was arranging itself into a circle again. Footsteps sounded down the corridor.

"This is the Chair of Final Submission," L'Index said. "Goodbye, my love." And he clamped her head back.

"Oh no," she said. "Wait. Don't . . ."

A clumsy bolt and bit arrangement was thrust into her mouth, chipping a tooth and reducing her words to infantile sobs and gobblings.

The footsteps advanced and the Encyclopaedia parted to make a passage. Shiny steel chinked slyly in a leather bag. L'Index leaned over and whispered in her ear.

"Remember, you may always consult me . . ."

She bucked and slammed in the chair but it was fixed to the floor by heavy bolts.

"Oh my sweet," L'Index said. "Don't lose heart now. Remember what you were: alone, lonely and discontented. You will never be lonely again." His breath stank of peppermint and sperm. "Now you can pass into a new world where nothing is forbidden but virtue."

A bag snapped open. A needle was withdrawn. It rang faintly, eight inches long.

"Give yourself up now to the world of the Braille Encyclopaedia! Knowledge shared only by these few, never communicated. Knowledge gained by sense of touch alone."

And she finally understood then, just before the needles punctured her eardrums. Her bladder and her bowels let go and the odors of her own chemical wastes were the last things she smelled before they destroyed that sense also. Finally her tongue was amputated and given to the angel to play with.

"Now go," L'Index said, unheard. There was sadness in his voice. His tragedy was to be forever excluded from the Empire of the Senseless. "Join the Encyclopaedia."

Released from the chair, The Meat Chamber stumbled into the arms of her fellow entries in the Braille Encyclopaedia. Bodies fell together. Blind hands stroked sensitized skin. They embraced her and licked her wounds and made her welcome.

She screamed for a very long time but only one person there heard her. Finally she stopped, exhausted.

And then she began to read.

And read.

And read.

THE POISONED STORY
Rosario Ferré

Rosario Ferré is a Puerto Rican writer whose first book, *Papeles de Pandora*, was praised throughout Latin America. She is also the author of two books of essays; a collection of poetry, *Fabulas de la garza desangrada*; and a novella, *Maldito amor*. In 1991, the University of Nebraska Press brought out Ferré's excellent collection *The Youngest Doll and Other Stories* in an English translation. "The Poisoned Story" comes from this collection, and was also published in *Green Cane Juicy Flotsam*, a recommended anthology of short stories by Caribbean women published in 1991 by Rutgers University Press.

Ferré, an avid reader of folk and fairy tales, has also published four books of children's tales based on stories told to her as a child by her nanny. In her essay "The Writer's Kitchen," she relates how, after the failure of her first writing attempts, she completed her first successful story, "The Youngest Doll," by drawing upon these oral narratives of childhood. In the following story, Ferré draws upon the classic fairy-tale theme of conflict between stepmother and child, with a nod to the Arabian tales of *A Thousand and One Nights*.

—T.W.

And the King said to Ruyán the Wise Man:
"Wise Man, there is nothing written."
"Leaf through a few more pages."
The King turned a few more pages, and before long the poison began to course rapidly through his body. Then the King trembled and cried out:
"This story is poisoned."

—*A Thousand and One Nights*

Rosaura lived in a house of many balconies, shadowed by a dense overgrowth of crimson bougainvillea vines. She used to hide behind these vines, where she could read her storybooks undisturbed. Rosaura, Rosaura. A melancholy child, she had few friends, but no one had ever been able to guess the reason for her sadness. She was devoted to her father, and whenever he was home she used to sing and laugh around the house, but as soon as he left to supervise the workers in the canefields, she would hide once more behind the crimson vines and before long she'd be deep in her storybook world.

I know I ought to get up and look after the mourners, offer my clients coffee and serve cognac to their unbearable husbands, but I feel exhausted. I just want to sit here and rest my aching feet, listen to my neighbors chatter endlessly about me. When I met him, Don Lorenzo was an impoverished sugar-cane planter, who only managed to keep the family afloat by working from dawn to dusk. First Rosaura, then Lorenzo. What an extraordinary coincidence. He loved the old plantation house, with its dozen balconies jutting out over the canefields like a windswept schooner's. He had been born there, and the building's historic past had made his blood stir with patriotic zeal: It was there that the criollos' first resistance to the invasion had taken place, almost a hundred years before.

Don Lorenzo remembered the day very well, and he would enthusiastically reenact the battle scene as he strode vigorously through halls and parlors—war whoops, saber, musket and all—thinking of those heroic ancestors who had gloriously died for their homeland. In recent years, however, he'd been forced to exercise some caution in his historic walks, as the wood-planked floor of the house was eaten through with termites. The chicken coop and the pigpen that Don Lorenzo was compelled to keep in the cellar to bolster the family income were now clearly visible, and the sight of them would always cast a pall over his dreams of glory. Despite his economic hardships, however, he had never considered selling the house or the plantation. A man could sell anything he had—his horse, his cart, his shirt, even the skin off his back—but one's land, like one's heart, must never be sold.

I mustn't betray my surprise, my growing amazement. After everything that's happened, to find ourselves at the mercy of a two-bit writer. As if my customers' bad-mouthing wasn't enough. I can almost hear them whispering, tearing me apart behind their fluttering fans: "Whoever would have thought it; from charwoman to gentlewoman, first wallowing in mud, then wallowing in wealth. But finery does not a lady make." I couldn't care less. Thanks to Lorenzo, their claws can't reach me anymore; I'm beyond their "lower my neckline a little more, Rosita dear, pinch my waist a little tighter there, Rosita darling," as though alterations to their gowns were no work at all and I didn't have to get paid for them. But I don't want to think about that now.

When his first wife died, Don Lorenzo behaved like a drowning man in a shipwreck. He thrashed about desperately in an ocean of loneliness for a while, until he finally grabbed on to the nearest piece of flotsam. Rosa offered to keep him afloat, clasped to her broad hips and generous breasts. He married her soon afterwards and, his domestic comfort thus reestablished, Don Lorenzo's hearty laugh could once again be heard echoing through the house, as he went out of his way to make his daughter happy. An educated man, well-versed in literature and art, he found nothing wrong with Rosaura's passion for storybooks. He felt guilty about the fact that she had been forced to leave school because of his poor business deals, and perhaps because of it on her birthday he always gave her a lavish, gold-bound storybook as a present.

This story is getting better; it's funnier by the minute. The small-town, two-bit writer's style makes me want to laugh; he's stilted and mawkish and turns everything around for his own benefit. He obviously doesn't sympathize with me. Rosa was a practical woman, for whom the family's modest luxuries were unforgivable self-indulgences. Rosaura disliked her because of this. The house, like Rosaura's books, was a fantasy world, filled with exquisite old dolls in threadbare clothes; musty wardrobes full of satin robes, velvet capes, and crystal candelabra which Rosaura used to swear she'd seen floating through the halls at night, held aloft by flickering ghosts. One day Rosa, without so much as a twinge of guilt, arranged to sell all the family heirlooms to the local antique dealer.

The small-town writer is mistaken. First of all, Lorenzo began pestering me long before his wife passed away. I remember how he used to undress me boldly with his eyes when I was standing by her sickbed, and I was torn between feeling sorry for him and my scorn for his weak, sentimental mooning. I finally married him out of pity and not because I was after his money, as this story falsely implies. I refused him several times, and when I finally weakened and said yes, my family thought I'd gone out of my mind. They believed that my marrying Lorenzo and taking charge of his huge house would mean professional suicide because my designer clothes were already beginning to earn me a reputation. Selling the so-called family heirlooms, moreover, made sense from a psychological as well as from a practical point of view. At my own home we've always been proud; I have ten brothers and sisters, but we've never gone to bed hungry. The sight of Lorenzo's empty cupboard, impeccably whitewashed and with a skylight to better display its frightening bareness, would have made the bravest one of us shudder. I sold the broken-down furniture and the useless knickknacks to fill that cupboard, to put some honest bread on the table.

But Rosa's miserliness didn't stop there. She went on to pawn the silver, the table linen, and the embroidered bedsheets that had once belonged to Rosaura's mother, and to her mother before her. Her niggardliness extended to the family menu, and even such moderately epicurean dishes as fricasseed rabbit, rice with guinea hen, and baby lamb stew were banished forever from the table. This last measure saddened Don Lorenzo deeply because, next to his wife and daughter, he had loved those criollo dishes more than anything else in the world, and the sight of them at dinnertime would always make him beam with happiness.

Who could have strung together this trash, this dirty gossip? The title, one must admit, is perfect: the unwritten page *will* bear patiently whatever poison you spit on it. Rosa's frugal ways often made her seem two-faced: she'd be all smiles in public and a shrew at home. "Look at the bright side of things, dear, keep your chin up when the chips are down," she'd say spunkily to Lorenzo as she put on her best clothes for mass on Sunday, insisting he do the same. "We've been through hard times before and we'll weather this one out, too, but there's no sense in letting our neighbors know." She opened a custom dress shop in one of the small rooms of the first floor of the house and hung a little sign that read "The fall of the Bastille" over its door. Believe it or not, she was so ignorant that she was sure this would win her a more educated clientele. Soon she began to invest every penny she got from the sale of the family heirlooms in costly materials for her customers' dresses, and she'd sit night and day in her shop, self-righteously threading needles and sewing seams.

The mayor's wife just walked in; I'll nod hello from here, without getting up. She's wearing one of my exclusive models, which I must have made over at least six times just to please her. I know she expects me to go over and tell her how becoming it looks, but I just don't feel up to it. I'm tired of acting out the role of high priestess of fashion for the women of this town. At first I felt sorry for them. It broke my heart to see them with nothing to think about but bridge, gossip, and gadflying from luncheon to luncheon. Boredom's velvet claw had already finished off several of them who'd been interned in mainland sanatoriums for "mysterious health problems," when I began to preach, from my modest workshop, the doctrine of "salvation through style." Style heals all, cures all, restores all. Its followers are legion, as can be seen by the hosts of angels in lavishly billowing robes that mill under our cathedral's frescoed dome.

Thanks to Lorenzo's generosity, I subscribed to all the latest fashion magazines, which were mailed to me directly from Paris, London, and New York. I began to write about the importance of line and color to a successful business, and not only for advertisement, but for the spiritual well-being of the modern entrepreneur. I began to publish a weekly column of fashion advice in our local gazette, which kept my clientele pegged to the latest fashion trends. Whether the "in" color of the season was obituary orchid or asthma green, whether in springtime the bodice was to be quilted or curled like a cabbage leaf, whether buttons were to be made of tortoise shell or mother-of-pearl, it was all a matter of dogma to them, an article of faith. My shop turned into a beehive of activity, with the town's most well-to-do ladies constantly coming and going from my door, consulting me about their latest ensembles.

The success of my store soon made us rich. I felt immensely grateful to Lorenzo, who had made it all possible by selling the plantation and lending me the extra bit of money to expand my workshop. Thanks to him, today I'm a free woman; I don't have to grovel or be polite to anyone. I'm sick of all the bowing and scraping before these good-for-nothing housewives, who must be constantly flattered to feel at peace. Let the mayor's wife lift her own tail and smell her own cunt for a while. I much prefer to read this vile story rather than speak to her, rather than tell her "how nicely you've got yourself up today, my dear, with your witch's shroud, your whisk-broomed shoes, and your stovepipe bag."

Don Lorenzo sold his house and his land and moved to town with his family. The change did Rosaura good. She soon looked rosy-cheeked and made new friends, with whom she strolled in the parks and squares of the town. For the first time in her life she lost interest in her storybooks, and when her father made her his usual birthday gift a few months later, she left it half read and forgotten on the parlor table. Don Lorenzo, on the other hand, became more and more bereaved, his heart torn to pieces by the loss of his canefields.

Rosa, in her workshop, took on several seamstresses to help her out and now had more customers than ever before. Her shop took up the whole first floor of the house, and her clientele became more exclusive. She no longer had to cope with the infernal din of the chicken coop and the pigpen, which in the old days had adjoined her workshop and cheapened its atmosphere, making elegant conversation impossible. As these ladies, however, took forever to pay their bills, and Rosa couldn't resist keeping a number of the lavish couturier models for herself, the business went deeper and deeper into debt.

It was around that time that she began to nag Lorenzo constantly about his will. "If you were to pass away today, I'd have to work till I was old and gray just to pay off our business debts," she told him one night with tears in her eyes, before putting out the light on their bedside table. "Even if you sold half your estate, we couldn't even begin to pay them." And when she saw that he remained silent, his gray head slumped on his chest, and refused to disinherit his daughter for her sake, she began to heap insults on Rosaura, accusing her of not earning her keep and of living in a storybook world, while she had to sew her fingers to the bone in order to feed them all. Then, before turning her back to put out the light, she told him that, because he obviously loved his daughter more than anyone else in the world, she had no choice but to leave him.

I feel curiously numb, indifferent to what I'm reading. A sudden chill hangs in the air; I've begun to shiver and I feel a bit dizzy. It's as though this wake will never end; they'll never come to take away the coffin so the gossipmongers can finally go home. Compared to my clients' sneers, the innuendos of this strange tale barely made me flinch; they bounce off me like harmless needles. After all, I've a clear conscience. I was a good wife to Lorenzo and a good mother to Rosaura. That's the only thing that matters. It's true I insisted on our moving to town, and it did us a lot of good. It's true I insisted he make me the sole executrix of his estate, but that was because I felt I was better fit to administer it than Rosaura while she's still a minor, because she lives with her head in the clouds. But I never threatened to leave him, that's a treacherous lie. The family finances were going from bad to worse and each day we were closer to bankruptcy, but Lorenzo didn't seem to care. He'd always been capricious and whimsical, and he picked precisely that difficult time in our lives to sit down and write a book about the patriots of our island's independence struggle.

From morning till night he'd go on scribbling page after page about our lost identity, tragically maimed by the "invasion" of 1898, when the truth was that our islanders welcomed the Marines with open arms. It's true that, as Lorenzo wrote in his book, for almost a hundred years we've lived on the verge of civil war, but the only ones who want independence on this island are the romantic and the rich; the ruined landowners who still dream of the past as of a paradise lost; the frustrated, small-town writers; the bitter politicians with a thirst for power and monumental ambitions. The poor of this island have always been for commonwealth or statehood, because they'd rather be dead than squashed once again under the patent leather boot of the bourgeoisie. Each country knows which leg it limps on, and our people know that the rich of this land have always been a plague of vultures. And today they're still doing it; those families are still trying to scalp the land, calling themselves pro-American and friends of the Yankees to keep their goodwill, when deep down they wish they'd leave, so they would graze once again on the poor man's empty guts.

On Rosaura's next birthday, Don Lorenzo gave his daughter the usual book of stories. Rosaura, for her part, decided to cook her father's favorite guava compote for him, following one of her mother's old recipes. As she stirred the bubbling, bloodlike syrup on the stove, the compote's aroma gradually filled the house. At that moment Rosaura felt so happy, she thought she saw her mother waft in and out of the window several times, on a guava-colored cloud. That evening, Don Lorenzo was in a cheerful mood as he sat down to dinner. He ate with more relish than usual, and after dinner he gave Rosaura her book of short stories, with her initials elegantly monogrammed in gold, and bound in gleaming doe-heart's skin. Ignoring his wife's furrowed brow, he browsed with his daughter through the exquisite volume, whose thick gold-leaf edges and elegant bindings shone brightly on the lace tablecloth. Sitting stiffly, Rosa looked on in silence, an icy smile playing on her lips. She was dressed in her most luxurious opulent lace gown, as she and Don Lorenzo were to attend a formal dinner at the mayor's mansion that evening. She was trying hard to keep her patience with Rosaura because she was convinced that being angry made even the most beautifully dressed woman look ugly.

Don Lorenzo then began to humor his wife, trying to bring her out of her dark mood. He held the book out to her, so she might also enjoy its lavish illustrations of kings and queens, all sumptuously dressed in brocade robes. "They could very well inspire some of your fashionable designs for the incoming season, my dear. Although it would probably take a few more bolts of silk to cover your fullness than it took to cover theirs, I wouldn't mind footing the bill because you're a lovable, squeezable woman, and not a stuck-up, storybook doll," he teased her, as he covertly pinched her behind.

Poor Lorenzo, you truly did love me. You had a wonderful sense of humor, and your jokes always made me laugh until my eyes teared. Unyielding and distant, Rosa found the joke in poor taste and showed no interest at all in the book's illustrations. When father and daughter were finally done admiring them, Rosaura got up from her place and went to the kitchen to fetch the guava compote, which had been spreading its delightful perfume through the house all day. As she approached the table, however, she tripped and dropped the silver serving dish, spattering her stepmother's skirt.

I knew something had been bothering me for a while, and now I finally know what it is. The guava compote incident took place years ago, when we still lived in the country and Rosaura was almost a child. The small-town writer is lying again; he's shamelessly and knowingly altered the order of events. He gives the impression the scene he's retelling took place recently, that it actually took place only three months ago, but it's been almost six years since Lorenzo sold the farm. Anyone would think Rosaura was still a girl, when in fact she's a grown woman. She takes after her mother more and more; she fiddles away her time daydreaming, refuses to make herself useful, and lives off the honest sweat of those of us who work.

I remember the guava compote incident clearly. We were on our way to a cocktail party at the mayor's house because he'd finally made you an offer on the sale of the hacienda, which you had nostalgically named "The Sundowns," and the people of the town had rebaptized "Curly Cunt Downs," in revenge for your aristocratic airs. At first you were offended and turned him down, but when the mayor suggested he would restore the house as a historic landmark, where the mementos of the sugar-cane-growing aristocracy would be preserved for future generations, you promised to think about it. The decision finally came when I managed to persuade you, after hours of endless arguments under our bed's threadbare canopy, that we couldn't go on living in that huge house, with no electricity, no hot water, and no adequate toilet facilities; and where one had to move one's bowels on an antique French Provincial latrine, which had been a gift to your grandfather from King Alphonse XII. That's why I was wearing that awful dress the day of Rosaura's petty tantrum. I had managed to cut it from our brocade living-room curtains, just as Vivien Leigh had done in *Gone With the Wind*, and its gaudy frills and garish flounces were admittedly in the worst of taste. But I knew that was the only way to impress the mayor's high-flown wife and cater to her boorish, aristocratic longings. The mayor finally bought the house, with all the family antiques and *objets d'art*, but not to turn it into a museum, as you had so innocently believed, but to enjoy it himself as his opulent country house.

Rosa stood up horrified and stared at the blood-colored streaks of syrup that trickled slowly down her skirt, until they reached the silk embossed buckles of her shoes. She was trembling with rage, and at first couldn't get a single word out. When her soul finally came back to her body, she began calling Rosaura names, accusing her shrilly of living in a storybook world, while she, Rosa, worked her fingers to the bone in order to keep them all fed. Those damned books were to blame for the girl's shiftlessness, and as they were also undeniable proof of Don Lorenzo's preference for Rosaura, and of the fact that he held his daughter in higher esteem than his wife, she had no choice but to leave him. Unless, of course, Rosaura agreed to get rid of all her books, which should immediately be collected in a heap in the backyard, where they would be set on fire.

Maybe it's the smoking candles, maybe it's the heavy scent of all those myrtles Rosaura heaped on the coffin, but I'm feeling dizzier. I can't stop my hands from trembling and my palms are moist with sweat. The story has begun to fester in some remote corner of my mind, poisoning me with its dregs of resentment. As soon as she ended her speech, Rosa went deathly pale and fell forward to the floor in a heap. Terrified at his wife's fainting spell, Don Lorenzo knelt down beside her and begged her in a faltering voice not to leave him. He promised he'd do everything she'd asked for, if only she'd stay and forgive him. Pacified by his promises, Rosa opened her eyes and smiled at her husband. As a token of goodwill at their reconciliation, she allowed Rosaura to keep her books and promised she wouldn't burn them.

That night Rosaura hid her birthday gift under her pillow and wept herself to sleep. She had an unusual dream. She dreamt that one of the tales in her book had been cursed with a mysterious power that would instantly destroy its first reader. The author had gone to great lengths to leave a sign, a definite clue in the story which would serve as a warning, but try as she might in her dream, Rosaura couldn't bring herself to remember what that sign had been. When she finally woke up she was in a cold sweat, but she was still in the dark as to whether the story worked its evil through the ear, the tongue, or the skin.

Don Lorenzo died peacefully in his bed a few months later, comforted by the cares and prayers of his loving wife and daughter. His body had been solemnly laid out in the parlor for all to see, bedecked with wreaths and surrounded by smoking candles, when Rosa came into the room, carrying in her hand a book elegantly bound in red and gold leather, Don Lorenzo's last gift to Rosaura. Friends and relatives all stopped talking when they saw her walk in. She nodded a distant hello to the mayor's wife and went to sit by herself in a corner of the room, as though in need of some peace and quiet to comfort her in her sadness. She opened the book at random and began to turn the pages slowly, pretending she was reading but really admiring the illustrations of the fashionably dressed ladies and queens. As she leafed through the pages, she couldn't help thinking that now that she was a woman of means, she could well afford one of those lavish robes for herself. Suddenly, she came to a story that caught her eye. Unlike the others, it had no drawings, and it had been printed in a thick, guava-colored ink she'd never seen before. The first sentence took her mildly by surprise, because the heroine's name was the same as her stepdaughter's. Her curiosity kindled, she read on quickly, moistening the pages with her index finger because the guava-colored ink made them stick to each other annoyingly. She went from wonder to amazement and from amazement to horror, but in spite of her growing panic, she couldn't make herself stop reading. The story began . . . "Rosaura lived in a house of many balconies, shadowed by a dense overgrowth of crimson bougainvillea vines . . . ," and how the story ended, Rosa never knew.

BLOOD

Janice Galloway

Janice Galloway was born in Ayrshire, Scotland, where she taught for ten years. Her first book, *The Trick is to Keep Breathing*, won a Scottish Arts Council Book Award and was shortlisted for the Whitbread First Novel Award and the Scottish First Book of the Year. She is working on another novel. "Blood" is from her collection of the same title and also appeared in *The New Gothic*.

The word "blood" is a powerful one. It's loaded with connotations, particularly when juxtaposed with an adolescent girl. Although the blood in this story is from a tooth extraction, the power of the piece resides in all the symbolic and literal meanings of the word.

—E.D.

He put his knee up on her chest getting ready to pull, tilting the pliers. Sorry, he said. Sorry. She couldn't see his face. The pores on the backs of his fingers sprouted hairs, single black wires curling onto the bleached skin of the wrist, the veins showing through. She saw an artery move under the surface as he slackened the grip momentarily, catching his breath; his cheeks a kind of mauve color, twisting at something inside her mouth. The bones in his hand were bruising her lip. And that sound of the gum tugging back from what he was doing, the jaw creaking. Her jaw. If you closed your eyes it made you feel dizzy, imagining it, and this through the four jags of anesthetic, that needle as big as a power drill. Better to keep her eyes open, trying to focus past the blur of knuckles to the cracked ceiling. She was trying to see a pattern, make the lines into something she could recognize, when her mouth started to do something she hadn't given it permission for. A kind of suction. There was a moment of nothing while he steadied his hand, as if she had only imagined the give. She heard herself swallow and stop breathing. Then her spine lifting, arching from the seat, the gum parting with a sound like uprooting potatoes, a coolness in her mouth and he was holding something up in the metal clamp; great bloody lump of it, white trying to surface through the red. He was pleased.

There you go eh? Never seen one like that before. The root of the problem ha ha.

All his fillings showed when he laughed, holding the thing out, wanting her to look. Blood made a pool under her tongue, lapping at the back of her throat and she had to keep the head back instead. Her lips were too numb to trust: it would have run down the front of her blazer.

Rinse, he said. Cough and spit.

When she sat up he was holding the tooth out on a tissue, roots like a yellow clawhammer at the end, one point wrapping the other.

See the twist? Unusual to see something like that. Little twist in the roots.

Like a deformed parsnip. And there was a bit of flesh, a piece of gum or something nipped off between the crossed tips of bone.

Little rascal, he said.

Her mouth was filling up, she turned to the metal basin before he started singing again. *She's leaving now cos I just heard the slamming of the door* then humming. He didn't really know the words. She spat dark red and thick into the basin. When she resurfaced, he was looking at her and wiping his hands on something like a dishtowel.

Expect it'll bleed for a while, bound to be messy after that bother. Just take your time getting up. Take your time there. No rush.

She had slid to the edge of the chair, dunting the hooks and probes with having to hold on. The metal noise made her teeth sore. Her stomach felt terrible and she had to sit still, waiting to see straight.

Fine in a minute, he said. Wee walk in the fresh air. Wee walk back to school.

He finished wiping his hands and grinned, holding something out. A hard thing inside tissue. The tooth.

You made it, you have it haha. There you go. How's the jaw?

She nodded, and pointed to her mouth. This almost audible sound of a tank filling, a rising tide over the edges of the tongue.

Bleed for a while like I say. Don't worry though. Redheads always bleed worse than other folk. Haha. Sandra'll get you something: stop you making a mess of yourself.

Sandra was already away. He turned to rearrange the instruments she had knocked out of their neat arrangement on the green cloth.

Redheads, see. *Don't take your love to town.*

Maybe it was a joke. She tried to smile back till the blood started silting again. He walked over to the window as Sandra came back with a white pad in her hand. The pad had gauze over the top, very thick with a blue stripe down one side. Loops. A sanitary towel. The dentist was still turned away, looking out of the window and wiping his specs and talking. It took a minute to realize he was talking to her. It should stop in about an hour or so he was saying. Maybe three at the outside. Sandra pushed the pad out for her to take. If not by six o'clock let him know and they could give her a shot of something ok? Looking out the whole time. She tried to listen, tucking the loops at the ends of the towel in where they wouldn't be obvious, blushing when she put it up to her mouth. It was impossible to tell if they were being serious or not. The dentist turned back, grinning at the spectacles he was holding between his hands.

Sandra given you a wee special there. Least said haha. Redheads eh? *Oh Roooobeee*, not looking, wiping the same lens over and over with a cloth.

The fresh air was good. Two deep lungfuls before she wrapped her scarf round the white pad at her mouth and walked. The best way from the surgery was past the flats with bay windows and gardens. Some had trees, crocuses, and bits of cane. Better than up by the building site, full of those shouting men. One of them always shouted things, whistled loud enough to make the whole street turn and look. Bad enough at the best of times. Today would have been awful. This way was longer but prettier and there was nothing to stop her taking her time. She had permission. No need to worry about getting there for some particular ring of some particular bell. Permission made all the difference. The smell of bacon rolls at the café fetched her nose coffee and chocolate. They spoiled when they reached her mouth, heaped up with sanitary towel and the blood still coming. Her tongue wormed toward the soft place, the dip where the tooth had been, then back between tongue root and the backs of her teeth. Thick fluid. A man was crossing the road, a greyhound on a thin lead, a woman with a pram coming past the phone box. Besides, girls didn't spit in the street. School wasn't that far though, not if she walked fast. She clutched the tooth tight in her pocket and walked, head down. The pram was there before she expected it; sudden metal spokes too near her shoes before she looked up, eyes and nose over the white rim of gauze. The woman not even noticing but keeping on, plowing up the road while she waited at the curb with her eyes on the gutter, trying hard not to swallow. Six streets and a park to go. Six streets.

The school had no gate, just a gap in the wall with pillars on either side that led into the playground. The blacked-out window was the staff room; the others showed occasional heads, some white faces watching. The music block was nearest. Quarter to twelve. It would be possible to wait in the practice rooms till the dinner bell in fifteen minutes and not shift till the afternoon. She was in no mood, though, not even for that. Not even for the music. It wouldn't be possible to play well. But there was no point in going home either because everything would have to be explained in triplicate when the mother got in and she never believed you anyway. It was all impossible. The pad round her mouth was slimy already, the wet going cold farther at the far sides. She could go over and ask Mrs. McNiven for another towel and just go anyway, have a lie-down or something but that meant going over to the other block, all the way across the playground again and the faces looking out knowing where you were going because it was the only time senior girls went there. And this thing round her mouth. Her stomach felt terrible too. She suddenly wanted to be in the music rooms, soothing herself with music. Something peaceful. Going there made her feel better just because of where it was. Not like at home. You could just go and play to your heart's content. That would be nice now, right now this minute, going up there and playing something: the Mozart she'd been working on, something fresh and clean. Turning, letting the glass door close, she felt her throat thicken, closing over with film. And that fullness that said the blood was still coming. A sigh into the towel stung her eyes. The girls' toilets were on the next landing.

Yellow. The light, the sheen off the mirrors. It was always horrible coming here. She could usually manage to get through the days without having to, waiting till she got home and drinking nothing. Most of the girls did the same, even just to avoid the felt-tip drawings on the girls' door—mostly things like split melons only they weren't. All that pretending you couldn't see them on the way in and what went with them, GIRLS ARE A BUNCH OF CUNTS still visible under the diagonal scores of the cleaners' Vim. Impossible to argue against so you made out it wasn't there, swanning past the word CUNTS though it radiated like a black sun all the way from the other end of the corridor. Terrible. And inside, the yellow lights always on, nearly all the mirrors with cracks or warps. Her own face reflected yellow over the nearside row of sinks. She clamped her mouth tight and reached for the towel loops. Its peeling away made her mouth suddenly cold. In her hand, the pad had creased up the center, ridged where it had settled between her lips and smeared with crimson on the one side. Not as bad as she had thought, but the idea of putting it back wasn't good. She wrapped it in three paper towels instead and stuffed it to the bottom of the wire bin under the rest, bits of paper and God knows what, then leaned over the sinks, rubbing at the numbness in her jaw, rinsing out. Big, red drips when she tried to open her mouth. And something else. She watched the slow tail of red on the white enamel, concentrating. Something slithered in her stomach, a slow dullness that made it difficult to straighten up again. Then a twinge in her back, a recognizable contraction. That's what the sweating was, then, the churning in her gut. It wasn't just not feeling well with the swallowing and imagining things. Christ. It wasn't supposed to be due for a week yet. She'd have to use that horrible toilet paper and it would get sore and slip about all day. Better that than asking Mrs. McNiven for two towels, though, anything was better than asking Mrs. McNiven. The cold tap spat water along the length of one blazer arm. She was turning it the wrong way. For a frightening moment, she couldn't think how to turn it off then managed, breathing out, tilting forward. It would be good to get out of here, get to something fresh and clean, Mozart and the white room upstairs. She would patch something together and just pretend she wasn't bleeding so much, wash her hands and be fit for things. The white keys. She pressed her forehead against the cool concrete of the facing wall, swallowing. The taste of blood like copper in her mouth, lips pressed tight.

The smallest practice room was free. The best one: the rosewood piano and the soundproofing made it feel warm. There was no one in either of the other two except the student who taught cello. She didn't know his name, just what he did. He never spoke. Just sat in there all the time waiting for pupils, playing or looking out of the window. Anything to avoid catching sight of people. Mr. Gregg said he was afraid of the girls and who could blame him haha. She'd never understood the joke too well but it seemed to be right enough. He sometimes didn't even answer the door if you knocked or made out he couldn't see you when he went by you on the stairs. It was possible to count yourself alone, then, if he was the only one here. It was possible to relax. She sat on the piano stool, hunched over her stomach, rocking. C-major triad. This piano had a nice tone, brittle and light. The other two made a fatter, fuzzier noise altogether. This one was leaner, right for the Mozart anyway. Descending chromatic scale with the right hand. The left moved in the blazer pocket, ready to surface, tipping something soft. Crushed tissue, something hard in the middle. The tooth. She had almost forgotten about the tooth. Her back straightened to bring it out, unfold the bits of tissue to hold it up to the light. It had a ridge about a third of the way down, where the glaze of enamel stopped. Below it, the roots were huge, matte like suede. The twist was huge, still bloody where they crossed. Whatever it was they had pulled out with them, the piece of skin, had disappeared. Hard to accept her body had grown this thing. Ivory. She smiled and laid it aside on the wood slat at the top of the keyboard, like a misplaced piece of inlay. It didn't match. The keys were whiter.

Just past the hour already. In four minutes the bell would go and the noise would start: people coming in to stake claims on the rooms, staring in through the glass panels on the door. Arpeggios bounced from next door. The student would be warming up for somebody's lesson, waiting. She turned back to the keys, sighing. Her mouth was filling up again, her head thumping. Fingers looking yellow when she stretched them out, reaching for chords. Her stomach contracted. But if she could just concentrate, forget her body and let the notes come, it wouldn't matter. You could get past things that way, pretend they weren't there. She leaned toward the keyboard, trying to be something else: a piece of music. Mozart, the recent practice. Feeling for the clear, clean lines. Listening. She ignored the pain in her stomach, the pressure of paper towels at her thighs, and watched the keys, the pressure of her fingers that buried or released them. And watching, listening to Mozart, she let the music get louder, and the door opened, the abrupt tearing sound of the doorseals seizing her stomach like a fist. The student was suddenly there and smiling to cover the knot on his forehead where the fear showed, smiling fit to bust, saying, Don't stop, it's lovely; Haydn isn't it? and she opened her mouth not able to stop, opened her mouth to say Mozart. It's Mozart—before she remembered.

Welling up behind the lower teeth, across her lips as she tilted forward to keep it off her clothes. Spilling over the white keys and dripping onto the clean tile floor. She saw his face change, the glance flick to the claw roots in the tissue before he shut the door hard, not knowing what else to do. And the bell rang, the steady howl of it as the outer doors gave, footfalls in the corridor gathering like an avalanche. They would be here before she could do anything, sitting dumb on the piano stool, not able to move, not able to breathe, at this blood streaking over the keys, silting the action. The howl of the bell. This unstoppable redness seeping through the fingers at her open mouth.

DOGSTAR MAN
Nancy Willard

Nancy Willard has won the O. Henry Award and the Newbery Award for her novel *A Visit to William Blake's Inn*. She has also published several volumes of short stories and poetry, picture books for children, and the adult novel *Things Invisible to See*. Willard lives in Poughkeepsie, New York, where she teaches in the English department at Vassar.

"Dogstar Man" is a quiet and moving story of American magic realism, set on the outskirts of Madison, Wisconsin. It comes from the pages of *Full Spectrum 3*.

—T.W.

When I was twelve years old, my father, who rarely touched anything stronger than 7UP, got mildly drunk with a man named Olaf Starr who kept a dog team. This happened in Madison, Wisconsin, where I grew up. My father, Carl Theophilus, owned the Treble and Bass Music Store there. Maybe you've heard of it. The store carried accordions, drums, trumpets, harmonicas, guitars, pitch pipes, tambourines, and sheet music. Five free lessons came with all the instruments, except the harmonica, and my father built a tiny soundproof practice room in the back. Saturday mornings a boy from Madison High School came to give the free lessons to languid young girls, who emerged from the practice room sweaty and bright-eyed, all of them promising to practice. My father also repaired instruments. By the time I was in high school, he'd sold the business and was doing repairs full time and making lutes, dulcimers, and Irish harps on commission.

He kept shelves of exotic woods, rosewood and purple heart, teak and lignum vitae. One man ordered a guitar made of lignum vitae for his son, who played in a rock band and smashed his instrument every night, but by God, he wouldn't be smashing this one. Mainly my father stocked the commoner varieties, basswood and oak and black cherry and ash, which he used for the curved bodies of the lutes and the harps. He also had a few odd pieces of golden chinkapin and water tupulo, hornbeam and hackleberry, for which there wasn't much demand except when he did inlay work on the sound holes of the lutes. You never knew, he said, what a customer would ask for. He wouldn't work with ivory, out of respect for the elephants, though he has always loved Chinese ivory carvings, especially those

313

that keep the shape of the tusk. I believe there's not a book on Asian art in the Madison public library that my father hasn't checked out.

Olaf Starr lived outside of Madison on land that his father had once farmed. All the Starr Cheese in Wisconsin was made there, and it was a big business in the thirties and forties. That ended when Olaf took over. Forty years later, when I was growing up, the house was gone and the barn that stood in the north acre was in ruins; snow had caved in the roof, leaving a confusion of broken timber in its wake that made me feel I was peering into the stomach of a vast beast. The windows of the stable were broken, and stars winked through the holes left by shingles that had blown or rotted off. Over the stalls, you could still read the names of horses: Beauty; Misty; Athena. Behind the stable, Olaf Starr parked his pickup truck.

On the south acre, Olaf had built himself a log cabin and a dog yard, with seven small cabins, low to the ground, for his dogs. After a heavy snowfall, he would hitch them up and drive to a general store just in town. No one else in Madison drove a dogsled. Mornings when I went out cross-country skiing on the golf course behind our house, I might catch a glimpse of him on the horizon, his dogs strung out in a thin line, like Christmas lights, with Olaf Starr standing on the back runners of the sled. I called him the dogstar man, and I half expected to see him drive into the heavens. He was a big man, with white hair, who carried a knapsack and wore the same Levi's, suspenders, down jacket and boots, day after day, shedding the jacket in summer, resurrecting it at the first snowfall.

My father said that the dogstar man's wife had left long ago for a more comfortable life of her own, so during the one night I spent at the cabin I never met or saw any evidence of her. I was in sixth grade and trying to write a report on cheese as part of a unit on agriculture. I did not like agriculture, which was a vast general thing. You could not put anything in the report about how cows look, standing in a rolling field, though that is so important it should come first. From far away, they look like ciphers that someone has written with a thick brown pen, and I wished I could write my whole report using the ponderous alphabet of cows. And you could not put in anything about the hiss of milk in the pail, or the salt licks that rise in the fields like dolmens or ancient shrines, and you could not put in the peculiar appetites of goats for wind-dried bedsheets on the line and children's sunsuits and anything scented with human use.

So I asked the teacher, Mrs. Hanson, if I could write a story about cheese, and she said, yes, but it could not be a fairy tale. The cheese must not talk or sing or dance or have adventures. The story must be about how cheese is made. I could write that story.

I did not know the first thing about how cheese is made. My father told me to go to the library and find a book that would tell me. But my mother said, "Go and watch somebody making it. That's better than a book." My father agreed and suggested I call the Wisconsin Wilderness processing plant to see if they gave tours.

Suddenly my parents had the same thought at the same time and said almost in unison.

"Olaf Starr makes cheese. He'd be glad to show you."

The dogstar man had no phone, so on Saturday afternoon my father drove out to the farm. Ten inches of snow had fallen a week ago, and the cold had kept it on the ground, though the main roads were clear. My father turned off I-90 and took the road less traveled. The dogsled track cut a deep ribbon across the white fields on either side of us, and where the road ended at the broken barn and we got out of the car, the sled track disappeared into a pine woods.

You could hear the dogs yapping and yelping. A hundred seemed a modest estimate.

"We should've brought our skis," said my father.

That would have been far easier than walking in, which took us twice as long. I'd seen the outside of the dogstar man's house in summer but not in winter, and I'd never seen the inside.

In the dog yard, seven hounds sat on the roofs of their houses and barked at us, and the hair on my neck prickled in a primitive response to danger.

"They're tied," said my father.

Only when I saw that they could not spring far from the stakes to which they were leashed did I begin to savor the adventure of doing something entirely new. I thought of our yard, so small and neat that when my mother bought two metal lawn chairs and a patio umbrella, my father complained of the clutter. The dogstar man's yard was a sprawl of empty cable spools, old oil drums, ropes, ski poles, harnesses and the dogsled itself, which hung from a row of pegs on the cabin wall. The grass on the sod roof was blond.

The dogstar man, hearing the racket, opened the door. He knew my father as a man who ordered firewood from him; he was surprised to see both of us on his doorstep. His face remained perfectly impassive as my father explained our errand while I stared at Olaf Starr with the greatest interest, as if I were examining a hawk or an otter, some wild creature always seen in motion and from a distance.

A brief silence marked the end of my father's speech, and when the dogstar man was quite certain it *was* the end, he nodded and motioned us into his house. It was not so much a house as a lair, a den, that an animal might make and stock with all that instinct told him would carry him through the winter. Firewood was stacked solid against one wall. Against the opposite wall stood five fifty-gallon drums of water, a shelf of dishes and crocks and large cooking pots, a treadle sewing machine, and a dozen huge bags of dog food.

From under the four burners on the surface of the wood stove shone a thin rim of fire. The flame in the oil lamp on the table danced in its glass chimney with such shifting brilliance that the air in the cabin seemed to be alive and breathing, steadily and quietly.

My father and I drew two stools up to the table.

The dogstar man took down a large crock and set it on the table between us.

"The secret of cheese is patience," he said. "Cheese has taught me everything I know about life."

He set three spoons and three brass bowls of different sizes on the table.

"I traded a year's supply of firewood to a professor at the university for these. And when I got them home, I made a discovery. Listen."

He brushed his hand over the rim of the largest and a deep hum filled the room.

He brushed the smallest and a higher hum, a fifth above the first, spun out of it. He brushed the last bowl, and it sent forth a note that completed the triad. But if I say the bowls hummed, I do not tell you *how* they hummed. Not like a cat or a spinning wheel, but like a planet whirling down the dark aisles of the galaxy.

"The best way to make cheese is, put it in singing bowls," said the dogstar man. "This is also the best way to eat it."

He dipped a spoon into the crock and began to ladle cottage cheese from the crock into the bowls.

"Also," he said, "the voice of the bowls quiets the dogs."

My father, astonished into silence by all these marvels, found his voice.

"But these are singing bowls from Tibet," he exclaimed. "I'm sure they're worth a good deal of money. If you ever want to sell them, come to me with a price."

"But I won't sell them," said the dogstar man. "I'll trade them for something I need."

"What do you need?" asked my father.

"Nothing now," he said, "but next week, dog food. I buy dog food by the ton. Ground barley is good," he mused, "and fish meal."

He spooned cottage cheese from the crock into the bowls.

"When I was at the university, I didn't study at all."

"You went to the university?" exclaimed my father.

"For one year, in 1927. And when my father asked me what I was majoring in I told him I wanted to major in philosophy. Philosophy! He didn't understand about philosophy. I told him that philosophers consider problems of time and what is the true good. I told him it was like majoring in cheese; something solid emerges from what is thin and without definition."

The whole of our visit, he talked and talked—and not one word about how to make cheese. The next day my mother took me to the public library where the Encyclopaedia Britannica revealed to me the secret of making cheese. In my report, I mentioned rennet and casein. I did not mention singing bowls, and I did not write a story. I got my report back with praise from Mrs. Hanson written across the top: *Good work, Sam! You put in a lot of information and you stuck to your subject.*

The next afternoon the dogstar man appeared in my father's music store. He admired the guitars, the accordions, the new shipment of tambourines, and asked him if he could make a whistle that the dogs could hear from a great distance.

"How great a distance?" asked my father.

The dogstar man opened his pack, drew out a map of the United States, and spread it out on the counter.

"Here," he said. "I'm planning to visit my sister, and I want my dogs to know I'm thinking of them."

And he put his thumb down on the whole state of Florida.

In three days, my father finished the whistle, and the dogstar man drew from his pack the largest singing bowl and gave it to him. It was as if an honored guest had moved in with us. My father made a little house for the bowl to sit in, a replica of a Tibetan spirit house, he said. This he put on top of the china cabinet.

Once a day the bowl was played. Sometimes my mother played it, sometimes I played it, and sometimes he played it himself. Often I dreamed of whales singing, a music I did not yet know existed.

A week later the dogstar man returned and said he wanted to exchange the whistle that called dogs for one that called birds. So many of the birds he loved had gone south. He wanted to let them know he'd welcome them back any time, if the warm countries weren't to their liking.

"Why did you tell me to make a whistle that calls dogs if you wanted one that calls birds?" asked my father.

The dogstar man was interested in more practical questions.

"Can you fix it so it will call both?"

My father said he would try. He added a section of wingwood with a dovetail joint that was nearly invisible, and the dogstar man was very pleased and said it was exactly what he wanted. He reached into his knapsack and pulled out the medium-sized singing bowl. My father closed the shop and carried it home at once and nested it in the other bowl, in the little spirit house.

The bowls were not beautiful but they were immensely present, and when we ate in the dining room we were always aware of them, and we did not complain about the cold weather or who should have taken out the garbage the night before. No, we were pleasant to one another, in the way that people are pleasant before a guest or stranger to whom they wish to show their best side.

A postcard arrived from Paradise, Florida, showing the roseate spoonbill in glorious flight. The dogstar man's message was brief: "It works!"

Three days before Christmas, the dogstar man appeared again, holding the whistle.

"This whistle," he said. "I wonder if you could fix it."

"In what way is it broken?" asked my father.

"It's not broken," the dogstar man assured him. "I just wonder if you could improve it."

"Improve it?"

"I was wondering," said the dogstar man, "if you could fix it so it would call stars."

"Stars!"

"I thought I'd get me in some ice fishing. The fish do like clear nights best."

My father took the whistle back. The section he added this time was purely ornamental. He cut it from coral, which has no resonating properties, and he vowed to go the dogstar man one better. He added a link of hornbeam, on which young stags love to rub their budding antlers; and a link of alder, which beavers prefer above all other trees for building dams; and a link of mulberry, whose small dark fruit the wood mouse loves. He did not cut these links into simple rings but joined them in interlocking shapes, pieced with bits of shell and horn, bone and silver.

On a Saturday morning, when I was helping my father put new price stickers on the sheet music, the dogstar man arrived, and my father gave him the improved whistle and waited for some sign of praise, a whistle of admiration, perhaps.

But the dogstar man said nothing about my father's exquisite workmanship. He tucked the whistle into his breast pocket and reached into his knapsack and took out the smallest singing bowl and set it on the counter.

Then he looked at me and said,

"Do you like books?"

"Sure," I said. I never say no to a book.

Out of his knapsack he pulled a volume bound in leather softer than the chamois my father used to polish the violins. When he put it into my hands, I felt he had just given me a small animal seldom seen and beautiful to the blind who see with their fingers.

I opened it to the title page: *Palmer Cox's Juvenile Budget, Containing Queer People with Paws, Claws, Wings, Stings, and Others Without Either.*

"This book was mine when I was your age," he said. "Merry Christmas."

I flipped through the book and thought, What a god-awful present. The stories, all of them in poetry and small print, were crammed on the yellowing pages, and the illustrations, done in scratchy pen and ink, crowded into the text as best they could. Still, I was the kind of kid who would read anything, and I knew I would have a go at the *Juvenile Budget.* But I could not say it gladdened my heart.

"Thank you," I said.

My father had the habit of carrying the spirit house, with its nested singing bowls, from room to room, to keep them near him. On Christmas Eve he put them on the mantel to watch over the tree. Of course I did not believe in Santa Claus, but I played the game and so did my mother and father. Growing up is watching faith descend to the level of a beloved ritual.

At nine o'clock I put my two presents under the tree: a Sheaffer pen, which I bought at the drugstore, and a pillow with the name Jerry Garcia embroidered on it, which I made in school after the principal went to a conference on new trends in education and became convinced that boys should take home ec for one semester while the girls took shop. I was not convinced. I would never make one of those sleek, useful projects the teacher recommended. I would not even make a pattern. The pillow turned out to be the size of an overgrown pincushion, nothing you'd choose to sit on, unless you had hemorrhoids. I knew Mother would love it because it looked handmade.

The card said, "For Mother and Father," as the pen and pillow were suitable for both.

At ten o'clock, when I announced I was going up to bed, so as not to displease Santa, my mother looked relieved. She had all the presents to wrap yet. I hung my stocking under the singing bowls and was halfway up the stairs when the doorbell rang and the door, which was unlocked, burst open.

The dogstar man filled the front hall with his enthusiasm. He'd spent the day ice fishing on Waubesa Lake. He'd pulled from the still, chill bottom of the lake three bass, two trout, a sunfish, and a pike, and he was the first person in the county to catch a two-point buck with a fishhook. He'd brought in enough meat to feed himself the rest of the winter.

He pulled out a bottle of schnapps and presented it to my father and lingered, waiting for him to open it.

I could not possibly go to bed now. I might miss something.

My father and the dogstar man sat down at the dining room table and drank. That is to say, the dogstar man drank a lot and my father nursed a single shot glass, which was nevertheless enough to skew his judgment. He did not even remember to bring his singing bowls with him.

"All I own of value in this world is my sled and my dogs," said the dogstar man, "and when I am gone, no man is worthier to have them than yourself. Give me pen and paper, and I will write my will."

Every shred of scrap paper, which usually cluttered around the telephone, had vanished from sight, and my father could find nothing better than a circular for a grand sale at Happy Jack's—"Everything must go, to the bare walls." The dogstar man turned it over, and on the blank side wrote his will, making my father heir to seven dogs. He ended by writing out the names of the dogs, along with their rank in harness.

> Swing dogs: Eleanor Roosevelt and John Kennedy
> Team dogs: Lou Gehrig and Babe Ruth
> Wheel dogs: Finn McCool and Melville
> Lead dog: Hermes

Then he turned to me and my mother.

"I've left space for you to sign. Two witnesses."

To humor him, my mother signed. I signed because I'd never been asked to witness anything before and I did not want to pass up this opportunity. Without reading it over, the dogstar man pocketed his will, shook hands with each of us and took his unsteady leave, and my father and mother thought no more on the matter.

At midnight on Christmas Eve, the snow started falling, and it did not stop until the next afternoon. And then, quite unexpectedly, it turned warm.

The day before New Year's Eve, the dogstar man disappeared. A skier, hearing the howling and baying of seven ravenous huskies, called the police. Because the snow around the dog yard was deep and undisturbed by human tracks, the police broke into the dogstar man's cabin. The presence of the will on the kitchen table suggested suicide, but the circumstances of his death convinced them otherwise. At the lake they found the dogstar man's pickup truck. On the ice they found the shelter he'd built. The current ran strong under the thin ice where the shore curved toward the jagged hole in the ice, through which they concluded he had fallen. They did not find the man himself. It is hard to grieve for a man who has disappeared and who might return someday. I think my father and mother expected to receive another postcard from him. We did not really believe he was dead until the sheriff stopped by our house and asked my father to come and fetch his dogs.

Seven dogs at a stroke! Neither my father nor my mother knew the first thing about caring for dogs. Days of lawn chairs and umbrellas, farewell! My father bought a book called *Your Sled Dogs and How to Care for Them* and hired a man to put in seven tethering stakes and help him move the sled and bags of dog food and the doghouses into the backyard. Then he phoned a veterinarian, Dr. James Herrgott, and told him what had befallen us.

Dr. Herrgott made a house call and examined the dogs. From the kitchen window, we watched him, a tall lean figure in a wool cap and down jacket and boots and Levi's with holes in the knees. One by one, he knelt before each dog, examined its fur, its eyes, the lining of its mouth.

Wrapped in an aura of cold air, he sat down at our kitchen table and told us what we owned. Finn McCool and John Kennedy and Melville and Eleanor Roosevelt and Babe Ruth and Lou Gehrig were young dogs, between two and three years old, all mixed-breed huskies. Hermes was at least five years old and part Siberian husky.

"One of the big old-style freighting dogs," he observed. "Most mushers nowadays like the smaller breeds."

My father looked terrified. For the first time, I perceived a weakness in him and a superior strength in myself, and I took on the job of feeding the dogs in the morning. This meant rising at six instead of seven; ten minutes' snoozing and I'd miss the school bus. The front door slamming shut in the milky light before dawn would wake them, and by the time I'd hauled the big canister of dog food into the yard, they would be yapping and tugging at their chains and stretching, their tails switching and waving like flags. The smell of their food—a thin yellow gruel of ground barley and fish meal and fat, which I ladled into deep tin bowls—made my father nauseous.

After school I fed them again and fetched a shovel and cleaned the dog yard.

My mother assigned herself the task of putting fresh hay in the doghouses. That was a fragrant and pleasant occupation; the dogs would crawl into the hay and move round and round, hollowing it into a nest.

Sometimes my father ran the dogs and sometimes I did it, but soon he relinquished that job too, because I enjoyed doing it and he did not. The intricate maneuvers of running dogs in harness daunted him. He could never remember who hated whom and what dogs got on well together.

After school I slipped their harnesses on and hitched them to the sled and we headed for the golf course behind the house. I never saw snow so deep that Hermes could not break a trail in it. When we crossed the frozen stream at the back of the course, the clicking of their toenails on the ice always startled them. I loved the crossing; the shadow we cast on that bright surface made a grand sight.

In February the temperature fell to thirty-five below and stayed there. My mother could not bear to leave any animal outside in that weather. My father reminded her that we had no basement, no garage, no shed of any kind.

"We have a big living room," she said. "We could partition it. Half for the dogs and half for us."

She kept after him till he put a chain-link fence down the middle of the living room, while my mother took out the rug and the furniture. From then on, the dogs slept indoors. A maze of smaller fences separated them from each other. The gates on these fences were never locked. When I stayed up to watch the Saturday-night movie in the living room with my parents, the loping and breathing and snuffling and growling did not bother my mother or me, but it drove my father wild. I think he could have gotten used to this, but something happened to me that changed everything for all of us.

I got the flu, the kind that keeps you in bed for two weeks. I felt as if someone had sucked all the strength out of me and left me on the small white shore of my bed to find my way back to health. My father took over my tasks and did them, in his own way.

He exercised the dogs, but he did not take out the sled. He walked them singly. Of course, as he pointed out to me, he could not walk seven dogs every day. My mother walked them when she had time, but she reminded him that the dogstar man had willed them to my father, not to us.

He fed the dogs, but he refused to handle the fish meal and fat, and he bought canned meat and dehydrated chicken kibbles in hundred-pound bags that scarcely lasted a week. Soon the dogs were demanding four meals a day and howling at night. My mother found that if she opened the gate in the living room fence, the dogs grew quiet. After everyone was in bed, they would leave their quarters and gather in my room.

It is not easy sleeping with seven dogs, even when you love them. In the safety of my bedroom they went on dreaming of their old fears, just as I went on dreaming of mine. Roused by a remembered injury, Lou Gehrig would leap out of sleep and sink his teeth into John Kennedy's neck, and I would fly out of bed to part them. When sled dogs fight, generations of jackals and wolves snarl in their blood. All night part of my mind stayed awake, listening for the low growl that signaled the beginning of a quarrel. When morning came, I never felt rested.

And Melville got sick. His fur fell out in odd patches, though my mother washed him with Castile soap and sponged his legs, chest, face, and tail with a special foam that Dr. Herrgott recommended for shedding animals.

A thaw surprised us in February, and my mother agreed to let the dogs sleep in the yard again. But the dogs had caught the scent of being human and could not get enough of it. From darkness till dawn they howled. I was back in school but not strong enough to take over caring for the dogs, and I suppose it was the howling and complaints from the neighbors that finally drove my father to make what he warned me was an important announcement.

"I'm going to sell Olaf's dogs. I can't afford to keep them."

We had just sat down to dinner, and he looked at me to see how I would take his words. I said nothing.

"We'll only sell them to someone who can really take care of them," said my mother.

That night I fell asleep to the howling of the dogs. What woke me was a silence so sinister that I jumped out of bed and hurried to the window, certain they'd been poisoned. My heart nearly thudded through my chest when I saw someone was indeed in the yard. He was unchaining them. First John Kennedy, then Babe Ruth, then Hermes.

I never thought of calling my father. No, I pulled on my clothes, snatched my jacket from the bedpost, and marched out into the yard. When the thief turned his face toward me, I was speechless with fright.

"I've come for my dogs," said the dogstar man. "They miss me, and I miss them."

"You're dead," I whispered. My teeth were chattering. "You fell through the ice and drowned."

"That's true," said the dogstar man. And he went on unchaining them. They were lining up, letting him slip the harnesses over them, taking their old places. Hermes first, then Finn McCool and Melville in the second spot, then Lou Gehrig and Babe Ruth, and in the last position, Eleanor Roosevelt and John Kennedy.

"If you're dead, how are you going to take your dogs?"

"Easy," said the dogstar man. "They can cross over. Didn't you know that? Didn't they teach you *anything*?"

The dogsled was leaning against the back of the house, and he pulled it down, hitched the dogs to it, and took his place on the back runners. He beckoned me over.

"For you," he said. "I don't need this where I'm going."

And he dropped the whistle my father had made into my hand.

PERSISTENCE OF MEMORY

Joanne Greenberg

Joanne Greenberg's numerous published works include *Founder's Praise*, *The King's Persons*, *Simple Gifts*, *In This Sign*, *Age of Consent*, and *Of Such Small Differences*. She is perhaps best known as the author of *I Never Promised You a Rose Garden* (under the name "Hannah Green"). Her most recent collection of short fiction, *With the Snow Queen*, includes the following dark and complex fantasy tale, "Persistence of Memory." Within the structure of fantasy, Greenberg explores a very real dilemma; all too many people quietly choose to give up pieces of their memory, and then find that in the bargain they have given away large chunks of heart and soul as well.

—T.W.

Jurgen had come to Leonard on the yard and told him there was a visitor. "I don't think it's a relative," he said, and he looked at Leonard oddly. Leonard got up and followed, happy for the change in routine. Media had tapered off; if it was a woman, he might be able to touch her for money. He needed money. With the same odd look, Jurgen let him wash up before he went in. The visitors' room was large and bare, divided by a Plexiglas barricade. There was one person there, his visitor, the oldest, ugliest woman he had ever seen, skeletal, lipless, and wrinkled. Her fingers were working, working over her face and body, touching it, moving, picking, bunching at the ragged dress she wore. He was glad for once he couldn't see clearly. A former visitor had plastered her side of the Plexiglas partition with kisses and the mess hadn't been cleaned off yet. He sat down and looked at her from a lowered head. It was what he did with the press.

The woman watched him and then, to his horror, opened her mouth and gave a piercing cry. On both sides of the barrier the guards turned, but things like that happened here and they turned back. "Lady," Leonard said, "I don't know you. There's been a mistake." She unnerved him.

She gave a cough, trying with physical wrenchings and swallowings to suppress the weeping. She gulped air, and forced back another cry. He was transfixed like a bystander at a fatal wreck. "I need you," she said. "I and the others—all the others—need you," and her hands, like spiders, ran up and down up and down her face, hair, body.

Leonard was revolted and fascinated in his revulsion. "What is it? Who are you?"

"Gehenna," she said.

"Well, Mrs. Gehenna."

Her laughter was more horrifying than her cry. It was a shriek. For the first time in his experience, Leonard saw the guards shiver. On both sides of the barrier they retreated behind the doors and watched through the glass. The woman took another breath. "There's no time for screaming," she said. "It's too late to laugh or scream. Listen. Gehenna is not who I am, although," and a laugh like a hiccup escaped, "Gehenna is where I'm from. It's the other side, and the souls of the punished seethe and fire falls from the sky and nests in our hair. Listen. One day a week, from Sabbath eve to sundown Sabbath day, the law relents, and we are free of it, and Hell rejoices more than Heaven."

"What is all this—" Leonard said. The woman must be mad.

"Listen. On Sabbath eve the fire stops, the lake of flame dries up, and we are free and we can go into the world. Listen—What do you imagine we do, hung upside down the six-days-forever? How do we endure, sheaved like bats in an attic where rags of flame burn us as they light on our fur?" Leonard was silent. She leaned forward and whispered through the speaking holes in the Plexiglas. "We tell stories. In the first millennium we tell our own lives, all the proofs, justifications, over and over. We cry the unfairness of our damnation, we revisit the woundings that we bore and those we gave others again and again and again."

"What do you want from me?"

"Listen! Listen! Why do you think God made man? It was the story He loved. In Gehenna, the instruments of music incinerate or freeze and the notes burn in the mouths of the players. Fine art goes to stinking smoke; sculptors' marble burns to lime. Only the story—Listen! We say 'Listen,' and we tell stories."

"I'm going back on the yard," Leonard said and got up. "I think you're crazy."

"I can get you out of here," the woman said.

Leonard stopped. At the level at which he stood, the Plexiglas was less stained and scratched. He saw her face. Then, he believed what she said. There were no scars on the flesh, only fresh burns, made from a point so close they looked like powderburns, made and remade endlessly. "How can you get me out?"

Her voice was gritty. "You're serving fifteen years, parole in seven and a half. Aggravated robbery."

"It wasn't the money," Leonard said. "You wouldn't understand. It was a statement against a repressive society, against a society that values property rights above human rights."

"Listen. There's no time for that, for all the reasons and the justifications. I have only this small sabbath, a sabbath you waste, a sabbath of no value to you.

You have 2,737 days to serve, and you've served 364, so that including leap years you have 2,375. For every day of those days, I can offer you what you yearn for—unconsciousness, nothingness, or dreams—long, lovely dreams. While you are away, you'll function here in this world and you won't incur the risks or dangers of this place. Listen! You can be conscious for just the time it takes to give to us . . . what we need. It will happen at a time before the prison wakes up in the morning. Then you will decide which of your memories you will give us. It will be your part of what we need, use, desire . . ."

"Memory? Which of my memories?"

"Our own memories burn and sear. The bad ones are all those years of reasons endlessly repeated. Even the good ones get tainted in Gehenna. It's to close those away, to drown them out, that we hang in anguish and cry other stories, take other days and dreams, see other roads, live in other houses. Listen, we say, and we wrap our burning flesh in your sensations, your evocations. Keep what you want; save what you want. Give me, us, the humiliating moments, the times of weakness, cowardice, the fights with friends, the abuse by the ones supposed to love you. For these incidents and the sensations connected with them, for every one, you can have a day of consciousness removed from here, from the hatred, the hostility, from the boredom and danger of this place."

She was silent then, but her body thrummed with impatience, her hands picking, smoothing, finding the sparks of her burning world as though to extinguish them before they set her afire.

"Is this . . . job . . . for me alone?"

She laughed. "Gehenna is all day and all night the six-day-forever, and the need never ends. There's a lady in New Jersey who gives all the ugliness she's ever known—a wretched childhood, a hideous rape—and she dreams herself off on a Hawaiian vacation with an ideal lover every time her husband's family comes to visit. There is a man in a Cuban jail—compared to his, your days are days of heaven. We have children . . ."

"Children?"

The old wrinkles drew up her mouth. He couldn't tell if it was a laughter or a moan. "What makes you think children have lives they want to live completely, or that they have no memories with which to pay us? Their sensations are more intense, their memories less blunted. Small ones stand closer to the coiled snake sunning or the peony on its stem. I love their fresher passions, brighter than the later passions, for color, taste, bright red, sweet sugar—yes . . ."

"Why did you choose me?"

"We listen—we can't help listening. The world's everyday sound is a vast roar, but there are voices now and then, that we can single out. Maybe one of us was passing and heard you curse. . . . Listen, time is short; will you or won't you?"

Before him the body began to tremble and the fingers that had been picking by habit for seeds of fire, maggots of fire, went wild over the face and body, trembling and jittering.

"You're willing to offer me . . ."

"Anesthesia against present pain."

"And my body will function here . . ."

"Better than you could function. There'd be no emotion to get in the way."

"Let me think about it."

"That is one thing we can't give. Look at the day—the clock is ticking—there are shadows now that weren't here fifteen minutes ago, and no time. You have no time. Ringnose wants his money and if he doesn't get it, he may kill you."

Leonard gaped at her. It was her knowledge more than her physical presence that made him believe she had power that had not arisen from his need, boredom, or jailhouse fever. He had been stymied by his debt to Ringnose. When he had first come on the tier, the big man had offered him some hash and, being new and frightened, Leonard had taken it, terrified of Ringnose's menace. Now, Leonard owed him for it; money, services, what? He had been hoping for something to change this. He had written to his parents begging for money, but they were too frightened to break the law by trying to smuggle it in to him. He kept hoping that something might happen, someone from the movement whose media had praised him as a hero "making our rotting institutions pay as they go." "You didn't set me up with Ringnose, did you?" he asked her.

"Time—there's no time for that. Listen, you can hear water dropping from the leaky spigot. Each drop is a second, each second rides the world from east to west and drops off, gone. Give us a memory and we will give you a day off—nothingness, escape, Ringnose paid."

"Any memory?"

"Any memory strong enough, any incident you can see in your mind, feel in your head or your vitals, conjure in vision, know. Sort among the sensations, the horrors, the joys if you want to lose those, too. There are plenty you will want to let go of."

Leonard thought he had had enough bad experiences to supply years of blanking out. "When do I start?"

The Spirit's arms shot up in exultation and her eyes shone. "Tonight. Get us one. I'll come to you tomorrow, at dawn, into your mind, evoke it, take it, and the day will be rubbed out, erased."

He lay in his bunk that evening, suddenly conscious that for the first time since his imprisonment, he was interested, even fascinated by what he was doing. It felt good to care about something, to choose, to have means.

His name had been Leonard Futterman; he had changed it to Len Future when he was a college freshman. He had wanted a life without past entanglements, nothing to render unclear the loyalty he felt for the group he was joining, a revolutionary group that wanted a new world. His parents had marveled at his energy. They did not know how far it had gone until his arrest. The jittery movements of the Spirit had reminded him slightly of his parents' terror as they faced him in jail and heard his arguments and the fury he brought to the positions he took. By then he had come to despise their timidity and weakness. Memory. Incident. Choose.

Grandfather Herrman had left a small glass factory in Germany to emigrate to South America in 1932, a year after his father's birth. Leonard remembered his grandparents as nervous and furtive, eternal strangers. He had sometimes marveled as he thought of the old people, how pale and frightened they must have been among the colorful, loud inhabitants of Brazil. They had spent three years there and had come to the United States and were foreign here as well. They had been shamed, Leonard learned, in some mysterious way. Memory: Grandfather on porch, Brooklyn, 1963, crying for his dead wife. It had made Leonard embarrassed even then because it seemed so babyish. That memory was well let go. He wondered if he could recreate it fully enough. He put himself on the porch. He remembered how its gray painted railing was chipped here and there and in the chips showed its hundred undercoats in thirty colors. He heard the sound of the old man's sobs—"Oh, God, oh, God, what will I do?"—shrill as a woman's in the hot, still afternoon. In the bunk beneath him, Milburn Waycross, huge and angry, muttered hate in his evening routine, shot his urges across the back wall of the cell, and withdrew into sleep. Tomorrow, Milburn Waycross and Ringnose and the food and the waiting and the stink and the noise would be gone. If the memory was complete enough, all he needed to do was evoke it and she—they could have it and give it to the fire that sent them burning away on its wind. Remember.

He woke as usual before the buzz-clang wake-up. For the first time since his imprisonment, he felt expectation, even excitement. Would she come walking through the walls? As he lay waiting, her urgent voice whispered in his head, "Memory! Memory!" and then Leonard let her have what he had prepared, the porch, the look of his grandfather in detail, the sense of shame and anger, the time of the year, the smell of the painted wood, oily in the heat of his hand. He seemed to slip back into a doze and again the voice cried, "Memory! Memory!" Mrs. Farney, his third-grade teacher—Fly-Face Farney, who pulled and pulled him to the principal's office, who never let any of them walk but always pulled, pushed, tugged at them, and whose rasping "chil*dren*" was the stuff of nightmare. The essence of her bloomed in his mind and he gave the days, two separate ones, and dozed again and woke, and again, and again.

It occurred to Leonard that he might be being cheated. He felt he had awakened, given a memory, and slipped back to sleep for a moment, and then given another. When the voice came again, he said, "How can I be sure days are passing?"

She said, "You yourself will leave proof." Every time he woke thereafter, a different color rubber band was around his wrist, or a thread or a shoelace. Then he turned, stretched, sought memory, found it, gave it, and again, and again. Sometimes the memory was fragmentary and her voice, or another voice, would scream out of the place in fire, "Give it, remember!" and he would try harder or give another. On the sabbath, the voices were still, and Leonard used his rest to dream away the time in fantasy while his body went to his work and served his sentence.

In forty days Leonard had decimated most of his childhood. At first he had imagined he had endless memories to give—his playmates, teachers, Mrs. Teel, Paulie Malone. There was the day he wet his pants because he had played too long at recess and misjudged the time. There were school trips and days home sick and the way the afternoon light lay long knives of shadow across his bed. He had thought all that would fill years. Once, waking, it occurred to him that dreams were memories, too, and for a while he lived off his store of childhood dreams and adolescent sex fantasies, those which were complete enough for her to take.

It was now winter and his wakings to the drip of melting icicles from fifth tier's overhang or the feathery fall of snow past the window made him know that Gehenna was keeping its part of the bargain. He had moments of anxiety about his part of it. Eighty days had gone from 2,375. He had 2,295 left. Did he have as many memories? Did he have a thousand? A hundred more?

His wakings came to be edged with anxiety. Then he discovered he could get better access to his memory if he gave himself simple nouns: pine tree, apple, street. He could remember specific things connected with those. He had sixty more days, but on the sixty-first he hit the blank wall of his bankrupt past. It happened with the word *caramel corn*. He was remembering a carnival he had gone to, a day for which he had waited, he and . . . he and . . . silence. Nothing. The day had been shared by someone, someone eager, happy, waiting. He and *someone* had gone in the car, laughing and joking, had ridden the rides, eaten the caramel corn. The memory with the loss of that someone lay deflated, spent. Although he got the day, childhood intensity of hot sun and the cooking-sugar smell of the caramel and the oily smell of the popping corn, carnival music, and the colors all around them, he had seen the end. The memories were not to be shared, but given, and when there were no more, he would hit the wall, blank, total, with no face or scenes he knew. There would, when it was all over, be no evocation of anything, no memory at all.

It was too late to stop. The few moments of waking, stretching, formulating his memory were horrible to him, unbearable to smell and see. His cell was small, two bunks, one very low toilet, the high sink over it—a man had to wash sometimes with the stink of a stopped up commode directly under him. The walls were full of graffiti so that the eye was caught by the ugly screed of words scratched in the thousand angers of a thousand cons. He was buying his way out of it with something that had, only one hundred forty-one days ago, seemed less valuable than the smallest coin made. Remember. It caught. They were at the beach, his aunt and uncle, mother and father of . . . the wall again. He remembered his aunt who, for the beach, always wore a kerchief, a white one with red dots. . . . He realized he was working hard, trying to squeeze detail out of a resisting past without giving too much. Memories could be divided, saved, husbanded. The day at the beach, though, was it one or a distillation of many such days? In either case it must be rationed, given in segments like an orange, because like an orange, part by part, his mind was being eaten. The wall told him so. There had once been someone connected with him for whom there was now no evocation of any kind.

On day 150 (2,225 days remaining), Leonard awoke and begged for a rest. The Spirit howled from hell: "Do you know how to lie in fire, to freeze in the shame of your pleasant past?"

"I don't have anything more to give—"

"Then live the rest of your sentence."

"No, please . . . I can't do that."

"Try harder. We fixed it with Ringnose and no one bothers you now. We have done well by you."

"You're eating me alive."

"Listen! You have relatives, friends, you went to school, camp, you are *middle class*. Never in human history have people had more novelty of experience, trips, visits, outings, vacations. It is novelty on which memory is based. Listen!"

"Give me time to go to the library, to get some books, pictures . . ."

"Give it—give it!" she cried.

Some time later he woke and found himself holding his high school and college yearbooks. He opened them greedily, no longer caring to separate the pleasant from the unpleasant, the whole from the fragmented. He knew he would give all he had, wherever 2,225 memories were stored. He started with *The Cougar*, his high school yearbook.

The teams; there were the coaches, the clubs, the green springtimes and the blue-wind autumns. He had once thought he might save the best of these, a simple memory of Willie Madigan, Joe Sperber, Clem Jones, and himself, walking across the far end of the track after school. It was the day they had all decided to quit football. Willie and Clem were first string, Joe and Leonard were third, where no one cared. They were, that day, amazed and proud of Willie and of their friendship. They had made a decision, the first that pitted them against the adult world of expectation. It was a heady moment. The trees across the road were bare, the wind almost cold and whipping the school flags so that their sound was like applause. They were dressed for the cold—Willie was in his letterman's blue and white, he himself was in a trainman's coat he had gotten secondhand and wore like a dare. Such were their bodies then that they could have gone coatless and not really minded. They felt this somehow to be their strength. They gave none of the credit to their youth. Invincible, they were making the choice to step down. For Willie and Clem this had not been possible until they knew they were capable of first-string play. Caught in that memory, Leonard paused a moment in a pain almost great enough to stop it, and then he let it go, evoked it, and it was taken and he slept again.

*   *   *

He used up the high school yearbook in thirty days. He could read it from cover to cover and evoke nothing, no one. Junior high had gone months ago. Grade school was a fitful flicker like lightning at the horizon reflecting itself against clouds—seen and gone before it could be caught.

College. Relatively few of the cons had gone to college and there was a certain envy, felt and sometimes expressed by them. One of the blacks Leonard had bunked with had said: "You jivin', everybody be the same, you be robbin' banks for the poor. That's after you done got all you can get."

Leonard had answered, "Everyone gets what he can," but he had stopped defending himself and then he had stopped trying to alter his speech to be more like theirs.

College was where Leonard felt he had come into his own. It was the time of his greatest excitement and awakening. His activities didn't appear in the yearbook, the arguments, the commitments, the people. Nowhere were there pictures of Anthony Lorenzo, of all the talking and the listening that had formed his political awareness, of Barbara and Teri, Don Miller, Ken Seybright. Still, the scenes of the campus, the dorms, and student center brought back many of the memories of their meetings, bull-sessions, the organizing and defining by themselves as a serious political group and by the other students as radicals. Leonard had liked the term *radical*. He enjoyed being unique, separated. Lorenzo was a brilliant leader, a patriot in a way that didn't make Leonard want to gag at the word. He was Len, now, Len Future, and he and Lorenzo and Seybright and Barb and Teri were going to do what the books only talked about. They would shatter and remake, explode and rebuild. They held protests and marches and when they turned around they saw others marching with them. They began to think of more direct forms of action.

In the beginning Leonard had thought he would keep those memories as his own, but now he told himself it would be foolish and romantic to save what had no practical use and what was an unnecessary possession, a mental photo album as trite and bourgeois as the yearbooks he now held. He spent the next wakings on his later days, the robberies.

How Gehenna loved the robberies. There were other voices now, a gabble of them, and when the memory was interesting or special they moaned like lovers. For the slack or incomplete memories, they urged and pulled. "The day, what was it like?"

"It was the night we planned the second bank job," Leonard said. He had a sudden spasm of guilt about giving up the names and faces, invoking them in his mind-voice. They had sworn secrecy. . . .

"Memory! Memory—" They gibbered like bats.

He hesitated. Miller was doing time here, too, but in another building, and they seldom met. Lorenzo had copped a plea, Seybright had escaped, and as far as Leonard knew was still free. The loyalty they had sworn . . . He dove into the memory.

It was a summer night, hot and muggy. They had all felt powerful, in command. Action against property was righteous, Lorenzo had said. Leonard's part had been to map the bank, detail the exits, and later watch how it opened.

"Give us all of it!"

He tried to give the details he knew they craved. Lorenzo's apartment, dank but cool. They drank beer, having sworn off drugs until after the job. Leonard had laid out the bank's floor plan. They were all on a high, a quiet high, like rafting on fast water. . . . That made him remember rafting, another memory, another day's respite, and he slept and woke and gave them the water, sun-glinted as he came toward the rapids, the mile-long sinews contracting and stretching against his boat. I remember . . . and then he slept.

"About the robbery . . ." she said. The robbery itself had been a comedown because they had been off stride that day; he knew it waking up, but couldn't remember specifically enough, and the job had only one strong memory, the moment of their being in the bank, of his dropping the attaché case and having to pick it up. He tried to tell her—them—in his mind-voice that it should have been funny, clumsiness when grace was called for—a robbery was, after all, a public appearance—and how he had almost said "oops," but it wasn't funny. The onlookers had been terrified; thwarting him might result in his firing his gun and a red-splattered—"Oh, God!" a woman had cried, and fainted. A new voice demanded that minute and Leonard tried, picturing humor gone cold, the smell of the air just at that moment, hot day, cold sweat, and how they were off rhythm so that no one had thought to plan who went through the door first so there was a scramble and Lorenzo nearly fell.

"Feelings, what were your feelings?"

He knew what they wanted by now, shame, rage, triumph, joy. He had had none of those. "You try for nothingness, no emotion. There's too much else to think of." He remembered the belly-clutch of fear just then. The door. Then he remembered seeing how ordinary the street looked, how out on that ordinary street they had gone back to their plan to split up. He gave them bright sun, dislocation, fear, relief within seconds. They took that moment.

On the 210th day, Leonard suffered a kind of breakdown. He woke up and there was nothing. He felt no sensation, saw no picture in his mind—none. They came: "Remember. Remember!"

"I have nothing." There was a cry from hell—anguish and rage, the cry of the addicted. Leonard felt their terror and then his own. "I'm dried up. I can't . . ." and then there was only the prison day, bearing down.

For the first time in seven months, Leonard rose resident in his body, heard the wake-up coughs and hawks of the men on the tier, men pissing, groaning, cursing.

He smelled the smells. The seven months he had escaped into memory had blunted his ability to protect himself from the onslaught of his senses. He dressed, fumbling, almost weeping, was walked to breakfast, recoiled in the ugly impacted hate and rage of the men around him, paranoid spew, fume of ungratified sex, their sounds their smells their hair-trigger touchiness or obtunded despair. Now and then men came to him and said things, things pertaining to the life his surrogate self shared with them. He answered as well as he could. Once or twice he saw puzzlement on their faces. It was masked quickly as everything was, and he yearned almost to tears for the salvation he was losing—why couldn't he remember? There must be more. During the evening break he went to the library and looked at cookbooks for memories, at catalogues, at pictures, for any clue that would open the magic door again, door through which he had once walked so easily. The day passed. Another, another.

Leonard's search became desperate because somehow he wasn't able to adjust to prison life as he had before. The possibility of an alternative had destroyed his ability to tighten himself against the assaults of its boredom, danger, and ugliness. Three days. She came to the visitors' room again.

If anything, she was skinnier, more withered, tighter. Her hands never stopped their pinching, picking, spidering in her ragged clothes.
   "I've lost it," he said. "There is no more."
   "Nonsense. Of course there's more. Look around. You don't want to be here— find something. Listen!"
   "I'm played out. Done."
   Her eyes lit. "You need a vacation," she said.

It was a car ad he had seen years before, a gracious old house among big trees. There was a wide veranda with a rocker on it. A sports car was in front of the house, and in it were scuba things and picnic baskets.
   "Wonderful," she said, "go there and rest. The house has everything you'll need."
   "How long?"
   "A week. We have Ringnose now, for what he's worth, Luchese, Kent. Enjoy yourself."

All the days were sun-dappled. He lay in the meadow in front of the house or rocked and read magazines on the porch. Twice he took the car to the lake with the people who came by, owners of the gear and the picnic things. They were pretty laughing girls and clean-limbed young men, but they were ad people—they had no pasts, no futures, no hopes, no memories. They took him scuba-diving but the lake was silted and the company boring. He made love to the girls and forgot it immediately after doing it. He had vowed he would rest from memory, but a few times he tried it gingerly, like a neurology patient testing for the paralysis that might or might not still be there. There was no remembering and in the old brass bed, open-window cool in the moonlight, he heard rats scrabbling in the walls.

And the days there were unchanging. It never rained; there was no sense of movement through a season, no old flowers dying or new ones in bud.

"You've rested. Let's begin. There's more—of course there's more."

"Something has let go . . ." he said, "I can feel it."

"Only memories."

"Don't lie. I felt it *there*, lazing in the sun, reading, riding, making love. I've sold you my soul, haven't I?"

She laughed the screeching laugh that drove the guards behind the doors. "No one, not even you, gives up his soul."

"What do I give up, besides those memories? I felt something stop and break away and flow away inside me."

"Oh, that—that's not serious—it's not a vital need."

"What is it?"

"If it's gone, it would have been the ability to change, to recreate yourself. It's more of a choice than a need, and you've never wanted change in yourself."

"I'm pledged to work for change. The movement . . ."

"Your bunch wants everyone else to change—society."

"How do people change?" Leonard asked.

For a moment she slowed and went quieter. "They start with changing their own stories, by retelling them with new shadings. Are there gentler moments in memory? Are there crueler? By stroke and stroke, memory by memory, over time they remodel their pasts and then themselves, their ideas of who they were, then are, and then, of who they will be."

"And I have no past. I gave it all to you."

"You hated it; it's gone."

"I'm walking streets without markers . . ."

"Losing *memories* doesn't mean losing your *memory*. Back then, didn't you recognize a friend even when you had forgotten some of the things you did together? You still have the friend, you just don't have the memory."

"And changing . . ."

"You'll get old like everyone else, but you'll no longer have to labor at rewriting your past or remodeling yourself. Give us memory, now, give it. Remember!"

"I can't take prison. I can't stand these days . . ."

"Find the stories for us. They're there—hundreds, thousands more. You don't want them, you don't use them. Give us—give us—and we'll see you're comfortable, sleeping, reading, rocking on the porch—"

He went back to his cell and lay on his bunk ransacking. Friends, all gone, foods, names, flowers. He got ten things on a list and another ten that might yield—flowerpot, a broken flowerpot. Where was it? When did it happen? He went to the screaming cafeteria, writing all the associations he had, desperately seeking—

plaid shirt—madras shirt—whose? It was a kid in school, Prentice. There had to be more. The evening dragged. A washcloth—*injuries*. When? Where? Ten more memories, another ten. Remember the time I shut my finger in the car door and my dad was . . . he slept.

On the 250th day he woke in a dry, familiar desperation, went through a list of one hundred words seeking to evoke—there—nothing to give now. He tried another hundred, hoping for the eye-corner phantom that runs for safety before it can be seen and identified, a moment, a girl, a friend . . .

The past was bare, a twilit plain without the beauty of twilight, and unchanging.

To the screams of anguish he said, "It's over."

"Find it—find it!"

"I'm done."

He rose into the prison morning. There he lay and counted the time remaining to him, the two thousand one hundred days before he could be accepted for parole. Each of those days would be a prison day, a day through which he would walk skin-stripped at the mercy of his senses, uninsulated. He would not be clever because vulnerable people aren't clever and because of that he might be beaten, stabbed, made a victim again. He wanted to cry but the wake-up sounded, raw in his ears. Then the whole tier groaned, and rose in hate. It occurred to Leonard that simpler than what the Spirit had said about recasting life, every prisoner had a small place of refuge through the day. The refuge was memory. The man at the laundry basket piling and sorting clothes might be fishing on a once-seen lake, or simply cruising the main drag in Coffeeville on a Saturday night, with the car radio on and a girl in a tight sweater. Leonard, whose experiences had been more varied than most of the prisoners, had, by choice, given away the geography of his childhood and adolescence. There was nothing left to glow behind the hideous moment and make it bearable.

The days, taken raw, went hour by hour. He had begun to think of suicide. Then Rimper on tier three had a heart attack. Leonard put in for the job at the power plant and got it, there being no other con who wanted it.

The work was simple. He checked the gauges that monitored the lights, heat, and power. Years ago, the job had been vital and heavy with perks. Now, all the systems were on backup and auxiliary power and the job was only boring. Leonard wanted it because it let him be alone, free of having to fake the self he had been while his real self slept.

May. His parents came. They were, as always, cowed by the prison. They huddled and shrank. His mother brought bribe food, and spoke in whispers. "Are you all right?" He told them he was. They began to talk about family news: Aunt Essie had had a stroke. Cousin Brian was getting married. Births and Bar Mitzvahs. For none, not one, had Leonard a memory. He recognized his parents, but they had lost definition and it was hard to follow their simplest talk. "It takes me in the feet—you know me and my feet, all the years standing . . ." And Leonard didn't have a clue to what his father meant or to his mother's sighed, "Betty's upset, naturally. You'd think after all her troubles . . ."

He sat and watched them suffer behind the Plexiglas. He had given away all the cousins and the aunts and the days, landmarks of his childhood, mountains, seashores, clouds, spiderwebs from which hung . . . wait . . . from which dew hung . . . He saw it with perfect, pristine clarity, a memory without defensiveness or self-serving, a simple, stunning picture infused with childhood's awe. The dew was suspended in such a way on that perfect web that each drop carried, weighing and trembling lightly on the suspension cables of the web, a little rainbow. He saw it again, how the light brimmed in the tiny prisms, and prism and drop and web hung in the spring morning where he stood close to the smell of the wet grass, because he was a little kid. Grass touched his knee, cold-green with the morning's cold dew. Then there was a little breeze and the web trembled and the drop suddenly shuddered and the prism scattered rainbow and fell from the web like tears. "I remember," he said. They thought he was speaking of Aunt Essie and nodded.

The ruined landscape had yielded up a survivor. Where there was one there might be others. One by one, they might creep from under the rubble. Hadn't he been seeing someone home drunk one night in college? Didn't he pretend to be drunker than he was so he might look up at the vast spread of stars and yes, yes, he had been wearing a . . . it was a wool jacket, heavy, and a blue knit watch-cap and his friend—a shadow now—had still some part of him that had not been given away. Web and starry-night, warm-jacket shadow friend would be his to use, to remake himself, bit by bit, year by year. His friend was singing away in his ear. He couldn't capture the tune and there was a destination he couldn't place, but the memory, wind and cold and gin and being tired and the stars and the singing . . . dew in the web—Thank God. "Did you ever have long hair?" he asked his drawn, huddled mother; "Was it ever held with two curved combs at the sides of your head?"

YOU'LL NEVER EAT LUNCH ON THIS CONTINENT AGAIN

Adam Gopnik

The following story is pure California, albeit the West Coast of two hundred million years ago. This wickedly funny fantasia comes from *The New Yorker*, where Adam Gopnik works as a staffer, and which has published a number of his other pieces.

—T.W.

Angiosperms (flowering plants) first evolved toward the end of the dino-saurs' reign. Many of these plants contain psychoactive agents, avoided by mammals today as a result of their bitter taste. Dinosaurs had neither means to taste the bitterness nor livers effective enough to detoxify the substances.

—Stephen Jay Gould.

Scientists poking through volcanic rubble in the mountains of Antarctica have stumbled upon the 200 million-year-old remains of dinosaurs, marking the first time the extinct beasts have been found so far south. . . . The scientists said they think they have found the remains of at least two different dinosaurs, and said the fossils may be a snapshot of a drama of death played out 200 million years ago, when Antarctica was warm, mild and part of the Southern super-continent known as Gondwanaland.

—*The Washington Post*.

Here's my theory, she thought, we *are* the missing link. We are halfway between our animal selves and wherever it is that we're going. . . .

Besides, we need our space. The soul was invented as an arbiter between the two, and drugs can be very helpful in spiritual and territorial terms.

—Julia Phillips.

Mostly, she blamed the mammals. She watched herself watching her talons dry in the sun and all the news washed over her—a litany of chaos, lies, and despair. Am I the only one who can't tell them apart, she wondered. For a while she had thought, O.K., the new game, and she had tried to keep up with all the varieties: lemurs, lorises, shrews, some of them swinging and some of them climbing but really all the same—the chattering, the placentas, the four-chambered hearts. She could never flash on this sleeping thing they did. What was it? A counter to that restless scheming and humping all day long? They were everywhere on the West Coast now, with their fuzzy little coats, and their big night-seeing eyes, and the thumbs. Those opposable thumbs! Her group, out on the beach, used to have such contempt for the mammals, the way they scurried around on the floor. "Hey, squashed another furball," Stego would say, stamping down with his beautiful, muscular, to-die-for back foot when they were all in a circle, weekending around La Brea, flowered out, and he wouldn't even bother to look back and see what kind he had put out of its nipple-sucking misery. To imagine these things taking over the Coast. No way on earth. Not in a million years.

Which is about what it had taken. She knew what they said about her—that it was the flowers, as simple as that. Yeah, right. As though she hadn't always had this spiritual striving to get out-of-bodied on the whole incredible scene and view it from high up. From a safe distance, whatever that was. No, it was the mammals who had driven her away. Creatures that young weren't as spiritual as her crowd had been. Creatures that young were afraid to be alone—they eschewed eccentricity. It was all part of the larger picture: the diminished vision, the bankrupt dreams.

None of it had ever been about continental domination or territory, not for her, anyway—she was always telling that to the other big lizards. The territorialism, the bellowing around the tar pits, the aggressive predation—that hadn't meant anything at all to her. It had been another game for her, a spiritual game—that old notion, held over from her infancy, that if she moved fast enough she would survive extinction. That they would *all* survive extinction. "Hell of a belief for a cold-blooded creature," Stego had said, squinting at her with his funny little double-lidded eyes. Which was true, God knows. There was always something cosmic about Stego. Maybe a little *too* cosmic. She blamed him a lot, too.

The game, the way she had learned it, had been species extension. How long have you been on earth? How long can you stay here? Macho boy-lizard penis-extension stuff, O.K., but she had been the first girl lizard in it. They had dreams, her kind: they saw the world as a majestic, single-file parade of major creatures—creatures who took millions of years of development, *classic* creatures. Now, with the mammals in charge, there was nothing worth a second look; it was all just spinoffs and syndication. "Speciation"—that was their code word for it, meaning just more mammals with minor, half-assed spins on the same basic, dumb, low-budget, tree-climbing, milk-sucking idea. Branching. Variation. Scads of shrewlike creatures running around humping, producing their own sequels.

The boasting! "See that four-footed feline?" you could hear them saying to each other down there in the valley. "Give him a development deal and a few thousand generations, and, I promise you, you're looking at a major, major predator." Some of her old group had "adapted"—that was their word for it. Take the twelve-step program, be a good lizard, begin to change: in a few generations your scales become feathers, and your ten rows of razor teeth a dainty little beak, and off you go, flying to your new little nest. But then what were you? *Who* were you? One more cunning little creature with a development deal and a "niche" in the "ecology." When you used to rule the earth.

One of the lemurs had explained the new deal-making to her, working his thumbs like mad. (Nervous, they were always so nervous around her. It was that spiritual thing she still had, she guessed.) "Punctuated equilibrium," that was the jargon for it. Wait around, make variations, keep the bottom line low. Then, when there's a crack in the old order, grab your chance. "You get in on the back end, and then you have moments. Adapt or die, baby." Then he had given her a lecture on what makes a great species, a hit species. As though her kind hadn't been walking the earth for—oh, what was it, sixty million years? Fifty million years? The flowers cut down on your memory. "It's adaptability that matters," he said. A few years later, that sucker got blown away by one of the last remaining pterodactyls with night vision. Adapt or die. Right.

"Too dumb to taste the bitterness." That was what she knew the furballs told each other under their breaths, exchanging those wizened, knowing little toothy grins. Seeing her kind reeling around with that wild blissed-out look you got after a really righteous flower. Hey, that's right, furball. Ever felt a thousand flowers exploding like pinwheels inside your consciousness, rushing down there to the brain at the base of your spine and letting loose?

Dumb, her kind were dumb. "Stego's got a brain the size of a walnut, in the base of his spine." "The bronto's got a brain the size of a navel orange." As if their cranial capacity weren't exactly right for animals of their size. And they had no idea what a joy it had once been—the heaven-shaking sound as we met to intertwine necks and pound the ground and roar. Hey, ever wonder why they called us thunder lizards? *We ruled the effing earth.*

The mammals, really, had driven her to the flowers. She remembers the first time the weird-looking lizard with the crooked grin and all the plates up and down his muscular back showed her how to extract the pollen. "Don't suck it so hard," he said softly. "Hold the pollen in your teeth and let it out slowly through your nose." Hey, just a minute, plate-face. Who do you think you're dealing with here? But she went along with him anyway. Oh, baaaby, baaaby. She even wondered briefly if this was going to be the Big One. The Ultimate. Death. Extinction. The Fate of all Living Things. But it had kept on and on, like a glimpse of eternity held in your hand.

Yeah, right. Too dumb to taste the bitterness.

*   *   *

She had taken a meeting with one of them in the middle of her most intense period. Her high period. One of the little thumbsters she had seen once or twice around the flower beds at La Brea back when it was still thrilling to be young and twenty feet high and cold-blooded and living in California. She was burning the residue from one of those big sunflowers, angiospermed-out, when this primate from the old days comes to call, running up the side of a palm tree and nestling by her ear. "Hey, my lady," he says, panting the way they do.

"Hey, furball," she said. "Long time no speak." A put-down once. Now you could call them hairball, fuzzette, body heat. They didn't care. They had the upper hand.

"Yeah, well, not because your name doesn't come up from time to time among us all." (Right—as in, That bitch still alive?) "I'll get right to the point." Busy, busy little mammal. Places to go, other mammals to hump. She hears that now they're starting to do it face to face. *Yuck.* "Listen, down there on the floor a lot of us are asking, 'Is this really a happy lady?' And I'm hearing—what I'm hearing is no, not really. So a lot of us were thinking, What about a partnership? A start-up situation. You know, coproduction. You dominate the high ground, we take the jungle floor. Hey—you'll still be an independent entity, only within this *larger* entity. Together we could dominate this continent for a major, major time frame."

She nods slowly. She shows more enthusiasm for this concept than she really feels. What they want is she should sell out everything her kind had believed in for millennia—sell out her birthright—and she isn't even supposed to feel the pain. Isn't even supposed to recognize that there *is* any pain. Just one entity within a larger entity. This was the new epoch for you: absolute corruption without a single identifiable moment of compromise.

"Yeah, what do you take out of the front end?" she asks, shutting her first, translucent lids. Which always freaks them out, the mammals—that tearlike, semi-opaque lid dropping down in the middle of their pitch. Hey, they think, the panic growing in their heaving little chests. She could turn. One bite from those monster jaws and I'm an article in *Natural History.*

"There's just one condition," the furball says, scampering back down the branch. "Just don't embarrass us in public, you know." That injured innocence all of them have. He laughs. Looks more feral than ever. Jagged, yellowing teeth emphasizing all the molelike aspects of his demeanor. Chewing on sugarcane, probably. She recalled what Stego had said when they first started noticing them. "No matter how big the cranial capacity, remember what they were when they started out. *Moles.* You can't let them ever forget it."

But she just goes on with her flower. "Hey, you want some?" She offers to blow some pollen his way. The perfect hostess.

Oh, that sends the little fucker scurrying. "Hey, no. I mean—you know, it tastes . . ." He cuts himself off. Blushing, the way they do—all the hot blood pumping up in their arteries toward their lying little faces.

She blames her mother, too. She had always made her think that it could just go on. Her mother had forced all this girl-lizard thing on her—this dainty, chewing-the-palm-leaves thing. And when she was young, and lit by some inner ambition, she played along with it. But her mother had screwed her up in her relationships with all the other women. So was it any surprise that the last straw for her had been when the furball pointed out that little dopey simian swinging its arms, and said, "See that one? Lucy, they call her. Unlimited potential. Give her a thousand generations, she'll be walking erect, using tools, making deals. She could become the hottest thing on earth since—well, since you, my lady." That had cut it. Another woman, like herself. Thanks, Mom.

So head south, young female. The babe from the Antarctic Commission said that they were desperate for production, for any kind of creatures at all, and with the land bridge it was just a couple of long days' walks away. She had taken the plate-back along with her, for the sex mostly, though he was good company in a kind of lowriding, grungeball way. There would be plenty of empty space down there, and no mammals, just a lot of weird, retro-looking birds. Black and white, all black and white—kind of an art-house look, she guessed.

On the way south, she lies under the stars, awake in the middle of the night, unable to think anything but "I am going to die, he is going to die." Staring numbly at the stars, knowing that she is but a speck of sand under the fingernail of a larger being who is but a speck of sand under the fingernail of a larger being. Et cetera, et cetera, as they used to say when things just went on forever and her kind ruled the earth. Old plate-back tosses and turns while she looks at the stars. He hasn't eaten all day.

They were in business together. Go out, get some out-of-country money. Maybe those penguins liked basic action-adventure, monosyllable grunt stuff. That was usually big in the foreign markets—a couple of monster lizards writhing around and biting at each other. O.K., she could do that. Hey, she was adapting, wasn't she? She had been clean for a couple of weeks, and they were in business together. Plate-back rolls over, his stomach grumbles, and she almost likes him. Hey, they have a working relationship, they have an understanding, they have a deal. You could live with it. Just don't ask why.

THE GLAMOUR
Thomas Ligotti

Thomas Ligotti was born in 1953 in Michigan. His early stories (mostly from small-press magazines) have been collected in *Songs of a Dead Dreamer*.

Ligotti's baroque style is demanding on the reader. He has a unique voice in today's horror fiction. "The Glamour," from his new collection *Grimscribe*, is a marvelous illustration of Ligotti's ability to project dread and unease in his stories, making readers start at sudden noises and glance around while reading his subtly disquieting narratives.

—E.D.

It had long been my practice to wander late at night and often to attend movie theaters at this time. But something else was involved on the night I went to that theater in a part of town I had never visited before. A new tendency, a mood or penchant formerly unknown to me, seemed to lead the way. How difficult to say anything precise about this mood that overcame me, because it seemed to belong to my surroundings as much as to my self. As I advanced farther into that part of town I had never visited before, my attention was drawn to a certain aspect of things—a fine aura of fantasy radiating from the most common sights, places and objects that were both blurred and brightened as they projected themselves into my vision.

Despite the lateness of the hour, there was an active glow cast through many of the shop windows in that part of town. Along one particular avenue, the starless evening was glazed by these lights, these diamonds of plate glass set within old buildings of dark brick. I paused before the display window of a toy store and was entranced by a chaotic tableau of preposterous excitation. My eyes followed several things at once: the fated antics of mechanized monkeys that clapped tiny cymbals or somersaulted uncontrollably; the destined pirouettes of a music-box ballerina; the grotesque wobbling of a newly sprung jack-in-the-box. The inside of the store was a Christmas-tree clutter of merchandise receding into a background that looked shadowed and empty. An old man with a smooth pate and angular eyebrows stepped forward to the front window and began rewinding some of the toys to keep them in ceaseless gyration. While performing this task he suddenly looked up at me, his face expressionless.

I moved down the street, where other windows framed little worlds so strangely picturesque and so dreamily illuminated in the shabby darkness of that part of town. One of them was a bakery whose window display was a gallery of sculptured frosting, a winter landscape of swirling, drifting whiteness, of snowy rosettes and layers of icy glitter. At the center of the glacial kingdom was a pair of miniature people frozen atop a many-tiered wedding cake. But beyond the brilliant arctic scene I saw only the deep blackness of an establishment that kept short hours. Standing outside another window nearby, I was uncertain if the place was open for business or not. A few figures were positioned here and there within faded lighting reminiscent of an old photograph, though it seemed they were beings of the same kind as the window dummies of this store, which apparently trafficked in dated styles of clothing. Even the faces of the mannequins, as a glossy light fell upon them, wore the placidly enigmatic expressions of a different time.

But in fact there actually were several places doing business at that hour of the night and in that part of town, however scarce potential customers appeared to be on this particular street. I saw no one enter or exit the many doors along the sidewalk; a canvas awning that some proprietor had neglected to roll up for the night was flapping in the wind. Nevertheless, I did sense a certain vitality around me and felt the kind of acute anticipation that a child might experience at a carnival, where each lurid attraction incites fantastic speculations, while unexpected desires arise for something which has no specific qualities in the imagination yet seems to be only a few steps away. Thus my mood had not abandoned me but only grew stronger, a possessing impulse without object.

Then I saw the marquee for a movie theater, something I might easily haved passed by. For the letters spelling out the name of the theater were broken and unreadable, while the title on the marquee was similarly damaged, as though stones had been thrown at it, a series of attempts made to efface the words that I finally deciphered. The feature being advertised that night was called *The Glamour.*

When I reached the front of the theater I found that the row of doors forming the entrance had been barricaded by crosswise planks with notices posted upon them warning that the building had been condemned. This action was apparently taken some time ago, judging by the weathered condition of the boards that blocked my way and the dated appearance of the notices stuck upon them. In any case, the marquee was still illuminated, if rather poorly. So I was not surprised to see a double-faced sign propped up on the sidewalk, an inconspicuous little board that read: ENTRANCE TO THE THEATER. Beneath these words was an arrow pointing into an alleyway which separated the theater from the remaining buildings on the block. Peeking into this dark opening, this aperture in the otherwise solid façade of that particular street, I saw only a long, narrow corridor with a single light set far into its depths. The light shone with a strange shade of purple, like that of a freshly exposed heart, and appeared to be positioned over a doorway leading into the theater. It had long been my practice to attend movie theaters late at night— this is what I reminded myself. But whatever reservations I felt at the time were easily overcome by a new surge of the mood I was experiencing that night in a part of town I had never visited before.

The purple lamp did indeed mark a way into the theater, casting a kind of arterial light upon a door that reiterated the word "entrance." Stepping inside, I entered a tight hallway where the walls glowed a deep pink, very similar in shade to that little beacon in the alley but reminding me more of a richly blooded brain than a beating heart. At the end of the hallway I could see my reflection in a ticket window, and approaching it I noticed that those walls so close to me were veiled from floor to ceiling with what appeared to be cobwebs. These cobwebs were also strewn upon the carpet leading to the ticket window, wispy shrouds that did not scatter as I walked over them, as if they had securely bound themselves to the carpet's worn and shallow fibers, or were growing out of it like postmortem hairs on a corpse.

There was no one behind the ticket window, no one I could see in that small space of darkness beyond the blur of purple-tinted glass in which my reflection was held. Nevertheless, a ticket was protruding from a slot beneath the semicircular cutaway at the bottom of the window, sticking out like a paper tongue. A few hairs lay beside it.

"Admission is free," said a man who was now standing in the doorway beside the ticket booth. His suit was well fitted and neat, but his face appeared somehow a mess, bristled over all its contours. His tone was polite, even passive, when he said, "The theater is under new ownership."

"Are you the manager?" I asked.

"I was just on my way to the rest room."

Without further comment he drifted off into the darkness of the theater. For a moment something floated in the empty space he left in the doorway—a swarm of filaments like dust that scattered or settled before I stepped through. And in those first few seconds inside, the only thing I could see were the words REST ROOM glowing above a door as it slowly closed.

I manuevered with caution until my sight became sufficient to the dark and allowed me to find a door leading to the auditorium of the movie theater. But once inside, as I stood at the summit of a sloping aisle, all previous orientation to my surroundings underwent a setback. The room was illuminated by an elaborate chandelier centered high above the floor, as well as a series of light fixtures along either of the side walls. I was not surprised by the dimness of the lighting nor by its hue, which made shadows appear faintly bloodshot—a sickly, liverish shade that might be witnessed in an operating room where a torso lies open on the table, its entrails a palette of pinks and reds and purples . . . diseased viscera imitating all the shades of sunset.

However, my perception of the theater auditorium remained problematic not because of any oddities of illumination but for another reason. While I experienced no difficulty in mentally registering the elements around me—the separate aisles and rows of seats, the curtain-flanked movie screen, the well-noted chandelier and wall lights—it seemed impossible to gain a sense of these features in simple accord with their appearances. I saw nothing that I have not described, yet . . . the round-backed seats were at the same time rows of headstones in a graveyard; the aisles were endless filthy alleys, long desolate corridors in an old asylum, or the dripping passages of a sewer narrowing into the distance; the pale movie screen was a dust-blinded window in a dark unvisited cellar, a mirror gone rheumy with age in an abandoned house; the chandelier and smaller fixtures were the facets of murky crystals embedded in the sticky walls of an unknown cavern. In other words, this movie theater was merely a virtual image, a veil upon a complex collage of other places, all of which shared certain qualities that were projected into my vision, as though the things I saw were possessed by something I could not see.

But as I lingered in the theater auditorium, settling in a seat toward the back wall, I realized that even on the level of plain appearances there was a peculiar phenomenon I had not formerly observed, or at least had yet to perceive to its fullest extent. I am speaking of the cobwebs.

When I first entered the theater I saw them clinging to the walls and carpeting. Now I saw how much they were a part of the theater and how I had mistaken the nature of these long pale threads. Even in the hazy purple light, I could discern that they had penetrated into the fabric of the seats in the theater, altering the weave in its depths and giving it a slight quality of movement, the slow curling of thin smoke. It seemed the same with the movie screen, which might have been a great rectangular web, tightly woven and faintly in motion, vibrating at the touch of some unseen force. I thought: Perhaps this subtle and pervasive *wriggling* within the theater may clarify the tendency of its elements to suggest other things and other places thoroughly unlike a simple theater auditorium, a process parallel to the ever-mutating images of dense clouds. All textures in the theater appeared similarly affected, without control over their own nature, but I could not clearly see as high as the chandelier. Even some of the others in the audience, which was small and widely scattered about the auditorium, were practically invisible to my eyes.

Furthermore, there may have been something in my mood that night, given my sojourn in a part of town I had never visited before, that influenced what I was able to see. And this mood had become steadily enhanced since I first stepped into the theater, and indeed from the moment I looked upon the marqee advertising a feature entitled *The Glamour*. Having at last found a place among the quietly expectant audience of the theater, I began to suffer an exacerbation of this mood. Specifically, I sensed a greater proximity to the point of focus for my mood that night, a tingling closeness to something quite literally *behind the scene*. Increasingly I became unconcerned with anything except the consummation or terminus of this abject and enchanting adventure. Consequences were evermore difficult to regard from my tainted perspective.

Therefore I was not hesitant when this focal point for my mood suddenly felt so near at hand, as close as the seat directly behind my own. I was quite sure this seat had been empty when I selected mine, that all the seats for several rows around me were unoccupied. And I would have been aware if someone had arrived to fill this seat directly behind me. Nevertheless, like a sudden chill announcing bad weather, there was now a definite presence I could feel at my back, a force of sorts that pressed itself upon me and inspired a surge of dark elation. But when I looked around, not quickly yet fully determined, I saw no

occupant in the seat behind me, nor in any seat between me and the back wall of
the theater. I continued to stare at the empty seat because my sensation of a vibrant
presence there was unrelieved. And in my staring I perceived that the fabric of the
seat, the inner webbing of swirling fibers, had composed a pattern in the image
of a face—an old woman's face with an expression of avid malignance, floating
amidst wild shocks of twisting hair. The face itself was a portrait of atrocity, a
grinning image of lust for sites and ceremonies of mayhem. It was formed of those
hairs stitching themselves together.

All the stringy, writhing cobwebs of that theater, as I now discovered, were the
reaching tendrils of a vast netting of hairs. And in this discovery my mood of the
evening, which had delivered me to a part of town I had never visited before and
to that very theater, only became more expansive and defined, taking in scenes of
graveyards and alleyways, reeking sewers and wretched corridors of insanity as well
as the immediate vision of an old theater that now, as I had been told, was under
new ownership. But my mood abruptly faded, along with the face in the fabric of
the theater seat, when a voice spoke to me. It said:

"You must have seen her, by the look of you."

A man sat down one seat away from mine. It was not the same person I had
met earlier; this one's face was nearly normal, although his suit was littered with
hair that was not his own.

"So did you see her?" he asked.

"I'm not sure what I saw," I replied.

He seemed almost to burst out giggling, his voice trembling on the edge of a
joyous hysteria. "You would be sure enough if there had been a private encounter,
I can tell you."

"Something was happening, then you sat down."

"Sorry," he said. "Did you know that the theater has just come under new
ownership?"

"I didn't notice what the showtimes are."

"Showtimes?"

"For the feature."

"Oh, there isn't any feature. Not as such."

"But there must be . . . something," I insisted.

"Yes, there's something," he replied excitedly, his fingers stroking his cheek.

"What, exactly. And these cobwebs . . ."

But the lights were going down into darkness. "Quiet now," he whispered. "It's
about to begin."

The screen before us was glowing a pale purple in the blackness, although I
heard no sounds from the machinery of a movie projector. Neither were there any
sounds connected with the images which were beginning to take form on the
screen, as if a lens were being focused on a microscopic world. And in some way
the movie screen might have been a great glass slide that projected to gigantic
proportions a landscape of organism normally hidden from our sight. But as these
visions coalesced and clarified, I recognized them as something I had already seen,
more accurately *sensed*, in that theater. The images were appearing on the screen
as if a pair of disembodied eyes were moving within venues of profound morbidity

and degeneration. Here was the purest essence of those places I had felt were superimposing themselves on the genuinely tangible aspects of the theater, those graveyards, alleys, decayed corridors, and subterranean passages whose spirit had intruded on another locale and altered it. Yet the places now revealed on the movie screen were without an identity I could name: they were the fundament of the sinister and seamy regions which cast their spectral ambience on the reality of the theater but which were themselves merely the shadows, the superficial counterparts of a deeper, more obscure realm. Farther and farther into it we were being taken.

The all-pervasive purple coloration could now be seen as emanating from the labyrinth of a living anatomy: a compound of the reddish, bluish, palest pink structures, all of them morbidly inflamed and lesioned to release a purple light. We were being guided through catacombs of putrid chambers and cloisters, the most secreted ways and waysides of an infernal land. Whatever these spaces may once have been, they were now habitations for ceremonies of a private sabbath. The hollows in their fleshy, gelatinous integuments streamed with something like moss, a fungus in thin strands that were threading themselves into translucent tissue and quivering beneath it like veins. It was the sabbath ground, secret and unconsecrated, but it was also the theater of an insane surgery. The hair-like sutures stitched among the yielding entrails, unseen hands designing unnatural shapes and systems, weaving a nest in which the possession would take place, a web wherein the bits and pieces of the anatomy could be consumed at leisure. There seemed to be no one in sight, yet everything was scrutinized from an intimate perspective, the viewpoint of that invisible surgeon, the weaver and webmaker, the old puppet-master who was setting the helpless creature with new strings and placing him under the control of a new owner. And through her eyes, entranced, we witnessed the work being done.

Then those eyes began to withdraw, and the purple world of the organism receded into purple shadows. When the eyes finally emerged from where they had been, the movie screen was filled with the face and naked chest of a man. His posture was rigid, betraying a state of paralysis, and his eyes were fixed, yet strikingly alive. "She's showing us," whispered the man who was sitting nearby me. "She has taken him. He cannot feel who he is any longer, only her presence within him."

This statement, at first sight of the possessed, seemed to be the case. Certainly such a view of the situation provided a terrific stimulus to my own mood of the evening, urging it toward culmination in a type of degraded rapture, a seizure of panic oblivion. Nonetheless, as I stared at the face of the man on the screen, he became known to me as the one I encountered in the vestibule of the theater. The recognition was difficult, however, because his flesh was now even more obscured by the webs of hair woven through it, thick as a full beard in spots. His eyes were also quite changed and glared out at the audience with a ferocity that suggested he indeed served as the host of great evil. But all the same, there was something in those eyes that belied the fact of a *complete* transformation—an awareness of the bewitchment and an appeal for deliverance. Within the next few moments, this observation assumed a degree of substance.

For the man on the movie screen regained himself, although briefly and in limited measure. His effort of will was evident in the subtle contortions of his face, and his ultimate accomplishment was modest enough: he managed to open his mouth in order to scream. Of course no sound was projected from the movie screen, which only played a music of images for eyes that would see what should not be seen. Thus, a disorienting effect was created, a sensory dissonance which resulted in my being roused from the mood of the evening, its spell over me echoing to nothingness. Because the scream that resonated in the auditorium had originated in another part of the theater, a place beyond the auditorium's towering back wall.

Consulting the man who was sitting near me, I found him oblivious to my comments about the scream within the theater. He seemed neither to hear nor see what was happening around him and what was happening to him. Long wiry hairs were sprouting from the fabric of the seats, sliding along their arms and along every part of them. The hairs had also penetrated into the cloth of the man's suit, but I could not make him aware of what was happening. Finally I rose to leave, because I could feel the hairs tugging to keep me in position. As I stood up they ripped away from me like stray threads pulled from a sleeve or pocket.

No one else in the auditorium turned away from the man on the movie screen, who had lost the ability to cry out and relapsed into a paralytic silence. Proceeding up the aisle I glanced above at a rectangular opening high in the back wall of the theater, the window-like slot from which images of a movie are projected. Framed within this aperture was the silhouette of what looked like an old woman with long and wildly tangled hair. I could see her eyes gazing fierce and malignant at the purple glow of the movie screen. And from these eyes were sent forth two shafts of the purest purple light that shot through the darkness of the auditorium.

Exiting the theater the way I had come in, it was not possible to ignore the words REST ROOM, so brightly were they now shining. But the lamp over the door in the alley was dead; the sign reading ENTRANCE TO THE THEATER was gone. Even the letters spelling out the name of the feature that evening had been taken down. So this had been the last performance. Henceforth the theater would be closed to the public.

Also closed, if only for the night, were all the other businesses along that particular street in a part of town I had never visited before. The hour was late, the shop windows were dark. But how sure I was that in each one of those dark windows I passed was the even darker silhouette of an old woman with glowing eyes and a great head of monstrous hair.

THE PEONY LANTERN

Kara Dalkey

Minneapolis writer Kara Dalkey is the author of four magical novels including *Euryale*, a mannered and lyrical tale set in Greece, and *The Nightingale*, a poignant retelling of Hans Christian Andersen's fairy tale transplanted to the courts of ancient Japan. Dalkey returns to Japan for the following story, first published in *Pulphouse* magazine, about which she writes:

"I came across the idea for this story from a book of woodblock prints by a nineteenth-century Japanese artist, Yoshitoshi. The book was called *Thirty-Six Ghosts*, and it contained thirty-six beautiful prints, each based on a Japanese ghost story or other theme of the supernatural. . . . Plate number 27 was *The Peony Lantern*."

—T.W.

The autumn wind blows through flame-boughed trees and they sigh like parted lovers, or mourners for the year that is dying. The wind brings me memories.

I come from a family of lantern makers, and that is my trade now. It is a good trade, even for an old man such as I am. But not long ago, I had the excellent fortune to be in the service of a young samurai. His name was Shinzaburo and he was but a younger son of a lesser branch of the Taira clan. Still, I was proud to be Chamberlain of the Wardrobe for his household, and he was a kind and just lord.

My skills were not wasted in his service. Shinzaburo was courting the Lady Tsuyu, and as a gift for her I made a peony lantern. I still believe it was the finest I ever made. The petals were of the sheerest pink silk and they glowed with the light from the candle within. I was told the Lady Tsuyu adored the gift and I felt well rewarded.

But those pleasant days melted away, as cherry blossoms before the heat of summer. Our lord Shinzaburo was called to war—the Taira clan again went to the battlefield against the voracious Minamoto. Only our lord's standard bearer went with him. The rest of us stayed behind, and kept his house, and waited.

And then we learned of the terrible defeat of the Taira. Our lord Shinzaburo and his standard bearer, we were told, died valiantly, though futilely, on the shores of Lake Biwa.

In sorrow, the household dispersed. His goods were taken to distant relatives and the other servants found other work. It was my sad task to inform the Lady Tsuyu of Shinzaburo's fate.

I remember kneeling on her veranda in the autumn rain. As I was but a lowly servant, it was not seemly that I should speak to a lady of Tsuyu's quality face to face. She sat behind cloth and wood blinds, and I could smell the chrysanthemum scent of her kimonos, hear them rustling with her small movements, see the trailing edge of one golden silk sleeve. The separation should have eased my discomfort, yet I was unable to find the proper words. I am no poet, but I passed to her under the blinds a blood-red leaf. "Our dear Shinzaburo is such as this," I said to her, "fallen, yet in passing, glorious."

I heard her sigh and knew she understood, but I did not hear her faint or weep. Her soft, young voice was steady as she thanked me for my message. She seemed resolute, her feet upon a path already chosen. I wished that I knew the appearance of her face, so that I could imagine her brave countenance. I asked if there was any service I could do for her. She politely said there was none and bade me go.

I returned the next morning to Tsuyu's house to see if there was yet anything I might do, for I knew my lord had loved her dearly, and would wish that she be looked after. But when I arrived, I found the lady's house deserted and empty. A neighbor said the whole household had packed up and stolen away in the middle of the night. I found myself wondering if Tsuyu had taken my peony lantern with her. As I passed the house one last time, I saw on one white shoji panel many spots of a dark red stain. *Ah,* I thought, *where the lady has gone she will have no need of lanterns.*

After this time, the only one of my lord's servants whom I kept as friend was Gyunyuko, Shinzaburo's old nursemaid. She was, and still is, a woman of grace and strength. Though she was very distressed to hear of our lord's death, yet her faith was strong and she was certain our lord sat among lotus petals in the Pure Land. She had no other family, having outlived them all, so I became as a nephew to her. She went to live in a nearby village while I stayed in Heian Kyo, and from time to time I would send her some of what I earned from my lantern making. Once a month we would meet in the marketplace and exchange news and pleasantries. I expected this was the way we would each live out the rest of our days.

Then, two years later, Gyunyuko came rushing up to greet me in the market-place. I still remember her white hair flying, her face like a child's on New Year's Day. "I have wonderful news!" she cried, grasping my arms.

"Don't tell me," I said, "You have just learned that you have a long-lost grandchild."

She grinned and beat a fist lightly against my arm. "Nearly as good! I have news of our lord Shinzaburo. He is not dead! A man in the village saw him return on a ship. Our lord should be here in Heian Kyo by now. Let us look for him!"

I cautioned her against listening to wild rumors, particularly those that give hope, but she would not be dissuaded. We sought out relatives of our lord. Those that would speak to us claimed not to have seen him. We went to all the places an itinerant samurai might be found, gambling dens, the willow district, the Rashomon. He was not there and none had seen him. At last, as evening threw its purple curtain across the sky, Gyunyuko and I wearily wandered back to the old house where we had served him.

And there he was. He stood staring at the now-dilapidated house, unmoving. The war had changed him. His face was more gaunt and pale, and his clothes were tattered. We rushed to Shinzaburo and bowed very low before him, exclaiming how pleased we were that he lived and had returned. We offered—no, begged—to again be in his service.

He regarded us with gentle, distant surprise. "I am sorry, my good friends," he said. "It gives me joy to see you. But I cannot keep you in my service. I am ronin, now. Go, please."

Gyunyuko and I pleaded that payment did not matter. We had each been frugal and had some savings. We would be happy enough with the honor of serving him.

At last, he said with a small, rueful smile, "Well, since I seem unable to send you away, I suppose you must have your wish."

With joy, Gyunyuko and I set about making the ruin of the old house livable, as much as our aging bones would let us. We swept and cleared three rooms whose partitions and screens were still intact, brought in braziers to ward off the chill. Shinzaburo seemed to take little interest in our activities, instead sitting quietly in contemplation of the night.

Naturally, I had to tell him about the Lady Tsuyu. He nodded solemnly, saying he had heard rumors of her fate. Then he changed the subject and I said no more about her.

For several days we tried to regain some of the contentment of past times. In the early morning, Shinzaburo would go off in search of work, while Gyunyuko and I spent the day making little improvements and repairs on the house. Gyunyuko would mend his clothes, exclaiming how filthy they were. I patched the torn and weather-stained shoji panels, and found the job similar to making a very large lantern.

In the evening, Shinzaburo would come back. There was no news of employment, but he never seemed disheartened. Even then, in fact, I had the feeling he was waiting for something. To his credit, unlike other ronin, he did not take to gambling or drinking away his troubles. Instead he would spend his nights alone, painting, or writing poetry, or staring out thoughtfully at the moonlight.

On the eve of the first day of O-Bon, Festival of the Dead, Gyunyuko asked our lord Shinzaburo what sort of fruits or vegetables he wished her to buy for offerings to his ancestors, and what sort of brazier or lantern to use for the last-night fire.

To our surprise, Shinzaburo shook his head. "You need get nothing, Gyunyuko. I will not be celebrating O-Bon this year." When we gasped in shock, he added, "I have no wish to see the ghosts of my ancestors. I feel too much shame. And I have no wish to celebrate death, for I have seen too much of it. Let there be no lights or feasts. You two may go join in the parades and dancing if you wish."

Gyunyuko did not protest further, but she retired to another room. After she left, I said softly, "No lights at all, Shinzaburo-sama? People will wonder. Neighbors will talk."

He was silent a moment, then said to me, "Do you remember that peony lantern you once made?"

"I remember it well, my lord."

"Could you make another? Not as elaborate, I cannot afford the silk. But from paper, perhaps?"

I said that I could and was pleased to see my lord smile.

The following day, the first day of O-Bon, I bought the paper and bamboo and spent the entire day making the peony lantern. I carefully fitted the bamboo struts together, pasted the paper peonies to the crown, and tied wide paper streamers to the sides. That evening, I hung the lantern on the gate post to dry. I hoped, also, that the neighbors might see it there and know that our household was not ignoring the proper festivities.

Shinzaburo stayed in that evening, as always. Gyunyuko retired to her room early, still worried, I think, about Shinzaburo. I went out to the veranda which overlooked a busy street and sat to watch the people go by.

Some bustled past carrying baskets of fruit to place on their household shrines. A group of men passed, carrying great taiko drums that boomed like thunder. Ladies of the willow districts strutted by in bright kimonos.

Most of all, I noticed the lanterns. It seemed half the people who passed carried one, gathering them for the last night of O-Bon. I could tell by the size, shape, and type of paper or silk used, which of my competitors had made which lanterns. Some had been made by the monks at local temples. I even recognized a few of my own, made in years past.

In all, I found the parade quite pleasing to watch. After the sun had set, the evening air had become cooler and less oppressive. The sky darkened to a deep purple and a few stars winked overhead. The passers-by in the street became fewer. Some children went laughing past, leaving a profound silence behind them. I began to consider rising and dragging my old bones to bed.

I saw a pink light bobbing in the distance down the road and it held my eye for a moment, then it was hidden behind the neighbor's hedge. A few moments later, I heard women's voices softly exclaiming at our gate. I turned and saw two women staring at my peony lantern. The taller one, who was dressed in kimonos the colors of moonlight, gaped at it in amazement. The smaller one of them was pointing at it, and in her hand she held another peony lantern precisely like it.

I rushed down to the gate and in my surprise blurted rudely, "Where did you get that lantern?"

The two ladies stepped back, startled. The taller one raised her sleeves demurely to cover the lower part of her face. The smaller one said, "Please pardon us, sir. This lantern was a present to my lady from Lord Shinzaburo. He used to live here, I think. We were very surprised to see another lantern like ours."

And then I realized that the smaller woman was Lady Tsuyu's serving maid, Yone. And the taller woman must be none other than the Lady Tsuyu herself. I gasped and bowed very low.

"Please pardon me, Lady Tsuyu," I said. "Had I recognized you, I would not have been so rude."

She laughed, and said, in a voice very like what I had heard two years ago, but more whispery and faint, "How could you recognize me when we have never seen one another?"

"Yes. And we had heard—oh, my lady, I have wonderful news for you. My lord Shinzaburo lives! He has returned home at last and is within."

Lady Tsuyu was so surprised, she lowered her sleeves from her face. "Truly?" she whispered.

I politely looked away, but not before noticing that her face was beautiful, but pale, and more delicate than a snowflake.

Shinzaburo must have heard our voices, for he then looked out from behind the blinds. "What is it—Ah!" He caught sight of the lady at once and scrambled onto the veranda. "Tsuyu-chan!" he cried.

The two women were equally astonished to see Shinzaburo. He called for her to join him and she and Yone readily came through the gate, smiling at my paper lantern as they passed it. Lady Tsuyu let Shinzaburo help her onto the veranda.

I decided it would be intruding for me to join the reunited lovers and so I went inside the house and sought out Gyunyuko.

"That cannot be," she said when I told her the news.

"It is true. Come look for yourself." I guided her to the blinds and we peeked out around the edge at the lovers and Yone sitting on the veranda. Shinzaburo must have commented on her appearance, for the Lady Tsuyu coughed gently behind her sleeve and said, "Yes, I am sure I must look different. Forgive me. I have been ill."

Yone bowed low in shame. "It is our great sorrow that we cannot appear in the finery of old times. Our family has become poor since the fall of the Taira, and I fear I am a very poor seamstress."

Shinzaburo said, "It does not matter. None of it matters. The love in my heart is no poorer and I am happy to share its wealth."

I let the blind fall silently back into place and Gyunyuko and I stepped down the hallway. "You see?" I said.

Gyunyuko only nodded, her ancient face very serious and thoughtful.

The following night, the second night of O-Bon, Lady Tsuyu returned and sat on the veranda, with Shinzaburo and me. She had again brought my peony lantern. She seemed even more delicate and pale than before, somehow. Her eyes were ever so slightly sunken into her face, so that in the light of my lantern, it suggested the face of a skull. No, I thought, *I am imagining things.* Yet I found myself wishing that I had noticed, as she climbed onto the veranda, whether the Lady Tsuyu had feet.

I shuddered and felt a need to leave. Murmuring about the cool wind and hinting that perhaps the Lord and Lady would like some privacy, I excused myself and withdrew behind the blinds into the house.

I stood in the dark hallway for some moments, trying to recapture my breath. *This is what he had been waiting for,* I realized. *He knew she would come. That is why he asked me to make the paper peony lantern. To guide her here.* I saw light approaching down the hallway. I started and then chided myself. It was only Gyunyuko carrying a candle.

"She has come again," she said, shuffling up to me, "hasn't she?"

"Yes!" I said, hoping enthusiasm might cover my apprehension. "Isn't it wonderful? It will be like the old times again."

Gyunyuko frowned at me in concern. "I know what is upsetting you. And it upsets me too. Lady Tsuyu has indeed come back to us . . . as a ghost."

I tried to laugh but could not. "But, that is foolishness."

"Look at her again. Look carefully."

I turned around and went to the blind. Pushing it aside just a little, I peered at Lady Tsuyu. She raised her face to gaze sweetly at Shinzaburo, and I saw between her lifted chin and the collar of her kimono a long white scar slashing down across her neck.

I looked away and let the blind fall back into place.

"You saw the scar?" Gyunyuko asked.

"Yes. But it was only a rumor that—"

"No. Her neighbors found the knife. And the blood."

"Yes," I said softly. "I saw the blood too."

"Then you know it is true."

I grasped her shoulders. "He loves her, Gyunyuko. What shall we do?"

Gyunyuko lowered her eyes and thought a moment. "She is not a vengeful ghost, so he is in no immediate danger. We can leave them be for now. But tomorrow we must speak to a priest. He can tell us what to do."

The following morning, after our lord had left on his usual search for employment, Gyunyuko and I went off to a temple. I had suggested we visit the Great Eastern Temple, Toji, but Gyunyuko shook her head and said it was more appropriate to visit the temple of Lady Tsuyu's former home.

It was a tiny neighborhood temple, but quite tidy and well-kept. The little graveyard beside it showed much tending. As we walked the step-stone path up to the temple, we came to a stone basin in front of a small statue of Kwannon, goddess of mercy. An inscription on the basin declared it to be a repository for prayers to those whose graves were far away or of unknown location. But what held my eyes was a little pink silk peony attached to a wooden prayer tag that lay at one side of the basin. With trembling hands, I picked up the tag. The prayer upon it asked the Amida to reunite the petitioner with a lost loved one. No name was on the tag, yet I knew with a certainty who had left it. "Poor Lady Tsuyu," I murmured.

"Poor Tsuyu!" Gyunyuko hissed. "Pah. She chose her path. Our duty is to protect our lord."

"I think he knows what she is. Is he not choosing his own path as well? Do we have the right to interfere?"

A gentle cough behind us made me jump like a guilty child caught stealing a piece of fruit. A bald priest stood there with a patient expression, as if people fished about in the prayer basins all the time. Though it was quite improper, I held up the prayer tag and said, "Could you possibly tell us who left this? We think it might have been . . . a relative of ours."

The priest looked at me dubiously, but answered, "It is interesting that you picked that one. It was left some nights ago by a mysterious woman in pale kimonos. The priest who saw her was quite astonished as, he said, she resembled a woman who was rumored to be two years dead. He tried to speak to her, but she hid her face and hurried off into the night. If she is, indeed, a relative of yours, you might put that poor priest's mind at rest by telling us who she is."

Gyunyuko then said, with a glare at me, "Forgive our misstatement, holy one. The woman who left this is not our relative. She was betrothed to our lord, Shinzaburo, and she has indeed been dead for two years. She is a ghost."

The priest's eyes widened. "Is it so? Well, that is not reassuring at all. Are you certain?"

"She is so pale and delicate, she hardly seems a creature of this world—"

"Many women try for such an effect," the priest said.

"But when we saw her up close, we saw her death scar on her neck."

"Ah," said the priest.

Gyunyuko said, "We have come to ask how we may protect our lord from her—"

"Or if he needs to be protected," I added.

"Well," said the priest, "if she is a ghost, then your lord should be protected. For though her visit may be for love, still she will drain his life from him, for she needs it to remain in this world."

"I am bothered that our lord does not see the danger himself."

"Well, it is said that ghosts have the power to delude those who love them. No doubt your lord thinks her the beauty he once knew. But this is a very inauspicious time for her visitation. On the last night of O-Bon, she must leave this world and return to the Hollow Land."

Gyunyuko sucked her breath between her teeth. "Then it must be that she intends to take our lord with her when she leaves. Please tell us, holy one, how may we protect him?"

"You must be sure that they are not together the last night of O-Bon."

"That is tomorrow night, holy one. How might we safely accomplish this?"

The priest rubbed his cheek, then brightened. "Wait here," he said, and strode back into the temple.

Gyunyuko said nothing to fill the silence he left behind. I think she was angry that I lied to the priest, or that I doubted what we were doing. I looked down and saw that I still held Lady Tsuyu's prayer tag. I gently placed it back in the basin beneath the statue of Kwannon.

Some while later, the priest returned, a bundle of old scrolls in his arms. "Here you are," he said, handing them to me. "We have extra copies of these sutras. You may have them for your lord's protection. Cover all the entrances to your house with these. Then, so long as the entrances are closed, no ghost may enter. This will keep her out on O-Bon night. And if she returns on the next," the priest shrugged for emphasis, "then you know she is not a ghost."

We thanked the priest and bowed to him many times, and carried the sutras home. We hid them behind the household shrine, and planned what we should do. The rest of that day, and that evening, we did nothing different. Even when Lady Tsuyu came again, we treated her as an honored guest. It was difficult for me to dissemble, though. Lady Tsuyu seemed more pale and ghastly than the night before. *Perhaps*, I thought, *because of our visit to the priest I am no longer burdened with delusions and I see her true form.* There was so much love in her eyes for our lord, however, that I could not hate her. Shinzaburo seemed to sense something was wrong with Gyunyuko and me, for he gave us strange glances. Still, we left him and the lady alone that night and I prayed their last night together would be a joyous one.

The following day, just before sunrise, Gyunyuko and I huddled in the kitchen to stay warm. We heard Shinzaburo and Tsuyu departing, our lord escorting her to the gate of the house. He sounded happy and hearty as ever. *Love can work such wonders*, I thought. I imagined them walking through the wild garden together, surrounded by morning mist. It was painful to think that it must end.

As soon as we were certain that Shinzaburo had left, we began our chore. The edge of very blind, every shoji, was covered with a sutra. I pasted the paper down carefully as Gyunyuko chanted the prayers. It was like building a giant temple lantem, and I wished I could take more joy in the process. At one point, I thought I saw Yone, Tsuyu's handmaid, peering through the garden gate. I called out to her, but she ran away. I wondered if she were a ghost too. It took nearly all day to finish covering all the entrances to the house. We left only one spot uncovered at the front entrance.

Just after sunset, Shinzaburo returned. He strode confidently through the open shoji where Gyunyuko, as always, knelt in welcome. As soon as he was inside, she slammed the shoji home and slapped a sutra over the remaining spot, sealing the house safe from any ghost who might try to enter.

Shinzaburo looked around at the holy prayers plastered all over the walls. He turned on Gyunyuko. "What have you done?" he demanded.

Gyunyuko bowed very low. "Our duty, Shinzaburo-sama. We are protecting you."

"Protecting me! From what?"

"It is our belief," I said, also bowing low, "that your Lady Tsuyu is a ghost. We had heard that she had killed herself—"

"Foolishness!" Shinzaburo shouted. "Tsuyu is not a ghost! I have held her in my own arms!"

"Please excuse our presumption, my lord, but we spoke to a priest today. He said that ghosts have the power to cast delusions over those who love them."

Shinzaburo bared his teeth, breathing rapidly in anger. "I knew I should never have hired you again. I should—"

We heard movement at the garden veranda and Lady Tsuyu calling, "Shinza-buro? Shinzaburo-chan?"

"Do not go to her, I beg you," said Gyunyuko. "This one night, do not go to her."

"Shinzaburo!" Tsuyu's voice cried. "Yone told me something may be wrong and I hurried here. What is it? What is wrong?"

"Nothing, Tsuyu-chan. I shall be there in a moment."

But Gyunyuko got to the veranda shoji first, scuttling quicker than I had ever seen her move. She knelt between Shinzaburo and the shoji, saying, "You must not let her in."

"Shinzaburo!" cried Lady Tsuyu. "Please, you promised! I must be with you tonight. We must be together! Don't leave me alone out here!"

"You see!" Gyunyuko hissed. "She will take you to the Land of Darkness with her."

"Old fool," Shinzaburo growled.

"My lord," I said, "Let it be for this one night. If your lady is here again tomorrow night, then it is proven she is not a ghost and you may do with us as you wish. Indulge us, please, this one foolishness. It is for your sake."

"Please!" Tsuyu shrieked behind the shoji. Her fingernails gashed the paper of the panels, like the claws of some wild animal, stopping where they came against the sutras.

Shinzaburo went to the simple wooden stand on which hung his long and short swords. He took up the short wakazashi and slowly drew it from its wooden scabbard. "Get away from the shoji," he said, his voice soft and deadly, his eyes bright with rage. Gyunyuko bowed her head and did not move.

I knew that Gyunyuko would die for her duty if I did not act. As Shinzaburo stepped forward, I grabbed Gyunyuko's arm and pulled her away from the shoji, sliding it open with my other hand. I spared Lady Tsuyu only one quick glance— she was a horror, with dark, sunken eyes, wild unkempt hair, and her face powder smeared and streaked. I hurried Gyunyuko out of the room and ran with her down the hallway to the farthest room of the house. There we huddled together in the dust.

"He has chosen his path," I said to her, stroking her white hair as she sobbed on my shoulder. In the distance, I could hear my lord and lady moaning, but I could not tell if they were cries of ecstasy or despair.

I must have slept, somehow, for I awoke to the sound of a scream. Sunlight was streaming in through the window slats, blinding me. I rose and staggered down the hallway to my lord's chamber. I arrived just as Gyunyuko stepped out, her face blank with shock.

"We never saw him in full daylight," she murmured. "I never saw him eat."

I grabbed her shoulders. "What are you saying? What has happened? Is our lord gone?"

Gyunyuko clutched at my sleeves and she stared up at me in terror and sorrow. "We were wrong!" She pointed into Shinzaburo's chamber. "We should have been protecting her!"

I looked in and saw the thin, pale, and freshly dead body of Lady Tsuyu lying amid the bleached bones of my lord Shinzaburo, who had indeed died two years before on the shores of Lake Biwa.

We later learned from Yone, the handmaid, that Lady Tsuyu had attempted sepukku the night after I gave her the news of Shinzaburo's death. She had not cut deep enough and her relatives were able to save her life. But she lost the child she was carrying, and had remained ill ever afterward.

Gyunyuko, burdened with shame, became a nun at a nearby Shinran temple, hoping to forget this world. I returned to my family trade of lantern making, at which I expect I shall work until I, too, leave this world.

It must be the melancholy autumn wind that brings me such thoughts. The trees sigh and whisper together. Fallen leaves chase one another playfully past my feet. I hope my lord and lady now dwell in joy, wherever their karma has taken them. Someone is bowing to me—I turn, but no. It is only the peony lantern nodding in the wind.

TO BE A HERO
Nancy Springer

"To Be a Hero" by Nancy Springer (whose short story "In Carnation" can be found elsewhere in this volume) comments on storytelling . . . and on life. It comes from *Weird Tales* magazine.

—T.W.

It always happens to ordinary guys like me
With maybe a secret sorrow
A missing father, a crippled arm
A fragile mother to support
A need for the services of a hero

And of course there is a woman I worship
Passionate and beautiful with wild wild hair
Who does not care about me at all.
Whether she would make me happy
Seems to be parenthetical.

So he comes out of nowhere, tall and dark
A fugitive from his own sad perilous past
He has been a gangster maybe or a jewel thief
Or a spy. He chooses me as a friend
Because I have all the innocence he has ever lost.

He is silent, handsome, he dresses in black
At first sight she falls hard in love with him
And he soft and wary and careful with her.
It is of course necessary that I should be blond
With blue eyes and a boyish grin.

When we fight over her he takes my blows
And won't hurt me even though I know
At least once he has killed a man.
Sooner or later he finds out about my father
Or I lose the farm or my mother dies
And I end up crying on his shoulder.

Or maybe he helps me save the home place
Or maybe I do it myself. I am after all
White hat to his black. He casts a long shadow,
By his side I catch the sun. Just knowing him
Has made me worthy to be a hero.

When his past tracks him down, when he goes away again
And we all know he can never come back,
Because he has made a man of me
He can hand the girl to me on a platter
But what does it matter. I don't want her anymore.
It's him I love.

THE SAME IN ANY LANGUAGE
Ramsey Campbell

Campbell sold his first story to August Derleth when he was sixteen years old and his first collection was published by Arkham House two years later. Since then he has written ten novels and numerous short stories and won both the British and World Fantasy Awards. His novel *The Count of Eleven* was recently published in the U.S., as was his story collection *Waking Nightmares*.

"The Same in Any Language" takes place on the exotic Greek island of Crete, is understated, well told, and makes the skin crawl—what more could one want?

—E.D.

The day my father is to take me where the lepers used to live is hotter than ever. Even the old women with black scarves wrapped around their heads sit inside the bus station instead of on the chairs outside the tavernas. Kate fans herself with her straw hat like a basket someone's sat on and gives my father one of those smiles they've made up between them. She's leaning forwards to see if that's our bus when he says, "Why do you think they call them lepers, Hugh?"

I can hear what he's going to say, but I have to humour him. "I don't know."

"Because they never stop leaping up and down."

It takes him much longer to say the first four words than the rest of it. I groan because he expects me to, and Kate lets off one of her giggles I keep hearing whenever they stay in my father's and my room at the hotel and send me down for a swim. "If you can't give a grin, give a groan," my father says for about the millionth time, and Kate pokes him with her freckly elbow as if he's too funny for words. She annoys me so much that I say, "Lepers don't rhyme with creepers, Dad."

"I never thought they did, son. I was just having a laugh. If we can't laugh we might as well be dead, ain't that straight, Kate?" He winks at her thigh and slaps his own instead, and says to me, "Since you're so clever, why don't you find out when our bus is coming?"

"That's it now."

"And I'm Hercules." He lifts up his fists to make his muscles bulge for Kate and says, "You're telling us that tripe spells A Flounder?"

"Elounda, Dad. It does. The letter like a **Y** upside-down is how they write an **L**."

"About time they learned how to write properly, then," he says, staring around to show he doesn't care who hears. "Well, there it is if you really want to trudge around another old ruin instead of having a swim."

"I expect he'll he able to do both once we get to the village," Kate says, but I can tell she's hoping I'll just swim. "Will you two gentlemen see me across the road?"

My mother used to link arms with me and my father when he was living with us. "I'd better make sure it's the right bus," I say, and run out so fast I can pretend I didn't hear my father calling me back.

A man with skin like a boot is walking backwards in the dust behind the bus, shouting "Elounda" and waving his arms as if he's pulling the bus into the space in line. I sit on a seat opposite two Germans who block the aisle until they've taken off their rucksacks, but my father finds three seats together at the rear. "Aren't you with us, Hugh?" he shouts, and everyone on the bus looks at him.

When I see him getting ready to shout again I walk down the aisle. I'm hoping nobody notices me, but Kate says loudly, "It's a pity you ran off like that, Hugh. I was going to ask if you'd like an ice cream."

"No thank you," I say, trying to sound like my mother when she was only just speaking to my father, and step over Kate's legs. As the bus rumbles uphill I turn as much of my back on her as I can, and watch the streets.

Agios Nikolaos looks as if they haven't finished building it. Some of the tavernas are on the bottom floors of blocks with no roofs, and sometimes there are more tables on the pavements outside than in. The bus goes downhill again as if it's hiccuping, and when it reaches the bottomless lake where young people with no children stay in the hotels with discos, it follows the edge of the bay. I watch the white boats on the blue water, but really I'm seeing the conductor coming down the aisle and feeling as if a lump's growing in my stomach from me wondering what my father will say to him.

The bus is climbing beside the sea when he reaches us. "Three for leper land," my father says.

The conductor stares at him and shrugs. "As far as you go," Kate says, and rubs herself against my father. "All the way."

When the conductor pushes his lips forwards out of his moustache and beard my father begins to get angry, unless he's pretending. "Where you kept your lepers. Spiny Lobster or whatever you call the damned place."

"It's Spinalonga, Dad, and it's off the coast from where we're going."

"I know that, and he should." My father is really angry now. "Did you get that?" he says to the conductor. "My ten-year-old can speak your lingo, so don't tell me you can't speak ours."

The conductor looks at me, and I'm afraid he wants me to talk Greek. My mother gave me a little computer that translates words into Greek when you type them, but I've left it at the hotel because my father said it sounded like a bird which only knew one note. "We're going to Elounda, please," I stammer.

"Elounda, boss," the conductor says to me. He takes the money from my father without looking at him and gives me the tickets and change. "Fish is good by the harbour in the evening," he says, and goes to sit next to the driver while the bus swings round the zigzags of the hill road.

My father laughs for the whole bus to hear. "They think you're so important, Hugh, you won't be wanting to go home to your mother."

Kate strokes his head as if he's her pet, then she turns to me. "What do you like most about Greece?"

She's trying to make friends with me like when she kept saying I should call her Kate, only now I see it's for my father's sake. All she's done is make me think how the magic places seemed to have lost their magic because my mother wasn't there with me, even Knossos where Theseus killed the Minotaur. There were just a few corridors left that might have been the maze he was supposed to find his way out of, and my father let me stay in them for a while, but then he lost his temper because all the guided tours were in foreign languages and nobody could tell him how to get back to the coach. We nearly got stuck overnight in Heraklion, when he'd promised to take Kate for dinner that night by the bottomless pool in Agios Nikolaos. "I don't know," I mumble, and gaze out the window.

"I like the sun, don't you? And the people when they're being nice, and the lovely, clear sea."

It sounds to me as if she's getting ready to send me off swimming again. They met while I was, our second morning at the hotel. When I came out of the sea my father had moved his towel next to hers and she was giggling. I watch Spinalonga Island float over the horizon like a ship made of rock and grey towers, and hope she'll think I'm agreeing with her if that means she'll leave me alone. But she says, "I suppose most boys are morbid at your age. Let's hope you'll grow up to be like your father."

She's making it sound as if the leper colony is the only place I've wanted to visit, but it's just another old place I can tell my mother I've been. Kate doesn't want to go there because she doesn't like old places—she said if Knossos was a palace she was glad she's not a queen. I don't speak to her again until the bus has stopped by the harbour.

There aren't many tourists, even in the shops and tavernas lined up along the winding pavement. Greek people who look as if they were born in the sun sit drinking at tables under awnings like stalls in a market. Some priests who I think at first are wearing black hat boxes on their heads march by, and fishermen come up from their boats with octopuses on sticks like big kebabs. The bus turns round in a cloud of dust and petrol fumes while Kate hangs onto my father with one hand and flaps the front of her flowery dress with the other. A boatman stares at the tops of her boobs which make me think of spotted fish and shouts "Spinalonga" with both hands round his mouth.

"We've hours yet," Kate says. "Let's have a drink. Hugh may even get that ice cream if he's good."

If she's going to talk about me as though I'm not there I'll do my best not to be. She and my father sit under an awning and I kick dust on the pavement outside until she says, "Come under, Hugh. We don't want you with sunstroke."

I don't want her pretending she's my mother, but if I say so I'll only spoil the day more than she already has. I shuffle to the table next to the one she's sharing with my father and throw myself on a chair. "Well, Hugh," she says, "do you want one?"

"No thank you," I say, even though the thought of an ice cream or a drink starts my mouth trying to drool.

"You can have some of my lager if it ever arrives," my father says at the top of his voice, and stares hard at some Greeks sitting at a table. "Anyone here a waiter?" he says, lifting his hand to his mouth as if he's holding a glass.

When all the people at the table smile and raise their glasses and shout cheerily at him, Kate says, "I'll find someone and then I'm going to the little girls' room while you men have a talk."

My father watches her crossing the road and gazes at the doorway of the taverna once she's gone in. He's quiet for a while, then he says, "Are you going to be able to say you had a good time?"

I know he wants me to enjoy myself when I'm with him, but I also think what my mother stopped herself from saying to me is true—that he booked the holiday in Greece as a way of scoring off her by taking me somewhere she'd always wanted to go. He stares at the taverna as if he can't move until I let him, and I say, "I expect so, if we go to the island."

"That's my boy. Never give in too easily." He smiles at me with one side of his face. "You don't mind if I have some fun as well, do you?"

He's making it sound as if he wouldn't have had much fun if it had just been the two of us, and I think that was how he'd started to feel before he met Kate. "It's your holiday," I say.

He's opening his mouth after another long silence when Kate comes out of the taverna with a man carrying two lagers and a lemonada on a tray. "See that you thank her," my father tells me.

I didn't ask for lemonada. He said I could have some lager. I say, "Thank you very much" and feel my throat tightening as I gulp the lemonada, because her eyes are saying she's won.

"That must have been welcome," she says when I put down the empty glass. "Another? Then I should find yourself something to do. Your father and I may be here for a while."

"Have a swim," my father suggests.

"I haven't brought my cossy."

"Neither have those boys," Kate says, pointing at the harbour. "Don't worry, I've seen boys wearing less."

My father smirks behind his hand, and I can't bear it. I run to the jetty the boys are diving off, and drop my T-shirt and shorts on it and my sandals on top of them, and dive in.

The water's cold, but not for long. It's full of little fish that nibble you if you only float, and it's clearer than tap water, so you can see down to the pebbles and the fish pretending to be them. I chase fish and swim underwater and almost catch an octopus before it squirms out to sea. Then three Greek boys about my age swim over, and we're pointing at ourselves and saying our names when I see Kate and my father kissing.

I know their tongues are in each other's mouths—getting some tongue, the kids at my school call it. I feel like swimming away as far as I can go and never coming back. But Stavros and Stathis and Costas are using their hands to tell me we should see who can swim fastest, so I do that instead. Soon I've forgotten my father and Kate, even when we sit on the jetty for a rest before we have more races. It must be hours later when I realise Kate is calling, "Come here a minute."

The sun isn't so hot now. It's reaching under the awning, but she and my father haven't moved back into the shadow. A boatman shouts "Spinalonga" and points at how low the sun is. I don't mind swimming with my new friends instead of going to the island, and I'm about to tell my father so when Kate says, "I've been telling your dad he should be proud of you. Come and see what I've got for you."

They've both had a lot to drink. She almost falls across the table as I go to her. Just as I get there I see what she's going to give me, but it's too late. She grabs my head with both hands and sticks a kiss on my mouth.

She tastes of old lager. Her mouth is wet and bigger than mine, and when it squirms it makes me think of an octopus. "Mmm*mwa*," it says, and then I manage to duck out of her hands, leaving her blinking at me as if her eyes won't quite work. "Nothing wrong with a bit of loving," she says. "You'll find that out when you grow up."

My father knows I don't like to be kissed, but he's frowning at me as if I should have let her. Suddenly I want to get my own back on them in the only way I can think of. "We need to go to the island now."

"Better go to the loo first," my father says. "They wouldn't have one on the island when all their willies had dropped off."

Kate hoots at that while I'm getting dressed, and I feel as if she's laughing at the way my ribs show through my skin however much I eat. I stop myself from shivering in case she or my father makes out that's a reason for us to go back to the hotel. I'm heading for the toilet when my father says, "Watch out you don't catch anything in there or we'll have to leave you on the island."

I know there are all sorts of reasons why my parents split up, but just now this is the only one I can think of—my mother not being able to stand his jokes and how the more she told him to finish the more he would do it, as if he couldn't stop himself. I run into the toilet, trying not to look at the pedal bin where you have to drop the used paper, and close my eyes once I've taken aim.

Is today going to be what I remember about Greece? My mother brought me up to believe that even the sunlight here had magic in it, and I expected to feel the ghosts of legends in all the old places. If there isn't any magic in the sunlight, I want there to be some in the dark. The thought seems to make the insides of my eyelids darker, and I can smell the drains. I pull the chain and zip myself up, and then I wonder if my father sent me in here so we'll miss the boat. I nearly break the hook on the door, I'm so desperate to be outside.

The boat is still tied to the harbour, but I can't see the boatman. Kate and my father are holding hands across the table, and my father's looking around as though he means to order another drink. I squeeze my eyes shut so hard that when I open them everything's gone black. The blackness fades along with whatever I wished, and I see the boatman kneeling on the jetty, talking to Stavros. "Spinalonga," I shout.

He looks at me, and I'm afraid he'll say it's too late. I feel tears building up behind my eyes. Then he stands up and holds out a hand towards my father and Kate. "One hour," he says.

Kate's gazing after a bus that has just begun to climb the hill. "We may as well go over as wait for the next bus," my father says, "and then it'll be back to the hotel for dinner."

Kate looks sideways at me. "And after all that he'll be ready for bed," she says like a question she isn't quite admitting to.

"Out like a light, I reckon."

"Fair enough," she says, and uses his arm to get herself up.

The boatman's name is Iannis, and he doesn't speak much English. My father seems to think he's charging too much for the trip until he realises it's that much for all three of us, and then he grins as if he thinks Iannis has cheated himself. "Heave ho then, Janice," he says with a wink at me and Kate.

The boat is about the size of a big rowing-boat. It has a cabin at the front and benches along the sides and a long box in the middle that shakes and smells of petrol. I watch the point of the boat sliding through the water like a knife and feel as if we're on our way to the Greece I've been dreaming of. The white buildings of Elounda shrink until they look like teeth in the mouth of the hills of Crete, and Spinalonga floats up ahead.

It makes me think of an abandoned ship bigger than a liner, a ship so dead that it's standing still in the water without having to be anchored. The evening light seems to shine out of the steep rusty sides and the bony towers and walls high above the sea. I know it was a fort to begin with, but I think it might as well have been built for the lepers. I can imagine them trying to swim to Elounda and drowning because there wasn't enough left of them to swim with, if they didn't just throw themselves off the walls because they couldn't bear what they'd turned into. If I say these things to Kate I bet more than her mouth will squirm—but my father gets in first. "Look, there's the welcoming committee."

Kate gives a shiver that reminds me I'm trying not to feel cold. "Don't say things like that. They're just people like us, probably wishing they hadn't come."

I don't think she can see them any more clearly than I can. Their heads are poking over the wall at the top of the cliff above a little pebbly beach which is the only place a boat can land. There are five or six of them, only I'm not sure they're heads; they might be stones someone has balanced on the wall—they're almost the same colour. I'm wishing I had some binoculars when Kate grabs my father so hard the boat rocks and Iannis waves a finger at her, which doesn't please my father. "You keep your eye on your steering, Janice," he says.

Iannis is already taking the boat toward the beach. He didn't seem to notice the heads on the wall, and when I look again they aren't there. Maybe they belonged to some of the people who are coming down to a boat bigger than Iannis's. That boat chugs away as Iannis's bumps into the jetty. "One hour," he says. "Back here."

He helps Kate onto the jetty while my father glowers at him, then he lifts me out of the boat. As soon as my father steps onto the jetty Iannis pushes the boat out again. "Aren't you staying?" Kate pleads.

He shakes his head and points hard at the beach. "Back here, one hour."

She look as if she wants to run into the water and climb aboard the boat, but my father shoves his arm around her waist. "Don't worry, you've got two fellers to keep you safe, and neither of them with a girl's name."

The only way up to the fort is through a tunnel that bends in the middle so you can't see the end until you're nearly halfway in. I wonder how long it will take for the rest of the island to be as dark as the middle of the tunnel. When Kate sees the end she runs until she's in the open and stares at the sun, which is perched on top of the towers now. "Fancying a climb?" my father says.

She makes a face at him as I walk past her. We're in a kind of street of stone sheds that have mostly caved in. They must be where the lepers lived, but there are only shadows in them now, not even birds. "Don't go too far, Hugh," Kate says.

"I want to go all the way round, otherwise it wasn't worth coming."

"I don't, and I'm sure your father expects you to consider me."

"Now, now, children," my father says. "Hugh can do as he likes as long as he's careful and the same goes for us, eh, Kate?"

I can tell he's surprised when she doesn't laugh. He looks unsure of himself and angry about it, the way he did when he and my mother were getting ready to tell me they were splitting up. I run along the line of huts and think of hiding in one so I can jump out at Kate. Maybe they aren't empty after all; something rattles in one as if bones are crawling about in the dark. It could be a snake under part of the roof that's fallen. I keep running until I come to steps leading up from the street to the top of the island, where most of the light is, and I've started jogging up them when Kate shouts, "Stay where we can see you. We don't want you hurting yourself."

"It's all right, Kate; leave him be," my father says. "He's sensible."

"If I'm not allowed to speak to him, I don't know why you invited me at all."

I can't help grinning as I sprint to the top of the steps and duck out of sight behind a grassy mound that makes me think of a grave. From up here I can see the whole island, and we aren't alone on it. The path I've run up from leads all round the island, past more huts and towers and a few bigger buildings, and then it goes down to the tunnel. Just before it does it passes the wall above the beach, and between the path and the wall there's a stone yard full of slabs. Some of the slabs have been moved away from holes like long boxes full of soil or darkness. They're by the wall where I thought I saw heads looking over at us. They aren't there now, but I can see heads bobbing down towards the tunnel. Before long they'll be behind Kate and my father.

Iannis is well on his way back to Elounda. His boat is passing one that's heading for the island. Soon the sun will touch the hills. If I went down to the huts I'd see it sink with me and drown. Instead I lie on the mound and look over the island, and see more of the boxy holes hiding behind some of the huts. If I went closer I could see how deep they are, but I quite like not knowing—if I was Greek I expect I'd think they lead to the underworld where all the dead live. Besides, I like being able to look down on my father and Kate and see them trying to see me.

I stay there until Iannis's boat is back at Elounda and the other one has almost reached Spinalonga, and the sun looks as if it's gone down to the hills for a rest. Kate and my father are having an argument. I expect it's about me, though I can't hear what they're saying; the darker it gets between the huts the more Kate waves her arms. I'm getting ready to let my father see me when she screams.

She's jumped back from a hut which has a hole behind it. "Come out, Hugh. I know it's you," she cries.

I can tell what my father's going to say, and I cringe. "Is that you, Hugh? Yoo-hoo," he shouts.

I won't show myself for a joke like that. He leans into the hut through the spiky stone window, then he turns to Kate. "It wasn't Hugh. There's nobody."

I can only just hear him, but I don't have to strain to hear Kate. "Don't tell me that," she cries. "You're both too fond of jokes."

She screams again, because someone's come running up the tunnel. "Everything all right?" this man shouts. "There's a boat about to leave if you've had enough."

"I don't know what you two are doing," Kate says like a duchess to my father, "but I'm going with this gentleman."

My father calls to me twice. If I go with him I'll be letting Kate win. "I don't think our man will wait," the new one says.

"It doesn't matter," my father says, so fiercely that I know it does. "We've our own boat coming."

"If there's a bus before you get back I won't be hanging around," Kate warns him.

"Please yourself," my father says, so loud that his voice goes into the tunnel. He stares after her as she marches away; he must be hoping she'll change her mind. But I see her step off the jetty into the boat, and it moves out to sea as if the ripples are pushing it to Elounda.

My father puts a hand to his ear as the sound of the engine fades. "So every bugger's left me now, have they?" he says in a kind of shout at himself. "Well, good riddance."

He's waving his fists as if he wants to punch something, and he sounds as if he's suddenly got drunk. He must have been holding it back when Kate was there. I've never seen him like this. It frightens me, so I stay where I am.

It isn't only my father that frightens me. There's only a little bump of the sun left above the hills of Crete now, and I'm afraid how dark the island may be once that goes. Bits of sunlight shiver on the water all the way to the island, and I think I see some heads above the wall of the yard full of slabs, against the light. Which side of the wall are they on? The light's too dazzling; it seems to pinch the sides of the heads so they look thinner than any heads I've ever seen. Then I notice a boat setting out from Elounda, and I squint at it until I'm sure it's Iannis's boat.

He's coming early to fetch us. Even that frightens me, because I wonder why he is. Doesn't he want us to be on the island now he realizes how dark it's getting? I look at the wall, and the heads have gone. Then the hills put the sun out, and it feels as if the island is buried in darkness.

I can still see my way down—the steps are paler than the dark—and I don't like being alone now that I've started shivering. I back off from the mound, because I don't like to touch it, and almost back into a shape with bits of its head poking out and arms that look as if they've dropped off at the elbows. It's a cactus. I'm just standing up when my father says, "There you are, Hugh."

He can't see me yet. He must have heard me gasp. I go to the top of the steps, but I can't see him for the dark. Then his voice moves away. "Don't start hiding again. Looks like we've seen the last of Kate; but we've got each other, haven't we?"

He's still drunk. He sounds as if he's talking to somebody nearer to him than I am. "All right, we'll wait on the beach," he says, and his voice echoes. He's gone into the tunnel, and he thinks he's following me. "I'm here, Dad," I shout so loud that I squeak.

"I heard you, Hugh. Wait there. I'm coming." He's walking deeper into the tunnel. While he's in there my voice must seem to be coming from beyond the far end. I'm sucking in a breath that tastes dusty, so I can tell him where I am, when he says, "Who's that?" with a laugh that almost shakes his words to pieces.

He's met whoever he thought was me when he was heading for the tunnel. I'm holding my breath—I can't breathe or swallow—and I don't know if I feel hot or frozen. "Let me past," he says as if he's trying to make his voice as big as the tunnel. "My son's waiting for me on the beach."

There are so many echoes in the tunnel I'm not sure what I'm hearing besides him. I think there's a lot of shuffling; and the other noise must be voices, because my father says, "What kind of language do you call that? You sound drunker than I am. I said my son's waiting."

He's talking even louder as if that'll make him understood. I'm embarrassed, but I'm more afraid for him. "Dad," I nearly scream, and run down the steps as fast as I can without falling.

"See, I told you. That's my son," he says as if he's talking to a crowd of idiots. The shuffling starts moving like a slow march, and he says, "All right, we'll all go to the beach together. What's the matter with your friends, too drunk to walk?"

I reach the bottom of the steps, hurting my ankles, and run along the ruined street because I can't stop myself. The shuffling sounds as if it's growing thinner, as if the people with my father are leaving bits of themselves behind, and the voices are changing too—they're looser. Maybe the mouths are getting bigger somehow. But my father's laughing, so loud that he might be trying to think of a joke. "That's what I call a hug. No harder, love, or I won't have any puff left," he says to someone. "Come on then; give us a kiss. They're the same in any language."

All the voices stop, but the shuffling doesn't. I hear it go out of the tunnel and onto the pebbles, and then my father tries to scream as if he's swallowed something that won't let him. I scream for him and dash into the tunnel, slipping on things that weren't on the floor when we first came through, and fall out onto the beach.

My father's in the sea. He's already so far out that the water is up to his neck. About six people who look stuck together and to him are walking him away as if they don't need to breathe when their heads start to sink. Bits of them float away on the waves my father makes as he throws his arms about and gurgles. I try to run after him, but I've got nowhere when his head goes underwater. The sea pushes me back on the beach, and I run crying up and down it until Iannis comes.

It doesn't take him long to find my father once he understands what I'm saying. Iannis wraps me in a blanket and hugs me all the way to Elounda, and the police take me back to the hotel. Kate gets my mother's number and calls her, saying she's someone at the hotel who's looking after me because my father's drowned; and I don't care what she says, I just feel numb. I don't start screaming until I'm on the plane back to England, because then I dream that my father has come back to tell a joke. "That's what I call getting some tongue," he says, leaning his face close to mine and showing me what's in his mouth.

TERATISMS
Kathe Koja

Koja, whose story "Angels in Love" also appears in this volume, depicts a hellish vision of the nuclear family gone mad in "Teratisms." It's reminiscent of the artificially created family in the film *Near Dark*; the dysfunction is so massive that the family virtually cannibalizes itself from within.

—E.D.

"Beaumont." Dreamy, Alex's voice. Sitting in the circle of the heat, curtains drawn in the living room: laddered magenta scenes of birds and dripping trees. "Delcambre. Thibodaux." Slow-drying dribble like rusty water on the bathroom floor. "Abbeville," car door slam, "Chinchuba," screen door slam. Triumphant through its echo, "Baton Rouge!"

Tense hoarse holler almost childish with rage: "Will you shut the fuck *up?*"

From the kitchen, woman's voice, Randle's voice, drawl like cooling blood: "Mitch's home."

"You're damn right Mitch is home." Flat slap of his unread newspaper against the cracked laminate of the kitchen table, the whole set from the Goodwill for thirty dollars. None of the chairs matched. Randle sat in the cane-bottomed one, leg swinging back and forth, shapely metronome, making sure the ragged gape of her tank top gave Mitch a good look. Fanning herself with four slow fingers.

"Bad day, big brother?"

Too tired to sit, propping himself jackknife against the counter. "They're all bad, Francey."

"Mmmm, forgetful. My name's Randle now."

"Doesn't matter what your name is, you're still a bitch."

Soft as dust, from the living room: "De Quincy. Longville." Tenderly, "Bewelcome."

Mitch's sigh. "Numbnuts in there still at it?"

"All day."

Another sigh, he bent to prowl the squat refrigerator, let the door fall shut. Half-angry again, "There's nothing in here to eat, Fran—Randle."

"So what?"

"So what'd you eat?"

More than a laugh, bubbling under. "I don't think you really want to know." Deliberately exposing half a breast, palm lolling beneath like a sideshow, like a street-corner card trick. Presto. "Big brother."

His third sigh, lips closed in decision. "I don't need this," passing close to the wall, warding the barest brush against her, her legs in the chair as deliberate, a sluttish spraddle but all of it understood: an old, unfunny family joke; like calling names; nicknames.

The door slamming, out as in, and in the settling silence of departure: "Is he gone?"

Stiff back, Randle rubbing too hard the itchy tickle of sweat. Pushing at the table to move the chair away. "You heard the car yourself, Alex. You know he's gone."

Pause, then plaintive, "Come sit with me." Sweet; but there are nicknames and nicknames, jokes and jokes; a million ways to say I love you. Through the raddled arch into the living room, Randle's back tighter still, into the smell, and Alex's voice, bright.

"Let's talk," he said.

Mitch, so much later, pausing at the screenless front door, and on the porch Randle's cigarette, drawing lines in the dark like a child with a sparkler.

"Took your time," she said.

Defensively, "It's not that late."

"I know what time it is."

He sat down, not beside her but close enough to speak softly and be heard. "You got another cigarette?"

She took the pack from somewhere, flipped it listless to his lap. "Keep 'em. They're yours anyway."

He lit the cigarette with gold foil matches, JUDY'S DROP-IN. An impulse, shaming, to do as he used to, light a match and hold it to her fingertips to see how long it took to blister. No wonder she hated him. "Do you hate me?"

"Not as much as I hate him." He could feel her motion, half a head-shake. "Do you know what he did?"

"The cities."

"Besides the cities." He did not see her fingers, startled twitch as he felt the pack of cigarettes leave the balance of his thigh. "He was down by the grocery store, the dumpster. Playing. It took me almost an hour just to talk him home." A black sigh. "He's getting worse."

"You keep saying that."

"It keeps being true, Mitch, whether you want to think so or not. Something really bad's going to happen if we don't get him—"

"Get him what?" Sour. No bitter. "A doctor? A *shrink*? How about a one-way ticket back to Shitsburg so he—"

"Fine, that's fine. But when the cops come knocking I'll let you answer the door," and her quick feet bare on the step, into the house. Tense unconscious rise of his shoulders: Don't slam the door. Don't wake him up.

Mitch slept, weak brittle doze in the kitchen, head pillowed on the Yellow Pages. Movement, the practiced calm of desire. Stealth, until denouement, a waking startle to Alex's soft growls and tweaks of laughter, his giggle and spit. All over the floor. All over the floor and his hands, oh God Alex your *hands*—

Showing them off the way a child would, elbows turned, palms up. Showing them in the jittery bug-light of the kitchen in the last half hour before morning, Mitch bent almost at the waist, then sinking back, nausea subsiding but unbanished before the immensity, the drip and stutter, there was some on his mouth too. His chin, Mitch had to look away from what was stuck there.

"Go on," he said. "Go get your sister."

And waited there, eyes closed, hands spread like a medium on the Yellow Pages. While Alex woke his sister. While Randle used the washcloth. Again.

Oxbow lakes. Flat country. Randle sleeping in the back seat, curled and curiously hot, her skin ablush with sweat in the sweet cool air. Big creamy Buick with all the windows open. Mitch was driving, slim black sunglasses like a cop in a movie, while Alex sat playing beside him. Old wrapping paper today, folding in his fingers, disappearing between his palms. Always paper. Newsprint ink under his nails. Glossy foilwrap from some party, caught between the laces of his sneakers. Or tied there. Randle might have done that, it was her style. Grim droll jokery. Despite himself he looked behind, into the back seat, into the stare of her open eyes, so asphalt blank that for one second fear rose like a giant waiting to be born and he thought, Oh no, oh not her too.

Beside him Alex made a playful sound.

Randle's gaze snapped true into her real smile; bared her teeth in burlesque before she rolled over, pleased.

"Fucking bitch," with dry relief. With feeling.

Alex said, "I'm hungry."

Mitch saw he had begun to eat the paper. "We'll find a drive-through somewhere," he said, and for a moment dreamed of flinging the wheel sideways, of fast and greasy death. Let someone else clean up for a change.

There was a McDonald's coming up, garish beside the blacktop; he got into the right lane just a little too fast. "Randle," coldly, "put your shirt on."

Chasing the end of the drive-through line, lunchtime and busy and suddenly Alex was out of the car, leaned smiling through the window to say, "I want to eat inside." And gone, trotting across the parking lot, birthday paper forgotten on the seat beside.

"Oh God," Mitch craning, tracking his progress, "go after him, Randle," and Randle's snarl, the bright slap of her sandals as she ran. Parking, he considered driving off. Alone. Leaving them there. Don't you ever leave them, swear me.

You have to swear me, Michie. Had she ever really said that? Squeezed out a promise like a dry log of shit? I hope there is a hell, he thought, turning off the car, I hope it's big and hot and eternal and that she's in it.

They were almost to the counter, holding hands. When Randle saw him enter, she looked away; he saw her fingers squeeze Alex's, twice and slow. What was it like for her? Middleman. Alex was staring at the wall menu as if he could read. "I'll get a booth," Mitch said.

A table, instead; there were no empty booths. One by one Alex crumbled the chocolate-chip cookies, licked his fingers to dab up the crumbs. Mitch drank coffee.

"That's making me sick," he said to Randle.

Her quick sideways look at Alex. "What?" through half a mouthful, a tiny glob of tartar sauce rich beside her lower lip.

"That smell," nodding at her sandwich. "Fish."

Mouth abruptly stretched, chewed fish and half-smeared sauce, he really was going to be sick. Goddamned *bitch*. Nudging him under the table with one bare foot. Laughing into her Coke.

"Do you always have to make it worse?"

Through another mouthful, "It can't get any worse." To Alex, "Eat your cookies."

Mitch drank more coffee; it tasted bitter, boiled. Randle stared over his head as she ate: watching the patrons? staring at the wall? Alex coughed on cookie crumbs, soft dry cough. Gagged a little. Coughed harder.

"Alex?" Randle put down her sandwich. "You okay? Slap his back," commandingly to Mitch, and he did, harder as Alex kept coughing, almost a barking sound now and heads turned, a little, at the surrounding tables, the briefest bit of notice that grew more avid as Alex's distress increased, louder whoops and Randle suddenly on her feet, trying to raise him up as Mitch saw the first flecks of blood.

"Oh *shit*," but it was too late, Alex spitting blood now, spraying it, coughing it out in half-digested clots as Randle, frantic, working to haul him upright as Mitch in some stupid reflex swabbed with napkins at the mess. Tables emptied around them. Kids crying, loud and scared, McDonald's employees surrounding them but not too close, Randle shouting, "*Help* me, you asshole!" and Mitch in dumb paralysis watched as a tiny finger, red but recognizable, flew from Alex's mouth to lie wetly on the seat.

Hammerlock, no time to care if it hurts him, Randle already slamming her back against the door to hold it open and Alex's staining gurgle hot as piss against his shoulder, Randle screaming, "Give me the keys! Give me the keys!" Her hand digging hard into his pocket as he swung Alex, white-faced, into the back seat, lost his balance as the car jerked into gear and fell with the force of motion to his temple, dull and cool, against the lever of the seat release.

And lay there, smelling must and the faint flavor of motor oil, Alex above collapsed into silence, lay a long time before he finally thought to ask, "Where're we going?" He had to ask it twice to cut the blare of the radio.

Randle didn't turn around. "Hope there's nothing in that house you wanted."

*   *   *

Night, and the golden arches again. This time they ate in the car, taking turns to go inside to pee, to wash, the rest rooms small as closets. Gritty green soap from the dispenser. Alex ate nothing. Alex was still asleep.

Randle's lolling glance, too weary to sit up straight anymore. "You drive for a while," she said. "Keep on I-10 till you get—"

"I know," louder than he meant; he was tired too. It was a chore just to keep raising his hand to his mouth. Randle was feeling for something, rooting slowly under the seat, in her purse. When he raised his eyebrows at her she said, "You got any cigarettes?"

"Didn't you just buy a pack?"

Silence, then, "I left them at the house. On the back of the toilet," and without fuller warning began to weep, one hand loose against her mouth. Mitch turned his head, stared at the parking lot around them, the fluttering jerk of headlights like big fat clumsy birds. "I'm sick of leaving stuff places," she said. Her hand muffled her voice, made it sound like she spoke from underwater, some calm green place where voices could never go. "Do you know how long I've been wearing this shirt?" and before he could think if it was right to give any answer, "Five days. That's how long. Five fucking days in this same fucking shirt."

From the back seat Alex said, "Breaux Bridge," in a tone trusting and tender as a child's. Without turning, without bothering to look, Randle pistoned her arm in a backhand punch so hard Mitch flinched watching it.

Flat-voiced, "You just shut up," still without turning, as if the back seat had become impossible for her. "That's all you have to do. Just shut up."

Mitch started the car. Alex began to moan, a pale whimper that undercut the engine noise. Randle said, "I don't care what happens, don't wake me up." She pulled her T-shirt over her head and threw it out the window.

"Randle, for God's sake! At least wait till we get going."

"Let them look." Her breasts were spotted in places, a rashy speckle strange in the greenish dashlight, like some intricate tattoo the details of which became visible only in hard daylight. She lay with her head on his thigh, the flesh beneath her area of touch asleep before she was. He drove for almost an hour before he lightly pushed her off.

And in the back seat the endless sound of Alex, his rustling paper, the marshy odor of his tears. To Mitch it was as if the envelope of night had closed around them not forever but for so long there was no difference to be charted or discerned. Like the good old days. Like Alex staggering around and around, newspaper carpets and the funnies especially, vomiting blood that eclipsed the paler smell of pigeon shit from the old pigeon coop. Pigeonnier. Black dirt, alluvial crumble and sprayed like tarot dust across the blue-tiled kitchen floor. Wasn't it strange that he could still remember that tile, its gaudy Romanesque patterns? Remember it as he recalled his own nervous shiver, hidden like treasure behind the mahogany boards. And Randle's terrified laughter. Momma. Promises, his hands between her dusty palms; they were so small then, his hands. Alex wiping uselessly at the scabby drip of his actions, even then you had to watch him all the time. Broken glasses, one after another. Willow bonfires. The crying cicadas, no, that was happening now, wasn't it? Through the Buick's open windows. Through the hours and hours of driving until the air went humid with daylight and the reeking shimmer of exhaust, and Randle stirring closed-eyed on the front seat beside him and murmuring, anxious in her sleep, "Alex?"

He lay one hand on her neck, damp skin, clammy. "Shhhh, he's all right. It's still my turn. He's all right."

And kept driving. The rustle of paper in the back seat. Alex's soft sulky hum, like some rare unwanted engine that no lack of fuel could hamper, that no one could finally turn off.

And his hands on the wheel as silent as Randle's calmed breathing, as stealthy as Alex's cities, the litany begun anew: Florien, Samtown, Echo, Lecomte, drifting forward like smoke from a secret fire, always burning, like the fires on the levees, like the fire that took their home. Remember that? Mouth open, catching flies his mother would have said. Blue flame like a gas burner. What color does blood burn?

And his head hanging down as if shamefaced, as if dunned and stropped by the blunt hammer of anger, old anger like the fires that never burned out. And his eyes closing, sleeping, though he woke to think, Pull over, had to, sliding heedless as a drunken man over to the shoulder to let himself fall, forehead striking gentle against the steering wheel as if victim of the mildest of accidents. Randle still asleep on the seat beside. Alex, was he still saying his cities? Alex? Paper to play with? "Alex," but he spoke the word without authority, in dreams against a landscape not welcome but necessary: in which the rustle of Alex's paper mingled with the slower dribble of his desires, the whole an endless pavane danced through the cities of Louisiana, the smaller, the hotter, the better. And he, and Randle too, were somehow children again, kids at the old house where the old mantle of protection fell new upon them, and they unaware and helpless of the burden, ignorant of the loss they had already and irrevocably sustained, loss of life while living it. You have to swear me, Michie. And Randle, not Randle then, not Francey but Marie-Claire, that was her name, Marie-Claire promising as he did, little sister with her hands outstretched.

The car baked slow and thorough in the shadeless morning, too far from the trees. Alex, grave as a gargoyle chipped cunningly free, rose, in silence the back door handle and through the open windows his open palms, let the brownish flakes cascade down upon Mitch and Randle both, swirling like the glitter-snow in a paperweight, speckles, freckles, changing to a darker rain, so lightly they never felt it, so quiet they never heard. And gone.

The slap of consciousness, Randle's cry, disgust, her hands grubby with it, scratching at the skin of her forearms so new blood rose beneath the dry. Scabbed with blood, painted with it. Mitch beside her, similarly scabbed, brushing with a detached dismay, not quite fastidious, as if he were used to waking covered with the spoor of his brother's predilections.

"I'm not his mother!" Screaming. She was losing it, maybe already had. Understandable. Less so his own lucidity, back calm against the seat; shock-free? Maybe he was crazier than she was. Crazier than Alex, though that would be pushing it. She was still screaming, waves of it that shook her breasts. He was getting an erection. Wasn't that something.

"I'm sick of him being a monster. I can't—"

"We have to look for him."

"You look! You look! I'm tired of looking!" Snot on her lips. He grabbed her by the breasts, distant relish, and shoved her very hard against the door. She stopped screaming and started crying, a dry drone that did not indicate if she had actually given in or merely cracked. Huh-huh-huh. "Put your shirt on," he said, and remembered she didn't have one, she had thrown it away. Stupid bitch. He gave her his shirt, rolled his window all the way down. Should they drive, or go on foot? How far? How long had they slept? He remembered telling her it was his turn to watch Alex. Staring out the window. Willows. Floodplain. Spanish moss. He had always hated Spanish moss. So *hot*, and Randle's sudden screech, he hated that too, hated the way her lips stretched through mucus and old blood and new blood and her pointing finger, pointing at Alex. Walking toward them.

Waving, extravagant, exuberant, carrying something, something it took both hands to hold. Even from this distance Mitch could see that Alex's shirt was soaked. Saturated. Beside him Randle's screech had shrunk to a blubber that he was certain, this time, would not cease. Maybe ever. Nerves, it got on his nerves, mosquito with a dentist's drill digging at your ear. At your brain. At his fingers on the car keys or maybe it was just the itch of blood as he started the car, started out slow, driving straight down the middle of the road to where he, and Randle, and Alex, slick and sticky to the hairline, would intersect. His foot on the gas pedal was gentle, and Alex's gait rocked like a chair on the porch as he waved his arms again, his arms and the thing within.

Randle spoke, dull through a mouthful of snot. "Slow down," and he shook his head without looking at her, he didn't really want to see her at this particular moment.

"I don't think so," he said as his foot dipped, elegant, like the last step in a dance. Behind Alex, the diagonal shadows of willow trees, old ones; sturdy? Surely. There was hardly any gas left in the car, but he had just enough momentum for all of them.

THE LIFE OF A POET
Kobo Abe

Kobo Abe is a Japanese writer known for highly inventive stories that spin the reader sideways from the familiar into the surreal. His books include *The Prize of S. Karma*, *Secret Rendezvous*, *The Ruined Map*, *The Face of Another*, and *Inter Ice Age 4*. The film version of his novel *The Woman in the Dunes* won the Jury Prize at the Cannes Film Festival.

Abe was born in Tokyo, grew up in Manchuria, and now lives in Tokyo with his wife, an artist and stage designer. Translator Juliet Winters Carpenter has lived in Japan for eighteen years, and is now an associate professor at Doshisha Women's College, Kyoto. "The Life of a Poet" is part fable and part contemporary fairy tale; it comes from Abe's collection *Beyond the Curve*, published in Winters' English language translation in 1991. The story's original Japanese language publication (as "Shijin no Shogai") was in 1951.

—T.W.

Whir click clatter. Whir click clatter. From early morning until late at night, the thirty-nine-year-old crone went on pumping the shiny, oil-blackened spinning wheel, cutting back on her already scanty sleep and toiling like a machine in human guise. All so that twice a day she might fill her stomach-shaped oilpan with noodle-shaped oil, and keep the machinery inside her from ever stopping.

On and on and on she worked, until eventually, it came to her. She realized that the machine made of parched flesh and yellow bone was overflowing with the dust of her weariness. And she was seized with doubt.

"What have my innards got to do with me?" she wondered. "Why have I got to go on working this spinning wheel for their sake, when they're a mystery to me? If it's only to feed the weariness inside me, there's no point in going on, for Weariness, you've grown too large for me to hold." *Whir click clatter.* "Ah me, I'm as tired as if I'd turned to cotton."

Just as she was thinking this under the yellow, thirty-watt bulb in her tenement workroom, the crone ran out of fiber. She issued a command to the machinery inside her to stop. But strange to tell, the spinning wheel kept right on moving of its own accord, showing no sign of slowing.

Implacably, the wheel spun round and round, grasping with the last bit of thread for a loose fiber with which to continue its work. Realizing there was no such fiber to be found, the loose end stuck fast to the young crone's skin, winding around her fingers. And so from the fingertips on, her body, so limp and bone-weary it resembled nothing so much as a wad of cotton, began to elongate, unravel, and wind onto the wheel. Only after she was completely turned to thread, and the thread was wrapped entirely around the bobbin, did the machine finally slow to a stop with a light, moist *rattle rattle rattle*.

"First you fired fifty workers and made us do their work in addition to our own. Then, with those people gone—the ones who had the courage and the conviction to speak out against your injustice—you forced us to work even harder, and earned a profit of fifty million yen! We demand a raise!"

The son of the thirty-nine-year-old crone had been fired for distributing hand-bills printed with such inflammatory words. For the sake of his unfortunate com-rades left behind, he had spent one entire day stenciling words of purest oxygen with which to rekindle the dying flames in the furnaces of their hearts, and another turning them out on the mimeograph machine. Then, exhausted, he had lain down and fallen fast asleep at his mother's feet, his bare midriff covered with old newspaper, as she pumped the foot-treadle of the spinning wheel with a *whir click clatter*.

With the final *rattle rattle rattle* he opened his eyes, just in time to see the tips of her toes slipping away, through her black, dirt-encrusted work clothes. He watched, horrified, as her toes stretched out longer and thinner, only to disappear through the narrow hole on the spinning wheel.

"Mother!" The old son of the young crone sat cross-legged with his arms around his knees and his fingers laced, tightening his grip until the nails turned purple. Whenever he encountered something too taxing for his mind to contemplate, or too overwhelming for his heart to feel, he unconsciously assumed this position. After a time, he cast aside the newspapers, laid his mother's empty clothes across his midriff, and stretched out again, succumbing to the wave of exhaustion that swept over him—an inescapable law of physical existence. When this man who owned nothing but his cast-off bonds once gave himself over to sleep, nothing could deter him.

The next morning brought the footsteps of the woman next door, who was as poor as he was. She had come to collect the thread that her neighbor had spun the night before. She used it to weave jackets in order to stimulate the metabolism of her family of five, which tended to grow sluggish on her husband's meager salary.

—Where's your mother, out? Now where could she have got off to so early in the morning? Oh no, just look at all this thread not rewound. What'll I do? I'm in a hurry, so I'll take it as is. But tell her I've got to add on a little service charge, will you?

The aged youth stifled a yawn, sat cross-legged, and laced his fingers over his knees again.

—I have a feeling it's not such a good idea for you to take that away.

—Oh, you do, do you? Well, that's all very fine. Tell me, have you invented a magic formula so we can fill our bellies on air? When you do that, don't look so mopy, will you?

—That's my trouble, ma'am, I don't know how I should look.

—Of course not. If you did, I'd give you the back of my hand! Oh, go on. What a boy you are to tease me like this, so early in the morning!

In three days, the crone was woven into a jacket.

The woman who had woven it went out on the street carrying it over her arm. On the corner by the factory, she called out to a passer-by.

—Mister, how about a nice jacket? It's good and warm. You won't catch any colds with this on.

—Why, maybe you're right. It's even warm to the touch.

—Of course it is. This is one hundred percent wool, I'll have you know! Clipped from live sheep.

—It almost seems as if someone was wearing it until this moment.

—Nonsense. This is no second-hand item. I just finished weaving it myself.

—Are you sure something else isn't mixed in with it?

—Come closer and feel it again. The wool is from a live ewe.

—Maybe so. Hey, did you hear that funny noise? When I pinched it, it yelped. Is that because the wool is from a live ewe, too?

—Don't be silly. All you heard was the growling of your own belly. You must have eaten some rotten beans.

Inside the jacket, the young crone fought back her tears. Seeking to become the jacket completely, she thought with a brain of cloth and felt with a heart of cloth.

The crone's son came by.

—Ma'am, are you going to sell that jacket? I have a feeling it's not such a good idea.

—Oh, you do, do you? Well, I have a feeling you'd better not stick your nose in my business! That's all I need, to be teased by a pauper like you.

—Jackets are made to be sold, aren't they, he mused.

—And don't forget it. Anyone who thinks they're made to be worn has got another thing coming. Say, mister, come take a look! This would look terrific on you. All the girls'll give you the eye. And you'll never catch cold.

But try as she would, she found no takers. It wasn't that the jacket was poorly made. The knitting needles she'd been using for the last thirty years were by now extensions of her fingers, and with them she had woven a sturdy, practical garment. Nor was it the season, for soon it would be winter.

The problem was simply that everyone was too poor.

The people who needed her jacket were too poor to buy it. Those who could afford it were members of the class that wore expensive, imported jackets. So the jacket ended up in a pawnbroker's storehouse, in exchange for thirty yen.

All the pawnshops were already full of jackets. And all of the houses in town were full of people who owned no jackets. Why didn't they complain? Had they forgotten that there even were such things as jackets?

Crushed by poverty like so many pickles at the bottom of life's barrel, the bags of skin surrounding their flesh had been drained of dreams, souls, and desires.

Ownerless and unprotected, these dreams and souls and desires hung now in the air like invisible ether. They were what had needed jackets. Yes, that was it. The same poverty that kept people from buying jackets had robbed them of anything inside requiring the protection of one.

The sun stooped, shadows lengthened and paled, winter arrived. Traces of the escaped dreams, souls, and desires of the poor gathered in the sky as clouds, cutting off the sunlight and making the winter bitterly cold.

Trees shed their leaves, birds molted, and the air became as smooth and slippery as glass. People walked hunched over, ends of noses turned red, and words and coughs froze in the air like clouds of cigarette smoke, causing suspicious teachers to whip their students, and foremen their laborers, out of misplaced zeal. The poor feared the coming of night and mourned the coming of dawn. Men in foreign jackets spent all their time cleaning and polishing their hunting rifles, and women in foreign jackets pirouetted before their mirrors thirty times a day, adjusting expensive furs around their necks. Skiers melted wax for their skis, and skaters oiled grindstones to sharpen their skates. The last swallow flew away, and the first coal-seller stood on the streetcorner, rubbing his hands to keep warm.

All of this, along with the normal changes attendant on the coming of winter, chilled the cloud of dreams and souls and desires within and without until each dream, each soul, each desire froze and crystallized. And one day, they began falling to earth as snow.

In such orderly fashion did the snow fall, filling all crevices, that when you stared hard it seemed rather as if space itself was flowing heavenward. The snow soaked up all sounds of ordinary life in the streets. In the strange quiet, late at night, you could hear the soft jingle of snowflake brushing snowflake, like the chiming of tiny silver bells in a great, soundproofed room.

Naturally, this snow of crystalline dreams, souls, and desires was no ordinary snow. The crystals were wonderfully large, complex, and beautiful. Some had the frigid whiteness of fine, thin porcelain, and others the faint off-white glow of ivory shavings made with a microtome; still others bore the seductive gleam of thin, polished fragments of white coral. Some looked like an elaborate arrangement of thirty swords, others like seven varieties of plankton in layers, and still others like the most beautiful crystals of ordinary snow, seen through a kaleidoscope and magnified eightfold.

And this snow was colder than liquid air, for someone witnessed a flake of it fall into liquid air and vaporize with a puff of steam. It was also unusually hard. Those sword-shaped crystals could have shaved whiskers.

When automobiles passed over it, far from melting in accordance with the law of regelation, the snow jingled underneath and its sharp edges slashed the tires to ribbons. Nearly every substance known to science would either be cut to pieces before it could grind down one of those snowflakes, or freeze before it could melt one away.

What examples should one give to illustrate such coldness? In imitation of Verlaine, should one speak of the snow that fell on the brows of lovers sitting cheek-to-cheek in a wintry park—and left them hard and unmoving as a painted

Dali sculpture? Or of the snow that fell on the brow of a man with a temperature of 106, as he lay groaning on his deathbed—freezing him midway between life and death, unable to stir in either direction? Or of the snow that fell on a beggar's oilcan stove as it burned feebly by a tumbledown wall, freezing the flames motionless as glasswork?

Hour after hour, day after day, night after night . . . on and on fell the snow, ceaseless as the conveyor belt in a Ford factory. Endlessly, softly it fell, with a jingle as of tin on wood floors, falling

   on branches of roadside trees,
     on mailboxes,
       on empty swallows' nests,
        on roofs,
         on roads,
          on sewers,
           down manholes,
            on streams,
             on railway bridges,
              on tunnel entrances,
              on fields,
               on birdhouses,
                on charcoal burners' lodges,
and on the pawnshop storehouse where the jacket lay. . . .

And then fresh snow fell on the old, covering and softening the hard edges and turning the whole town into soft slopes and gentle curves until, in a matter of days or perhaps hours, as if the gears of a movie projector had suddenly ground to a halt, the entire town stopped cold. The axis of time disappeared from Minkowski's theory of space-time, and only space, as represented by a single plane, moved against the direction of the falling snow.

A worker carrying his lunch sack leaned partway out the door to gaze up at the sky, and froze that way. A ball thrown by children playing in an empty lot froze in midair, as if caught in an invisible spider's web. A pedestrian about to light a cigarette froze with his head tilted to one side, holding in his hand a match lit with a still, glasslike flame. A clump of smoke came crawling out of a large factory smokestack like a mischievous imp with a black cloth over its head, and froze motionless, like gelatin that had hardened in cold water. And—before it had a chance to hold fast in midair like the ball—a sparrow fell to earth, shattering like a light bulb into a thousand pieces.

The snow continued to fall.

The mercury column plunged lower and lower until there were no calibrations left, and the thermometer itself began to shrink.

From time to time, cracks raced across the surface of the town, raising great swirls of snow as they went. But these, too, were soon buried under falling snow.

Even so, in the beginning a few families managed to keep from freezing. They were the families wearing imported jackets. The imported jackets themselves had no great warmth, mind you, but their owners, being wealthy, all had roofs impervious to snow, and blazing stoves. In time, however, even these people noticed the growing emptiness of their larders. Gathered around their hot, glowing stoves, family members began to keep sharp watch on the size of one another's portions at mealtimes. Fuel ran short and sofas gave way to wooden chairs, then orange crates; then people sat on the floor, and then one by one the floorboards were carefully ripped out. Electric lights gave way to oil lamps, then to candles, and finally to darkness. The ladies who had worn sleek furs shriveled into dried-out foxes, and the gentlemen who had polished their hunting rifles while thinking of their bank stocks turned into hairless, rheumatic dogs. Their college-aged sons, once absorbed in detective stories, armed themselves with pistols and raided their mothers' hoards of canned goods stored carefully away in bedrooms.

From out of the darkened windows, in place of dignified voices scolding the maid, or the gentle, refined laughter of victorious gamblers, there began to issue curses, screams, the thud of heavy objects falling, sounds of ripping cloth, and loud, heartbreaking moans.

Heads of families consulted hysterically with one another over independently powered, cordless telephones, and finally decided to appeal for foreign aid. This was the response to their inquiry over the wireless:

—Buy another five thousand jackets. New design. Ideological tiger-crest, mottled black and white. Or would you prefer fifty or so atom bombs?

It became apparent to them all that the only solution was to get the poor in motion again, get the factories operating again, and start a war.

One resourceful fellow made a bundle of sticks, fastened bent wire on the end, stuck it out through a crack in the window, and tried to hook one of the frozen pedestrians outside. For an instant, all the families in imported jackets stopped fighting and held their breaths, glued to their binoculars and cordless telephones. But the pedestrian only crumbled silently to pieces.

Then came the final, self-destructive burst of hysteria. People were undone, like toys with broken springs. Despairing, they sought the quickest route to becoming meaningless matter. Open a window, stick an arm out into the snow, and freeze yourself—this, it seemed, was the last remaining option of a rational being.

Strangely enough, just when it seemed that every imaginable creature was frozen solid, there was still one mouse whose life went on as before. She lived in the storehouse of the pawnshop where the crone's jacket was stored. She was looking for material to make a warm nest for her five babies, soon to be born.

Unlike humans, the mouse knew nothing of poverty that could bar the fulfillment of one's deepest desires; when she found the wonderful jacket, she didn't hesitate a moment. Taking it in her mouth, she gnawed off a piece. All at once, blood flowed from the severed place. The mouse's teeth had sunk in just over the crone's cloth heart. Uncomprehending, the mouse fled back to her nest in astonishment, and promptly miscarried.

The crone's blood spilled out quietly and spread into every corner of the jacket, staining it bright red.

The snow suddenly stopped. It is likely that the limits of cold had been reached, freezing the very falling of the snow and so making further precipitation impossible.

Then the red jacket, still glossy with blood, rose lightly into the air as if it had been donned by some invisible creature, and glided outside. Through the unmoving snow-space, where day was indistinguishable from night, it glided and swam.

Before long the crone-jacket located a young man in the snow. It was her son, frozen by the factory gate with a wad of handbills stuffed under one arm, caught in the act of handing one to a worker, who stood frozen with a hand outstretched to receive it.

The jacket stopped in front of the youth and wrapped itself around his aged body. He blinked. Then he moved his head gingerly from side to side, and shook his body little by little. He looked around in wonder, then down at his red jacket. All at once it came to him that he was a poet, and he nodded, smiling.

He gathered the melodious snow in his hands and gazed at it. Now he could touch it without freezing. Had it become even colder than the snow, then, that gleam in his eye? He scooped up snow like sand at the seashore and poured it from palm to palm, without injury. Had it become harder than steel, then, the skin of his hands? He was confused. He had to remember. How had this transformation come about?

Frowning, he tried hard to focus his thoughts. Yes, there was something that he must remember. Something that every pauper knew, if memory were not suspended, frozen. Where had this snow fallen from?

Even if he didn't know the answer, perhaps he could feel it. Look at these crystals of snow, he told himself, so marvelously large, complex, and beautiful. What are they if not the forgotten words of the poor? Words of their dreams . . . souls . . . desires. Hexagonal, octagonal, duodecadonal, flowers lovelier than flowers, the very structure of matter . . . the molecular arrangements of souls of the poor.

The words of the poor are not only large, intricate, and beautiful, but succinct as mineral, and rational as geometry. It stands to reason that none but souls of the poor can become crystalline.

The youth in the red jacket listened to the snow-words with his eyes. He decided to write them down on the backs of the handbills under his arm.

He grabbed a handful of snow and threw it in the air. It flew up with a jingle jingle, but when it fell back down the sound changed to "jacket, jacket." The youth laughed. His happiness escaped through his barely parted lips as a quiet, cheerful melody, and disappeared into the distant sky. As if in answer, the snow all around him began to hum "jacket, jacket."

After that he began a precise, detailed investigation of each separate crystal. He wrote everything down, decided on his notation, compiled and analyzed statistics, made graphs, and listened again, even more carefully. He could hear it—the words of the snow, the voices of the dreams, souls, and desires of the poor. With tireless, amazing energy, he went on working.

Gradually, the snow started to melt. Having finished speaking to him, evidently it had no further reason to exist. In the order that they finished speaking, those crystals of snow so cold they had frozen flames now melted away without a trace, like the snows of early spring that vanish the moment they light on the black, moist earth.

In fact, it was almost spring. With every word that he wrote in his notebooks, as if the pages were calendar leaves, spring crept ever closer.

One day, through a crack in the clouds, the sun thrust out a ray of light like the arm of a mischievous little girl. And then, as if groping for a golden ring let fall by mistake into the bottom of a water pitcher filled with old, foaming brew, slowly it shook the town from its slumber.

One could sense creatures stirring. A man came reeling forward, half-paralyzed, saw the young man and laughed, holding out a hand in greeting. Touching the arm of the youth, he muttered "Jacket," and ran away. Before long the youth was surrounded by a large group of people, new ones joining all the time; "Jacket," each one would whisper, laying a hand on his arm, and then go off, smiling. These people spread throughout the town.

All around, the unattended storehouses were opened, and countless jackets were carted off. "Jacket!" The joyful, powerful paean was sung out ringingly to all the messengers of spring: to the heavy, moist black earth; to the babbling stream, tumbling and racing along like a three-year-old just learning to run; and to the pale green jewels poking out from between the lingering islands of snow. Though it was spring, there was still a chill in the air, so how beautiful, how wonderful it was to see those poor people clothing themselves in jackets!

The last flake of snow gone, the youth's work was done. The factory whistle sounded, and all around him, crowds of people wearing jackets set off to work, smiling. Returning their greetings, he closed the last page of his poetry collection, now complete.

And vanished into that page.

THE WITCH OF WILTON FALLS
Gloria Ericson

Gloria Ericson sold fiction and nonfiction to various magazines in the sixties and seventies, dropped out of writing to pursue other business interests, and in the last three years returned to writing. She lived in the New York metropolitan area for many years and has lived near Washington, D.C., since 1984.

"The Witch of Wilton Falls" has an interesting history. It was written in the mid-sixties, sent to an original (non-genre) anthology where the editor suggested Ericson try it on *Alfred Hitchcock's Mystery Magazine*. The story was bought and published in 1964. It was reprinted in 1991 and made such an impression on me that I didn't care if it was twenty-five years old. Despite the title, the story has no supernatural element in it. Ericson reports that she is writing a novel version of the story.

—E.D.

As I scanned the rest of my mail, I absentmindedly opened the one letter my secretary had left sealed, thinking it might be personal. Absorbed as I was, I failed to notice the return address, so its message came as rather a shock: *Since we could find no evidence of next-of-kin, and you seemed to be her only correspondent and visitor, we thought you would want to know that Miriam Winters passed away quietly in her sleep on the 25th.*

The sun pouring through the Venetian blinds of my office seemed suddenly chilled. I had been standing while I opened the letter, but now I sat, swung the big leather chair around, and gazed out the window. So she had died—at last. *Her only visitor.* I wasn't even that. When was the last time I had seen her—five years ago? Six? I remembered receiving a card from her this past Christmas and making sure Meg sent one in return. How lonely she must have been these last years. Suddenly I was filled with the worst kind of remorse—the kind you feel when someone's gone and it's too late to make up any neglect.

I was only a kid, no more than sixteen, when they let Old Man Winters out and, since I was the one responsible for his release, I went around that summer swaggering like a damn hero. It wasn't until later that I came to think differently of myself. I haven't been back to Wilton Falls in a good many years, and I wonder if they still tell their kids and their grandchildren about that summer. I wonder if they still tell it the wrong way, too—making Miriam Winters out to be some sort of witch. Well, they're wrong. She wasn't a witch. I talked to her enough later (*too* late) to know.

Swinging my chair back to the desk, I looked at the letter again. It was strange, but I was probably the only living person who had ever heard the full details of her side of the story. Certainly the newspapers had never given her her due. They were too busy making sensational copy out of the horror she had perpetrated— and it *was* horror. I have never denied that, or condoned what she did, but it was my fate to get a more rounded picture than anyone else, and so I always have felt differently about Miriam Winters. . . .

Miriam stopped to wipe the perspiration from her brow. There were two more shirts to iron. Harry was due home tonight, and he'd ask about them first thing. He had a lot of shirts, enough to last him four weeks on the road while an equal number were being done up at home. A salesman had to be well-groomed, Harry always said. Still, it seemed that he took more shirts than necessary. Miriam, after her first blunder, never mentioned it when she found lipstick or powder smudges on any of them.

She looked fearfully at the clock over the kitchen sink. Why had she waited until the last minute? Well, it had been a difficult month. Bobby had been sick, and then she'd had so many of those awful headaches. Ever since Harry had knocked her against the stove the last time he'd been home, she had been bothered by the headaches and that funny confused feeling that came over her from time to time. She put down the iron and rubbed her head. She didn't mind the headaches so much, but worried about the confused feeling. She wondered if she blacked out at such times and fervently hoped not. Bobby was pretty self-sufficient for a four-year-old, but who could tell what he would do if he found his mother unconscious someday?

Fortunately she had just put the final touches on the last shirt when she heard Harry's car drive into the old barn behind the house. He came banging in—a big man, a good twenty years older than Miriam—set down his luggage without an answer to her quavering "hello," and went out again. He returned with a couple of paper bags which he carefully placed on the kitchen table. Miriam's heart sank. It hadn't been a good trip, then. She could always tell by the amount of whisky he brought back with him to ease the few days' rest at home before he started off again.

"I have your supper all ready," said Miriam, poking at the pots on the stove.

Harry, fussing with the seal on one of the whisky bottles, stopped only long enough to glare at her. "My shirts done?"

"Yes—oh, yes—all of them. Now just you sit down and I'll dish out your supper."

He grunted and seated himself heavily at the wooden table.

Two hours later he was wildly drunk.

He would not allow her to go to bed, and although she was able to avoid his drunken lunges for a while, he finally had her backed into a corner. The whisky fumes of his breath and the feel of his fumbling hands at her clothes sickened her. "No, no, H-Harry . . ." Her voice involuntarily rose in a crescendo.

Then there were other hands plucking at her, and she looked down at Bobby. Aroused by the noise, he had come weeping into the kitchen. "Mama, Mama," he said, trying to pull her away.

Miriam swallowed and tried to speak calmly. "You must go back to bed, Bobby. Come, I'll take you."

But Harry held her firm. "You'll do no such thing. You can just stop being the damn mother for once. When a man comes home from the road he wants a little comfort—a little wifely comfort." Then to the child, who still clung, "G'wan, dammit. Get to bed."

But the weeping child did not move, and swift as lightning the big hand of the man swung out. The body of the small boy seemed to fly through the air before landing in a crumpled heap at the base of the sink. From the gash on the forehead blood spurted first, then flowed in a horrible red sheet down the face of the child. His mouth opened but no sound came out.

Even Harry seemed stunned by the sight and made no move to stop Miriam as she tore from his arms with a strange animal-like sound. The child's breath had come back, and his sobs mingled with hers as she rocked him in her arms and sponged at his face with a wet dish towel. There was no hope of outside help in this emergency, for there was no phone and Harry was too drunk to drive to a doctor. The house itself was isolated, situated as it was on the edge of a meadow. Beyond that stretched a wooded area. The nearest neighbor, Miriam knew, was at least a mile away.

Finally, thankfully, the flow of blood lessened and then stopped. As Miriam gently swabbed her son's head, she noted how wide the gash was and how frighteningly near his eye. Tomorrow morning she would have a doctor look at it, but now bed, probably, was the best therapy. She picked the child up and went past Harry, who had again settled himself at the table, silently drinking. She improvised a clumsy bandage, and tucked the still faintly sobbing child in bed. He did not want her to go, so she sat on the edge of the bed until, with a last convulsive shudder, he allowed himself to be overtaken by sleep.

She went quietly back to the kitchen. Harry had succumbed finally, and sat sprawled at the table, his head on his arms. Miriam shook him, but when he did not respond, she went to the knife drawer and selected the largest, sharpest knife she had. She shut the drawer and went and stood behind her husband, hefting the knife, gauging the angle of thrust that would be best . . .

It was odd. Her role in life up to this minute had been that of follower. She was ever stumbling after some stronger-willed person, often hating it but never knowing how to break away; indecisive. That's why it was odd that suddenly she should know just what to do. She didn't have to agonize over her decision or consult someone else. Harry must be done away with. It was *right*. She *knew* it.

What stayed her hand, then?

A haunting phrase from her childhood Sunday school: *Thou shalt not kill?* An awareness of how difficult it would be to dispose of a dead body? Perhaps. But more probably it was the sudden image that flashed across her mind, an image of herself behind bars and Bobby alone. Murderers were always caught, weren't they? She had made no plans to cover her "crime," nor had she any belief that even if she did, the police wouldn't find out sooner or later. She was not *that* clever— merely right.

Slowly she lowered her hand. Perhaps she could not kill Harry, but he must be restrained in some way—the thing tonight was too close. Miriam shivered as she recalled the bloodied face of her child. No, just as wild beasts must be killed or locked up . . .

Locked up? She thought a moment. Of course. That was the answer. The big old house with its large expanse of fenced-in grounds had been purchased less than a year ago from former kennel owners. They had been breeders of Great Danes, as a matter of fact, and in the cavernous cellar one area had been sectioned off with sturdy cyclone fencing set in concrete. The area was about nine by nine feet, with the fencing extending even across the top. This "cage" had been used for whelping bitches and their puppies. Harry in such a cage would never be able to hurt Bobby or herself again.

She stared at Harry's bulk. Tomorrow she would wonder how she had been able to drag such a heavy man across the kitchen, down the cellar steps, and into the cage, but tonight she merely knew that it must be done.

Harry stirred and moaned once or twice in the tortuous journey but never fully awakened from his drunken stupor. Perspiration trickled down Miriam's back and between her breasts, and by the time she had hauled her unconscious husband into the caged area she was wringing wet. A wooden platform, raised a few inches from the floor, took up a portion of the cage. Apparently the dogs had slept on this. Miriam went upstairs and dragged two blankets from their bed and threw them in on the platform. Then she closed the cage door. There was a heavy padlock on the latch. She clicked it shut. She had no key for it, but that did not matter because she did not expect to open it again—ever.

The first few days were terribly noisy, of course. It was fortunate the house was so isolated or surely Harry's bellows of disbelief, anger, and frustration would have been heard. Miriam took Bobby to the doctor the next day to have his wound attended. The doctor was aghast and wanted to know why she hadn't come when it happened, and how *did* it happen?

"He fell against the latch of the sink cabinet last night and it would have been too difficult to come all this way on foot in the dark. My husband isn't home with the car," Miriam lied, confident that Bobby would not refute her story, and he did not. He was a quiet, obedient child, solemn beyond his years.

When they returned from the doctor's, they could hear Harry's shrieks of rage as they walked in the door. Bobby shrank against his mother. Miriam sat down on the straight chair near the door and took her son onto her lap. "Listen, Bobby, you mustn't let those noises in the cellar bother you. It's only . . ." She paused a moment, suddenly thinking of a different approach. "You remember those fairy tales we were reading the other night?"

Bobby nodded.

"Do you remember the one about the prince being turned into a frog?"

"Yes . . ."

"Well, something like that has happened, I think, to your father. He has been turned into a bear, a great shaggy bear, as punishment, I imagine, for not—for not being more kind. Well, anyway, he's in a cage in the cellar so he cannot hurt us."

Bobby's eyes were round. A particularly loud bellow rose from below at this point, and the child trembled. "He-he c-can't get out . . ." he quavered.

"No." Miriam's voice was firm. "He absolutely can't get out—and after a while he'll probably stop making so much noise." She slid the child from her lap and stood up. Then she added, "By the way, Bobby, you mustn't tell *anybody* at *all* about this, or they will make us let him out."

Glancing down at him, she saw his eyes widen with horror at the thought. She smoothed down her dress, satisfied. Bobby would never tell.

Miriam allowed three days to pass before she went down to Harry. He was lying down, seemingly exhausted by three days of shouting, but at her approach he sprang up and clutched with trembling fingers at the heavy cage meshing. Miriam stopped a few feet from the cage and set down on the floor the plate of food and shallow bowl of milk she was carrying. Then, as if repeating something she had rehearsed many times, she picked up a broom that lay nearby and shoved first the plate and then the bowl toward the "gate" of the cage, which cleared the floor by about three inches.

Harry's lips twitched. "All right, you, what's this all about?"

She did not answer but continued to shove the food toward him.

Harry's voice was shrill. "Dammit, Miriam, let me out! Miriam—Miriam, do you hear me . . ." His voice became uncertain. Her silence seemed to unnerve him. Was this the same woman whom he had browbeaten so long? The same woman who had heretofore quaked at his every command? He tried again, a conciliatory tone suddenly in his voice. "Listen, Miriam, I admit you may have a beef. Look, I know I had too much to drink, but you can't keep me locked up here forever, can you?"

She answered him then. She straightened up and looked with her unblinking clear blue eyes into his. "Yes," she said.

He was taken aback. "W-What?"

"Yes," she repeated. "I can keep you locked up forever. I can and I must." She indicated the food with her foot. The two dishes were half under the gate. "Here's some food. I'll bring you more tomorrow night." Then she turned and started up the stairs.

He was apparently shocked into silence for a moment, but then an outraged bellow of venomous anger escaped him. "You'll never be able to get away with it, Miriam!" he screamed. "People'll find out. Don't you realize, you idiot, you can't get away with something like this. You'll be arrested . . ."

The young woman on the stairs continued ascending as if she heard nothing. At the top she switched off the cellar light and shut the door carefully, quietly, behind her.

Every evening she took him food, seldom speaking herself, letting his increasingly hysterical screams of abuse cascade over her with no comment. When the stench in the cage became unbearable she employed the same means of cleaning it the former kennel owners apparently had used. She coupled a hose on a nearby spigot and hosed off the cage floor, the water and filth easily channeling themselves into the slight gully in the cement floor outside the cage. The gully led to an open drain in the floor, and this she kept sanitary by a periodic sprinkling with disinfecting powder. Several times a week she also slid a shallow basin of soapy water in to him so that he might clean himself if he wished.

As the weeks passed, Harry's vilification, his threats, became less. He tried a new tack. It was just a matter of time, he assured her. His company would be checking up soon. And, anyway, how long did she think she could hold out by herself? How would she live? How would she earn money? If his questions did not seem to disconcert her, it was only because she had given those same questions great thought herself.

For instance, Miriam had already telephoned Harry's company. She was sorry, she told them, but her husband had taken another job and wished to terminate his employment with them. As Harry had never been one of their better salesmen, they were not overly upset. Fine, they said, they wished him luck, but would he please send back his sample case and stock book. Miriam said she'd see that they were in the mail that day, and they were. Thus the company, which the man in the cage so desperately counted on to start a hullabaloo over his disappearance, quietly washed its hands of him.

The weeks immediately following Harry's incarceration were idyllic ones for Miriam and Bobby. They went to the nearby fields to pick wild strawberries, they frolicked in the woods. Never had Miriam been so happy. Her childhood had consisted of one indifferent foster home after another. Her marriage to Harry, which she had thought would be an escape, had merely had the effect of putting her in a new foster home with a new foster parent—and a more brutal one, at that. But now she was free—free for the first time in her life. Even her headaches and that confused feeling seemed to be bothering her less. In the fall Bobby would be starting school, and she must then consider her future. Harry's remarks about her inability to support herself were not lost on her, but there was enough money in the savings account for the present, and she was determined not to worry about anything until the fall.

In the fall her decision not to worry was completely justified because things fell into place beautifully for her. Old Mrs. Jenkins, the town librarian, died, and Miriam, ever a lover of books, applied for the position. There were few applicants for the job, and Miriam, although a comparative newcomer to town, made by far the best appearance. She was quiet, neat, and seemingly conscientious. Also, her implication that her salesman husband had abandoned her didn't hurt her chances. If anything, it aroused the town board's sympathies, and they gave her the job. The position didn't pay much, but Miriam's wants were few: merely enough money to maintain Bobby and herself and to feed the "Shaggy Bear" in the basement. The latter epithet had become particularly appropriate, for Harry had grown quite a beard and there were times when Miriam had difficulty recognizing the shaggy lumbering creature in the cage as her husband—so much difficulty that she soon stopped trying. He was merely the "Bear" who must be fed nightly and ignored as much as possible the rest of the time.

Ignoring him became more difficult during the winter months, for a change came over him. Until then he had been an abusive, vilifying creature, shaking the cage mesh violently, slamming his metal dishes around, screaming deprecations upon her head. But one night she went down with his food to find him holding onto the mesh and whimpering. He saw her, and a great tear rolled down his cheek and glistened on the rough beard. It was followed by others. The Bear was crying! "Miriam, Miriam," it sobbed.

How strange that a bear should know her name. But then, she must remember, it really was Harry in that bear suit.

"Miriam, please—please set me free. I know I haven't been good to you, but I promise I'll go away and never bother you again. Just set me free . . ." Great sobs shook the creature's frame.

Miriam felt tears well up in her own eyes. She was a sensitive person and could feel great sympathy for this caged creature. Carefully she set the dishes down for the Bear. "I'm sorry," she said softly before turning back to the stairs.

That night she had difficulty sleeping. What sadness there was in the world! How sorry she felt for that poor Bear. If only there were something she could do to ease his unrest, but of course there wasn't. Many was the time in the years to come that she had to remind herself that, sorry as she was for the Bear, there was nothing she could do about it, really.

Bobby, destined to grow up in such an unusual household, knew without asking that he must never bring boys home from school to play with him. His friends soon came to accept this eccentricity, just as the townspeople came to accept the fact that their sweet-faced librarian, although friendly enough at the library, lived a rather hermit-like existence with her son, and never asked anyone to visit.

Surely Bobby could not have long believed the father-turned-into-a-bear story. There must have come a day when curiosity overcame him and he peeked into one of the cellar windows. While still quite young, he may have been fooled by the sight of the shaggy creature, thinking it really was a bear, even as his mother had come to think of it as a bear. But as he grew older he must have looked again and known, and knowing, what could he do? Go to the police? Have his father, whom he only dimly remembered as a bellowing brute, freed? And where would his gentle mother be sent? To a jail—to a madhouse? No, no. He did not know— could not *afford* to know—what was in the cellar.

However slowly the years may have passed for the Bear, they passed quickly enough for Miriam and Bobby. Grammar school. High school. *War!* War was in the air. Hitler was marching through Czechoslovakia . . . Poland . . . Then Pearl Harbor. Bobby enlisted the next day in the navy. He kissed his mother's tearstained face and hugged her comfortingly. It would all be over soon, now that he was in it, he said to make her smile, but she did not smile. Her whole life was leaving.

Miriam told the Bear about it that evening. Over the years she had developed the habit of sitting outside the cage in an old rocking chair in the evenings when Bobby was at a basketball game or at some other school activity. She enjoyed chatting with the Bear—now that he had learned not to talk about the possibility of his freedom and instead quietly listened to her tell of things in the outside world: Bobby's athletic exploits, incidents at the library, and so on. It was quite cosy, really. She had placed an old floor lamp next to the rocker and sometimes she would read aloud from books she brought home from the library. The Bear seemed to appreciate that. This evening, when she told him of Bobby's leaving, he seemed most sympathetic.

"Miriam," he said, his voice rusty with disuse, "l-let me out now. Let me take care of you while Bobby's away."

She looked at him, stunned. After all this time and he still didn't understand—still could bring that up! Sorrowfully she got up from the rocker, snapped off the lamp, and started up the stairs. At the top she shut the door quietly but firmly on his pleadings. After all these years he still didn't understand that you don't let wild beasts loose. No matter how sorry you feel for the lions and tigers in the zoos and no matter how tame they seem, you just don't go around letting them loose on society.

Soon there were long newsy letters from Bobby, which she read to the Bear at night. (He had apparently learned his lesson after his last outburst and had become more docile and quiet than ever.) It didn't seem long at all before Bobby was home on his first leave, healthy, bronzed, wonderful to look at. Miriam wished the Bear could see him.

Bobby used his leave to good advantage, too, by painting the house and making other repairs that were needed. The morning before he left he stood staring out the kitchen window. Miriam went over to him, and he looked down at her thoughtfully. "Mom, I noticed some kids cutting across the back lot yesterday. The fencing must be down back there."

Miriam nodded. "I dare say. After all, it's pretty old fencing."

Bobby shifted his weight and frowned. "I don't like it—kids cutting across the property. I'm going to town today and get some new posts and barbed wire."

He worked all that day and until it was time for him to leave the next evening. He came in hot and sweaty, but looking satisfied. "I put 'No Trespassing' signs up and strung the fencing real tight. I'd like to see any kid get through all those strands of barbed wire." He came over and put his arm around his mother. "It'll be good for years, Mom. Long after I come back . . ."

But he didn't come back. She was at the library when the telegram arrived. Everyone was terribly kind. There were offers of lifts home, but she refused them all, preferring to walk the two miles by herself—the last mile over the now overgrown private road that led to her house. She did not break down until she had sought out the Bear, and then she slumped down on the cold cement outside his cage and sobbed over and over, "Bobby's gone, Bear. Bobby's gone." Through the heavy wire mesh the claw-like fingers with the unclipped nails pushed, as if trying to stroke her. Tears rolled down the shaggy beard, but whether the Bear was shedding tears over the loss of his son or over the futility of his own life is not known.

Life goes on. By spring Miriam had come to accept with a kind of dull resignation Bobby's passing. She continued her job at the library, of course, for without Bobby's allotment check she was again the sole support of herself and the Bear.

Bobby's insurance money she did not touch. Someday she might be unable to work and would need it.

The days in the old house at the end of the overgrown road established themselves in a seldom-varying pattern. The Bear had become quite trustworthy, and on weekends when the weather was nice Miriam even dared open from the outside the small window over his cage. It gave her much pleasure to see him rouse himself from his usual slump on the wooden platform and stand directly under the open window, inhaling great breaths of fresh air. Sometimes he would suddenly fling his arms up but then as suddenly drop them as they contacted the meshing on the top of his cage. Sometimes he rose on tiptoes as if straining to see out, but of course he could not. Often she brought him bouquets of flowers picked from the meadow, and he seemed to like that, burying his face in the blooms and sniffing hungrily. She was glad to do these things, for she had become quite fond of him, really, and more and more her prime concern in life became his comfort and contentment.

The years, one by one, passed slowly, quietly by. There were a few times of crisis, of course—the time the Bear was so sick, for instance. It was sheer torture for Miriam to listen to him call out hoarsely for a doctor and know that she could not possibly get one. She could do nothing but pray, and eventually her prayers were answered. The Bear stopped sweating and moaning, finally, and began to get better. Then there was the time she herself was sick. It was one summer during her vacation. She was too ill to go to the doctor and had no way to summon him to the house, nor would it have been advisable for her to do so even if she could for, as keeper, she was in a sense as much a prisoner as the Bear. The fever raged through her for several days and the only thing that kept her from succumbing was the distant sound of the Bear's plaintive calls. It would be so easy just to let go and die, but she could not. The Bear was hungry—needed her . . . So she fought, and lived to see the Bear fall upon the food she finally weakly brought to him. It was worth the fight.

Perhaps the worst time of all was when the pan of hot grease caught fire in the kitchen. With frantic efforts she managed to put it out, scorching her arms quite badly in the process. It was not the pain in her arms that left her trembling, though, but the thought of what might have happened had the fire spread. The Bear would have been trapped, burned alive. The thought left her weak. She wracked her brain for a solution to the possibility of such a thing's happening again, and suddenly remembered that Harry, her former husband (she had not thought of him in years), had owned a revolver. She went upstairs and found it in an old cupboard. She felt much better. This way the Bear was assured of a quick, merciful death.

The time the furnace broke down required even more ingenuity on her part, and the coffee she offered the Bear at that time was heavily laced with sleeping pills. When he fell into a deep, drugged sleep she threw dropcloths over the cage, ranged discarded furniture against it, and called the repairmen. The men worked for an hour over the furnace, completely unaware that within a few feet of them a creature, once-man, slept.

And the years ticked on . . .

*   *   *

I was kind of at loose ends that summer I was sixteen, anyway. Having lost my mother and father in an automobile accident only a few months before, I was spending some time with my grandfather in his "hunting shack" at Wilton Falls. My grandfather was a judge downstate and normally used the shack only once or twice in the fall for hunting, but this year he had taken time off in the early summer and come up with me. Guess he thought some fishing and general rambling in the woods would be good for me; get my mind off my loss.

I was out in the woods by myself that day, though, when I came across the rusted barbed wire that surrounded the Winters place. I tested it with my foot and it gave way. Nimbly I leaped over the broken strands and soon found myself in a choked meadow, on the edge of which perched a weatherbeaten Victorian house. I regarded the apparition with surprise. Was it occupied? Probably not; much too neglected-looking. I sauntered over to observe more closely, and then bent to peer through one of the cellar windows. The cellar was quite dark and it was a moment before my eyes accustomed themselves to the feeble light. Almost directly under the window there was a cagelike arrangement, with a hulking shape in one corner. A shadow? No, it seemed to move, and suddenly I was looking at a matted tangle of hair, out of which stared the deadest, most vacant eyes I had ever seen. My heart gave a sickening lurch. What I was seeing was impossible. I stayed a moment longer, as if riveted by those terrible dead-man eyes. Then the shaggy head turned away and I was released—released to run across the sunny unreal meadow, over the broken strands of barbed wire that tore at my clothes, through the adjoining woods. I had slowed down somewhat by the time I reached my grandfather's cabin and was a little ashamed of myself. After all, I was no kid—ye gods, I was *sixteen*— and here I was running like a scared rabbit. Then the memory of those eyes returned in full force and I felt cold sweat pop out all over me.

My grandfather, looking strangely unjudgelike in his plaid shirt and denim pants, was fussing at the stove when I came in. "Hello there," he said. "I was wondering where you were. Lunch is almost ready."

I stood, my back against the door, still breathing hard. "Gramp," I said, and there was, despite myself, a quiver in my voice.

My grandfather looked up then. His glance sharpened. "Something the matter, son? You look upset."

I tried to wave my hand deprecatingly but failed in that gesture, too. "Gramp, who lives in that big old house at the edge of the meadow?"

My grandfather frowned. "At the edge of the meadow . . . Oh, you must mean Mrs. Winters' place. Why?"

"I was just over there now and I saw—"

"Over there? That place is posted. You shouldn't have gone there."

"But the fencing is all rusted and I didn't see any No Trespassing signs . . ."

"Well, maybe the signs *are* too weathered to read any more, but everyone around here knows it's posted."

"Well, I didn't know, and I looked in one of the cellar windows. Gramp, there's something in a big cage there. A–A man, I think it is . . ."

My grandfather pulled out a chair and seated himself at the table. "Now, let's hear this from the beginning. What are you talking about—a cage, and a man—you-think in it?"

I told him the whole thing, but I could see he wasn't convinced.

"You're sure your eyes, and imagination, weren't playing tricks on you, son? I mean, everyone knows Mrs. Winters lives there all by herself. She's had a very tragic life, actually. First her husband abandoned her and she had to bring up their son all alone. Then he was killed in the war. I wouldn't want any wild rumors circulated by a grandson of mine to hurt her."

"But it's no wild rumor, Gramp, it's *true*. Please, Gramp, you've got to go look yourself."

I guess the urgency in my voice decided him. He stood up. "Okay. Best to squelch this now. You'll see it was just your imagination . . ."

By nightfall all Wilton Falls was in a state of shock. The police had sawed off the old padlock and led a stumbling, half-blind Harry Winters into the fresh air of freedom, and the town's gentle middle-aged librarian had been taken into "protective custody." She did not seem to mind. Her only concern seemed to be that "The Bear" be taken care of. When assured that he would be, she went along docilely enough. Actually, both of them were taken to the county hospital for observation—but to different wings.

How the town did buzz the next couple of weeks. The story made even the downstate papers with a banner headline: HUSBAND KEPT IN CAGE 30 YEARS BY WIFE. Under my picture it said: *He dared to look in the Witch's dungeon.* Under Mr. Winters' picture it said: *Caged like a beast for 30 of his 75 years.* And under Mrs. Winters' picture: *The Witch of Wilton Falls—She turned her husband into a "Bear."* It was all pretty heady stuff for me, being hero-of-the-hour, as it were. But then I looked more closely at the pictures of Mr. and Mrs. Winters and suffered my first feeling of disquietude. They both had the look of puzzled children on their faces as they were led away.

Miriam Winters, of course, was sent to the state mental hospital, but deciding what to do with Harry Winters was more of a problem. The county psychiatrists had difficulty testing him due to his refusal (or was it *inability*?) to talk, and finally came to the frustrated conclusion that although his mind had undoubtedly been affected by his imprisonment, he was harmless enough, and could be released to proper care. But what was "proper care"? There was a great outcry against sending him to the county home, for it was felt that in the few years that were left to him he deserved to be "free." The public conscience was stirred on this point and it was finally arranged that the old man go back to his own house. A volunteer committee of townspeople was set up in which one member every day would check on the old man, bring him groceries, take away laundry, etc. Part of the volunteers' duties included "socializing"—but that aspect was dropped as soon as it became evident that Harry Winters had no desire to chat with *anybody*.

Just what did Harry Winters' freedom mean to him after all those years? I found out, unfortunately, one hot August night about six weeks after his reinstatement in his old home. I had been into town and decided to take a shortcut past the old Winters place on the way back. As I approached the house, I noted that it was unlighted except for a faint glow from the cellar windows. I recalled rumors I had heard in town. Nothing in the house ever seemed disturbed, they said—even the bed not slept in. Could it be that after all these years Harry Winters only felt comfortable sleeping in his cage and returned there each night?

Stealthily I crept up to a cellar window and peered in. In the dim light I could make out the outlines of the cage. Next to it was the rocking chair that Miriam Winters had used, but it was a moment before I realized that the hulking shape nearby was Harry Winters himself. He was sitting on the floor with his chin resting on one of the rocker's arms. There was a familiarity about the scene which I could not at first place, but then it came to me. In my grandfather's house there was a large painting in one of the bedrooms called *The Shepherd's Chief Mourner.* It showed a large dog mournfully resting his chin on the draped coffin of a deceased shepherd, his master. The sudden analogy between that painting and the tableau below sent a shaft of pain to my heart. I could not stand to see more, but as I prepared to rise, the mourning hulk suddenly moved. The shaggy head raised up, the throat arched, the mouth opened, and from it rose a cry of such utter anguish, such complete despair, that my hands flew instinctively to my ears to shut it out. But I could not shut it out. Again and again it came—a cry of longing—the longing of a tame bear for its gentle keeper.

I ran then. Even as I had once fled over a sun-choked meadow, now I flew over a moon-silvered one. This time, too, I was chased by horror, but this time the horror was of my own making and I knew I would never be able to outrun it.

They found Harry Winters the next morning in his cage—dead. His heart had given out, they said.

It was after my grandfather and I went downstate that I began to have the nightmares, though. Perhaps I cried out during them, because one morning at breakfast Grandfather remarked quietly, "I hope you don't feel guilty about reporting Miriam Winters, son. It *had* to be done."

I nodded my head. "Yes, I know . . ."

My lack of conviction must have shown, for my grandfather became emphatic. "It's time we laid this ghost away," he said. "You and I are going to the state mental hospital to see Miriam Winters."

Although I went reluctantly, the visit turned out to be surprisingly pleasant. Miriam was delighted to have company and chatted cheerfully. She had heard that the Bear was dead, which was sad, but then, she added philosophically, he was pretty old. She knew that if he became sick again she would have to put him to sleep permanently anyway.

My grandfather looked at me pointedly at this revelation. Surely I needed no more proof that we had done the right thing in reporting the Winters affair. From his standpoint the visit was a success, but in a way it backfired, for Miriam was a kindly, warmhearted woman. She said I made her think of her son Bobby, and she hoped I'd come to see her again. To my own amazement I found myself promising I would.

And I did, many times. Was it my way of assuaging the faint guilt I still felt over disrupting the Winters couple's strangely compatible life together? I don't know, but I do know that in chatting with her I gradually learned the full story of the events leading to Harry Winters' imprisonment.

I went to my grandfather. "She shouldn't be in a mental institution," I complained. "She's not really insane, except of course about the 'Bear,' and he probably caused that insanity, beating her and all . . ."

My grandfather stared at me and sighed. "That ghost is still not laid, hmmm?" He thought a moment. "The county home in Wilton Falls is a well-run place. I'll see what I can do."

Miriam was transferred to the county home three weeks later, and I felt more at peace than I had for a long time. I still went to see her, but less frequently, as it was a longer run up to Wilton Falls. Then I went away to college—later began working—got married—moved farther away. Visits became replaced by letters, letters by a Christmas card, and now . . .

I looked down at the letter in my hand. Now there would not even be any need for that. Miriam Winters had paid her debt to society, and presumably society was satisfied. But I knew that, for *my* part, could I but relive that long-ago summer day, this time I would stare into the almost-blind eyes of Harry Winters and go quietly on my way.

HOME BY THE SEA
Pat Cadigan

Some of the best writers today are working hard and well to stretch the boundaries of the genres in which they choose to write. Pat Cadigan's short fiction is certainly a good example of this. Her SF stories "Pretty Boy Crossover" and "Angel," and novella "Fool to Believe" were nominated for major awards as was her horror story "The Power and the Passion." Cadigan's most recent novel, *Synners*, was nominated for a Nebula Award and a new novel, *Fools*, will be out this October.

"Home by the Sea," published in A *Whisper of Blood*, was born at the 1990 World Science Fiction Convention in the Hague, the Netherlands. That's where Cadigan and friends sat watching the gray horizon on a cloudy day at the resort district of Scheveningen. Cadigan, who has written about vampires and vampirism before, used this setting to paint her own peculiar view of the end of the world, a visceral yet haunting evocation of a possible apocalypse for our time.

—E.D.

There was no horizon line out on the water.

"Limbo ocean. Man, did we hate this when I was a commercial fisherman," said a man sitting at the table to my left. "Worse than fog. You never knew where you were."

I sneaked a look at him and his companions. The genial voice came from a face you'd have expected to find on a wanted poster of a Middle Eastern terrorist, but the intonations were vaguely Germanic. The three American women with him were all of a type, possibly related. A very normal-looking group, with no unusual piercings or marks. I wondered how long they'd been in Scheveningen.

I slumped down in my chair, closed my eyes, and lifted my face to where I thought the sun should be. It was so overcast, there wasn't even a hot spot in the sky. Nonetheless, the promenade was crowded, people wandering up and down aimlessly, perhaps pretending, as I was, that they were on vacation. It was equally crowded at night, when everyone came to watch the stars go out.

Of course *we're on vacation*, a woman had said last night at another of the strange parties that kept congealing in ruined hotel lobbies and galleries. This had been one of the fancier places, ceilings in the stratosphere and lots of great, big ornate windows so we could look out anytime and see the stars die. *It's an enforced vacation. Actually, it's the world that's gone on vacation.*

No, that's not it, someone else had said in an impeccable British accent. It always surprised me to hear one, though I don't know why; England wasn't that far away. *What it is, is that the universe has quit its job.*

Best description yet, I'd decided. *The universe has quit its job.*

"Hey, Jess." I heard Jim plop down in the chair next to me. "Look what I found."

I opened my eyes. He was holding a fan of glossy postcards like a winning poker hand. Scheveningen and The Hague as they had been. I took them from him, looked carefully at each one. If you didn't know any better, you'd have thought it had been a happy world, just from looking at these.

"Where'd you find them?"

"Up a ways," he said, gesturing vaguely over his shoulder. He went *up a ways* a lot now, scavenging bits of this and that, bringing them to me as if they were small, priceless treasures. Perhaps they were—souvenirs of a lost civilization. Being of the why-bother school now, myself, I preferred to vegetate in a chair. "Kid with a whole pile of them. I traded him that can of beer I found." He stroked his beard with splayed fingers. "Maybe he can trade it for something useful. And if he can't, maybe he can fill a water pistol with it."

What would be useful, now that the universe had quit its job? I thought of making a list on the back of one of the postcards. Clothing. Shelter. Something to keep you occupied while you waited for the last star to go out—a jigsawpuzzle, perhaps. But Jim never showed up with one of those, and I wasn't ambitious enough to go looking myself.

My old hard-driving career persona would have viewed that with some irony. But now I could finally appreciate that being so driven could not have changed anything. Ultimately, you pounded your fist against the universe and then found you hadn't made so much as a dent, let alone reshaped it. Oddly enough, that knowledge gave me peace.

Peace seemed to have settled all around me. Holland, or at least this part of Holland, was quiet. All radio and TV communications seemed to be permanently disrupted—the rest of the world might have been burning, for all we knew, and we'd just happened to end up in a trouble-free zone. Sheerly by accident, thanks to a special our travel agency had been running at the time. We joked about it: *How did you happen to come to Holland? Oh, we had a coupon.*

A kid walked by with a boombox blaring an all-too-familiar song about the end of the world as we know it and feeling fine. The reaction from the people sitting at the tables was spontaneous and unanimous. They began throwing things at him, fragments of bricks, cups, cans, plastic bottles, whatever was handy, yelling in a multitude of languages for him to beat it.

The kid laughed loudly, yelled an obscenity in Dutch, and ran away up the promenade, clutching his boombox to his front. Mission accomplished, the tourists had been cheesed off again. The man at the next table had half risen out of his chair and now sat down again, grinning sheepishly. "All I was gonna do was ask him where he found batteries that work. I'd really like to listen to my CD player." He caught my eye and shrugged. "It's not like I could hurt him, right?"

Jim was paying no attention. He had his left hand on the table, palm up, studiously drawing the edge of one of the postcards across the pad below his thumb, making deep, slanted cuts.

"I wish you wouldn't do that," I said.

"Fascinating. Really fascinating." He traced each cut with a finger. "No pain, no pain at all. No blood and no pain. I just can't get over that."

I looked toward the horizonless ocean. From where I was sitting, I had a clear view of the tower on the circular pier several hundred feet from the beach, and of the woman who had hanged herself from the railing near the top. Her nude body rotated in a leisurely way, testifying to the planet's own continuing rotation. As I watched, she raised one arm and waved to someone on the shore.

"Well," I said, "what did you expect at the end of the world?"

"You really shouldn't deface yourself," I said as we strolled back to the hotel where we were squatting. If you could really call it a hotel—there was no charge to stay there, no service, and no amenities. "I know it doesn't hurt, but it doesn't heal, either. Now you've got permanent hash marks, and besides not being terribly attractive, they'll probably catch on everything."

Jim sighed. "I know. I get bored."

"Right." I laughed. "For the last twenty years, you've been telling me I should learn how to stop and smell the roses and now *you're* the one who's complaining about having nothing to do."

"After you've smelled a rose for long enough, it loses its scent. Then you have to find a different flower."

"Well, self-mutilation *is* different, I'll give you that." We passed a young guy dressed in leather with an irregular-shaped fragment of mirror embedded in his forehead. "Though maybe not as different as it used to be, since it seems to be catching on. What do you suppose *he's* smelling?"

Jim didn't answer. We reached the circular drive that dead-ended the street in front of our hotel, which had gone from motorcycle parking lot to motorcycle graveyard. On impulse, I took Jim's hand in my own as we crossed the drive. "I suppose it's the nature of the end of time or whatever this is, and the world never was a terribly orderly place. But nothing makes sense anymore. Why do we still have day and night? Why does the earth keep turning?"

"Winding down," Jim said absently. "No reason why the whole thing should go at once." He stopped short in the middle of the sidewalk in front of the hotel. "Listen."

There was a distant metallic crashing noise, heavy wheels on rails. "Just the trams running again. That's something else—why does the power work in some places and not in others?"

"What?" Jim blinked at me, then glanced in the general direction of the tram yard. "Oh, that. Not what I meant. Something I've been wondering lately"— there was a clatter as a tram went by on the cross street "—why we never got married."

Speaking of things that didn't seem important anymore—it wasn't the first time the subject had come up. We'd talked about it on and off through the years, but after eighteen years together, the matter had lost any urgency it might have had, if it had ever had any. Now, under a blank sky in front of a luxury hotel where the guests had become squatters, it seemed to be the least of the shadow-things my life had been full of, like status and career and material comforts. I could have been a primitive tribeswoman hoarding shiny stones for all the real difference those things had ever made. They'd given me nothing beyond some momentary delight; if anything, they'd actually taken more from me, in terms of the effort I'd had to put into acquiring them, caring for them, keeping them tidy and intact. Especially the status and the career. And they sure hadn't stopped the world from ending, no more than our being married would have.

But I was so certain of what Jim wanted to hear that I could practically feel the words arranging themselves in the air between us, just waiting for me to provide the voice. *Well, dear, let's just hunt up a cleric and get married right now.* Add sound and stir till thickened. Then—

Then what? It wasn't like we actually had a future anymore, together or singly. The ocean didn't even have a horizon.

"I think we *are* married," I said. "I think any two people seeing the world to its conclusion together are married in a way that didn't exist until now."

It should have been the right thing to say. Instead, I sounded like a politician explaining how a tax increase wasn't really a tax increase after all. After two decades, I could do better than some saccharine weasel words, end of the world or no.

Say it, then. The other thing, what he's waiting for. What difference does it make? The question I had to answer first, maybe the question Jim was really asking.

The edges of the cuts he'd made in his hand moved against my skin. They felt like the gills of an underwater creature out of its element, seeking to be put back in.

No pain at all. No blood and no pain.

It's not like I could hurt him, right?

Right. It's the end of the world as we know it, and I feel nothing. So we can go ahead now, do all those things that used to be so dangerous. Self-mutilation, bonding rituals, any old hazard at all.

Jim's eyes were like glass.

"Better get into the lobby now if you want to see it."

It was the Ghost of Lifetimes Past; that was what Jim and I had been calling her. She stood a respectful distance from us, a painfully thin blond woman in a dirty white tutu and pink satin ballet shoes. The most jarring thing about her was not her silly outfit, or the way she kept popping up anywhere and everywhere, but that face—she had the deep creases of someone who had lived seventy very difficult years. Around the edge of her chin and jawbone, the skin had a peculiar strained look, as if it were being tightened and stretched somehow.

"The crucifixion," she said, and gave a small, lilting giggle. "They're probably going to take him down soon, so if you want a look, you'd better hurry." Her gaze drifted past us and she moved off, as if she'd heard someone calling her.

"You in the mood for a crucifixion?" I said lightly. It was a relief to have anything as a distraction.

"Not if we can possibly avoid it."

But there was no way we could. Pushing our way through the small crowd in the lobby, we couldn't help seeing it. I vaguely recognized the man nailed directly to the wall—one of the erstwhile millionaires from the suites on the top floor. He was naked except for a wide silk scarf around his hips and a studded collar or belt cinched wrong side out around his head in lieu of a crown of thorns. No blood, of course, but he was doing his best to look as if he were in pain.

"God," I whispered to Jim, "I hope it's not a trend."

He blew out a short, disgusted breath. "I'm going upstairs."

Somehow, I had the feeling that it wasn't really the crucifixion he was so disgusted with. I meant to follow him but suddenly I felt as nailed in place as the would-be Christ. Not that I had any real desire to stand there and stare at this freak show, but it held me all the same. All that Catholic schooling in my youth, I thought, finally catching up with me after all these years, activating a dormant taste for human sacrifice.

Ersatz-Christ looked around, gritting his teeth. "You're supposed to mock me," he said, the matter-of-fact tone more shocking than the spikes in his forearms. "It won't work unless you mock me."

"You're a day late and a few quarts low," someone in the crowd said. "It won't work unless you shed blood, either."

The crucified man winced. "Shit."

There was a roar of laughter.

"For some reason, that never occurs to them. About the blood."

I looked up at the man who had spoken. He smiled down at me, his angular face cheerfully apologetic. I couldn't remember having seen him around before.

"This is the third one I've seen," he said, jerking his head at the man on the wall. The straight black hair fell briefly over one eye and he tossed it back. "A grand gesture that ultimately means nothing. Don't you find it rather annoying, people who suddenly make those grand risky gestures only after there isn't a hope in the hell of it mattering? Banning the aerosol can after there's already a hole in the ozone layer, seeking alternate sources of power after nuclear reactors have already gone into operation. It's humanity's fatal flaw—locking the barn after the horse has fled. The only creature in the universe who displays such behavior."

I couldn't place his accent or, for that matter, determine if he actually had an accent—I was getting tone-deaf in that respect. He didn't look American, but that meant nothing. All the Americans were getting a European cast as they adopted the local face.

"The universe?" I said. "You must be exceptionally well traveled."

He laughed heartily, annoying ersatz-Christ and what sympathizers he had left. We moved out of the group, toward the unoccupied front desk. "The universe we know of, then. Which, for all intents and purposes, might as well be all the universe there is."

I shrugged. "There's something wrong with that statement, but I'm no longer compulsive enough to pick out what it is. But it might be comforting to know that if there is a more intelligent species somewhere, its foibles are greater than ours, too."

"Comforting?" He laughed again. "It would seem that in the absence of pain, no comfort is necessary." He paused, as if waiting for me to challenge him on that, and then stuck out his hand. "I'm Sandor."

"Jess." The warmth of his unmarked, uncut hand was a mild shock. Fluctuations in body temperatures were as nonexistent as blood in these nontimes. Which would only stand to reason, since blood flow governed skin temperature. Everyone was the same temperature now, but whether that was something feverish or as cold as a tomb was impossible to tell with no variation. Perhaps I just hadn't been touching the right people.

"Odd, isn't it," he said, politely disengaging his hand from mine. I felt a rush of embarrassment. "They wanted to investigate it at the hospital, but I wouldn't let them. Do you know, at the hospital, people are offering themselves for exploratory surgery and vivisection? And the doctors who have a stomach for such things take them willingly. Yes. They cut them open, these people, and explore their insides. Sometimes they remove internal organs and sew the people up again to see how they manage without them. They manage fine. And there is no blood, no blood anywhere, just a peculiar watery substance that pools in the body cavity.

"And hidden away in the hospital, there is a doctor who has removed a woman's head. Her body is inactive, of course, but it does not rot. The head functions, though without air to blow through the vocal cords, it's silent. It watches him, they say, and he talks to it. They say he is trying to get the head to communicate with him in tongue-clicks, but it won't cooperate. *She* won't cooperate, if you prefer. And then there's the children's ward and the nursery where they keep the babies. These babies—"

"*Stop* it," I said.

He looked dazed, as if I'd slapped him.

"Are you insane?"

Now he gave me a wary smile. "Does sanity even come into it?"

"I mean . . . well, we just met."

"Ah, how thoughtless of me."

I started to turn away.

That strangely warm hand was on my arm. "I do mean it. It *was* thoughtless, pouring all that out on someone I don't know. And a stranger here as well. It must be hard for you, all this and so far from home."

"Oh, I don't know." I glanced at the crucified man. "It's all so weird, I think maybe I'd just as soon not see it happen anyplace familiar. I don't really like to think about what it must be like back home." I jerked my thumb at the man nailed to the wall. "Like, I'd rather that be some total stranger than one of my neighbors."

"Yes, I can see that. Though it must be a little easier to be with someone you're close to, as well." He looked down for a moment. "I saw you come in with your companion."

I gave him points for perception—most people assumed Jim was my husband. "Are you from here?" I asked.

"No. As I'm sure you could tell."

"Not really. Is Sandor a Polish name?"

He shrugged. "Could be. But I'm not from there, either."

There was a minor commotion as the police came in, or rather, some people dressed in police uniforms. Scheveningen was maintaining a loose local government—God knew why, force of habit, perhaps—with a volunteer uniformed cadre that seemed to work primarily as moderators or referees, mostly for the foreigners. They pushed easily through the thinning crowd and started to remove the crucified man from the wall, ignoring his protests that he wasn't finished, or it wasn't finished, or something.

"*Ite missa est,*" I said, watching. "Go, the Mass is over. Or something like that."

"You remember the Latin rite. I'm impressed."

"Some things hang on." I winced at the sound of ersatz-Christ's forearm breaking. "That sounded awful, even if it didn't hurt."

"It won't heal, either. Just goes on looking terrible. Inconvenient, too. At the hospital, they have—" He stopped. "Sorry. As you said, some things hang on."

"What do you suppose they'll do with him?" I asked as they took him out. "It's not like it's worth putting him in jail or anything."

"The hospital. It's where they take all the mutilation cases bad enough that they can't move around on their own. If they want mutilation, they can have plenty there, under better conditions, for better reasons, where no one has to see them."

Finally, I understood. "Did you work there long?"

"Volunteered," he said, after a moment of hesitation. "There are no employees anymore, just volunteers. A way to keep busy. I left—" He shrugged. "Sitting ducks."

"Pardon?"

"That's the expression in English, isn't it? For people who leave themselves open to harm? In this case, literally open."

"If it doesn't hurt and it doesn't kill them, and this is the end of it all as we know it," I said slowly, "how can they be leaving themselves open to harm?"

"A matter of differing cultural perspectives." He smiled.

I smiled back. "You never told me what culture you were from."

"I think you could say that we're all from here now. Or might as well be. There's an old saying that you are from the place where you die, not where you were born."

"I've never heard that one. And nobody's dying at the moment."

"But nothing happens. No matter what happens, nothing happens. Isn't that a description of a dying world? But perhaps you don't see it that way. And if you don't, then perhaps *you* aren't dying yet. Do you think if you cut yourself, you might bleed? Is it that belief that keeps *you* from mutilating yourself, or someone else? Do you even wonder about that?"

I looked from side to side. "I feel like I'm under siege here."

He laughed. "But *don't* you wonder? Why there aren't people running through the streets in an orgy of destruction, smashing windows and cars and each other? And themselves."

"Offhand, I'd say there just doesn't seem to be much point to it." I took a step back from him.

"Exactly. No point. No reward, no punishment, no pleasure, no pain. The family of humanity has stopped bickering, world peace at last. Do you think if humans had known what it would take to bring about world peace, that they'd have worked a lot harder for it?"

"Do you really think it's like this everywhere in the world?" I said, casually moving back another step.

"Don't you?" He spread his hands. "Can't you feel it?"

"Actually, I don't feel much." I shrugged. "Excuse me, I'm going to go catch up on my reading."

"Wait." He grabbed my arm and I jumped. "I'm sorry," he said, letting go almost immediately. "I suppose I'm wrong about there being no pleasure and pain. I'd forgotten about the pleasure of being able to talk to someone. Of sharing thoughts, if you'll pardon the expression."

I smiled. "Yeah. See you around." I shook his hand again, more to confirm what I'd felt when he'd grabbed my arm than out of courtesy, and found I'd been right. His skin definitely felt cooler. Maybe *he* was the one who wasn't dying and I had sucked whatever real life he had out of him.

Only the weird survive, I thought, and went upstairs.

No matter what happens, nothing happens. Jim was curled up on the bed, motionless. The silence in the room was darkening. Sleep canceled the breathing habit, if "sleep" it actually was. There were no dreams, nothing much like rest—more like being a machine that had been switched off. Another end-of-the-world absurdity.

At least I hadn't walked in to find him slicing himself up with a razor, I thought, going over to the pile of books on the nightstand. Whatever had possessed me to think that I would wait out the end of the world by catching up with my reading had drained away with my ambition. If I touched any of the books now, it was just to shift them around. Sometimes, when I looked at the covers, the words on them didn't always make sense right away, as if my ability to read was doing a slow fade along with everything else.

I didn't touch the books now as I stretched out on the bed next to Jim. He still didn't move. On the day—if "day" is the word for it—the world had ended, we'd be in this room, in this bed, lying side by side the way we were now. I am certain that we both came awake at the same moment, or came to might be a better way to put it. Went from unconscious to conscious was the way it felt, because I didn't wake up the way I usually did, slowly, groggily, and wanting nothing more than to roll over and go back to sleep for several more hours. I had never woken up well, as if my body had always been fighting the busy life my mind had imposed on it. But that "day," I was abruptly awake without transition, staring at the ceiling, and deep down I just *knew*.

There was no surprise in me, no regret, and no resistance. It was that certainty: *Time's up*. More than something I knew, it was something I *was*. Over, finished, done, used up . . . but not quite gone, as a bottle is not gone though emptied of its contents. I thought of Jim Morrison singing "The End," and felt some slight amusement that in the real end, it hadn't been anywhere near so dramatic. Just . . . *time's up*.

And when I'd finally said, "Jim . . . ?" he'd answered, "Uh-huh. I've got it, too." And so had everyone else.

I raised up on one elbow and looked at him without thinking anything. After awhile, still not thinking anything, I pulled at his shirt and rolled him over.

Sex at the end of the world was as pointless as anything else, or as impossible as bleeding, depending on your point of view, I guess. The bodies didn't function; the minds didn't care. I felt some mild regret about that, and about the fact that all I *could* feel was mild regret.

But it was still possible to show affection—or to engage in pointless foreplay— and take a certain comfort in the contact. We hadn't been much for that in this no-time winding-down. Maybe passion had only been some long, pleasant dream that had ended with everything else. I slipped my hand under Jim's shirt.

His unmoving chest was cadaver-cold.

That's it, I thought, *now we're dying for real*. There was a fearful relief in the idea that I wouldn't have to worry about him mutilating himself any further.

Jim's eyes snapped open and he stared down at my hand still splayed on his stomach, as if it were some kind of alien, deformed starfish that had crawled out of the woodwork onto his torso.

"You're warm," he said, frowning.

And like that, I was lost in the memory of what it was to feel passion for another human being. What it was to *want*, emotions become physical reactions, flesh waking from calm to a level of response where the edge between pleasure and pain thinned to the wisp of a nerve ending.

I rolled off the bed and went into the bathroom. Behind me, I heard Jim rolling over again. Evidently he didn't want to know about my sudden change in temperature if I didn't want to tell him. A disposable razor sat abandoned on the counter near the sink. If I took it and ran my fingertip along the blade, would I see the blood well up in a bright, uneven bead? I didn't want to know, either.

The exploding star was a fiery blue-white flower against the black sky. Its light fell on the upturned faces of the crowd on the promenade, turning them milky for a few moments before it faded.

"Better than fireworks," I heard someone say.

"Ridiculous," said someone else. "Some kind of trick. The stars are thousands and millions of light-years away from us. If we see them exploding now, it means the universe actually ended millions of years ago and we're just now catching up with it."

"Then no wonder we never made any contact with life on other planets," said the first voice. "Doesn't *that* make sense? If the universe has been unraveling for the last million years, all extraterrestrial life was gone by the time we got the technology to search for it."

I looked around to see who was speaking and saw her immediately. The Ghost of Lifetimes Past was standing just outside the group, alone as usual, watching the people instead of the stars. She caught my eye before I could look away and put her fingertips to her mouth in a coy way, as if to stifle a discreet giggle. Then she turned and went up the promenade, tutu flouncing a little, as an orange starburst blossomed in the west.

If Jim had come out with me, I thought, weaving my way through the crowd, I probably wouldn't have been doing something as stupid as following this obviously loony woman. But he had remained on the bed, unmoving, long after it had gotten dark, and I hadn't disturbed him again. I had sat near the window with a book in my lap and told myself I was reading, not just staring until I got tired of seeing the same arrangement of words and turning a page, while I felt myself fade. It had been a very distinct sensation, what I might have felt if I had been awake when the world had ended.

The Ghost of Lifetimes Past didn't look back once but I was sure she knew I was following her, just as I knew she had meant for me to follow her, all the way to the Kurhaus. Even from a distance, I could see that the lights were on. Another party; what was it about the end of the world that seemed to cry out for parties? Perhaps it was some kind of misplaced huddling instinct.

I passed a man sitting on a broken brick wall, boredly hammering four-inch nails into his chest. If we hung notes on them, I thought, and sent him strolling up and down the promenade, we could have a sort of postal service-cum-newspaper. Hear ye, hear ye, the world is still dead. Or undead. Nondead. Universe still unemployed after quitting old job. Or was it, really?

The Ghost flounced across the rear courtyard of the Kurhaus without pausing, her ballet shoes going scritch-scritch on the pavement. Light spilled out from the tall windows, making giant, elongated lozenges of brightness on the stone. One level up, I could see people peering out the galleria windows at the sky. When the sun went, I thought suddenly, would we all finally go with it, or would it just leave us to watch cosmic fireworks in endless night?

They made me think of birds on a nature preserve, the people wandering around in the lobby. Birds in their best plumage and their best wounds. A young, black-haired guy in a pricey designer gown moved across the scuffed dusty floor several yards ahead of me, the two chandelier crystals stuck into his forehead above the eyebrows, catching the light. Diaphanous scarves fluttered from holes in his shoulder blades. Trick or treat, I thought. Or maybe it was All Souls' Day, every day.

At the bar island, someone had used the bottles on the surrounding shelves for target practice and the broken glass still lay everywhere like a scattering of jewels. I saw a woman idly pick up a shard lying on the bar and take a bite out of it, as if it were a potato chip. A man in white tie and tails was stretched out on the floor on his stomach, looking around and making notes on a stenographer's pad. I wandered over to see what he was writing, but it was all unreadable symbols, part shorthand, part hieroglyphics.

There was a clatter behind me. Some people were righting one of the overturned cocktail tables and pulling up what undamaged chairs they could find. It was the group that had been sitting near me on the promenade that day, the man and his three women companions, all of them chattering away to each other as if nothing was out of the ordinary. They were still unmarked and seemed oblivious to the freak show going on around them—I half expected the man to go to the bar and try to order. Or maybe someone would sweep up some broken glass and bring it to them on a tray. Happy Hour is here, complimentary hors d'oeuvres.

The Ghost reappeared on the other side of the bar. She looked worse, if that were possible, as if walking through the place had depleted her. A tall man on her left was speaking to her as he ran a finger along the wasted line of her chin while a man on her right was displaying the filigree of cuts he'd made all over his stomach, pulling the skin out and displaying it like a lace bib. The skin was losing its elasticity; it sagged over the waistband of his white satin pajama pants. The layer of muscle underneath showed through in dark brown.

I turned back to the group I'd seen on the promenade, still in their invisible bubble of normalcy. The man caught sight of me and smiled a greeting without a pause in what he was saying. Maybe I was supposed to choose, I thought suddenly; join the freaks or join the normalcy. And yet I had the feeling that if I chose the latter, I'd get wedged in among them somehow and never get back to Jim.

They were all staring at me questioningly now and something in those mild gazes made me think I was being measured. One of the women leaned into the group and said something; it was the signal for their intangible boundary to go back up again. Either I'd kept them waiting too long, or they didn't like what they saw, but the rejection was as obvious as if there had been a sign over their heads.

I started for the side door, intending to get out as fast as I could, and stopped short. The boy standing near the entrance to the casino might have been the same one who'd had the boombox, or not—it was hard to tell, there were so many good-looking blond boys here—but the man he was talking to was unmistakably Jim. He hadn't bothered to change his rumpled clothes or even to comb his hair, which was still flat on one side from the way he'd been lying on the bed.

Jim was doing most of the talking. The kid's expression was all studied diffidence, but he was listening carefully all the same. Jim showed him his hand and the kid took it, touching the cuts and nodding. After a few moments, he put his arm around Jim's shoulders and, still holding his hand, led him around the front of the closed, silent elevator doors to the stairs. I watched them go up together.

"Do you wonder what that was all about?"

I didn't turn around to look at him. "Well. Sandor Whoever from Wherever. The man who can still raise the mercury on a thermometer while the rest of us have settled at room temperature. If you start talking about interesting things people are doing in the hospital, I might take a swing at you."

He chuckled. "That's the spirit. Next question: Do you wonder how they get the power on in some places when it won't work in others?"

"In a way."

"Do you want to find out?"

I nodded.

He didn't touch me even in a casual way until we reached his room on the fourth floor. It was the first time I'd ever been higher than the galleria level. The lights in the hallway shone dimly, glowing with what little power was left from whatever was keeping the lobby lit up, and his hand was like fire as he pulled me out of the hallway and into the room.

His body was a layer of softness over hard muscle. I tore his clothing to get at it; he didn't mind. Bursts of light from the outside gave me fleeting snapshots of his face. No matter what I did, he had the same expression of calm acceptance. Perhaps out of habit, covering the secret of his warmth—if the rest of us pod creatures knew he was the last (?) living thing on earth, what might we not do for this feeling of life he could arouse?

Already, his flesh wasn't as warm as it had been. That was me, I thought, pushing him down on the bed. I was taking it from him and I couldn't help it. Or perhaps it was just something inherent in the nature of being alive, that it would migrate to anyplace it was not.

Even so, even as he went from hot to cool, he lost nothing. Receptive, responsive, accommodating—in the silent lightning of dying stars, calm and accepting, but not passive. I was leading in this pas de deux, but he seemed to know how and where almost before I did, and was ready for it.

And now I could feel *how* it was happening, the way the life in his body was leached away into my own un-alive flesh. I was taking it from him. The act of *taking* is a distinctive one; no one who had ever taken anything had taken it quite like I took Sandor.

He gave himself up without resistance, and yet *give up* was not what he was doing, unless it was possible to surrender aggressively. It was as if I wanted him because his purpose was to be wanted, and he had been waiting for me, for someone to provide the wanting, to want him to death. Ersatz-Christ in the lobby had had it wrong, it never could have worked. Humans didn't sacrifice themselves, they were sacrificed to; they didn't give, they were alive only in the act of taking—

Somehow, even with my head on fire, I pulled away from him. He flowed with the movement like a storm tide. I fought the tangle of sheets and cold flesh against warm, and the violence felt almost as good as the sex. If I couldn't fuck him to death, I'd settle for beating his head in, I thought dimly. We rolled off the bed onto the carpet and I scrambled away to the bathroom and slammed the door.

"Is there something wrong?" The puzzlement in his voice was so sincere I wanted to vomit.

"*Stop it.*"

"Stop what?"

"Why did you let me do that to you?"

He might have laughed. "Did *you* do something to me?"

A weak pain fluttered through my belly. There was a wetness on my thighs.

"Turn on the light," he said. "You can now, you know. It'll work for you, now that you're living."

I flipped the switch. The sudden brightness was blinding. Turning away from the lights over the sink, I saw myself in the full-length mirror on the door. The wetness on my thighs was blood.

My blood? Or his?

The pain in my belly came again.

"Jess?"

"Get away. Let me get dressed and get out of here. I don't want this."

"Let me in."

"No. If you come near me, I'll take more from you."

Now he did laugh. "What is it you think *you* took?"

"Life. Whatever's left. You're alive and I'm one of the fading ones. I'll make you fade, too."

"That's an interesting theory. Is that what you think happened?"

"Somehow you're still really alive. Like the earth still turns, like there are still stars. Figures we wouldn't all fade away at once, us people. Some of us would still be alive. Maybe as long as there are still stars, there'll still be some people alive." The sound of my laughter in the small room was harsh and ugly. "So romantic. As long as there are stars in the sky, that's how long you'll be here for me. Go away. I don't want to hurt you."

"And what *will* you do?" he asked. "Go back to your bloodless room and your bloodless man, resume your bloodless wait to see what the end will be? It's all nothing without the risk, isn't it? When there's nothing to lose, there's really nothing at all. Isn't that right?"

The lock snapped and the door swung open. He stood there holding on to either side of the doorway. The stark hunger in the angular features had made his face into a predator's mask, intent, voracious, without mercy. I backed up a step, but there was nowhere to go.

He lunged at me and caught me under the arms, lifting me to eye level. "You silly cow," he whispered, and his breath smelled like meat. "*I* didn't get cooler, *you* just got *warmer*."

He shoved me away. I hit the wall and slid down. The pain in my shoulders and back was exquisite, not really pain but pure sensation, the un-alive, undead nerve endings frenzied with it. I wanted him to do it again, I wanted him to hit me, or caress me, or cut me, or do anything that would make me *feel*. Pain or pleasure, whatever there was, I wanted to live through it, get lost in it, die of it, and, if I had to die of it, take him with me.

He stood over me with the barest of smiles. "Starting to understand now?"

I pushed myself up, my hands slipping and sticking on the tiled wall.

"Yeah." He nodded. "I think maybe you are. I think you're definitely starting to get it." He backed to the sink and slid a razor blade off the counter. "How about this?" He held the blade between two fingers, moving it back and forth so it caught the light. "Always good for a thrill. Your bloodless man understands that well enough already. Like so many others. Where do you think he goes when he takes his little walks up the promenade, what do you think he does when he leaves you to sit watching the hanging woman twist and turn on the end of her rope?" He laughed and popped the blade into his mouth, closing his eyes with ecstasy. Then he bared his teeth; the blood ran over his lower lip onto his chin and dripped down onto his chest.

"Come on," he said, the razor blade showing between his teeth. "Come *kiss* me."

I wasn't sure that I leaped at him as much as the life in him pulled me by that hunger for sensation. He caught me easily, holding me away for a few teasing seconds before letting our bodies collide.

The feeling was an explosion that rushed outward from me, and as it did, I finally did understand, mostly that I hadn't had it right at all, but it was too late to do anything about it. The only mercy he showed was to let the light go out again.

Or maybe that wasn't mercy. Maybe that was only what happened when he drained it all out of me and back into himself, every bit of pain and pleasure and being alive.

He kept the razor blade between his teeth for the whole time. It went everywhere, but he never did kiss me.

The room was so quiet, I thought he'd left. I got up from where I'd been lying, half in and half out of the bathroom, thinking I'd find my clothes and go away now, wondering how long I'd be able to hide the damage from Jim—if damage it was, since I no longer felt anything—wondering if I would end up in the hospital, if there was already a bed with my name on it, or whether I'd be just another exotic for nightly sessions at the Kurhaus.

"Just one more thing," he said quietly. I froze in the act of taking a step toward the bed. He was standing by the open window, looking out at the street.

"What's the matter?" I said. "Aren't I dead enough yet?"

He laughed, and now it was a soft, almost compassionate sound, the predator pitying the prey. "I just want to show you something."

"No."

He dragged me to the window and forced my head out. "See it anyway, this one time. A favor, because I'm so well pleased." He pulled my head back to make me look up at the sky. A night sky, very flat, very black, featureless, without a cloud and with no stars, none at all.

"A magic lantern show, yes," he said, as though I'd spoken. "*We* put the signs and wonders in the sky for you. So you wouldn't see *this*."

He forced my head down, digging his fingers more deeply into my hair. Below, in the courtyard, people wandered among a random arrangement of cylindrical things without seeing them. They were pale things, silent, unmoving; long, ropy extensions stretched out from the base of each one, sinking into the pavement like cables, except even in the dim light, I could see how they pulsed.

While I watched, a split appeared in the nearest one. The creature that pushed its way out to stand and stretch itself in the courtyard was naked, vaguely female-looking, but not quite human. It rubbed its hands over the surface of the cylinder, and then over itself. I pulled away.

"You see, that's the other thing about your kind besides your tendency toward too little, too late," he said conversationally as I dressed. If I tucked my shirt into my pants I could keep myself together a little better. "You miss things. You're blind. All of you. Otherwise, you'd have seen us before now. We've always been here, waiting for our time with you. If even one of you had seen us, you might have escaped us. Perhaps even destroyed us. Instead, you all went on with your lives. And now we're going on with them." He paused, maybe waiting for me to say something. I didn't even look at him as I wrapped my shirt around the ruin of my torso. "Don't worry. What I just showed you, you'll never see again. Perhaps by the time you get home, you'll even have forgotten that you saw anything."

He turned back to the window. "See you around the promenade."

"First time's the worst."

The Ghost of Lifetimes Past fell into step beside me as I walked back along the promenade. She was definitely looking worse, wilted and eaten away. "After that," she added, "it's the natural order of things."

"I don't know you," I said.

"I know you. We all know each other, after. Go home to your husband now and he'll know you, too."

"I'm not married."

"Sure." She smiled at me, her face breaking into a mass of lines and seams. "It could be worse, you know. They like to watch it waste me, they like to watch it creep through me and eat me alive. They pour life into us, they loan it to us, you could say, and then they take it back with a great deal of interest. And fascination. They feed on us, and we feed on them, but considering what they are, we're actually feeding on ourselves. And maybe a time will come that will really be the end. After all, how long can we make ourselves last?"

She veered away suddenly, disappearing down a staircase that led to one of the abandoned restaurants closer to the waterline.

As I passed the tower, the hanging woman waved a greeting. There would be no horizon line on the ocean again today.

I had thought Jim would know as soon as he saw me, but I didn't know what I expected him to do. He watched me from where he lay on the bed with his arms behind his head. Through the thin material of his shirt, I could see how he'd been split from below his collarbone down to his navel. It seems to be a favorite pattern of incision with them, or maybe they really have no imagination to speak of.

He still said nothing as I took a book from the stack on the nightstand and sat down in the chair by the window, positioning myself with my back to the room. The words on the pages looked funny, symbols for something I no longer knew anything about.

The mattress creaked as Jim got up and I heard him changing his clothes. I didn't want to look—after all, it wouldn't matter what I saw—and still not wanting to, I put the unreadable book aside and turned around.

The incision was actually very crude, as if it had been done with a jagged shard of glass. I wanted to feel bad at the sight, I wanted to feel sorry and sad and angry at the destruction, I wanted of feel the urge to rush to him and offer comfort. But as Sandor had pointed out, in the absence of pain, no comfort was necessary.

Abruptly, Jim shrugged and finished dressing, and I realized he'd been waiting for something, maybe for me to show him my own. But I had no desire to do that yet.

"I'm going for a walk up the promenade," he said, heading for the door. "You can come if you want." He didn't look back for a response.

"Do you think," I heard myself say just before he stepped out into the hall, "they're everywhere? Or if we could just get home somehow . . ."

"Jess." He almost smiled. "We *are* home."

I followed him at a distance. He didn't wait for me, walking along briskly but unhurriedly, and I didn't try to catch up with him. The sky seemed darker and duller, the sounds of the people on the promenade quieter, more muffled. The trams didn't run.

I stayed out until dark. The dying-stars show was especially spectacular, and I watched it until Sandor finally got around to coming back for me.

PISH, POSH, SAID HIERONYMUS BOSCH

Nancy Willard

Nancy Willard, whose short story "Dogstar Man" is published elsewhere in this volume, is also the author of deliciously magical poetry such as "The Ballad of Biddy Early" and the poem on the following pages.

"Pish, Posh, Said Hieronymus Bosch" introduces the harried housekeeper of Hieronymus Bosch, a Dutch artist of the fifteenth century known for his brilliantly bizarre and fantastical paintings. Willard's poem is reprinted from a sumptuous children's picture-book edition, beautifully illustrated by Leo, Diane, and Lee Dillon.

—T.W.

Once upon a time there was an artist
named Hieronymus Bosch who loved odd creatures.
Not a day passed that the good woman who looked
after his house didn't find a new creature
lurking in a corner or sleeping in a cupboard.
To her fell the job of
    feeding them,
    weeding them,
    walking them,
    stalking them,
    calming them,
    combing them,
    scrubbing and tucking in all of them—
until one day . . .

"I'm quitting your service, I've had quite enough
of your three-legged thistles asleep in my wash,
of scrubbing the millstone you use for a dish,
and riding to shops on a pickle-winged fish."

"Pish, posh,"
said Hieronymus Bosch.

"How can I cook for you? How can I bake
when the oven keeps turning itself to a rake,
and a beehive in boots and a pear-headed priest
call monkeys to order and lizards to feast?

"The nuns were quiet. I'd rather be bored
and hang out their laundry in sight of the Lord,
than wrestle with dragons to get to my sink
while the cats chase the cucumbers, slickity-slink."

"They go slippity-slosh,"
said Hieronymus Bosch.

"Take us under your wing, take us up on your back,"
they howled, while the claws murmured, "clickety-clac."

"They're not what I wished for. When women are young
they want curly-haired daughters and raven-haired son.
In this vale of tears we must take what we're sent,
feathery, leathery, lovely, or bent."

That night she awoke to a terrible roar.
Her suitcase yawned and unleashed on the floor
a mole in a habit,
  a thistledown rabbit,
    a troop of jackdaws,
      a three-legged dish,
the pickle-winged fish, and a head wearing claws.

With a pain in her back and a fog in her head,
she walked twenty-two miles and collapsed into bed.

She packed her fur tippet, her second-best hat.
(The first was devoured by a two-headed bat.)

"I don't mind the ferret, I do like the bee.
All witches' familiars are friendly to me.
I'd share my last crust with a pigeon-toed rat,
and some of my closest relations are cats."

"My aunt was a squash,"
said Hieronymus Bosch.

Hieronymus rose from a harrowing night,
saw salvation approaching, and crowed with delight.

With her suitcase and tippet secure on the dish,
she clambered aboard the pickle-winged fish.

"The dragon shall wear a gold ring in his nose
and the daws stoke the fire and the larks mend our clothes
forever and ever, my nibble, my nosh,
till death do us part," said Hieronymus Bosch.

"My lovey, my dear, have you come back to stay?
Let the crickets rejoice and the mantises pray,
let the lizards do laundry, the cucumbers cook.
I shall set down new rules in my gingerbread book."

THE ASH OF MEMORY, THE DUST OF DESIRE

Poppy Z. Brite

Another young, talented writer whose stories first appeared in small-press horror magazines, Poppy Brite started winning attention with the publication of stories like "His Mouth Will Taste of Wormwood" in the first *Borderlands* anthology. Her first novel, *Dead Souls*, has been published in a limited edition by Borderlands Press and will be appearing in a mass-market edition in October.

"The Ash of Memory, the Dust of Desire" is from the anthology *Dead End: City Limits*, and although the impetus for the events in the story could happen anywhere, the horror lies in the contrast between the hard, abandoned detritus of an industrial society and the soft, vulnerable human body and soul.

—E.D.

Once, I thought I knew something about love.

Once, I could stand on the roof of the tallest skyscraper in the city and look out across the shimmering candyscape of nighttime lights without thinking of what went on down in the black canyons between the buildings: the grand melodramatic murders, the willful and deliberate hurt, the commonplace pettiness. To live is to betray. But why do some have to do it with such pleasure?

Once, I could look in the mirror and see the skin of my throat not withered, the hollows of bone not gone blue and bruised around my eyes.

Once, I could part a woman's legs and kiss the juncture like I was drinking from the mouth of a river, without seeing the skin of the inner thighs gone veined and livid, without smelling the salt scent and the blood mingled like copper and seawater.

Once, I thought I knew something about love.

Once, I thought I wanted to.

Leah met me in the bar at the Blue Shell. It was six o'clock, just before dinnertime, and my clothes were still streaked with the dill-cream soup and Dijon dressing we had served at lunch. The fresh dill for the soup had come on a truck that morning, in a crate, packed secure between baby carrots and dewy lettuces. I wondered how many highways it had to travel between here and its birthplace,

417

how many miles of open sky before the delivery man lugged it up to the twenty-first floor of the posh hotel. "The Blue Shell on Twenty-one" read the embossed silver matchbooks the busboys placed on every table, referring not to avenue number but to floors above street level. Way up here they kept it air-conditioned, carefully chilled . . . except in the heart of the kitchen, where no amount of circulated air could compete with the radiant heat of a Turbo Ten-Loaf bread oven. In addition to the residue of lunch, I felt sheathed in a layer of dry sweat like a dirty undershirt gone wash-gray with age.

The bar on ground floor was as cool as the rest of the hotel, though, and Leah was cool too. As cool as the coffee cream when I took it out of the refrigerator first thing every morning. For her appointment today she had dressed carefully, in the style affected by all the fashionable girls this year. Leah was one of the few who could get away with it: her calves were tight and slender enough for the clunky shoes and the gaudy, patterned hose, her figure spare enough for the sheath-snug, aggressively colored (or, for a very special occasion, jet black) dresses, the planes of her face sufficiently delicate to sport the modified beehive hairdo, swept up severely in front, but with a few long strands spiraling carefully down the back. "There was a long waiting line," she told me, toying with the laces of her shoestring bodice. I imagined her sitting in one of the anonymous chairs at the clinic, hugging herself the way she did when she was defensive or less than comfortable— an unconscious gesture, I was sure. My cool Leah would never have chosen to do something that so exquisitely exposed her own vulnerability.

I was supposed to feel guilty. I was supposed to feel neglectful because I hadn't been able to get anyone to work lunch for me; thus I had sent fragile Leah into a dangerous situation unprotected, into a situation of possible pain without the male stability she craved. Something in me cringed at the accusation, as if on cue. Until now I had only sipped at the boilermaker I'd ordered; now I drank deeply, and was vaguely surprised to see it come away from my lips half-drained. The taste was good, though, the sour tangy beer washing down and the sweet mash of the whiskey lingering. Bushmills. The kitchen staff drank free after getting off a shift, and the bar brands were damn tasty.

"They hurt me," she said next. "I don't see why I had to have a pelvic. Jilly didn't have to have a pelvic when she went to her private doctor. They just tested her pee, and when they called her on the phone later, the nurse already had an appointment set up for her."

"Jilly's boyfriend designs software," I told her. "Jilly can afford to see a private doctor."

"Yes, but listen." She spoke excitedly, mouthing her words around the various straws and skewers they'd put in her drink. She drank fruity, frothy stuff, drinks you couldn't taste the alcohol in, drinks that more properly belonged on a dessert plate with a garnish of whipped cream. A dark red maraschino cherry bobbed against her lips. "Cleve went with me today. He says he's got some money saved up from his last gallery show. If you help too, I'll have enough. I can have the operation at a private doctor's office—the clinic's going to call and make me an appointment." Her hand set her drink down on the bar, found mine, tightened over it.

I noticed the way she said *operation* before I thought of anything else. Casual, with no more pain in the twist of her mouth than if she were saying *new dress* or *boyfriend* or *fuck*. Like something she was used to having, that she couldn't get used to the idea of not having whenever she wanted it. It wasn't until my next swallow of whiskey that I registered the name she'd spoken.

"Cleve went with you?"

Again the casual twist of the lips, not quite a smile. "Yes, Cleve went. You couldn't get off work. I didn't feel like doing it alone."

I remembered standing in the kitchen two days ago, slicing a carrot into rounds and then chopping the rounds into quarters. I kept my eyes fixed on the big wooden cutting block, on the knife slicing through the crisp orange meat of the carrot, but in the corner of my vision I could see Cleve twisting his battered old hat in his hands. Between his long fingers, the hat was like an odd scrap of felt. Cleve's hands were large enough to fit easily around my throat; Cleve stood a head and a half taller than me, and his arms might have been strong enough to throw me half the length of the kitchen. But I knew he would let me kick his ass if I wanted to. If I was hurting so bad that I wanted to pound his head against the floor or punch him in the face until his blood ran, then he was prepared to let me. That was how deep his guilt went. And that was how bad he still wanted Leah.

"I can't work for you Wednesday," he'd told me. "Any other day I'd do it, you know that. I've got to see this gallery owner, it's been set up for weeks."

He wouldn't meet my eyes. I thought he was just upset at the idea of me having to run the kitchen alone, having to make the thousand little decisions that go with the lunch rush while all the time I worried about Leah . . . imagining her getting off the bus at the last stop before the clinic, having to walk through blocks of the old industrial district. Other parts of the city were more dangerous, but to me the old factories and mills were the most frightening places. The places where abandoned machinery sat silent and brooding, and twenty-foot swaths of cobweb hung from the disused cogs and levers like dusty gray curtains. The places that everyone mostly stayed away from, mostly left alone with the superstitious reverence given all graveyards. But once in a while something would be found in the basement of a factory or tucked into the back room of a warehouse. A head, once, so badly decomposed that no one could ever put a face to it. The gnawed bones and dried tendons and other unpalatable parts of a wino, jealously guarded by a pack of feral dogs. This was where the free clinic was; this was where certain doctors set up their offices, and where desperate girls visited them.

And while Leah was making her way through this blasted landscape, while I was slicing goat cheese for the salads or making a delicate lemon sauce to go over the fresh fish of the day, Cleve would be ensconced in some art gallery far uptown. I pictured it like the interior of a temple: lavish brocade and beaded curtains, burning sachets of sandalwood and frankincense, carpet lush and rich enough to silence even the tread of Cleve's steel-toed cowboy boots. There Cleve would be, kicking back in some cool dim vast room, trying to say the right things about the colorful paintings that came from some secret place in his brain, about the sculptures he shaped into being with the latent grace of his big hands. I liked the idea of Cleve bullshitting some spotless hipper-than-thou gallery owner, someone who attended the right parties to see and be seen, someone who had never been to the old industrial district or any of the rough parts of town except for a quick slummy thrill, someone who never got mustard all over his shirt or scalded his hands in hot dishwater.

But Cleve hadn't been bullshitting anyone except me.

Leah extricated her hand from mine and adjusted the hem of her skirt over her knee. Her fingernails were painted the cool blue of a blemishless autumn sky; her movements were guarded and deliberate. I caught the glimmer of her frosted eyelids, but in the semidarkness of the bar I could not see her eyes.

I took a long drink of my boilermaker. Warm rancid beer; the flat taste of whiskey settling spiderlike over my tongue.

One of Cleve's passions was his collection of jazz and blues records, most of them the original pressings. No digital techno-juju or perfect plastic sound, just the old cardboard sleeves whose liner notes told the stories of entire lives. Just the battered vinyl wheels that could turn back time and rekindle desire, just the dark sorghum voices. Billie and Miles, Duke and Bird . . . and more obscure ones. "Titanic" Phil Alvin, Peg Leg Howell. I had given him a bunch of them, and he knew I loved them too. One night he willed them to me over a case of Dixie beer. (Cleve had made a special trip to New Orleans when the Dixie brewery finally closed, and there were still a few cases stashed in his studio closet; I had helped him drink another five or six.) "Jonny, if I got jumped by a goddamn kid gang on my way home—" he paused to light a Chesterfield "—or if I walked in front of a bus or something, you'd have to take 'em, man." He gestured around the room at a series of little jewel-box watercolors he was doing at the time. "My paintings could go their own way—shit, they can take care of themselves. But you have to take the records. You're the only one who loves 'em enough."

The records were Cleve's sole big indulgence. The rest of his extra money went to buy paints and canvas and an occasional luxury like groceries. He never collected them out of any kind of anal retentiveness, and desire to possess and catalog. It was just the feel of good heavy vinyl in the hands, the fragrant dust that sifted from the corners of the dog-eared cardboard, the music that spun you back to some grand hotel ballroom where you danced beneath a crystal chandelier . . . or some smoky little dive renting space in the basement of a whorehouse. The records were magic rabbit holes that led to the past, to a place where there was still room for romance. And I loved them as much as Cleve did.

And right then, in that moment at the bar as Leah withdrew her hand from mine, I could have taken a hammer and smashed the records all to bits.

We walked the four blocks from the hotel to the train tunnel half-staggering, almost drunk off our one drink apiece. Leah had not eaten because of her appointment; I, after wracking my brain to concoct delicious menus day after day, could hardly eat at all. Forsaking a free dinner at the Blue Shell meant we would go to bed hungry. Our refrigerator at home was empty of all but the last parings of our life together: an old rind of cheese on the shelf, a vegetable or two that neither of us would ever cook withering in the drawer, a flask of vodka I had stashed in the freezer.

As we left the hotel behind, the street grew shabbier. The buildings along here were old row houses of brick and wood, once fashionable, now unrenovated and nearly worthless. Children and teenagers sat on some of the stoops, hardness aging their faces, their grim eyes urging us past. Most unnerving were the houses that stood vacant: I could not imagine what face would look out from the dirty darkness behind the windows. Leah pulled my arm around her. I felt her skin and muscles moving under the thin dress. I thought of that strength moving with me, around me, like snakes wrapped in cool velvet. We had not had sex in three weeks, had not made love in so much longer than that. Whenever I was not with either Cleve or Leah, I imagined them together, drowning in ecstasy, dying their little deaths into each other.

Cleve had told me first, as soon as he realized that Leah didn't intend to. Away from the kitchen, away from work, in a neutral bar with a fresh beer in front of me, he confessed in a hesitant voice, telling me what a dumbfuck he was and how anyway there was only *lust* between them, no love, not seeing how that would hurt the worst. He bought me another beer before I finished my first one. Maybe he just wanted to know where both of my hands were.

Leah was in bed but not asleep when I went home. She'd heard me coming up the stairs and fumbling with my key, and rolled over when I came in. Some nights she slept naked; tonight she was wearing something as sheer and weightless as ectoplasm. I saw the line of her shoulder silhouetted in filmy silver-white, some-how more erotic than the curve of her hip or breast. I sat on the edge of the bed.

"I waited up for my story," she said. It was our custom for me to tell her a tale before we fell asleep at night: sometimes just a shred of hotel gossip or a memory from childhood, sometimes a dream, one of the plans I only told her and Cleve, one of my schemes to get away from the kitchen and into a grander, larger, more leisurely world. These were made of the finest ego-spun gossamer and collapsed in the telling; nonetheless it was pleasurable to tell her, like placing a drop of my heartblood on her lips.

"I'm not telling you a story tonight," I said. "Tonight it's your turn."

She didn't move then, only looked up at me with her eyes dark in the darkness of the room: she knew I knew. And four weeks later she finally came up with a story to tell me in return for all the ones I'd given her. She was carrying a living, breathing, bloodsucking piece of meat inside her, and it might be Cleve's meat, and it might be mine.

Leah always liked to feel passive when she had sex. No, it wasn't just that she *liked* to: she *needed* to feel passive, needed to feel she was being acted upon. I could kiss her anywhere, manipulate her knees and elbows and the strong curve of her back, pretend she was a department-store mannequin I was posing for some pornographic window display. She would press her face into a pillow and whimper, enjoying the power of pretended helplessness. I could dine on her tangy juices all night if I wished, I could stay inside her as long as I pleased, come when I wanted to. Only when I asked her what *she* wanted would Leah get angry. She had to be the little girl; she had to have someone take control.

Not on the morning of her operation. I woke in the still, stuffy light of predawn, unsure what had caused me to surface. I thought I had heard a distant sound, something separate from the intermittent cacophony of voices and sirens that punctuated the night. A train whistle miles away, or a telephone ringing in a far-off room.

Then, before I even knew Leah was awake, she sat up and in one liquid movement was straddling me. I had not felt her body close to mine in so long that it startled me into immobility. Even when I pressed up against the urgent sharpness of her nipples, up into the syrupy heat of her crotch, I wasn't ready.

She tensed above me. In the waxing light I saw surprise on her face, and faint annoyance. She began to grind against me. In the unfamiliar position I could not think how to respond. Leah hardly ever got on top—maybe five or six times in the three years we had been together. It didn't fit her penchant for being acted upon, and it played up the fact that she was almost as tall as me. She had told me that one of the things she liked best about Cleve was his bigness. His hands could enfold hers as if her hands were baby birds. Her bones felt more delicate when she pressed them against the solid bulk of him.

My overactive imagination served me up plenty of Leah-and-Cleve snapshots, plenty of inevitable intimate moments, generous helpings of feverish speculation. I was helpless to push these out of my mind once they held sway, but that was not the worst thing about them.

The worst thing about them was that occasionally—usually when I was feeling low and tired and ugly—these thoughts would give me a moment of masochistic excitement.

I thought of Leah's flower-stem spine pressed flush against Cleve. I thought of him kneeling above her, his back covering hers, his big hands cupping the tender weight of her breasts. I knew Cleve preferred to fuck doggy-style. He was a confirmed butt man, loved to ride between those sweet snowy globes. I thought of him just barely entering her, the petals of her opening for him, slicking him with her juice. Cleve had a thick penis, heavily veined and solid-looking; he told me the only time a girl had blatantly propositioned him was once when he had been modeling for an art class.

Imagining it going into Leah, searching out the fruit of her heaven, I began to get hard too.

She grabbed me and then suddenly I was deep inside her. One thrust upward and I felt I was pushing at the heart of her womb. She came the way women do when they only need one good deep touch: quick and hard, with an animal groan instead of the little feathery noises she often made. I thought of the lump of meat that grew inside her, thought of bathing it with my sperm, melting away its rudimentary flesh, melting away the past few months and their caustic veneer of pain. Then I did come. The sperm didn't reach far enough: it pulsed out in long, aching spasms that flowed back down over us, into the sticky space between our thighs. The months of pain did not melt away. The lump of meat remained—it would have to be scraped away, not drowned in the seed of sorrow.

As she was pulling away from me, the telephone did ring. The noise jarred something in me, a faint, grating edge of déja vu: I wondered again what had woken me. Leah hunched over the receiver. "Yes," she said. "Wait—let me get something—" She grabbed a pen from the bedside table, a glossy magazine from the clutter on the floor. Her breasts hung ripe as eggs when she leaned over. She scratched something on the cover of the magazine. I rolled my head sideways on the pillow and looked. *217 Payne Street,* she had written—the doctor's address, which the clinic wouldn't divulge until the morning of the abortion. An address in the disused industrial district of the city.

"Thank you," said Leah, "yes . . . thank you." Gently she placed the receiver back in its cradle. The weak light was growing brighter behind the dirty curtains. Leah got out of bed and hurried to the bathroom. I was still lying there when she came out thirty minutes later. She did not look at me. She pulled fishnet stockings the color of smoke up over her long smooth thighs, fastened a wisp of a garter belt around her waist, zipped up a sleeveless, black-lace shift. Then she sat on the edge of the bed and cried.

I held her hand and touched her face with all the tenderness I could summon. Her mascara did not run—some new waterproof kind, I supposed. Her lipstick was perfect. I tried to comfort her, and all I could see in my mind was Leah lying back on a stainless steel operating table, some black-rubber vacuum-tube apparatus snaking up into her. Her labia were stretched wide as a screaming mouth and she was wearing nothing but the lacy garter belt and the fishnet stockings.

It was an image Cleve would have appreciated.

"Yes, Jonny, I know you try to be sweet to me. You're a saint, Jonny. But you know what you have? Only that damned *little-boy* sweetness. You can't take care of me. You could cook me a million gourmet dinners and when I finished them I'd still be lonely. Cleve has a special kind of sweetness—"

"I know, I know. Cleve's sweet the way a dumb dog is sweet. You like 'em big and stupid, right?" When I was with Cleve I could not hate him. Only my arguments with Leah could convince me that Cleve had ever meant me any harm, and only then could I say cruel things about him. We had started arguing on the way to the doctor's office. Walking through the abandoned factory district made me tense—the landscape was falling to waste, long stretches of broken glass gleaming dully here and there like quicksilver sketched onto a monochromatic gray photograph. The silence in the empty, shabby streets seemed deafening. Leah mistook my own silence for indifference: I wasn't listening to her gloomy prattle, wasn't even thinking of the ordeal about to happen to her.

The buildings here loomed low and oppressive, blotting out the sun. Years ago this place had been a toxic hell of factories and mills. We passed smokestacks blackened halfway down their towering stalks with soot and char. We passed burned-out lots that made me think of cremation grounds. The smell of death was here too—the odor of burning crude oil is somehow as humanly filthy as the odor of corrupted flesh. These places had been abandoned over the past twenty or thirty years, as the heart of the city's industry gradually moved north to the silicon suburbs. Out there you could live your whole life shuttling between a superhighway, an exit sign, a gleaming building made of immaculate silver glass, a house and a yard and a wide-screen TV and the superhighway again.

More frightening to me than the empty lots, more oppressive than the huge corrugated-steel Dumpsters that overflowed with thirty years' forgotten trash, were the dead husks of the buildings. Some of them went on for blocks and blocks, and I could not help but imagine what it would be like to walk through them—endless mazes of broken glass and spiderweb and soft sifting ash, with the corners laved in shadow, with the pipes and beams zigzagging crazily overhead. I thought of a poem I had written once for some long-ago college class, in some idealistic day when the city was far away and I only cooked the food I wanted to eat. A few lines came back to me: *When the emptiness in you grows too large/You fill its vaulted chamber with the ash of memory/ With the dust of desire.*

"I don't want to fight," Leah said suddenly. "There's not enough time, it's too soon. Hold me, Jonny. Help me—" She pressed me back against a wall and covered my mouth with hers. Her lips were lush, her tongue was moist and searching, and again I was reminded of loving her. Not the sterile and functional fuck this morning, but the real love we had once shared: the soft friction of skin, the good long thrusts, the liquid sounds of pleasure. But these memories were receding rapidly. Soon they would be just a point of brightness on a dark horizon, and I knew now that they could never return. As I kissed Leah I became conscious of the rough bricks at my back, of the vast empty space behind me. I grasped her shoulders and gently pushed her away. "Come on," I said. "You can't be late. What are we looking for—Payne Street?"

She nodded, didn't speak. We kept walking. In all the blocks since we'd gotten off the train, we had only seen two or three other people: sad silent cases who walked with their heads down, who looked like they might vanish from existence as soon as they turned the corner. Now it seemed we were alone. The streets grew ever shabbier and emptier; a few of them had signs whose letters were half-obliterated, spelling out cryptic messages, pointing to nowhere. None of them looked like they might have ever said Payne Street. At one corner, a long spray of dirt lay across the sidewalk. Leah could not quite step all the way over it, and when we were past I saw a dark crumb stuck to the heel of her shoe. The delicate tired lines around her mouth and eyes seemed etched in dust. I began to feel that the landscape was encroaching upon her; she would leave here forever marked.

If it could erase the mark of Cleve from her, or rather the mark of her love for Cleve, then I would bless this blasted landscape. Maybe then I could love her again.

I thought I wanted to.

Soon it was obvious that we were getting to the fringes of the industrial section. The buildings here were more cramped and ramshackle. If anything walked here, it would be the wraith of a drudge worked to death in the sweatshops, dead of blood poisoning from a needle run through her finger. Or perhaps a tattered ghost, a hungry soul mangled by machinery from a time that knew no safety regulations. The sidewalk was fissured with deep cracks and broken into shards, as if someone had gone at it with a sledgehammer. I saw weeds sprouting at the edges of the vacant lots, leaves barely tinged with green, as furtive and sunless as mushrooms.

"You think the doctor's office burned down?" I said.

The look from beneath Leah's eyelashes was pure sparkling hate. Leah disliked getting around the city, and when she had to find a place by herself, she got panicky and sometimes mean. "He said we should come out of the tunnel and turn left. It was supposed to be three blocks down past the cotton factory."

"They had cotton *mills*, Leah, not factories, and any one of those buildings we passed could have been the one you want. By the time we walk all the way back there, we'll be a half hour late." A little flame of rage snapped in my chest. If she didn't have her directions straight, and if we arrived too late, we could miss the appointment. Appointments with a private doctor who would perform this particular operation were difficult to get, so difficult that if Leah missed this chance, she might be too far along by the time she could get another.

Without a word, she wheeled and started walking back the way we had come. I had to hurry to keep up with her; despite my anger, there was still the old reflexive fear that she might twist her ankle in one of the cracks or break into a run and escape from me or fall into a giant hole that would open like a mouth in the ground beneath her feet. You hold onto what you have; you do not give it up easily, even when you know it is poisoning you.

We walked quickly for a long time. Leah was sure we had turned at a certain corner; I didn't remember, and we argued over that. Somehow she managed to bring Cleve's name into it. "If you were with *Cleve*," I said furiously, "you wouldn't be bitching at him. You'd be all contrite and saying how stupid you were to get lost. You'd whine until you tricked him into taking care of you."

Leah spun on her heel. "Well, Cleve *isn't* here, is he? He had to hang his stupid gallery show today—he couldn't come! I'm stuck with you!"

"He was never going to go. He said you and I should go alone—said maybe that would help you decide. Make you quit stringing me along, I guess he meant."

"Yes, that was what he said he told you. But Jonny, I was going to meet him this morning. I was going to tell you I wanted to go by myself, that I'd decided I had to do it alone. Then I was going to meet Cleve at the train station. But when I called him this morning, the bastard backed out. He decided to spend the day playing with his damned pictures."

Only the fact that I was still somehow pitifully, stupidly in love with Leah allowed me to do what I did then. I turned and ran from her. If I had stayed I could not have kept my fingers from round her throat; in my head I would have been choking her and Cleve at once. Never mind the total illogic of it; never mind that both Leah and Cleve knew I would never have let her go off alone; never mind that I did not really believe Cleve would betray me so completely, not even for Leah, not even though I knew he was pitifully in love with her too. Something had woken me up this morning at the first pale light of dawn; it could have been a cry down in the street, or a jet plane arrowing through the smog far overhead. Or it could have been Leah murmuring into the phone, cursing her conspirator in a whisper when she realized he wasn't coming. Then replacing the receiver ever so gently—wanting to slam it down—and flowing over on top of me. Making love to me to spite Cleve, even if only in her head.

I had the spreading cancer of jealousy in me; it had been eating away inside me for a long time. Now at last I thought I was in its death throes, suffering its final agony. And, like any dying man, I tried to run from it.

We had already lost the way we had come by. Now I ran deeper into the maze of streets, not looking or caring which way I went. For a few moments I sprinted, desperate to get away, wanting nothing but to run and run. Then the sound of Leah's heels ticking frantically behind me began to slow me down, began to pull me back to here and now and what I thought I wanted. I walked fast, jogging when she got too close, not letting her catch up with me but not completely losing her. I was afraid I might never find her again; I was afraid of having nothing to crawl back to.

Then I turned a corner and didn't look over my shoulder soon enough. When I did glance back, Leah was gone.

I froze. How could I have lost her, not meaning to? I waited a few seconds to see if she might follow. If I ran back around the corner and she was still coming, my game would be up—it would be as good as admitting that I hadn't wanted to run away at all. But if she'd gotten disgusted and started back to the train station, I had to catch her. I had to get her to that appointment if I still could. If she needed dragging there, I would drag her.

I came around the corner and the sidewalk was empty. For a moment I vacillated between anger and the stark terror of abandonment. But farther up the street, at the mouth of a narrow alleyway, I saw a smudge on the sidewalk—darker than the drifting ash, and shiny. I walked back to it. The smudge on the sidewalk was blood, twin patches of it ground into the cement. A few feet away, half-hidden beneath a blackened flake of newspaper, lay a tube of scarlet lipstick.

Leah had tripped over her heels, fallen, spilled her purse, skinned her knees brutally on the broken sidewalk. But where had she gone after that?

I looked down the alleyway. No one there. Nothing—

—except a sign.

I hadn't seen it at first. No one walking quickly past would have noticed it; it had been placed only three or four feet up the wall, at waist level instead of eye level. And it was so faded, the edges of the letters seeming to blend into the dusty brick, that it could hardly be read. But I imagined Leah sitting up after her fall, her smoky fishnets torn and the raw ganglia of her kneecaps screaming, her eyes filling with tears. She would have sat there for a moment, dazed, not quite able to get up. And the sign might have caught her eye.

Pain Street, it said.

The alleyway led between two empty factory buildings.

Suddenly the sky seemed too wide and bright and heavy, the silence too big. A fragment of sidewalk shifted under my foot. I saw little drifts of refuse piled against either wall of the alley—soot and ash, more bits of charred paper, the razor confetti of broken glass. I did not know if I could set foot in the alley; I did know, however, that I could not go home alone.

One wall was blank and featureless all the way to the back of the alley, where more trash was heaped. At my approach, a bottle rolled lazily down but did not shatter. I thought I had walked into a cul-de-sac until I came to the end of the alley. There, set back in an alcove of crumbling mortar, was a heavy steel door wedged open with half a brick.

Someone had taken a nail or a shard of glass and scratched the number 217 on the door.

The door made a gritty ratcheting noise as I pulled it open, but there was no trash in front of it, and the hinges swung easily. Someone had opened it before me. I paused for a moment, drinking in what little dirty sunlight managed to filter into the alley. Then I stepped inside. It was easy. Leah always led me to the places I feared most, and I always followed.

The air inside the building was as cool and dim and stagnant as the air in a sarcophagus. In the dark rafters and pipes of the ceiling it hung like a cloud of bats waiting to fly, rustling their parchment wings, exuding their arid spice smell. *The ash of memory*, I thought dreamily, *the dust of desire*. Walking in this air was like moving through a syrup of fermented ages; the silence in here could wrap you up like cloth and preserve you for a thousand years. As my eyes adjusted to the light, shapes began to resolve themselves around me: a huge mesh of Gigeresque machinery, cogs hanging in the air like dull toothy moons, rubber belts and hoses gone brittle with dust, steel spires soaring up to the apex of the great vaulted chamber. And a row of hooks as long as my leg, sharp metal hooks that looked oddly organic, as if they should be attached to the wrist-stump of some enormous amputee.

I walked a few steps into the chamber, and my foot punched through something dry and papery. A giant vegetable bulb, I thought, like an onion or a shallot kept too long in a root cellar, rotten and desiccated from the inside. Not until I pulled my foot back did the fragile rib cage crumble, collapsing the swollen shell of the belly and exposing the scrimshaw beadwork of the spine.

A younger woman than Leah, almost a child, half-buried and half-dissolved into the grime and ash of the factory floor. Most of the face was gone. I saw scattered teeth gleaming in the dust like fragments of ivory. But the curve of the cheekbone—the tiny hand—surely she could not yet have been sixteen. And I wondered why she had come at all, with the once-ripe swell of her belly; she had been too far along in her pregnancy to have hoped to live through an abortion.

I could go no further. I could not walk that gauntlet of machinery, not even to find Leah. I could not turn my back on it either. I stood over the husk of the young girl, and the machinery stretched out mutely as far as I could see, and time hung motionless inside the old factory, not disturbed by me or Leah or anything in the city. It seemed impossible that just a few miles away the trains were still running, the drugs were still changing hands, the endless frantic party went on as if time could not be stopped.

Very nearby, magnified by furtive echoes, I heard the click of a high heel. "Leah," I called, not knowing if I hoped to save her or if I wanted her to save me. "Leeeeah . . ." When she walked into the far end of the chamber, I could no longer be ashamed of the pleading note in my voice. Her face was smeared with tears and makeup. The blood from her scraped knees had begun to cake, gluing her torn stockings to her legs. Her face twisted with relief and she started toward me, her arms out as if in supplication. In that moment Cleve might never have touched her, never have tasted her. We might have gone home together, might have slept in each other's arms again. I might have rested my cheek on the burgeoning mound of her belly, and found peace.

Then the machinery kicked on.

It had not been used in a long time, long enough to let the young girl fall away nearly to bare bones, and it filled the air with dust as thick as whipped cream. Only dimly did I see the first hook lifting Leah up and away from me, as if she had raised her arms and flown. I stood there dumbly for several minutes, unable to grasp what had happened even as her blood fell upon my face and my out-stretched hands. A high-heeled shoe dropped to the floor in front of me, missing my head by an inch. I did not move. I stared up, up at the swirling clouds of dust, up at the figure that hung suspended like an angel in black lace. When the dust cleared Leah was slumped over limp, her head hanging upside down, her hair like a bright banner in the dusk of the room. The hook had punched into her back and out through the soft flesh of her abdomen, but her face was perfectly calm. I was calm, too, an absolute calm like the equilibrium of particles in a solution. Should I have been frightened? Perhaps. But somehow I knew that even if I walked up to one of the machines and touched it, I would not be hurt. They did not want me.

The metal of the hook was beaded with bright blood. On its sharp tip was a thick gobbet, darker than the rest and more solid-looking. It looked like nothing but a piece of meat—meat that had ceased to live or breathe or suck.

I no longer thought I knew something about love.

Now I *knew* what love was all about.

I have described the scene to Cleve as well as I could, and asked him to paint it for me. When he has captured it as closely as possible in the jeweled watercolor tones that he loves—the soft gray dust, the banner of her hair, the red so clear and vital it hurts the eye to see it—he will mat and frame it and we will hang it on the wall.

Cleve's work has become somewhat fashionable among the gallery crowd, and he has begun getting shows uptown, where the art patrons don't think they've gotten their money's worth unless they pay upwards of five hundred for a piece. We have both cut back to half time at the Blue Shell. Whenever we have a night off, we try to work our way through the last of the Dixie beer, and we listen to Sarah Vaughan or Mingus or Robert Johnson, and when the music ends we sit and stare at each other, and a thousand secrets pass between our eyes.

I hate to look in the mirror. I hate to see the beginnings of an old man's face. I hate the loose skin of my throat and the hollows around my eyes. But I know what Leah's eyes must look like by now.

Sometimes we talk about magic.

In a city of millions, an ancient city overcrowded and mean enough, a kind of magic could evolve.

Ancient by American standards isn't very old. Two or three hundred years at most . . . and the abandoned mills and factories are no more than sixty years old. But I think of New Orleans, that city mired in time, where a whole religion evolved in less than two hundred years—a slapdash recipe concocted of one part Haitian graveyard dust, one part juju from the African bush, a jigger of holy Communion wine, and a dash of swamp miasma. Magic happens when and where it wants to.

In a great, cruel, teeming city, one could create one's own magic . . . intentionally or otherwise. Magic to fulfill desires that should remain buried in the deepest pit of the soul, or just to get through the desperate hustle of staying alive from day to day. And out of the desperation, out of the hunger for bread or love, out of the secret hard bright joy at the madness of it all—out of these things something else could be born. Something made of bad dreams and lost love, something that would use as its agent the abandoned, the forgotten, the all-but-useless.

The obsolete engines, the rusted cogs . . . and the steel hooks that stay honed sharp and shiny. The machinery of a forsaken time.

The love that no one wanted anymore.

I go up to the roof of Cleve's building and I look out over the city, and I think about all the power waiting to emerge from its black womb, and I wonder who else will tap into this homegrown magic, and I howl into the wind and rejoice at the emptiness within me.

And nowhere else on the horizon have I ever seen so many billions of lights . . . or so many patches of darkness.

THE PAVILION OF FROZEN WOMEN

S. P. Somtow

As does S. P. Somtow's other story in this collection, "The Pavilion of Frozen Women" takes place in an exotic setting, reflecting Somtow's wide travels and understanding of other cultures. "The Pavilion of Frozen Women" is a powerful and moving murder mystery set in Sapporo, Japan, during the annual snow festival. Most of the main characters are "outsiders" to Japan—Afro-Americans, Native Americans, Ainus—and their interactions reflect the uneasy relationship the Japanese have with those who are not Japanese. But more importantly, the story is about the accommodations a minority culture makes to the majority in order to succeed on the majority's terms, and the effects such accommodations have on the individual. This story first appeared in the anthology *Cold Shocks*.

—E.D.

1

"Alles Vergängliche
Ist nur ein Gleichnis. . . ."

—Faust

She was draped against the veined boulder that jutted up from the snow and gravel in the rock garden of Dr. Mayuzumi's estate. One hand had been placed demurely over her pubes—the Japanese have a horror of pubic hair that has caused it to become the last taboo of their pornography—the other was flung against her forehead. A trickle of blood ran from the side of her lip down her slender neck, past one breast, to a puddle beside her left thigh.

When I got there with my notebook and my camera, they were milling around in the cloister that ran all the way around the rectangular rock garden. Their breath hung in the still cold air, and no one had touched the body yet, not even the police.

I hadn't come to Sapporo to cover a slasher; I'd come there for the Snow Festival. I'd only been in town for a couple of hours. I'd only just started unpacking when I got the phone call from the Tokyo office and had to grab a taxi to this estate just outside town. I didn't even have time to put on a coat.

To say that it was cold doesn't begin to describe it. But I'd been feeling this cold since I was just a *winchinchala* back at the Pine Ridge Reservation in South Dakota. I stood there in my Benetton sweatshirt and my Reeboks and looked out of place. I ignored the cold.

A police officer was addressing the press. They weren't like stateside reporters; there was a pecking order—the Yomiuri and Asahi Shimbun people got the best places, the tabloids hunched down low in the back and spoke only when spoken to—gravely, taking turns, scribbling solemnly in notebooks. They all wore dark suits.

I'd had Japanese at Berkeley, but I couldn't follow much, so I just stood there staring at the corpse. There wasn't a strand of that stringy blond hair that was out of place. It was the work of an artist.

It was the hair that jolted me into remembering who she was. So this wasn't just another newspaper story after all.

The snow was beginning to obliterate the artist's handiwork—powdering down her hair, whitening away her freckles. She'd been laughing all the way from San Francisco to Narita Airport. I still had her card in my purse.

I snapped a picture. When the flash went off they all froze and turned toward me all at once, like a many-headed monster. It's uncanny the way they can do that. Then they all smiled that strained, belittling smile that I'd been experiencing ever since I'd arrived in Japan a week before.

"Look," I said at last, "I'm with the Oakland *Tribune*." Suddenly I realized that there wasn't a single woman among all those ranked reporters. In fact, there were no other women there at all. I felt even more self-conscious. No one spoke to me at all. It didn't matter that what I was wearing stood out against the black-white-and-gray like a peacock in a hen coop. I was a woman; I was a *gaijin*; I wasn't there.

Presently the police officer murmured something. They all laughed in unison and turned back to their note-taking. One reporter, perhaps taking pity on me, said, "American consulate will be here soon. You talk to *them*."

"Yeah, right," I said. I wasn't in the mood for bullshit. "Listen, folks, I *know* this woman. I can *i-den-ti-fy* her, *wakarimashita?*"

The many-headed monster swiveled around again. There was consternation behind the soldered-on smiles. I had the distinct impression they didn't feel it was my place to say anything at all.

At that moment, the people from the consulate arrived. There was a self-important bald man with a briefcase and a slender black woman. A few flashbulbs went off. The woman, like me, hadn't planned on a visit to the Mayuzumi estate on a snowy afternoon. She was dressed to the gills, probably about to hit one of those diplomatic receptions.

"I'm Esmeralda O'Neil," she said to the police officer. "I understand that an American citizen's been—" She stopped when she saw the corpse.

The policeman spoke directly to the bald man. The bald man deferred to the black woman. The policeman couldn't seem to grasp that Esmeralda O'Neil was the bald man's boss.

"Look here—" I said. "I can tell you who she is."

This time I got more attention. More flashes went off. Esmeralda turned to me. "You're Marie, aren't you? Marie Wounded Bird. They told us you were coming, and to take care of you," she said. "I was hoping to meet you at the reception tonight."

"I didn't get invited," I said testily.

"Who is she?" she said. She was a woman who recovered quickly—a real diplomat, I decided.

"Her name's Molly Danzig. She's a dancer. She sat next to me on the flight from San Francisco. She works—worked—at a karaoke bar here in Sapporo— the rooftop lounge at the Otani Prince Towers."

"You know anything else about her, darlin'?"

"Not really."

She looked at the corpse again. "Jesus fucking Christ." She turned to the police officer and began talking to him in rapid Japanese. Then she turned back to me. "Look, hon," she said, "all hell's gonna break loose in no time flat; CNN's already on their way. Why don't you come to the reception with us?" Then, taking me by the arm so that her aide couldn't hear her, she added, "You don't know what it's like here, hon. Machismo up the wazoo. I'd give anything for an hour of plain old down-home girl talk. So—reception?"

"I'm not sure . . . I'd feel a bit like trespassing."

"Why darlin', you've already gone and done *that*! This is the Mayuzumi estate we're standing in now . . . and the reception is Dr. Mayuzumi's bash to welcome the foreign dignitaries to the Snow Festival." I had heard of this Mayuzumi vaguely. Textiles, beer, personal computers. Finger in every pie.

The Japanese reporters were already starting to leave. They filed out in rows, starting with the upscale newspapers and ending with the tabloids. It was only then that I noticed the man with the sketch pad.

At first I thought he must be an American. Even from the other side of the rock garden I could see that he had the most piercing blue eyes. He was kneeling by the railing of the cloister. In spite of the cold he was just wearing jeans and a T-shirt. He had long black hair and a thick beard. He was hairy . . . bearlike, almost. Asians are hardly ever hairy.

The policeman barked an order at him. He backed off. But there was something in his body language, something simultaneously deferential and defiant, something that identified him as a member of a conquered people, a kind of hope-lessness. It was so achingly familiar it made me lose my cool and just gape at him. That was how my mother always behaved when the social worker came around. Or the priest from the St. Francis Mission. Or whenever they'd come around to haul my dad off to jail for the weekend because he'd guzzled down too much *mniwakan* and made himself a nuisance. All my aunts and uncles acted that way toward white people. The only one who never did was Grandpa Mahtowashté. And that was because he was too busy communicating with the bears to pay any attention to the real world.

My grandfather had taken me to my first communion. Nobody else came. He knelt beside me and shouted out loud: "These damned priests don't know what this ritual really means." They made him wait outside the church.

God I hated my childhood. I hated South Dakota.

The man stared back at me with naked interest. I hadn't seen that here before either. People never looked you in the eye here. I had become an invisible woman. It occurred to me then that we were invisible together, he and I.

I stopped listening to Esmeralda, who was babbling on about the social life of the city of Sapporo—explaining that it wasn't all beer, that the shiny-modern office buildings and squeaky-clean avenues were no more than a veneer—and just stared at the man. Although he was looking straight at me, he never stopped sketching.

"Anyway, hon, I'll give you my card . . . and . . . here's where the reception's going to be . . . the Otani Prince Towers . . . rooftop, with a mind-boggling view of the snow sculptures being finished up." Esmeralda made to leave, and I said something perfunctory about seeing her again soon.

Then I added, "Do you know who that man is?"

"That's Ishii, the snow sculptor. Aren't you here to interview him?"

It showed how confused I'd become after seeing my fellow traveler lying dead in the snow. Aki Ishii was one of the grand masters on my list of people to see; I had his photograph in my files. It had been black and white, though. I couldn't have expected those eyes.

And he was already walking toward me, taking the long way around the cloister.

He said to me: "Transience and beauty . . ." He was a softspoken man. "Transience and beauty are the cornerstones of my art. It was Goethe, I think, who said that all transient things are only metaphors . . . should we seize this moment, Miss Wounded Bird? Or is the time not yet ripe for an interview?"

"You know me?" I said. I had suddenly, unaccountably, become afraid. Perhaps it was because there were only the two of us now . . . even the corpse had been carried off, and the Americans had tramped away down the cloister.

The temperature fell even more. At last I started to shiver.

"I know you, Miss Wounded Bird—perhaps you will let me call you 'Marie'— because the *Tribune* was kind enough to send me a letter. I knew who you were at once. Something about your body language, your sense of displacement; you were that way even with your fellow countrymen. I understand that, you see, because I am Ainu."

The Ainu . . . it began to make sense. The Ainu were the aboriginal inhabitants of this island—blue-eyed neolithic nomads pushed into the cold by the manifest destiny of the Japanese conquerors. There were only 15,000 pure-blooded Ainu left. They were like the Lakota—like my people. We were both strangers in our own land.

It occurred to me that I was on the trail of a great story, an important story. Oh, covering the festival would have been interesting enough—there's nothing quite like the Sapporo Snow Festival in all the world, acres and acres of snow being built up into vast edifices that dissolve at the first thaw. It's all some Zen-like affirmation of beauty and transience, I had been told . . . and now I was hearing the grand master himself utter those words over the site of a sex murder . . . hearing them applied with equal aptness to both art and reality.

"Perhaps I could escort you to the reception, Marie?" he said. Behind his

Japanese accent there was a hint of some other language, perhaps German. I seemed to remember from his dossier that he had, in his youth, studied in Heidelberg under a scholarship from the Goethe-Institut. It was quaint but kind of attractive. I started to like him.

We left the rock garden together. He had an American car—a Mustang—parked by the gate. "I know the steering wheel is on the wrong side," he said apologetically, "but I'll drive carefully, I promise."

He didn't. The thirty kilometers back into downtown Sapporo were terrifying. We lurched, we hydroplaned, we skidded, past tiny temples enveloped in snow, past ugly postmodernist apartments, past row houses with walls of rice paper crammed along alleyways. Snow bent the branches of the trees to breaking. The sunset glittered on roofs of glossy tile, orange-green or cobalt blue. I was glad he was driving with such abandon. It made me think less of Molly Danzig, laughing over how she'd been fleecing the rubes at the karaoke bar, trading raunchy stories about men she had known, wolfing down airline food in between giggles . . . Molly Danzig, who in death had become part of an ordered elegance she had never evinced in the twelve hours I had sat beside her on the plane from San Francisco.

The reception was, of course, a massive spectacle. These people really knew how to lay on a spread. The top floor of the hotel had been converted into a Styrofoam and plastic replica of the winter wonderland outside. Three chefs worked like maniacs behind an eighty-foot sushi bar. Elsewhere, cooks in silly pseudo-French uniforms sliced patisseries, carved roasts, and ladled soup out of swan-shaped tureens. Chandeliers sparkled. Plastic snowflakes rained down from a device in the ceiling. You could have financed a feature film by hocking the clothes on these people's backs—Guccis, Armanis, Diors—a few of those $5,000 kimonos. Although Aki had thrown on a stylish black leather duster, I found myself hopelessly underdressed for this shindig. It didn't help that everyone was studiously ignoring us. Aki and I seemed to be walking around in a private bubble of indifference.

One wall was all glass. You could see down into Odori Park, on the other side of Sapporo's three-hundred-feet-wide main drag. The snow sculptures were taking shape. Once the festival started they would be floodlit. Now they were ghostly hulks haunching up toward the moon. This year's theme was "Ancient Times"; there was a half-formed Parthenon at one end of the park, a Colosseum in the foreground, an Egyptian temple complete with Sphinx, a Babylonian ziggurat . . . all snow.

A huge proscenium filled one end of the lounge, and on it stood a corpulent man who was crooning drunkenly into a microphone. The song appeared to be a disco version of "Strangers in the Night." There was no band.

"Jesus!" I said. "They should shoot the singer."

"That would hardly be wise," Aki said. "That man is Dr. Mayuzumi himself."

"Karaoke?" I said. There's only one karaoke bar in Oakland and I'd never been to it. This fit the description all right. As Dr. Mayuzumi left the stage to desultory applause, someone else was pushed up onto the stage amid gales of laughter. It turned out to be Esmeralda O'Neil. She began singing a Japanese pop song, complete with ersatz Motown gestures and dance steps.

"Oh," Aki said, "but this is the club where your . . . friend . . . used to work. Miss . . . Danzig." He pronounced her name *Danjigu*.

"Let's get a stiff drink," I said at last.

We went and sat at the sushi bar. We had some hot sake, and then Aki ordered food. The chef pulled a pair of live jumbo shrimp out of a tank, made a few lightning passes with his knife, and placed two headless shrimp on the plate. Their tails wiggled.

"It's called *odori*." Aki said, "dancing shrimp . . . hard to find in the States."

I watched the shrimp tails pulsing. Surely they could not feel pain. Surely it was just a reflex. A lizard's tail goes on jerking after you pull it off the lizard.

Aki murmured something.

"What did you say?"

"I'm apologizing to the shrimp for taking its life," he said. He looked around shiftily as he said it. "It's an Ainu thing. The Japs wouldn't understand." It was the kind of thing my grandfather did.

"Eat it," Aki said. His eyes sparkled. He was irresistible.

I picked up one of them with my chopsticks, swished it through the soy sauce dish, popped it in my mouth.

"What do you feel?" he said.

"It's hard to describe." It had squirmed as it went down my throat. But the way all the tastes exploded at once, the soy sauce, the horseradish, the undead shrimp with its toothpastelike texture and its exquisite flavor . . . there'd been something almost synaesthetic about it . . . something joyous . . . something obscene.

"It's a peculiarly Japanese thing," said the Ainu snow sculptor, "this almost erotic need to suck out a creature's life force . . . I have been studying it, Marie. Not being Japanese, I cannot intuit it; I can only listen in the shadows, pick up their leavings as I slink past them with downcast eyes. But you, Marie, you I can look full in the face."

And he did. The way he said my name held the promise of dark intimacy. I couldn't look away. Once again this man's body language evoked something out of my childhood. It was my father, reaching for me in the winter night, in the bedroom with the broken window, with his liquor breath hanging in the moonlit air. And me with my eyes squeezed tight, calling on the Great Mystery. Jesus, I hated my father. Although I hadn't thought of him in ten years, he was the only man in my life. I felt resentful, vulnerable, and violated, all at once. And still I couldn't look away. Then Esmeralda breezed over and came to my rescue.

"You never stop working for a moment, do you, hon?" she said, and ordered a couple of *odori* for herself.

I said, "What about Molly Danzig? Any word about—"

"Darlin', that girl's just vanished from the universe as far as anyone can see. The press aren't talking. Nothing on TV. Even CNN's been put on hold for a few days. Total blackout . . . even the consulate's being asked to wait on informing the next of kin . . . it's that festival, you know. It's a question of face."

"Doesn't it make you mad?"

"Hell no! I'm a career diplomat, darlin'; this girl doesn't rock any boats." She bit down on the wriggling crustacean with relish. "Mm-mm, good." No squeamishness, no regret.

I looked around. The partygoers were still giving us a wide berth, but now and then I thought I could see stares and hear titters. Was I paranoid? "Everyone knows about it, don't they?" I said.

"It?" said Esmeralda ingenuously.

"It! The murder that no one can talk about! That's why they're all avoiding me like yesterday's fish; they know that I knew her. I stink of that girl's death."

"It's nothing, hon." She took a slug of sake.

Aki tugged at my elbow. "I can see you're getting uncomfortable here," he whispered. "Would you care to blow this joint—I believe that's how you Americans call it?"

I could see where this was leading. I was attracted to him. I was afraid of him. I had a story to write and I knew that a good story sometimes demands a piece of your soul. How big a piece? I didn't want to give in yet, so I said, "I'd love to see the snow sculptures. Now, when the park's deserted, in the middle of the night."

"Your wish is my command," he said, but somehow I felt that it was I who had been commanded. Like a vampire, Aki had to be invited before he could strike.

In the moonlight, we walked past the Clock Tower, the only Russian building left on Hokkaido, toward the TV tower which dominated the east end of Odori-Koen. The park was long and narrow. Mountains of snow were piled along the walkways.

They had brought in extra snow by the truckload. There were a few men working overtime shoveling paths and patting down banks of snow. A man on a ladder was shaping the entablature of a Corinthian column with his hands. Fog roiled and tendriled about our feet. I didn't ask Aki why the park and the zombie shrimp had the same name; I had a feeling the answer would unnerve me too much.

We walked slowly up the mile-long park toward the tableau that was Aki's personal creation—I knew from my notes that this was to be the centerpiece of the festival, a classical representation of the Judgment of Paris.

"What do you think of Sapporo?" Aki asked me abruptly.

"It's—"

"You don't have to tell me. It's an ugly town. It's all clean and shopping-mall-ridden and polished till it shines, but still it's a brand-new city desperately looking for something to call a soul."

"Well, the Snow Festival—"

"Founded in 1950. Instant ancient culture. A Disneyland of the Japanese sensibility."

It was not what I'd come to hear. I'd had the article half written before I'd even boarded the plane. I'd wanted to talk about tradition, the old reflected in the new. We walked on.

People go to bed early in Japan. You could hardly hear any traffic. A long line of trucks piled high with snow stretched the length of the park and turned north at the Sosei River end. It took three hundred truckloads of snow for the average snow sculpture. The snow came from the mountains.

Most of the sculptures had been cordoned off. Now and then we passed artisans who would turn from their work, bow smartly, and bark out the word *sensei*. Aki walked ahead. We did not touch. Public displays between the sexes are frowned on here. I had been relieved to learn that.

"It was a shame about that Danjigu girl," Aki said. "I have seen her many times, at the karaoke club; Mayuzumi rather liked her, I think."

Molly had said something about fat rich businessmen. I wished he would change the subject. I said, "Tell me something about your art, Aki."

"Is this the interview?" Our footsteps echoed. Ice tinkled on the trees. "But I have already talked about beauty and transience."

"Is that why you were sketching Molly's corpse? I thought it was kind of . . . macabre."

He smiled. No one was watching us. His hand brushed against mine for a fleeting second. It burned me. I walked ahead a few steps.

"So what are you looking for in your art, Mr. Ishii?" I asked him in my best girl-reporter voice.

"Redemption," he said. "Aren't you?"

I did not want to think about what I was looking for.

"I feel a bit like Faust sometimes," he said, "snatching a few momentary fragments of beauty out of the void, and in return giving up . . . everything."

"Your soul for beauty?" I said. "Kind of romantic."

"Oh, it's all those damned Germans, Goethe, Schiller: death, transfiguration, redemption, weltschmerz—going to school there can really fill you with Teutonic portentousness."

I had to laugh. "But what about being Ainu?" I said. "Doesn't that contribute to your artistic vision too?"

"I don't want to talk about that."

So we were alike, always running away from who we were. He strode purposefully ahead now, his shadow huge and wavery in the light of the full moon.

A wall of snow towered ahead of us. Here and there I could see carved steps. "I'll help you up," he said. He was already climbing the embankment. My Reeboks dug into the snow steps. "Don't worry," he said, "my students will smooth them out in the morning. Come."

The steps were steep. Once or twice he had to pull me up. "There will be a ramp," he said, "so the spectators can cluster around the other side."

We were standing on a ledge of snow now, looking down onto the tableau he had created. Here, at the highest point in the park, there was a bitter breeze. It had stopped snowing and the air was clear, but the sky was too bright from the city lights to see many stars. The artificial mountain wrapped around us on three sides; the fourth was the half-built viewer's ramp; the area formed a kind of open-air pavilion.

Aki said, "Look around you. It's 1200 B.C. We're on the slopes of Mt. Ida, in the mythological dawn. Look—over there—past the edge of the park—the topless towers of Ilium." It was the Otani Prince Towers, glittering with neon, peering up through twin peaks. It was an optical illusion—the embankment no more than thirty feet high, a weird forced perspective, the moonlight, the fog swirling—that somehow drew the whole city into the fantasy world. "Come on," he said, taking my hand as we descended into the valley. A ruined rotunda rose out of a mound of rubble. A satyr played the panpipe and a centaur lay sleeping against a broken wall. It was hard to believe it was all made of snow. On the wall, sculpted in bas-relief, was the famous judgment: Paris, a teenaged version of Rodin's *Thinker*, leaning forward as he sat on a boulder; the three goddesses preening; the golden apple in the boy's hand.

"Now look behind the wall," Aki said.

I saw a cave hollowed out of the side of the embankment. At its entrance, sitting in the same attitude as the bas-relief, was a three-dimensional Paris; beyond, inside the cave, you could make out three figures, their faces turned away.

"But—" I said. "You can't see the tableau from the spectator's ramp! At best, you'd see the back of Paris's head, the crook of Athena's arm. You can only see the relief on the ruined wall."

"But that is what this sculpture is all about, Marie," Aki said. He was talking faster now, gesticulating. "I hold the mirror up to nature and within the mirror there's another mirror that mirrors the mirrored nature I've created . . . reflections within reflections . . . art within art . . . the truth only agonizingly, momentarily glimpsed . . . and that which is most beautiful is that which remains unseen. Come on, Marie. You will get to see my hidden world. Come. Come."

He seized my hand. I climbed down beside him. A system of planks, concealed by snowy ridges, led to the grotto. Like a boy with an ant farm, Aki became more intense, more nervous as we neared the center of his universe. When he reached the sculpture of Paris, he became fidgety. He disregarded me completely and went up to the statue, reshaping a wrinkle in the boy's cloak, fussing with his hair. Paris had no face yet.

Curious to see how the grand master had visualized the three beautiful goddesses, I turned away from him toward the interior of the cave. The chill deepened as I stepped away from the entrance. The tunnel appeared to descend into an infinite darkness; another illusion perhaps, a bend, a false perspective . . . unless there was really an opening into some labyrinthine underworld.

The goddesses were not finished yet. Two had no faces. The third—Hera, goddess of marital fidelity and orthodoxy—had the face of Molly Danzig.

I thought it must be some trick of the moonlight or my frazzled nerves. But it was unmistakable. I went up close. The likeness was uncanny. If the snow had started to breathe I would not have been more startled. And the eyes . . . what were they? . . . some kind of polished gemstone embedded in the snow . . . snow-moistened eyes that seemed to weep . . . I could feel my heart pounding.

I backed away. Into Aki's arms. "Jesus," I said, "this is sick, this is morbid—"

"But I have already explained to you about beauty and transience," Aki said softly. "I have been watching this girl ever since she started at the karaoke club; her death by violence is, how would you say it, synchronicity. Perhaps a sacrifice for giving my art the breath of life."

Molly Danzig shook her head. I think. Her eyes shone. Or maybe caught the moonlight. She breathed. Or maybe the wind breathed into her. Or my fear. I was too scared to move for a moment and then—

"Kiss me," he whispered. "Don't you understand that we are both bear people? You are the first I have met."

"No!" I twisted free from him and ran. Down the icy pathway, with the moist wind whipping at my face, past the Parthenon and the Colosseum and the Sphinx. Past the piled-up snow. Snow seeping into my sneakers and running down my neck. It was snowing again. I crossed the street. I was shivering. It was from terror, not from cold.

Jesus, I'm getting spooked by illusions, I told myself when I reached the façade of the Otani. I took a deep breath. Objectivity. Objectivity. I looked around. There was no one in sight. I stood on the steps for a moment, wondering where to get a taxi at one in the morning.

At that moment, Esmeralda and her portly aide swept through the revolving doors and glided down the steps. She was wearing a fur stole, the kind where you'd be mugged by conservationists if you tried to wear it on the street in California. She saw me and called out, "Marie, darlin', you need a ride to your hotel?"

I nodded dumbly. A limousine pulled up. We piled in.

As we started to move down the street, I saw him again. Standing at the edge of the park. Staring intently at us. Sketching. Sketching.

2

"Das Unzulängliche
Hier wird's Erreignis."

—Faust

Bear people—

When I was a child I saw my grandfather speaking to bears.

The hotel I was staying at was a second-class *ryokan*, a traditional-style hotel, because I wanted to get the real flavor of the Japanese way of life. The smell of tatami. The masochistic voyeurism of communal bathing. I tossed and turned on the futon and wished for a water bed in San Mateo. And the roar of the distant surf. But my dreams were not of California.

In my dream I was a *winchinchala* again. In my dream was my father's shack. Midnight and the chill wind whining through the broken pane. I'm twisting on the pee-stained mattress on the floor. Maybe there's a baby crying somewhere. A damp hand covers my mouth.

"Gotta see to the baby, *até*." I'm whispering.

"*Igmu yelo*," says my father. *It's only a cat.* The baby's shrieking at the top of his lungs. Dad crushes me between his thighs. Even his sweat is turning to ice. I ooze through his fingers. I run down stairs that lead down down down down caverns down down to—

"*Don't!*"

From the dirt road that runs alongside the frozen creek next to the outhouse you can see a twisted mountain just past the edge of the Badlands. The top is sheared off. I wish myself up to the ledge where I'm going to stand naked in the wind and I'm going to see visions and know everything that's to come and I'm going to stand and become a frozen woman like the other women who have stood there and dreamed until they dreamed themselves into pillars of red and yellow stone.

"*Tunkashila!*" I'm screaming. "Grandpa!"

I'm running from the wind that's my dad's breath reeking of *mniwakan*.

Suddenly I know that the man who's chasing me is a bear. I don't look back but I can feel his shadow pressing down on me, on the snow. I'm running to my grandfather because I know I'll be safe with him, he'll draw a circle in the ground and inside everything will be warm and far from danger and he'll put down his pipe inside the sacred circle and say to the bear: *Be still, my son, be still.*

I'm running from the cold but I might as well run from myself. I'm going to be frozen right into the mountain like all the other women from now back to the beginning of the universe, women dancing in a slow circle around the dying fire. I'm running through the tunnel that becomes—

The tunnel beneath the sea. I'm riding the bullet train, crossing to Hokkaido island, to the Japan no one knows, the Japan of wide open spaces and desolate snowy peaks and spanking-new cities that have no souls. I'm staring out as the train shrieks, staring at the concrete cavern. I see Molly Danzig's eyes and I wonder if they're real, I wonder if Aki has plucked them from the corpse and buried them in the snow woman's face.

The frozen woman shakes her head. Her eyes are deep circles drawn in blood. "No, *até*, no, *até*," I whisper.

Be still, my son, my grandfather says to the bear who rears up over the pavilion of frozen women. My grandfather gives me honey from a wooden spoon. He puts his pipe back in his mouth and blows smoke rings at the bear, who growls a little and then slinks, cowed, back into the snowy forest.

Circles. Circles. I'm running in circles. There's no way out. The tunnel has twisted back on itself. I will turn to snow.

Molly Danzig's card: an apartment building a few blocks west of the Sapporo Brewery. It was about a fifteen-minute ride on the subway from my *ryokan*. The air was permeated with the smell of hops. Snow piled against a Coke machine with those slender Japanese Coke cans. At the corner, a robocop directed traffic. Its metal arms were heaped with snow. The first time I'd seen one of those things I'd thought it must be a joke; my Tokyo guide told me, self-importantly, that they'd had them for twenty years.

The afternoon was gray. The sky and the apartment building were the same dead shade, gray gray gray.

I took the elevator to the tenth floor. I don't know what I expected to find. I told myself, Hey, sister, you're a reporter, maybe there *is* a gag order on this story now but it won't last out the week. I had my little Sure Shot in my purse just in case.

The hall: shag carpet, dull modern art by the elevator. This apartment building could be anywhere. The color scheme was nouveau "Miami Vice." I followed the apartment numbers down the corridor. Hers, 17A, should be at the end. There it was with the door ajar. An old man in overalls was painting the door.

Painting out the apartment number. Painting out Molly's name. A brushstroke could obliterate a life.

I pushed my way past him into the apartment. I'd had a notion of what Molly's place would look like. Molly was always laughing so I imagined there'd be outrageous posters or funky furniture. She loved to talk about men—I don't—so I imagined some huge and blatant phallic statue standing in the middle of the room. It wasn't like that at all. It was utterly still.

The windows were wide open. It was chillier here than outside. A wind was sighing through the living room and the tatami floor was peppered with snow. No furniture. No Chippendales pinups on the walls. The wind picked up a little. Snowflakes flecked my face.

The kitchen: two bowls of cold tea on the counter. The stove was still lit. I turned it off. A half-eaten piece of sushi lay in a blue-and-white plate. I took a few snapshots. I wondered if the police had come by to dust the tea bowls for prints.

I heard a sound. At first I thought it must be the wind. The wind blew harder now and behind the sighing I could hear someone humming. A woman.

I stepped into the living room. Snow seeped through my sneakers. I was shivering. It was a contralto voice, eerie, erotic. I could hear water dripping, too. It came from behind a *shoji* screen door. A bedroom, I supposed.

I knew I was going to have to go in. I steeled myself and slid the *shoji* open.

Snowflakes whirled. The wind was really howling here. Through a picture window I could see the Sapporo Brewery and the grid of the city, regular as graph paper, and snowy mountains far beyond it. I smelled stale beer on the snow that settled on my cheeks.

The humming grew louder. A bathroom door was ajar. Water dripped.

"Molly?"

I could feel my heart pounding. I flung the bathroom door wide open.

"Why—Marie darlin'—I sure wasn't expecting *you.*" Esmeralda looked up at me from the bathtub, soaping herself lazily.

"You knew who she was the whole time," I said.

"It's my business to know that, hon," she said. "Not too many American citizens in Sapporo, as you might have noticed, but I keep tabs on 'em all. Hand me that washcloth? Pretty please?"

I did so numbly. Why had she asked me who the dead woman was if she already knew her? "You tricked me!"

"In diplomacy school, Marie, they teach you to let the other person do all the talking. Oftentimes they end up digging their own grave that way."

"But what are you doing here?"

"This is my apartment. Molly Danzig used to sublet. I've got a suite in the consulate I usually end up crashing out at, but the hot water in our building never works right."

She reached for a towel and slid out of the tub. She steamed; she was firm and magnificent and had a way of looking fully clothed even when she was naked; I guessed it was her diplomatic comportment. The Lakota are a modest people. I was embarrassed.

"Believe me, this ain't St. Louis. I mean, girl," she said, reaching for the hair dryer, "here's me, on a GS salary with perks up the wazoo, housing allowance, no mouths to feed . . . but if it weren't for all those receptions with all that free food, I'd be lining up at a fucking soup kitchen. Let's forget this and just go shopping somewhere, Marie."

"All right." I couldn't see where I could go with the story at this point. I had three or four pieces, but they didn't seem to fit together—maybe they didn't even belong in the same puzzle. Perhaps I just needed to spend a mindless afternoon buying souvenirs.

Esmeralda drove me to the Tanuki-koji arcade, a labyrinthine underground mall that starts somewhere in the middle of town and snakes over and under, taking in the train station and the basement of the Otani Prince. She parked in a loading zone ("*Gaimusho* tags, darlin'—they're not going to tow any of us diplomats, no way!") and although it was afternoon, we descended into a world of neon night.

When you're confused and pushed to the limits of your endurance and you think you're going to crack up, sometimes shopping is the only cure. I never went shopping when I was a kid. Yes, sometimes we'd take the pickup and lurch toward Belvedere or Wall, where at least you could watch the mechanical jackalopes for 25¢ or gaze at the eighty-foot fake dinosaur as it reared up from the knee-high snow. Shopping was a vice I learned from JAPs and WASPs in Berkeley. But I had learned well. I could shop with passion. So could Esmeralda. It was an hour or two before I realized that, for her as well as me, the ability to shop effusively was little more than a defense mechanism. As we warmed to each other a little, I could see that she spoke two different languages, with separate lexicons of gesture and facial expression; they were as different as English and Lakota were for my parents, except they were both English, and she could slide back and forth between them with ease.

We moved from corridor to corridor, past little noodle stands with their glass cases of plastic food in front, past *I Love Kitty* emporia and kimono rental stores and toy stores guarded by mechanical Godzillas, past vending machines that dispensed slender cans of Sapporo beer and iced coffee. People shuffled purposefully by. The concrete alleyways were slick with mush from above ground. Glaring neons blended into chiaroscuro.

By six or so we were laden down with shopping bags. Junk mostly—fans, hapi coats, orientalia for my apartment in Oakland, postcards showing the Ainu in their native costume, with ritual tattoos and fur and beads—not that there were any to be seen in the antiseptic environs of Sapporo.

"What do you know about the Ainu?" I asked Esmeralda.

"They're wild people. Snow people, kind of like Eskimos maybe—they worship bears, have shamanistic rituals—only for tourists—the Japanese forced them all to take Japanese names and they can't speak Ainu anymore."

It was a story I knew well. My grandfather Mahtowashté had told me the same story. "I can speak to bears," he said, "because once, when I was a boy, a bear came to me in a dream and gave me my name." And he'd give me a piece of bread dipped in honey and I'd say, "*Tunkashila*, make it so I can get out of here . . . make it all go away."

"There're more Ainu around than you might think. A lot of them have interbred with the Japanese. They don't *look* Ainu anymore, but . . . people still feel prejudiced. They don't advertise, unlike our friend Aki. Most of them just try to blend in. They'd lose their social standing, their credit rating, their influence . . ."

I knew all about that. I'd spent my whole life escaping, blending.

"Come on," Esmeralda said, "time for coffee."

We stopped at a coffee shop and squeezed ourselves into tiny armchairs and we each ordered a cup of Blue Mountain at ¥750 a pop. Tiny cups of coffee and tall glasses of spring water.

"Help me, Esmeralda," I said. "Jesus, I'm lost."

"This isn't the place you thought it would be." A neon blue-and-pink reproduction of Hokusai's "Wave" flashed on and off in the window. The alley beyond was in shadow. You could hear the whoosh of the subway trains above the New Age muzak and the murmur of conversation. I wondered whether the sun had already set in the world above. "You're thinking dainty little geishas, tea ceremonies, samurai swords . . . cute gadgets . . . crowds. And you're on Hokkaido, which isn't really Japan at all, which looks more like Idaho in January, where the cities are new and the people are searching for new souls . . ."

"You sound like that sculptor sometimes, Esmeralda."

"Oh, Aki. Did you fuck him yet, honey? He's a good lay."

"I'm not easy," I said testily. Actually, in a way, I was a virgin.

Oh God, I remembered the two of us in the cavern, I remembered the eyes of Molly Danzig, I remembered how he'd stared straight into my eyes, as though he were stalking me. A hairy beast of a man. Lumbering. A grizzly bear tracking me through the snow.

"Marie? Are you all right?" She sipped her coffee. "They don't give refills either—five bucks and no fucking refill." She drained it. "But you know, you should get to know him. You know how hard it is for a red-blooded American girl to get laid here? These people don't even know you're there—oh, they're polite and all, but they know we're not human. Blacks, Indians, whites, Ainu, we all look alike to them . . . we *all* niggers together. Besides, everyone here *knows* that all Americans have AIDS."

"AIDS?" I said.

"Stick around here, hon, and you'll know how a Haitian feels back home. Hey, I screwed Mayuzumi once—but I might as well have been one of those inflatable dolls." She laughed, a bit too loudly. A schoolgirl at the next table tittered and covered her mouth with her hand. "Molly Danzig now . . . he liked her a lot . . . actually he was paying her rent, you know. He liked to have her around whenever he needed to indulge his secret vice . . . I guess he thought it was kind of like bestiality."

"Molly was—"

"Shit, darlin', we all whores, one way or another!" she added. I felt I was being backed into a corner.

"Aki frightens me."

"Don't he! But he's the only man in this whole godforsaken country who has the common decency not to roll over and fall asleep right after they come."

The neon wave flashed on and off. Suddenly *he* was there. In the window. The blue-and-pink light playing over his animal features. "It's him!" I whispered.

Aki's eyes sparkled. He had his sketch pad. His hand was constantly moving in tiny meticulous strokes.

"What does he want?" I said. "Let's get out of here before—"

"What do you mean, hon? I told him to meet us here." Aki was closing his sketch pad and moving into the coffee shop. A waitress hopped to attention and bowed and rapped out a ceremonial greeting like a robot. His gaze had not once left my face.

"But—he *knew* her, don't you see? He knows you—he knows me—and she's *dead* and one of the three goddesses in his sculpture has her face . . . and the other two are blank . . ."

Esmeralda laughed. It was the first time I had ever voiced this suspicion . . . or even admitted to myself that I *had* a suspicion. I realized how preposterous it must sound.

I felt ashamed. I looked away. Stared into the brown circle of my coffee cup as though I could hypnotize myself into the phantom zone. I could hear his footsteps, though. Careful, stalking footsteps.

He stood above me. I could feel his breath. It smelled of honey and cigarettes. He said, "I understand, Marie. It's spooky there in the moonlight. You are in the middle of a city of a million people, yet inside my snow pavilion you are also inside my art, a sculpted creation. It's frightening." He touched my neck. Its warmth shot through me. I tingled.

"It was nothing to do with you," I found myself saying. "It's something else—out of my past—that I thought I'd forgotten."

"Ah," he said. Instead of moving his hand, he began to caress my neck in a slow, circular motion. I had a momentary vision of him snapping off my head. I wanted to panic but instead I found myself relaxing under his gentle pressure . . . sinking into a well of dark eroticism . . . I was trembling all over.

"Culture tonight!" Aki said. "A special performance of a new *bunraku* play, *Sarome-sama*, put on by the Mayuzumi foundation for the edification of the . . . foreign dignitaries."

"*Bunraku?*" The last thing I wanted was to go to a puppet show with him and Esmeralda. I had heard of *bunraku* in my Japanese culture class at Berkeley—it was all yodeling and twanging and wooden figures in expensive costumes strutting across the stage with excruciating elegance.

But she wouldn't hear of it. "Darlin', *everyone* will be there. And this is a really *weird* new show . . . it's the traditional puppet theater, sure, but the script's adapted from Oscar Wilde's *Salome*—translated into a medieval Japanese setting—oh, honey, you'll never see anything like it."

"But my clothes—" I said. I felt like a puppet myself.

"And what," she said, putting her hands on her hips, "are credit cards for, girl?"

Weird did not begin to describe the performance we witnessed at the Bunka Kaikan cultural center. The weirdness began with the opening speeches, one by Dr. Mayuzumi, the other by a cultural attaché of the German Embassy, which belabored endlessly the concept of cultural syncretism and the union of East and West. What more fitting place than Hokkaido, an island so rich in cross-cultural resonances, whose population was in equal parts influenced by the primitive culture of the enigmatic Ainu, by Japan, by Russia, and—in this modern world— by—ah—the "Makudonarudo Hambaga" chain . . .

Polite laughter; I had a vision of Ronald McDonald prancing around with a samurai sword.

I thought the preamble would end soon; it turned out to be interminable. But they had promised a vast buffet afterwards at the expense of the Mayuzumi Foundation. I saw Mayuzumi himself, sitting alone in a box on the upper tier, like royalty. Esmeralda and I were near the front, next to the aisle, with Aki between us. We were both wearing Hanae Mori gowns that we'd splurged on at the underground arcade.

The lights dimmed. The twang of a *shamisen* rent the air; then a spotlight illumined an ancient man in black who narrated, chanted, and uttered all the characters' lines in a wheezing singsong. We were in for cultural syncretism indeed; the set—Herod's palace in Judaea—had been transformed into a seventeenth-century Japanese castle, King Herod and his manipulative wife into a shogun and a geisha, and Salome into a princess with hair down to the floor. John the Baptist, for whom, in Oscar Wilde's revisionist text, Salome was to conceive an illicit and finally necrophiliac passion, was a Jesuit missionary. The centerpiece of the stage was the massive cistern in which John lay imprisoned. It was such a fascinating interpretation that it was hard to remember that I was sitting next to a man whom I suspected of murder.

In *bunraku*, the puppeteers are dressed in black and make no attempt to conceal themselves as they operate their characters. There were three operators to each of the principals. It took only minutes for the puppeteers to fade into the background . . . it made you think there *was* something to this ninja art of invisibility. The characters flitted about the stage, their eyelids fluttering, craning their necks and arching the palms of their hands, shrieking in paroxysms of emotion.

An American audience wouldn't be this silent, I thought.

The eerie rhythms entranced me. The rasp of the *shamisen*, the shrill, sustained wailing of the flute, the hollow *tock-tock-tock* of the woodblock did not meld into a soothing, homophonous texture as in Western music. Each sound was an individual strand, stubbornly dissonant. The narrator sang, or sometimes spoke in a lisping falsetto. In one scene, as Salome, his voice crescendoed to a passionate shriek that seemed the very essence of a woman's desire, a woman's frustration. He knows me, I thought . . . he has seen me running from my father, bursting with terror and love. I could hardly believe that a man could portray such feelings.

At the back of the auditorium, aficionados burst into uproarious cheering. From the context I guessed it was the moment when Salome demands to kiss John's mouth and he rebuffs her, and idea of demanding his severed head first germinates in her mind . . . for the Salome puppet threw herself across the floor of the stage, the three operators manipulating wildly as she flailed about in savage mimicry of a woman's despair.

Jesus, I thought. I've been there.

I looked at Aki and found that he was looking behind us, up at Mayuzumi's box. As applause continued, Mayuzumi made a little gesture with his right index finger. Aki whispered in Esmeralda's ear. She said, "Gotta go, darlin'—be right back." The two of them slipped into the aisle.

Was there some kinky triangle ménage between them? I could see Aki and Esmeralda in leather and Mayuzumi all tied up—the slave master playing at being the slave . . . Esmeralda wasn't inhibited like me. Maybe they had become so aroused they'd slipped away to one of those notorious coffee shops, the ones with the private booths.

I didn't want to think about it too much, and after a while I became thoroughly engrossed in the play. I couldn't follow the Japanese—it was all archaic—but I knew the original play, and the whole thing was in such a slow-motion style that you had plenty of time to figure things out.

There was the dance of the seven veils—not the Moroccan restaurant variety, but a sinuous ballet accompanied by drum and flute, and a faster section with jerky movements of the head and eyebrows and the arms obscenely caressing the air . . . the seven veils were seven bridal kimonos of embroidered brocade . . . the demand for the saint's severed head with which to satiate Sarome-sama's lust . . . the executioner, his katana glittering in the arclight, descending into the cistern . . . I gulped . . . how could they be wood and cloth when I could feel their naked emotions tearing loose from them? A drum began to pound, step by pounding step as the headsman disappeared into the oubliette.

The drums crescendoed . . . the flute shrilled . . . the shamisen snarled . . . I heard screaming. It was my own.

A head was sailing out of the cistern, shooting up toward the stage flies . . . a human head . . . Esmeralda's head.

For a split second I saw her torso pop from the cistern. Blood came spurting up. The puppets' kimonos were soaking. The torso thrashed and sprayed the front seats with blood. The claque began to applaud.

O Jesus Jesus it's real—

The head thudded onto the stage. Its lifeless eyes stared up into mine. I was the only one screaming. Wildly I looked about me. People turned away from me. It was as if I were somehow to blame because I had screamed. An announcement started coming over a loudspeaker. There was no panic. The audience was filing slowly out by row number, moving with purposeful precision, like ants. No panic, no shrieks, no nervous laughter. It was numbing. Jesus, I thought, they're aliens, they're incapable of feeling anything. Only the foreign guests seemed distraught. They stood in little huddles, blocking the traffic as the rest of them politely oozed around them. The stagehands were scurrying across the stage, moving props about.

The Salome puppet flopped against the castle walls with its doll-neck wrung into an impossible angle.

I stared up at Mayuzumi's box. Mayuzumi was gone.

Esmeralda's head was gone. They were mopping up the blood. I could hear a police siren in the distance.

Then, up the center aisle, framed in the doorway between two columns of departing theatergoers, I saw Aki Ishii appear as if in a puff of smoke.

Sketching.

Sketching *me*.

Jesus Christ—maybe he'd lured her away to kill her! I couldn't control my rage. I started elbowing my way toward him. The audience backed away. Oh yes. We *gaijin* all have AIDS. Aki backed slowly toward the theater entrance. There was a shopping bag on his arm. The doors were flung wide and the snow was streaming down behind him and I was shivering in my Hanae Mori designer dress that wasn't designed for snow or serial killers.

He backed into the street. The crowd parted. Men with stretchers trotted into the theater and a police siren screeched. I started to pummel him with my fists.

"Am I next?" I screamed. "Is that it? Are you sucking out our souls one by one to feed your art that's going to turn to mush by Friday?"

He held his hands up. "It's not like that at all," he said.

The wind howled. I was hysterical by now. Fuck these people and their propriety. I shouted at a passing policeman, "Here's your goddamn sex murderer!" He ignored me. "That shopping bag! The head's in the shopping bag!" I tried to wrest it from him. I could feel something squishy inside it. There was blood on everything.

"How could you be so wrong?" Aki said. "How could you fail to understand me? I told you the truth. It's not me—it's—it's—" His eyes glowed. That odor of honey and tobacco again . . . startled, I remembered where I'd smelled it before . . . on my grandfather's breath. I kept on hitting him with my fists but my blows were weak, dampened by snow and by my own bewilderment. You've got no right, I was thinking, no right to bring me those bad dreams . . . no right to remind me . . .

He grabbed my wrists. I struggled. His sketch pad flew into the snow. The wind flipped the pages and I saw face after face . . . beautiful women . . . beautiful and desolate . . . my own face. "My art," Aki said. There was despair in his voice. "You knocked my art out of my—" He let go abruptly. Scurried after the sketch pad, his black duster flailing in the wind like a Dracula cape. He found it at last. He cried to me across the shrieking wind: "We're both bear people. You should have understood." And he ran off into the darkness. He vanished almost instantly, like one of those puppeteers with their ninja arts.

It was only then that I realized that my dress was dripping with blood. It was caking against my arms, my neck. The wind and the sirens were screaming all at once.

No one's going to ignore *this* killing, I thought. A consular officer . . . a public place . . . a well-known artist hanging around near the scene of both crimes . . .

But as I watched the audience leaving in orderly rows, as I watched the policemen solemnly discoursing in hushed tones, I realized that they might well ignore what had happened.

I was going to have to go to someone important. Someone powerful. Power was all these people understood.

3

"Das Unbeschreibliche,
Hier ist's getan . . ."

—Faust

Midnight and the snow went on piling. I walked. Snow smeared against the blood on my clothes. I walked. I had some notion of finding my way back to the *ryokan*, making a phone call to the Tokyo office, maybe even to Oakland. I could barely see where I was going.

Bear people . . .

No one in the streets. The wind whistled. Sushi pennants flapped against restaurant entrances. I breathed bitter liquid cold. At last I saw headlights . . . a taxi.

By two in the morning I was outside the Mayuzumi estate. There were wrought-iron gates. The gates had been left open and the driveway had been recently shoveled. He let me off in front of the mansion.

A servant woman let me in, rubbing her eyes, showed me where to leave my shoes, and fetched clean slippers. She swabbed at my bloodstains with a hot towel. Then she handed me a clean *yukata* and watched while I tried to slip it on over my ruined gown.

It was clear that I—or someone—was expected. Perhaps there was a local geisha club that made house calls.

"*Mayuzumi-san wa doko*—?" I began.

"*Ano . . . o-furo ni desu.*"

She led me up to the steps to the tatami-covered foyer. She slid aside a *shoji* screen, then another and another. We walked down a succession of corridors—I walked, rather, and the maid shuffled, with tiny muffled steps, pausing here to fuss with a flower arrangement, there to incline her head toward a statue of the Amida Buddha. Beyond the Buddha image was a screen of lacquered wood on which were painted erotic designs. She yanked the screen aside and then I was face-to-face with Dr. Mayuzumi . . . naked, sitting in a giant bath, being methodically massaged by a young girl who sang as she kneaded.

He was a huge man. He was, I could see now, remarkably hirsute, like Aki Ishii; his eyes were beady and set closely together; he squinted when he looked at me, like a bear eyeing a beehive.

Behind Dr. Mayuzumi, the shoji screens had been drawn aside. The bathroom overlooked the rock garden where Molly's body had been. Snow gusted behind him and clouds of steam tendriled between us.

"Ah," he said, "Marie Wounded Bird, is it not? The reporter. I had thought we might meet in less . . . informal surroundings, but I am glad you are here. Tomichan! Food for our guest! You will join me for a light supper," he said to me. It was an order.

"You have to help me, Dr. Mayuzumi," I said. "I know who the killer is."

He raised an eyebrow. With a gesture, he indicated that I should join him in the bath. I knew that the Japanese do not find mixed bathing lewd, but I had never done it before; I balked. Two maids came and began to disrobe me. They were politely insistent, and the hot water seemed more and more enticing, and I found myself being scrubbed with pumice stone and led down the tiled steps . . . the water was so hot it hurt to move. I let it soak into my pores. I watched the snowflakes dance around the stone lantern in the cloister at the edge of the rock garden.

"No one will do anything," I said. "But there's a pattern. The victims are white and black . . . people who don't belong to the Yamato race . . . maybe that's why none of you people think it's important. The victims are all subhuman . . . like me . . . and I think I'm next, don't you see? The three goddesses . . . the Judgement of Paris . . . and the killer is subhuman too . . . an Ainu."

"What are you trying to say?" Mayuzumi said. "You would not be attempting to pin the blame on Aki Ishii, the grand master of snow sculpting?"

I gasped. "You knew all along. And you knew that I would come here."

Just as the heat was becoming unbearable, one of the serving maids fetched a basket of snow from outside. She knelt down at the edge of the bath and began to sprinkle it over my face, my neck. I shuddered with agony and delight. Another maid held out a lacquerware tray in front of me and began to feed me with chopsticks.

It was a lobster salad—that is, the lobster was still alive, its spine broken, the meat scooped out of its tail, diced with cucumbers and a delicate *shoyu* and vinegar dressing, and replaced in the splayed tail-shell with such artistry that the lobster continued to wriggle, it claws clattering feebly against the porcelain, its antennae writhing, its stalk-eyes glaring. I had already started to chew the first mouthful before I saw that my food was not quite dead. But it was too delicious to stop. And knowing I was draining the creature's life force only heightened the frisson. "I'm sorry," I whispered.

"Ah," Dr. Mayuzumi said, "you're apologizing to the lobster for—"

"Taking its life," I said. Wasn't that what Aki had said about the shrimp?

"How well you understand us." I was conscious of a terrible sadness in him. There was more to him than just being a millionaire with a finger in every pie. "I, too, am sorry, Marie Wounded Bird." He ordered the maid to remove the lacquer trays. "Yet you did not come to dine, but to accuse."

"Yes."

"You have proof, I hope; a man of Mr. Ishii's standing is not indicted lightly. His reputation . . . indeed, the reputation of the Snow Festival itself . . . would be at stake. You can understand why I sought to discourage the press from . . . ah . . . untimely revelations."

"But he's *killing* people!" I said.

"Mr. Ishii is a great artist. He is very precious to us. His foibles—"

I recoiled. "How can you—"

"In the grand scheme, in the great circle of birth and rebirth, what can a few lives matter?" he said. "But Mr. Ishii's art . . . does matter. And now you are here, blowing across our fragile world like *kamikaze*, the wind of the gods, irresistible and unstoppable. You would melt us down, just as the spring sun will soon melt the exquisite snow sculptures which 1.6 million tourists are about to see."

I couldn't believe this. It was the most familiar line of bullshit in the world. I was soaking in 110°, in the nude, eating live animals and listening to the Mayor of Amity shtick right out of *Jaws I*. My own life was on the line, for God's sake! I remembered Aki's eyes . . . the way he had run his fingers along the nape of my neck . . . his long dark hair flecked with snow . . . the quiet intensity with which he spoke of beauty and transience and voiced his resentment of the conquering Japanese. Could he really be one of those Henry Lee Lucas types? I knew he had had sex with Molly and Esmeralda. I knew he had been tracking me. Sketching. Sketching. Smelling of tobacco and honey, like my grandfather.

God I wanted him and I hated myself for wanting him. For a moment, standing in the snow amid his creation, listening to him—Jesus, I think I *loved* him.

"Goddammit, I can prove it," I said. "I'll show you fucking body parts. I'll show you eyeballs buried in snow and skeletons under the ice."

I was doomed to betray him.

"All right," said Dr. Mayuzumi. "I feared it would come to this."

The limousine moved rapidly toward downtown Sapporo. We sat in the backseat each hunched into an opposite corner. It was still snowing. We didn't speak until we were within a few blocks of Odori Park.

At last, Dr. Mayuzumi said, "Why?"

I said, "I don't know, really, Dr. Mayuzumi. Maybe he's sending a message to the Japanese people . . . about discrimination, about the way you treat minorities." I didn't want to think of Aki just as an ordinary mad slasher. We had too much in common for that. But there was just too much evidence linking him to Molly and Esmeralda . . . and me. Four minorities. Lepers in a land that prized homogeneity above all things. I had a desperate need to see the killings as some political act . . . it might not justify them, but I could understand such killings. Like the Battle of Little Big Horn . . . like the second siege at Wounded Knee. "Politics," I said bitterly.

"Perhaps." He did not look into my eyes.

The chauffeur parked at the edge of the park.

We began walking toward the "Judgment of Paris" tableau. Dr. Mayuzumi strode swiftly through the slush, his breath clouding about his face. I struggled to keep up. I became angrier as we walked. I had come to see him with information and now it seemed he had known all along, that his coming with me now was merely the working out of some preordained drama.

The full moon lengthened our shadows. Even the snow-shoveling workmen were gone; the empty trucks were parked in neat rows along the Odori.

Dr. Mayuzumi strode past the snow Sphinx and the Pyramids of Gizeh; I trudged after him, awkward in the short coat that one of the servants had lent me.

I was determined not to let him take the lead. I brushed by him. I was furious now. It seemed that this whole town had been built on lies. Snow gusted and flurried. Ice-shards lanced my face. I walked. Snow metropolises rose and fell around me. I didn't look at them. I tried to quell the cold with sheer anger.

We passed the columns of the Temple of Poseidon at Sounion, the icy steps of a Babylonian ziggurat, a Mexican pyramid atop which sat a gargoyle god ripping the heart out of a hapless child. Moonlight fringed the ice with spectral colors. Had the buildings grown taller somehow? Were the sculptures pressing in, narrowing the pathway, threatening to crash down over me? A skull-shaped mountain grinned down. Trick of the light, I told myself. I stared ahead. My shoes were waterlogged.

At length we came to Mt. Ida. I marched uphill. They could fix the footprints later. Dr. Mayuzumi followed. We crossed the terrace with its classical friezes, its nymphs and shepherds gesturing with Poussin-like languor.

In a moment we stood inside Ishii's secret kingdom, the cave that the audience could not see. The mirror of mirrored mirrors.

There had been more tunneling. The walls were lit by reflected moonlight and the cave seemed to stretch forever into blackness, though I knew it was an illusion. Like Wile E. Coyote, we are easily fooled by misdirecting signposts . . . a highway median that leads to the edge of a cliff . . . a tunnel painted onto the side of a sandstone mountain. It seemed we stood at the entry to an infinite labyrinth.

Dr. Mayuzumi took out a flashlight and shined it on the interior of the cave.

There were the three statues. Molly Danzig stood with her arms outstretched. It was her—but dead she was more beautiful somehow, more perfect . . . the statue of Athena had the face of Esmeralda O'Neil. She glowered; she was anger personified. It was just as I had imagined. The third goddess had no face yet . . . and neither did the boy Paris who was to choose between them.

I could be beautiful too, I thought. Cold and beautiful. I was tempted. I told myself: I hate the cold. I hate my childhood. That's why I went away to California.

Dr. Mayuzumi said, "Look at their eyes . . . as though they were still alive . . . look at them."

Molly's eyes: a glint of blue in the gloom. They stared straight into mine. Esmeralda's looked out beyond the entrance. The Athena statue held a spear and a gorgon-faced shield. God, they were beautiful. But I knew the deadly secret of their verisimilitude.

"How long can the cold preserve a human organ, an eye, for example?" I said. "Doesn't this snow-clad beauty hide death? Tell me there are no human bones beneath . . ."

"You would destroy this masterwork?"

It was too late. Before he could stop me I had plunged my fingers into Molly's face. I wanted to pull the jellied eyeballs out of the skull, to thrust them in Dr. Mayuzumi's face.

The face caved in. There was nothing in my fists but snow, flaking, crumbling, melting against the warmth of my hands. And then, when the snow had melted, two globes of glass and plastic. Two marbles.

I looked at Dr. Mayuzumi. His look of indignation turned to mocking laughter.

All my resentment exploded inside me. I smashed my fists against the statues of my two friends. Snow drenched me. The statues shattered. There were no bones beneath, no squishy organs. Only snow. Tears came to my eyes and melted the snow that had clung to my cheeks.

"A *gaijin* philistine with a stupid theory," said Mayuzumi.

I beat my arms against the empty snow, I buried myself elbow deep. I wept. I had understood nothing at all. The marbles slipped from my fingers and skated over a stretch of ice.

I felt Dr. Mayuzumi's hand on my shoulder. He pulled me from the slush. There was so much sadness in him. "And I thought you understood us . . ."

He gripped me and would not let go. His hands held no comfort. His fingernails dug into my flesh . . . like claws.

"I thought you understood us!" he rasped. His teeth glinted in reflected moonlight . . . glistened with drool . . . his eyes narrowed . . . his mouth smelled of honey and tobacco.

I thought you understood us . . . what did that mean?

And all at once I knew. When he had greeted me in the bath, when I mumbled *I'm sorry* at the writhing lobster, had he not said *How well you understand us?* I had completely missed it before . . . "You're an Ainu too, one who's been able to pass for a Yamato," I said. "You've blended with the Japanese . . . you've climbed up to a position of power by hiding from yourself . . . and it's driven you mad!"

"I'm sorry . . . oh, I'm sorry," he said. His voice was barely human. Still he would not let go. In the dark I could not see his face.

"Why are you apologizing?" I said softly.

"I need your soul."

Then I realized that he was going to kill me.

The flashlight illuminated him for a moment. His face was caving in on itself. Dark hair was sprouting up through the skin. I felt bristles push up from his palms and prick my shoulders. I was bleeding. I struggled. His nose was collapsing into a snout . . .

"Bear people!" I whispered.

He could not speak. Only an animal growl escaped his throat. He had become my father. I was caught inside the nightmare that had haunted me since I was *winchinchala*. I kicked and screamed. He roared. As his body wrenched into a new shape, I slipped from his grasp. The cavern shook and rumbled. Snow crashed over the entrance. I could hear more snow piling up. The cave was contracting like a womb. We were sealed in. The whine of the wind subsided.

The flashlight slid across the snow. I dived after it. I waved it in the air like a light saber. Its beam was the only illumination. It moved across the eyes . . . the teeth . . . I could smell the fetid breath of a carnivore. I was choking on it. "What are you?" I screamed.

He roared and the walls shook and I knew he no longer had the power of human speech. He began to lumber toward me. There was no way to escape. Except by stepping backwards . . . backwards into the optical illusion that suggested caves within caves, worlds within worlds . . .

I backed into the wall. The wall pulsated. It seemed alive. The very snow was living, breathing. The wall turned into a fine mist like Alice's mirror . . . I could hear the tempest raging, but it was infinitely far away.

I was at the edge of an icy incline that extended downward to darkness.

The bear-creature that had been Dr. Mayuzumi fell down on all fours. He pounced. I tripped over something . . . a plastic bag . . . its contents spilled onto my face. In the torchlight I saw that it was Esmeralda's head. The severed trachea snaked into the snow. There were no eyes. I bit down on human hair. I retched. There was blood in my throat. The bear-creature reared up. I screamed, and then I was rolling down the slope, downward, downward—

And then I was in a huge cavern running away from the were-bear my father with his rancid breath and the wind whistling through the broken windowpane and—

Darkness. I paused. Strained to listen. The bear paused, too. I could hear him breathing, a savage purr deep as the threshold of human hearing, making the very air vibrate.

I swung the flashlight in an arc and saw—

The fangs, the knife-sharp claws poised to strike and—

There was music. The dull thud of a drum. The shriek of the bamboo flute and the twang of the *shamisen*, and—

The bear sprang! The claws ripped my cheeks. I was choking on my own blood. I fell and fell and fell and my mouth was stopped with snow and I was numb all over from the cold and I was sliding down an embankment with the bear toying with me like a cat with a mouse and I screamed over and over, screamed and tasted blood and snow and—

I heard a voice: *Be still, my son.* The voice of my grandfather.

I was slipping away from the bear's grasp.

Into a circle of cold blue light.

In the circle stood Aki Ishii. He was naked. His body was completely covered in tattoos: strange concentric designs like Neolithic pottery. His long black hair streamed in a wind that seemed to emanate from his lips and circle around him; I felt no wind. Smoke rose from a brazier, fragrant with tobacco and honey.

"*Tunkashila* . . ." I murmured. I crawled toward him. Clutched at his feet in supplication.

The bear reared up at the edge of the circle. In the pale light I saw him whole for the first time. His face still betrayed something of Mayuzumi; his body still contained the portly outline of the magnate; but his eyes burned with that pure unconscionable anger that comes only in dreams.

"Be still," said Aki Ishii. "You may not enter the circle. It is I who am the shaman of the bear people. You cannot gain true power by taking men's souls; you must give in equal measure of your own."

And then I saw, reflected in the wall of ice behind us, miragelike images of Molly Danzig and Esmeralda O'Neil. They were half human, half cave painting. They too were naked and covered with tattoos. They had become Ainu, but I saw that they were also *my* people . . . they were also the Greek goddesses . . . Molly, who had fled from her home and herself and sought solace in the arms of strangers, had been incarnated as domesticity itself; Esmeralda, whose diplomatic career belied her bellicose nature, had become the goddess of war. What was I then? There was only one goddess left: the goddess of love.

But I was incapable of love, because of what my father had done. I hated him, but he was the only man I had ever loved.

Three musical instruments materialized in the smoke of the incense burner. Molly plucked the *shamisen* of domestic tranquility out of the air; Esmeralda seized the war drum. One instrument remained: the phallic bamboo flute of desire. I took it and held it to my lips. Of its own accord it began to play, a melody of haunting and erotic sweetness. And the drum pounded and the *shamisen* sounded . . . three private musics that could not blend . . . until we faced the bear together.

"My son," said Aki Ishii softly, "you must now reap the fruits of your own rage."

The bear exploded. His head split down the middle and the mingled brains and blood gushed up like lava from a volcano. His belly burst open and his entrails writhed like snakes. The drumbeats were syncopated with the cracking of the bear's spine. Shards of tibia shredded the flesh of his legs. Blood spattered the ceiling. The walls ran red. Blood rained down on us. Each piece of the bear ate away at itself, as though dissolving in acid. The smoke from the brazier turned into a blood-tinged mist. And all the while Aki Ishii stood, immobile, his face a mask of tragedy and regret.

I didn't stop playing until the last rag of blood-drenched fur had been consumed. Small puddles of blood were siphoning into the snow. The images of my dead friends were swirling into the mist that was the honey-tinged breath of Aki Ishii, shaman of the bear people. Only the eyes remained, resting side by side on an altar of snow. Aki nodded. I put down the flute and watched it disappear into the air. I knelt down and picked up the eyes. They were hard as crystal. The cold had marbled them.

"I'm sorry," Aki said. The light was dimming.

"Are you going to kill me?" I whispered, knowing that was what an apology presaged.

"I'm not going to take anything from you that you will not give willingly," said the snow sculptor. He took me by the hand. "The war between the dark and the light is an eternal conflict. Dr. Mayuzumi wanted what I wanted . . . but his magic is a magic of deceit. He was content with the illusion of power. But for that illusion, he had to feed on real human lives. This is not really the way of bear people."

"The dead women—"

"Yes. I planted a piece of those women into the snow sculptures. We made love. I captured a fragment of their joy and breathed it into the snow. Dr. Mayuzumi devoured them. They were women from three races the Japanese find inferior, but each race had done what the Ainu have not done—they have fought back—the blacks and the reds against the white men, the whites against the Japanese themselves. That was what made him angry. Our people have had their souls stolen from them. By stealing a piece of each of the three women's souls, tearing them violently from their bodies in the moment of death, he sought to give himself a soul. But a soul cannot be wrested from another person; it is a gift."

He took my other hand. And now I saw what it was that I had feared so much. I thought I had locked it up and thrown away the key, but it was still there . . . my need to be loved, my need to become myself.

"Now," said Aki Ishii to me, "you must free yourself, and me."

I held out the bear's two marble eyes. He took one from me. We each swallowed an eye in a single gulp. It had no taste. It was like communion. And then he kissed me.

We made love as the light faded from the cavern, and when we emerged from the wall of ice, the statues were whole again, and the goddess of love had my face; but the face of Paris was still blank.

4

"Das Ewig-weibliche
Zieht uns hinan!"

—Faust

It was a beautiful festival. By night, thousands upon thousands of paper lanterns lit the way for the million and a half tourists who poured into the city for the first week of February. The deaths of two foreign women were soon forgotten. Dr. Mayuzumi's bizarre suicide aroused much sympathy when his Ainu origins were revealed; it was only natural that a man in his position would be unable to cope with his own roots.

The death of grand master Ishii was mourned by some; but others agreed that it was only fitting for an artist to die after creating his masterpiece. He was found in the cavern, nude, gazing at the statues of the three goddesses; he had replaced the image of Paris with himself. It was agreed that he had sacrificed his life to achieve some fleeting epiphany comprehensible only to other artists, or, perhaps, other Ainu.

I can't say I understood it at all. I had stood at the brink of some great and timeless truth, but in the end it eluded me.

It was a beautiful festival, but to me it no longer seemed to have meaning. I was there in a plastic city of right-angled boulevards, a city that had robbed the land of its soul; a city that stood over the bones of the Ainu, that mocked the dead with its games of beauty and impermanence. Like Rapid City with its concrete dinosaurs . . . like Deadwood with its mechanical cowboys and Indians battling for 25¢ and all eternity . . . like Mount Rushmore, forever mocking the beauty of our Black Hills by its beatification of our conquerors.

You can't understand about being oppressed unless you're born with it. It is something you have to carry around all the time, like soiled underwear that's been soldered to your skin.

I know now that I'm not one of you. You own my body, but my soul belongs to the mountains, to the air, to the streams, the trees, the snow.

I think I will go back to Pine Ridge one day. Perhaps my grandfather will teach me, before he dies, the language of the bears.

I think I will even see my father. Perhaps I can be the angel of his redemption, as I think I was for Aki Ishii.

Perhaps I will even forgive him.

MOON SONGS

Carol Emshwiller

Carol Emshwiller's stories have been published in literary, feminist, and science fiction magazines. Her first novel, *Carmen Dog*, was published in 1990.

"Moon Songs" is from the slightly different American edition of her World Fantasy Award–winning collection *The Start of the End of It All*, first published by The Women's Press in Great Britain. The story contains the wit and subtle hard-edge that all great satires possess.

—E.D.

Carol Emshwiller is one of America's finest contemporary fiction writers. In her stories, elements of fantasy and surrealism are employed to comment on the real world we live in—with style, compassion, and a wit that bites.

—T.W.

A tiny thing that sang. Nothing like it mentioned in any of my nature books, and I had many. At first no name we gave it stuck. Sometimes we called it Harriet, or Alice, or Jim. Names of kids at school. All ironies. More often we just called it Bug. This mere mite—well, not really that small, more the size of a bee— pulled itself up by its front legs, the back ones having been somehow bent. Or so it seemed to us. Perhaps it happened when we caught it.

How can such a tiny thing have such a voice? Clear. Ringing out. Echoing as though in the mountains or in some great resonating hall. Such a wonderful other-worldly sound. We felt it tingling along our backbones and on down into the soles of our feet.

My sister kept it in a cricket cage. Fed it lettuce, grains of rice, grapes, but never anything of milk or butter, "in order to keep down the phlegm," she said, even though we didn't know how it made its sounds. We asked ourselves that first day, "Is it by the wings? Is it the back legs? Is it, after all, the mouth?" We looked at it through a magnifying glass, but still we couldn't tell. Actually we didn't look at it long that time, for (then) we didn't like the look of it at all. There were hairs or

457

barbels hanging down from its mouth and greenish fur at the corners of its eyes. We didn't mind the yellow fur on its body as that seemed cuddly and beelike to us. "Does it have a stinger?" my sister asked, but I couldn't say yes or no for sure, except that it hadn't stung us yet . . . me yet, for that first day I was the one that held it.

"I would suppose not," I told my sister. "Maybe it has its voice to keep it safe, and besides, if it had a stinger it would have used it by now." I did look carefully, though, but could see no sign of one.

To make it sing you had to prick it with a pin. It would sing for ten or fifteen minutes and then would need another prick. We knew enough to be gentle. We wanted it to last a long time.

How we discovered the singing was by the pricking, actually. The thing lay as though dead after we first caught it and we wanted to know for sure was it or wasn't it, so we pricked it. One prick got a little motion. Two, and it sat up, struggling to pull its poor back legs under itself. Three, and it began to sing and we knew we had something startling and worthwhile—a little jewel—better than a jewel, a jewel that sang.

My sister insisted she had seen it first and that, therefore, it was hers alone. She always did like tiny things, so I supposed it was right that she should have it, but I saw it first, and I caught it, and it was my hand first held it for she was frightened of it . . . thought it ugly before she heard it sing. But she had always been able to convince me that what I knew was true, wasn't.

She was very beautiful and it was not just I who thought so. Heads turned. She had pale skin and dark eyes and looked at everything with great concentration. Her hair was black and hung out from her head in a sort of fan shape. She wore a beaded head band she'd made herself with threads and tiny beads.

We were in the same school, she, a full-blown woman about to graduate, and I in the ninth grade, still a boy . . . still in my chubby phase before I started to grow tall. I felt awkward and ugly. I *was* awkward and, if not exactly ugly, certainly not attractive. Her skin was utter purity, while I was beginning to get pimples. For that reason alone, I believed that everything she said was right and everything I said was wrong. It had to be so because of the pimples.

Beautiful as she was, my sister wasn't popular, yet popularity or something akin to it . . . something that looked like it, was what she wanted more than anything, and if that were impossible, then fame. She wanted to make a big splash in school. She wanted to sing, and dance, and act, but she had a small, reedy voice and, although graceful as she went about her life, she was awkward when on stage. Something came over her that made her like a puppet—a self-conscious stiffness. She was aware of this and she had gone from the desire to be on stage to the desire not to expose herself there because she knew how, as she said, ridiculous she looked—how, as she said, everyone would laugh at her, though I knew they wouldn't dare laugh at her any more than I dared. People were afraid of her just as I was. They called her "The Queen," and they joked that she had taken vows of chastity. They called me "Twinkie." Sometimes that was expanded to "Twinkle Toes," for no reason I could tell except that the words went together. I certainly wasn't light on my feet, though perhaps I did twinkle a bit. I was so anxious to please. I smiled and agreed with everyone as though they were all my sister and I always agreed with her. It was safer to do so. I don't remember when I first figured that out. It was as though I'd always known it as soon as I began to realize anything at all.

"I wish it would have beginnings and ends to its singing instead of being all middles, middles, middles," my sister said and she tried hard to teach it to have them. Once she left it all day with the radio tuned to a rock and roll station while she was at school. It was so exhausted—even we could tell—by the end of the day that she didn't do anything like that again. Besides, it had learned nothing. It still began in the middle and ended in the middle, almost as though it sang to itself continuously and only switched to a louder mode when it was pricked and then, when let alone again, lapsed back into its silent music.

I wouldn't have known the first time my sister took the mite to school, had I not sat near her in the cafeteria. She never wanted me to get close to her at school and I never particularly wanted to. Her twelfth graders were nothing like my ninth graders. She and I never nodded to each other in the halls though she always flashed me a look. I wasn't sure if it was a greeting or warning.

But this time I sat fairly close to her at lunch and I noticed she was wearing the antique pearl hat pin we'd found in the attic. She had it pinned to her collar, which was also antique yellowed lace, as though we'd found that in the attic, too. She could laugh a tense, self-conscious wide-mouthed laugh. (She was never relaxed, not even with me. Probably not even with herself, though, now that I think about it. Sometimes when we lay back, she on her bed and I in her chair, and listened to the mite sing . . . sometimes then she was, I'm sure, relaxed.) She was laughing that laugh then, which was why I looked at her more closely than I usually allowed myself to do when in school. I was wondering what had brought on that great, white-toothed derision, when I saw the hat pin and knew what it was for, and then I saw the tiny thread attached to her earring. No, actually attached to her earlobe along with the earring, right through the hole of her pierced ear, and I saw a little flash of yellow in the shadow under her hair, and I thought, no, our mite (for I still thought of it as "ours" though it seemed hers now), our mite should stay safely at home and it should be a secret. Anything might happen to it (or her) here. There were boys who would rip it right out of her ear if they knew what it could do, or perhaps even if they didn't know. And the hat pin made it clear that she was thinking of making it sing. I wondered what would happen if she did.

Also I worried that it wouldn't be easy for her to control her pricking there by her ear. She'd have to hold the mite in one hand and try to feel where it was and prick it with the other, and she couldn't be sure where she would be pricking it— in the eye for all she knew.

I wanted to object, but instead, when we were home again and alone, to let her know I knew, I asked her if she was hearing it sing to her all through school? If, tethered that close to her ear, she could hear its continuous song, but she said, no, that sometimes she heard a slight buzzing, and she wasn't even sure it came from it. It was more like a ringing in her ear. Still, she said, she did like the bug being there, close by. It made her feel more comfortable in school than she'd ever felt before. "It's my real friend," she said.

"What about if it stings? What if it *does* have a stinger? We don't know for sure it doesn't."

"It would have stung already, wouldn't it? Why would it wait? *I'd* have stung if *I* had a stinger."

And I thought, she's right. It hadn't been so well treated that it wouldn't have thought to sting if it could have.

So we lay back then and listened to it. We could feel the throbbing of its song down along our bodies. We shut our eyes and we saw pictures . . . landscapes where we floated or flew as though we were nothing but a pair of eyes. Sometimes everything was sunny and yellow and sometimes everything was foggy and a shiny kind of gray.

It was strange, she and the mite. More and more she'd had only male names for it: George, Teddy, Jerry—names of boys at school—but now Matt. Matt all the time though there was no Matt that I knew of. I began to feel that she was falling in love with it. We would sit together in her room and she'd let it out of the cage . . . let it hobble around on her desk, flutter its torn wings, scatter its fairy dust. She was no longer squeamish about studying it in the magnifying glass. She watched it often, though not when it sang. Then she and I would always lie back and shut our eyes to see the visions.

And then she actually said it. "Oh, I love you, love you. I love you so much."

It had just sung and we were as though waking up from the music.

"Don't," I said. And I felt a different kind of shiver down my spine, not the vibrations of the song, but the beat of fear.

"What do you mean, don't. Don't tell *me* don't. You know nothing. Nothing of love and nothing of anything. You're too young. And what's so bad about having barbels? You don't even shave yet."

I was beneath contempt though I was her only companion—not counting the mite, of course. She had no friend but me and yet I was always beneath contempt. I did feel, though, that should I be in danger, she'd come to my aid . . . come to help me against whatever odds. She'd not hesitate.

She wore the mite to school every day after that first day. As far as I could tell she told no one, for if she'd told even one person it surely would have gotten back to me. Such things always did in our school. I began to relax. Why not take it to school if it gave her such pleasure to do so? It wasn't until I saw the list of finalists in the talent show that I understood what she was up to. She'd already used it in the tryouts. She (not she and her mite), *she* was listed as one of the seven finalists.

She was a sensation. She left her mouth open all the time as though in a sort of open-mouthed humming. She moved just as awkwardly as always, as though deciding to hold out one arm and then the other, alternating them, and deciding to smile now and then as she pretended to sing, but she looked beautiful anyway. The music made it so . . . made it flowing. Also she was dressed in gray (with yellow earrings and beads) as though to make herself a part of that landscape we often saw as we listened. I knew nobody would make fun of her, whisper about her afterward, or imitate her behind her back.

She was accompanied on the piano by the leader of the chorus, who was pretty good at improvising around what the mite was doing. I thought it was a good thing she had the accompaniment, for it made the music a little less strange and that seemed safer. There was less chance of the mite's being discovered.

Everybody sat back, just as the two of us always did, feeling the vibrations of it and no doubt seeing those landscapes. After ten or so minutes of it they clapped and shouted for more and my sister pricked the mite once again and pretended to sing for ten more minutes and then said that was all she could do. Afterward everybody crowded around and asked her how she had learned to do it. Of course she got first prize.

After that she didn't exactly have friends, but she had people who followed her around, asked her all sorts of questions about her singing, interviewed her for the school paper. Some people wanted her to teach them how to do it, but she told them she had a special kind of throat, something that would be considered a defect by most, but that she had learned to make use of it.

Because of her I became known at school, too. I became the singer's brother. I became the one with the knowledge of secrets, for they did sense a secret. There was something mysterious about us both. You could see it in their eyes. Even I, Twinkle Toes, became mysterious. Talented because close to talent.

After that she was asked to sing a lot though she always said she couldn't do it often. "Keep them wanting more," she told me, "and keep them guessing." Sometimes she would come down with a phony cold just when she'd said she would sing and the auditorium was already filled with people who'd come just to hear her.

But something stranger than love . . . more than love began to happen between my sister and the mite. Or, rather, the mite was the same, but my sister's relationship with it changed. That first performance she'd pricked it too hard. A whitish fluid had come out of it, dripped down one side and dried there, making the yellow fur matted . . . less attractive. She felt guilty about that and said so. "I'm such a butcher," she said, and she seemed to be trying to make up for it by finding special foods that it might like. She even brought it caviar, which it wouldn't touch. And she *wanted* punishment. Sometimes she would ask it to sting her. "Go ahead," she'd say. "I deserve it. And you have a right to do it and I don't care if you do, I'll love you just the same. Matt, Matt, Matt, Matty," she said, and it occurred to me perhaps it was a name she'd made out of mite. She had called it sometimes Mite, Mite, and now had made it clearly male with Matt. "My Matt," she said, "all mine." I was out of it completely except as watcher and listener. Its song had not suffered from the wounding. It just had more difficulty moving itself about. My sister had tried to wash the white stuff off, but that had only smeared it around even more, so that the mite was now an ugly, dull creature with, here and there, one or two yellow hairs that stuck out. "Sting me," my sister said, "bite me. I deserve it."

Now she would lie on her bed with her blouse pulled up and let it crawl on her stomach. It moved with difficulty, but it always moved, except now and then when it seemed to sit contentedly on her belly button. "I don't deserve you," she'd say. "I don't deserve one like you." And sometimes she'd say, "Take me. I'm yours," spread-eagled on her bed and laughing as though it were a joke, but it wasn't a joke. Sometimes she'd say, "You love me. Do you really? Don't you? Do you?" or, "Tell me what love is. Is it always small things that once could fly? Is it small things that sting?"

I sat there watching. She hardly seemed to notice me but I knew it was important that I be there. Even though beneath contempt, I was the observer she needed. I saw how she let it crawl up under her blouse or down her neck and inside her bra, how she giggled at its tickle or lay, serious, looking at the ceiling.

In the cricket cage she'd placed a velvet cushion and she'd hung the cage over her bed by a golden-yellow cord.

"I'm your only friend," she'd say. "I'm your keeper, I'm your jailer, I'm your everything, I'm your nothing," and then she'd carefully place the mite in its cage and I would know it was time for me to leave.

At school she became known as an artist with a great future and she walked around as though it were true, that she *was* an artist, that she could dress differently from anyone else, that she was privileged and perhaps a little mad. "I live for my art," she'd say, "and only for that." She stopped doing her homework and said it was because she practiced her music for hours every day.

I told her she might be found out. "Can you live with this secret forever?"

"Not to sing is to die," she said and it was as though she had forgotten it wasn't she who sang. "I will die," she said, "if I can't sing."

"What if *it* dies or stops singing? It might. It's not that healthy by the looks of it."

"Why are you asking me this? Why do you want to hurt me?"

"I'm scared of what's happening."

"Love always scares people who don't know anything about it, and art does too. I'll always be this . . . in the middle of the song in the middle of my life. In the middle. No end and no beginning. I had a dream of such a shining rain, such silver, such glow, as if I were on the moon, or I were a moon myself. Do you know what it's like to be a moon? I was a moon."

But I knew that she was frightened too . . . of herself and of her love, and I thought that if I weren't there she'd not be this way, that I was the audience she played to, that without me she'd not believe in her drama. Without me there'd be no truth to it. That night . . . the night I thought of this, I stayed away from our evening of music. I went back to my nature books and, it was true, she did need me. She brought me back with a bribe of chocolate. I even think her sexual dreams, as she ignored me and stared at the ceiling, were of no pleasure to her without me there to be ignored. I did come back, but I wasn't sure how long I would keep doing it.

And she was, in her way, nice to me then. To show her gratefulness, she bought me a little book on bees. The next night she threw it at me while I sat, again, in her chair and she lay on her bed. "It's nothing," she said, "but *you* might like it."

"I do," I said, "I really do," because I knew she needed me to say it and I did like it.

"I'm going to give a program all my own," she told me then. "It's at school, but it's for everybody in town and they're charging for it and I'm to get a hundred dollars even though it's a benefit for band uniforms. It's already beginning and I haven't even tried. I just sat here and didn't do my homework and everything's beginning to come true just as I've always wanted it to."

I began to feel even more frightened thinking of her giving a whole program. We'd never had the mite sing more than about forty minutes at a time at the very most. "Well, I won't be there," I said. I had never challenged her directly before, but now I said, "And I won't let you do this, but if I can't stop you, I won't be there."

"Give me back that book," she said.

I was sorry to lose it, but I gave it back. I would be sorrier to lose her. It was odd, but the higher she went with this artist business, and the higher she got in her own estimation, the more she, herself, seemed to me like the mite: torn wings, broken legs, sick, matted fur . . .

"It's just like you," she said. "This is my first really big moment and you want to take my pleasure in it from me." But I knew that she knew it wasn't at all like me. "You're jealous," she said, and I wondered, then, if that were true. I didn't think I was but how can you judge yourself?

The mite inched along her desk as we spoke and I had in mind that I should squash it right then. Couldn't she see the thing was in pain? And then I saw that clearly for the first time. It *was* in pain. Maybe the singing was all a pain song. I couldn't stand it any longer, but she must have seen something in my face for she jumped up and pushed me out the door before I hardly knew myself what I was about to do . . . pushed me out the door and locked it.

I thought about it but there was no way that I could see how to stop her. I could tell everybody about the mite, but would they believe me? And wouldn't they just go and have the concert anyway even if they knew it was the mite that sang? Maybe that would be an even greater draw. I had lost my chance to put the creature out of its misery. My sister wouldn't let me near it again. Besides, I wasn't sure if what she said wasn't true, that she'd die if she couldn't sing . . . if she couldn't, that is, be the artist she pretended to be.

She was going to call her program MOON SONGS. There would be two songs with a ten-minute intermission between them. I decided I would be there, but that she wouldn't know it. I would stand in a dark corner in the wings after she had already stepped on stage.

The concert began as usual, but this time I was changed and I could hear the pain. It *was* a pain song. Or perhaps the pain in the song had gotten worse so that I could finally understand it. I didn't see how my sister could bear it. I didn't see how anyone in the audience could bear it, and yet there they sat, eyes closed already, mouths open, heads tipped up like blind people. As I listened, standing there, I, too, tipped my head up and shut my eyes. The beauty of pain caught me up. Tears came to my eyes. They never had before, but now they did. I dreamed that once everything was sun, but now everything was moon. And then I forced my eyes to open. I was there to keep watch on things, not to get caught up in the song.

We . . . she never made it to the intermission. After a half hour, the song became more insistent. It was louder and higher pitched and I could see my sister vibrating as though from a vibrato in her own throat that, then, began to shake her whole body. Nobody else saw it. Though a few had their eyes open, they were looking at the ceiling. The song rose and rose and I knew I had to stop it. My sister sank to her knees. I don't think she pricked the mite at all any longer. I think it sang on of its own accord. I came out on the stage then and no one noticed. I wanted to kill the mite before it shook my sister to pieces, before it deafened her with its shrieking, but I saw that the string that held it to her earlobe was turned and led inside her ear. I pulled on it and the string came out with nothing tied to it. The mite was still inside. My sister was gasping and then she, too, began to make the same sound of pain. The song was coming from her own mouth. I saw the ululations of it in her throat. And I saw blood coming from her nose. Not a lot. Just one small trickle from the left nostril, the same side, where the mite had been tied to the left ear.

I slapped her hard, then, on both cheeks. I was yelling, but I don't think anybody heard me, least of all my sister. I shook her. I hit her. I dragged her from the stage into the wings and yet still the song went on and the people sat in their own dream, whatever it was. Certainly not the same dream we'd always seen before. It couldn't be with this awful sound. Then I hit my sister on the nose directly and the song faltered, became hesitant, though it was still coming from her own mouth and nowhere else. Her eyes flickered open. I saw that she saw me. "Let me go," she said. "Let *us* go. Let us both go." And the song became a sigh of a song. Suddenly no pain in it. I laid her down gently. The song sighed on, at peace with itself and then it stopped. Alive, then dead. With no transition to it . . . both of them, my sister and the mite, stopped in the middle.

I never told. I let them diagnose it as some kind of hemorrhage.

In many ways my life changed for the better after that. I lived for myself, or tried to, and, the year after, I became tall, and thin, and pale, and dark like my sister and nobody called me Twinkie ever again.

THE AFTERNOON OF JUNE 8, 1991

Ian Frazier

Ian Frazier graced the pages of *The Year's Best Fantasy and Horror: Fourth Annual Collection* with the hilarious legal spoof "Coyote v. Acme." He's back this year with a little tale of Satanism, reprinted from the pages of *The New Yorker*.

Frazier is the author of *Nobody Better, Better Than Nobody, Great Plains,* and *Dating Your Mom.*

—T.W.

Those who adopt satanism come from all walks of life. . . . They include doctors, lawyers, professors, university presidents.

—The magazine *Insight.*

Hello and welcome—is this on?—hello and welcome to the ssbt sbt zzzzbt alumni and friends of Brainard *bzzzt* Brainard University, zzzbt and to all the wheeee zzzzzzzzz families of the class of '91. And to all of you new graduates zzzzzzzzz ZAAA ZAAA AZAZEL AZAZEL zzzzzzzb sitting down front in your elegant black caps and gowns, let me add—you made it! Ssssbt zzzzbt zzzeee b'zeee b'zeee zzzzAMIEL this rain holds off awhile so we don't have to move the ceremony into the gym. *Wheeeeee Moloch, Moloch, serve him* a special welcome to all the faculty emeriti— it's good to have you back—nnnnnNERGAL BELIAL LAL-LAL-LAL also to the fiftieth anniversary class of '41. Your special reunion drive raised enough non-earmarked zzzzzzzzzzz sssssss SSSSSSAMMAEL SCRATCH SCRATCH funds for us to add some badly needed phet phet phet TOPHET phet phet to our physical plant. Many thanks from the entire Brainard University family.

-ily-ly-ly-ly eeeeeeee rely here at Brainard on the generosity of individual and corporate contributors sssssssSERPENT AHRIMANESsssss THAMUZzzzzzzz offset an alarming thirty-two-per-cent increase in costs *bbbbbbbbeeeeelzebubbbbbb* unfortunately, a projected shortfall of almost three million dollars. Your loyal support, which has had an enormous impact on our success, bab bab bab BAB BAB ABADDON enhance the quality of the learning experience at Brainard. Wheeeeeee wheeee eeeeee Old Nick Nick Nick a sombre note on this festive occasion, but in the face of unrelenting financial pressures bbbbbbbheeeee beasthood beasthood before the end of the fiscal year on June 30th.

Now for the good news. rrrrrr RRRRRRROOOOOAAAAARRRRRRITTT HOW-OW-OW-WOW-WOW-WOWrrrrrr rrrrrrOW rrrrrrrrOW rrrrRAHAB RAHAB BAB BAB BAAL BAALIM BAALBERITH rrrrRRROARRRrrrr awarded summa cum laude. OW OW OW POWERS-OF-THE-AIR magna cum laude, and nearly two hundred receiving the lesser but still very commendable degree of cum laude. In addition, we point with pride to the impressive number of graduates who will be receiving stipendiary hummm hummm hummmMMMMMMMMMMMELCHOM RIMMON ASMODEUS APOLLYON CHEM-OSH, ROBHES-THE-DOOR-DEMONNNNNNNNNNNNNN nearly half again as many as any university in the area. Again, oooooooooo eeeeeeeeee *Shedim Ahriman Eurony-mous Erl-King swarming, swarming,* many prestigious scholars in our tenured and non-tenured faculty.

[Takes drink of water.]

Bzip bzeeeeeeeeeee bzeeeeeeeeeeee *Beasssssst-Masssssster Beasssssst-Masssssss-ter* generous bequest of Mr. and Mrs. Harry E. WAAAAAHHHHEEE MAWWORM expansion of our media center and film department, construction to begin this hhhhhhhhhhhhhhhh. The reHHHOOOOOOOVESsss zzzzzzzzz, a matching grant from our friends at Electric Boat. Let's give them a round of rrreeeeee-rrrrreeeee-reeee *eee*EEEEEE EREBUS RHADAMANTHUS PRINCE-OF-DARKNESS HORNED-ONE UHN UHN UHN nnnnnn round of applause. We couldn't do it without you.

[Bubbling hellmouth opens in earth in front of podium, then closes.]

As I'm sure we all know only too well, the price of a college education HORROR THE HORROR-ROR-ROR-ROR over the last twenty years zzzz b'zzzzzzzz b'zzzzzzzz regrettable b'zzzzzzz *Pazuzu-Prince-of-Locustssss,* and will for the foreseeable future. Student tuitions actually cover only The-Insect-Inside-You-That-Wants-To-LIVE! which amounts to less than two-fifths of the actual sbt sbeeeee sbeee Baron SAMEDI-eeeeeeeee of every diploma awarded today. And of that two-fifths

[Deafening crack, as lightning hits overhead. Smell of sulfur.]

in long-term, interest-deferred federal tuition loans. Given the critical nature of the need, we have begun two highly lauded funding outreach programs. I wish I had more answers during this difficult ffffffffffffff Mephisto ffffffffft ft pht Astaroth pht ffffff

[Whirlwind touches down in center aisle. Sparks from p.a. system.]

introduce our commencement speaker, Dr. Howard Hall. Born in Springfield, Dr. Hall made his first dollar as a child of six, when he convinced a playmate to purchase a toy he had made. After attending the public schools he matriculated at Brainard where

> [Is skewered to floor by religious symbol falling from steeple of school chapel nearby. Prizes self loose, gets up.]

and went on to earn his Master's at CH-CH-CH-CHORONZON BLACK-RIDER and soon BEHEMOTH BELPHEGOR president of his own SEMJAZA BERALD BARALAMENSIS ADRAMMELECH-eck-eck private listings to realtors. BAL-BAL-BALDACHIENSIS PAUMA-CHIE APOLOROSEDES unaffected by the crash, luckily, ITEMON GENIO LUCIFUGE NAAMAHHHHHH after whom Hall Quadrangle is named. Please join me in giving him a nice

> [Explodes into smoke.]

GWYDION AND THE DRAGON

C. J. Cherryh

Hugo Award–winning Oklahoma writer Carolyn Cherryh has earned her place as one of the best-selling science fiction writers of our day with such hard-hitting novels as *Downbelow Station* and her recent *Heavy Time*. When, on occasion, she turns her hand to fantasy (as in the Russian historical novel *Russalka*) her storytelling touch is equally deft, evocative, and memorable.

"Gwydion and the Dragon" spins the familiar elements and characters of traditional Welsh legends into a brand-new fairy tale. Like the fairy tales of old it is complex and sensual, and meant for adult ears. This story first appeared in *Once Upon a Time*, the beautifully illustrated anthology.

—T.W.

Once upon a time there was a dragon, and once upon that time a prince who undertook to win the hand of the elder and fairer of two princesses.

Not that this prince wanted either of Madog's daughters, although rumors said that Eri was as wise and as gentle, as sweet and as fair as her sister Glasog was cruel and ill-favored. The truth was that this prince would marry either princess if it would save his father and his people; and neither if he had had any choice in the matter. He was Gwydion ap Ogan, and of princes in Dyfed he was the last.

Being a prince of Dyfed did not, understand, mean banners and trumpets and gilt armor and crowds of courtiers. King Ogan's palace was a rambling stone house of dusty rafters hung with cooking pots and old harness; King Ogan's wealth was mostly in pigs and pastures—the same as all Ogan's subjects; Gwydion's war-horse was a black gelding with a crooked blaze and shaggy feet, who had fought against the bandits from the high hills. Gwydion's armor, serviceable in that perpetual warfare, was scarred leather and plain mail, with new links bright among the old; and lance or pennon he had none—the folk of Ogan's kingdom were not lowland knights, heavily armored, but hunters in the hills and woods, and for weapons this prince carried only a one-handed sword and a bow and a quiver of gray-feathered arrows.

His companion, riding beside him on a bay pony, happened through no choice of Gwydion's to be Owain ap Llodri, the houndmaster's son, his good friend, by no means his squire: Owain had lain in wait along the way, on a borrowed bay mare—Owain had simply assumed he was going, and that Gwydion had only hesitated, for friendship's sake, to ask him. So he saved Gwydion the necessity.

And the lop-eared old dog trotting by the horses' feet was Mili: Mili was fierce with bandits, and had respected neither Gwydion's entreaties nor Owain's commands thus far: stones might drive her off for a few minutes, but Mili came back again, that was the sort Mili was. That was the sort Owain was too, and Gwydion could refuse neither of them. So Mili panted along at the pace they kept, with big-footed Blaze and the bownosed bay, whose name might have been Swallow or maybe not—the poets forget—and as they rode Owain and Gwydion talked mostly about dogs and hunting.

That, as the same poets say, was the going of Prince Gwydion into King Madog's realm.

Now no one in Dyfed knew where Madog had come from. Some said he had been a king across the water. Some said he was born of a Roman and a Pict and had gotten sorcery through his mother's blood. Some said he had bargained with a dragon for his sorcery—certainly there was a dragon: devastation followed Madog's conquests, from one end of Dyfed to the other.

Reasonably reliable sources said Madog had applied first to King Bran, across the mountains, to settle at his court, and Bran having once laid eyes on Madog's elder daughter, had lusted after her beyond all good sense and begged Madog for her.

Give me your daughter, Bran had said to Madog, and I'll give you your heart's desire. But Madog had confessed that Eri was betrothed already, to a terrible dragon, who sometimes had the form of a man, and who had bespelled Madog and all his house: if Bran could overcome this dragon he might have Eri with his blessings, and his gratitude and the faithful help of his sorcery all his life; but if he died childless, Madog, by Bran's own oath, must be his heir.

That was the beginning of Madog's kingdom. So smitten was Bran that he swore to those terms, and died that very day, after which Madog ruled in his place.

After that Madog had made the same proposal to three of his neighbor kings, one after the other, proposing that each should ally with him and unite their kingdoms if the youngest son could win Eri from the dragon's spell and provide him an heir. But no prince ever came back from his quest. And the next youngest then went, until all the sons of the kings were gone, so that the kingdoms fell under Madog's rule.

After them, Madog sent to King Ban, and his sons died, last of all Prince Rhys, Gwydion's friend. Ban's heart broke, and Ban took to his bed and died.

Some whispered now that the dragon actually served Madog, that it had indeed brought Madog to power, under terms no one wanted to guess, and that this dragon did indeed have another form, which was the shape of a knight in strange armor, who would become Eri's husband if no other could win her. Some said (but none could prove the truth of it) that the dragon-knight had come from far over the sea, and that he devoured the sons and daughters of conquered kings, that being the tribute Madog gave him. But whatever the truth of that rumor, the dragon hunted far and wide in the lands Madog ruled and did not disdain to take the sons and daughters of farmers and shepherds too. Devastation went under his shadow, trees withered under his breath, and no one saw him outside his dragon shape and returned to tell of it, except only Madog and (rumor said) his younger daughter Glasog, who was a sorceress as cruel as her father.

Some said that Glasog could take the shape of a raven and fly over the land choosing whom the dragon might take. The people called her Madog's Crow, and feared the look of her eye. Some said she was the true daughter of Madog and that Madog had stolen Eri from Faerie, and given her mother to the dragon; but others said they were twins, and that Eri had gotten all that an ordinary person had of goodness, while her sister Glasog—

"Prince Gwydion," Glasog said to her father, "would have come on the quest last year with his friend Rhys, except his father's refusing him, and Prince Gwydion will not let his land go to war if he can find another course. He'll persuade his father."

"Good," Madog said. "That's very good." Madog smiled, but Glasog did not. Glasog was thinking of the dragon. Glasog harbored no illusions: the dragon had promised Madog that he would be king of all Wales if he could achieve this in seven years; and rule for seventy and seven more with the dragon's help.

But if he failed—failed by the seventh year to gain any one of the kingdoms of Dyfed, if one stubborn king withstood him and for one day beyond the seven allotted years, kept him from obtaining the least, last stronghold of the west, then all the bargain was void and Madog would have failed in everything.

And the dragon would claim a forfeit of his choosing.

That was what Glasog thought of, in her worst nightmares: that the dragon had always meant to have all the kingdoms of the west with very little effort—let her father win all but one and fail, on the smallest letter of the agreement. What was more, all the generals in all the armies they had taken agreed that the kingdom of Ogan could never be taken by force: there were mountains in which resistance could hide and not even dragonfire could burn all of them; but most of all there was the fabled Luck of Ogan, which said that no force of arms could defeat the sons of Ogan.

Watch, Madog had said. And certainly her father was astute, and cunning, and knew how to snare a man by his pride. There's always a way, her father had said, to break a spell. This one has a weakness. The strongest spells most surely have their soft spots.

And Ogan had one son, and that was Prince Gwydion.

Now we will fetch him, Madog said to his daughter. Now we will see what his luck is worth.

The generals said, "If you would have a chance in war, first be rid of Gwydion."

But Madog said, and Glasog agreed, there are other uses for Gwydion.

"It doesn't *look* different," Owain said as they passed the border stone.

It was true. Nothing looked changed at all. There was no particular odor of evil, or of threat. It might have been last summer, when the two of them had hunted with Rhys. They had used to hunt together every summer, and last autumn they had tracked the bandit Llewellyn to his lair, and caught him with stolen sheep. But in the spring Ban's sons had gone to seek the hand of Madog's daughter, and one by one had died, last of them, in early summer, Rhys himself.

Gwydion would have gone, long since, and long before Rhys. A score of times Gwydion had approached his father King Ogan and his mother Queen Belys and begged to try his luck against Madog, from the first time Madog's messenger had appeared and challenged the kings of Dyfed to war or wedlock. But each time Ogan had refused him, arguing in the first place that other princes, accustomed to warfare on their borders, were better suited, and better armed, and that there were many princes in Dyfed, but he had only one son.

But when Rhys had gone and failed, the last kingdom save that of King Ogan passed into Madog's hands. And Gwydion, grief-stricken with the loss of his friend, said to his parents, "If we had stood together we might have defeated this Madog; if we had taken the field then, together, we might have had a chance; if you had let me go with Rhys one of us might have won and saved the other. But now Rhys is dead and we have Madog for a neighbor. Let me go when he sends to us. Let me try my luck at courting his daughter. A war with him now we may not lose, but we cannot hope to win."

Even so Ogan had resisted him, saying that they still had their mountains for a shield, difficult going for any army; and arguing that their luck had saved them this far and that it was rash to take matters into their own hands.

Now the nature of that luck was this: that of the kingdom in Dyfed, Ogan's must always be poorest and plainest. But that luck meant that they could not fail in war nor fail in harvest: it had come down to them from Ogan's own great-grandfather Ogan ap Ogan of Llanfynnyd, who had sheltered one of the Faerie unaware; and only faithlessness could break it—so greatgrandfather Ogan had said. So: "Our luck will be our defense," Ogan argued with his son. "Wait and let Madog come to us. We'll fight him in the mountains."

"Will we fight a dragon? Even if we defeat Madog himself, what of our herds, what of our farmers and our freeholders? Can we let the land go to waste and let our people feed this dragon, while we hide in the hills and wait for luck to save us? Is that faithfulness?" That was what Gwydion had asked his father, while Madog's herald was in the hall—a raven black as unrepented sin . . . or the intentions of a wizard.

"Madog bids you know," this raven had said, perched on a rafter of Ogan's hall, beside a moldering basket of a string of garlic, "that he has taken every kingdom of Dyfed but this. He offers you what he offered others: if King Ogan has a son worthy to win Madog's daughter and get an heir, then King Ogan may rule in peace over his kingdom so long as he lives, and that prince will have titles and the third of Madog's realm besides. . . .

"But if the prince will not or cannot win the princess, then Ogan must swear Madog is his lawful true heir. And if Ogan refuses this, then Ogan must face Madog's army, which now is the army of four kingdoms each greater than his own. Surely," the raven had added, fixing all present with a wicked, midnight eye, "it is no great endeavor Madog asks—simply to court his daughter. And will so many die, so much burn? Or will Prince Gwydion win a realm wider than your own? A third of Madog's lands is no small dowry and inheritance of Madog's kingdom is no small prize."

So the raven had said. And Gwydion had said to his mother, "Give me your blessing," and to his father Ogan: "Swear the oath Madog asks. If our Luck can save us it will save me and win me this bride; but if it fails me in this it would have failed us in any case."

Maybe, Gwydion thought as they passed the border, Owain was a necessary part of that luck. Maybe even Mili was. It seemed to him now that he dared reject nothing that loved him and favored him, even if it was foolish and even if it broke his heart: his luck seemed so perilous and stretched so thin already he dared not bargain with his fate.

"No sign of a dragon, either," Owain said, looking about them at the rolling hills.

Gwydion looked about him too, and at the sky, which showed only the lazy flight of a single bird.

Might it be a raven? It was too far to tell.

"I'd think," said Owain, "it would seem grimmer than it does."

Gwydion shivered as if a cold wind had blown. But Blaze plodded his heavy-footed way with no semblance of concern, and Mili trotted ahead, tongue lolling, occasionally sniffing along some trail that crossed theirs.

"Mili would smell a dragon," Owain said.

"Are you sure?" Gwydion asked. He was not. If Madog's younger daughter could be a raven at her whim he was not sure what a dragon might be at its pleasure.

That night they had a supper of brown bread and sausages that Gwydion's mother had sent, and ale that Owain had with him.

"My mother's brewing," Owain said. "My father's store." And Owain sighed and said: "By now they must surely guess I'm not off hunting."

"You didn't tell them?" Gwydion asked. "You got no blessing in this?"

Owain shrugged, and fed a bit of sausage to Mili, who gulped it down and sat looking at them worshipfully.

Owain's omission of duty worried Gwydion. He imagined how Owain's parents would first wonder where he had gone, then guess, and fear for Owain's life, for which he held himself entirely accountable. In the morning he said, "Owain, go back. This is far enough."

But Owain shrugged and said, "Not I. Not without you." Owain rubbed Mili's ears. "No more then Mili, without me."

Gwydion had no least idea now what was faithfulness and what was a young man's foolish pride. Everything seemed tangled. But Owain seemed not in the least distressed.

Owain said, "We'll be there by noon tomorrow."

Gwydion wondered, Where is this dragon? and distrusted the rocks around them and the sky over their heads. He felt a presence in the earth—or thought he felt it. But Blaze and Swallow grazed at their leisure. Only Mili looked worried—Mili pricked up her ears, such as those long ears could prick, wondering, perhaps, if they were going to get to bandits soon, and whether they were, after all, going to eat that last bit of breakfast sausage.

"He's on his way," Glasog said. "He's passed the border."

"Good," said Madog. And to his generals: "Didn't I tell you?"

The generals still looked worried.

But Glasog went and stood on the walk of the castle that had been Ban's, looking out over the countryside and wondering what the dragon was thinking tonight, whether the dragon had foreseen this as he had foreseen the rest, or whether he was even yet keeping some secret from them, scheming all along for their downfall.

She launched herself quite suddenly from the crest of the wall, swooped out over the yard and beyond, over the seared fields.

The dragon, one could imagine, knew about Ogan's Luck. The dragon was too canny to face it—and doubtless was chuckling in his den in the hills.

Glasog flew that way, but saw nothing from that cave but a little curl of smoke—there was almost always smoke. And Glasog leaned toward the west, following the ribbon of a road, curious, and wagering that the dragon this time would not bestir himself.

Her father wagered the same. And she knew very well what he wagered, indeed she did: duplicity for duplicity—if not the old serpent's aid, then human guile; if treachery from the dragon, then put at risk the dragon's prize.

Gwydion and Owain came to a burned farmstead along the road. Mili sniffed about the blackened timbers and bristled at the shoulders, and came running back to Owain's whistle, not without mistrustful looks behind her.

There was nothing but a black ruin beside a charred, brittle orchard.

"I wonder," Owain said, "what became of the old man and his wife."

"I don't," said Gwydion, worrying for his own parents, and seeing in this example how they would fare in any retreat into the hills.

The burned farm was the first sign they had seen of the dragon, but it was not the last. There were many other ruins, and sad and terrible sights. One was a skull sitting on a fence row. And on it sat a raven.

"This was a brave man," it said, and pecked the skull, which rang hollowly, and inclined its head toward the field beyond. "That was his wife. And farther still his young daughter."

"Don't speak to it," Gwydion said to Owain. They rode past, at Blaze's plodding pace, and did not look back.

But the raven flitted ahead of them and waited for them on the stone fence. "If you die," the raven said, "then your father will no longer believe in his luck. Then it will leave him. It happened to all the others."

"There's always a first," said Gwydion.

Owain said, reaching for his bow: "Shall I shoot it?"

But Gwydion said: "Kill the messenger for the message? No. It's a foolish creature. Let it be."

It left them then. Gwydion saw it sometimes in the sky ahead of them. He said nothing to Owain, who had lost his cheerfulness, and Mili stayed close by them, sore of foot and suspicious of every breeze.

There were more skulls. They saw gibbets and stakes in the middle of a burned orchard. There was scorched grass, recent and powdery under the horses' hooves. Blaze, who loved to snatch a bite now and again as he went, moved uneasily, snorting with dislike of the smell, and Swallow started at shadows.

Then the turning of the road showed them a familiar brook, and around another hill and beyond, the walled holding that had been King Ban's, in what had once been a green valley. Now it was burned, black bare hillsides and the ruin of hedges and orchards.

So the trial they had come to find must be here, Gwydion thought, and uneasily took up his bow and picked several of his best arrows, which he held against his knee as he rode. Owain did the same.

But they reached the gate of the low-walled keep unchallenged, until they came on the raven sitting, whetting its beak on the stone. It looked at them solemnly, saying, "Welcome, Prince Gwydion. You've won your bride. Now how will you fare, I wonder."

Men were coming from the keep, running toward them, others, under arms, in slower advance.

"What now?" Owain asked, with his bow across his knee; and Gwydion lifted his bow and bent it, aiming at the foremost.

The crowd stopped, but a black-haired man in gray robes and a king's gold chain came alone, holding up his arms in a gesture of welcome and of peace. Madog himself? Gwydion wondered, while Gwydion's arm shook and the string trembled in his grip. "Is it Gwydion ap Ogan?" that man asked—surely no one else but Madog would wear that much gold. "My son-in-law to be! Welcome!"

Gwydion, with great misgivings, slacked the string and let down the bow, while fat Blaze, better trained than seemed, finally shifted feet. Owain lowered his bow too, as King Madog's men opened up the gate. Some of the crowd cheered as they rode in, and more took it up, as if they had only then gained the courage or understood it was expected. Blaze and Swallow snorted and threw their heads at the racket, as Gwydion and Owain put away their arrows, unstrung their bows and hung them on their saddles.

But Mili stayed close by Owain's legs as they dismounted, growling low in her throat, and barked one sharp warning when Madog came close. "Hush," Owain bade her, and knelt down more than for respect, keeping one hand on Mili's muzzle and the other in her collar, whispering to her, "Hush, hush, there's a good dog."

Gwydion made the bow a prince owed to a king and prospective father-in-law, all the while thinking that there had to be a trap in this place. He was entirely sorry to see grooms lead Blaze and Swallow away, and kept Owain and Mili constantly in the tail of his eye as Madog took him by the arms and hugged him. Then Madog said, catching all his attention, eye to eye with him for a moment, "What a well-favored young man you are. The last is always best.—So you've killed the dragon."

Gwydion thought, Somehow we've ridden right past the trial we should have met. If I say no, he will find cause to disallow me; and he'll kill me and Owain and all our kin.

But lies were not the kind of dealing his father had taught him; faithfulness was the rule of the house of Ogan; so Gwydion looked the king squarely in the eyes and said, "I met no dragon."

Madog's eyes showed surprise, and Madog said: "Met no dragon?"

"Not a shadow of a dragon."

Madog grinned and clapped him on the shoulder and showed him to the crowd, saying, "This is your true prince!"

Then the crowd cheered in earnest, and even Owain and Mili looked heartened. Owain rose with Mili's collar firmly in hand.

Madog said then to Gwydion, under his breath, "If you had lied you would have met the dragon here and now. Do you know you're the first one who's gotten this far?"

"I saw nothing," Gwydion said again, as if Madog had not understood him. "Only burned farms. Only skulls and bones."

Madog turned a wide smile toward him, showing teeth. "Then it was your destiny to win. Was it not?" And Madog faced him about toward the doors of the keep. "Daughter, daughter, come out!"

Gwydion hesitated a step, expecting he knew not what—the dragon itself, perhaps: his wits went scattering toward the gate, the horses being led away, Mili barking in alarm—and a slender figure standing in the doorway, all white and gold. "My elder daughter," Madog said. "Eri."

Gwydion went as he was led, telling himself it must be true, after so much dread of this journey and so many friends' lives lost—obstacles must have fallen down for him, Ogan's Luck must still be working. . . .

The young bride waiting for him was so beautiful, so young and so—kind— was the first word that came to him—Eri smiled and immediately it seemed to him she was innocent of all the grief around her, innocent and good as her sister was reputed cruel and foul.

He took her hand, and the folk of the keep all cheered, calling him their prince; and if any were Ban's people, those wishes might well come from the heart, with fervent hopes of rescue. Pipers began to play, gentle hands urged them both inside, and in this desolate land some woman found flowers to give Eri.

"Owain?" Gwydion cried, looking back, suddenly seeing no sign of him or of Mili: "Owain!"

He refused to go farther until Owain could part the crowd and reach his side, Mili firmly in hand. Owain looked breathless and frightened. Gwydion felt the same. But the crowd pushed and pulled at them, the pipers piped and dancers danced, and they brought them into a hall smelling of food and ale.

It can't be this simple, Gwydion still thought, and made up his mind that no one should part him from Owain, Mili, or their swords. He looked about him, bedazzled, at a wedding feast that must have taken days to prepare.

But how could they know I'd get here? he wondered. Did they do this for all the suitors who failed—and celebrate their funerals, then . . . with their wedding feast?

At which thought he felt cold through and through, and found Eri's hand on his arm disquieting; but Madog himself waited to receive them in the hall, and joined their hands and plighted them their vows, to make them man and wife, come what might—

"So long as you both shall live," Madog said, pressing their hands together. "And when there is an heir Prince Gwydion shall have the third of my lands, and his father shall rule in peace so long as he shall live."

Gwydion misliked the last—Gwydion thought in alarm: As long as he lives.

But Madog went on, saying, "—be you wed, be you wed, be you wed," three times, as if it were a spell—then: "Kiss your bride, son-in-law."

The well-wishes from the guests roared like the sea. The sea was in Eri's eyes, deep and blue and drowning. He heard Mili growl as he kissed Eri's lips once, twice, three times.

The pipers played, the people cheered, no few of whom indeed might have been King Ban's, or Lugh's, or Lughdan's. Perhaps, Gwydion dared think, perhaps it was hope he brought to them, perhaps he truly had won, after all, and the dreadful threat Madog posed was lifted, so that Madog would be their neighbor, no worse than the worst they had had, and perhaps, if well-disposed, better than one or two.

Perhaps, he thought, sitting at Madog's right hand with his bride at his right and with Owain just beyond, perhaps there truly was cause to hope, and he could ride away from here alive—though he feared he could find no cause to do so tonight, with so much prepared, with an anxious young bride and King Madog determined to indulge his beautiful daughter. Women hurried about with flowers and with torches, with linens and with brooms and platters and plates, tumblers ran riot, dancers leaped and cavorted—one of whom came to grief against an ale-server. Both went down, in Madog's very face, and the hall grew still and dangerous.

But Eri laughed and clapped her hands, a laughter so small and faint until her father laughed, and all the hall laughed; and Gwydion remembered then to breathe, while Eri hugged his arm and laughed up at him with those sea-blue eyes.

"More ale!" Madog called. "Less spillage, there!"

The dreadful wizard could joke, then. Gwydion drew two easier breaths, and someone filled their cups. He drank, but prudently: he caught Owain's eye, and Owain his—while Mili having found a bone to her liking, with a great deal of meat to it, worried it happily in the straw beneath the table.

There were healths drunk, there were blessings said, at each of which one had to drink—and Madog laughed and called Gwydion a fine son-in-law, asked him about his campaign against the bandits and swore he was glad to have his friends and his kin and anyone he cared to bring here: Madog got up and clapped Owain on the shoulder too, and asked was Owain wed, and, informed Owain was not, called out to the hall that here was another fine catch, and where were the young maids to keep Owain from chill on his master's wedding night?

Owain protested in some embarrassment, starting to his feet—

But drink overcame him, and he sat down again with a hand to his brow, Gwydion saw it with concern, while Madog touched Gwydion's arm on the other side and said, "The women are ready," slyly bidding him finish his ale beforehand.

Gwydion rose and handed his bride to her waiting women. "Owain!" Gwydion said then sharply, and Owain gained his feet, saying something Gwydion could not hear for with all the people cheering and the piper starting up, but he saw Owain was distressed. Gwydion resisted the women pulling at him, stood fast until Owain reached him, flushed with ale and embarrassment. The men surrounded him with bawdy cheers and more offered cups.

It was his turn then on the stairs, more cups thrust on him, Madog clapping him on the shoulder and hugging him and calling him the son he had always wanted, and saying there should be peace in Dyfed for a hundred years . . . unfailing friendship with his father and his kin—greater things, should he have ambitions. . . .

The room spun around. Voices buzzed. They pushed him up the stairs, Owain and Mili notwithstanding, Mili barking all the while. They brought him down the upstairs hall, they opened the door to the bridal chamber.

On pitch dark.

Perhaps it was cowardly to balk. Gwydion thought so, in the instant the laughing men gave him a push between the shoulders. Shame kept him from calling Owain to his rescue. The door shut at his back.

He heard rustling in the dark and imagined coils and scales. Eri's soft voice said, "My lord?"

A faint starlight edged the shutters. His eyes made out the furnishings, now that the flare of torches had left his sight. It was the rustling of bedclothes he heard. He saw a woman's shoulder and arm faintly in the shadowed bed, in the scant starshine that shutter let through.

He backed against the door, found the latch behind him, cracked it the least little bit outward and saw Owain leaning there against his arm, facing the lamplit wall outside, flushed of face and ashamed to meet his eyes at such close range.

"I'm here, m'lord," Owain breathed, on ale-fumes. Owain never called him lord, but Owain was greatly embarrassed tonight. "The lot's gone down the stairs now. I'll be here the night. I'll not leave this door, nor sleep, I swear to you."

Gwydion gave him a worried look, wishing the two of them dared escape this hall and Madog's well-wishes, running pell-mell back to his own house, his parents' advice, and childhood. But, "Good," he said, and carefully pulled the door to, making himself blind in the dark again. He let the latch fall and catch.

"My lord?" Eri said faintly.

He felt quite foolish, himself and Owain conspiring together like two boys at an orchard wall, when it was a young bride waiting for him, innocent and probably as anxious as he. He nerved himself, walked up by the bed and opened the shutters wide on a night sky brighter than the dark behind him.

But with the cool night wind blowing into the room he thought of dragons, wondered whether opening the window to the sky was wise at all, and wondered what was slipping out of bed with the whispering of the bedclothes. His bride forwardly clasped his arm, wound fingers into his and swayed against him, saying how beautiful the stars were.

Perhaps that invited courtly words. He murmured some such. He found the courage to take Madog's daughter in his arms and kiss her, and thereafter—

He waked abed with the faint dawn coming through the window, his sword tangled with his leg and his arm ensnared in a woman's unbound hair—

Hair raven black.

He leaped up trailing sheets, while a strange young woman sat up to snatch the bedclothes to her, with her black hair flowing about her shoulders, her eyes dark and cold and fathomless.

"Where's my wife?" he cried.

She smiled, thin-lipped, rose from the bed, drawing the sheets about her like royal robes. "Why, you see her, husband."

He rushed to the door and lifted the latch. The door did not budge, hardly rattled when he shoved it with all his strength. "Owain?" he cried, and pounded it with his fist. "Owain!"

No answer came. Gwydion turned slowly to face the woman, dreading what other shape she might take. But she sat down wrapped in the sheets with one knee on the rumpled bed, looking at him. Her hair spread about her like a web of shadows in the dawn. As much as Eri had been an innocent girl, this was a woman far past Eri's innocence or his own.

He asked, "Where's Owain? What's become of him?"

"Guesting elsewhere."

"Who are you?"

"Glasog," she said, and shrugged, the dawn wind carrying long strands of her hair about her shoulders. "Or Eri, if you like. My father's elder daughter and younger, all in one, since he has none but me."

"Why?" he asked. "Why this pretence if you were the bargain?"

"People trust Eri. She's so fair, so kind."

"What do you want? What does your father want?"

"A claim on your father's land. The last kingdom of Dyfed. And you've come to give it to us."

Gwydion remembered nothing of what might have happened last night. He remembered nothing of anything he should have heard or done last night, abed with Glasog the witch, Madog's raven-haired daughter. He felt cold and hollow and desperate, asking, "On your oath, *is* Owain safe?"

"And would you believe my oath?" Glasog asked.

"I'll see your father," Gwydion said shortly. "Trickery or not, he swore me the third of his kingdom for your dowry. Younger or elder, or both, you're my wife. Will he break his word?"

Glasog said, "An heir. Then he'll release you and your friend, and your father will reign in peace . . . so long as he lives."

Gwydion walked to the open window, gazing at a paling, still sunless sky. He feared he knew what that release would be—the release of himself and Owain from life, while the child he sired would become heir to his father's kingdom with Madog to enforce that right.

So long as his father lived . . . so long as that unfortunate *child* might live, for that matter, once the inheritance of Ogan's line and Ogan's Luck passed securely into Madog's line—his father's kingdom taken and for no battle, no war, only a paltry handful of lies and lives.

He looked across the scorched hills, toward a home he could not reach, a father who could not advise him. He dared not hope that Owain might have escaped to bring word to his father: I'll not leave this door, Owain had said—and they would have had to carry Owain away by force or sorcery. Mili with him.

It was sorcery that must have made him sleep and forget last night. It was sorcery he must have seen when he turned from the window and saw Eri sitting there, rosy-pale and golden, patting the place beside her and bidding him come back to bed.

He shuddered and turned and hit the windowledge, hurting his hand. He thought of flight, even of drawing the sword and killing Madog's daughter, before this princess could conceive and doom him and his parents. . . .

Glasog's voice said, slowly, from Eri's lips, "If you try anything so rash, my father won't need your friend any longer, will he? I certainly wouldn't be in his place then. I'd hardly be in it now."

"What have you done with Owain?"

Eri shrugged. Glasog's voice said, "Dear husband—"

"The marriage wasn't consummated," he said, "for all I remember."

It was Glasog who lifted a shoulder. Black hair parted. "To sorcery—does it matter?"

He looked desperately toward the window. He said, without looking at her: "I've something to say about that, don't you think?"

"No. You don't. If you wouldn't, or couldn't, the words are said, the vows are made, the oaths are taken. If not your child—anyone's will do, for all men know or care."

He looked at her to see if he had understood what he thought he had, and Glasog gathered a thick skein of her hair—and drew it over her shoulder.

"The oaths are made," Glasog said. "Any lie will do. Any child will do."

"There's my word against it," Gwydion said.

Glasog shook her head gravely. "A lie's nothing to my father. A life is nothing." She stood up, shook out her hair, and hugged the sheets about her. Dawn lent a sudden and unkind light to Glasog's face, showing hollow cheeks, a grim mouth, a dark and sullen eye that promised nothing of compromise.

Why? he asked himself. Why this much of truth? Why not Eri's face?

She said, "What will you, husband?"

"Ask tonight," he said, hoping only for time and better counsel.

She inclined her head, walked between him and the window, lifting her arms wide. For an instant the morning sun showed a woman's body against the sheets. Then—it might have been a trick of the eyes—black hair spread into the black wings, something flew to the window and the sheet drifted to the floor.

What about the dragon? he would have asked, but there was no one to ask.

He went to the door and tried it again, in case sorcery had ceased. But it gave not at all, not to cleverness, not to force. He only bruised his shoulder, and leaned dejectedly against the door, sure now that he had made a terrible mistake.

The window offered nothing but a sheer drop to the stones below, and when he tried that way, he could not force his shoulders through. There was no fire in the room, not so much as water to drink. He might fall on his sword, but he took Glasog at her word: it was the form of the marriage Madog had wanted, and they would only hide his death until it was convenient to reveal it. All the house had seen them wed and bedded, even Owain—who, being honest, could swear only what he had seen and what he had guessed—but never, never to the truth of what had happened and not happened last night.

Ogan's fabled Luck should have served him better, he thought, casting himself onto the bedside, head in hands. It should have served all of them better, this Luck his greatgrandfather had said only faithlessness could break—

But was Glasog herself not faithlessness incarnate? Was not Madog?

If that was the barb in greatgrandfather's blessing—it had done nothing but bring him and his family into Madog's hands. But it seemed to him that the fay were reputed for twists and turns in their gifts, and if they had made one such twist they might make another: all he knew was to hew to the course Ogan's sons had always followed.

So he had come here in good faith, been caught through abuse of that faith, and though he might perhaps seize the chance to come at Madog himself, that was treachery for treachery and if he had any last whisper of belief in his luck, that was what he most should not do.

"Is there a child?" Madog asked, and Glasog said, "Not yet. Not yet. Be patient."

"There's not," Madog said testily, "forever. Remember that."

"I remember," Glasog said.

"You wouldn't grow fond of him—or foolish?"

"I?" quoth Glasog, with an arch of her brow. "I, fond? Not fond of the dragon, let us say. Not fond of poverty—or early dying."

"We'll not fail. If not him—"

"Truly, do you imagine the dragon will give you *anything* if the claim's not legitimate? I think not. I do think not. It must be Gwydion's child—and *that*, by nature, by Gwydion's own will. That *is* the difficulty, isn't it?"

"You vaunt your sorcery. Use it!"

Glasog said, coldly, "When needs be. If needs be. But it's myself he'll have, *not* Eri, and for myself, not Eri. That's my demand in this."

"Don't be a fool."

Glasog smiled with equal coldness. "This man has magical protections. His luck is no illusion and it's not to cross. I don't forget that. Don't you. *Trust* me, Father."

"I wonder how I got you."

Glasog still smiled. "Luck," she said. "You want to be rid of the dragon, don't you? Has my advice ever failed you? And isn't it the old god's bond that he'll barter for questions?"

Her father scowled. "It's *my* life you're bartering for, curse your cold heart. It's my life you're risking with your schemes—a life from each kingdom of Dyfed, *that's* the barter we've made. We've caught Gwydion. We can't stave the dragon off forever for your whims and your vapors, Daughter. Get me a grandson—by whatever sorcery—and forget this foolishness. Kill the dragon . . . do you think I've not tried that? All the princes in Dyfed have tried that."

Glasog said, with her grimmest look: "We've also Gwydion's friend, don't we? And isn't he of Ogan's kingdom?"

Gwydion endured the hours until sunset, hungry and thirsty and having nothing whatever to do but to stare out the slit of a window, over a black and desolate land.

He wondered if Owain was even alive, or what had become of Mili.

Once he saw a raven in flight, toward the south; and once, late, the sky growing dimly copper, he saw it return, it seemed more slowly, circling always to the right.

Glasog? he wondered—or merely a raven looking for its supper?

The sky went from copper to dusk. He felt the air grow chill. He thought of closing the shutters, but that was Glasog's access. So he paced the floor, or looked out the window or simply listened to the distant comings and goings below which alone told him that there was life in the place.

Perhaps, he thought, they only meant him to die of thirst and hunger, and perhaps he would never see or speak to a living soul again. He hoped Glasog would come by sunset, but she failed that; and by moonrise, but she did not come.

At last, when he had fallen asleep in his waiting, a shadow swept in the window with a snap and flutter of dark wings, and Glasog stood wrapped only in dark hair and limned in starlight.

He gathered himself up quickly, feeling still that he might be dreaming. "I expected you earlier," he said.

"I had inquiries to make," she said, and walked to the table where—he did not know how, a cup and a silver pitcher gleamed in reflected starlight. She lifted the pitcher and poured, and oh, he was thirsty. She offered it, and it might be poisoned for all he knew. At the very least it was enchanted, and perhaps only moondust and dreams. But she stood offering it; he drank, and it took both thirst and hunger away.

She said, "You may have one wish of me, Gwydion. One wish. And then I may have two from you. Do you agree?"

He wondered what to say. He put down the cup and walked away to the window, looking out on the night sky. There were a hundred things to ask: his parents' lives; Owain's; the safety of his land—and in each one there seemed some flaw.

Finally he chose the simplest. "Love me," he said.

For a long time Glasog said nothing. Then he heard her cross the room.

He turned. Her eyes flashed at him, sudden as a serpent's. She said, "Dare you? First drink from my cup."

"Is this your first wish?"

"It is."

He hesitated, looking at her, then walked away to the table and reached for the shadowy cup, but another appeared beside it, gleaming, crusted with jewels.

"Which will you have?" she asked.

He hoped then that he understood her question. And he picked up the cup of plain pewter and drank it all.

She said, from behind him, "You have your wish, Gwydion."

And wings brushed his face, the wind stirred his hair, the raven shape swooped out the window.

"Owain," a voice said—the raven's voice, and Owain leaped up from his prison bed, such as he could, though his head was spinning and he had to brace himself against the wall. It was not the raven's first visit. He asked it, "Where's my master? What's happened to him?"

And the raven, suddenly no raven, but a dark-haired woman: "Wedlock," she said. "Death, if the dragon gets his due—as soon it may."

"Glasog," Owain said, chilled to the marrow. Since Madog's men had hauled him away from Gwydion's door he had had this dizziness, and it came on him now. He felt his knees going and he caught himself.

"You might save him," Glasog said.

"And should I trust you?" he asked.

The chains fell away from him with a ringing of iron, and the bolts fell from the door.

"Because I'm his wife," she said. Eri stood there. He rubbed his eyes and it was Glasog again. "And you're his friend. Isn't that what it means, friendship? Or marriage?"

A second time he rubbed his eyes. The door swung open.

"My father says," Glasog said, "the dragon's death will free Prince Gwydion. You may have your horse, your dog, your armor and your weapons—or whatever you will, Owain ap Llodri. But for that gift—you must give me one wish when I claim it."

In time—Gwydion was gazing out the window, he had no idea why, he heard the slow echo of hoofbeats off the wall.

He saw Owain ride out the gate; he saw the raven flying over him.

"Owain," he cried. "Owain!"

But Owain paid no heed. Only Mili stopped, and looked up at the tower where he stood.

He thought—Go with him, Mili, if it's home he's bound for. Warn my father. There's no hope here.

Owain never looked back. Gwydion saw him turn south at the gate, entirely away from home, and guessed where Owain was going.

"Come back," he cried. "Owain! No!"

It was the dragon they were going to. It was surely the dragon Owain was going to, and if Gwydion had despaired in his life, it was seeing Owain and Mili go off in company with his wife.

He tried again to force himself through the window slit. He tried the door, working with his sword to lift the bar he was sure was in place outside.

He found it and lifted it. But it stopped with the rattle of chain.

* * *

They found the brook again, beyond the hill, and the raven fluttered down clumsily to drink, spreading a wing to steady herself.

Owain reined Swallow in. He had no reason to trust the raven in any shape, less reason to believe it than anything else that he had seen in this place. But Mili came cautiously up to it, and suddenly it was Glasog kneeling there, wrapped only in her hair, with her back to him, and Mili whining at her in some distress.

Owain got down. He saw two fingers missing from Glasog's right hand, the wounds scarcely healed. She drank from her other hand, and bathed the wounded one in water. She looked at Owain and said, "You wished to save Gwydion. You said nothing of yourself."

Owain shrugged and settled with his arm around Mili's neck.

"Now you owe me my wish," Glasog said.

"That I do," he said, and feared what it might be.

She said, "There's a god near this place. The dragon overcame him. But he will still answer the right question. Most gods will, with proper sacrifice."

Owain said, "What shall I ask him?"

She said, "I've already asked."

Owain asked then, "And the answers, lady?"

"First that the dragon's life and soul lies in his right eye. And second that no man can kill him."

Owain understood the answer then. He scratched Mili's neck beneath the collar. He said, "Mili's a loyal dog. And if flying tires you, lady, I've got a shoulder you can ride on."

Glasog said, "Better you go straightaway back to your king. Only lend me your bow, your dog, and your horse. *That* is my wish, ap Llodri."

Owain shook his head, and got up, patting Mili on the head. "All that you'll have by your wish," Owain said, "but I go with them."

"Be warned," she said.

"I am that," said Owain, and held out his hand. "My lady?"

The raven fluttered up and settled on his arm, bating as he rose into the saddle. Owain set Swallow on her way, among the charred, cinder-black hills, to a cave the raven showed him.

Swallow had no liking for this place. Owain patted her neck, coaxed her forward. Mili bristled up and growled as they climbed. Owain took up his bow and drew out an arrow, yelled, "Mili! Look out!" as fire billowed out and Swallow shied.

A second gust followed. Mili yelped and ran from the roiling smoke, racing ahead of a great serpent shape that surged out of the cave; but Mili began to cross the hill then, leading it.

The raven launched itself from Owain's shoulder, straighter than Owain's arrow sped.

A clamor rose in the keep, somewhere deep in the halls. It was dawn above the hills, and a glow still lit the south, as Gwydion watched from the window.

He was watching when a strange rider came down the road, shining gold in the sun, in scaled armor.

"The dragon!" he heard shouted from the wall. Gwydion's heart sank. It sank further when the scale-armored rider reached the gate and Madog's men opened to it. It was Swallow the dragon-knight rode, Swallow with her mane all singed; and it was Mili who limped after, with her coat all soot-blackened and with great sores showing on her hide. Mili's head hung and her tail drooped and the dragon led her by a rope, while a raven sat perched on his shoulder.

Of Owain there was no sign.

There came a clattering in the hall. Chain rattled, the bar lifted and thumped and armed men were in the doorway.

"King Madog wants you," one said. And Gwydion—

"Madog will have to send twice," Gwydion said, with his sword in hand.

The dragon rode to the steps and the raven fluttered to the ground as waiting women rushed to it, to bring Princess Glasog her cloak—black as her hair and stitched with spells. The waiting women and the servants had seen this sight before—the same as the men at arms at the gate, who had had their orders should it have been Owain returning.

"Daughter," Madog said, descending those same steps as Glasog rose up, wrapped in black and silver. Mili growled and bristled, suddenly strained at her leash—

The dragon loosed it and Mili sprang for Madog's throat. Madog fell under the hound and Madog's blood was on the steps—but his neck was already broken.

Servants ran screaming. Men at arms stood confused, as if they had quite forgotten what they were doing or where they were or what had brought them there, the men of the fallen kingdoms all looking at one another and wondering what terrible thing had held them here.

And on all of this Glasog turned her back, walking up the steps.

"My lady!" Owain cried—for it was Owain wore the armor; but it was not Owain's voice she longed to hear.

Glasog let fall the cloak and leaped from the wall. The raven glided away, with one harsh cry against the wind.

In time after—often in that bitter winter, when snows lay deep and wind skirled drifts about the door—Owain told how Glasog had pierced the dragon's eye; and how they had found the armor, and how Glasog had told him the last secret, that with the dragon dead, Madog's sorcery would leave him.

That winter, too, Gwydion found a raven in the courtyard, a crippled bird, missing feathers on one wing. It seemed greatly confused, so far gone with hunger and with cold that no one thought it would live. But Gwydion tended it until spring and set it free again.

It turned up thereafter on the wall of Gwydion's keep—King Gwydion, he was now—lord of all Dyfed. "You've one wish left," he said to it. "One wish left of me."

"I give it to you," the raven said. "Whatever you wish, King Gwydion."

"Be what you wish to be," Gwydion said.

And thereafter men told of the wisdom of King Gwydion as often as of the beauty of his wife.

A STORY MUST BE HELD

Jane Yolen

In addition to writing fiction for children and adults, Jane Yolen is a poet, fairy tale scholar, anthologist, and the editor of Jane Yolen Books, an imprint of Harcourt Brace Jovanovich. Yolen's lyrical, mythical poetry has appeared in numerous magazines and collections. The following poem, "A Story Must Be Held," draws on Yolen's experiences both as a writer of stories and as an oral storyteller. It comes from *Colors of a New Day: Writing for South Africa*, a benefit collection featuring the works of a number of English and American writers compiled by Sarah Lefanu and Stephen Hayward.

—T.W.

A story must be held
tightly in the hand,
fingers cupping the weight of it.
Here is "Mr. Fox,"
dark, brooding,
a black rockfall of words
in the center of my palm

A story must be held
loosely in the heart,
black stone of it
a second chamber,
the beat of it an echo,
murmuration,
remembrance of a voice.

A story must be held
firmly in the mouth,
a pebble between teeth,
a graveled voice:
"This is the tale of Mr. Fox

as it is told in England,
as it is spoke on the moors."

I shall tell you the tale right now:
with my mouth,
with my heart,
with my hand,
my thumbprint on
a thousand others
already whorled into the stone.

THE OGRE'S WIFE

Pierrette Fleutiaux

"The Ogre's Wife" is a French fairy tale—but not one for children, or for the faint of heart. This dark, complex story—like the very best fairy tales—works on many different metaphorical levels at once. It is a dazzling, disturbing work of magical prose.

Pierrette Fleutiaux is the author of the novel *Nous sommes eternels*, which recently won the Prix Femina. She was born in a very small town in central France during World War II where, as she writes, "there was no TV and few entertainments, and I spent my childhood reading books or running around the countryside." Fleutiaux now resides in Paris. Translator Leigh Hafrey resides in Massachusetts and teaches at the Harvard Business School.

"The Ogre's Wife" comes from the pages of *Grand Street* (#37), where it was published in an English translation by Leigh Hafrey.

—T.W.

In reading fairy tales such as "Jack and the Beanstalk" and "Little Poucet," I've always wondered about the "giant's" or "ogre's" wife. Who was she? Where did she come from? How did she deal with the bad habits (not to mention size) of her husband? "The Ogre's Wife" in this story (based on "Little Poucet") was seduced by an angel who turns into a monster overnight. Isn't that an apt commentary on the sex act and sexual relationships through time. . . .

—E.D.

The Ogre's wife doesn't like preparing flesh, although she doesn't know it. Something comes over her when the smell fills the house and there isn't a pure breath of air to be had. She pulls out a haunch, dunks it in the fire, which hisses, she eats it, eats another, getting drunk on the smell of charred meat. Then the meat seems to swell up inside her; she feels it pressing against the walls of her stomach. It is as if a new, thick, stubborn life were taking shape in the ruins of that violated flesh, in the black depths of her intestines within her own frightened flesh.

The woman then goes out to the backyard, where she has piled the viscera and entrails by the dung heap. She looks at them, she gags, she vomits all the meat she has eaten in a tremor that resembles a sob.

Then she goes to the well, draws a pail of clear water, bathes her face, her eyes, and at the end cups her hands and drinks deeply. She feels the cool water sliding along the irritated walls of her stomach. The redness leaves her eyes, the nausea leaves her throat, the heavy throbbing leaves her temples. She takes a quick look around, and when she's certain there's nobody there she lifts her skirt and washes her legs, her genitals, and after that her arms and armpits, where she has hair, too. Then she throws out the dirty water, draws another pail, and drinks again.

Now the woman is like the well: inside, a silent coolness surrounded by a body set like laid stone, and the chill of the water with which she has just washed lingering on the outside like a thin film of ice.

She returns to the big kitchen. Now she can tend to the dead beasts, rinse the dishes, set the table. She neither sees nor smells the hairy, greasy, bloody, brownish, greenish, winy, livid, insipid, rank morsels of meat. Smells and colors do not tumble down her, they stop short at her rim, and she rests in the somber depths of the water, which reflects no image.

The seven little ogresses come to the table, as rowdy as they are hungry. The wife feeds them, calms the fidgety ones, soothes the anxious ones: each will have her carefully apportioned share of raw meat, and if necessary the wife will offset a greater width by trimming the thickness, and will also remove the bone splinters and the nerves. Then she puts them to bed, having made sure each of them has brushed her teeth, having scraped their gums herself, removing the little shreds of flesh that hang between their sharp teeth.

She puts them to bed and goes back downstairs to wash the rest of the raw meat from their plates. By the time the Ogre comes home, she has set the table again, with a pile of bloody joints built into a handsome pyramid at the center. The Ogre takes his seat, the wife hers, but in her stomach she stirs the well water, making tiny cascades. The Ogre chews, crunches, and swallows; she doesn't hear him.

"Aren't you eating?" the Ogre says.

"I ate with the children," the woman says, smiling like a nymph.

When the Ogre has finished eating and smoked his pipe, he goes up to his daughters' bedroom to count them. He runs his hand over their heads, where the hair has stopped growing and stands up like hedgehog spines or the iron spikes on a gate. When he comes to the end of the row, he calls out to his wife:

"How many of them are there?"

"Seven," she says.

"Right," he says.

Then he goes back down the row of beds, unscrewing a little graduated bar with a number from each one, because the beds are also scales.

"How much meat?" he calls to his wife.

"What you told me."

"Right," says the Ogre.

And when he has counted his daughters and verified the amount of meat they've eaten, he stretches out in his big bed, grumbling a little because their hair has pricked his hand, and, satisfied, immediately starts snoring.

The Ogre's wife waits a little longer, and then, when she is sure not a soul stirs in this house where, with smothered tearing sounds, flesh is obscurely transferring its allegiance, she releases the banister and returns to her kitchen. There she puts on the light and feels she is finally emerging from the deep well into which she had withdrawn. The kitchen is spotless; not a trace of blood or bone or flesh remains. Without the Ogre's knowing, the windows have been left open and have brought in the balmy night air. The other life of the Ogre's wife begins.

A gentle hunger wakes in her. From beneath a trapdoor she pulls the red potatoes that she grows in a hidden clearing in the forest, picks lettuce and leeks from the pots where they pass for houseplants, and takes artichokes from a vase where their leaves look like the petals of a big, angry rose. She cleans her vegetables meticulously and puts them in a pot on the stove. The water simmers sweetly, emitting delicate, scented vapors in the room, and it seems to her that all these things are arranging themselves in a big, loose, soft nest she will curl up in.

Once the vegetables are cooked, she eats them slowly with a bit of the butter she keeps in a little jar marked "body cream," and she can feel her stomach opening up and welcoming these foods like a tender paste, telling her when it is full without hiccuping or gagging. Afterward, the woman gathers the peels and throws them out at the edge of the forest, where she knows birds and all sorts of small creatures with which she is familiar will come and make them disappear. Then, walking slowly along the path where the soft grass muffles the sound, she goes back to her kitchen, sits down on the doorstep, and smokes a cigarette while she watches the great, shadowy forest that begins just a few yards from the house. And that is how she falls asleep, her back against the doorpost, carrying the great, dark forest beneath her eyelids, which never quite close. Later, the dawn will wake her, and she will quickly go upstairs to the Ogre so he won't notice she's been gone.

She is sleeping—but is she really? The great forest is right there before her still half-open eyes. In that dim mass, branches snap, axes ring out against the trees, something flees through the undergrowth, voices cry out, weep, shout, wolves howl, and then there is that sound that has been casting about in the night for some time, now close, now far away, as though searching for an opening in this giant net of vegetation. It is a small and persistent sound, the Ogre's wife must hear it when she sleeps like that on the doorstep, she must hear it deep inside her head where the forest moves.

Two ogre friends come to dine with her husband, the Ogre. On such occasions, the wife isn't required to sit at the table or pretend to eat. She has too much to do serving these giants, moving mountains of meat, rolling barrels of blood. That said, the ogres aren't monsters; they would like to help the slim woman push her excessively heavy loads, but she won't let them, she doesn't want them to notice her, she doesn't want them to see her. The truth is, she doesn't want to be there. Let them do their feasting, let her do her chores. But there is something else, which is that she likes to listen to them when they talk between rounds of gorging themselves. The ogres have seven-league boots, they have traveled all over the world, and when they aren't talking about their ungodly hunts, listening to their crude and colorful phrases is like going to the movies. The Ogre's wife has only her own two legs, and they are not very strong, but she knows a multitude of things exist beyond her forest, and the ogres' rough descriptions work their way into her and stir up memories. Once she too went far away, to the edge of a big blue sea that wasn't contained like a well but stretched to the far horizon like a bath for all the creatures of the earth.

The Ogre's wife remembers. She was walking alone, sadly bent beneath her load—she has forgotten what the load was, but she knows she had been carrying it since childhood. It was winter, her feet sank into the ruts—what the ruts were from she can't recall either, but they had always been there. The snow began to fall, the little girl could no longer see the path. She stopped walking and started to pray. Almost immediately, a shape appeared against the blurred backdrop of the horizon, a completely white shape that flew over the hills and came toward her through the falling snow. "It's an angel," she told herself. "My prayers have been answered." When the angel reached her, she saw he was very large, with two intense eyes in a face covered with small ice crystals. He took her hand and looked at her closely.

"You're freezing," he said in his strange, otherworldly voice.

"I'm cold," the little girl murmured.

"Doesn't your blood flow in your veins?" the angel asked.

"My father says I have the blood of a turnip."

"The blood of a what?"

"A turnip," the girl said, taking heart.

She could hear the amazement in the angel's voice. "He feels sorry for me," she said to herself, and she who had never felt like anything at all suddenly felt very small, which was an enormous change and almost made her dizzy, but also gave her a will she'd never known.

"You're pale, is your blood pale too?"

"My father says I have the complexion of a rutabaga."

"A rutabaga?" the angel said, with revulsion.

"Yes," said the girl.

"You have skinny fingers."

"I'm nothing but skin and bones."

"Nothing but bones?" the angel said.

"No," said the little girl.

"And you're flat," the angel said, pulling back a flap of her thin coat.

"As flat as an endive leaf."

"And I can see through your skin."

"Like the skin of an onion."

"An onion?" the angel said, with increasing horror.

"That's what everyone says," the girl assured him, now making things up.

She could tell exactly what touched the angel, and she was ready to run through her father's whole garden if she had to, to keep him interested in her. Because he must be interested in her to ask so many questions. She was so thrilled by this that a little color finally came into her cheeks and her eyes began to shine. The angel, who had the delicacy of his kind, noticed this.

"Of course, your looks aren't that awful, are they?" he said, looking at her closely. "Only no one would want to eat you up, of course," he added in the same pensive tone.

The girl went up to him and timidly touched his big, snow-covered boots. "Take me to heaven," she said.

"What?" said the angel.

"I'd like to go to heaven with you," the little girl said, pressing up against him and looking him straight in the eye.

"There isn't much to you," said the angel, thunderstruck, "but you've got brass."

"I'd do anything for you," the girl said, more and more taken with the fact that she had startled an angel, and such a big angel at that.

"In that case . . . ," the angel said, hesitating.

"Oh please, won't you?" the little girl said, with her arms around his boots.

"It isn't done," the angel said.

"You've got the power," the girl said.

"True," the angel said.

"And besides," she said, "no one will see us."

And, in fact, the thick snow falling around them had covered the path. It lay heavily on the drooping branches of the trees and filled the air; there wasn't a sound, not a soul.

"Since you can fly," the girl said, "there won't be any footprints."

"True," the angel said, looking at his boots.

"And I don't weigh much," she added.

"But," the angel asked, "are you strong?"

So that's it, the little girl mused. He thinks I'm afraid to leave this earth, where everything is so heavy and where everyone makes fun of me. He thinks I'll scream and struggle and make trouble for him in heaven.

"Very strong," she answered, jumping onto his back and wrapping her arms firmly around his neck.

The angel flew over hills, forests, streams. Sometimes he dropped down and brushed the ground for a moment with the toe of his boot, then he quickly rose again and the little girl closed her eyes to avoid getting dizzy. The angel's broad head protected her, but she could hear the wind whipping around the sides. She was drunk with speed and height, her head seemed filled with a substance lighter than snow. When night fell, they stopped at the edge of a wood.

"Are we there?" the girl asked. Her body felt weightless to her, she felt nothing beneath her fingers, saw nothing around her but a transparent blackness and white highlights.

"No," he said, "but I know a shack nearby."

At the shack the angel squeezed her very tight, wrapped her in his warmth, penetrated her with his strength. Everything was the way she had heard it described by people of the faith, even when she didn't recognize each thing for what it was at first, and it was her great effort to recognize so much that was new that finally put her to sleep.

Wake up," said a hard voice the next morning.

The little girl woke with a start, and it wasn't like coming into a beautiful dream, but like leaving a terrible battle that had covered her in bruises. The angel's wings were no longer white, nor was his face or his flying boots. He was a big man in a black coat, with tousled hair, a beard, and very big, gaping shoes that gave off a terrible rotting smell.

He's the devil, the girl thought, and I'm being punished.

"What are you going to do to me?" she asked, trembling.

"What?" the devil said.

"Are you going to kill me?"

"I said I wouldn't eat you, didn't I?" said the devil.

"Well, then, what are you going to do to me?"

"Nothing I didn't already do last night."

"Last night?" she said.

She looked down at her legs, her stockings, and her skirt, and saw they were spotted with blood.

"Let's go," the devil said, and threw her over his shoulder like a sack.

The snow vanished; it got warm. Cautiously looking down, she suddenly saw an enormous well full of moving water, with a multitude of naked bodies around the rim, strewn this way and that beneath the burning sun. "This is hell," she said to herself, feeling the harsh glow of the colors against her face. She could already feel her skin cooking. When they touched down, the sand was burning hot; all around, the bodies were stuck to it and charred, like on a grill. "Even the water is boiling," she said to herself, and when the devil pushed her in she was already nearly dead with fear and exhaustion.

The water didn't burn her. It was fresh and not very deep, and when you stopped being afraid to look at it, it had the blue of real stained-glass windows. It wasn't boiling, but the little waves came lapping against her legs like minnows in a stream. The devil had moved off; now he had turned into a fish and was slicing through the water with big strokes of his fins. "Is he leaving?" she asked herself, astonished. She looked behind her, but her anxious gaze couldn't get beyond two little girls leaning over side by side on the damp strip of beach, busily digging a canal. The devil was coming back; in his hand he held a potbellied fish with black whiskers and red scales.

"I'll cook it for you," the girl said, suddenly ecstatic.

"Don't bother," the devil said.

And before her startled eyes he bit right into the fish, which quickly ceased struggling, and in five big bites had swallowed it.

"I don't like white flesh like that," he said, "but it's all they've got here."

He too was looking at the little girls, who were bent so far over their canal that all you saw were their round, golden buttocks. And as he looked at them a fit of hiccuping suddenly came over him, his face turned red, he couldn't breathe.

The girl plunged her hand down his throat. Her hand and wrist were so slim that they had no trouble going down the pipe, and in a second she had pulled out the fish's whiskers, which had stuck in the devil's esophagus.

"You saved my life," the devil said.

"You mean you can die?" the girl said.

"Just like anybody else, and often over something as trivial as that."

"So much the better," the little girl said.

"So much the better what?"

"That you owe me your life."

The devil looked at her in surprise; then, finding he could breathe freely, he cleared his throat just for the pleasure of it.

"You're not so bad after all," he said.

The Ogre's wife no longer believes in angels and devils. She has left all of that far behind. The life of an Ogre's wife has taken hold of her in the invisible way lives have of being always present, so that even if you want to get rid of them you can't, and you need another life—hungrier, tougher, or more cunning—to make the first one let go.

So now this is what happens. The Ogre comes home. He takes off his big boots and tosses his catch onto the table: breastplates with ribs jutting out like long curving teeth, but mostly hindquarters, legs and thighs of every size and shape, torn down the middle. The Ogre throws down these gaping, bleeding thighs with the fur still hanging from their sides; all at once he opens his fly, pulls out his huge ogreish member, and shoves it into the folds of flesh, where it instantly turns red. He grabs a thigh in each hand, squeezes them against his member, spreads them apart again; the bones crack. He groans with each back-and-forth movement of the thighs; his wife has to stay and watch, but the dead beast does not give him what he wants—he has brought home doe haunches and sow haunches, but their cold, slack vaginas are not what he needs. With a quick motion he flips his prey onto its belly, lifting the hind legs high as though they were flags, then slamming them roughly down and driving his member deep into the ruptured organs. He opens and closes the dislocated thighs; the broken bones tear at his member; he howls with his head thrust forward, as if the voice of the quartered animal were passing through his body and rising in a desperate appeal to the unfathomable god of the flesh. But he is still not satisfied.

One day he brings home the rump of a cow, and his wife stares in horror at the great white hind legs splattered with blood and dung. He makes her come to him and tosses her onto the cow, pulls up her skirt, and seizes her slender thighs. The woman trembles—someday, without thinking, he will spread them brutally apart as well and crack them with a single stroke; her belly will be ripped open, he will flip her over and thrust himself into her erupting entrails. The Ogre finds no satisfaction in her, either; her body is too tiny. He brings in a live bull, binds its hooves to the four corners of the kitchen, and impales his wife on its member. The animal's spasms, its bellowing and twisting, whip him into a frenzy, he breaks off its horns, shoves his member into its eyes, and crawls across the rough hide.

His wife is very white against the bull's black belly, he slobbers toward her, crying, "The last hope! The last hope!" He still has not had enough, he throws himself down on all fours and sinks his teeth into the animal's living flesh, where its limbs are stretched tight. Its agony causes the whole house to shake, and the wife atop its disintegrating body senses she has lost control; the monstrous member slides between her pale thighs and she doesn't know what to cling to.

"Stop!" she cries out suddenly. "Stop, stop!" The Ogre looks up, and their eyes meet for an instant.

"Up there," she says urgently.

At the head of the stairs, the seven little ogresses in their white nightgowns are crowded together, staring at their mother, naked atop the black beast, and at their father, on all fours with his penis in his hand and his mouth full of raw flesh. The seven little ogresses survey the carnage, but their faces show neither fear nor revulsion; their eyes are glittering.

"Go to bed!" the Ogre roars in a terrifying voice, and the disappointed ogrelettes retreat and vanish.

Pacified, the Ogre pulls his wife off the bull, politely stretches her out on the ground, finishes his business inside her with a modest convulsion, and then gets dressed again. He triumphantly summons his children and shows them the parts of the beast with care, giving them the names, the tastes, the scents; he quizzes each of them, and when they respond correctly he lets them throw themselves on the twitching mass with their pointy ogresses' teeth, their dozens of pointy little teeth.

"Put on your napkins!" their mother cries.

But they don't listen.

"Use your knives and forks!"

But they glance at their father and see him laughing, and they shrug off her recommendations.

"Don't take such big bites!" their upset mother cries, but the little ones throw themselves even more greedily onto the beast, which has finally finished dying.

"Chew!" their mother says.

No one listens.

"They'll choke!" she pleads with the Ogre.

Sensing their mother's helplessness, the ogresses continue even more eagerly, despite her despair. The Ogre finally deigns to hear her. "Go along with your mother now," he says.

And the wife takes them off to the well and washes them one by one. Weeping, she washes their little lamprey mouths that tear at flesh so eagerly. She talks to them, tells them their sharp teeth wound and cause suffering, but the ogrelettes laugh, they don't understand their mother's arguments, they make fun of her, they're aroused and euphoric. When they're clean, their mother puts each of them in a white nightgown that still shows sharp creases from ironing. The children tolerate it, and now their mother sees all seven of them, clear and distinct among the pails gleaming softly in the moonlight, their little feet all white in the evening dew on the grass. She sees their round cheeks, their pink lips, their air of good health, and a door closes inside her on the bloody scenes as though they belonged to another time, another life. She kisses her children tenderly, and when they are all in bed she begins telling them a story.

"Once upon a time, there was a little girl who lived in a village. Her mother and her granny loved her to distraction, and they had made her a little red ridinghood—"

"What color red?" the ogrelettes call out.

"Poppy," their mother says, thinking of the flowers she loves along the roadsides.

"No!" the children say.

"Strawberry," their mother says, thinking of the delights she has walking across the fields.

"No!" the children cry.

"Tomato," their mother says, seeing her secret garden in the clearing.

"No way!" the children cry; a tomato is to them what spinach is to others.

"Cherry," their mother says, looking at the little pink print on the curtain at the window.

"Oh, come on!" the children cry, practically choking with laughter.

And when the wife, bewildered, falls silent for a moment, the children immediately begin yelling, "Cow's blood, bull's blood, cow's blood, bull's blood!"

The woman sighs and continues her story. "Her mother and her granny had made her a little blood-red ridinghood. One day, when her mother had baked and decorated some cakes—"

"Yuck, yuck!" the children yell.

"What's wrong?" their mother asks.

"Not cakes, not cakes!"

"Then what?" their mother asks.

"Snakes, snakes!"

"Oh," their mother sighs.

"Trapped and skinned," the children say.

"Fine. So, one day when her mother had trapped and skinned some snakes, she said, 'Go see how your granny is doing and take her this snake and this little pot of jam . . . of ham.' "

"That's it, that's it!" the children encourage her.

Pleased to see their faces light up, the wife goes on. "As she was going through the woods, she met the Big Bad Wolf, who would have loved to eat her up."

"No!" the children yell.

"Well, what now?" their mother says.

"The Big Bad Wolf, whom she would have loved to eat!" the children yell, so excited they stand up in bed.

"Sit down," their mother says, "or I won't go on."

The children sit down again and she goes on.

"She met the Big Bad Wolf, whom she would have loved to eat only he didn't dare—"

"Only *she* didn't dare—"

"Only she didn't dare."

"Why not?" one of the ogresses cries.

"Because there were some woodcutters there," one of them answers.

"Because her granny was waiting for her," another says.

"Because her mother had told her she couldn't," the youngest says.

"Well, then, let her eat them all!" the eldest yells in a strident voice.

At these words, the ogresses look at their mother. Their round, opaque little eyes settle on her tender skin, on her rumpled collar, on her breasts, which show through her blouse in the moonlight, on her arms where the bull has bruised them. The children are silent and their focused eyes don't move.

Uneasy, their mother murmurs, "You shouldn't eat wolves."

Then, nervous, she goes on, "You shouldn't let wolves eat you."

Then, at a loss, "You should eat what is right."

The mother feels her thoughts tripping her up. She no longer knows which way to turn, fears lurk on all sides, the ogresses' eyes are glued to her skin. She is overcome by a tremendous fatigue, and she would like nothing better than to let herself slip to the ground and surrender to whatever happens, but she forces herself to continue her story.

"The little girl took the long way around, and had a good time gathering herbs—"

"Birds," the ogresses say.

"Had a good time gathering birds and chasing butterflies—"

"Frogs and flies," the ogresses say.

"And making posies of the little flowers that she found—"

"And making mush of the little slugs that she found."

"The wolf didn't waste any time getting to the granny's house."

"Wrong," the eldest says. "*She* got there first, and do you know why, sisters?"

"Because she had taken the Ogre's boots," the others answer.

"Terrific!" the youngest yells excitedly, and they all applaud.

The mother looks at them, sitting in their beds so cheerfully and clapping their hands the way children do. Her exhaustion goes away and a little joy returns: a joy that is worn and tattered like an old delusion, but that she has never thrown out for good and that now comes back to envelop her—still useful, if only for a moment. She wants to tell her children a story, to be there in that room with the seven little beds all in a line, talking softly in the dim light of the moon, while the curtain sways softly at the window in the shadow of the cherry tree and the room expands and contracts in time with all those small, attentive breaths as though all of them, she and her children, were being rocked upon a great warm bosom.

"I'll go on," she says. "The little girl got there first and told her granny what had happened. 'Put your snake, your birds, your frogs, your flies, and your slugs on the doorstep so the wolf can eat them,' her granny said. 'Then he won't be hungry anymore and he'll go away.'"

"No, no!" the ogresses cry.

"I don't understand," their mother says.

"She wants to eat the wolf," the youngest murmurs.

"And to eat him when he's good and fat," the eldest cries.

"I was forgetting," their mother says.

"Go on, go on," the ogresses say.

"All right," the mother says. "The little girl got into bed with her granny, and when the wolf arrived, she pounced on him."

"No, no," the children cry.

"That's not how it goes?" the mother asks, distraught.

"Details, give us details," the children say.

"I'll tell it," the eldest says. "The wolf ate everything on the doorstep, but that only made him more hungry, so he got into bed with Little Red Ridinghood, who was dressed up as her grandmother. He was pretty surprised to see how that granny looked in her negligee. 'Granny, what pretty eye shadow you have on!' he said."

" 'The better to seduce you, little wolf!' " all the ogresses but the youngest cry out.

" 'And what pretty lipstick you have on!' "

" 'The better to kiss you, little wolf.' "

" 'And what pretty arms!' "

" 'The better to squeeze you, little wolf.' "

" 'And what pretty breasts!' "

" 'The better to arouse you, little wolf.' "

"That's enough," their mother says. "It's time for bed. Now, here's the end of the story. 'Granny, what pretty pointy teeth you have,' said the wolf. 'The better to eat you with, little wolf!' And as she spoke those words the naughty little girl jumped on the poor little wolf and ate him up."

The ogresses are very dissatisfied with this ending, but since they can't tell why, they allow themselves to be put to bed. Their mother straightens the tips of their hair, which have become bent in the course of the story, pulls the curtain across the moon, and leaves, feeling chilly and numb.

The Ogre comes in his turn to the ogresses' room.

"How many?" he says.

"Seven," she says, leaning against the banister.

"Right," the Ogre says.

Eating a whole bull this evening has calmed him down. It doesn't even occur to him to check the graduated bars; he calls for his wife and goes to bed. The bull has calmed him down, and all he wants from her tonight are her slim thighs, which he will open without violence. He mounts her and moves without frenzy. The Ogre is so big his wife can't feel where his body ends. She can't touch his feet and she can't see his head, which lies well beyond her, rubbing and hitting the wall as though involved in something that has nothing to do with her, in a language she doesn't know. Her own head is against his ribs, and she looks for the most yielding spot to rest her face in and get a little air. All she knows of the Ogre are his lower rib cage pressing against her forehead; his stomach—she can hear the muffled echoes of the dead flesh battling inside—pressing against her ears; his enormous thighs, which immobilize her own and give her endless cramps; and his penis, which fortunately isn't so big, and moves inside her without her feeling it—an absence sometimes rubbery, sometimes hairy and sticky. It's just that the Ogre's head is so far from hers, and what he is doing so far from being what she might enjoy, that she never feels even the beginning of pleasure, never even a hope of a beginning.

When he's done, his mood sometimes softens for a few minutes, and the wife climbs up near his head and brushes aside his sweat-soaked locks.

"At least let me cook the flesh," she says.

"I can't," he says.

"Why not?"

"I have to have it raw, otherwise . . ."

"Otherwise?" the wife says.

"Otherwise my hunger is like a solid wall, a web of gray threads, parching illness, a constant grinding that drives me mad."

"Yes," the wife says.

"I need flesh that cries out. My hunger comes back in a rush, and I fill myself with what I need."

"Yes," the wife says.

"The wall opens, and everything that is parched and gray and grinding suddenly explodes, and I fill myself with what I need."

The woman continues to smooth his matted curls, but she knows she mustn't say a word, mustn't look him in the eye, or the Ogre will rise in anger and she will see that look he has when he brings home the beasts.

This evening, though, he goes on talking.

"Even the beasts," he says. "Their flesh is dull, they don't understand me. They can't share with me, they aren't with me. Soon I'll have to, I'll have to—"

Horrified, the wife puts out the light. "Let's go to sleep," he says.

In the night, the open window, at first cloudy, little by little becomes clear. The great forest looms up beyond in the pale light. The wife carries the great forest in her eyes, which are always half-open, and as she sleeps the little noise that has been hovering about for some time, now near, now far, comes back more loudly. Twigs can be heard breaking, leaves being crumpled, brambles crunching; something small and very determined is casting about, trying to get out of that great forest, trying to get into her head.

The wife is dreaming. The street is empty, she is sitting alone on the edge of the sidewalk. A little girl comes down the street, very little, almost an infant. There is a fairly high wall running along the sidewalk, and on the other side of the wall, down below, the wife knows there is a ledge covered with weeds and wildflowers. The ledge isn't very wide; there is nothing beyond it but sky, emptiness. Suddenly the little girl breaks away and jumps onto the wall. She has already thrown one leg over to the other side. The wife doesn't understand why no one is rushing up, why she herself doesn't budge. But she can't take her eyes off what is happening. The child moves with the deftness of a serpent, the control of a well-trained predator, and suddenly, just as her whole body is about to go over, she raises her face. The wife is stunned by the girl's expression. The child isn't just playing, she knows what she is doing, her baby eyes are set and full of fury. Her glance goes right through the wife, as though she were nothing but a vague shape made of mist on the sidewalk, but she doesn't know what feeling it fills her with. The face of that child on the wall, and that little leg sliding over! Then it's done. The wife listens for the dull thud of the child's fall onto the grassy ledge, but none comes, and she waits a long time, her heart repeating the same, pounding question: "But there was a ledge, wasn't there? There was a ledge?"

She wakes up expecting the noise, fearing the emptiness in which the noise doesn't come. And suddenly she hears a very soft snapping in front of the house. Her skin prickles. It is as though her dream has jumped tracks: the fall into the abyss beyond the ledge has happened, and now something—the remnants of the sound she didn't hear—is gently scratching at the membrane of silence and darkness around the house, around her sleep.

Trembling, she goes down into the kitchen, crosses to the door, and opens it suddenly. On the doorstep there is only a very small boy, scantily clothed, his whole body trembling.

"I want to come in," he says.

The woman looks at him, thunderstruck.

"I'm lost," he says. "My brothers and I are cold. Let us in."

"God help you," the wife murmurs. "Don't you know this is the Ogre's house?"

"The wolves will eat us too," the little boy whispers. "Let us in."

They debate it, the little boy numb with cold and the wife numb with fear. He won't retreat toward the forest and she can't retreat into her house. They walk in the garden, on the path, back and forth at the edge of the forest. The wife has never met such an obstinate and contentious person. She forgets her fear.

"The wolves mean death," he says.

"The Ogre means death as well," she says.

"The wolves mean a brute death, my screams will be lost in their rough fur, their jaws, their dirty black claws. There's nothing more brutal than that, there's nothing more terrible than my screams drowning in brute flesh."

The woman listens passionately. "How will it be different with the Ogre?" she asks, forgetting he's her husband, forgetting he's in her bed, forgetting he's there, close by, in the house.

"His eyes will look at me, they will return my screams and add something to them. The Ogre will understand me, there will be two of us at my death, we will share something."

"That's odd," the wife says. "The Ogre said that too."

"You see?" he says. "It will be better than with the wolves."

"It will be worse," says the wife, who can't understand where all these words are coming from. "You'll want to ask him for mercy."

"It's you I'll ask for mercy," he says. "You'll protect me, I know it."

"I won't be able to do anything," the wife says, "and my heart will break with sadness."

"We've been abandoned," he says. "I'll think of you suffering for me and I'll have that solace. With the wolves, all I'll have is the pain and the brutishness."

"You mean you want me to suffer?" the wife says.

"Maybe that's what you need," the little boy says. "How long have you been living here?"

"A long time," the wife murmurs.

She sees the child in her dream just as its legs slide over the wall, its face turned toward her with those eyes full of something she doesn't understand. She is seized with fury.

"Why have you come here?" she cries.

"Because of the wolves," he says.

"But there aren't any more wolves," she cries.

"Why are you shouting?"

"Because you're here," the wife says.

"But I'm here because you're here," he says.

They walk faster and faster at the edge of the forest, coming and going rapidly. The wife is completely absorbed in this argument that rises and falls around them, looping and knotting and binding them so completely they don't want to get loose. Caught up in their argument, they talk more and more loudly, so loudly that they hear nothing around them, nothing of what is going on at the same time across the garden, in the house.

Thumbkin's six brothers had gone into the house. They were cold and they couldn't stand waiting anymore; their little brother was palavering and not coming back. They went in and went upstairs one after the other. Drawn by the heat, they found the ogresses' bedroom, and each one slipped into a bed without thinking, without even undressing, they were so tired and frozen.

In his bed, the Ogre is having a bad night. He has talked too much this night, and the words have muddled his brain like bad wine. He wakes in a storm cloud and immediately smells fresh flesh, very much alive and fragrant with the scent of the outdoors. He rises, reeling, and follows the smell to the ogresses' bedroom. The boys hear the floor shaking as though trees were falling in the forest. They quickly slide under the beds and wait, holding their breath. The Ogre comes into the room and bends over his daughters; he smells the smell that is driving him mad in their sheets, on their skin.

"Get up!" he cries.

Startled from their sleep, the ogrelettes rise like little serpents. They too catch the scent, and a thrill runs through them. They gather and sniff at each other like a pack of jackals, their eyes shining in the night. The Ogre places his big hands on them, bends over to catch the scent too, and they turn on him suddenly and bite his hand with their pointy little teeth. The Ogre growls.

The little boys have fled during this commotion, crawling into the darkness. They have found another pocket of warmth—now they're in the Ogre's big bed, snuggling and squeezing against one another; half-asleep, half-awake, they listen to the growling and hissing that comes from beyond the staircase.

The Ogre has withdrawn his bloody hand, and, retreating with a growl, he goes back to his room. The horde of ogresses follow him. They smell the wild odor in the bed where their father has lain down again, they mill around him, sniffing, and climb onto him with their little pointy teeth unsheathed and gleaming like razor blades.

The little boys had thrown themselves under the bed, and now they flee toward the other bedroom, slithering like little beasts. The ogresses and the Ogre race from one room to the other. The smell grows stronger all the time, they circle one another, their little teeth sink in farther and farther, the Ogre's hands squeeze at random, blood flows, bones crack, the scent in the air baffles them, drives them mad, blinds them, the ogresses are upon their father like a pack, he shakes his enormous arms and bites to the right, to the left, crushes and tears. When the noise finally dies down and the little boys venture out again, there is nothing left but a mangled heap at the head of the stairs between the two rooms. They go downstairs and find themselves a place in the kitchen near the hearth, where a little bit of heat still lingers, and then, finally at peace, they fall asleep with the scent of the forest wafting over them through the open door.

When the wife returns, still debating with Thumbkin, she sees his six brothers lying there asleep.

"You see?" Thumbkin says. "Nothing happened."

"You win," the wife says. "Lie down beside them."

Then she goes out on the doorstep as is her wont and sits there bolt upright. Her mind is compact as a stone, as though the world had just changed and there was no room yet for many murmuring thoughts. When Thumbkin and his brothers leave at dawn, she hardly moves. She remains alone in the house with the corpses she hasn't yet seen.

The wife has the house to herself. The first few days, she comes and goes. When she thinks of the ogrelettes in their white nightgowns by the well, she weeps. When she thinks of their pointy teeth and the shreds that hung between their pink lips, her tears stop. And the Ogre? The memory of him leaves a black hole that swallows up thought. They are all under the earth now, and no one in the village complains about them anymore; in their dead-and-buried state they have become like everybody else, and now they can be forgotten. At the cemetery, the big tomb and the seven little ones lie there as submissively as all the others. People say the ogrelettes' hair has grown up through the ground and become the hedge of spiky bushes against the wall at the back. For a long time the wife comes to straighten the thorns into a proper crown at the head of the tombs, but one day she no longer sees her children's hair in them and leaves them to disorder.

The wife no longer vomits. Once, in town, she saw magazines with animals and whips and leather instruments and vampires. She came home, and ever since she has found herself laughing, suddenly laughing midway up the stairs, laughing at the thought of those magazines, at her memories, which insert themselves between the pages, making the printed images pale by comparison. In the middle of her kitchen, she raises her skirt and looks at her long white thighs, no longer bruised or cramped. She has sold the salting tubs, the mincers, the slaughtering pens; she has sold the guns, the hooks, and the big jugs saturated with indelible brown stains. Her garden is full of fruit and handsome green plants that grow in broad daylight, her stomach feels better, she has little to say. She receives newspapers, all the newspapers that come to the village—she reads incessantly. Massacres, carnage, killings, and crime; torture in basements, booby-trapped summer homes, deranged gunmen, explosions; and children, children burned, children gunned down like clay pigeons, raped, cut up, as well as children in uniforms with guns in their hands, and children in gangs with chains. The Ogre's wife clips these articles and pastes them on big sheets of cardboard, which she puts up here and there around the house—it doesn't matter where, since no one comes to visit—and now and again she comes to a stop before one of them and falls into a revery, an anxiety, an oblivion.

Days pass. One morning, the Ogre's wife opens a cupboard and sees the Ogre's big boots standing there. She turns around. Beyond the windows (which are almost always open now), beyond the garden, she can see the great forest drawn like a thick black line against the clear and empty sky. She comes back down as she used to long ago and sits on the kitchen doorstep. Night falls. The dim tangle of the forest twines firmly around her gaze, and when she drifts off, the branches, the twigs, the leaves enter her half-open eyes, and in the depths of her sleep a small noise begins casting about.

The following day, the wife returns to the cupboard, takes out the boots, and slides her feet into them. Being enchanted, the boots immediately settle against her skin, feel their way along her toes, her heels, her ankles, then find their marks and take on the shape of the feet of the Ogre's wife.

She goes outside. With one step she is already at the other end of her garden, another step and she is at the edge of the forest. Then the Ogre's wife takes a very deep breath, squares her timid shoulders, flexes her slim thighs, and suddenly she takes off in a great leap over the forest.

She is flying, flying over the forest in her seven-league boots. In the dim undergrowth, Thumbkin is wandering once again, followed by his six sniveling brothers, still tripping over roots, filled with the chimerical desire to find their parents and with a neurotic fear of wolves. Thumbkin lets them talk. He's got other things to think about: once was enough to shatter his universe. Being deserted a second time, having to march again among these enormous black trunks, where each branch seems to snap beneath his skin like an unknown organ exploding, sending unheard-of sounds along his nerves—all this, instead of stamping Thumbkin into the soil of the forest, has freed him from it forever. He doesn't want to go back, but where can he go, and what should he do with the six whiners who are holding him back?

Thumbkin climbs a tree. He scans peaks and valleys, and then, in the misty distance, he notices a shape that seems to be flying toward him. His heart beats quickly, he waves wildly from his branch, he shouts and struggles. Oh, if only she will see him and come over, he will know how to hold her.

She has seen him, and in two strides she is beside him. He has grown, she has changed—they greet each other eagerly.

"I'm taking you with me," she says.

"What about the others?" he asks, pointing at the six crybabies sitting in a circle at the foot of the tree.

The Ogre's wife bends down, pushing aside two or three branches.

"It's you I want, not them," she says.

How she has changed, Thumbkin muses, and he admires her so much he'd like to jump into the pocket of her blouse right now and never leave it.

"They are my brothers," he says reluctantly, "and they don't know how to care for themselves."

The Ogre's wife takes a package out of her bag.

"Here's everything they'll need," she says, throwing it through the branches. "Let's go."

"Right," Thumbkin says. He listens to the sound of the falling package and to his brothers' voices as they howl like puppies at the moon. Then he jumps into the big pocket of the wife's blouse and off they fly over the great forest, through the pale air, which slowly clears, lights up, bursts into flame.

Inside the pocket, Thumbkin doesn't stir. Sometimes he very gently rests his head on the wife's breast. The wife feels this pressure on her breast at the same time as she feels the thrill of flight in her legs and the warmth of the sun on her cheeks. How close her lover's head is to her heart, how swift their flight, how vast and open the earth!

They stop at nightfall in a clover patch. Thumbkin comes out of her pocket, stretches his folded limbs, but he doesn't leave the wife's body. He settles in the other pocket, lays his head on the other breast, and his heat radiates softly through the wife's body. They sleep that way. The next day, Thumbkin moves into the big pocket on her skirt, he stretches his legs in the hollow of her thigh, he rests his head and his open arms against the wife's rounded belly. Come evening, he settles on the other side, and the heat in the wife's body continues to grow.

They pass through the countryside, camping out wherever they like, leaping over borders, sight-seeing and visiting, always body to body. Thumbkin has moved from her front to her back, from one shoulder to the other, from one buttock to the other, he has stopped in the small of her back, beneath her armpits, at the bend in her arms, he feels her sweat running in rivulets around him, and the wife's body continues gently heating up. One evening, they come to a great city spread out along a river. The river makes a bend downtown, a space full of gardens with bridges radiating out and a hotel at the back sparkling with lights and surrounded by multicolored flags trembling in the breeze. The place looks like a big butterfly at the heart of the city, and the wife lands on its back. They have a room in the shining hotel, with a bay window overlooking the river at the point where it forks. Thumbkin searches the wife's body in the places he couldn't reach when they were flying across the countryside in the seven-league boots. He places himself between her legs and gently spreads them, he spreads the great purple lips and lays himself down in the middle of that wet and odorous bed, his head on the little pillow at the top and his arms extended in the fur. The window is wide open, and the river waters flow with a strong and steady sound. They remain this way a long time, until all the heat that has been dispersed, forgotten, extinguished in the wife's body rises to the surface, gathers into a compact, vibrant beam, and then Thumbkin starts to move, following the lines of force from that beam as it hesitates and casts about. In the dim undergrowth of her body, the Ogre's wife hears a small noise like something gliding through leaves and branches; as she follows it, all the energy contained in her body rises into that vibrant beam and suddenly explodes, sweeping away her troubles, her memories, her fears, sweeping away all the vines and brambles and deadwood, flowing like the great river outside that shimmers and undulates at the center of the city.

She sleeps, and Thumbkin, who has brought this woman, so big and beautiful and strong, to climax—Thumbkin changes. He feels himself growing by the minute. Nothing will ever abandon him again. He thinks of his brothers, who are probably still following one another Indian file through some ravine with no sky, he thinks of the city with that big river he can see through the window, and the ancient hunger that has tormented him for so long changes inside him and flows throughout his body like a fine, placid water with which he will wash down big, sugary slices of the countryside, waiting while he rests.

Thumbkin's head lies by the wife's and his feet lie by hers. The wife dreams she is on the back of the world, which is a big, bright, velvety butterfly, flitting through space where it is king.

The seven-league boots fell under the feet of a passing mosquito, and, being enchanted, they immediately shrank to its modest scale and vanished with the tiny creature, fading into thin air like a mirage before dazzled eyes.

English translation by Leigh Hafrey.

Honorable Mentions:
1991

Abe, Kobo, "Intruders," *Beyond the Curve.*
——, "Record of Transformation," *Ibid.*
——, "The Irrelevant Death," *Ibid.*
Akhurst, Julia, "Small Pieces of Alice," *Darklands.*
Albright, Dawn, "Black Ribbon," *Marion Zimmer Bradley's Fantasy Magazine* #14.
Alcalá, Kathleen J., "Sweetheart," *Isaac Asimov's Science Fiction Magazine,* March.
Aldiss, Brian W., "FOAM," *New Worlds* #1.
Allyn, Doug, "Speed Demon," *Ellery Queen's Mystery Magazine,* Oct.
Amery, Francis, "Self-Sacrifice," *Interzone* 54.
Anderson, Dana M., "Cafe Purgatorium," *Cafe Purgatorium.*
Antczak, Steve, "Break Down the Walls of the World," *After Hours* #9.
Antieau, Kim, "Medusa's Child," *Final Shadows.*
Armstrong, Michael, "The Kikituk," *Cold Shocks.*
Arnzen, Michael A., "Brazilian Night," (poem) *Dreams and Nightmares.*
——, "Eye for an Eye," *Outlaw Bikers Tattoo Review* #16.
Athkins, D. E., "Blood Kiss," *Thirteen.*
Atwood, Margaret, "Death by Landscape," *Wilderness Tips.*
Austin, A. J., ". . . But Fear Itself," *Aboriginal SF,* Dec.
Ballard, J. G., "Dream Cargoes," *Omni* Feb.; *War Fever.*
Bankier, William, "A Lot of Hurt Feelings," *EQMM,* June.
Barker, A. L. "I'll Never Know," *Winter's Tales: New Series 7.*
Bechard, Gorman, "Tabith Watching," *After Hours* #11.
Beckert, Christine, "Baggage," *After Hours* #12.
Beckett, Chris, "La Macchina," *Interzone* 46.
Beechcroft, William, "Torrent," *Alfred Hitchcock's Mystery Magazine,* Nov.–Dec.
Berry, Michael, "Kessel's Party," *Psycho-Paths.*
bes Shahar, Eluki, "Spellbinder," *Sword & Sorceresses VIII.*
Betancourt, John Gregory, "Tap Dancing," *Weird Tales,* Spring.
Bishop, Michael, "Life Regarded as a Jigsaw Puzzle of Highly Lustrous Cats," *Omni,* Sept.
——, "Thirteen Lies About Hummingbirds," *Final Shadows.*
Bisson, Terry, "Press Ann," *IASFM,* Aug.
Blackburn, Eric, "Wild Thing," *Newer York.*
Blaylock, James P. and Powers, Tim, "The Better Boy," *IASFM,* Feb.
Bloch, Robert and Kuttner, Henry, "The Grab Bag," *Weird Tales,* Spring.
Block, Lawrence, "Something to Remember You By," *New Mystery Magazine* #1.

Boston, Bruce and Frazier, Robert, "Holos at an Exhibition," *Amazing Stories*, July.

Boyle, T. Coraghessan, "Hope's Rise," *Harper's*, March.

Bradfield, Scott, "Didn't She Know," *The New Gothic*.

Brandner, Gary, "Darke Street," *Invitation to Murder*.

———, "Milestone's Face," *Masques IV*.

———, "The Ice Children," *Cold Shocks*.

———, "To Have and to Hold," *Hotter Blood*.

Branham, R. V., "Chango Chingamadre, Dutchman, & Me," *Full Spectrum 3*.

Brantingham, Juleen, "Patterns," *Weird Tales*, Summer.

———, "Something About Camilla," *Final Shadows*.

Braunbeck, Gary A., "For Want of A Smile," *Not One of Us #8*.

———, "Don't Sit Under the Apple Tree with Anyone Else but Me," *Eldritch Tales* 25.

Brennan, Joseph Payne, "Where Nettles Cling," (poem) *Weirdbook* 26.

Brown, Molly, "Neon Nightsong," *After Hours #10*.

Brown, Warren, "Mayfly Night," *Ibid*.

Bryant, Edward, "Colder Than Hell," *Cold Shocks*.

———, "Country Mouse," *Copper Star*.

———, "Down Home," *Obsessions*.

———, "Fetish," Axolotl Press chapbook.

———, "The Great Steam Bison of Cycad Center," *Fires of the Past*.

Bryant, Taerie, "The Vampire Child," *Prisoners of the Night* 5.

Buchanan, Carl, "Kidsgame," (poem) *Xenophilia* 3.

Budz, Mark, "The War Inside," *Pulphouse Weekly*, June 6.

Burros, Deborah, "Masks," *Swords and Sorceresses VIII*.

Cadger, Rick, "Through a Glass," *Fear #29*.

Cady, Jack, "A Sailor's Pay," *Final Shadows*.

———, "The Sons of Noah," *Omni*, Jan.

Cail, Carol, "Where is it Now?" *Hawaii Review*, Spring.

Campbell, Ramsey, "A Street Was Chosen," *Weird Tales*, Summer.

———, "Another World," *Iniquities*, Spring.

———, "Wrapped Up," *Cemetery Dance*, Fall.

Carpenter, Leonard, "Torso," *IASFM*, Nov.

Carroll, Jonathan, "The Moose Church," *A Whisper of Blood*.

Carter, Angela, "The Merchant of Shadows," *The New Gothic*.

Castle, Mort, "Love, Hate, and the Beautiful Junkyard Sea," *Masques IV*.

Caves, Sally, "Fetch, Felix," *The Magazine of Fantasy & Science Fiction*, July.

Chappell, Fred, "Alma," *More Shapes Than One*.

———, "Ancestors," *Chronicles: Magazine of American Culture*, March.

Charnas, Suzy McKee, "Now I Lay Me Down to Sleep," *A Whisper of Blood*.

———, and Yarbro, Chelsea Quinn, "Advocates," *Under the Fang*.

Cirone, Patricia B., "The Sweet Taste of Her Skin," *Pulphouse Wkly*, June 1.

Cisneros, Sandra, "Eyes of Zapata," *Woman Hollering Creek and Other Stories*.

———, "Little Miracles, Kept Promises," *Ibid*.

Clegg, Douglas, "People Who Love Life," *The Scream Factory* #6.
———, "Where Flies Are Born," *Tekeli-li* #2.
Clemence, Bruce, "No Way Street," *Pulphouse Short Story Paperback* #15.
Collingbourne, Huw, "Blue Narcissus," *Fear* #30.
Collins, Nancy A., "Dancing Nitely," *Under the Fang.*
———, "Demonlover," *Hotter Blood.*
———, "How it Was With the Kraits," *Cold Blood.*
———, "Iphigenia," *There Won't Be War.*
———, "Raymond," *The Ultimate Werewolf.*
———, "The One-Eyed King," *The Fantastic Adventures of Robin Hood.*
Connolly, David T., "Julia's Touch," *Masques IV.*
Constantine, Storm, "In the Dark Storm," (poem) *Now We Are Sick.*
Cooney, Caroline B., "Where the Deer Are," *Thirteen.*
Coulson, Joseph and Relling, William, Jr., "Mama's Little Soldier," *Cemetery Dance*, Spring.
Counsil, Wendy, "Stigmata," *F & SF*, April.
Cover, Arthur Byron, "A Murder," *Pulphouse Weekly*, Aug. 17.
Coyne, John, "Burn this Flag," *2AM*, Spring.
Crispin, A. C. and O'Malley, Kathleen, "Pure Silver," *The Ultimate Werewolf.*
D'ammassa, Don, "Wake Up Call," *Eldritch Tales* 25.
Daniel, Tony, "Words," *IASFM*, Feb.
Dann, Jack, "Voices," *Omni*, Aug.
deCormier-Shekerjian, Regina, "Ritual," (poem) *The Nation*, March 11.
Dedman, Stephan, "But Smile No More," *Aurealis* #12.
Del Carlo, Eric, "Up Round the Bend," *After Hours* #10.
de Lint, Charles, "The Boys of Goose Hill," (lyrics) *Authors Choice Monthly* #22.
———, "Coyote," *Desert Moments.*
———, "Death Leaves an Echo," *Cafe Purgatorium.*
———, "The Graceless Child," *Halflings, Hobbits, Warrows & Weefolk.*
———, "Pity the Monsters," *The Ultimate Frankenstein.*
———, "We Are Dead Together," *Under the Fang.*
———, "Winter Was Hard," *Pulphouse* #10.
DeMarinis, Rick, "Rudderless Fiction: Lesson One," *The Voice of America.*
Denton, Bradley, "Blackburn and the Blind Man," *Pulphouse Wkly.*, Aug. 17.
———, "Rerun Roy, Donna, and the Freak," *F & SF*, Oct./Nov.
———, "Skidmore," *F & SF*, May.
Donnelly, Marcos, "Tracking the Random Variable," *Full Spectrum 3.*
Dorr, James S., "Milk Carton Monsters," *New Mystery Magazine* #1.
———, "Romance Unlimited," *Borderlands 2.*
———, "When the Cats Are Away," *Haunts*, Fall-Winter.
———, "The Wellmaster's Daughter," *Alfred Hitchcock's Mystery Magazine*, Nov.
Dowling, John, "Pandemonium," *After Hours* #11.
Duggins, David, "Black Coffee," *Fear* #27.
Dunham, Jere, "East of the Dawn," *Swords and Sorceresses VIII.*

Dunn, J. R., "The Other Shore," *Omni*, Dec.
Dyer, S. N., "The July Ward," *IASFM*, April.
Easter, Richard, "Amy," *Dark Voices 3*.
Egan, Greg, "Appropriate Love," *Interzone 50*.
———, "Blood Sisters," *Interzone 44*.
———, "Fidelity," *IASFM*, Sept.
———, "The Infinite Assassin," *Interzone 48*.
Elflandsson, Galad, "The Good Ship 'Revenge' or, What the Crew Don't Know
   Won't Hurt Me," *Now We Are Sick*.
Elliott, Tom, "Roadkill," *Cemetery Dance*, Spring.
———, "The Web on Creque Bayou," *Haunts*, Spring.
Ely, David, "The Children," *Always Home*.
Emshwiller, Carol, "If the Word Was to the Wise," *The Start of the End of It
   All*.
———, "There Is No Evil Angel But Love," *Ibid.*
Engstrom, Elizabeth, "The Pan Man," *F & SF*, July.
Epperson, S. K., "The Son Also Rises," *Cemetery Dance*, Spring.
Evans, Elizabeth, "Blood and Gore," *The Quarterly* 17.
Farrington, Geoffrey, "Little St. Hugh," *Tales of the Wandering Jew*.
Felice, Cynthia, "Second Cousin Twice Removed," *IASFM*, Dec.
Finch, Marina, "The Scarecrow's Bride," *Pulphouse* #10.
Frazier, Robert, "He Who . . ." (poem), *Grue* #12.
———, "Stigmata," (poem) *Omni*, July.
———, "What Lives After," *Newer York*.
Friesner, Esther M., "The Shoemaker and the Elves," *F & SF*, March.
Frost, Gregory, "Attack of the Jazz Giants," *There Won't Be War*.
Gaiman, Neil and Jones, Stephen, "Now We Are Sick," (poem) *Now We Are
   Sick*.
Gallagher, Stephen, "DeVice," *Hotter Blood*.
———, "Magpie," *Final Shadows*.
Galloway, Janice, "The Meat," *Blood*.
Gardner, Craig Shaw, "Day of the Wolf," *The Ultimate Werewolf*.
Garton, Ray, "The Picture of Health," *Hotter Blood*.
Gibbons, Richard Patrick, "The Two Senoras," *EQMM*, Feb.
Gilden, Mel, "Moonlight on the Gazebo," *The Ultimate Werewolf*.
Gluckman, Janet, "Castoff," *Midnight Zoo* #3.
Goldstein, Lisa, "A Traveler at Passover," *Pulphouse* #10.
Gores, Joe, "Sleep the Big Time," *EQMM*, April.
Gorman, Ed, "Deathman," *Dark Crimes*.
———, "Duty," *Under the Fang*.
———, "The Coming of Night, the Passing of Day," *Masques IV*.
Grant, Charles L., "Girl of My Dreams," *Obsessions*.
———, "Peacemaker," *Borderlands 2*.
———, "One Life in an Hourglass," *The Bradbury Chronicles*.
———, "Make a Wish Upon the Moon," *Dead End: City Limits*.
Grealy, Lucy, "In the Nick of Time," *The Sonoran Review* #21.

Greenbaum, Jessica, "The Yellow Star that Goes with Me," *The New Yorker*, March 25.

Greenland, Colin, "The Stone Face," *Final Shadows*.

———, "You're Deceased, Father William," (poem) *Now We Are Sick*.

Grey, Robert, "Lullaby," *After Hours* #10.

———, "Sing I Die," *Prisoners of the Night*.

Griffin, Peni R., "Books," *IASFM*, Nov.

Griffith, Nicola, "Wearing My Skin," *Interzone* 50.

Haber, Karen, "The Dark Places In Between," *Final Shadows*.

Haldeman, Joe, "Images," *F & SF*, May.

Hall, Melissa Mia, "The Looking Glass Hand," *Dead End: City Limits*.

Hambly, Barbara, "Changeling," *Once Upon a Time*.

Hand, Elizabeth, "The Bacchae," *Interzone* 49.

———, "Snow on Sugar Mountain," *Full Spectrum 3*.

Harrington, Barry, "The Competition," *Aberrations* #1.

Harrington, Joyce, "Frankie Baby," *The Ultimate Frankenstein*.

Hautala, Rick, "Sources of the Nile," *Masques IV*.

Heaven, Alan, "The Hauler-in Susie M.," *Interzone* 53.

Hendee, Barb, "Full Moon Hearth," *Deathrealm* #14.

Henderson, C. J., "Whose Turn Is It?" *Obsessions*.

Hightower, Lynn S., "The Magic House," *Final Shadows*.

———, "The Rose Elf," *F & SF*, March.

Higney, Gene Michael, "Comes the Night Wind, Cold, and Hungry," *Cemetery Dance*, Spring.

Hill, Richard, "Auntie Ethel," (poem) *Now We Are Sick*.

Hodge, Brian, "Androgyny," *Borderlands 2*.

———, "Cancer Causes Rats," *Cold Blood*.

———, "Midnight Sun," *Under the Fang*.

Hoffman, Nini Kiriki, "An Invasion of Angels," *Pulphouse* #10.

———, "A Painting Lesson," *Amazing Stories*, Jan.

———, "Unleashed," *The Ultimate Werewolf*.

———, "Voices in a Shelter Home," *Amazing Stories*, March.

———, "Zits," *Iniquities*, Autumn.

Hoing, David, "City of the Dreadful Night," *F & SF*, Aug.

Holder, Nancy, "Bring Me the Head of Timothy Leary," *Cold Shocks*.

———, "Have You Seen Me?" *Cemetery Dance*, Summer.

———, "Lady Madonna," *Obsessions*.

———, "Woman's Little Wound," *Noctulpa 5: Guignoir and Other Furies*.

Hood, Martha A., "Dust to Dust to . . ." *Interzone* 52.

———, "Fun Flesh," *Tales of the Unanticipated* #8.

Hoppe, Stephanie T., "Old Night," *Tales of Magic Realism by Women*.

Hopper, Jeannette M., "Swelter," *Copper Star*.

Horvitz, Leslie Alan, "His N' Hers," *New Mystery* #2.

Howard, Clark, "Dark Conception," *EQMM*, Oct.

Infante, Guillermo Cabrero, "The Phantom of the Essoldo," *A Hammock Beneath the Mangoes*.

Irwin, Robert, "Waiting for the Zaddik," *Tales of the Wandering Jew.*
Jablokov, Alexander, "Living Will," *IASFM*, June.
Jafek, Bev, "The Statistician," *The Black Warrior Review*, Spring/Fall.
Janifer, Laurence M., "Learning Experience," *Newer York.*
Johnson, Kij, "I ♥ MY♭" *Tales of the Unanticipated* #8.
Kaaberbol, Lene, "Puss," *Dark Voices 3.*
Kilpatrick, Nancy, "When Shadows Come Back," *The Standing Stone Short Fiction Contest 1991.*
Kilworth, Garry, "Hamelin, Nebraska," *Interzone* 48.
Kimbriel, Katharine Eliska, "Triad," *F & SF*, Aug.
Kisner, James, "Fugyu," *Night Visions 9.*
———, "Splatter Me an Angel," *Masques IV.*
Klein, Robert William, "Haunts Come Out," *AHMM*, April.
Knapp, Kevin, "Egypt/Egypt," (poem) *Nyctalops*, April.
Koja, Kathe, "Impermanent Mercies," *Dark Voices 3.*
———, "The Neglected Garden," *F & SF*, April.
Laidlaw, Marc, "Gasoline Lake," *F & SF*, Oct./Nov.
Lane, Joel, "Common Land," *Darklands.*
Langford, David, "Encounter of Another Kind," *Interzone* 54.
Lansdale, Joe R., "In the Cold, Dark Time," *Obsessions.*
Law, Stephen, "He Who Laughs," *Dark Voices 3.*
Layefsky, Virginia, "This Place Belongs to You," *EQMM*, Jan.
Laymon, Richard, "The Tub," *Hotter Blood.*
Lee, Michael, "Stranger in the Green Chair," *F & SF*, April.
Lee, Tanith, "The Mermaid," *Final Shadows.*
———, "Venus Rising On Water," *IASFM*, Oct.
Lepovetsky, Lisa, "Ghost," (poem) *Grue* #14 supplement.
———, "Tracks," *Grue* #14 supplement.
Lethem, Jonathan, "The Happy Man," *IASFM*, Feb.
Ligotti, Thomas, "Miss Plarr," *Weird Tales*, Winter/*Grimscribe.*
———, "Mrs. Rinaldi's Angel," A *Whisper of Blood.*
———, "Netherscurial," *Weird Tales*, Winter/*Grimscribe.*
———, "The Cocoon," *Ibid.*
———, "The Dreaming in Nortown," *Ibid.*
———, "The Night School," *Ibid.*
Linaweaver, Brad, "Clutter," *Psycho-Paths.*
Lipinski, Miroslaw, "The Cult of Puke," *Twisted* #6.
Little, Bentley, "Bumblebee," *Cold Blood.*
Lovesey, Peter, "Supper with Miss Shivers," *EQMM*, Mid-Dec.
Lumley, Brian, "The Picknickers," *Dark Voices 3.*
Lutz, John, "Mr. Lucrada," *The Ultimate Dracula.*
MacLeod, Ian R., "The Family Football," *Interzone* 53.
———, "The Giving Mouth," *IASFM*, March.
Malzberg, Barry N., "Folly for Three," A *Whisper of Blood.*
———, "How I Managed to Blunt the Alien Invasion," *Omni*, April.
Mapes, Diane, "Remnants," *Interzone* 50.

Markham, Marion M., "There Are Fantasies in the Park," *AHMM*, Jan.

Markham, Robert J., "On the Edge," (poem) *Plexus*, Oct.

Marr, Michelle, "Rope Trick," *The Sterling Web* #6.

Massie, Elizabeth, "Hot Orgy of the Caged Virgins," *Iniquities*, Spring.

————, "M is for the Many Things," A *Whisper of Blood*.

Masterton, Graham, "Pig's Dinner," *Cemetery Dance*, Winter.

————, "Rococo," *Hotter Blood*.

————, "The Heart of Helen Day," *Masques IV*.

————, "The Sixth Man," *Cold Shocks*.

Mayhar, Ardath, "Lonesome Canefield Blues," *New Mystery Magazine* #1.

McCaffery, Simon P., "The Deep End," *AHMM*, Dec.

McDevitt, Jack, "Valkyrie," *There Won't Be War*.

McDonald, Ian, "Fragments of an Analysis of a Case of Hysteria," *Tales of the Wandering Jew*.

McGrath, Patrick, "The Other Psychiatrist," *Winter's Tales: New Series 7*.

————, "Cleave the Vampire, or, A Gothic Pastorale," *I Shudder At Your Touch*.

McLaughlin, Mark, "Leave Her Alone," *Not One of Us* #7.

McNaughton, Brian, "Caput Mortuum," *Weirdbook* 26.

Mecklem, Todd, "The Newt Fisher," *BBR* #19.

Miller, Rex, "Dead Issue," *Borderlands 2*.

Miller, Wayne G., "God Can Be a Cruel Bastard," *Chilled to the Bone*.

Misha, "The Stone Badger," *Fiction International* 20.

Monteleone, Thomas F., "Prodigal Sun," *Under the Fang*.

————, "The White Man," *Dead End: City Limits*.

Moon, Elizabeth, "Clara's Cat," *Catfantastic II*.

Morlan, A. R., "St. Jackaclaws," *Cold Shocks*.

Morrow, Bradford, "The Road to Nadĕja," *The New Gothic*.

Mosiman, Billie Sue, "Pretty Boy," *Invitation to Murder*.

Moss, David, "On the Rocks," *After Hours* #11.

Murakami, Haruki, "The Elephant Vanishes," *The New Yorker*.

Murphy, Earl, "Even Steven," *2AM*, Spring.

Murphy, Pat, "South of Oregon City," *The Ultimate Werewolf*.

————, "Traveling West," *IASFM*, Feb.

Murphy, Warren and Cochran, Molly, "A Nice Place to Visit," *Newer York*.

Muth, Jon J., "Four Poems," *Words Without Pictures*.

Nabors, Cecily, "Wolf's Bane," *After Hours* #9.

Nasir, Jamil, "Mr. and Mrs. Smith," *Tales of the Unanticipated* #8.

Natsuki, Shizuko, "Harder Than to Die," *New Mystery* #2.

Neilson, Robert, "Pleasing Mister Ross," *Fear* #34.

Nelson, Resa, "Lovepets," *Pulphouse* #11.

Newland, Mike, "The Carrion Eaters," *Copper Star*.

Noble, Carol T., "Sign," *Not One of Us* #7.

Nolan, William F., "Babe's Laughter," *Cold Blood*.

————, "Blood Sky," (chapbook).

————, "Broxa," *Weird Tales*, Fall.

Nutman, Philip, "Churches of Desire," *Borderlands* 2.
———, "Pavlov's Wristwatch," *Darklands*.
Oates, Joyce Carol, "The Guilty Party," *Glamour*, July.
Oliver, Chad, "A Lake of Summer," *The Bradbury Chronicles*.
Olson, Paul F., "Down the Valley Wild," *Borderlands* 2.
O'Driscoll, Mike, "Prince of the Dying Night," *Fear* #25.
O'Toole, John M., "Playing the Game," *EQMM*, June.
Paradise, Sandra, "The Honeymoon," *Aboriginal SF*, Jan./Feb.
Partridge, Norman, "Eighty-Eight Sins," *Amazing Stories*, Dec.
———, "Guignoir," *Noctulpa 5: Guignoir and Other Furies*.
———, "The Hollow Man," *Grue* #13.
Peake, Tony, "Necessary Appendages," *Winter's Tales: New Series 7*.
Pendleton, Jan, "Teeth," *The Quarterly* 17.
Perry, Stephani, "The Key," *Pulphouse* #11.
Perry, Steve, "Chrome Bimbo," *Pulphouse Magazine 5*.
Person, Lawrence, "Details," *IASFM*, April.
Philbrick, W. R., "The Dark Rising," *The Ultimate Dracula*.
Pickard, Nancy, "The Scar," *A Woman's Eye*.
Pilkington, Ace G., "Theseus Beyond the Labyrinth," (poem) *Weirdbook* 26.
Pisacreta, Sharon, "The Subscription," *EQMM*, Jan.
Powell, James, "Winter Hiatus," *EQMM*, Oct.
Pritchard, John, "Nights," *Fear* #26.
Pronzini, Bill, "Thirst," *Cemetery Dance*, Winter.
Ptacek, Kathryn, "Sounds," *Masques IV*.
Rains, Richard, "The Atonement," *Borderlands* 2.
Raisor, Gary L., "Stigmata," *Ibid*.
Rathbone, Wendy, "The Host," *Prisoners of the Night 5*.
Reed, Diana, "Master Finlayson's Boy," *BBR* #19.
Reed, Kit, "Calling Hours," *Fires of the Past*.
———, "The Protective Pessimist," *The Texas Review*, Vol. XI, Nos. 1 & 2.
———, "River," *IASFM*, Sept.
Reeves-Stevens, Garfield, "Part Five," *The Ultimate Frankenstein*.
Reichert, Mickey Zucker, "The Eranis Pipe," *Halflings, Hobbits . . . .*
Relling, William, Jr., "The Injuries That They Themselves Procure Must Be Their Schoolmasters," *Dead End: City Limits*.
Relton, Peter, "The Ninth Mask," *Dark Horizons* #32.
Rendell, Ruth, "For Dear Life," *The New Gothic*.
———, "Mother's Help," *The Copper Peacock*.
Resnick, Mike, "Winter Solstice," *F & SF*, Oct./Nov.
Reynolds, Barry H., "The Trashman of Auschwitz," *Writers of the Future VII*.
Rich, Mark, "Limits," *Tales of the Unanticipated*, Winter–Summer.
Richards, Tony, "Hamadryad," *AHMM*, Dec.
Roberson, Jennifer, "Riding the Nightmare," *Horse Fantastic*.
Roberts, Keith, "The Will of God," *IASFM*, July.
Rodgers, Alan, "Sleep," (poem) *New Life for the Dead*.
Romath, Mike, "Electricity," *New York Press*, April 17–23.

Royle, Nicholas, "Crispy Notes," *Obsessions*.
———, "Moving Out," *Skeleton Crew*, Jan.
———, "Parallax," *Final Shadows*.
Rusch, Kristine Kathryn, "Children of the Night," *The Ultimate Dracula*.
———, "Dancers Like Children," *F & SF*, Sept.
———, "Self-Protection," *Obsessions*.
———, "The Life and Deaths of Rachel Long," *Invitation to Murder*.
Russell, Ray, "The Collapse of Civilization," *Masques IV*.
Russo, Richard Paul, "Celebrate the Bullet," *IASFM*, Mid-Dec.
Sallee, Wayne Allen, "For Their Wives Are Mute," *Borderlands 2*.
———, "With the Wound Still Wet," *Cemetery Dance*, Summer.
———, and Lynch, H. Andrew, "The Pain Detail," *Iniquities*, Autumn.
Salmonson, Jessica Amanda, "Small Repulsive Man," *Nyctalops*, April.
———, "How Death Came to Inyar the Shepherd," *Weirdbook* 26.
Sarrantonio, Al, "Richard's Head," *Obsessions*.
Sanders, Kate, "Jim's Angel," *Revenge*.
Schimel, Lawrence, "There Are Heroes Wrapped in Seaweed," (poem) *Dreams & Nightmares*.
Schow, David J., "A Week in the Unlife," *A Whisper of Blood*.
———, "Scoop Bites the Dust," *Pulphouse Weekly #2*.
Schwader, Ann K., "Blood Rights," (chapbook).
Schweitzer, Darrell, "After the Night," (poem) *Grue #13*.
———, "Savages," *Masques IV*.
Scliar, Moacyr, "The Plagues," *A Hammock Beneath the Mangoes*.
Sellers, Peter, "This One's Trouble," *AHMM*, July.
Sheffield, Charles, "Eighth Trimester," *Starshore*, Spring.
Sherman, Delia, "Blood Kin," *Vampires*.
Sheriff, John Paxton, "Fifth Time Dead," *AHMM*, June.
Shirley, John, "Just Like Suzie," *Cemetery Dance*, Summer.
———, "Pearldoll," *Hotter Blood*.
———, "Woodgrains," *Obsessions*.
Shwartz, Susan, "Dreaming in Black and White," *Psycho-Paths*.
Siddall, Sylvia M., "Thylacine, Thylacine," *Interzone* 44.
Silva, David B., "Alone of His Kind," *Obsessions*.
———, "Slipping," *Borderlands 2*.
———, "Bleed Red, Bleed White," *Cold Blood*.
Simmons, Dan, "All Dracula's Children," *The Ultimate Dracula*.
———, "The Counselor," *Obsessions*.
———, "My Private Memoirs of the Hoffer Stigmatic Pandemic," *Masques IV*.
Skinner, Brian, "De Natura Vana Perceptionis," *2AM*, Spring.
Slater, Judith, "Water Witch," *The Sonoran Review #20*.
Slesar, Henry, "Deuce," *F & SF*, June.
———, "Home Again," *EQMM*, Nov.
Smythe, George W., "Under the Sun: Spotted," *Argonaut #15*.
Snider, Clifton, "Aphrodite," *Blue Mesa Review #3*.
Som, T. G., "Correctional Justice," *After Hours #9*.

Soukup, Martha, "Dog's Life," *Amazing Stories*, March.
———, "Ties," *Newer York*.
Springer, Nancy, "The Most Magical Thing About Rachel," *Horse Fantastic*.
Spruill, Steven, "Ysex," *Cemetery Dance*, Fall.
Stableford, Brian, "Slumming in Voodooland," *Pulphouse Short Story Paperback #26*.
Stanton, Mary, "The Czechoslovakian Pigeon Farmer and the Pony that Wasn't a Paint," *Horse Fantastic*.
Straub, Peter, "The Kingdom of Heaven," *The New Gothic*.
Strickland, Brad, "And the Moon Shines Full and Bright," *The Ultimate Werewolf*.
Stuart, Kiel, "Do Me Baby," *Aberrations #1*.
———, "Juice," *Hotter Blood*.
St. Aubin de Teran, Lisa, "The Spider's Web," *Revenge*.
Takashi, Atoda, "Woman With a Hobby," *New Mystery Magazine #1*.
Taylor, Eleanor Rossi, "Kitchen Fable," (poem) *The New Yorker*, March 11.
Taylor, Lucy, "Atrocities," *Hotter Blood*.
———, "Blessed Be the Bound," *Noctulpa 5: Guignoir and Other Furies*.
Taylor, Joe, "Welcome to the Pleistocene and Land," *Subtropical Speculations*.
Tem, Melanie, "Daddy's Side," (chapbook).
———, "Fry Day," *Final Shadows*.
———, "Secrets," *Cemetery Dance*, Spring.
———, "Sitting with the Driver," *Copper Star*.
———, "The Ice Downstream," *Cold Shocks*.
Tem, Steve Rasnic, "Hearts," *Haunted Library*.
———, "Adleparmeun," *Cold Shocks*.
———, "Brutes," *Iniquities*, Autumn.
———, "Celestial Inventory," (chapbook).
———, "Cutlery," *Absences: Charlie Goode's Ghosts*.
———, "Daddy's an Actor," *New Mystery Magazine #1*.
———, "Jesse," *Psycho-Paths*.
———, "Plainclothes," *Cemetery Dance*, Fall.
———, "Robin in the Mists," *The Fantastic Adventures of Robin Hood*.
———, "The Regulars," *After Hours #10*.
———, "The Secret Flesh," *Pulphouse #11*.
———, "Wanderlust," *Tales of the Wandering Jew*.
———, and Tem, Melanie, "This Icy Region My Heart Encircles," *The Ultimate Frankenstein*.
Tepper, Sheri S., "The Gourmet," *F & SF*, Oct./Nov.
Tessier, Thomas, "Infidel," *A Whisper of Blood*.
———, "The Dreams of Dr. Ladybank," *Night Visions 9*.
Thompson, James, "It's Gary's Shambling Show," *Tekeli-li #1*.
Tillman, Lynne, "A Dead Summer," *The New Gothic*.
Tilton, Lois, "The Other Woman," *Masques IV*.
———, "The Soldier's Bride," *F & SF*, Aug.
Travis, Tia, "Five in Whiskey Dog," *Noctulpa 5: Guignoir and Other Furies*.

Twigg, Malcolm, "Digger," *Fear* #5.

Urban, Scott H., "The Chute," *Noctulpa 5: Guignoir and Other Furies.*

Vachss, Andrew, "Anytime I Want," *Invitation to Murder.*

Van Helden, E. R., "The Tourist," *Aurealis* #3.

Van Hollander, Jason, "The Hell Book," *Weird Tales*, Fall.

Vandermeer, Jeff, "Flesh," *Fear* #6.

———, "Welcome to the Masque," *Deathrealm* #15, Fall/Winter.

Vernon, Steve, "Honey Jew, Hooney Jew," *Not One of Us* #8.

Wagner, Karl Edward, "The Slug," A *Whisper of Blood.*

Wakefield, Tom, "Dance of the Vipers," *Winter's Tales: New Series 7.*

Waldrop, Howard, "Fin de Cyclé," *Night of the Cooters: More Neat Stories.*

Watson, Ian, "The Talk of the Town," *Fires of the Past.*

Watt-Evans, Lawrence, "Parade," *Dead End: City Limits.*

Webb, Don, "Avocation," *Figment* #6.

———, "Letters from Sarah," *IASFM*, Feb.

Webb, Wendy, "The Boarder," *Final Shadows.*

Wentworth, K. D., "Due Process," *Aboriginal SF*, Dec.

———, "The Ronnie," *AHMM*, Aug.

West, Paul, "Banquo and the Black Banana: The Fierceness of the Delight of the Horror," *The New Gothic.*

West, Suzi, K., "Eat In or Carry Out," *After Hours* #10.

White, Ellen Emerson, "The Boy Next Door," *Thirteen.*

White, G. Kyle, "Where the Sky Never Cries," *Cemetery Dance*, Fall.

Wiggins, Marianne, "Eso Es," *Bet They'll Miss Us When We're Gone.*

Wilber, Rick, "The Impaler in Love," (poem) A *Whisper of Blood.*

Williams, Walter Jon, "Erogenoscape," *IASFM*, Nov.

Williams, Sidney and Pettit, Robert, "Does the Blood Line Run on Time?" *Under the Fang.*

Williamson, Chet, "First Kill," *Cold Shocks.*

———, "The Bookman," *Obsessions.*

Willis, Connie, "Jack," *IASFM*, Nov.

Wiloch, Thomas, "Marionettes," *World Letter* Volume 1.

Wilson, Andrew J., "In the Maze of Faces," *Fear* #34.

Wilson, F. Paul, "Home Repairs," *Cold Blood.*

———, "The November Game," *The Bradbury Chronicles.*

Wilson, Gahan, "Sea Gulls," *Masques IV.*

———, "Them Bleaks," *Psycho-Paths.*

Windsor, Patricia, "A Little Taste of Death," *Thirteen.*

Wisman, Ken, "Jamie's Hands," *Midnight Zoo.*

Witcover, Paul, "Lighthouse Summer," *IASFM*, April.

Wittington, Mary Kay, "Avhel," *Vampires.*

Wolfe, Gene, "The Seraph from Its Sepulcher," *Sacred Visions.*

Womack, Jack, "Lifeblood," A *Whisper of Blood.*

Yamada, Amy, "Kneel Down and Lick My Feet," *Monkey Brain Sushi.*

Yarbro, Chelsea Quinn, "Confession of a Madman," *Psycho-Paths.*

———, "A Writ of *Habeas Corpus*," *The Ultimate Frankenstein.*

Yolen, Jane, "Angels Fly Because They Take Themselves Lightly," (poem) *IASFM*, Mid-Dec.

———, "Great Gray," *Fires of the Past*.

Zambreno, Mary Frances, "Miss Emily's Roses," *Vampires*.

Zilinskaite, Vytaute, "Sisyphus and the Woman" (translated by Debra Irving), *Soviet Women Writing*.

About the Editors

ELLEN DATLOW has been Fiction Editor at *Omni* for over a decade, and in that time has published award-winning stories by many of the finest writers in science fiction, fantasy, and horror. She has also edited a number of anthologies, including *Blood Is Not Enough, Alien Sex, The Omni Books of Science Fiction* and *A Whisper of Blood*, and has co-edited the previous four volumes in the *Year's Best Fantasy and Horror* series with Terri Windling. She lives in New York.

TERRI WINDLING developed the innovative Ace Fantasy list in the late 1970s. Since leaving Ace, she has worked as a consulting editor for Tor books, and is the creator and ongoing packager of the *Fairy Tales* series of adult fantasies inspired by traditional folklore. She is also the creator of the *Borderlands* urban fantasy series of anthologies and novels, which is in production as a Winter 1992 feature, and has edited or co-edited a number of fiction anthologies. She also runs the Endicott Studio, specializing in book publishing projects and art for exhibition. She lives in Arizona.

About the Artist

THOMAS CANTY is one of the most distinguished artists working in the fantasy field. He has won the World Fantasy Award for his distinctive book jacket and cover illustrations, and is a noted book designer working in a number of diverse fields, as well as with various small presses. He has also created children's picture-book series for St. Martin's Press and Ariel Books. He lives in Massachusetts.

About the Packager

JAMES FRENKEL has been a publisher, packager, and editor for over twenty years. Editor of Dell's science fiction imprint in the late 1970s, he published Bluejay Books, a major trade publisher in the field in the mid-1980s. He is currently a consulting editor for Tor Books. He also edits the Collier Nucleus series of classic SF and fantasy reprints. He lives in New York with his wife, Joan D. Vinge, with whom he is collaborating on several fiction anthologies.

About the Media Critic

EDWARD BRYANT is a major author of horror and science fiction. He has won Hugo and Nebula Awards for short fiction. He also works in radio, writes book reviews for major journals and newspapers, and is a charming and able speaker. He lives in Colorado.